THRONE

OF STARS

EMPIRE OF MAN by
DAVID WEBER & JOHN RINGO

March to the Sea • *March to the Stars*
Empire of Man (omnibus) • *March Upcountry*
We Few • *Throne of Stars* (omnibus)

THRONE OF STARS

DAVID WEBER
JOHN RINGO

THRONE OF STARS

March to the Stars copyright © 2003 by David Weber & John Ringo. We Few copyright © 2005 by David Weber & John Ringo.

A Baen Books Original

Baen Publishing Enterprises
P.O. Box 1403
Riverdale, NY 10471
www.baen.com

ISBN: 978-1-4767-3666-2

Cover art by David Seeley

First Baen paperback printing, August 2014

Distributed by Simon & Schuster
1230 Avenue of the Americas
New York, NY 10020

Library of Congress Cataloging-in-Publication Data

Weber, David, 1952-
[Novels. Selections]
Throne of stars / by David Weber and John Ringo.
    pages cm
"A Baen Books original"--T.p. verso.
 ISBN 978-1-4767-3666-2 (paperback)
1. Princes--Fiction. 2. Life on other planets--Fiction. 3. Kings and rulers--Succession--Fiction. 4. Space warfare--Fiction. I. Ringo, John, 1963- II. Weber, David, 1952- March to the stars. III. Weber, David, 1952- We few. IV. Title.
 PS3573.E217T47 2014
 813'.54--dc23
                                    2014014385

Printed in the United States of America

10 9 8 7 6 5 4 3 2 1

CONTENTS

THRONE of STARS

MARCH TO THE STARS

PROLOGUE

The body was in a state of advanced decomposition. Time, and the various insect analogues of Marduk, had worked their way with it, and what was left was mostly skeleton with a few bits of clinging tendon and skin. Temu Jin would have liked to say it was the worst thing he'd ever seen, but that would have been a lie.

He turned over one of the skeletal hands and ran a sensor wand across it. The catacomblike tomb was hot and close, especially with three more team members and one of the gigantic Mardukans packed into it with him. The heat on Marduk was always bad—the "temperate" regions were a fairly constant thirty-five degrees—but in the tomb, with the remnant stink of decomposition (not to mention the smell of the unwashed assholes he'd arrived with), it was like an antechamber to Hell.

One that was already inhabited.

There was no question that its occupants had been Imperial Marines. Or, at least, people with Marine nano packs. The trace materials and surviving nanites were coded, and the sensor practically screamed "Imperials." But the questions were how they had gotten here . . . and *why* they were here. He could think of several reasons, and he liked the stink of all of them even less than he did the stench in this room.

"Ask them again, geek," Dara said in a tight voice. The survey

3

team leader choked for a second—again—then hawked, spat, and finished by blowing out his nose on the floor. Marduk was hell on his sinuses. "Talk gook. Make sure this is all there was."

Jin looked up at the towering Mardukan and ran the translation through his "toot." The tutorial implant, lodged just inside his mastoid bone, took his chosen words, translated them into the local Mardukan dialect, and adjusted his speaking voice to compensate.

"My illustrious leader wishes to ensure, once again, that there were no survivors."

Mardukan expressions were not the same as those of humans. Among other things, their faces had fewer muscles, and much of their expressiveness came from eloquent gestures of their four arms. But the body language of this Mardukan was closed, as well. Part of that might be from the fact that he was missing one arm from the elbow down. Currently, there was a rather nice prosthetic hook in its place, razor-sharp on both sides. So Dara had to be either stupid, arrogant, or both to ask, for the fifth time, if the Voitan representative was lying.

"Alas," T'Leen Targ said with a sorrowful but cautious sweep of his arms (and hook), "there were no survivors. A few lasted a pair of days, but then they, too, succumbed. We did all we could for them. That we had been only a day sooner! The battle was great; your friends warred upon more Kranolta than the stars in the sky! They stacked them against the walls of the city and cut them down with their powerful fire-lances! Had our relief force but been sooner, some might have survived! Woe! But we were too late, alas. However, they did break the power of the Kranolta, and for that Voitan was and is eternally thankful. It was because of that gratitude that we interred them here, with our own honored dead, in hopes that someday others of their kind might come for them. And . . . here you are!"

"Same story," Jin said, turning back to the team leader.

"Where's the weapons? Where's the gear?" Dara demanded. Unlike the commo-puke's, his toot was an off-the-shelf civilian model and couldn't handle the only translation program available. It was loaded with the local patois used around the distant starport, but handling multiple dialects was beyond its capability, and Jin's system couldn't cross load the translation files.

"*Some* of that stuff should have survived," the team leader continued. "And there were supposed to be more of them at the last city. Where'd the rest of 'em go?"

"My illustrious leader asks about our dear friends' weapons and equipment," Jin said. The communications technician had had fairly extensive dealings with the natives, both back at the distant starport and on the hellish odyssey to this final resting place of the human castaways. And of them all, this one made him the most nervous. He'd almost rather be in the jungles again. Which was saying a lot.

Marduk was an incredibly hot, wet, and stable planet. The result was a nearly worldwide jungle, filled with the most vicious predators in the known worlds. And it seemed that the search team—or assassination team, depending on how one viewed it—had run into all of them on its journey here.

The starport's atmospheric puddle-jumpers had flown them to the dry lakebed where the four combat shuttles had landed. There was no indication, anywhere, of what unit had flown those shuttles, or where they had come from. All of them had been stripped of any information, and their computers purged. Just four Imperial assault shuttles, totally out of fuel, in the middle of five thousand square kilometers of salt.

There had, however, been a clear trail off the lakebed, leading up into the mountains. The search team had followed it, flying low, until it reached the lowland jungles. After that it had just . . . disappeared into the green hell.

Dara's request to return to base at that point had been denied. It was unlikely, to say the very least, that the shuttle crews might survive to reach civilization. Even taking the local flora and fauna out of the equation, the landing site was on the far side of the planet from the starport, and unless they had brought along enough dietary supplements, they would starve to death long before they could make the trip. But unlikely or not, their fate had to be known. Not so much because anyone would ever ask, or care, about them. Because if there was *any* shred of a possibility that they could reach the base, or worse, get off planet, they had to be eliminated.

That consideration had been unstated, and it was also one of the reasons that the tech wasn't sure he would survive the mission. The "official" reason for the search was simply to rescue the survivors. But the composition of the team made it much more likely that the real reason was to eliminate a threat. Dara was the governor's official bully-boy. Any minor "problem" that could be fixed with a little muscle or a discreetly disappearing body tended to get handed to the team leader. Otherwise, he was pretty useless. As demonstrated by his inability to see what was right in front of his eyes.

The rest of the team was cut from the same cloth. All fourteen of them—there'd been seventeen . . . before the local fauna got a shot at them on the trek here—were from the locally hired "guard" force, and all were wanted on one planet or another. Aware that maintaining forces on Class Three planets was difficult, at best, the distant Imperial capital allowed local governors wide latitude in the choice of personnel. Governor Brown had, by and large, hired what were still known as "Schultzes," guards who could be trusted to see, do, and hear nothing. Still, there were those special occasions when a real problem cropped up. And to deal with those problems, he had secured a "special reaction force" composed of what could graciously be called "scum." If, of course, one wanted to insult scum.

Jin was well aware that he was not an "official" member of the Special Force. As such, this mission might be a test for entry, and in many ways, that could be a good thing. Unfortunately, even if it was an entry test, there was still one huge issue associated with the mission: It might involve fighting the Marines. He had several reasons, not the least of which was the likelihood of being blasted into plasma, to not want to fight Marines, but the mission had been angling steadily that way.

Now, however, it seemed all his worry had been for naught. The last of the Marines had died here, in this lonely outpost, overrun by barbarians before their friendly "civilized" supporters could arrive to save them!

Sure they did, he thought, and snorted mentally. Either they wandered off and these guys are covering for them . . . or else the locals finished them off themselves and are graciously willing to give these "Kranolta" the credit. The only problem at this point is figuring out which.

"Alas," the local said yet again. He seemed remarkably fond of that word, Jin thought cynically as Targ gestured in the direction of the distant jungle somewhere outside the tomb. "The Kranolta took all their equipment with them. There was nothing left for us to give to their friends. That is, to you."

And you can believe as much or as little of that as you like, Jin thought. But the answer left a glaring hole he had to plug. And hope his efforts never came to light.

"The scummy says the barbs threw all the gear into the river," he mistranslated.

"Poth!" Dara snarled. "That means it's all trashed. *And* we can't trace the power packs! Even trashed, we could've gotten something for them."

What an imbecile, Jin thought. Dara must have been hiding behind the door when brains were given out.

When a body is looted, the looters very rarely take *every scrap* of clothing. Nor was that the only peculiarity. There was one clinging bit of skin on the corpse before him which had clearly been cut away in an oval, as if to remove a tattoo after the person was dead . . . and there were no weapons or even bits of weapons anywhere in sight. For that matter, the entire battle site had been meticulously picked over to remove every trace of evidence. Some of the scars from plasma gun fire had even been covered up. The barbarians, according to the locals' time line, could not possibly have swept the battlefield that well, no matter how addicted to trophy-taking they might be, before the "civilized" locals arrived to finish driving them off.

The last city they'd passed through had also been remarkably reticent about the actions the objects of the search team's curiosity had taken on their way through. The crews of the downed shuttles had apparently swept into town, destroyed and looted a selected few of the local "Great Houses," and then swept out again, just as rapidly. According to the local king and the very few nobles they'd been permitted to question, at least. And in that town, the search team had been followed everywhere by a large enough contingent of guards to make attempts to question anyone else contraindicated.

All of that proved one thing to Jin, and it took a sadistic, snot-filled idiot like Dara not to see it.

The bodies had been sterilized.

Somebody wanted to make *damn* sure no one could determine who these Marines had been without a DNA database. The dead Marines' toots were already a dead issue, of course. Their built-in nanites had obediently reduced them to half-crumbled wreckage once their owners were dead. That was a routine security measure, but the rest of this definitely went far beyond "routine." Which meant these particular people were something other than standard Marines. Either Raiders or . . . something else. And since the locals were covering for them so assiduously, it was glaringly obvious that all of them *hadn't* died.

All of which meant that there was a short company—from the number of shuttles, Jin had put their initial force at a company—of an Imperial special operations unit out there wandering in the jungle. And the only reasonable target for their wandering was a certain starport.

Lovely.

He pushed aside a bit of the current corpse's hair, looking for any clue. The Marine had been female, with longish, dishwater blond hair. That was the only thing about the skeletal remains which would have been recognizable to anyone but a forensic pathologist, which Jin was not. He had some basic training in forensics, but all he could tell about this corpse was that a blade had half-severed the left arm. However, under the cover of the hair, there was a tiny earring. Just a scrap of bronze, with one ten-letter word on it.

Jin was unable to keep his eyes from widening, but he didn't freeze. He was far too well trained to do something so obvious. He simply moved his hand in a smooth motion, and the tiny earring was ripped from the decaying ear, a scrap of skin still dangling from it.

"I'm not finding anything," he said, getting to his feet as he willed his face to total immobility.

He looked at the native, who returned his regard impassively.

The local "king" was named T'Kal Vlan. He'd greeted the search team as long-lost cousins, all the time giving the impression that he wanted to sell them a rug. For T'Leen Targ, though, it always seemed to be a toss-up between selling them a rug and burying them in one. Now the local scratched his horn with his hook and nodded . . . in a distinctly human fashion.

"I take it that you did not find anything," Targ said. "I'm *so* sorry. Will you be taking the bodies with you?"

"I think not," Jin replied. Standing as they were, the team leader was behind the local. Jin reached out with his left hand, and the Mardukan took it automatically, another example of acculturation to Terrans. Jin wondered if the Marines had realized how many clues they were unavoidably leaving behind. Given who they apparently were, it was probable, for all the proof of how hard they'd worked to avoid it. As he shook the Mardukan's slime-covered hand, a tiny drop of bronze was left behind, stuck in the mucus.

"I don't think we'll be back," the commo tech said. "But you might want to melt this down so nobody else finds it."

In the palm of the native's hand, the word "BARBARIANS" was briefly impressed into the mucus.

Then it disappeared.

CHAPTER ONE

"It's a halyard."

"No, it's a stay. T'e headstay."

The thirty-meter schooner *Ima Hooker* swooped closehauled into aquamarine swells so perfect they might have been drawn from a painting by the semimythical Maxfield Parrish. Overhead, the rigging sang in a faint but steady breeze. That gentle zephyr, smelling faintly of brine, was the only relief for the sweltering figures on her deck.

Julian mopped his brow and pointed to the offending bit of rigging.

"Look, there's a rope—"

"A line," Poertena corrected pedantically.

"Okay, there's a line and a pulley—"

"T'at's a block. Actually, it's a deadeye."

"Really? I thought a block was one of those with cranks."

"No, t'at's a windlass."

Six other schooners kept formation on *Hooker*. Five of them were identical to the one on whose deck Julian and Poertena stood: low, trim hulls with two masts of equal height and what was technically known as a "topsail schooner rig." What that meant was that each mast carried a "gaff sail," a fore-and-aft sail cut like a truncated triangle with its head set from an angled yard—the "gaff"—while the foremast also carried an entire set of conventional square sails. The after gaff sail—the "mainsail," Julian mentally corrected; after all, he had to get *something* right—had a boom; the forward gaff sail did not. Of course, it was called the foresail whereas the lowest square sail on that mast was called the "fore *course*," which struck him as a weird name for any sail. Then there were the "fore topsail," "fore topgallant," and "fore royal," all set above the fore course.

The second mast (called the "mainmast" rather than the "aftermast," for some reason Julian didn't quite understand, given that the ship had only two masts to begin with and that it carried considerably less canvas than the foremast) carried only a single square topsail, but compensated by setting a triangular "leg of mutton" fore-and-aft sail above the mainsail. There were also staysails set between the masts, not to mention a flying jib, outer jib, and inner jib, all set between the foremast and the bowsprit.

The seventh schooner was different—a much bigger, less agile, somehow unfinished-looking vessel with a far deeper hull and no less than five masts—and, at the insistence of Captain Armand Pahner, Imperial Marines, rejoiced in the name of *Snarleyow*. The smaller, more nimble ships seemed to regard their larger sister with mixed emotions. No one would ever have called *Snarleyow* anything so gauche as *clumsy*, perhaps, but she was clearly less fleet of foot, and her heavier, more deliberate motion almost seemed to hold the others back.

All of the ships carried short-barreled cannon along their sides. *Snarleyow* mounted fifteen of them to a side, which gave her a quarter again the broadside armament of any of her consorts, but all of them carried a single, much larger cannon on a pivot mount towards the bow, as well. And every single one of them had ropes everywhere. Which was the problem.

"Okay." Julian drew a deep breath, then continued in a tone of massive calm. "There's a line and a pu—block. So why isn't it a halyard?"

"Halyard hauls up t'e sail. T'e stay, it hold t'e pocking mast up."

The Pinopan had grown up around the arcane terminology of the sea. In fact, he was the only human member of the expedition (with the exception of Roger, who had spent summers in Old Earth's blue-water recreational sailing community) who actually understood it at all. But despite the impression of landsmen—that the arcana existed purely to cause them confusion—there was a real necessity for the distinct terminology. Ships constantly encounter situations where clear and unambiguous orders may mean the difference between life and death. Thus the importance of being able to tell hands to pull upon a certain "rope" in a certain way. Or, alternatively, to let it out slowly, all the while maintaining tension.

Thus such unambiguous and unintelligible orders as "Douse the mainsail and make fast!" Which does *not* mean throw water on it to increase speed.

"So which one's the halyard?" Julian asked plaintively.

"Which halyard? Countin' t'e stays'ils, t'ere's seventeen pocking halyards on t'is ship. . . ."

Hooker's design had been agreed upon as the best possible for the local conditions. She and her consorts had been created, through human design and local engineering, to carry Prince Roger and his bodyguards—now augmented by various local forces—across a previously unexplored ocean. Not that there hadn't, as always, been the odd, unanticipated circumstance requiring last-minute improvisation. The fact that a rather larger number of Mardukan allies than originally anticipated had been added to Roger's force had created the need for more sealift capacity. Especially given the sheer size of the Mardukan cavalry's mounts. *Civan* were fast, tough, capable of eating almost anything, and relatively intelligent. One thing they were *not*, however, was petite. Hardly surprising, since the cavalrymen who rode into battle on their backs averaged between three and three and a half meters tall.

Carrying enough of them to sea aboard the six original schooners had turned out to be impossible once the revised numbers of local troopers had been totaled up. So just when everyone had thought they were done building, they—and somewhere around a quarter of the total shipbuilding force of K'Vaern's Cove—had turned to to build the *Snarleyow*. Fortunately, the local labor force had learned a lot about the new building techniques working on the smaller ships, but it had still been a backbreaking, exhausting task no one had expected to face. Nor had Poertena been able to spend as much time refining her basic design, which was one reason she was ugly, slabsided, and slow, compared to her smaller sisters. She was also built of green timber, which had never been seasoned properly and could be expected to rot with dismaying speed in a climate like Marduk's. But that was all right with Prince Roger and his companions. All they really cared about was that she last long enough for a single voyage.

Although she was scarcely in the same class for speed or handiness as Poertena's original, twin-masted design, *Snarleyow* was still enormously more efficient than any native Mardukan design. She had to be. The nature of the local weather was such that there was an almost unvarying wind from the northeast, yet that was the very direction in which the ships had to sail. That was the reason for their triangular sails. Their fore-and-aft rig—a technology the humans had introduced—made it possible for them to sail much more sharply into the wind than any local vessel, with its clumsy and inefficient, primitive square-rigged design, had ever been able to do. Similar ships had sailed the seas of Earth all the way up to the beginning of the Information Age, and they remained the mainstay for water worlds like Pinopa.

"Now I'm really confused," Julian moaned. "All right. Tying something down is 'making fast.' A rope attached to a sail is a 'sheet.' A rope tied to the mast is a 'stay.' And a bail is the iron thingamajig on the mast."

"T'e boom," Poertena corrected, wiping away a drop of sweat. The day, as always, was like a steambath, even with the light wind that filled the sails. "T'e bail is on t'e boom. Unless you're taking on water. T'en you bail it out."

"I give up!"

"Don' worry about it," the Pinopan said with a chuckle. "You only been at t'is a few weeks. Besides, you got me an' all t'ose four-armed monstrosities to do t'e sailing. You jus' pull when we say 'heave,' and stop when we say 'avast.'"

"And hold on when you say 'belay.'"

"And hold on *tight* when we say belay."

"I blame Roger for this," Julian said with another shake of his head.

"You blame Roger for what?" a cool female voice asked from behind him.

Julian looked over his shoulder and grinned at Nimashet Despreaux. The female sergeant was frowning at him, but it slid off the irrepressible NCO like water off a duck.

"It's all Roger's fault that we're in this predicament," he replied. "If it wasn't for him, I wouldn't have to learn this junk!"

Despreaux opened her mouth, but Julian held up a hand before she could retort.

"Calmly, Nimashet. I know it's not Roger's fault. It was a joke, okay?"

Despreaux's frown only underscored the classical beauty of her face, but it was dark with worry.

"Roger's . . . still not taking Kostas' death very well, Adib. I just don't . . . I don't want anybody even *joking* about this being his fault," she said, and Poertena nodded in agreement.

"T'e prince didn't maroon us here, Julian. T'e Saints an' whoever set t'at pocking toombie on us marooned us." The diminutive armorer shrugged. "I guess it wasn't very pocking punny."

"Okay," a chagrined Julian said. "You've got a point. Roger has been sort of dragging around, hasn't he?"

"He's been in a funk, is what you mean," Despreaux said.

"Well, I'm sure there's some way you could cheer him up," Julian suggested with an evil grin.

"Oh, pock," Poertena muttered, and backed up quickly. After a crack like that the fecal matter was about to hit the impeller.

"Now this is a mutinous crew, if ever I've seen one." Sergeant Major Eva Kosutic said, joining them. She looked from Despreaux's furious face to Julian's "butter-wouldn't-melt-in-my-mouth" expression and frowned. "All right, Julian. What did you say this time?"

"Me?" Julian asked with enormous innocence but little real hope of evading the consequences. The sergeant major had an almost miraculous sense of timing; she always turned up just as the action was hottest. Which come to think of it, described her in bed as well. "What would I have said?"

Now he looked from the sergeant major to the fulminating Despreaux, decided that coming clean offered his best chance of survival, and shrugged with a repentant expression.

"I just suggested that there might be a way to cheer Roger up," he admitted, then, unable to help himself, grinned again. "I guarantee I'm right. God knows *I've* been more cheerful lately."

The sergeant major rolled her eyes and crossed her arms.

"Well if that's your attitude, you'll damned well be less cheerful for a while!" She looked at the three noncoms and shook her head. "This is a clear case of His Evilness' finding work for idle hands. Poertena, I thought you were supposed to be conducting a class in rigging."

"I was trying to get Julian up to speed, Sergeant Major," the Pinopan said, tossing a length of rope to the deck. "T'at's not going too good."

"I've got all the stuff loaded in my toot," Julian said with a shrug. "But some of the data seems to be wrong, and the rest just seems to be hitting and bouncing. I mean, what's 'luff' mean?"

"It's when the sail flaps," Kosutic replied, shaking her head. "Even *I* know that, and I *hate* sailing. I guess we should've known better than to try to teach Marines to be sailors."

"We don't really need them, Sergeant Major," Poertena told her. "We've got plenty of Mardukans."

"We need to work on our entry techniques, anyway," Julian pointed out. "We've been engaging in all these open-field maneuvers, but when we take the spaceport, it's going to be mostly close quarters. Whole different style, Smaj. And we haven't really done any of that since Q'Nkok."

The sergeant major frowned, then nodded. She was sure Julian had come up with that because it was more fun than learning to sail. But that didn't mean he was wrong.

"Okay. Concur. If we wanted sailors, we should've left you on the *DeGlopper* and brought Navy pukes. I'll talk the change over with the

Old Man. If he approves, we'll start working on close combat techniques for the rest of the voyage."

"Besides," Poertena pointed out gloomily, "we might need them before t'en. I've never seen a place like t'is t'at *didn't* have pirates."

"And then there's the 'fish of unusual size.'" Julian chuckled and gestured out over the emerald waters. "So far, so good, right?"

"Don't laugh," Despreaux muttered. "I read that log. I do *not* want to tangle with something big enough to bite a boat in half, even a small one."

"Well," Kosutic said, with a tug on her earlobe. "If worse comes to worst, we can always give Roger a pocket knife and throw him at it."

"Ooooo!" Julian shook his head. "You haven't even *met* one of these little fishies and you hate them *that* much?"

Prince Roger Ramius Sergei Alexander Chiang MacClintock, Heir Tertiary to the Throne of Man, turned away from the creaming waves to look across the shipboard bustle. The sergeant major had just broken up the huddle around Julian, and the four NCOs were headed in four different directions. He took a moment extra to watch Despreaux make for the fo'c'sle. He knew his depression was beginning to affect her, and that he needed to snap out of it. But the loss of Kostas was the one wound that would not seem to heal, and he'd had too much time to think about it since the frenetic haste of getting all seven ships built had eased into the voyage itself. For the first time in what seemed forever, he wasn't engaged in frantic efforts to train native troops, fight barbarian armies, build ships, or simply hike through endless jungle. For that matter, nothing was actively attempting to kill him, devour him, assassinate him, or kidnap him, and a part of him was distantly amazed to discover just how much having that respite depressed him. Having time to think, he had learned, was not always a good thing.

He supposed he could pull up the list of casualties on his implanted toot. But there wouldn't be much point. When they'd first landed, the Marines of Bravo Company, Bronze Battalion of the Empress' Own Regiment, had been just so many faces. And the officers and crew of the Assault Ship *DeGlopper,* long since expanding plasma, had just been blurs. But since some time after the pilots of the shuttles had brought them to deadstick landings on this backward hell, some time between the internecine fighting that had erupted at the first city they'd visited and the furious battles with the Kranolta barbarians, the Marines had become more than faces. In many ways, they had become more than family—as close as a part of his own body.

And each loss had been like flaying skin.

First the loss of half the company in Voitan, fighting the Kranolta. Then the constant low-level seepage as they battled their way across the rest of the continent. More good troops killed in Diaspra against the Boman, and then a handful more in Sindi against the main Boman force. The ones who fell to the damnbeasts and the vampire moths. And the crocs. The ever-be-damned damncrocs.

And one of those fallen had been Kostas.

Kostas. Not a Marine, or even one of the Navy shuttle pilots. Not one of the Mardukan mercenaries who had become welded to the Bronze Barbarians. Roger could, to an extent, justify their losses. The entire purpose of Bravo Company, and of the mercenaries, was to protect the once lily-white skin of Prince Roger Ramius Sergei Alexander Chiang MacClintock, and they'd all known it when they signed on. But that wasn't Kostas' purpose. He was just a valet. A nobody. A nonentity. Just . . . Kostas.

Just the man who had stood by Roger when the rest of the universe thought he was a complete loss. Just the man who, thrown the responsibility for feeding and clothing the company on its march, had taken it on without a qualm. Just the man who had found food where there was none, and prepared sumptuous dishes from swamp water and carnivores. Only the man who had been a father figure to him.

Only Kostas.

And not even lost to enemy action. Lost to a damn croc, five meters of rubbery skin and teeth. One of the innumerable hazards of the damned jungles of Marduk. Roger had killed the croc almost immediately, but it had been too late. He'd killed dozens of them since, but all of them were too late for Kostas. Too late for his . . . friend.

He hadn't had many friends growing up. Even as the least little scion of the Imperial Family, Roger had faced a future of power and wealth. And from the youngest age, there had been sycophants aplenty swarming around the prince. The innumerable Byzantine plots of Imperial City had sought constantly to co-opt one self-absorbed prince. And from the time he was a teenager, it had been Kostas—cautious, mousey Kostas—who had helped him thread the rocks and shoals. Often without Roger ever knowing it.

And now, he was gone. Just . . . gone. Like Hooker and Bilali and Pentzikis and . . . gods. The list went on and on.

Oh, they'd left a few widows on the other side in their wake. They'd made alliances when and where they could, even passed without a ripple in a few places. But more often than not, it had been plasma guns and bead rifles, swords and pikes and a few thousand years of technical and tactical expertise, blasting a swath of destruction a blind man could track because they had no choice. Which created its own problems, because they scarcely needed to be leaving any bread crumb trails behind them. Especially when they already knew they didn't face only "casual" enemies on the planet. True, there were more than enough foes who had become dangers solely because they felt . . . argumentative when the company had needed to cross their territory, but beyond them, Roger and the Barbarians faced the sworn enemies of the Empire and the Imperial House.

The planet Marduk was, technically, a fief of the Empire of Man. In fact, officially it was personally held by the Empress herself, since it had been discovered a few hundred years before by the expanding Empire and promptly claimed in the name of the House of MacClintock. For over a century, the planet had been no more than a notation on a survey somewhere, though. Then, early in the reign of Roger's grandfather, plans had been advanced for the Sagittarius Sector. Settlers were going to be sent out to the planets in the region, and a "new day of hope" would dawn for the beleaguered poor of the inner worlds. In preparation for the projected wave of expansion, outposts had been established on several of the habitable planets and provided with bare-bones starports. The Imperial government had put some additional seed money into establishing a limited infrastructure and offered highly attractive concessions to some of the Empire's biggest multistellar corporations to help produce more, but by and large, the planets in this sector had been earmarked strictly as new homes for the "little people" of the Empire.

Roger supposed the plans had spoken well for his grandfather's altruistic side. Of course, it was that same misplaced altruism and his tendency to trust advisers because of what he *thought* their characters were that had created most of the problems Roger's Empress Mother had been dealing with, first as Heir Primus and then as Empress, for longer than Roger had been alive. And it had also been an altruism whose hopes had been frustrated more often than not.

As they had been in the case of the Sagittarius Sector project.

Unfortunately for Grandfather's plans, the "poor" of the inner worlds were relatively comfortable with their low-paid work or government stipends. Given a choice between a small but decent apartment in Imperial City or Metrocal or New Glasgow or Delcutta and a small but decent house in a howling wilderness, the "poor" knew which side of their bread was buttered. Especially when the howling wilderness in question was on a planet like Marduk. For one thing, even in Delcutta, people rarely had to worry about being eaten.

So, despite all of the government's plans (and Emperor Andrew's), the sector had languished. Oh, two or three of the star systems in the area had attracted at least limited colonization, and the Sandahl System had actually done fairly well. But Sandahl was on the very fringe of the Sagittarius Sector, more of an appendage of the neighboring Handelmann Sector. For the most part, the Sagittarius planetary outposts and their starports had discovered that they were the designated hosts for a party no one came to. Except for the Saints.

One of the less altruistic reasons for the effort to colonize the sector in the first place had been the fact that the Cavaza Empire was expanding in that direction. Unfortunately, the plan to build up a countervailing Imperial presence had failed, and eventually, as the

Saints continued their expansion, they had noticed the port installed on the small, mountainous subcontinent of Marduk.

In many ways, Marduk was perfect for the Saints' purposes. The "untouched" world would require very little in "remedy" to return it to its "natural state." Or to colonize. With their higher birthrate, and despite their "green" stand, the Saints were notably expansionist. It was one of the many little inconsistencies which somehow failed to endear them to their interstellar neighbors. And in the meantime, the star system was well placed as a staging point for clandestine operations deeper into the Empire of Man.

Roger and his Marines were unsure of the conditions on the ground. But after their assault ship/transport, HMS *DeGlopper*, had been crippled by a programmed "toombie" saboteur, they had needed the closest port to which they could divert, and Marduk had been elected. Unfortunately, they had arrived only to be jumped by two Saint sublight cruisers which had been working in-system along with their globular "tunnel-drive" FTL carrier mother ship. The presence of Cavazan warships had told the Marines that whatever else was going on here, the planetary governor and his "locally" recruited Colonial Guards were no longer working for the Empire. That could be because they were all dead, but it was far more likely that the governor had reached some sort of accommodation with the Saints.

Whatever the fate of the governor might have been, the unpalatable outlines of the Bronze Barbarians' new mission had been abundantly clear. *DeGlopper* had managed to defeat the two cruisers, but she'd been destroyed in action with all hands herself in the process. Fortunately, the prince and his Marine bodyguards had gotten away undetected in the assault ship's shuttles while she died to cover their escape and conceal the secret of Roger's presence aboard her. *Un*fortunately, the only way for the Marines to get Roger home would be to take the spaceport from whoever controlled it and then capture a ship. Possibly in the face of the remaining Cavazan carrier.

It was a tall order, especially for one understrength Marine company, be it ever so elite, shipwrecked on a planet whose brutal climate ate high-tech equipment like candy. The fact that they'd had only a very limited window of time before their essential dietary supplements ran out had only made the order taller. But Bravo Company of the Empress' Own was the force which had hammered fifteen thousand screaming Kranolta barbarians into offal. The force which had smashed every enemy in its path across half the circumference of the planet.

Whether it was turncoat Colonial Guards or a Saint carrier wouldn't matter. The Bronze Barbarians, and His Highness' Imperial Mardukan Guards, were going to hammer them into dust, as well.

Which didn't mean all of the hammers were going to survive.

Armand Pahner chewed a sliver of mildly spicy *bisti* root and watched the prince out of one eye as Kosutic approached. She was probably going to suggest a change in the training program, and he was going to approve it, since it had become abundantly clear that they were never going to make the Marines "real" sailors in the short voyage across the Northern Sea.

They were just about on the last leg of the journey they had begun so many months before, and he couldn't be more pleased. There would be a hard fight at the end. Taking the spaceport and, even more important, a functional ship would take some solid soldiering. But compared to the rest of the journey, it ought to be a picnic.

He chuckled grimly to himself, not for the first time, at how easily and completely a "routine" voyage could go wrong. Assuming they got back to report, this would definitely be one for the security school to study. Murphy's fell presence was obvious everywhere, from the helpless saboteur secreted within the loyal ship's company and driven to her suicidal mission by orders programmed into her toot, to the poor choices of potential emergency diversion planets, to the presence of Saint forces in the supposedly loyal system.

Once they'd reached the planet's actual surface, of course, things had only gone downhill. The sole redeeming quality of the trip was that they had left Earth guarding what was surely the weakest link in the Imperial Family. Now . . . he wasn't. The foppish, useless prince who had left Earth had died somewhere in the steaming jungles of Marduk. The MacClintock warrior who had replaced him had some problems of his own: the most serious of them, a tendency to brood and an even more dangerous tendency to look for answers in the barrel of a gun. But no one could call him a fop anymore. Not to his face, at least. Not and survive.

In a way, looked at with cold logic, the trip had been enormously beneficial, shipwreck, deaths, and all. Eventually, the old prince—unthinking, uncommitted, subject to control or manipulation by the various factions in the Imperial Palace—would probably have caused the deaths of far more than a company of Marines. So the loss of so many of Pahner's Barbarians could almost be counted as a win.

If you looked at it with cold enough logic.

But it was hard to be logical when it was *your* Marines doing the dying.

Kosutic smiled at the company commander. She knew damned well what he was pondering, in general, if not specifically. But it never hurt to ask.

"Penny for your thoughts, Captain."

"I'm not sure what his mother is going to say," the captain replied. It wasn't exactly what he'd been thinking about, but it was part and parcel of his thought process.

"Well, initially, she'll be dealing with disbelief," Kosutic snorted. "Not only that we, and Prince Roger in particular, are alive, but at the change in him. It'll be hard for her to accept. There've been times it seemed the Unholy One Himself was doing the operational planning, but between you and me, the prince is shaping up pretty well."

"True enough," Pahner said softly, then chuckled and changed the subject. "Speaking of shaping up, though, I take it you don't think we can turn Julian into a swabbie?"

"More along the lines of it not being worth the trouble," Kosutic admitted. "Besides, Julian just pointed out that we've gotten awful shabby at close combat work, and I have to agree. I'd like to set the Company to training on that, and maybe some cross-training with the Mardukan infantry."

"Works for me," Pahner agreed. "Despreaux took the Advanced Tactical Assault Course," he added after double-checking with his toot implant. "Make her NCOIC."

"Ah, Julian took it, too," the sergeant major said. Pahner glanced at her, and she shrugged. "It's not official, because he took it 'off the books.' That's why it's not in his official jacket."

"How'd that happen?" Pahner asked. After this long together, he'd thought he knew everything there was to know about the human troops. But there was always another surprise.

"ATAC is taught by contractors," Kosutic pointed out. "When he couldn't get a slot for the school, he took leave and paid his own way."

"Hmmm." Pahner shook his head doubtfully. "I don't know if I can approve using him for an instructor if he didn't take it through approved channels. Which contractor was it?"

"Firecat, LLC. It's the company Sergeant Major Catrone started after he got out."

"Tomcat?" Pahner shook his head again, this time with a laugh. "I can just see him teaching that class. A couple of times in the jungle, it was like I heard his voice echoing in my head. 'You think *this* is hot? Boy, you'd best wait to complain in HELL! And that's where you're gonna be if you don't get your head out of your ass!'"

"When in the Unholy One's Fifth Name did you deal with Sergeant Major Catrone?" Kosutic asked. "He'd been retired for at least a decade when I joined the Raiders."

"He was one of my basic training instructors at Brasilia Base," Pahner admitted. "That man made duralloy look soft. We swore that the way they made ChromSten armor was to have him eat nails for breakfast, then collect it from the latrines, because his anus compressed it so hard the atoms got crushed. If Julian passed the course with Tomcat teaching it, he's okay by me. Decide for yourself who should lead the instruction."

"Okay. Consider it done." Kosutic gave a wave that could almost have been classified as a salute, then turned away and beckoned for the other NCOs to cluster back around her.

Pahner nodded as he watched her sketching a plan on the deck. Training and doctrine might not be all there was to war, but it was damned well half. And—

His head jerked up and he looked towards the *Sea Skimmer* as a crackle of rifle fire broke out, but then he relaxed with a crooked, approving grin. It looked as if the Marines weren't the only ones doing some training.

CHAPTER TWO

Captain Krindi Fain tapped the rifle breech with a leather-wrapped swagger stick.

"Keep that barrel down. You're missing high."

"Sorry, Sir," the recruit said. "I think the roll of the ship is throwing me off." He clutched the breech-loading rifle in his lower set of hands as the more dexterous upper hands opened the mechanism and thumbed in another greased paper cartridge. It was an action he could perform with blinding speed, given the fact that he had four hands, which was why his bright blue leather harness was literally covered in cartridges.

"Better to miss low," the officer said through the sulfurous tang of powder smoke. "Even if you miss the first target, it gives you an aiming point to reference to. And it might hit his buddy."

The shooting was going well, he thought. The rifles were at least hitting *near* the floating barrel. But it needed to be better, because the Carnan Rifles had a tendency to be in the thick of it. Which was a bit of a change from when they had been the Carnan Canal Labor Battalion.

The captain looked out at the seawater stretching beyond sight in every direction and snorted. His native Diaspra had existed under the mostly benevolent rule of a water-worshiping theocracy from time out of mind, but the few priests who'd accompanied the Diaspran infantry to K'Vaern's Cove had first goggled at so much water, then balked at crossing it when the time came. So much of The God had turned out to be a bad thing for worship.

He stepped along to the next firer to watch over the private's shoulder. The captain was tall, even for a Mardukan. Not as tall or as massive as his shadow Erkum Pol, perhaps, but still tall enough to see over the shoulder of the private as the wind swept the huge powder bloom aside.

"Low and to the left, Sardon. I think you've got the aim right; it's the motion of the ship that's throwing you off. More practice."

"Yes, Sir," the private said, and grunted a chuckle. "We're going to kill that barrel sooner or later," he promised, then spat out a bit of *bisti* root and started reloading.

Fain glanced towards the back of the ship—the "stern" as the sailors insisted it be called. Major Bes, the infantry commander of the Carnan Battalion—"The *Basik*'s Own," as it was sometimes called, although any resemblance between the human prince it served and the harmless, cowardly herbivorous *basik* was purely superficial— was talking with one of the human privates assigned to the ship. The three humans were "liaisons" and maintained communications via their Terran systems. But unlike most of the few remaining humans, these were still uncomfortable around Mardukans, and the team leader seemed particularly upset about the quality of the food. Which just went to show that humans must be utterly spoiled. The food which had been available since joining the army was one of the high points for most of the Mardukans.

"I like the food," Erkum rumbled discontentedly behind him. "The human should keep his opinions to himself."

"Perhaps." Fain shrugged. "But the humans are our employers and leaders. We've learned from them, and they were the saviors of our home. I'll put up with one of them being less than perfect."

There was more to it than that, of course. Fain wasn't terribly introspective, but he'd had to think long and hard before embarking on this journey. The human prince had called for volunteers from among the Diaspran infantry after the Battle of Sindi. He'd warned them that he could promise little—that they would be paid a stipend and see new lands, but that that was, for all practical purposes, it.

The choice had seemed clear cut to most of the Diasprans. They liked the humans, and their prince perhaps most of all, but things were happening at home. The almost simultaneous arrival of the Boman hordes and the humans had broken the city out of its millennia-old stasis. New industries were being built every day, and there were fortunes to be made.

As a veteran officer of the Sindi campaign, Fain was bulging with loot to invest, and his family had already found a good opportunity, a foundry that was being built on the extended family's land. A tiny bit of capital could see a handsome return. In fact, he could probably have retired on the income.

Yet he'd found himself looking to the west. He hadn't known what was calling to him at the time. Indeed, he hadn't even begun to understand until days after he'd volunteered for the expedition. But some siren song had been pulling him into the train of the humans, and he'd found the answer in an offhand comment from one of those same humans. Fain had made a pronouncement about the status of "his" company, and Sergeant Julian had cocked his head at him and smiled. "You've got it bad," the NCO had said.

And that was when Fain had realized he'd been bitten by the command bug.

The command bug was one of the most pernicious drugs known to any sentient race. To command in battle was both the greatest and most horrible activity in which any adult could participate. Any good commander felt each death as if it were his own. To him, his men were his children, and holding one of his troops while he died was like holding a brother. But to command well was to know that whatever casualties he'd taken, more lives would have been lost under an inferior commander. And Fain had commanded well.

Handed a company out of the gray sky, he'd taken them into the most complicated environment possible—as outnumbered skirmishers on the flank of a large force—and managed to perform his duty magnificently. He'd lost troops, people he'd known for months and even years. But he'd also been in a few other battles, both before and since, and he'd known that many more of those people would have died under the commander he'd replaced. He'd kept his head, been innovative, and known when and how to cut his losses.

So when the choice came, to give up command and return to a life of business and luxury, or to take a command into the unknown, following an alien leader, he'd taken only a moment to decide. He'd sent most of his accumulated funds, the traded loot of four major and minor battles, to his family for investment, raised a true-hand, and sworn his allegiance to Prince Roger MacClintock and the Empire of Man.

And, to no one's amazement (except, perhaps his own), most of his company had followed him. They'd follow him to Hell.

Most of his troops were aboard the *Ima Hooker* with Sergeant Knever, but there was also a small detachment here on *Sea Skimmer*, and today was one of its twice-weekly riflery drills.

Fain made it a point to supervise those drills in person, because he'd learned the hard way that good marksmanship was an important factor in the sort of warfare the humans taught. The Carnan Rifles' entire battalion had gradually segued into a rifle skirmisher force, following the lead of its most famous captain, and with skirmishers, excellent marksmanship was paramount. They were supposed to get out in front of conventional forces and snipe the leaders of approaching formations. They had to be able to hit something smaller than the broad side of a temple to do that job, and the Carnan Rifles were proving they could do just that.

Well, most of them.

Then there was Erkum.

At almost four meters in height, the big Mardukan dwarfed even his captain. Mardukans generally ran to three meters or so, from their broad, bare feet to their curved double horns, so Erkum was a giant even for them. And, except mentally, he wasn't slow, either, despite his size. Fain had seen him catch spears in flight and outrun *civan* for short bursts.

But he couldn't hit a *pagathar* with a rifle at ten paces. If it was headed straight for him.

At a walk.

Erkum had attached himself to the captain before that particular weakness became apparent. Before, in fact, Fain had been anything but a junior pike NCO. But everything seemed to have worked out. Erkum protected the captain's back, and that wasn't long-range work. As long as Fain's enemies came within five meters or so, the hulking private could usually hit them. And even if he hit them only with the butt of his weapon, they tended to stay down. More than that, he had acquired what was probably the perfect tool for his chosen spot.

The weapon was more cannon than gun. It was the brainchild of the same inventor who'd come up with the standard Mardukan rifle, and it used metallic cartridges similar to the ones developed for the bolt action rifles that had replaced the Marines' bead rifles as their sophisticated ammunition ran out. But its barrel diameter was nearly three times that of the standard rifles, and it fired "semi-automatically." A barlike magazine protruded vertically from the top of the weapon. It held seven short, stubby cartridges, each as long as a Mardukan hand, and as each round was fired, the bar slid downward to expose the next cartridge to the firing mechanism and hammer. The weight of the dropping "magazine" both cocked the weapon and brought the next round into position.

It had been originally intended as a quick-firing swivel gun to mount on the schooners' bulwarks as an anti-sea monster defense, but in the end, it had been replaced for that function by the pintle-mounted harpoon cannons. As part of its original design concept, however, it had been designed to fire either buckshot or conical slugs, and Erkum carried a pair of reloads for each ammunition type on his person at all times.

The breech-bar reloads were a meter long by themselves, and could be lifted by a human only with difficulty. Erkum, on the other hand, reloaded one-handed, and fired the rounds as fast as he could pull the trigger. Of course, being near his line of fire was rather unhealthy. But it was a decent weapon for a combat-environment bodyguard. Even one who couldn't hit a mountain if it was falling on him.

Unfortunately, he had the damnedest time admitting his lack of marksmanship.

"These youngsters, they don't know how to hit nothing," the big

Mardukan growled. If he were a season older than most of the recruits and privates, Fain would have been astonished.

"It's okay, Erkum," the captain said, knowing what was coming. "Really. They're doing fine."

"They need to be showed how to really shoot," Erkum rumbled, taking the semiportable cannon off his back.

"You don't have to do this," Fain muttered. But although Erkum was easy to control in most areas, he was inordinately proud of his lack of skill with the damned gun.

"None of you *biset* could hit the side of a temple!" he yelled to the riflemen lining the rail. "I will now show you how it is done!"

The gun had a double shoulder rest with a lower support/stock that rested on the hips. It was held and "gross" aimed with the lower false-hands and "fine" aimed with the upper true-hands. Now the private shouldered the weapon, dropped in one of the magazine bars, and opened fire.

The gun really was a small cannon, and emitted the smoke level of one. But even with the smoke, the slow-moving shot could be tracked visually as it lofted through the air and fell beyond the barrel. The private wasn't able to use that information to adjust, however, because he'd already triggered two more bruising, smoke-spewing blasts from the weapon during its time of flight.

Fain coughed on the stinking cloud of smoke and tried not to laugh. Judging by the splashes, the rounds were falling all around the barrel and even tracking far enough off to be a hazard to the longboat that had dropped the target. None of them, however, were coming within a reasonable distance of the barrel itself.

He glanced over his shoulder at a semi-sensed movement, then clapped his lower hands as one of the humans surreptitiously hefted her own bead rifle and cracked off a single, irreplaceable round.

The hypervelocity bead was impossible to see, and the sound of the single shot was buried under the ongoing blasts from Erkum's cannon. The effect, however, was easy to discern as the barrel shattered into a thousand pieces.

"Hah!" Erkum grunted as he threw the gun over his back once more in satisfaction. "And they say I can't shoot."

He snorted magnificently, picked up the expended magazine, and slid it into one of the holders on his harness.

Fain shook his head in a gesture copied from the humans, and clapped his lower hands.

"No question," he agreed. "You're getting better."

"Me and my gun, we'll protect you, Krindi." Erkum rubbed a horn and shook his own head. "Did you see how it just exploded? I can't wait to get to use it for real."

Krindi looked to the stern of the ship and smiled as the human lifted her visor and gave a sardonic salute. And because the Mardukan was looking in that direction, he was one of the few to see the ocean open up behind the ship.

The opening was at least twenty meters across, a yawning cavern in the abruptly surfacing snout of a piscine easily as long as *Sea Skimmer* herself. The giant predator was an ambush hunter, like the terrestrial stonefish, and the snap-opening of its tooth-filled maw created a low-level vacuum that literally stopped the ship in her tracks.

Then the schooner dropped.

There were screams, human and Mardukan, throughout the ship as it first stopped dead in the water, then dropped backwards to scrape its copper-sheathed hull across the beast's lower teeth. And there were more screams as the maw snapped shut. The jaws shattered the ship, cutting it nearly in half, and pulling the mainmast over backwards as they clamped down on the stays.

Krindi bit down his own scream as the schooner staggered backwards and he saw the human sergeant and Major Bes tumble off the stern of the ship and down the creature's gullet. There was nothing wrong with his reflexes, however, and his left true-hand lashed out and grasped a line just before the beast bit down.

Erkum bellowed in rage as the impact of the thing's jaws on the deck flipped them both into the air like toys. Instead of grabbing a rope, though, the big private was clawing at his cannon even as he roared his fury, and then everything came back down and the beast pulled back with a twist of its massive head that reduced the already shattered transom to splinters.

What remained of the truncated ship started to settle by the stern, the deck sloping precariously down to the water, masts shattered and over the side. Anyone who hadn't already grabbed a rope was left to scramble for lines as they slid towards the frothing green water, and Krindi cursed and grabbed his own flailing cable with a stronger false-hand. He heard screams and cries from below decks, and knew that any of his detachment he hadn't lost in the first tremendous bite were probably doomed. But for the moment, all he could think about was whether or not he, personally, would survive.

He snatched at Erkum as the still-cursing private slid past. Somehow, Pol had gotten his gun back off of his back, and now he was trying to fit a magazine into place. What he thought he was going to do with it was more than Fain could have said, but the captain wasn't about to let him die just because he was being an idiot.

Krindi glanced at the water and hissed in anger as he saw the shadow of the beast, surrounded by a pool of red, whip around and come back. Apparently, the first taste hadn't been good enough, and it wanted the rest of the ship.

Unfortunately, there wasn't much the Diasprans could do about that.

Roger had been leaning on the ship's rail, looking at nothing in particular, when the beast surfaced. It wasn't in his direct line of sight, but movement draws the human eye, and as the company had found out, a combination of natural genetics and engineering had left Roger with reactions that were preternaturally quick. Which let him get his head around in time to watch the giant fish eat half the ship and a good bit of one of his better battalions.

The thing submerged after half a moment, swirling off to the ship's port side, its massive gills opening and closing. The gills obviously doubled as strainers, and the water went crimson behind it as it pulsed out a trail of shattered wood and blood. It nosed around to the stern and picked off a few of the flailing Mardukans on the surface by sucking them under with comparatively delicate inhalations. Then it dove once more, apparently lining up for another run at the beleaguered ship.

The sight was enough to give anyone pause, but Roger and most of the surviving Marines were still alive because they'd proven they were the fastest, luckiest, and—above all—deadliest of an already elite group. Shock no longer noticeably slowed them.

The prince heard commands from behind him—crisp and clear over the company net from Pahner, slightly louder and more shrill from the surprised Mardukan officers. But that was for others. In his case, there was only one action that made sense. He reached over his shoulder for his own rifle.

That weapon went everywhere with him, even aboard *Hooker*. It was an anachronism, a "smoke pole," as the Marines had derided it when they first landed. They'd thought he hadn't heard the sniggers and comments. The antique weapon of a spoiled rich boy. A "big game hunter" who'd never faced a real threat in his life.

Most of the bodyguards hadn't been with him for very long at that point. Guarding the original, patented, spoiled-rotten Prince Roger had been a rotating assignment for the Bronze Battalion's personnel. It had also been the equivalent of Purgatory, and anyone who'd been able to avoid it had done so . . . with alacrity. Which meant that very few of his current crop of babysitters had realized that he habitually shucked his bodyguards whenever he hunted. Or that many of the *things* he had hunted over the years would have made their blood run cold. The four-meter-long, gold-threaded Arcturian hypertiger in his trophy room was not a gift . . . and it had been taken with that same "smoke pole."

The Marines used hypervelocity bead guns, which were good weapons for killing people and overcoming conventional body armor. But the prince's rifle was for killing *animals,* and big animals, at that. When they'd first landed, the Marines had assumed the major threats would be the hostile natives, and so it had turned out. But they'd discovered that the wildlife was no picnic, either. And that was where the prince, and his "pocking leetle rifle," as Poertena had christened it, came in. There was no question in anyone's mind that the casualties due to wildlife, especially an ugly creature called the damnbeast, had been at least halved by the prince and his pocking rifle.

And now, once again, he proved why.

The prince had the old-fashioned, dual-action rifle off his shoulder, with a round chambered, and aimed faster than most people could draw and fire a bead pistol. The beast had submerged even more quickly, though. It was no more than a green-gray shadow in the aquamarine water, and he weighed his options as he watched it over his sights. He could see it coming around for another run, and he considered shooting through the waves. He'd made shallow-water shots often enough on the trek upcountry, and the relatively low velocity bullets of the rifle would penetrate where the hypervelocity beads shattered on the surface or skipped off. But the bullets also lost most of their energy in the first meter or so. Unless the creature was right at the surface, and basically raising a water-foot, shooting it submerged would be pointless.

Even as he considered that, another part of his brain was pondering shot placement. The fish was huge, with a body nearly as long as one of the schooners and a head twice as wide. In fact, it looked somewhat like one of the fish that was a staple in K'Vaern's Cove, their port of embarkation. If it really was something like a giant *coll*, then shot placement was going to be a bitch.

Coll were traditionally served whole, since there was a "pearl" that formed at the rear of the skull and collecting it was part of the ritual of the meal. Because of that, and because he'd been to more dinners in K'Vaern's Cove then he cared to count, he had a fair idea of the fish's anatomy. The opalescent jewel was of varying quality, but it rested directly above the spot where the fish's spinal cord connected to its skull. Given the angle from which Roger would be firing, if he tried for a spinal shot—not impossible for him, even from the moving deck—the round would probably bounce off the ersatz armoring of the pearl. If he tried for a heart shot, however, even he was likely to miss. That organ was deep in the body, and the round would have to travel through several meters of flesh to reach it. But any other body shot would be useless.

The rear of the head would be the best shot, then. The head was wide, and it was bone, but it was also filled with cavities. Rather than being primarily for armoring the brain, it was based upon the mechanics of the huge jaws. If he put the shot right at the rear of the skull, it should penetrate to the brain and "pith" the fish. Given the disparity in size between the bullets and the target, it was the best chance he'd have.

The entire train of thought flashed through his mind in a moment, and he took a breath and timed the roll of the ship as the fish started to surface for another tremendous bite.

Fain suddenly realized that although Erkum sounded incoherent, his actions made perfect sense. The private was not an intellectual, by any means, but he was—in that wonderfully ambiguous human term—"good with his hands." Fain had been in far too many fights for his few years, and he'd long since discovered that Erkum was a good person to have by your side, be it with hands, pipes, or guns. He might not be able to hit the broad side of a temple at any sort of range, but he instinctively acted in ways that kept him alive when it all fell into the pot. He left the thinking to Fain, but when it came to up close and personal mayhem, Erkum was as good as it got.

And he was about to lay down some mayhem. Fain had grabbed one of the feet of the furiously cursing private, preventing him from falling into the water, but Erkum could have cared less. He'd finally gotten a magazine of solid shot lined up, and he was waiting for his turn at the big fish. Fain suspected that the private had known he would be grabbed, trusted his boss to do the right thing, just as Fain trusted him, and now Erkum waited for the thing to surface.

Fain risked a look around and saw that Pol was not the only one planning a probably hopeless defense. A few of the remaining riflemen, those who'd had the presence of mind to grab a line or rail, instead of slipping down the rapidly tilting deck, were already pointing their rifles at the water. But several others were simply holding on for dear life. Couldn't have that.

"Company! Prepare to volley fire!" he called, trying to fumble out his own pistol with the fourth hand that wasn't occupied holding onto ropes or Erkum.

They were only going to get one shot.

CHAPTER THREE

"Move it! We're only going to get one shot!"

Kosutic turned from the harpoon gun crew to watch the Marines fanning out along the starboard rail. The ships hadn't come about, and the shattered schooner, which had been in the lead position, was slowly falling astern. If the harpoon gun didn't get into action quickly, it might not get a shot. Not unless they came around for one, and Pahner would never agree to that. He was trying to get the prince's ship away from that . . . that . . . *thing* as fast as he could.

At least the harpoon gear had been set up, ready, by the gun when all hell broke loose. It was against normal practice to pile charges for the ship's guns on deck. Partly that was because black powder was too dangerous. Sparks or open flame weren't the only things that could set it off; even the friction of grinding a few loose or spilled grains underfoot could do that, under the wrong conditions. But mostly it was because it would have been too easy for the powder to become wet and useless. But this particular weapon had been designed for just this contingency, and the need to get it into action as quickly as possible had dictated ready availability of ammunition. The humans had empty stores containers, plasteel boxes that maintained temperature and humidity, and one of those had been pressed into duty as a standby magazine.

Now the Mardukan gun crew threw back the lid and snatched

out the first cartridge. The charge bag was small, only half a kilo or so of powder. But it would throw the harpoon far enough, and without shattering the hardwood shaft.

As the gunner shoved the charge into the muzzle, the assistant gunner assembled the harpoon. Fitting the steel head to the shaft took only a moment, then the coiled line was attached with a human-designed clip. Last, the plug-based shaft was shoved down the barrel of the cannon, acting as its own ramrod.

But drilled and quick as the gun crew was, all of that took time. Time *Sea Skimmer* didn't have.

Krindi Fain had often wondered if he was going to die. He'd wondered the time a stone wall fell on the crew he was working with. That time, he'd been sheltered by a few sticks of scaffolding, and he'd survived. He'd wondered again, as a private in his first pike battle, by the canals of Diaspra. And he'd wondered repeatedly while fighting the Boman inside and outside of Sindi. But he hadn't *known* he was going to die.

Until now.

The beast opened up its maw, and he grunted in anger as he saw it surging up behind the sinking ship once again. He could see bits of wood and cloth, and red flesh, sticking to the thousands of teeth lining the inside of the fish's mouth. But he still didn't scream. He was frightened. God of Water knew he was! But he was going to go to his God as a soldier and a leader, not a coward.

And so, instead of screaming, he paused for a moment. That brief pause, so necessary for everyone to get fully lined up. And then, he yelled "*Fire!*"

Five of his men were still more or less on their feet, with their wits sufficiently about them to obey his command, but they were almost incidental. The two things that drove the fish off were Erkum and the prince.

The five rifle bullets all impacted on various places in and around the mouth. Two of them even penetrated up into the skull of the fish, but none of them did any vital damage, nor did they particularly "hurt."

Erkum's round, on the other hand, hurt like hell.

The sixty-five-millimeter bullet penetrated the roof of the mouth and traveled upward, blowing a massive tube through the skull of the sea monster. By coincidence—it could have been nothing else, given the quality of the marksman—the huge slug severed the right optical nerve, blinding the fish on that side, and blew out the top of its skull in a welter of gore.

At almost the same moment, the prince's round entered the *back* of the beast's head.

It wasn't the pith shot Roger had been trying for, but the round was much higher velocity than anything the Mardukans had, and it generated a significant "hydrostatic shock" cavity—the region in a body that was damaged by the shock wave of a bullet. In this case, the prince had missed his shot down and slightly to the right, but the region that the shot passed through was directly beneath the spinal cord, and the shock wave slapped against that vital nerve.

The combined result was that instead of slurping down the rest of the *Sea Skimmer*, the fish thrashed away to port and dove. But it did so wildly, uncontrolled. It was half-blind, there was damage to its spinal cord, and half its muscles weren't responding properly.

This food had spines.

"*Pentzikis*, come about to port and engage. *Sea Foam*, come to starboard and engage. *Tor Coll*, prepare depth charges."

Pahner glanced at the prince, who was still tracking the thrashing shadow. He didn't know if Roger had gotten off another impossible shot, or if it was the flurry of blasts from the sinking ship. But whichever it had been, it had at least momentarily dissuaded the fish. Now to put it down.

"Grenadiers to the rigging. Set for delay—I want some penetration on this thing, people," Pahner continued, cutting off a fresh slice of *bisti* root and slipping it into his mouth. The general outline of this fight had been worked out in advance—as well as it could be, at least, when no one had ever actually seen whatever it was that ate ships in this stretch of ocean. Well, never seen it and lived to report it, at any rate. But, as usual, the enemy wasn't playing by the plans. It had been assumed that they'd at least get a glimpse of the beast before it struck, which should have given them at least some chance of driving it off first. Now, all they could do was fight for the remaining six ships and hope to rescue a few of the survivors.

Sea Skimmer was sinking fast by the stern, but she was going down without a list. If they could finish the fish off in a few shots and send in boats, they might save most of those on her deck. The ones below deck were doomed, unless they could fight their way to the main hatch or swim out. It was still a hell of a way to lose a quarter of a battalion, its commander, and probably a damned fine junior officer with them. But there hadn't been many *good* places to die on this damned trek.

He glanced at Roger again, and shook his head. The prince had headed for the shrouds and was trying to get a better vantage point. Give him credit for trying, but Pahner doubted the prince's rifle was going to win this round.

As he thought that, the first harpoon gun boomed.

"I doubt that even *you* can do anything with a pistol, cousin," Honal said with a handclap of grim humor. His cousin, the former crown prince of Therdan, had drawn all four pistols at the first cry and had them trained over the side before the warning's echoes had faded.

"True," Rastar said now, and reholstered three of the percussion revolvers. "But if it comes after us, I'll at least let it know I'm here."

"Best stand clear, whatever else you do," Honal said dryly. "Our fine sailor friends are about to see if a harpoon is better than a pistol!"

"Well, that depends on the harpoon and the pistol," Rastar grunted in laughter. "After all, it's not what you use; it's how you use it!"

"And I intend to use it well!" the chief of the gun crew called. "But if you're in the way of the line as it flies, you'll be a red smear! Clear!"

The gun was fitted with a percussion cap hammer lock. Now the gun captain gave Honal and Rastar a heartbeat to duck to the side, then took a deep breath and yanked the firing lanyard.

The bang wasn't really all that loud, but the smoke cloud covered the entire foredeck, and there was a *whippity-thwhip!* as the coil of hawser at the base of the pintle reeled out. Then there was a cry from the rigging.

"*Target!*"

"Rig the line!" the gun captain bellowed, and the crew warped the five-centimeter hawser around a bollard as the rope began to scream and smoke.

"Prepare to come about on the port tack!" *Pentzikis'* captain shouted.

"Rig the line into the clamps!" the gun crew chief called. "The damn thing is going to go right under the keel! If the captain's not careful, it'll take us right over on our side!"

"Let that line run!" the ship's captain barked. "Come onto it when we're on tack!"

"Haul away!" the gunner cried. "We're getting slack!"

"Hold on!" Rastar shouted. "The *Tor Coll* is about to run across the rope!"

"Contact!" Sergeant Angell called over the company net from *Tor Coll*'s afterdeck. "Sir, we have solid contact."

"Right," Pahner acknowledged, glancing at the formation. "Have your captain keep falling off to port. I want you to take a heading of nearly due south and try to drag this thing off *Sea Skimmer*. *Sea Foam*, take another shot. All units, engage with care. Try to get some rounds on it, but don't hit the other ships."

Hooker's own harpoon gun boomed behind him as the schooner came around to starboard. It wasn't, strictly speaking, proper. The ship with the prince on it should be sailing out of harm's way, not into it. But with the fish pinned, it was probably safe enough.

Tor Coll passed above the thrashing shadow, and a huge white and green waterspout appeared behind the schooner. The depth charges used a combination of a grenade detonator and local blasting powder. Pahner hadn't been sure they would function as intended, but it turned out that they worked just fine. Bilali's very first drop scored a direct hit, and the monster fish flopped a few more times, then drifted gently to the surface, belly-up. Its underside was apparently covered in chromatospores, since it was flickering through a riot of colors when it broke the waves. It rippled a dozen shades of violet, then through the spectrum until it began flickering green, and finally stopped and slowly turned a cream color.

"Get that target longboat alongside *Sea Skimmer*. Launch all the ships' boats, and let's start recovering survivors. Warrant Officer Dobrescu!"

"Yes, Captain?" a calm tenor replied. Pahner glanced over his shoulder, and saw the speaker standing beside the mainmast while he gazed at the floating monster with an air of almost detached contemplation.

Chief Warrant Officer Dobrescu had been one of *DeGlopper*'s shuttle pilots. Flying a shuttle was a relatively safe job, although it hadn't quite worked out that was this time around. But in a previous life, he had been a Raider Commando medic, a person trained not only to stabilize a combat casualty, but to repair one if necessary. His accidental inclusion on the trip had been, literally, a lifesaver. A factor he was sometimes at pains to point out, not to mention complain about.

"I want you to prepare to receive casualties. If there are none, or if they're limited, I'll want your input on our little find here."

"Yes, Sir," the medic replied. "Of course, I'm a shuttle pilot, not a xenobiologist, but it looks like a *coll* fish to me. And that's my professional opinion."

"It's a *coll* fish," Captain T'Sool said. *Ima Hooker*'s captain rubbed his horns, then clapped his hands. "It's impossible, but may the White Lady damn me if it isn't one."

One of the *Hooker*'s sailor's held up a dripping bag in both true-hands. The oil-filled sac was common to the *coll* fish, part of its buoyancy system. But in normal-sized ones, the sac was the size of the last joint of a human thumb and filled with what, to Mardukans, was a deadly poison. As it had turned out, that oil was possibly the only substance on the planet that the Marines' nanites packs could convert into the numerous lipid-based vitamins and amino acids the planet's food lacked.

"Well," Kosutic said. "At least we've got plenty of feed for the *civan*. And that's enough *coll* oil to keep us for quite a while," she added, gazing at an oil sac that was at least a meter across.

"It's still a net zero," Pahner growled. "We lost an entire ship getting it, along with half of its crew, damned near two full companies of infantry, and three more Marines. I don't like losing troops."

"Neither do I," Kosutic agreed. "And this trip says it all. His Putridness' hand has certainly been over us the whole time."

"What just happened?" Eleanora O'Casey asked, as she climbed up through the main hatch to the deck.

The prince's chief of staff was the only remaining "civilian" caught on the planet with him. Although none of the shuttle pilots had been as prepared for the conditions here as the Marines, they'd at least had some background in rough conditions survival and a basic military nanite pack. But prior to the crash landing of the shuttles on the backside of the planet, the chief of staff had never set foot outside a city, and her nanites—such as they were—were designed for a nice, safe, *civilized* environment.

The "adventure" had had some benefits for her. She was in the best shape she'd ever been in her life. But her stomach, never the most robust, had not taken the journey well, and it was taking the voyage aboard ship even worse. Now the short brunette turned her head from side to side, counting masts.

"Aren't we missing one ship?" she asked.

"Not quite yet," Pahner said dryly. "But it won't be long now." He pointed over the side, to where *Sea Skimmer*'s shattered hull was beginning its final plunge. "We've discovered what ate the other expeditions," he added.

O'Casey walked to the side of the gently rocking schooner, and her eyes widened.

"Ooooooh!" she gasped, and quickly ran to the far rail, where she wouldn't get anything on the Mardukans butchering the vast fish.

"Well, I guess she won't be coming to dinner," Kosutic observed with a shake of her head.

* * *

"I guess this stuff gets tougher as it gets older."

Julian bounced the tines of his fork off of the slab of *coll* fish on his plate to emphasize his point.

There'd been no more attacks on the ship, and soundings indicated that the area in which *Sea Skimmer* had been ambushed was a seamount. Dobrescu theorized that a line of such seamounts might be the haunt of the gigantic *coll* fish. If he was right, it might be possible to create an industry to harvest the species, once its habits were better understood. The profit would certainly be worth it, if it didn't involve losing a ship every time.

"It probably does," the medic agreed now. "Not that anyone in K'Vaern's Cove ever saw a *coll* fish this big to give us any sort of meter stick." He rolled the head-sized opalescent pearl back and forth on the table top, and the bright, omnipresent cloud-light of Marduk made it seem to float above the surface.

"On the other hand, this thing seems to be identical to the ones from the smaller fish," he went on, rapping the pearl with a knuckle. "It's a hell of a lot bigger, of course, and it has more layers. There's a bone directly under it that's layered as well, and I'd suspect from the markings that the layers indicate its age. And these things must grow fast as hell, too. If I've figured out how to calculate its age properly, this fish was less than five times as old as the ones we ate in K'Vaern's Cove."

"How can that be?" Roger asked while he sawed at the tough flesh. He wasn't particularly hungry, and the meat was both oily and unpleasantly fishy, unlike the normally dry and "white" *coll* fish. But he'd learned that you just ate. You never knew if there would be worse tomorrow. "This thing was at least a hundred times that size!"

"More like forty or fifty, Your Highness," Despreaux corrected. She and Julian were relatively junior, but both of them had become a regular part of the command conferences. Julian by dint of his background in intelligence, and Despreaux because she kept Roger calm. Of course, her background in communications and tactics helped.

"The layers indicate massive growth spurts," Dobrescu said with a shrug, "but the genetic material is identical. These things could interbreed with the K'Vaern's Cove variety; ergo they're the same species. I suspect that studying their life-history would be difficult. At a guess, they probably breed inshore, or even in freshwater. Then, as they grow, they begin jockeying for territories. If they get the territory of a larger version, they grow very fast to 'fill' the territory." He paused and rolled the pearl again. "I also suspect that if we went back through this area, we wouldn't run into another specimen this large. But there would still be some damned big *coll* fish around."

"And in a few years . . ." Pahner said with a nod. "By the way, Your Highness, nice shot."

"Excuse me?" Roger gave the fish another stab, then gave up. He wasn't the first to do so, by any means.

The heavyset red and black striped beast occupying the entire corner of the compartment knew its cue. Roger had picked the pet up quite by accident at the village of D'Nal Cord many months before. The lizardlike creatures fulfilled the role of dogs among Cord's people, although Roger had seen no sign of any similar species elsewhere on their travels.

Now Dogzard stood up and gave a vertebrae-popping stretch that extended her practically from one end of the compartment to the other. Being the only scavenger in a group that had blasted its way through endless carnivore-infested jungles had been good for the former "runt," and if she ever returned to her village, she would be double the size of any of the ones that had stayed behind.

Now she flipped out her tongue and regarded Roger's plate carefully as he held it towards her. After a brief moment verifying that, yes, this was food and, yes, she was permitted to have it, her head snapped forward in one of its lightning fast strikes, and the chunk of meat disappeared from the plate.

Satisfied that that was all for now, she returned to the corner to await the next meal. Or to fight. Whichever.

"There was a good solid crack on that vertebra," Dobrescu replied for Pahner in response to Roger's question. "One of the reasons, at least, that it didn't come back at that ship was your shot."

Dobrescu flicked his own lump of fish towards the prince's pet.

The chunk of meat never came within a meter of the deck before it disappeared.

"There was also a fist-sized hole through the roof of its mouth," the warrant officer continued, and raised an eyebrow in question as he glanced at the junior Mardukan at the foot of the table.

Fain was desperately trying to figure out the tableware. He'd tried watching Honal, Rastar, Chim Pri, and Cord, but that wasn't much help. The Mardukan officers had never quite mastered the knife and fork, either, and Roger's *asi*—technically, a slave, although Fain rather doubted that anyone would ever make the mistake of treating D'Nal Cord as anyone's menial—refused to use them at all.

In Cord's case, at least, Fain suspected, the refusal was mostly a pose. The old Mardukan shaman took considerable pains to maintain his identity as a primitive tribesman, but it was obvious to the Diaspran that the *asi*'s knowledge—and brain—were more than a match for any Water Priest he'd ever met. In the others' case, the captain was less certain. Honal had hacked off a chunk of the rubbery meat and was gnawing on it, while Rastar and Pri had lifted slightly larger chunks and were doing much the same. The human ability to hold the meat down with a fork and cut off small pieces was apparently beyond them.

Now, trapped by the medic's implied question, Krindi cleared his throat and nodded in a human gesture many of the mercenaries had picked up.

"That would be Erkum," he said. "At least one shot, perhaps more. It was very . . . confused on board, of course."

"Not so confused that you lost your head," Pahner noted, and took a sip of water. "You had everyone with a weapon fire a volley. I doubt most of the Marines would have kept control of their units that well."

"Thank you, Sir." Fain rubbed a horn. "But from what I've seen, I will politely disagree. Certainly, you and Prince Roger kept control of yours."

"No, I didn't," Roger said. He reached for the pitcher of water and poured himself another glass. "I should have been giving orders, not shooting myself. But I got angry. Those were good troops."

"Hmmm." Kosutic frowned. "I don't know, Your Highness. Let the cobbler stick to his last, as it were." The slight frown became a smile. "I have to admit that having you with a weapon in your hand never seems to be a *bad* idea."

Pahner smiled at the chuckles around the table, then nodded.

"Whether His Highness should've been shooting or ordering, we need to find a berth for Captain Fain. The infantry side was already short, so I'm just going to consolidate your personnel into a combined company. We lost Turkol Bes on the *Sea Skimmer* along with your boys, so we need a replacement for Captain Yair, who will be promoted to major and take Bes' place. Initially, I'm going to attach you to His Highness as a sort of aide-de-camp. The bulk of your company's survivors are already aboard the *Hooker*. We'll work them into the rest of her detachment, and giving you a little experience with the 'staff' will give you a chance to see how things run. Hopefully, we'll have you fully on board by the time we land. Clear?"

"Yes, Sir." Fain kept his face placid, but seeing "his" company lose its identity was not pleasant, however necessary its survivors' absorption might be. "One question . . ."

"Yes, you can hang onto Pol," Roger said with a very Mardukan grunt of laughter.

"Please do," Captain—no, Major—Yair endorsed. "You're the only one who can handle him."

"We don't know how many more of these things there might be," Pahner continued in a "that's settled" tone of voice, and gestured at the pearl Dobrescu was still fondling. "Or any damned thing else about threats along the way. But we've found out we can kill them, at least. Any suggestions about how to keep them from doing this again?"

"Mount a cannon at the rear. Maybe a couple," Fain said without thinking, then stopped when everyone looked at him.

"Go on," Roger said, nodding. "Although I think I know where you're going."

"Keep them loaded," Fain continued. "Ready to fire, with a crew to man them at all times. When it surfaces, fire. You have about a second and a half from when they appear to when you have to shoot."

"You'd have to have somebody being very vigilant on a continuous basis." Julian shook his head. "Then you'd have to make sure the powder didn't get wet and misfire. I don't think we have the technical capability to do that without modifications we'd need a shipyard to carry out."

"But a defense at the rear . . ." Roger rubbed a fingertip on the table, obviously intrigued by the notion. Then a sudden, wicked grin lit his somber face like a rising sun. "Who says it has to be a *local* cannon?" he demanded.

"Ouch!" Kosutic laughed. "You've got an evil mind, Your Highness."

"Of course!" Julian's eyes gleamed with enthusiasm. "Set up a plasma cannon on manjack mode. If something disturbs the sensor area: Blam!"

"Bead," Pahner corrected. Julian looked at him, and the captain waggled one hand palm-down above the table. "Those things get too close for a plasma cannon. We'd torch the ship."

"Yeah, you're right." Julian nodded. "I'll get it set up," he said, then wiped his mouth and looked unenthusiastically down at the chunk of meat still sitting on his plate. "You want me to break out some ration packs?" he asked in a decidedly hopeful voice.

"No." Pahner shook his head. "We need to eat what we've got. Until we know how long this journey is going to be, we still need to conserve our off-world supplies." He paused and took a breath. "And we also need to shut down the radios. We're getting close enough to the ports that we have to worry about radio bounce. They're low-intercept, but if the port has any notion that we're here, we're in the deep."

"So how do we communicate between the ships, Sir?" Despreaux asked. The sergeant had been particularly quiet all evening, but she was one of the two NCOs in charge of maintaining communications. With Julian setting up the weapons, it was her job to plan a jury-rigged replacement com net for the flotilla's units.

"Com lasers, flags, guns, flashing lights," Pahner said. "I don't care. But no radios."

"Yes, Sir," Despreaux said, making a note on her toot. "So we can use our tac-lights, for example?"

"Yes." Pahner paused again and slipped in a strip of *bisti* root while he thought. "In addition, the sailors in K'Vaern's Cove reported that piracy is not an unknown thing on Marduk. Now, why am I not surprised?"

Most of the group chuckled again. Practically every step of the journey had been contested by local warlords, barbarians, or bandits. It would have been a massive shock to their systems if it turned out these waters were any different.

"When we approach the far continent, we'll need to keep a sharp lookout for encroaching ships," Pahner continued. "And for these fish. And for anything else that doesn't look right."

"And His Dark Majesty only knows what's going to come next," Kosutic agreed with a smile.

CHAPTER FOUR

"Land ho!"

The lookout's cry rang out only two days after the attack by the giant *coll*. No one was really surprised by it, though. The evidence of an approaching landfall had been there for at least a day—a thin gray smoke on the horizon, and a golden alpenglow before dawn.

Julian swarmed up the ratlines to *Hooker*'s fore topmast crosstrees with an agility which might have seemed at odds with his determinedly antiseaman attitude. He took his glasses with him. They were considerably better than his helmet visor's built-in zoom function, and he spent several minutes beside the Mardukan seaman already perched there, studying the distant land. Then he zoomed the glasses back in and slid back down to the deck.

"Active volcano, sure enough," he reported to Pahner. "The island looks deserted, but there's another in the chain just coming over the horizon."

Pahner consulted his toot and nodded. "It doesn't appear on the map," he said, "but at this resolution, it wouldn't."

"But there *is* a line of mountains on the eastern verge of the continent," Roger pointed out, projecting a hologram from his pad. He pointed at the light-sculpture mountains for emphasis. "They could be volcanic in nature. Which would *probably* make this a southern extension of that chain."

"Hullo, the deck!" the lookout still at the crosstrees called. "'Nother to the south! We're sailing between them."

None of the islands were visible from deck-level, yet, but Captain T'Sool, more accustomed to the shallow, relatively confined waters of the K'Vaernian Sea than the endless expanse of the open ocean, looked nervous.

"I'm not sure I like this," he said. "We could hit shoals anytime."

"Possibly," Roger conceded, with a glance at the azure water over the side. "It's more likely that we're still over a subduction trench or the deep water around one. Water tends to be deep right up to the edge of volcanic formations. I'm glad to see our first landfall be volcanoes, actually. You might want to slow the flotilla and get some depth lines working, though."

"What are these 'volcanoes' you keep speaking of?" T'Sool asked. Roger checked his toot and realized that it had used the Terran word because there was no local equivalent.

"Have you ever heard of smoking mountains?" he asked.

"No," the seaman said dubiously.

"Well, you're in for a treat."

"Why does smoke come from the mountain?" Fain asked in awe.

The flotilla had slowed as it approached the chain, and now it proceeded cautiously between two of the islands. The one to the south was wreathed in thick, leafy, emerald-green foliage that made it look like a verdant paradise. Of course, as the Marines had learned the hard way, it was more likely to be a verdant hell, Mardukan jungles being what they were.

The island to the north, however, was simply a black hunk of basalt, rising out of the blue waters. Its stark, uncompromising lines made it look bigger than it actually was, and the top—the only portion formed into anything resembling a traditional cone—trailed a gentle plume of ash and steam.

"I could tell you," Julian replied with a grimace. "But you'd have to believe me rather than your religion."

Fain thought about that. So far, he'd found nothing that directly contradicted the doctrines of the Lord of Water. On the other hand, the dozens of belief systems he and the other infantry had encountered since leaving Diaspra had already indicated to him that the gospel of the priests of Water was not, perhaps, fundamentally correct. While there was no question that the priests understood the science of hydraulics, it might be that their overall understanding of the world was less precise.

"Go ahead," he said with a handclap of resignation. Then he chuckled. "Do your worst!"

Julian smiled in response and gestured at the vast expanse of water stretched out around the flotilla.

"The first thing you have to accept is that the priests' description of the world as a rock floating in eternal, endless waters isn't correct."

"Since we're intending to sail to the far side, I'd already come to the conclusion that 'endless water' might not be exactly accurate," Fain admitted with another handclap.

"What the world really is, is a ball floating in nothingness," Julian said, and raised both hands as Fain started to protest. "I know. How is that possible? Well, you're going to have to trust me for now, and check it out later. But what matters right now is that the center of the ball—the world—is very, very hot. Hot enough to melt rock. And it stays that way."

"That I have a hard time with," Fain said, shaking his head. "Why is it hot? And if it is, when will it cool?"

"It's hot because there's . . . stuff in there that's something like what makes our plasma cannon work," Julian said, waving his hands with a sort of vague frustration as he looked for an explanation capable of crossing the technological gulf yawning between his worldview and Fain's. "Like I said," he said finally. "You'll just have to trust me on some of this. But it is—hot, I mean—and somewhere under that mountain, there's a channel that connects to that hot part. That's why it smokes. Think of it as a really, really big chimney. As for when the inside of the world will cool, that won't happen for longer than I can explain. There will no longer be humans—or Mardukans— when it starts to cool."

"This is too strange," Fain said. "And how do I explain it to my soldiers? 'It's that way because Sergeant Julian said so'?"

"I dunno," Julian replied. "Maybe the sergeant major can help you out. On the other hand . . ."

Roger watched Bebi's team begin the entry. The team had already worked on open area techniques. Now they were working on closed . . . and they looked like total dorks.

There was nowhere to create a real shooting environment on the flotilla's ships, so the troopers were using the virtual reality software built into their helmet combat systems and their toots. The "shoot house" was nothing more than the open deck of a schooner, but with the advanced systems and the toots' ability to massage sensory input, it would be as authentic to the participants as if there were real enemies.

But since their audience could see that they were standing on nothing more than an unobstructed stretch of deck planks, the "entry team" looked like a group of warrior-mimes.

The virtual reality software built into the troops' helmets would have been a potent training device all by itself, and its ability to interface with the Marines' toots was sufficient to make the illusion perfect. Now Macek smoothed thin air as he emplaced a "breaching charge" on the fictitious door he could both "see" and "feel" with total fidelity, then stepped to the side and back. As far as he could tell, he was squatting, nearly in contact with a wall; to everyone else, he looked as if he were getting ready to go to the bathroom on the deck.

The sergeant major next to Roger snorted softly.

"You know, Your Highness, when you're doing this, one part of you knows how stupid you look. But if you don't ignore it, you're screwed. I think this is one of His Wickedness' little jokes on Marines."

Roger smoothed his ponytail and opened his mouth to say something, then closed it.

"Yes, Your Highness?" Kosutic said softly. "I take it there's something about that statement that bothers you?"

"Not about your observation," Roger said as Bebi triggered the notional charge and rushed through the resulting imaginary hole.

The prince had set his helmet to project the "shoot house" in see-through mode, and the team seemed to be fighting phantoms in a ghost building as he watched. Combined with his question, the . . . otherworldly nature of their opponents sent something very much like a shiver down his spine.

"It was that last comment," he said. "I've been wondering. . . . Why is Satanism the primary religion of Armagh? I mean, a planet settled by Irish and other Roman Catholic groups. That seems a bit . . . strange," he finished, and the sergeant major let out a chuckle that turned into a liquid laugh Roger had never heard from her before.

"Oh, Satan, is that all? The reason is because the winners write the history books, Your Highness."

"That doesn't explain things," Roger protested, pulling at a strand of hair. "You're a High Priestess, right? That would be the equivalent of—an Episcopal bishop, I guess."

"Oh, not a *bishop!*" Kosutic laughed again. "Not one of those evil creatures! Angels of the Heavens, they are!" Roger felt his eyes trying to cross, and she smiled at his expression and took pity on him.

"Okay, if you insist, Your Highness, here's the deal.

"Armagh was a slow-boat colony, as you know. The original colonists were primarily from Ireland, on Old Earth, with a smattering from the Balkans. Now, Ireland had a bloody history long before Christianity, but the whole Protestant/Catholic thing eventually got out of hand."

"We studied the nuking of Belfast at the Academy as an example of internal terrorism taken to a specific high," Roger agreed.

"Yes, and what was so screwed up about those Constables was that they killed as many—or more—of their own supporters as they did Catholics." She shrugged. "Religious wars are . . . bad. But Armagh was arguably worse, even in comparison to the Belfast Bomb.

"The original colonists were Eire who wanted to escape the religious bickering that was still going on in Ireland but keep their religion. They didn't want freedom from *religion,* only freedom from *argument* about it. So they took only Catholics.

"Shortly after landing, though, there was an attempted religious schism. It was still, at that time, a purely Catholic colony, and the schismatic movement was more on the order of fundamentalism rather than any sort of outright heresy. The schismatics wanted the mass in Latin, that sort of thing. But that, of course, threatened to start the arguments all over. So, as a result, to prevent religious warfare from breaking out again, they instituted a local version of the Papal College for the express purpose of defining what was religiously acceptable."

"Oh, shit," Roger said quietly. "That's . . . a bad idea. Hadn't any of them studied history?"

"Yes," she said sadly, "they had. But they also thought they could do things 'right' this time. The Inquisition, the Great Jihad of the early twenty-first century, the Fellowship Extinction, and all the rest of the Jihads, Crusades, and Likuds were beside the point. The worst of it was that those who founded the Tellers were good people. Misguided, but good. The road to Heaven is paved with good intentions, after all. Like most ardent believers, they thought God would make sure *they* got it right. That their cause was just, and that the other people who'd screwed up exactly the same idea before them had suffered—unlike them—from some fundamental flaw in their vision or approach."

"Rather than from just being human." Roger shook his head. "It's like the redistributionists that don't see the Ardane Deconstruction as being 'what will happen.'"

"The one thing you learn from history, Your Highness, is that we're doomed to repeat it. Anyway, where was I?"

"They set up an Inquisition."

"Well, that wasn't what they'd intended to set up, but, yes. That was what they got." Kosutic shrugged grimly. "It was bad. That sort of thing attracts . . . bad sorts. Not so much sociopaths—although it does attract them—but also people who are so sure of their own rectitude that they can't see that evil is evil."

"But you're a Satanist. You keep referring to 'His Wickedness,' so why does the concept of evil bother you?" Roger asked, his tone honestly perplexed, and Kosutic shrugged again.

"At first the organized opposition to the College was purely secular. The Resistance actually had a clause in its manifesto calling for an end to all religion, always. But the planet was too steeped in religious thought for that to work, and the Tellers, the Determiners of Truth, insisted on referring to anyone in the Resistance as 'minions of Satan.'"

"So instead of trying to fight the label, you embraced it for yourselves."

"And changed it," Kosutic agreed. "We won eventually, and part of the peace settlement was a freedom of religion clause in the Constitution. But by that time, the Satanists were the majority religion, and Christianity—or, at least, Armagh's version of it—had completely discredited itself. There's a really ancient saw that says that if Satan ever replaced God, he'd have to act the same. And to be a religion for the good of all, which was what we'd intended from the outset, we had to *be* good. The difference between Armaghan Satanism and Catholicism is a rejection of the supremacy of the Pope, a few bells and whistles we stole from Wicca, and referring to Satan instead of the Trinity. It really *is* Episcopalianism, for Satanists, which makes your bishop comparison even more humorous."

She'd been watching the training entry team as she spoke, and now she grimaced as Bebi flinched. The exercise was simple, "baby steps" designed to get the Marines back into the close-combat mode of thinking. But despite that, the team hadn't taken the simple security precaution of checking all corners of the room for threats, and the "enemy" hiding behind a pillar had just taken out the team leader.

"It's the little things in life," she muttered.

"Yep," Roger agreed. "They don't seem to be doing all that well."

He watched as Macek "responded" to the threat by uncovering his own area. At which point another hidden enemy took advantage of the lack of security to take out Berent. Kosutic's nostrils flared, and Roger grinned mentally as he pictured the blistering critique of the exercise she was undoubtedly compiling. But the sergeant major was one of those people for whom multitasking came naturally, and she resumed her explanation even as she watched Berent become a casualty.

"One of the big differences between the Church of Rome and

Armaghan Satanism is our emphasis on the Final Conflict and the preparations for it," she continued, her expression now deadly serious. "We believe that the Christians are dupes, that if God was really in charge, things would be better. It's our belief that Lucifer was cast out not by God, but by the other angels, and that they have silenced The One True God. It's our job, in the Final Conflict, to uphold the forces of good and win this time."

She turned to face the prince fully, and smiled at his widened eyes. It was not an especially winsome expression.

"We take that belief very seriously, Your Highness. There's a reason that Armagh, a low-population planet, supplies three percent of all the Imperial Marines, and somewhere around ten percent of all the elite forces. The Precepts of the Elders call for all good Satanists to be ready for the Final Conflict at all times. To uphold good in all their doings, and to be morally upright so that when the time comes to free God from the Chains of the Angels, we won't be found wanting."

She turned back to watch the training and shook her head.

"I mention this only to note that the Brotherhood of Baal would eat Bebi's team for lunch. The Brotherhood has used the Imperial freedom of religion clause to perform some tinkering on themselves that gives most of the rest of us Satanists cold chills. I doubt that any court would consider an abbott of Baal human if he or she didn't have documents to prove it. But you have to see them to believe it."

Roger watched as Bebi collected his "dead" and "wounded" and started the debrief.

"I imagine that Christians are . . . somewhat ambivalent about that approach."

"We don't preach," Kosutic said. "We don't proselytize. We certainly don't discuss our beliefs around the general public. And, frankly, we believe that as long as Christians and Jews and Muslims are being 'good,' they're violating the intent of their controllers. So we applaud them for it." She turned and gave him a truly evil smile. "It really confuses them."

Roger chuckled and shook his head as Despreaux began enumerating the team's faults. The plan had been good, but when they'd hit the door, they'd forgotten it and fought by the seat of their pants. They had, in fact, been fighting the way they would have fought Mardukans. But the next major conflict would probably put Bravo Company—what was left of it—up against humans. True, those humans would probably be pirate scum and garrison troopers, but standard colonial defenses called for space-intercept capable plasma cannon, monomolecular "twist" wire, and bunkers with interlocking fields of fire. And then they had to capture a ship.

It wasn't going to be a walk in the park.

"Well," Roger said with a sigh. "I just hope whoever the 'good guys' are, they're on our side."

Captain Pahner looked around the cramped cabin. The one fault of *Ima Hooker*'s design, which no one had considered in advance, was that the schooner had never been intended as a command ship. Poertena had recognized the necessity of designing around higher deckheads to allow more head room for the towering Mardukans of her crew. There was a limit to what he could do, but the final result— however claustrophobic the natives might still find it—was that even the tallest of the humans could stand upright without worrying about hitting his head on a deck beam. But however the ship might have been stretched vertically, there was only so much that could be done horizontally in a hull of *Hooker*'s length and beam. Despite the fact that Pahner, or Prince Roger, rather, had a minimal "staff," its members packed into the wardroom of the command schooner only with difficulty. Especially the Mardukans.

And that was before adding Roger's pet. Or his *asi* "bodyguard."

"All right," Pahner said with a grim smile. "We need to keep this meeting short, if for no other reason than so that Rastar can unbend his neck."

He looked over at Rastar Komas Ta'Norton, who stood hunched forward with his horns banging on the ceiling. The former prince of the Northern League wasn't large for a Mardukan, but he still towered over the humans.

"How're the *civan* doing?" the captain continued.

"As well as could be expected," the Northerner said with a shrug. The ostrichlike, omnivorous cavalry mounts were actually related to the vastly larger packbeasts, so they had leathery skin and were more capable of handling desiccation than the slime coated, amphibian-derived Mardukans. But they still weren't well-suited to a lengthy sea voyage. "They fit into these toys as well as we do, and they never had to deal with the pitching and rocking before. At least they have more head room aboard *Snarleyow* than we do here, and that outsized *coll* fish has stretched their feed supply nicely, but they aren't happy. We haven't lost any, yet, but we need to get to land soon."

"According to our map, we should," Julian commented. He tapped his pad, and an image of the large island or small continent they were approaching floated into view. "This is as detailed a zoom as I can get from the world map we had. It appears there's only one main river, and that it travels in a sort of semicircle through a good part of the continent. There should be a city on or near its mouth, and that *should* be less than three more days sailing from where we are right now—assuming this line of islands extends from the eastern chain."

"The spaceport is on the central plateau," O'Casey added, "and the continent is . . . extensively mountainous. In fact, it makes Nepal look flat—the province or the planet. Travel to the spaceport may take some time, and it could be arduous."

"Oh, no!" Roger chuckled. "Not an arduous march!"

Pahner grinned momentarily, but then shook his head.

"It's an important point, Your Highness. *Coll* oil or no, we're short on dietary supplements, and there won't be any more *coll* fish to get oil from once we head inland. That means we're short on time, too, so traveling through that region had better be fast."

"We have the additional problem of overhead coverage, Captain," Kosutic pointed out. "From here on out, we need to consider our emissions. If we're able to hear them, and we have been, then they can hear us, if they're listening. And they can also detect our heavy weapons. Plasma cannons especially."

"Also, Sir," Julian said diffidently, "it's likely that the people from the ships visit more than just the starport. There are always tourists, even on plancts where the local critters can't wait to eat them. We need to keep that in mind."

"Noted and agree." Pahner nodded. "Anything else?"

"The Diasprans," Despreaux commented. "They're . . . not happy."

Pahner turned to Fain. The infantry captain was still settling in to command Yair's old company (and the transferred survivors of his own, original command), but he was continuing to demonstrate an impressive capacity for assuming additional responsibilities. He was also working out well as Roger's aide-de-camp, and he'd ended up being the regular liaison to the human command conferences, despite being junior to the other two Diaspran commanders.

"Comments, Captain?" Pahner invited, and Fain rubbed a horn gently.

"It's the water. And . . . the space, I suppose."

"It's the lack of a chaplain," Kosutic snorted.

"Perhaps." Fain shrugged. "We probably should have brought a priest. But they didn't like the God in such abundance. It was troubling for them. And now, it's becoming troubling to the men, as well."

"The Diasprans are having a spiritual crisis, Captain," Kosutic explained.

"Not all that surprisingly," O'Casey snorted. The prince's chief of staff was a historian's historian, with a specialization in anthropology (human and nonhuman) and political history and theory. Those interest areas had made her an ideal choice as a tutor for a member of the Imperial Family, the position from which she had segued into the then-unenviable assignment as Prince Roger the Fop's chief of staff. They'd also made her absolutely invaluable in the trek across Marduk.

For all that, though, she'd been frustrated on more than one occasion by the tyrannical time pressure which had prevented her from spending long enough with any one of the cultures they'd encountered to feel that she'd truly had time to study it on its own terms. Too much of the expertise and analyses she'd been called upon to deliver had been based on little more than hurried, off-the-cuff analogies. That was the way *she* saw it, at least, although every Bronze Barbarian—and Roger—recognized the fact that her "off-the-cuff analogies" had done at least as much as the plasma cannons to get them this far alive.

This voyage, however, had finally offered her an opportunity to sit down and do some of the detailed study she loved so dearly, and Roger knew that one of the primary sources she'd spent hours with was *The Book of the Water*, the oldest and most sacred of the Diasprans' religious texts.

"It's not at all surprising that the Diaspran religion worked out the way it did," she said now. It was apparent to Roger that she was choosing her words and tone carefully, no doubt out of consideration for Krindi Fain's beliefs. "After all, they have historical—and accurate—proof that the God of Water is the only reason Diaspra exists."

"It is?" Despreaux asked.

"Yes," O'Casey confirmed, and nodded at Dobrescu. "Despite the inadequacies of our database on Marduk, Mr. Dobrescu and I have managed to confirm Roger's original observation on the day we first met Cord. It may seem ridiculous, given the climate we've encountered here, but this planet actually experienced a fairly recent period of glaciation. It produced the rock formations Roger observed then . . . and must also have killed off a substantial proportion of the planet's total population."

"Hell, yes!" Roger snorted, remembering how dreadfully vulnerable Cord and his nephews had been to the mountainous climate they had encountered crossing from Marshad to the Valley of Ran Tai. What humans regarded as little more than a pleasantly cool morning had been well-nigh fatal to the cold-blooded Mardukans.

"As you know," O'Casey continued, "this planet has only a very slight axial tilt, which gives it a relatively narrow equatorial belt. As nearly as Chief Dobrescu and I have been able to figure out, just about everyone outside that narrow zone must have been killed by the climatic changes involved when the glaciation set in. Geologically speaking, it was extremely recent, as well, which probably explains why the planetary population is so low, despite a climate—now— which permits several crops a year.

"There were, however, some isolated enclaves of Mardukans who survived outside the equatorial zone. The only one of those on which we have any specific documentation, so far, was Diaspra."

"The lake!" Roger said, snapping his fingers suddenly, and O'Casey nodded.

"Exactly. Remember how incredibly ancient the buildings around those volcanic springs looked?" She shrugged. "That's because the Diaspran priesthood is entirely correct about how old their city really is. There's been *a* city on that site since before the glaciers; it was the heat output of the volcanic springs that made it possible for that city's population to survive. No wonder they look upon water as the preserving miracle of all life!"

"That explains a lot," Kosutic said, tipping thoughtfully back in her chair. "Have you loaded *The Book of the Water* into your toot, Eleanora?" The chief of staff nodded. "Then can I get you to download a translation of it to mine after supper?"

"Of course," O'Casey agreed.

"Good! I'll be looking forward to reading it, because I'm pretty sure it will flesh out what I've already picked up from talking to people like Krindi here." She pointed at Fain with her chin. "In the meantime, though, I think I've already got enough of the handle on their theology to see where our current problem lies."

She turned her attention back to Roger and Pahner.

"Essentially, their cosmology calls for a piece of land floating in an eternal, endless body of water," she said. "It also calls for all water that hasn't been specifically contaminated to be 'good,' which means potable. So here we are, way out of sight of land, sailing over an apparently eternal body of . . . bad water."

"Water, water everywhere, and not a drop to drink," Pahner said with a slight grin, then looked serious again. "I can see where that would be a problem, Captain Fain. Do you have a suggestion for solving it?"

"As Sergeant Major Kosutic has just suggested, I've been discussing the problem with her, Sir," the Mardukan said diffidently. "I believe it would be useful for her to deal directly with the troops as a replacement for our usual priests. And, if possible, when the ships go back to K'Vaern's Cove, it would also be useful if, upon return, they brought a priest over with them."

Pahner gazed at him for a second, then shook his head in resignation.

"By the time they could get back here from K'Vaern's Cove, hopefully, we'll be well on our way to the port. If we're not, we might as well not have made the trip." The Marine tapped his fingers together while he thought, then gave Kosutic another slight grin. "Okay, High Priestess, you're on. Just no converting."

"No sweat," the sergeant major said. "I'll just point out to them that there's no problem, within their cosmology, with there being more than one 'world.' We're traveling across what is, technically, infinite water—a sphere *is* infinite, looked at in a certain way. For that matter, their definition practically cries out for multiple worlds, or, in fact, continents. And from what I've gleaned, there's nothing saying that all water is potable. In fact, they deal with certain types of nonpotable waters all the time. Waters that have been soiled by wastes, for example. And the God of Waters loves them just as much as he loves potable waters, and rejoices whenever they are restored to potability. Gets us into the concept of sin and redemption."

"The Prophet Kosutic," Roger said with a chuckle, and the sergeant major smiled at him.

"I'd invite you to a service, but I don't think the Empire is ready for that just yet."

"Now that we hopefully have that crisis dealt with," Pahner said, "there's another one to consider. Taking the port isn't going to be a picnic, and I've been watching the squad close-tactics training. It's not going well. Comments?"

"Train, train, train," Julian said. "We're barely scratching the surface yet, Sir. The teams *are* improving. Just not very rapidly."

"Sergeant Major?"

"Well . . ." Kosutic frowned. "I gotta say I don't feel like they're there, Julian. They're not concentrating. They're just going through the motions. We need to put some steel in their asses."

"With all due respect, Sergeant Major," Despreaux interjected,

"I don't think you can say any of us are lacking in 'steel.' I think our credentials on that are fairly clear."

"Maybe," Kosutic returned. "And maybe not. One thing about being in battle as long and as often as we have is that for just about everybody, after a while, the edge goes away. You can't be on Condition Red forever, and we've been on it for a helluva lot longer than is recommended. So I think that that steel, Sergeant, is starting to melt. And it couldn't come at a worse time. You do realize that after we take the port, we're going to have to take a *ship,* right?"

"Yes." Despreaux nodded, her eyes dark. "I do realize that."

"Obviously, we're not going to hit the port when we know there's a ship in orbit to watch us do it," Kosutic said. "But that means that whenever a ship *does* turn up, we're going to have to grab any shuttles it sends down the instant they hit dirt." She leaned forward and stabbed a rock-hard finger into the wooden table. "*And* prevent communication between them and their ship when we do it. Then, we'll have to send our own shuttles up, blow the hatches, and do a forced boarding. We'll have to blast our way through the whole ship without smashing *anything* that can't be fixed. And it's probably going to be a ship used to bad ports—to the idea of pirates trying to grab it. So its crew won't be sitting there with their guard down. Now how easy do you think that's going to be?"

"Sergeant Major," Roger said in mild reproof. "We're all aware that it's not going to be a walk in the park. But we'll get it done."

"Will we?" Kosutic asked. "It won't be Voitan or Sindi, Your Highness. We won't be in a fixed position waiting for the scummies to throw themselves onto our swords. It won't even be just a smash and grab, like Q'Nkok and Marshad. We'll have to move like lightning, in the boarding and taking the port. And we'll have to be precise, as well. And we're *not* moving like that right now."

"Can you take this ship without our help?" Rastar asked suddenly. "Isn't this what you brought us for? To fight by your side, your foes as ours?"

All the human heads in the cabin swiveled like turrets as their owners turned to look at him. Roger's mouth flapped for a moment before he could spit out a sentence. Then—

"It's . . . not that easy."

"This environment isn't one you want to fight in, Rastar," Eleanora said quietly. "You'll undoubtedly be involved in the taking of the port. But the ship will be another issue."

Roger nodded then leaned forward in the lamplight and placed his hand atop the Mardukan's.

"Rastar, there are very few people I would rather have by my side in a firefight. But you *don't* want to fight on shipboard. Onboard, if you press the wrong button, you can find yourself without any air to breathe, your breath stolen and your skin freezing until you die, quickly."

"There are . . . hazards, Rastar," Pahner agreed. "Hazards we would prefer not to subject your forces to. They aren't trained for that sort of environment. And despite the difficulty, a short platoon of Marines will be able to take most freighters. For that matter, since there will probably be functional armor at the spaceport, we can probably take a pirate down, as well. If, as the sergeant major has noted, we're trained to a fine edge."

He rubbed his cheek for a moment in thought.

"Who are the best at this sort of thing?" Roger asked. "I mean, of the troops we have."

"Probably myself and Despreaux, Your Highness," Julian answered.

"Don't count *me* out, boy," Kosutic said with a wink. "I was door-kicking when you were in swaddling clothes."

"Why don't we have a demonstration?" Roger asked, ignoring the byplay. "Set up a visible 'shoot-house' on the deck, made out of— I dunno, sails and stuff—and let the teams watch Despreaux and Julian do their thing. And the sergeant major, of course, if she's not too old and decrepit. Show them how it's done."

"Decrepit, huh?" The senior NCO snorted. "I'll show you *decrepit*, sonny!"

"That's 'Your Highness Sonny,'" Roger retorted with his nose in the air.

The comment elicited a general chuckle. Even Pahner smiled. Then he nodded more seriously.

"Good call, Roger. It will also give our allies a look at what we're doing. Since we're not going to be using live rounds, we can give them detectors and let them be the opposition. Let them see if they can stop the sergeant major's team."

"Surprise is the essence of an assault," Despreaux said quietly. "If they watch us prepare, they're not going to be too surprised."

"We'll train in the hold," Kosutic said, tugging at the skull earring dangling from her right ear. "Then duplicate the conditions on deck."

"That sounds good," Julian said, but his tone was a bit dubious. She cocked her head at him, and he shrugged. "You know how much of this is about muscle memory," he said. "Even with the helmet VR and our toots, we're still going to need at least some room to move in, if we're going to do it right. And, frankly, I don't think there's enough room in *Hooker*'s hold."

"He's got a point, Smaj," Roger said. The prince frowned for a moment, then shrugged. "On the other hand, there's a lot more room below decks on *Snarleyow*. I bet the *civan* have eaten enough of the forage to give us a lot more room in *Snarleyow*'s forward hold than we could find in any of the other ships."

"That's an excellent idea, Roger," Pahner approved. "Her between-deck spaces are even deeper than ours are, and she's got a lot more beam, as well."

"Still not as much room as I'd really like, but a lot better," Kosutic agreed.

"And we'll be the 'opposition'?" Rastar asked.

"Yes," Pahner said with a nod. "We'll set up a facility above decks on one of the other schooners. It may still be a little cramped for troopers the size of yours, but it should work out. As far as the demonstration itself goes, you'll know they're coming, but not quite when. And you'll be armed with your standard weapons, but no ammunition. The computer will be able to tell which shots hit and which miss, and the system will tell you with a buzzer if you're hit or killed."

"Can I participate also?" Fain asked.

"Certainly," Pahner said, then chuckled. "A sergeant major and two sergeants going after a prince and his officers. It should be interesting."

"Could I participate, too, instead of being the objective?" Roger asked. "I'd like to see how I'd do on this tac team."

Julian started to open his mouth in automatic protest, then thought about it. Every single time he had doubted the prince's abilities in a firefight, he'd been wrong. And so, after a moment more of thought, he shut his mouth, instead.

Kosutic frowned contemplatively. Then she nodded.

"We'll . . . introduce you to it, at least. It's more than just being able to shoot straight. Some people who aren't much good at other fighting are very good at close-quarters work, and vice versa. If you do well in the preliminary training, you'll participate in the final demonstration. If not, not."

"Fine," Roger said with a nod. "How long to set this up?"

"Start in the morning," Pahner said. "Captain T'Sool and I will get with *Snarleyow*'s skipper and have *Hooker*'s main deck set up to duplicate the conditions in *Snarleyow*'s hold. You do your prep down there, then do the assault on the deck. That way we can all watch."

"And make rude comments, I'm sure," Kosutic snorted.

"So are we going to play shirts and skins?" Julian ogled Despreaux luridly. "If so, I say *we* take skins."

The sergeant major's palm-strike would have been a disabling or even killing blow if it had landed a few inches farther forward on the side of his head, or if she'd used the base of her palm instead of the side. As it was, it just hurt like hell.

"You're toast, buddy," she said, chuckling as he rubbed the side of his head.

"Man," he protested. "Nobody around here can take a joke!"

"And don't let this interfere with your discussions with the Mardukans," Pahner reminded the sergeant major, ignoring the byplay. "I'm not sure that either takes precedence over the other."

The captain was still unsure and unhappy about the relationship between his senior NCO and his intel sergeant. They were discreet, and there wasn't a hint of favoritism, but small unit command was about managing personalities, and sex was one of the biggest destabilizers around. There were strict rules against the type and degree of fraternization the two of them were engaged in, and they knew it just as well as he did. But, he reminded himself yet again, none of the rules had contemplated a unit being cut off from all outside contact for over six months.

"Got it," the sergeant major nodded, noting his dark expression.

"Should we load anything else onto the list?" Roger asked, deliberately trying to reclaim a less serious mood. "I don't think Sergeant Major Kosutic has enough on her plate, yet."

"Ah, you just wait, Your Highness," the NCO told him with an evil smile. "As of tomorrow, you're just 'Recruit MacClintock.' You just keep right on joking."

"What's the worst that can happen?" Roger said with a smile. "Going back to Voitan?"

CHAPTER FIVE

"ARE YOU GOING TO KEEP AN EYE ON YOUR OWN SECTOR NEXT TIME, RECRUIT?"

"One hundred and twenty-seven. YES, SERGEANT MAJOR!"

There were several axioms, handed down from generation to generation by the noncommissioned officers who were the true keepers of the tribal wisdom, in which Sergeant Major Eva Kosutic firmly believed. "No plan survives contact with reality." "In battle, His Wickedness always has a hole card." "If the enemy is in range, so are you." All of them were rules the military forgot at its own peril, but the one that was currently paramount in her own mind was "The more you sweat, the less you bleed."

And at the moment, some people obviously needed to do a little more sweating than others, she thought bitingly.

Roger MacClintock had several things going for him when it came to close combat. He had been gifted, both naturally and through long ago manipulation of the MacClintock genotype, with the reactions of a pit viper. He was a natural-born shot, with the hand-eye coordination of a master marksman, and he had spent many a lonely hour building on that platform to perfect his aim. And he had a good natural combat awareness; in a fight, he always knew "where" he was and had a good feel for where the enemies and friendlies were

69

around him. That was an often underrated ability, but it was crucial in the sort of high-violence and sudden-death environment for which they were training.

But although he'd learned to be a "team player" in soccer, he'd never really had to perfect that in combat. Worse, perhaps, he tended to go his own way, as had been proven repeatedly on the long march from the shuttles' dry lakebed landing to K'Vaern's Cove. Roger was never one to integrate himself into a fire plan. Which made it a good thing that he always led from the front, since he also tended to kill anything that got in front of *him*.

"Your job, when we do an entry, is to watch my *back*! Not to watch where I am *going*! If I run into resistance, *I* will deal with it. But if I have to watch *your* sector at the same time, you are OFF THIS TEAM! Do I make myself perfectly clear?"

"CLEAR, SERGEANT MAJOR!" Roger hammered out his final push-up. "One fifty, Sergeant Major!"

"You just stay there in the front leaning rest position, Recruit MacClintock! I'll get to you when I'm ready."

"Yes, Sergeant Major!" the prince gasped.

The schooner *Snarleyow*'s forward hold was hotter than the hinges of hell and reeked of decaying filth in the bilges. But it was also the largest concealed open space aboard any vessel of the flotilla, which, from Eva Kosutic's perspective, made it the best possible place for training. It still didn't offer as much unobstructed area as she would have liked—not by a long chalk—but the cavalry's *civan* had already consumed the fodder which had originally been piled into it. And unlike the upper cargo deck, there were no *civan* in the hold itself.

Which was a very good thing. *Civan*, and especially the trained war-*civan* Prince Rastar and his men favored, were much more intelligent than most humans might have thought upon meeting them for the first time. But what they most definitely were *not* was cute or cuddly. In fact, any *civan* tended to have the temper of an Old Earth grizzly bear with a bad tooth. The temperament—and training—of those selected as cavalry mounts only exacerbated that natural tendency. Which was why the *civan* stalled along the sides of *Snarleyow*'s upper cargo deck were "tethered" (if that was the proper verb for it) not with halters or ropes, but with five-point chain tie-downs.

Even so, the Mardukans charged with their care and feeding were extremely careful about how close they got to the beasts' axlike jaws and razor-sharp, metal-shod fighting claws. For herself, Kosutic was delighted to have a training space, be it ever so hot, dank, and smelly, in which she didn't have to worry about losing a limb because she strayed too close to a *civan* in a worse mood than usual.

Of course, at the moment, *she* was in a worse mood than usual, and she shook her head, then gestured for the other two NCOs to follow her. She led them to the forwardmost end of the hold, then turned to face them.

"Options," she said quietly, and Julian wiped away a drop of sweat and shook his head.

"He's good, Smaj. Very good. But he won't stay focused on defense."

"He's too used to having us do that for him," Despreaux pointed out. "He's used to barreling through the opposition while we cover his back. Now *you're* barreling through the course, and he's supposed to cover *your* back." She shrugged ever so slightly. "He can't get used to it."

"Yeah, but a big part of it is that he's one aggressive son-of-a-bitch," Julian said with a quiet chuckle. "No offense intended to Her Majesty."

"There's that," Kosutic agreed, tugging at an earlobe. "I don't really want to switch him out for somebody else, either. He's got the moves to be better than just about anybody else in the company, if we can ever get them harnessed and coordinated, and only Macek might be able to equal him as it is. But I'm not going to get whacked because he's not covering his sector."

And that was exactly what had happened, three times so far.

When the helmet systems came on and their connection to the team's toots kicked in, the hold became a virtual shoot-house, and Kosutic had set the difficulty level very high. That meant that enemies weren't just in plain sight, on the route that the team took. Which, in turn, meant there had to be eyes turned in every direction . . . and

Roger insisted on facing forward, along the line of assault. Not only did that permit the "enemies" he would otherwise have neutralized a clear shot at the team, but in one case he'd managed to "shoot" the sergeant major in the back.

Something had to be done, and Despreaux furrowed her brow as all three of them considered the problem.

"We could . . ." she said, then stopped.

"What?" the sergeant major asked.

"You won't like it," Despreaux replied.

"I've done a lot of stuff I don't like," Kosutic sighed. "What's one more thing, by His Evilness?"

"All right," Despreaux said with a shrug. "We could put Roger on point."

"Uh," Kosutic said.

"Hmmm." Julian rubbed his jaw. "She's got a point. I think he might do pretty well."

"But . . ." the sergeant major said. "But—"

"'But that's *my* spot!'" Julian finished for her with a faint, humorous whine.

Kosutic looked daggers at him for a moment, then shook her head sharply.

"It's more than that, Adib. Do you really think the captain isn't going to use us? He put us together for more than just to show how it's done. My guess is that he's thinking of using us for something, as a team."

"What? His company's sergeant major, two of his squad leaders, and *the prince*?" Julian laughed. "You're joking, right?"

"No, I'm not," the sergeant major said seriously. "Just take it as a given that that might happen. Then think about putting Roger on point."

"Oh," Julian said.

"I can see your objection, Sergeant Major," Despreaux said carefully. "But I'm not sure it matters. Perhaps we should get Macek or Stickles instead of the prince. But if we *are* going to use him, I still think he should be on point. Frankly, I think, with all due respect, that he might be . . . a touch better even than you."

Despreaux gazed calmly at the sergeant major, waiting for the explosion, and Kosutic opened her mouth again. Then she closed it with a clop, fingered her earlobe for a moment, and shrugged.

"You might be right."

"I think she is, Smaj," Julian said with equal care. "The pocker is fast."

"Is that any way to talk about the Heir Tertiary to the Throne of Man?" Kosutic demanded with a grin. "But you're right. The pocker *is* fast. And he can shoot, too. But I hate to seem to . . . reward him for screwing up."

"You think point is a *reward*?" Julian shook his head.

Roger stood with his right elbow just touching the wood of the bulkhead, his head and body hunched and turned to his left. The wood was real, but just to his right was a large doorway that had been cut into it only recently. In his helmet systems, the doorway was visible only as an outline sketched on the wall with explosives. And the wall wasn't wood; it was plascrete. And in just a moment, the "explosives" were going to go off and blow a new door through it. And they would be going off less than a half-meter from his arm.

It was going to be an unpleasant experience. Roger rather doubted that even the sergeant major appreciated the full capabilities of his own toot. All the Marines were accustomed to using their implanted computers as both combat enhancers and training devices, and their toots' abilities in those regards far exceeded those of the hardware available to most citizens of the Empire. But Roger's toot was at least as much more capable than theirs as theirs were than the average civilian model. Which meant that the training simulation was even more "real" for him than for anyone else in the team. He'd considered kicking in the filters in an effort to spare himself some of the sergeant major's simulation's . . . energetic programming tricks, but he'd decided against it. He'd come to embrace the wisdom of another of Kosutic's beloved axioms: "Train like you're going to fight."

He pushed that thought away and concentrated on the moment at hand. Other than the initial walk-through of the simulated rooms, this was his first time on point, and he suspected that the sergeant major was going to be making a statement. In fact, it would be just her style to make the course unsurvivable. That would fit her passion for making training harder than real life could possibly be, and he'd already discovered from painful personal experience that she had an undeniable talent for doing her passion justice. On the other hand, this was supposed to be training for *her*, too, so whatever was waiting for him was waiting for her, as well. Of course, to get to her, it probably had to go through him first, and he couldn't help wondering what the simulator AI was going to throw at them. He hadn't bothered even to attempt to wheedle any more information out of the sergeant major. She wouldn't have told him, of course. But even if she might have, she probably couldn't. The way she'd set things up when she punched the basic scenario parameters into her computer to generate the simulation, not even she should know exactly what was on the other side of the wall.

But it was bound to be bad.

Despreaux quietly laid in the last bit of the simulated breaching charge and stood back. The explosion should fill the room beyond with flying fragments, along with a world's worth of overpressure, smoke, and noise. The Marines' helmets and chameleon suits would serve to reduce that same concussion, so it should give them a moment of surprise and shock in which to overcome whoever might be defending the room. Assuming that the defenders weren't outfitted with equipment similar to that of the Marines.

Despreaux held up a thumb, indicating that she was ready to go, and watched the rest of the team. Julian held up a thumb as well and hunched away from the blast area, followed by Kosutic.

Roger held up his own thumb and gripped his bead rifle tightly. The weapon was the standard issue field rifle for the Marines, but its "bullpup" design made it equally handy at close quarters. He'd become familiar with the weapon in the course of the battle across the continent, and it was now as much an extension of his body as his pistol or his personal rifle. In addition, his toot's combat pack had come with a slot for bead rifle, and he'd used the training system assiduously, building up his ability and confidence day by day. He'd never had much call for automatic weapons' training before, but he instinctively tended to be light on the trigger, so his bursts were always short and clean. With most targets, he'd tended to put two or three rounds into the upper chest, neck, or head. But except for the few targets which had presented themselves to "ass end Charlie" in the run-throughs, that had been against stationary targets. Now it was time to see if he really had what it took.

Despreaux took one more look at the team, hunched away herself, and triggered the breaching charge.

The suit systems—and toots—did the best they could to simulate the conditions, and that "best" was very good indeed. The helmets simulated a vast overpressure on their ears as they clamped onto the team's heads, their toots gave their sense of balance a hard jolt, and their chameleon suits went momentarily rigid and squeezed hard in kinetic reaction to the "pressure wave." But even before the cloth had started to settle again, Roger was through the door.

The room beyond was fairly small, no more than four or five meters square. A table in the center occupied much of its volume, and there was another door in the far wall. The scenario had called for no reconnaissance on the room, so the numbers or locations of hostiles had been unknown. But, as it turned out, there was plenty for a young prince to work on.

As he plunged through the smoke, he identified a hostile on the far side of the room. But that hostile was only just drawing a bead pistol, and something made Roger look to his right.

There was a human in the corner with a bead rifle trained right on him. The person wore the shoulder patch of a Colonial Garrison Trooper, but otherwise his equipment and uniform were identical to the Marines'. And it was clear that he'd reacted immediately to the detonation and entry. But as fast as the sim was reacting, "he" had never dealt with Prince Roger MacClintock.

Roger flipped the bead rifle sideways and "double-tapped" the defender in the corner off-hand, then flipped back to the left to engage another defender in the other corner. Only then did he engage and neutralize the first threat . . . who was just starting to level her bead pistol. Beads caromed off the floor and past his legs as that threat flew back against the far wall in a splash of red.

But by then, Roger was already gone.

Kosutic followed the prince through the smoke and covered left. In this case, she *did* know the layout and position of defenders, and she was shocked to see all three of them already dead. The two "sneaks" in the corners were both headless corpses, and the primary threat against the far wall had one round through the forehead and two more in her chest. The sergeant major was even more shocked as Roger threw a flashbang through the far door and followed it before it could detonate.

"*Roger!* Satan damn it, *SLOW DOWN!*"

The prince vaguely heard the sergeant major, but his helmet visor's heads-up display showed that so far the team had taken no casualties. That was how he intended to keep it. He followed the disarmed flashbang through the door, and, as he'd expected, all the defenders on the far side had hunched away in anticipation of the flash that never came. This room was larger, with an open door along the right wall, and a closed-door in the left wall. There were also quite a few defenders—seven, to be precise. For some reason the words "target-rich environment" came to mind. And also "Eva Kosutic is a bitch."

He shot two that were arrayed beside the door to his right, then took cover behind a handy workbench. From under the bench, he began single-tapping knees and shins as the other five defenders dropped to the floor and thus into view.

A grenade from one of the "wounded" defenders flew over the workbench, and it appeared to be the just and proper time to abandon his position. However, that wasn't all to the bad. The grenade was a standard issue frag, and the explosion, while unpleasant, would only manage to lift him over the bench a little faster. The chameleon suit was proof against all but high-velocity beads, and the shrapnel from the grenade wouldn't penetrate it. He wasn't sure if the combat simulator was designed to simulate shocked amazement on the part of the "enemy," but real ones would have stopped in dazed wonder at the front-flip that he managed over the workbench, riding the wavefront of the explosion.

★ ★ ★

Kosutic caught a flicker out of the corner of her eye as she came through the door, but realized it was the prince. Just then, a notional "grenade" went off to her right and slapped her against the wall. That was okay, but it threw off her first shot, and by the time she'd reacquired the two remaining defenders, they were both down with head and throat shots.

"Roger!"

Apparently there *had* been a purpose for all those saddle exercises they'd put him through in boarding school. Either his maneuver had temporarily locked up the simulation processor, or else it *was* designed to allow for amazed shock, because both of the remaining targets just sat there, frozen, clutching their wounds while he terminated them. The sergeant major was yelling about something, but *he* hadn't set up this nightmare, and he damned sure wasn't stopping or even slowing down until all the targets were cleared. He thumbed a frag grenade, set it for two-second detonation, and pitched it through the open door. Then he followed.

"*Roger!*" Kosutic shouted in exasperation. She'd seen the grenade go through the door, and he was following it far too closely, antiballistic chameleon suit or no. Putting him on point might make some sense; *she* could barely keep up with him, so Satan only knew what it would be like for the opposition! But it was just as clear that with him in the lead, His Wickedness was running wild.

The system finally threw Roger a curve and graded his bead rifle as damaged by the grenade explosion. It also graded his right hand as damaged, and his toot obliged the AI by sending a stab of all-too-genuine pain through the hand. That reduced his options considerably, so as the three targets in the room tried to recover from the slap of the fragmentation grenade, he reached across and drew his pistol with his left.

He also made a mental note to figure out a better way to enter rooms. Maybe it would be better not to follow his grenade "door knocker" *quite* as closely next time.

Despreaux shook her head over the carnage in the room. It was pretty clear that the sergeant major had intended to stack the deck. But apparently she hadn't stacked it well enough.

Nimashet had nothing to do as "ass-end Charlie," so she backed along, covering Julian now, and keeping the single closed door in the edge of her vision. If they were counterattacked, it would probably come from there. But it didn't pay to concentrate on only one threat axis. It was better to be open and ready to engage in any of "her" directions, she reminded herself.

Which reminder was of no damned use at all when the ceiling fell in.

Roger's new room had only the three defenders, and they were all down with double-taps before they recovered from the grenade. Unfortunately, the left end of the room was a plasteel wall with an armored gun-port. The cannon in it had been unable to engage as long as there were live defenders in its way, but as the last hostile fell, it opened up.

Roger managed to duck under the stream of bead-cannon rounds and crouched along the wall, sheltered from its fire. Unfortunately, there was a certain amount of ricochet, and Kosutic wasn't able to follow him through the door. He could hear a firefight going on in the other room, so he knew he couldn't stay where he was for long. And it looked as if there was just enough room to get a hand through the firing slot past the bead cannon.

He slipped a grenade from his pouch, and as he did, the indicators for Despreaux and Julian went to yellow, then orange. Both were wounded and would die without support.

Eva crouched behind the workbench Roger had abandoned and cursed. Despreaux and Julian were both down, and she herself was pinned by fire from the ceiling and the three heavily armored commandos who'd dropped through the hole. The targets were advancing cautiously, but their heavier armor was shrugging off most of her shots, even after she'd switched to armor piercing. It wasn't powered armor, just very heavy reactive plate, but if something didn't come through soon, they were going to lose this one.

Roger set the grenade to one second, flipped it into the bead cannon bunker, and dove for the door. If the damned simulator's AI didn't have the people in the bunker at least trying to get the grenade back out of their position, it wasn't very well written.

He wasn't punctured by the heavy weapon, so it appeared to have worked. But the situation in the far room sounded bad, and he was tired of going blind. He thought about it for just a moment, then flipped on his helmet's vision systems.

As it turned out, the "dead"—or at least "seriously wounded"—Julian had his head turned to the side. Roger looked in the same direction through the camera on his helmet and saw three heavily armored targets closing on the workbench he had flipped across on his own way through. He slipped a fresh magazine into the pistol and contemplated his right hand. It was still graded as "yellow" (and that damnably efficient toot of his was still giving him direct neural stimulation that hurt like hell to back up its "damage"), and he wasn't sure how much use he could make of it. But there was only one way to find out, so he drew a throwing knife and approached the door in a crouch.

This was going to take timing. Lots of timing.

Timing is everything, and in this case it was on the side of the righteous. Kosutic's HUD showed her the icon of the prince approaching the door, and she smiled. As the prince's actual figure appeared in the opening, she concentrated on the shooter in the ceiling.

Time to get some of their own back.

Roger stepped through the door as Kosutic started tearing into the ceiling with long, concentrated bursts of blind fire. His own firepower was more limited, but unlike her, he could actually see the shooter. He flipped up the knife and threw it towards the hole in the ceiling even as he fired at the three crouched targets in the room.

He saw the backs of each of their necks go red, then grunted in anguish as his chameleon suit hardened and the toot threw some more neural stimulation at him. Pain echoed through his chest, and his helmet's HUD flashed a brief schematic of his body with his torso outlined in yellow. But by then he had directed the pistol towards the ceiling, and before the shooter could get off another round, he was credited as a kill. The hostile fell through the hole to the deck, and Roger noted the knife blade buried in the bad guy's left arm.

Roger rotated to the right along the wall, trying to disregard the flashes of pain his toot obediently sent along his nerves each time he moved. At least one rib broken, he estimated. It hurt like hell, but his nanny pack was already deadening the pain—or, at least, his toot was grudgingly acting as *if* the nanites were doing their job—so he made himself ignore it as he reloaded his pistol.

Then he picked up Julian's bead rifle in place of his own, attached it to his harness' friction strap, and reloaded it, as well. Then he sidled towards the remaining closed door, cradling the rifle in his undamaged left hand.

He looked across at the sergeant major and gestured to the door and the hole in the ceiling, then shrugged. She grimaced back at him and gestured at the ceiling. He nodded, thumbed himself, then jabbed the same thumb upward. She grimaced again, but she also nodded and crouched down, setting her rifle on the floor and interlacing her fingers.

Roger let the friction strap pull Julian's rifle up, drew his pistol again, and stepped over to the sergeant major. He put one boot into her hands, leapt upward into the hole—

—and slammed into the intact deck overhead.

The next thing he knew, he was on the floor, clutching his head and neck in pain (which was not at all simulated) as Kosutic, Julian, and Despreaux tried not to laugh.

"Clear VR," the sergeant major said, and the simulator's AI obeyed, although Roger was half-surprised it could understand the command through her laughter. She leaned over him, and shook her head in an odd mixture of amusement and contrition.

"Satan and Lucifer," she got out. "I'm sorry about that, Your Highness. Are you okay?"

Roger lay on the floor of the poorly lit hold, clutching his neck and stared up at her—and the completely solid deckhead above her.

"Good Christ," he groaned. "What in hell happened?"

"I got so into the scenario, I forgot it wasn't real," Kosutic admitted. "*Snarleyow*'s big enough that I could build two or three rooms into the hold, but there wasn't anything I could do about the *vertical* limits, and I got so involved I forgot that there couldn't really be a hole in the 'ceiling.' That's the upper cargo deck planking. There's not even a *hatch*."

"Where's the targets?" Roger moaned pitifully. "Where's the *bead-cannon*? Where's the *door*? We were doing so welll!"

Julian rolled over on his side, still laughing, while Despreaux climbed to her feet.

"Fortunately," she observed with a disdainful glance at the giggling armorer, "*I'm* not dead."

"Oh, my head," Roger said, ignoring her. "I *hate* VR! Sergeant Major, did you just *piledriver* me into the ceiling?"

"That's more or less what I just said, Your Highness," Kosutic said, still chuckling.

"Oooo," Roger groaned. "Can I just lie here for a while?"

CHAPTER SIX

BAM!

"Man, I want my bead rifle back!" Julian muttered as his round plunked into the water, well clear of the floating target.

He and Roger stood side by side at *Ima Hooker*'s rail, between two of her starboard carronades. They'd just watched Rastar's team run through its own training on the schooner's main deck, and the experience had been fairly . . . ominous. They were due to have their "close contact" contest with the Mardukans the next morning, and it didn't look like it was going to be a walkover, even with Roger on point. The Vashin cavalry and selected Diaspran infantry who were going to act as the notional "guards" on key defenses of the spaceport would be graded as having light body armor. And since all the Vashin carried at least three weapons, it was going to be interesting.

"You're just jealous," Roger retorted as the floating barrel Julian had missed shattered from his own shot. "And it pains your professional ego to be shooting a 'smoke pole,'" he added with a grin.

The new rifles had been produced just in time for the battles around Sindi, and with their availability, the Marines had, for all practical purposes, put away their bead rifles until they reached the starport. The weapons had been designed using Roger's eleven-millimeter magnum Parkins and Spencer as a model, but modified in light of available technology.

The Parkins and Spencer's dual bolt-action/semi-automatic system had been impossible to duplicate, but the base for the bolt form was a modification of the ancient Ruger action, and *that* worked just fine. With the addition of scavenged battery packs from downchecked plasma rifles and various items of gear dead Marines no longer required, the electronic firing system built into the Parkins' cartridge cases also worked just fine. And since the prince had doggedly insisted on policing up his shooting stands whenever possible and dragging along the empty cases, there was sufficient brass to provide over two hundred almost infinitely reloadable rounds for each of the surviving Marines.

The black powder which was the most advanced form of explosives available on Marduk had made for a few compromises. One was that the rifles' slower-velocity bullets simply could not match the flat trajectory of a hypervelocity bead, which meant that at any sort of range, the barrel had to be elevated far beyond what any of the Marines were comfortable with. Which also explained why so many of their rounds tended to fall short.

"You can throw a rock faster than these bullets go," Despreaux growled from Roger's other side. "I still say that guncotton I made would have worked—and given us a hell of a lot better velocity, too!"

"Overpressure," Roger commented with a shake of his head. "And it was unstable as hell."

"I was working on it!" she snapped.

"Sure you were . . . and you're lucky you're not regrowing a set of fingers," Julian told her with another chuckle as he fired again. This time the round was on range for the second barrel, but off to the left. "Damn."

"Windage," Roger said laconically as he shattered that barrel, as well.

"Sight!" Julian snapped.

"Care to trade?" the prince offered with a smile.

"No," the Marine replied promptly, and glowered at Despreaux when she snickered.

While a good bit of it was the sight, most of it—as Julian knew perfectly well—was the sighter.

"Seriously," Roger said, gesturing for Julian's rifle. "I'd like to try. I turn the sight off from time to time, but it's not the same. And what happens if I lose it?"

Julian shook his head and traded rifles.

"It's going to be a bit tough to zero," he warned.

"Not really." The prince looked the rifle over. He'd checked them out when the first of them came off the assembly line, even fired a few rounds through one of them. But that had been months ago, and he took the time to refamiliarize himself with the weapon. Especially with the differences between it and his own Parkins.

Dell Mir, the K'Vaernian inventor who'd designed the detailed modifications, had done a good job. The weapons were virtually identical, with the exception of removing the optional gas-blowback reloading system—which Roger had to disengage anyway, when he used black-powder rounds in the Parkins—and the actual materials from which it was constructed.

It was fortunate that while the Mardukans' materials science was still in the dark ages, their machining ability was fairly advanced, thanks to their planet's weather. Whereas industrial technology had been driven, to a great extent, by advances in weaponry on Earth—and Althar, for that matter—the development of machining on Marduk had been necessitated by something else entirely: water. It rained five to ten times a day on this planet, and the development of any sort of civilization with that much rain had required advanced pumping technology. It was a bit difficult to drain fields with simple waterwheel pumps in the face of four or five meters of rain a year.

Production of the best pumps, the fastest and most efficient ones—and the ones capable of lifting water the "highest"—required fine machine tolerances and resistant metals. Thus, the Mardukans had early on developed both the machine lathe and drill press, albeit animal driven, as well as machine steel and various alloys of bronze and brass that were far in advance of those found at similar general tech levels in most societies.

But because they'd never developed electricity, there was no stainless steel, and no electroplating, so the rifle was made out of a strong, medium-carbon steel that was anything but rust-proof. And the stock, instead of a light-weight, boron-carbon polymer like the Parkins and Spencer's, was of shaped wood.

The weapon's ammunition was slightly different, as well. The cases were the same ones Roger had started with—as long as his hand, and thicker than his thumb, necking downward about fifteen percent to a bullet that was only about as thick as his second finger. The major changes were in the propellant and the bullet.

Roger's rifle used an electronic firing system that activated the center-point primer plug, and in the one operation that had been handled almost entirely by the Marines, Julian and Poertena had installed firing systems in each of the rifles created from spare parts for their armor, downchecked plasma rifles, and odd items of personal gear that hadn't been used up on the trek. Each of the weapons had the same basic design, although each had a few different parts. Mostly, though, it used parts from the plasma rifles, including the faulty capacitors which had made the off-world weapons unsafe to use. There was no problem using them for this application, since the energy being temporarily stored was far below that necessary to cause the spectacular—and lethal—detonations that had forced the weapons' retirement.

Julian had recommended, effectively, scrapping *all* of the plasma rifles and using their stocks for the base of as many of the black-powder rifles as possible, but Captain Pahner had nixed the idea. There hadn't been enough of the plasma rifles to provide all the black-powder weapons the company was going to require, so the majority of them would still have had to be made from native materials. Besides, he was still debating whether or not Julian and Poertena might be able to come up with a "fix" good enough to use the energy weapons for just one more battle. Given the probable difficulty of taking the starport, the plasma rifles might be the difference between success and failure, and he'd been unwilling to completely foreclose the possibility of using them.

The propellant in Roger's original rounds had been an advanced smokeless powder. From the perspective of the Marines with their electromagnetic bead rifles, long-range grenade launchers, and plasma rifles, that propellant had been a laughable antique.

Something dating back to the days when humans were still using steam to make electricity. But that same propellant was far, far out of reach of the Mardukans' tech base, so Dell Mir and the Marines had accepted that black powder was the only effective choice for a propellant.

Black powder, however, had its own peculiar quirks. One, which was painfully evident whenever someone squeezed a trigger, was the dense cloud of particularly foul-smelling smoke it emitted. Another was the truly amazing ability of black powder to foul a weapon with caked residue, and that residue's resistance to most of the Marines' cleaning solvents. Old-fashioned soap and water actually worked best, but the Bronze Barbarians' sensibilities were offended when they found themselves up to their elbows in hot, soapy water scrubbing away at their weapons with brushes and plenty of elbow grease.

But the biggest functional difference between black powder-loaded rounds and the ones Roger had brought out from Old Earth with him was that black powder exploded. More modern propellants *burned*—very rapidly, to be sure, but in what was a much more gradual process, relatively speaking, than black powder's . . . enthusiastic detonation. While nitro powders might well produce a higher absolute breech pressure, they did it over a longer period of time. For the *same* breech pressure, black powder "spiked" much more abruptly, which imposed a resultant strain on the breech and barrel of the weapon.

Not to mention a particularly nasty and heavy recoil.

Fortunately, the old axiom about getting what you paid for still held true, and the Parkins and Spencer was a very expensive weapon, indeed. Part of what Roger had gotten for its astronomical purchase price was a weapon which was virtually indestructible, which was a not insignificant consideration out in the bush where he tended to do most of his hunting. Another part, however, was the basic ammunition design itself. The Parkins' designers had assumed that situations might arise in which the owner of one of their weapons would find himself cut off from his normal sources of supply and be forced to adopt field expedients (if not quite so primitive as those which had been enforced upon the Marines here on Marduk) to reload their ammo. So the cases themselves had been designed to contain pressures which would have blown the breech right out of most prespace human firearms. And they had sufficient internal capacity for black-powder loads of near shoulder-breaking power.

In fact, the power and muzzle velocity of the reloaded rounds, while still far short of what Roger's off-world ammunition would have produced with its initial propellant, had been sufficient to create yet another problem.

The rounds Roger had started out with had jacketed bullets—old-fashioned lead, covered in a thin metal "cladding" that intentionally left the slug's lead tip exposed. On impact, the soft lead core mushroomed to more than half-again its original size and the cladding stripped back into a six-pronged, expanding slug. The main reason the cladding was necessary, however, was because the velocity of the round would have "melted" a plain lead bullet on its way up the barrel, coating the barrel and rifling in lead. Modern chemical-powered small arms ammunition was manufactured using techniques which were a direct linear descendent of technology which had been available since time immemorial: copper or some other alloy was added to the outside of lead bullets by a form of electroplating. But Mardukans didn't *have* electroplating, and it was a technology there'd been no time to "reinvent," so the humans had been forced to make do.

There'd been three potential ways to solve the problem. The first had been to reduce the velocity of the rounds to a point where they wouldn't lead the barrel, but that would have resulted in a reduction in both range and accuracy. The second choice had been to try to develop a stronger alloy to replace the lead, but since that wasn't something the Mardukans had ever experimented with, it would once again have required "reinventing" a technology. Finally, they'd settled on the third option: casting thin copper jackets for the rounds and then compressing the lead into them. There was an issue with contraction of the copper, but the compression injection—another technique garnered from pump technology—took care of that.

So the rounds were copper jacketed—"full-metal jacketed," as it was called. They weren't quite as "perfect" as Roger's original ammunition, of course. Every so often one of the bullets was unbalanced, and would go drifting off on its own course after departing the muzzle. But however imperfect they might have been by Imperial standards, they were orders of magnitude better than anything the Mardukans had ever had.

Now Roger cycled the bolt and popped up the ladder sight. The sight—a simple, flip-up frame supporting an elevating aperture rear sight and graduated for "click" range adjustment using a thumbwheel—was necessary for any accurate really long-range work. Elevating the rear sight forced the marksman to elevate the front sight, as well, in order to line them up, thus compensating for the projectile drop. It was another contraption the humans and Mardukans had sweated over, but once the design was perfected (and matched to the rounds' actual ballistic performance), the Mardukans had had no problem producing it.

But the sights weren't exactly a one-size-fits-all proposition, because everyone shot slightly differently, if only because everyone was at least slightly different in size, and thus "fitted" their weapons differently. As a result, the sights of any given rifle were "zeroed" for the individual to whom it belonged, which meant this rifle was zeroed for Julian, not Roger. Given that the range was about two hundred meters, the bullet could actually miss by up to a meter even if Roger's aim was perfect according to Julian's sight. But there was only one way to find out how bad it really was, so Roger calculated the wind, let out a breath, and squeezed the trigger.

The recoil was enough to make even him grunt, but he'd expected that, and he gazed intently downrange. Although the rounds were comparatively slow, they weren't so slow that he could actually watch them in flight. But the surface of the ocean swell was sufficiently smooth for the brief splash—to the left, and over by about half a meter—to be clearly visible.

"Told you it was the sight," Julian said with a slight snicker.

"Bet you a *civan* he makes the next one," Despreaux countered.

"As long as you're referring to the coin and not the animal, you're on," Julian replied. "Crosswind, rolling ship, bobbing barrel, and an unzeroed rifle. Two hundred meters. No damned way."

"You make a habit of underestimating the prince," Cord observed. Roger's *asi* had been standing behind Roger, leaning on his huge, lethal spear while he silently watched the children play with their newfangled toys. "You don't tend to underestimate enemies twice, I've noticed," the shaman continued, "which is good. But why is it that you persist in doing so where 'friendlies' are concerned?"

Julian glanced up at the towering native—the representative of what was little better than a hunter-gatherer society, who was undoubtedly the best-read and probably best educated Mardukan in the entire expedition. As always, his *facial* expression was almost nonexistent, but his amusement showed clearly in his body language, and Julian stuck out his tongue at him.

"That was my zero shot," Roger announced, ignoring the exchange between the Marine armorer and his *asi*. Then he put the rifle back to shoulder and punched out another round.

This time, the barrel was smashed.

Julian gazed at the bobbing wreckage for a moment, then reached into his pocket and pulled out a thin sheet of brass, which he handed over to Despreaux.

"I give."

Despreaux smiled and pocketed the brass, a K'Vaernian coin equal to a week's pay for a rifleman.

"It was a sucker bet, Adib. Have you *ever* won a shooting contest with Roger?"

"No," Julian admitted as Roger hefted the rifle once again. There were four more barrels scattered across the surface of the ocean, each floating amid its own cluster of white splashes as the Marines lining the schooner's side potted at them.

Roger lined up a shot at the most distant barrel, then shook his head when the round plunked into the sea well short.

"I'll admit that the scope does help," he confessed as he chambered another round. He brought the rifle back into firing position, but before he could squeeze the trigger, a shot rang out from the foredeck. Three more followed in rapid succession, and each bullet struck and shattered a barrel in turn.

Roger lowered Julian's rifle and looked forward as Captain Pahner lowered his own rifle and blew the gunsmoke out of the breech.

"I guess the captain wanted me to be sure who was king," the prince said with a smile.

"Well, Your Highness," Julian told him with a shrug, "when you've been doing this for fifty more years, you *might* be at the captain's level."

"Agreed, Julian," Roger said, leaning on the bronze carronade beside him. "I wonder if we'd have survived to this point with any old Bronze Battalion commander along. Captain Grades seemed—I don't know, 'okay.' But not at Pahner's level. Or am I wrong?"

"You're not," Despreaux said. "Pahner was a shoo-in for Gold Battalion. Hanging out at each level on the way there was just a formality."

"I thought he was going back to Fleet." Roger frowned.

"So did he," the sergeant replied. "I doubt it would've happened, though. Somebody was going to tell him to go on to Steel, and then to Silver. Most of the officers in those battalions didn't 'choose' to be there, you know."

"This is weird." Roger shook his head. "I thought the Regiment was voluntary."

"Oh, it is," Despreaux told him with a wink. " 'Captain Pahner, you just volunteered to take Alpha Steel. Congratulations on your new command.' "

"So does *Pahner* know this?"

"Probably not," Julian said. "Or, if he does, he's trying to ignore it. Even with rejuv, he's getting a bit long in the tooth to be a line commander. And he doesn't want to go higher. So he wants one last Fleet command before he retires. For him, Steel or even Gold would be a consolation prize."

Roger nodded with an understanding he could never have attained before marching halfway around the circumference of Hell with Pahner at his side. Then he chuckled softly.

"You know, when we get back Mother is going to owe me one huge favor. I'd thought about asking for a planetary dukedom as an alternative to hanging out at Imperial City, but maybe there's something else I should throw into the pot with it. Seems to me that if the captain wants a Fleet command, a 'friend at court' couldn't hurt his chances!"

"I'd guess not," Julian agreed with a grin, then cocked his head at the prince. "I'm glad to hear you're thinking beyond the end of the journey, Your Highness. But why a dukedom?"

"Because I want to be something more than the black sheep," Roger said with a much thinner smile. "Of course, you haven't asked me which planet I want."

"Oh, no!" Despreaux shook her head. "You've got to be joking!"

"Marduk has all of the requirements for a successful and productive Imperial Membership planet," Roger replied. "The fact that it's held directly in the Family's name would make it a lot simpler for Mother to designate it as such, and the Mardukans are fine people. They *deserve* a better life than that of medieval peons. And if one Roger Ramius Sergei Alexander Chiang MacClintock shepherds them from barbarism to civilization over five or ten decades, then that prince is going to be remembered for something more than being an unfortunate by-blow of the Empress."

"But . . ." Despreaux stopped and looked around at the ocean. "You want to raise *kids* on this planet? *Our* children?"

"Right, well, I'll just be going," Julian said as he stepped back. "Remember, no hitting, Nimashet. And no removing any limbs or vital organs."

"Oh, shut up, Adib," the sergeant said sharply. "And you don't have to leave. It's not like Roger's plans are any huge secret."

"Our plans," the prince corrected mildly. "And, yes, I think this would make a fine dukedom. Among other things, it would get you away from Imperial City's biddies—male and female, alike. I don't think they'll be able to handle having me marry one of my bodyguards as opposed to, say, one of their own well-trained, highly-qualified, and exquisitely-bred daughters. None of whom would have lasted ten minutes on Marduk. Princess of the Empire or not, some of those dragons will make your life Hell, given half a chance, and to be perfectly honest, neither you nor I really have the skills to respond in an appropriate—and nonlethal—fashion." He flashed her a wicked smile.

"And if you think I'm going to set up shop at K'Vaern's Cove or Q'Nkok, you're crazy," he went on. "I was thinking of the Ran Tai valley, frankly."

"Hmmm." Despreaux's expression was suddenly much more thoughtful. The valley was four thousand meters above the steamy Mardukan lowlands, and actually got chilly at night. It wasn't subject to the continuous rain of the jungles, either. All in all, it was a rather idyllic spot for humans. Which meant it was hell for Mardukans, of course.

"'Hmmm,' indeed," Julian said. "But you're assuming the Empress doesn't have some other task perfectly suited to you. She probably has a half dozen things she would've liked to throw your way if she'd trusted you before we left. Frankly, letting you 'languish in a backwater' is probably going to be at the bottom of her list."

"I may not give Mother the choice," Roger said darkly. "Frankly, I don't give a damn about Mother's needs at this point. My days of caring what Mother thinks ended in Marshad."

"She's your Empress, just as she is mine, Roger," Despreaux said. "And it's your Empire, just as it is mine. And our children's."

"One of these days, I will stop having to say this . . ." Cord began with a gesture that was the Mardukan equivalent of a resigned sigh.

"I know, I know," Roger answered. " 'I was born to duty.' I got it the first time."

"And it's a big cruel universe out there, Your Highness," Julian said with unwonted seriousness. "If you think the Boman and Kranolta were bad, you need to pay a little more attention to the Saints. There's not much worse than a 'civilized' society that considers human beings expendable. 'One death is a tragedy, a million is a statistic.' They *live* that philosophy. Also, 'The only problem with biospheres is that they occasionally develop sophonts.' I mean, these people aren't just into human extinction; they want to get rid of the Phaenurs and the Mardukans and the Althari, too. *All* sophonts. Except, of course, the best of the 'enlightened' Saint leadership, who—unlike any other enviro-destructive tool-using species—are capable of 'handling' the management of planets. Amazing how they think our pissant population growth rate is so bad when their Archon has six kids and nearly fifty grandkids."

"Okay, okay," Roger said. "I get the point. If Mother has something worthwhile she wants me to do, I'll do it. Okay?"

"Okay," Despreaux agreed. "Of course, that assumes we live to get off this mudball. But so far nothing's been able to stop our Rog," she added with a smile.

"Sail ho!" the Mardukan at the fore topmast crosstrees called suddenly. "Sail on the starboard bow, fine!" After a moment he leaned down and shouted again. "Looks like some more behind it!"

"And where there are sails, there are cities and trade," Julian observed.

"And where there's trade, there are pirates," Despreaux added. "And multiple sails means either a convoy, or . . ."

"Pirates," Roger said. The platform at the foremast crosstrees was crowded with four humans, D'Nal Cord, and Captain T'Sool. Fortunately, the Mardukan lookout had remained at his post at the fore topmast crosstrees, twelve meters above them. His greater height above sea level gave him a marginally better view, but the humans could see the oncoming sails themselves, and everyone who could had climbed the ratlines for a better look.

"Why pirates?" Pahner asked.

"The ship in the lead is carrying too much canvas for conditions," the prince replied. "They're running with the wind, but the breeze has been steadily increasing all afternoon. Between seeing another ship coming towards them—and I assume they've spotted us—and the increasing breeze, not to mention the way it's clouding up for a storm, she should have reduced sail by now. And she hasn't. So whatever she's sailing away from is more dangerous than risking a cracked mast or even capsizing."

The Marine glanced speculatively at the prince. Roger was still gazing out at the approaching ships, but he seemed to feel the weight of Pahner's eyes, and turned to meet them.

"So what's our call?" he asked the captain.

Pahner returned his own attention to the unknown ships and

dialed the magnification back up on his helmet systems as he pondered that. The safe bet was simply to avoid the entire situation. There was no upside to an engagement . . . except that they had almost no information about the continent towards which they were traveling.

If Roger's analysis was correct, and if they were able to make contact with the ship being pursued, it might be to their benefit. There appeared to be six of the—probable—pirate ships. Each was similar to an ancient cog, but with a pair of masts, not just one. Each mast carried only a single square sail, however, and their deep, rounded, high-sided hulls had clumsy-looking, castlelike foredeck citadels which undoubtedly mounted some of Marduk's massive, unwieldy bombards. They were scarcely the sleekest ships he'd ever seen, and he wondered why pirates, if that was what they were, didn't have ships a tad faster.

"What's an alternative to pirates?" he asked.

"Is this a trick question, Captain?" Kosutic inquired.

"I don't think so," Roger said. "I think his point is that if they *are* pirates, all well and good. If we blow the crap out of them, we establish our bona fides with the local powers that be. But if they're not pirates, announcing our intentions with a broadside might be a Very Bad Idea. We have to make peaceful and, hopefully, smooth contact with the local government. So what if they're harmless merchant ships which are supposed to be sailing in company, and the lead ship just has a lousy captain who's gotten too far ahead of the rest? In that case, blowing them away without a warning would *not* be a good way to make 'smooth' contact."

"Exactly," Pahner said. "So what are the other possibilities?"

"The boat in the lead could be a smuggler," Kosutic suggested. "Or something along those lines. And the ones behind could be revenue cutters. Well, revenue boats. Revenue tubs."

"And it could be even more complex than that," Roger pointed out. "They could be operating under letters of marque or some equivalent. So the ones in back could be both pirates *and* representatives of a government we need to contact. And if that's the case, asking the lead ship won't tell us so."

"All right," Pahner said with a nod. "We'll tack to intercept the group. We will not fire until fired upon. Get a helmet system for Ms. O'Casey so she can use the amplifiers for communication. We'll move alongside or send off a boarding party to make contact. If we take fire from either group, we'll respond with a single broadside. That should make the situation clear. If they continue to press it, we sink 'em."

"And if they *are* 'official' pirates?" Roger asked.

"We'll deal with that as we have to," Pahner answered. "We need intel on this continent . . . but we also need to live to use it."

CHAPTER SEVEN

Tob Kerr, master of the merchant vessel *Rain Daughter*, closed the glass and cursed. He wasn't sure where the strange ships had come from—there wasn't anything on that bearing but the Surom Shoals, and nobody actually lived in these demon-infested waters—but they were headed right for him. And sailing at least forty degrees closer to the wind than any tack he could take. He not only didn't recognize the origin of the ships, he couldn't even begin to identify their design, or imagine how sails like that could work.

However they did it, though, they obviously did a better job than his own ship could manage, and he wondered where they could possibly have sprung from.

The Lemmar Raiders behind him, on the other hand, were all too well known a quantity. With luck, they would only take his cargo. More likely, though, they would sell him and the crew into slavery, and sell his ship for a prize. Either way, he was ruined. So the best bet was to continue on course and hope for a gift from the Sar, because this was clearly a case of worse the devil you knew than the devil you didn't.

He looked back at the oncoming strangers. The more he studied them, the odder they looked. They were low, rakish, and almost unbelievably fast, and they carried an enormous sail area—one far larger than anything Kerr had ever seen before. It was amazing that they could sail the deep ocean at all; with so little freeboard, he had to wonder why the water didn't wash right over their decks. But it didn't. In fact, they rode the swells like *embera*, green foam casting up from their bows and their strange, triangular sails hard as boards as they sliced impossibly into the oncoming wind.

He grabbed a line and slid to the deck. The calluses of decades at sea made nothing of the friction, and his mate, Pelu Mupp walked over to him and flipped his false-hands in an expression of worry.

"Should we change course?" he asked.

It was a damnably reasonable question, Kerr thought grimly. The Lemmar Raiders had been in a fairly unfavorable position at the start. Well, as far as *Rain Daughter* was concerned. Certain other ships had been less fortunate, but Kerr had taken full advantage of the slim opportunity for escape the pirates' preoccupation with the convoy's other members had offered him. By the time they'd been free to turn their full attention to *Rain Daughter*, Kerr had managed to put enough distance between them to give him and his crew a better than even chance. A stern chase was always a long one, and under those conditions, victory could go to either side. The pirate ships were a bit faster than the merchantman, but the *Daughter* had a good lead, and any number of circumstances could have resulted in the Kirstian ship's escaping, especially if Kerr could only have kept clear of the Lemmar until darkness fell. But now, with the unknowns closing from almost dead to leeward, the trap seemed to have closed.

"No," Kerr said. "We'll hold our course. They *might* be friendly. And how much worse than the Raiders could they be?"

If the crew went into slavery, they would probably end up back in Kirsti, but as "guests" of the Fire Priests. And if that was the alternative, he preferred to throw himself over the side now.

"We'll hold our course, Mupp. And let the Lady of the Waters decide."

Roger pulled on a strand of hair and sighed.

"Captain, much as I hate making suggestions—" he began, only to stop dead as Pahner let loose an uncharacteristic bark of laughter that momentarily made him jump. Then the captain snorted.

"Yes, Your Highness?"

"Well, I *don't*," Roger retorted.

"I know you don't, Your Highness," Pahner said with a smile. "You tend to do something by yourself, and then ask me if it was okay later. That's different from making suggestions, I'll admit. So let's have it—what's the suggestion?"

"I was thinking about wind position," Roger continued, after deciding that it wasn't a good time for a discussion of whether one Prince Roger MacClintock had been making too many stupid mistakes lately. Most of the watchers had returned to the deck once the general outline of the approaching ships and their formation had been established. A Marine private was now perched at the fore topmast crosstrees beside the Mardukan lookout, using her helmet systems to refine the data. But at this point it was a matter of waiting nearly two hours as the ships slowly closed the intervening gap.

"They're coming in on our starboard bow, straight out of the wind, but the formation of six ships is spread to our west, and it takes a few minutes for us to wear around. If we stay on this course, when the pursuers come up to us, the most westerly ship will be in a position that would make it hard for us to completely avoid her."

"I'm . . . not quite getting this," Pahner admitted.

Roger thought for a moment, then did a quick sketch on his toot, detailing the human/K'Vaernian flotilla, the lead unknown, and the trailers.

"I'm sliding over a graphic," he said, flipping the sketch from his toot to the Marine's. "From the point of view of avoiding contact, we can break off from the lead ship easily. But if we decided to avoid the trailers, we'd have three choices. One would be to tack to starboard when we come up to them. That would put us in a position to take full advantage of the schooners' weatherliness to run past them into the wind and avoid contact handily. But it takes a bit of time to tack, and there's a small risk of getting caught in irons."

Pahner nodded at that. A couple of times, especially early in the voyage, when the native Mardukan captains were still getting accustomed to the new rig, one or more of the ships had been caught "in irons" while tacking, and ended up facing directly into the wind, effectively unable to move or maneuver until they could fall off enough to regather way. It was not a situation he wanted to be in with potential hostiles around.

"We don't want that to happen," he observed. "Go on."

"Our second choice would be to fall off to the west," Roger said, "opening out our sails and either sailing across the wind, or coming around to let it fill our sails from behind while we run almost away from it. That's a 'reach' or a 'broad reach.' The problem is, on either tack, the westernmost ship would have at least some opportunity to intercept us. We could probably show them our heels—I'd back any of ours, even *Snarleyow*, to outrun anything they've got. But there's a risk of interception."

"In which case, we blow away whatever unfortunate soul intercepts us," Pahner noted as he brought up the sketch on his implant and studied it.

"Yes, Captain, we can do that," Roger agreed, licking a salty drop of sweat off his upper lip. "But I submit that it would be better to be in a position where we can avoid contact altogether, if that's what we decide to do. Or control the maneuver menu if we decide to engage."

"Can we?" the captain asked. "And should we be discussing this with Poertena or the Skipper?"

"Maybe," Roger said. "Probably. But I was thinking. If we tack to starboard and put them on our port side, we've got all that maneuver room to starboard. It's a better wind position. Also, if we decide to jump in, we can get to windward for maneuvering better from that position. But we need to wait a bit, until we're a little closer."

"I'll talk it over with T'Sool," Pahner agreed. "But unless I'm much mistaken, that's a very good idea."

"They're wearing around," Pelu said.

"I can see that," Kerr answered. He rubbed his horns as he considered the small fleet's maneuvers. Its units were changing to an easterly heading on the port tack, and the maneuver was a thing of beauty for any seaman to watch. The sails seemed to float into position naturally, and in a remarkably short period of time, all five ships were hove over and flying before the wind.

"They're in a better position to drop on us from windward," Pelu worried. "Could they be some new ship type out of Lemmar?"

"If Lemmar could build ships like that," the captain snorted, "we'd already be in chains in Kirsti! And if they're in a better position to drop on us, they're also in a better position to *avoid* all of us. They can leave us in their wake any time they want to now, but before, they could have been cut off by the western Reavers. Actually, I think what they're doing now is a better sign."

"I wish we knew who they were," Pelu fretted.

"I wonder if they're wishing the same thing?"

"Ready for some more unsolicited input?" Roger asked with a grin.

"Certainly, Your Highness," Pahner replied with a slight smile. "Every fiber of my being lives to serve the Empire."

"Somehow, I think I detected just a tad of sarcasm attached to that answer," Roger said with an answering grin. "But I digress. What I was going to say is that we need to make contact with these folks."

"Agreed. And you have a suggestion?"

"Well, for first contact, we'll need someone who's well versed with the translator program and whose toot has enough capacity to run it. And that means either Ms. O'Casey or myself. And since it's a potentially dangerous situation . . ."

"You think it makes more sense to send the person I'm supposed to be guarding," Pahner finished. Then he shook his head. Firmly. "No."

"So you're going to send Eleanora?" Roger asked sweetly.

"Quit smiling at me!" Pahner snapped. "Damn it. I'm the commander of your bodyguard, Your Highness. I'm not supposed to be sending you into situations because they're too *dangerous* to send somebody else!"

"Uh-huh," Roger said. "So, you're sending Eleanora?"

"There is no way you're going over to that ship," Pahner said. "No. Way."

"I see. So . . . ?"

"Ah, freedom!"

Roger leaned back in the sailing harness, suspended from a very thin bit of rope less than an arm length above the emerald sea as the catamaran cut through the water at nearly sixteen knots. D'Nal Cord shifted and tried to get into something that felt like a stable position—difficult for someone his size on the deck of the flimsy craft—and rubbed a horn in exasperation.

"You have an unusual concept of freedom, Roger."

Most of the small boats of the flotilla were traditional "v" hulls, but both Roger and Poertena had insisted on at least one small "cat" for fast movement. Building it had required nearly as much human-provided engineering knowledge as the much larger schooners—light, fast catamarans require precise flexion in their crossbraces—but the result was a small craft that in any sort of decent weather was even faster than the schooners.

And it was *fun* to sail.

"I have to admit that this is sort of fun," Despreaux said, fanning her uniform top. "And the breeze is refreshing."

"Back on Earth, catting and skiing were as close as I ever got to being free," Roger pointed out, bounding forward in the harness to see if it improved the point of sail. "You guys would actually let me get away for a little bit."

"Don't complain," Kosutic replied. "Your lady mother's spent most of her life wrapped in cotton. As your grandfather's only child, there was no way the Regiment was willing to risk her at all. She rarely even got to leave the palace grounds."

"Frankly, I could care less about Mother's problems," Roger said coldly, swinging back in his harness as Poertena altered the cat's course slightly.

"Maybe not," the sergeant major replied. "But you've had more experience with 'real people' in the last six months than she has in her whole life. The closest she ever got to dealing with anyone but Imperial functionaries and politicians was the Academy. And even there, she spent the whole time still wrapped in cotton. They wouldn't

even *consider* having her do live zero-G drills—not out of
atmosphere, at least. It all had to be in simulators, where there was *no*
possibility of exposing her to death pressure. And if they never let
her do that, you can just imagine how much less likely they were to
let her do things like, oh—just as an example that comes from the
top of my head, you understand—leading a charge into a barbarian
horde. And no cut-ups like Julian were allowed within a kilometer of
her."

"And your point is?" Roger asked. He leaned further outward
and dangled his hand into the water as a slightly stronger puff of wind
hit the sail. "Speaking of risks, you do realize that if there are any of
those giant *coll* around, we're toast?"

"That sort of *is* the point," Kosutic said soberly. "Imperial City is
filled with professional politicians and noble flunkies, most of whom
have never had to scramble for money to supply a unit in the field.
Who've never been exposed to 'lower class' conditions. Who have
never slept on the ground, never gone to bed hungry. In some cases,
that means people who not only don't understand the majority of the
population of the Empire, but who also don't like them or care about
them. And in other cases—which I happen to think are worse—they
don't understand them, but they *idealize* them. They think there's a
special dignity to poverty. Or a special quality to being born into
misery and dying in it."

"Saint Symps," Despreaux said.

"And various soclibs," Kosutic agreed. "Especially the older style
pro-Ardane redistributionists."

"There's at least an argument there," Roger said. "I mean, too
much concentration of power, and you're not much better off than
under the Dagger Lords." He paused and grinned. "On the other
hand, I *know* you're all a bunch of low-lifes!"

"And if you live entirely by what you think is 'the will of the
people,' you get the Solar Union," Kosutic continued, pointedly
ignoring the prince's last comment.

"Pockers," Poertena growled, and spat over the side.

"Yeah, Armagh mostly sat that one out," the sergeant major
admitted. "But Pinopa got it bad."

"What really burned some of the early members of the Family was that the ISU used Roger MacClintock's policies as their 'model' for that idiocy," Roger said. "Prez Roger, that is. Roger the Unifier. But without accepting the societal sacrifices that were necessary. And then, when it all came apart, they tried to blame *us*!"

"I could kind of understand getting involved in planetary reconstruction," Despreaux commented. "Some of those planets were even worse off than Armagh. But leaving your main base completely uncovered was just idiotic."

"And why did they do that?" Kosutic asked, and proceeded to answer her own question. "They had to. They were already so wrapped up with social welfare programs that they couldn't build the sort of fleet and garrison force they needed and still be redistributionist. So they depended on bluff, sent the entire damned fleet off to try to do some planet-building, and the Daggers nipped in and ate the Solar System's lunch."

"The Daggers were very good at killing the golden goose," Roger said. "But we—the MacClintocks, that is—learned that lesson pretty well."

"Did we?" Kosutic asked. "Did we really?"

"Oh, no," Roger moaned. "This isn't another one of those 'let's not tell Roger,' things, is it?"

"No." The sergeant major laughed, but her eyes were on the native ship they'd come to meet, and her gaze was wary as Poertena wore around its stern, preparing to come alongside to port. "But take a good look at your grandfather's career," she continued, "and then tell me we've learned. Another person who'd never worked a day in his life and thought the lower classes were somehow magical. And, therefore, that they should be coddled, paid, and overprotected . . . at the expense of the Fleet and the Saint borders."

"Well, that's one mistake *I* would never make as Emperor," Roger joked as Poertena completed his maneuver. "I know you're all a bunch of lying, lazy pockers."

"Be about time to hail," Poertena said. The ship and the catamaran were about a hundred meters apart now, on near parallel headings, with the cat slightly to the rear of the much larger merchant ship. Since that put the wind at their stern, Poertena had brought the sail in until it was luffing and dangerously close to jibing, or falling over to the other side of the boat. It might make them a little anxious about collisons between things like heads and booms, but it also slowed them down enough that they wouldn't pass the slower Mardukan ship.

"Get us a little closer," Roger ordered as he unclipped the harness and secured it to the mast. "I need to be able to hear their reply. And I don't see any guns."

"Odd, that," Kosutic said. "I agree we need to get closer, but if those are pirates, or even letters of marque, chasing them, you'd think they would have defenses. And I don't even see a swivel gun."

"Something else to ask about," Roger said as Poertena fell off to starboard. The change quickly filled the sail, set as it was for a reach, and the cat began skipping across the rolling swell.

"Shit!" Despreaux flattened herself and tried to figure out where to move as it suddenly seemed obvious that the cat was about to go clear over on its side.

"*Hooowah!*" the prince said with a laugh, throwing his weight back outboard again to offset the heel. "Don't dunk us, for God's sake, Poertena! We're trying to show our good side."

"And *I* cannot swim," Cord added.

"Lifejackets!" Roger laughed. "I knew we forgot something!"

"T'is close enough?" Poertena asked as he brought the boat back to port with a degree more caution. They had closed to within sixty meters or so, and the Mardukan ship's crew was clearly evident, lining the side, many of them with weapons in their hands.

"Close enough," Roger agreed, then stood back up and grasped a line to stay steady. "Try not to flop us around too much."

"What? And have you get all wet and sloppy?" Despreaux said.

"Hea'en forbid!" Poertena laughed. "I try. Never know, though."

"You'd better," Kosutic growled. "Straight and steady."

"Just keep us on this heading," Kerr said to the helmsman. "They don't seem to be threatening us. And I don't see what they'd be able to do with that dinky little boat, anyway."

"Who are they?" Pelu asked.

"How the hell do I know?" Kerr shot back in exasperation. "They look like giant *vern*, but that's crazy."

"What do we do if they want to come aboard?"

"We let them," Kerr answered after a moment. "Their ships can run rings around us, and I think those ports showing on the sides are for bombards. If they are, there's not much we can do but heave to and do whatever they say."

"It's not like you just to give up," Pelu protested.

"They're not Lemmar, and they're not Fire Priests," Kerr pointed out. "Given the choice of them, or the Lemmar and the priests, I'll always take the unknown."

"Here goes nothing," Roger said.

"What language are you going to use?" Despreaux asked.

"The kernel that came with the program. It's probably taken from the tribes around the starport, and we're finally getting close to that continent. Hopefully it will at least be familiar to them for a change." He cleared his throat.

"Hullo the ship!"

"Oh, Cran," Pelu said.

"High Krath," Kerr muttered. "Why did it have to be High Krath?"

"Are they Fire Priests?" the helmsman asked nervously. "It can't be Fire Priests clear out here, can it?"

"It could be," Kerr admitted heavily. "Those could be Guard vessels."

"I never heard of the Guard having ships like that any more than the Lemmar," Pelu said. "Anyway, they would've used Krath, not High Krath. Most Guard *officers* can't speak High Krath."

"But they're not priests!" Kerr snarled, rubbing his horns furiously. "So where did they learn High Krath?"

"No response," Despreaux said. The unnecessary comment made it evident just how nervous the veteran NCO was.

"They're talking it over, though," Roger said. "I think the two by the helmsman are the leaders."

"Concur," the sergeant major agreed. "But they aren't acting real happy to see us."

"Oh, well," Roger sighed. "Time to up the ante. *Permission to come aboard?*"

"Well, at least they're asking," Pelu observed. "That's something."

"That's odd, is what it is," Kerr answered. He stepped to the rail and took a glance at the more distant ships. They had crossed his course almost a glass before, and then swung back to the west. At this point, they were still to his east and the range from them to *Rain Daughter* would have been opening as she ran past them on her southeasterly heading . . . except for how close they were to the wind. As it was, their nearest approach was still to come. But it didn't seem that they intended any harm. Either that, or they were jockeying for a good wind position.

"What do we do?"

"Let them board," Kerr said. His curiosity was getting the better of his good sense, and he knew it. But he didn't suppose, realistically speaking, that he had very many options, anyway. "One, I want to know who they are. Two, if we've got part of their crew on board, they're less likely to attack us."

He walked over to the rail and waved both true-hands.

"Come aboard!"

Roger caught the dangling line and swarmed up it. Technically, he should have let either Kosutic or Despreaux go first, and he could hear the sergeant major's curses even through the sound of rigging and water. But of the three of them, he was the most familiar with small boats, and he felt that even if it was a deliberate trap, he could probably shoot his way clear of the four-person welcoming party.

The scummies waiting for him were subtly different from those on the far continent. They were definitely shorter than the Vashin Northerners who made up the bulk of the cavalry, closer to the Diasprans in height. Their horns were also significantly different, with less of a curve and with less prominent age ridges. Part of that might have been cosmetic, though, because at least one of them had horns which had clearly been dyed. They were also wearing clothes, which, except for armor, had been a catch-as-catch-can item on the far continent. The "clothing" was a sort of leather kilt, evidently with a loincloth underneath. Otherwise (unless they were *very* unlike any of the other Mardukans the humans had met), certain "parts" would be showing under the kilt. The two leaders also wore baldrics which supported not only swords, but also a few other tools, and even what were apparently writing implements.

The leader of the foursome, the one who had waved for them to board, stepped forward. His horns were undyed and long, indicating a fairly good age for a Mardukan. He wasn't as old as Cord, though, or if he was, he was in better condition, because his skin was firm and well coated in slime, without the occasional dry spots that indicated advanced age in the locals.

Roger raised both hands in a gesture of peace. It wasn't taking much of a chance; he could still draw and fire before any of the four raised a weapon.

"I am pleased to meet you," he said, speaking slowly and distinctly and using the words available on the kernel that was the only Mardukan language the software had initially offered. "I am Prince Roger MacClintock. I greet you in the name of the Empire of Man."

"*Sadar* Tob Kerr . . . greet," the officer responded.

Roger nodded gravely while he considered what the toot was telling him. The language the local was using was similar to the kernel, but it contained words which were additional to the kernel's five-hundred-word vocabulary, combined with some that were clearly from another language entirely. It appeared that the leader was attempting to use the kernel language, but that it was a second language for him, not primary. The toot was flagging some of the words as probably being totally bogus. The captain—this Tob Kerr— clearly wasn't a linguist.

"Use your own language, rather than the one I'm using," Roger invited as Kosutic followed him over the side. If the others were on plan, Cord would be the next up, then Despreaux. Poertena would remain in the cat. "I will be able to learn it quickly," he continued. "But I must ask questions, if I may. What is the nature of your position, and who are the ships that pursue you?"

"We are a . . . from the Krath to the . . . base at Strem. Our . . . was . . . by Lemmar Raiders. The Guard ships were destroyed, and we are the only ship who has made it this far. But the Lemmar are . . . I do not think we'll . . . Strem, even if we can . . ."

Great, Roger thought. *What the hell is Krath?* Then he realized that the answer was lodged in the back of his brain.

"Krath is the mainland ahead?" he asked. The toot automatically took the words it had already learned from the language the captain was using where it had them, and substituted kernel words where it didn't. The sentence was marginally understandable.

"Yes," the officer replied. "The Krath are the . . . of the Valley. Strem is a recent acquisition. The . . . is attempting to subdue the Lemmar Raiders, but taking Strem means they have to supply it. We were carrying supplies and ritual . . . for the garrison. But the Lemmar came upon us in force and took our escorts. Since then, these six have been running down the survivors. I believe we are the last."

"Oh bloody hell," Roger muttered. "Are the rest between us and the mainland?"

"Yes," the local told him. "If you're making for Kirsti, then they are on your path. They're just below the horizon from the mast."

"Great. Just . . . great," Roger muttered again, then shook himself. "Tob Kerr, meet Sergeant Major Eva Kosutic, my senior noncommissioned officer." Cord dropped to the deck, and Roger rested his left hand lightly on the shaman's lower shoulder. "And this is D'Nal Cord, my *asi*." He had to hope that the translation software could explain what an *asi* was.

"I greet you, as well," Kerr said, then returned his attention to Roger and spoke earnestly. "Your ships can wear around and make sail for Strem. It's less than a day's sail from here, and you would surely make it. Those fine craft of yours are the fastest I've ever seen. But I cannot guarantee the garrison's greeting when you arrive there—this convoy was important to them."

"Are you getting this, Sergeant Major?" Roger asked, shutting off the translation circuit and slipping into Imperial.

"Yes, Your Highness," the NCO replied. Roger's toot had automatically updated her onboard software with its translations of the local language. As soon as he got back into proximity with the rest of the party, the updates would be transferred to them, as well, skipping from system to system. The Marine toots were well insulated against electronic attack, and while the greater capacity and power of Roger's toot made him the logical person to do the initial translation, his much more paranoid design required a manual transfer, rather than the automatic network of the Marines.

"I'm still not sure of *what* the Lemmar are," the prince continued. "But if this fellow is telling the truth, they're enemies of the continental forces. And there are apparently a stack of prize ships, with some crew to fight, between us and the continent. Again, if this guy is telling the truth."

"Pardon me," Kerr interrupted, "but I'd like to ask a question of my own, if I may. Who *are* you, and where did you come from?"

"We came across the Eastern Ocean." Roger trotted out the set response. "We are the first group we know of to actually make it, although others have tried. Our intent is to travel to the larger continent to the north—to Krath—and establish trade routes. But you say there are pirates between here and there?"

"Yes, both the six you see, and the prizes, some of whom are armed," Kerr said. "And as far as I know, you are indeed the first group to make the crossing. A few from our side have also attempted the crossing, including one large group of ships. It was assumed that there were very hostile people on the far side of the ocean. I take it that was wrong?"

"Oh, yeah," Kosutic broke in. "Your problem was very hostile and very large fish *between* here and there. *Coll* fish the size of a ship. We lost one of our vessels to one of them."

"We must make decisions and communicate with the other ships," Cord pointed out. Without a toot, the shaman was unable to understand anything Kerr had said, but, as always, he maintained his pragmatic focus on the matter in hand.

"You're right," Roger agreed. He nodded to his *asi*, then turned back to the merchantman's captain. "Tob Kerr, we must cross back to our own ships and advise them as to the situation. Then we will decide whether to turn for Strem or to go on."

"You cannot go on," Pelu broke in excitedly. "There are six of them—plus the armed prizes!"

Roger snorted, and Cord, standing at his back, sighed at the sound. Not so, the sergeant major.

"And your point is?" Eva Kosutic asked with a snort of her own.

"The Lemmar are an island nation," Roger said, pointing to the chart they had extracted from Tob Kerr. "They live in this volcanic archipelago that stretches down from the continent to this large island to the southeast. South from *that*, there's open ocean which is apparently also infested with killer *coll* fish. Nobody's ever come back to say 'aye or nay,' at any rate. But there's another archipelago to the southwest of it that stretches to the southern continent, and they're in contact with that continent on a fairly tenuous basis. This 'Strem Island' is apparently the crossroads of the trade between them, which makes it a rather rich prize. But while it can produce sufficient food, it also requires additional supply from the mainland. And it was a supply convoy that got hit. They were taking down weapons, new soldiers, and 'temple servitors,' and they would have brought back the goods—mostly spices—that have been stored at Strem awaiting safe transport."

"But the Lemmar changed their plans," Pahner said.

"Yes, Sir," the sergeant major answered. "The Lemmar are pirates, and there have been plenty of times in human history when pirates banded together into fairly large groups. But from what Tob Kerr says, having six of their 'large' ships pounce on the convoy simultaneously was a fairly bad surprise. And the Krath apparently aren't particularly good sailors—or, at least, their Navy is no great shakes. The Lemmar took out the three galleys that were supposed to guard the convoy without any ship losses of their own, then tore into the merchantmen like dire wolves on a flock of sheep. As far as Kerr knows, his ship's the only survivor."

"We have an opportunity here," Roger noted carefully.

"I'm aware of that, Your Highness," Pahner said. "Remember that little talk about going out on a limb, though? This is the classic Chinese sign for chaos: danger and opportunity mixed. Of course there's an opportunity . . . but my job is to pay attention to the danger, as well."

"If we take out the pirates," Roger pointed out, "and recapture most of the ships, the authorities on the continent should automatically treat us as the good guys."

"*Should*," Eleanora O'Casey interjected. "But that depends on the society, and there's no societal data at all in the database where these people are concerned. In fact, there's no societal data for *any* of the locals on this continent. Which, even allowing for the general paucity of data on this godforsaken planet, is a remarkable oversight.

"Without any information at all, it's impossible to say how they might actually react to our intervention. They could resent our showing our military prowess. They could be worried by it. They could even have an honor system under which saving their people would put *us* in *their* debt. There are a thousand possibilities that you haven't explored which could arise from recapturing those ships. And that assumes that, militarily, we can."

"Oh, I think we can," Pahner noted. He knew he was a landlubber, but it would take someone without eyes to miss the clear difference in capabilities between the ships. The pirate vessels were somewhat sleeker than the merchantman, and obviously had much larger crews—a common sign of pirates. But they mounted only a few clumsy swivel guns for broadside armament to back up the single large bombard fixed and pointed forward in their heavy bow "castles." *Sinking* them wouldn't be difficult, not with the flotilla's advantage in artillery. Reducing the crews, and then taking them by a boarding action, wouldn't even have been too costly in casualties, given all the bored Diasprans and Vashin they had on board. But there would be *some* casualties, and the end result had better be worth every one of them.

"Militarily, we can take these six fairly easily," the captain continued. "But we *will* take casualties, especially if we try to take them intact."

"How much are these ships worth?" Fain asked, with a slight clap of his hands that indicated mild humor. "I'm sorry to interrupt, but from the point of view of the people taking the casualties, there are only two things they're going to worry about. Will it prevent us from taking the starport—which is our big mission—and how much money will we get for those ships?"

"Mercenary," Roger said with a smile. "In most societies, ships cost a good bit. I'd say that if we can get them to port, and if the authorities permit us to sell them as a matter of standard prize rules, then there'll be a fair amount to spread around. Even if we take only one. And we may be able to claim most or all of the ships the pirates have already taken as legitimate prizes of war, assuming we manage to retake them, as well. If we can, it would be enough for an officer to retire on."

"Well, I already have that," Fain said. "But not all of the troops were in on the sack of Sindi. As one of the potential casualties, and if we can determine that we can sell them as prizes, my choice is to take the ships."

"T'ey going to slow us down sailing upwind to Krat'," Poertena pointed out. "We migh' be able to rig some jib sails, but t'ey still ain't gonna be as fast as us. Not enough keel, for one t'ing."

"That's something to think about quite a bit down the line," Pahner noted. "Taking these six warships is the significant issue. After that, we contact Kerr again and get his reaction. If it's favorable, we'll determine where to get sufficient prize crews, then sail on our way. If we encounter the rest of the prizes, we'll engage as seems most favorable at the time."

"In other words, we're going to play it by ear," Roger said with a grin. "Where in hell have I heard that operations order before?"

CHAPTER EIGHT

Cred Cies fingered his sword as five of the six ships changed course to windward. The biggest of the strangers held its initial course, heading to intercept—or protect—the fat merchantship *Rage of Lemmar* had pursued so long.

"They're going to engage us," Cra Vunet said. The mate spat over the side. "Six to five. The odds favor us."

Cies looked at the skies and frowned.

"Yes, they do. But no doubt they can count as well as we can, and they've obviously chosen to leave their biggest ship behind. I'm not sure I like the looks of that. Besides, it will be pouring by the time they get here. Only the bombard is sure to fire under those circumstances, and they seem to have nearly as many men aboard as we do. It will be a tough fight."

"And after it, we'll sail back to Lomsvupe with five ships of a new and superior design—six, after we scoop up the one that's hanging back!" the mate said with a true-hand flick of humor. "That will pay for a thousand nights of pleasure! Better than a single stinking landsman tub."

"On the other hand, they clearly think they can take *us*," Cies pointed out, still the pessimist. "And we'll have to wear around to engage, while they'll have the favor of the wind. If I'd been sure they

113

were going to attack before, I would have changed course to attack *them* from upwind, and with our bombard bearing. But I didn't. So, like I say, the fight will be a tough one. Tough."

"We're the Lemmar," Vunet said with another gesture of humor. "A fight is only worth bragging about if it's a tough one!"

"We'll see," Cies replied. "Wear ship to port; let's see if we can't get to windward of them after all before we engage."

"There they go," Roger said, leaning on the anti-*coll* bead cannon mounted on *Ima Hooker*'s afterdeck. "Wearing to port, just like I predicted."

"I don't get it," Pahner admitted. "Even if they manage to get to windward of us, it still leaves them in a position where we can rake their sterns."

"They don't think that way, Captain," Roger said. "They fight with fixed frontal guns, which means they don't have a concept of a broadside. They're expecting us to do what *they'd* do: turn to starboard just before we come opposite them, and try to sail straight into their sides. By that time, if they have the respective speeds figured right, they'll be slightly upwind and in a position to swing down on our flank. The worst that could happen is that we end up with both of us going at each other front-to-front and both broad-on to the wind, which isn't a bad point of sailing for one of those tubs.

"Now, the question is whether or not there's some way we can tap dance around out of range of those bombards while we get into a position to hammer them broadside-to-broadside."

"I thought the idea was to cross the enemy's 'T,'" Julian interjected as he watched the "tubs" wearing around. It was evident that the pirate vessels had extremely large crews for two reasons— both as fighters and because the squaresail ships just plain required more live bodies on the sheets and braces. "That's what they're always talking about in historical romances."

Roger turned towards him and lifted first his helmet visor and then an eyebrow.

"Historical *romances*?" he repeated, and Julian shrugged with a slightly sheepish expression.

"What can I say? I'm a man of many parts."

"I wouldn't have expected romance novels to be one of them," Roger commented, dropping the visor back as he returned his attention to observing the enemy. "But to answer your question, crossing the 'T' is an ideal tactic against an enemy who uses broadsides. But except for some swivel guns to discourage boarders, these guys don't have any broadside fire at all to speak of. Which isn't quite the case where those big, pocking bombards in the bows are concerned. So we're going to try very, very hard *not* to cross their 'T.'"

Pahner was uncomfortable. For the first time since hitting Marduk, it was clear that Roger's expertise, his knowledge, far exceeded the captain's own. On one level, Pahner was delighted that *someone* knew his ass from his elbow where the theory of combat under sail was involved. But "Colonel MacClintock" was still, for all practical purposes, a very junior officer. A surprisingly competent one, since he'd gotten over the normal "lieutenant" idiocy, but still very junior. And junior officers tended to overlook important details in combat operations. Often with disastrous consequences.

"So what plan do you recommend, Your Highness?" the captain asked after a moment.

Roger turned to look at him. The mottled plastic turned the prince's face into an unreadable set of shadows, but it was clear that his mind was running hard.

"I guess you're serious," Roger said quietly. He turned back to gaze at the distant ships and thought about it for perhaps thirty seconds. "Are you saying I should take command?" he asked finally, his voice even quieter than before.

"You're already in command," Pahner pointed out. "I'll be frank, Your Highness. I don't have a clue about how to fight a sea battle. Since you obviously do, you should run this one. If I see anything I think you've overlooked, I'll point it out. But I think this one is . . . up to you."

"Captain," Kosutic asked over the dedicated private command circuit, "are you sure about this?"

"Hold on a moment, Your Highness," Pahner said, turning

slightly away from the prince. "Gotta let 'em out of the nest eventually, Sergeant Major," he replied over the same channel.

"Okay. If you're sure," the noncom said dubiously. "But remember Ran Tai."

"I will," Pahner assured her. "I do."

He turned back to the prince, who was pacing back and forth with his hands clasped behind him, looking at the sky.

"I'm sorry, Your Highness. You were saying?"

"Actually, I wasn't." Roger stopped pacing, pulled out a strand of hair, and played with it as he continued to look at the sky. "I was thinking. And I'm about done."

"Are you going to take full command, Colonel?" the captain asked formally.

"Yes, I am," Roger replied with matching formality, his expression settling into lines of unwonted seriousness as the weight of responsibility settled on his shoulders. "The first thing we have to do is reef the sails before the squall sinks us more surely than the Lemmar."

"They're reducing sail," Cra Vunet said. The five other raider ships had completed their own turns before the wind from the storm hit and were following the *Rage* in line ahead.

"Yes," Cies said thoughtfully. "Those edge-on sails probably tend to push them over in a high wind. I imagine we'll be able to sail with it quite handily, compared to them."

"We'll lose sight of them soon!" Vunet yelled through the sudden tumult as the leading edge of the squall raced across the last few hundred meters of sea towards the *Rage*. "Here it comes!"

The squall was of the sort common to any tropical zone—a brief, murderous "gullywasher" that would drop multiple centimeters of rain in less than an hour. The blast of wind in front of the rain—the "gust front"—was usually the strongest of the entire storm, and as it swept down upon them, the placid waves to windward started to tighten up into an angry "chop" crested with white curls of foam.

The wind hit like a hurricane, and the ships heeled over sharply, even with their square sails taken up to the second reef. But the

Lemmar sailors took it with aplomb; such storms hit at least once per day.

"Well, they're gone!" Cies shouted back as the strange ships disappeared into a wall of wind, rain, and spray. "We'll stay on this course. Whether they fall off to windward or hold their own course, we'll be able to take them from the front. One shot from each ship, then we go alongside."

"What if they alter course?" Vunet shouted back.

"They're going to find it hard to wear around in this," Cies replied. "And if they try it, they'll still be settling onto course when we come on them. And the storm will probably be gone by then!"

"Come to course three-zero-five!" Roger shouted.

"I'm having a hard time punching a laser through to *Sea Foam*!" Julian yelled back over the roaring fury of the sea. "The signal's getting real attenuated by all this damned water!"

"Well, make sure you get a confirmation!" Pahner shouted, almost in the NCO's ear. "And we need a string confirmation on it!"

"Will do!"

Roger looked around the heeling ship and nodded his head. The Mardukan seamen were handling the lines well, and the situation, so far, was well in hand. The human-designed schooners had come well up into the wind, steering west-by-northwest, close-hauled on the starboard tack, in a course change which would have been literally impossible for the clumsy Mardukan pirates' rigs to duplicate. In many ways, the current conditions weren't that different from other storms they'd sailed through along the way, but they hadn't tried to maneuver in those. They'd simply held their course and hoped for the best. In this case, however, his entire plan depended upon their ability to maneuver *in* the storm.

It wouldn't be disastrous if they were unable to effect the maneuver he had in mind. It wouldn't be pleasant, but he was fairly certain that the schooners could take at least one or two shots from the pirates' bombards, assuming the simplistic weapons could even be fired under these conditions. But if they managed to pull off what he had in mind, they should suffer virtually no casualties. If he had to take losses, he would, but he'd become more and more determined to hold them to the absolute minimum as the trek went on.

The rain seemed to last forever, but finally he sensed the first signs of slackening in its pounding fury. That usually meant one more hard deluge, then the storm would clear with remarkable speed. Which meant it was almost time to start the next maneuver.

"Julian! Do you have commo?"

"Yes, Sir!" the sergeant responded instantly. "I got confirmations of course change from all ships."

"Then tell them to prepare to come to course two-seven-zero or thereabouts. And warn the gun crews to prepare for action to port, with a small possibility that it could be to starboard, instead. Tell the captains I want them to close up in line, one hundred meters of separation, as soon as the rain clears. I want them to follow us like beads on a string. Clear?"

"Clear and sent, Your Highness. And confirmed by all ships."

"Do you really have any idea where they are?" Pahner asked Roger over the helmet commo systems.

"Unless I'm much mistaken, they're over there," Roger said, gesturing off the port bow and into the blinding deluge.

"And what do we do when the other ships follow us 'like beads on a string'?" the captain asked curiously.

"Ah," Roger said, then glanced back at the commo sergeant. "To all ships, Julian. As soon as we clear the rain, send the sharpshooters to the tops."

The ship heeled hard to port as a fresh blast of wind from the north caught it, and Roger casually grabbed a stay.

"It's clearing," he observed. "Now to see where our other ships are."

"The *Foam* is right behind us," Julian said. "But they say some of the others are scattered."

The rain stopped as suddenly as it had begun, without even the slightest tapering off, and the rest of the K'Vaernian "fleet" was suddenly visible. The *Sea Foam* was some two hundred meters behind the *Hooker,* but the rest were scattered to the north and south— mostly south—of the primary course.

Roger looked the formation over and shrugged.

"Not bad. Not good, but not bad."

Pahner had to turn away to hide his smile. That simple "not bad" was a miracle. It was clear that getting the flotilla back together would take quite a few minutes, and any hope of simply turning and engaging the enemy whenever they appeared, was out of the airlock as a result. But the prince had simply shrugged and accepted that the plan would need revising. That was what a half a year of almost constant battle on Marduk had taught the hopeless young fop who'd first arrived here . . . and that, by itself, was almost worth the bodies scattered along the trail.

"Captain T'Sool," Roger said, "come to course two-seven-zero and take in the mainsail. We need to reduce speed until the rest of the fleet can catch up."

"Yes, Sir," the Mardukan acknowledged, and began shouting orders of his own.

"Julian," Roger turned back to the sergeant while T'Sool carried out his instructions. "To all ships: make all sail conformable with weather and close up in order. Get back in line; we have pirates to kill."

"Kral shit," Vunet said. Then, "Unbelievable!"

The rain had finally cleared, and the enemy fleet was once more visible . . . well upwind of their position, jockeying itself back into line. Neither he nor anyone else aboard the raiders' ships had ever heard of vessels that could do that. They must have tacked almost directly into the wind instead of wearing around before it! But it was clear that however well the individual ships might sail, they weren't well-trained as a group, and they'd gotten badly scattered by the storm.

The Lemmar ships, by contrast, were still in a nearly perfect line, and Cred Cies wasn't about to let the enemy have all day to get his formation back into order.

"Make a signal for all ships to turn towards the enemy and engage!"

"We'll be sailing almost into the teeth of the wind," Vunet pointed out.

"I understand that, Cra," Cies said with rather more patience than he actually felt. They wouldn't really be sailing into the "teeth of the wind," of course—it wasn't as if they were galleys, after all! And it was painfully evident that the strangers could sail far closer to the wind than any of his ships could hope to come. But if he edged as close to it as he could without getting himself taken all aback . . .

"We can still catch them before they reassemble," he told his mate. "Maybe."

Pahner tried not to laugh again as Roger folded his hands behind his back and assumed a mien of calculated indifference. The expression and posture of composed *sang-froid* was obviously a close copy of Pahner's own, and he'd seen more than one junior officer try it on for size. Roger was wearing it better than most, but then the prince smiled suddenly and swung his hands to the front, slamming a closed fist into the palm of his other hand.

"*Yes,*" he hissed. "You're mine!"

Pahner watched as the pirate ships swung up into the wind. Or, rather, *towards* the wind. It was obvious that they could come nowhere near as close to it as the schooners could, and the way their square sails shivered indicated even to his landsman's eye that they were very close to losing way. But for all that, it also brought those big, bow-mounted bombards around to line up on the *Ima Hooker*.

"Doesn't look so good to me," he opined.

"Oh, they're going to get some shots off at us," Roger admitted. "We may even take a few hits, although I doubt that their gunnery is going to be anything to write home about. But as soon as everyone is back in line, we're going to turn onto a reciprocal heading to put the wind behind us. We can put on more sail and really race down on them. They're going to get off one—at the most two—shots at us, and most of those are going to miss. If we lose a ship, I'll be astonished, and I don't even anticipate very many casualties. Then we'll be in among them, and we'll rip them up with both broadsides. They're about to get corncobbed."

"So this is a particularly good situation?" Pahner asked, looking back at the ships assembling behind the *Hooker*. The flagship was close-reaching on the starboard tack now, sailing about forty-five degrees off the wind. That was nowhere near as high as she had been pointing, but apparently it was still high enough for Roger's purposes, and Pahner could see that it gave the rest of the flotilla additional time to catch up. *Sea Foam* had reduced sail dramatically to conform to the flagship's speed, whereas *Prince John* had crammed on extra canvas now that the squall had passed and was driving hard to get into position. *Pentzikis* and *Tor Coll* were coming up astern of *Prince John,* and it looked like everyone would be back into formation within perhaps another fifteen minutes.

"Well, if they'd held to their original course and tried to continue past us, then work their way back up to windward behind us, it would have been a pain," Roger told the Marine. "They'd have played hell trying to pull it off, but to get this over within any short time frame, we have to sail in between them, where our artillery can hammer them without their bombards being able to shoot back, and their line was spaced a lot more tightly together than I liked. If they'd continued on their easterly heading, we'd have run the risk of getting someone rammed when we went through their line. By turning up towards us, they've effectively opened the intervals, because those ships are a lot longer than they are wide, and we're looking at them end-on now. In addition, at the moment we actually pass them, we'll be broadside-to-broadside. That means our guns will be able to pound them at minimum range, but that those big-assed bombards are going to be pointing at nothing but empty sea.

"The other choice would have been to sail around behind them, come up from astern, and pick them off one by one. That would keep us out of the play of their guns, too, but I don't want to still be fighting this thing come morning. Among other things, there're those other prize ships to chase down."

"We'll see," Pahner commented. "After this fight, and if Kerr's response is good. I don't want to do this sort of thing for nothing."

"What are they thinking?" Cies asked himself.

The lead enemy ship had waited patiently as the Lemmar ships put their helms down and headed up as close into the wind as they could. In fact, the entire enemy formation seemed to have deliberately slowed down, which didn't make any kind of sense Cies could see. It was painfully obvious to him that those sleek, low-slung vessels were far more weatherly than his own. He was edging as close into the wind as he could come, and by slowing down, the enemy was actually going to allow him to bring his artillery to bear on the last three or four ships in his line. He hadn't had to let Cies do that, and the raider captain was suspicious whenever an opponent provided opportunities so generously. His own ships would miss the lead enemy vessel by at least two hundred meters, but after they'd hammered the other ships and then boarded them, there would be plenty of time to deal with the leader. If it decided to run away, there wasn't much the Lemmar could do about it, given its obvious advantages in both speed and maneuverability. But if it tried to come back and do anything to succor its less fortunate consorts, it would have to reenter Cies' reach.

In which case there definitely *was* something he could do about it.

"Perhaps they're like the damned priests," Vunet said. Cies glanced across at him. He hadn't realized that he'd asked his rhetorical question aloud, but now his mate clapped his hands in a "who knows?" gesture. "Maybe they plan on sailing into our midst and trying to grapple us all together so they can board, like the priests would."

"If that's what they're thinking, they'll take a pounding," the captain replied. "We'll get off several shots as they close, then sweep their decks with the swivel guns as they come alongside."

"Julian, do we have hard communications in place?" Roger asked.

"Yes, Sir," the intel NCO answered. "Good fix on the *Foam* and the *Prince John*. We're all linked, and we're not emitting worth a damn."

"Okay, put me on."

Roger waited a moment, until each of the ship icons on his helmet's HUD flashed green, then spoke across the tight web of communications lasers to the senior Marine aboard each schooner.

"This needs to be relayed to all the ships' captains. On my mark, I want them to put their helms up, and we'll bear away ninety degrees to port. That will let us run directly downwind. Once we're on course, put on all sail conformable with the weather. I'm designating the enemy vessels one through six, starting from the most westerly. *Hooker* will pass between one and two; *Pentzikis* will pass between two and three; *Sea Foam* will pass between three and four; the *Johnny* will pass between four and five; and *Tor Coll* will pass down the starboard side of number six. If the enemy holds his course, we'll wear to port after we pass, and rake them from astern. Prepare to bear away on my mark. Flash when ready to execute."

He raised one arm as he stood beside Captain T'Sool and waited until all the HUD icons flashed green. It only took a moment, and then his arm came slashing down.

"All ships: execute!"

"They're actually doing it," Cies said in disbelief.

"I don't even see a forecastle," Vunet said in puzzlement. "Where the hell are their bombards?"

"How the hell do I know?" Cies growled back. "Maybe all they've got are those overgrown swivels on the sides!" He rubbed his horns, pleased that the enemy was being so stupid but anxious that it still might turn out that it wasn't stupidity at all, just something the enemy knew . . . and Cies didn't.

"Get aloft and direct the swivel guns. I don't want anything unexpected to happen."

"Right," Vunet grumped. "Something like losing?"

Roger walked down *Hooker*'s port side, greeting an occasional Mardukan gunner on the way. Most of the flotilla's gunners had been seconded from the K'Vaernian Navy and had served in the artillery at the Battle of Sindi. Roger had been away from the city for much of the battle, having his own set-to with a barbarian force that had refused to be in a logical place. But he'd arrived towards the end, after successfully protecting the main army's flank and annihilating the threat to its line of retreat, and he'd spent quite a bit of time around the artillerymen since. Most of them were native K'Vaernians, like the seamen, and figured that kowtowing to princes was for other people. But, like members of republics and democracies throughout the galaxy, they also had a sneaking affection for nobility, and they'd really taken a shine to Roger.

"Kni Rampol, where did you come from?" the prince asked as he reached up to clap one of the gun captains on his back. "I thought you were on the *Prince John*?"

"Captain T'Sool asked me to shift places with Blo Fal because he couldn't get along with the mate." The gunner stood up from his piece and caught a backstay to steady himself. The ship was running with the wind coming from astern, and with all sail set, she was swooping up one side of each swell, then charging down the other.

"Well, it's good to see you," Roger said with a modified Mardukan gesture of humor. "No playing poker during the battle, though!"

"I don't think so," the Mardukan agreed with a grunt of humor. "Before you know it, Poertena would find the game, and then I'd be out a month's pay!"

"Probably so, at that," Roger laughed. "In that case, better hang on to your money, keep the muzzle down, and keep firing until you're told to quit. This will be a solid battle to tell the children about."

"Good afternoon, Your Highness," Lieutenant Lod Tak said. The port battery commander was doing the same thing as Roger—walking the gun line, checking and encouraging his gun crews.

"Afternoon, Lod," Roger acknowledged. "You know the fire plan?"

"Load with grape and ball," Tak replied promptly. "Hold our fire until we bear, then a coordinated broadside at point blank, and go to individual fire. Grape if we're close enough; ball, if we're not. Sound good?"

"Sounds fine," Roger answered. "I don't think they'll know what hit them. The game plan is for us to wear round to the port tack after we pass side to side. That will bring us across their sterns, and we'll get a chance to give them a good, solid rake at close range that should take most of the fight out of them before we board. Grape shot should do the job just fine . . . and leave the damned ships in one piece as prizes, too!"

"That sounds good to me, Your Highness," the Mardukan agreed with cheerful bloodthirstiness. K'Vaern's Cove had always paid excellent prize money for enemy ships captured intact, and every member of *Hooker*'s crew knew exactly how this game was played.

Roger nodded to the lieutenant and continued forward, to where Despreaux stood beside the pivot gun. The bronze carronades along *Hooker*'s side threw eight-kilo shot, and their stubby tubes looked almost ridiculously small beside the towering Mardukans. But the pivot gun was a long gun—with a barrel as long as one of the three-meter natives was tall—and it threw a fifteen-kilo solid shot. Or a fifteen-*centimeter* explosive shell.

Despreaux and Gol Shara, *Hooker*'s chief gunner, had just finished fussing over loading the gun, and Shara's body language expressed an unmistakable aura of frustration.

"What's his problem?" Roger asked Despreaux, jabbing his chin at the gunner.

"He wanted to try the shells," she replied, never taking her eyes from the approaching enemy vessels.

"He did, did he?" Roger gave Shara a quick grin, which the Mardukan returned with complete impassivity, then turned back to admire Despreaux's aquiline profile. He decided that she would definitely *not* like to be told that she looked like a ship's warrior maiden figurehead. "The object is to take them as close to intact as we can get them," he pointed out mildly, instead.

"Oh, he *understands*; he just doesn't like it," Despreaux said, but still she never looked away from the Lemmar, and Roger frowned.

"You don't look happy," he said more quietly. He also thought that he would like to wrap her in foam and put her in the hold, where she wouldn't be exposed to enemy fire. But she was *his* guard, not the other way around, and any suggestion of coddling on his part would undoubtedly meet with a violent response.

"Do you ever wish it could just end, Roger?" she asked quietly. "That we could call over to them and say, 'Let's not fight today.'"

It took the prince a moment to think about that. It was a feeling that he'd had before his first major battle, at Voitan, where better than half the company had been lost, but he'd rarely experienced it since then. Rage, yes. Professional fear of failure, yes. But as he considered her question, he realized that the normal and ordinary fear of dying had somehow fallen behind. Even worse, in some ways, the fear of having to kill was doing the same thing.

"No," he said after the better part of a minute. "Not really. Not since Voitan."

"I do," she said still very quietly. "I do every single time." She turned to look at him at last. "I love you, and I knew even when I was falling in love with you, that you don't feel that way. But sometimes it worries me that you don't."

She looked deep into his eyes for moment, then touched him on the arm, and started back towards the stern.

Roger watched her go, then turned back to watch the oncoming enemy. She had a point, he thought. On Marduk, the only way to survive had been to attack and keep on attacking, but sooner or later, they would make it back to Earth. When they did, he would once again become good old Prince Roger, Number Three Child, and in those conditions, jumping down the throat of the *flar-ke* to kick your way out its ass was not an effective tactic. Nor would Mother appreciate it if he blew some idiotic noble's brains all over the throne room's walls, he supposed. Sooner or later, he'd have to learn subtlety.

At that moment, the lead Lemmar ship opened up with its bombard, followed rapidly by all five of its consorts.

Yes, she had a point. He had to admit it. One that bore thinking about. But for now, it *was* time to kick some ass.

CHAPTER NINE

"Prepare to run out!" Roger called, gauging the speed of the oncoming ships. The two formations sliced towards one another, the schooners moving much faster through the water than the clumsier raider vessels, and he frowned slightly. They were going to pass one another on opposite tacks, all right, but considerably more quickly than he had anticipated.

"I want to reduce sail as we pass through them, so we can get in more than one broadside."

"Agreed," Captain T'Sool said. *Hooker*'s Mardukan captain stood beside the prince, eyes narrow as he, too, calculated the combined approach speed. "I think taking in the middle and topmast staysails should be enough. If it isn't, we can always drop the mainsail and the inner jib, as well."

Despite the tension, Roger smiled faintly. There'd been no terms for those types of sails in any Mardukan language before Poertena had introduced them, so the diminutive armorer had been forced to use the human ones. It had worked—at least it precluded any possibility of confusing Mardukan words—but it was more than a bit humorous to hear a Mardukan make a hash of pronouncing "topmast staysail" . . . especially with a Pinopan accent. But T'Sool was almost certainly correct. What he'd suggested would reduce sail area significantly, and with it, *Hooker*'s speed, but the foresail was the real workhorse of the topsail schooner rig. Even if they did have to drop the mainsail, as well, her agility and handling would be unimpaired.

"I think just the staysails should be enough," he responded. "Julian, send that to the other ships along with the word that we'll be engaging shortly."

"Yes, Sir." The NCO grinned. "I think we can all figure out that last part on our own, though!"

Another boom echoed from the oncoming ships, and the ball from the nearest bombard was clearly visible as it flew well above the *Hooker*. It was audible, as well, even over the sounds of wind and sea. Roger was almost too intent to notice, but several people flinched as the whimpering ball sliced away several lines overhead. The two sides were little more than two hundred meters apart, with Roger's vessels swooping down upon the Lemmar.

"I think we're in range," Roger observed dryly.

"Indeed?" D'Nal Cord's tone was even drier. He stood directly behind Roger, leaning on his huge spear while guarding the prince's back, as any proper *asi* should when battle loomed. "And as Sergeant Julian is so fond of saying, you think this because . . . ?"

Roger turned to smile fiercely up at his *asi*, but other people on *Hooker*'s afterdeck had more pressing details to worry about.

"Srem Kol!" T'Sool shouted, and pointed upward when a Mardukan petty officer looked towards him. "Get a work party aloft and get those lines replaced! Tlar Frum! Stand by to reduce sail!"

Even as shouted acknowledgments came back to him, there was more thunder from the Lemmar line, and Roger heard a rending crash.

"*Prince John* just took a hit," Pahner said, and Roger looked over to see that the captain's gift for understatement hadn't deserted him. The third schooner in his own line had lost her foremast. It had plunged into the water on her starboard side, and the weight of the broken spars and sodden canvas was like an anchor. The ship swung wildly around to the right, exposing her broadside to the oncoming Mardukan raiders.

"Not much we can do about it now," Roger observed with a

mildness which fooled neither Pahner nor himself. "Nothing except smash the shit out of the scummies, anyway. And at least anybody who wants her is going to have to come close enough for her carronades to do a little smashing of their own. Still—" He looked at the Marine standing beside Cord. "Julian, tell the *Johnny* to concentrate on Number Four's rigging. *Sea Foam* and *Tor Coll* will have to hammer Number Three and Number Five to keep them off her."

"Got it," Julian acknowledged. The NCO had switched to a battle schematic on his pad and sent the updated plan to all five ships. "I've got a response from everyone except *Prince John*," he reported after a moment.

"I can see some damage aft." Pahner had the zoom dialed up on his helmet visor. "It looks like Number Four and Number Five were concentrating fire on her. She looks pretty beat up."

"I don't doubt it," Roger grunted. "Those are dammed big cannonballs." He shrugged. "But we'll settle their hash in a few minutes now. It's about time to open the ball. All ships—run out!"

"What do they think they're doing now?" Vunet demanded as *Rage of Lemmar*'s bombard thudded again.

"Just at a guess, I'd say they're finally getting ready to shoot back at us," Cred Cies said bitingly as the smooth sides of the strange, low-slung ships were suddenly barbed with what certainly looked like stubby bombard muzzles.

"With those tiny things?" the mate made a derisive gesture of contempt.

"With those tiny things," Cies confirmed.

"My son could hurt us worse with a toy sword," Vunet scoffed.

Given its angle of approach, the K'Vaernian flotilla could have opened fire with its forward pivot guns even before the Lemmar did. Roger, however, had chosen not to do so. Powerful as the pivot guns were, it was unlikely that they could have incapacitated any of the raider vessels by themselves without using the explosive shells, which would probably have destroyed their targets completely. Wooden ships waterproofed with pitch and covered with tarred rigging were tinderboxes, just waiting for any explosive shell to set them ablaze. And even if that hadn't been the case, Roger had had no interest in alerting the Mardukan pirates to the power of his vessels' weapons. The K'Vaernian Navy had been unimpressed by the carronades when they first saw them . . . and with considerably less excuse, since the K'Vaernians had already seen human-designed artillery in action at Sindi. The longer these scummies remained in ignorance about their capabilities, the better.

But the time for ignorance was about over. Especially for *Prince John*. Roger could see axes flashing on her forward deck as her crew frantically chopped away at the rigging holding the wreckage of the foremast against her side. If things worked out the way he planned, the raiders would be too busy to bother with the *Johnny* anytime soon, but if things *didn't* work out, it was going to be a case of God helping those who helped themselves.

In the meantime . . .

"Fire as you bear!"

Ima Hooker and her consorts each carried a broadside of twelve guns. Once upon a time, on a planet called Earth, those guns would have been described as eighteen-pounder carronades—short, stubby weapons with a maximum effective range of perhaps three hundred meters. Beside someone the size of a Mardukan, they looked even shorter and stubbier, and perhaps the pirate captains could be excused for failing to grasp the menace they represented. Certainly Roger had done everything he could to keep the Lemmaran crews from doing so . . . until now.

Despite the threat bearing down upon her, the *Prince John* did not fire first. Her guns, like those of every unit of the flotilla, had been loaded for a basically antipersonnel engagement, with a charge of grapeshot atop a single round shot. That was a marvelous combination for smashing hulls and slaughtering personnel at close range, but it left a bit to be desired in terms of long-range gunnery. The other schooners, continuing their race towards the enemy, were going to reach that sort of range far more quickly than any clumsy

Lemmaran tub was going to claw far enough up to windward for her to reach. So the *Johnny* held her fire, waiting to see what—if anything—got by her sisters and into her effective range.

Of course, even with their superior weapons, four schooners might find themselves just a bit hard-pressed to stop *six* raiders from getting past them.

Or perhaps not.

Cred Cies watched in disbelief as the side of the nearest enemy vessel disappeared behind a billowing cloud of dirty-white smoke. Those short, silly-looking bombards obviously threw far heavier shot than he had believed possible. The quantity of smoke alone would have made that obvious, but the hurricane of iron slamming into his vessel made it even more obvious. *Painfully* obvious, one might almost have said.

Those low-slung, infernally fast ships slashed down into the Lemmaran formation, and as they did, they showed him exactly why they'd adopted the approach they had. The raiders' bombards might have gotten off three or four unanswered shots each as the strangers drove in across their effective range, but the accuracy of those shots had left much to be desired. One of the enemy vessels had been crippled, and had clearly taken casualties, as well, but the others were unscathed.

Now they swept into the intervals in his own formation, and his teeth ground together in frustration as he realized that even as they did, they were actually reducing sail. They were slowing down, sacrificing their impossible speed advantage, and the shriek and crash of shot—the dreadful, splintering smash as round shot slammed into and through his own ship's timbers—was like a hammer blow squarely between the horns as he realized why.

"*All right!*" someone shrieked, and it took Roger a moment to realize that it had been him. Not that he was alone in his jubilation.

The endless hours of drill inflicted upon the K'Vaernian gunners had been worth it. The range to target was little more than fifty meters, and at that range, every shot went home. Jagged holes magically appeared in the stout planking of the raider ships. Grapeshot and splinters of their own hulls went through the massed troops, drawn up on the pirates' decks in obvious anticipation of a boarding action, like scythes. Bodies and pieces of bodies flew in grisly profusion, and the agonized shrieks of the wounded cut through even the thunder of the guns.

Roger wanted to leap to the rail to help serve one of the guns personally. The strength of the fierce, sudden temptation took him by surprise. It was as if the screams of his enemies, the sudden spray pattern of blood splashed across the lower edges of the square sails as wooden "splinters" two meters and more in length went smashing through the raider crews like ungainly buzz saws, closed some circuit deep inside him. It wasn't hunger . . . not precisely. But it was a *need*. It was something all too much like a compulsion, and deep inside him a silent, observing corner of his brain realized that Nimashet had been right to worry about him.

But there was no time for such thoughts, and it wasn't fear of his own inner demons which kept him standing by *Hooker*'s wheel as the artillery thundered and the enemy shrieked. It was responsibility. The awareness that he had accepted command for the duration of this battle and that he could no more abandon or evade that responsibility than Armand Pahner could have. And so he stayed where he was, with Julian poised at one shoulder and D'Nal Cord at the other, while someone else did the killing.

Hooker's carronades bellowed again and again. Not in the single, senses-shattering blast of the perfectly synchronized opening broadside but in ones and twos as the faster crews got off their follow-up shots. There was more thunder from overhead as sharpshooters—Marines with their big bolt-action rifles, and Mardukans, with their even bigger breech-loaders—claimed their own toll from the enemy.

The main "broadside" armament of the Lemmaran ships was composed of "swivel guns," which weren't much more than built-up arquebuses. They were about fifty millimeters in caliber, and they had the range to carry to the K'Vaernian schooners slicing through the Lemmaran formation, but without rifling, they were grossly inaccurate. On the other hand, the already short range was going to fall to zero when the flotilla finally closed to board the raider ships, and the swivels could still wreak havoc among the infantry who would be doing the boarding. So the sharpshooters were tasked with taking out the gun crews, as well as any obvious officers they could spot.

Even with the much more accurate rifles, the shots weren't easy to make. The ships were tossing in the long swells of the Mardukan ocean and simultaneously moving on reciprocal headings, so the targets were moving in three dimensions. Since the sharpshooters were perched on the fighting tops at the topmast crosstrees or lashed into the ratlines with safety harnesses, they were not only moving in three dimensions, they were moving *very broadly* in three dimensions, swaying back and forth, up and down, in a manner which, had they not become inured to it already, would have guaranteed seasickness. There were enough Mardukans on the raiders' decks to give each rifle shot an excellent chance of hitting someone, but despite all of their endless hours of practice, the odds against that someone being the target they'd *aimed* at were much higher. The sharpshooters claimed their own share of victims, but their best efforts were only a sideshow compared to the carnage wreaked by the carronades.

Each of the four undamaged schooners was engaged on both sides as they drove down between the Lemmaran vessels. The thundering guns pounded viciously at the stunned and disbelieving raiders, and Roger shook his head grimly as the first Lemmaran foremast went crashing over the side. A moment later, the hapless ship's mainmast followed.

"That's done for that one, Captain," he observed to Pahner, and the Marine nodded.

"What about supporting *Prince John*?" the captain asked, and Roger glanced at him. The Marine's tone made it clear that his question was just that—a question, and not a veiled suggestion. But it was a reasonable one, the prince thought, as he looked astern at the cloud of powder smoke rising above the crippled schooner. From the sound of her guns, though, the *Johnny* was firing with steady deliberation, not with the sort of desperation which might have indicated a close action.

"We've got time to settle these bastards first," Roger said, nodding at the incipient melee, and Pahner nodded again.

"You're in command," he agreed, and Roger took time to give him a quick, savage smile before he turned his attention back to T'Sool.

"Put your helm alee, Captain!" he ordered, and T'Sool waved two arms at his helmsman.

"Hands to sheets!" the Mardukan captain bellowed through the bedlam. "Off sheets!" Seamen who had learned their duties the hard way during the voyage scampered through the smoke and fury to obey his orders even as the gunners continued to fire, and T'Sool watched as the line-handlers raced to their stations, then waved at the helmsman again.

"Helm alee! Let go the sheets—handsomely there!" he thundered, and the helmsman spun the wheel.

Hooker turned on her heel like the lady she was, coming around to port in a thunder of canvas, with a speed and precision none of the raiders would have believed possible.

"Haul in and make fast!" T'Sool shouted, and the schooner settled onto her new heading, with the wind once more broad on her port beam. The sail-handlers made the sheets fast on the big fore-and-aft foresail, and her broadside spat fresh thunder as she charged back across her enemies' sterns.

There were *no* guns—bombards or swivels—to protect the raiders' sterns, and the carnage aboard the Lemmaran ships redoubled as the lethal grapeshot went crashing the entire length of the vessels. A single one of the iron spheres might kill or maim as many as a dozen—or even two dozen—of the raiders, and then the anti-*coll* bead cannon mounted on *Hooker*'s after rail opened fire, as well.

For the first time since the Marines landed on Marduk, their high-tech weapons were almost superfluous. The ten-millimeter, hypervelocity beads were incredibly lethal, but the storm of grapeshot and the flying splinters of the ships themselves spread a stormfront of destruction broader than anything the bead cannon could have produced. The beads were simply icing on the cake.

"Bring us back up close-hauled on the port tack, Captain T'Sool!" Roger snapped, and *Hooker* swung even further to port, riding back along a reciprocal of her original course that took her back up between the battered raider ships towards *Prince John*'s position. Both broadsides' carronades continued to belch flame with deadly efficiency, and Roger could clearly see the thick ropes of blood oozing from the Mardukan ships' scuppers.

The flotilla flagship broke back through the enemy's shattered formation with smoke streaming from her gun ports in a thick fog bank shot through with flame and fury. Another raider's masts went crashing over the side, and Roger sucked in a deep, relieved breath of lung-searing smoke, despite his earlier confident words to Pahner, as he saw *Prince John*.

The broken foremast had been cut entirely away; he could see it bobbing astern of her as she got back underway under her mainsail and gaff main topsail alone. It was scarcely an efficient sail combination, but it was enough under the circumstances. Or it should be, anyway. She wasn't moving very quickly yet, and her rigging damage had cost her her headsails, which meant the best she could do was limp along on the wind. But her speed was increasing, and at least she was under command and moving. Which was a good thing, since raider Number Four had somehow managed to claw her way through the melee.

The *Johnny* had seen her coming, and her carronades were already pounding at her opponent. The bigger, more heavily built raider vessel's topsides were badly shattered, and her sails seemed to have almost more holes in them than they had intact canvas, but she was still underway, still closing on the damaged schooner, and the big, slow-firing bombard protected by the massive timber "armor" of her forecastle was still in action. Even as Roger watched, it slammed another massive round shot into the much more lightly built schooner, and he swore viciously as splintered planking flew.

"It *would* be the *Johnny*," he heard Pahner say almost philosophically. He looked at the Marine, and the captain shrugged.

"Never seems to fail, Your Highness. The place you least want to get hit, is the one you can count on the enemy finding." He shook his head. "She's got quite a few of the Carnan aboard, and they already took a hammering when we lost *Sea Skimmer*."

"Don't count your money when it's still sitting on the table," Roger replied, then turned to Julian. "All ships," he said. "Close with the pirates to leeward and board. We'll go to *Johnny*'s assistance ourselves."

"Your Highness," Pahner began, "considering that our entire mission is to get you home alive, don't you think that perhaps it might be a bit wiser to let someone else go—"

Roger had just turned back to the Marine to argue the point when Pahner's helmet visor automatically darkened to protect the captain's vision. Roger didn't know whether or not *Prince John*'s Marine detachment had originally set up a plasma cannon for their anti-*coll* defense system. If they had, he thought with a strange detachment, they were probably going to hear about it—at length— from Pahner and the sergeant major. But it was also possible that they'd switched out the bead cannon at the last minute while the rest of the crew worked on repairs to the schooner's crippled rigging. Not that it mattered. Raider Number Four had managed to get around behind *Johnny*'s stern, where her deadly carronade broadside wouldn't bear. And in achieving that position of advantage, the pirate vessel had put itself exactly where the schooner's crew wanted it.

The Marines' plasma cannons could take out modern main battle tanks, and if *Hooker*'s bead cannon hadn't seemed to add much to her carronades' carnage, no one would ever say that about *Prince John*'s after armament. The round ripped straight down the center of the target ship, just above main deck level. It sliced away masts, rigging, bulwarks, and the majority of the pirates who had assembled on deck in anticipation of boarding. What was worse, in a way, was the thermal bloom that preceded the round. The searing heat touched the entire surface of the ship to flame in a tiny slice of a second, and the roaring furnace became an instant sliver of Hell, an inferno afloat on an endless sea that offered no succor to its victims. Those unfortunate souls below decks, "shielded" from the instant incineration of the boarding party, had a few, eternal minutes longer to shriek before the bombard's powder magazine exploded and sent the shattered, flaming wreck mercifully into the obliterating depths.

"I thought we wanted to capture the ships intact," Roger said almost mildly.

"What would you have done, Your Highness?" Pahner asked. "Yeah, we want to capture the ships, and recapture the convoy, if we can. But *Prince John*, obviously, would prefer to avoid being boarded herself."

"And apparently the Lemmar agree with that preference," D'Nal Cord observed. "Look at that."

He raised an upper arm and pointed. One of the six raider vessels drifted helplessly, completely dismasted while the blood oozing down her side dyed the water around her. Her deck was piled and heaped with the bodies of her crew, and it was obvious that no more than a handful of them could still be alive. Three more raiders each had one of the flotilla's other schooners alongside, and now that *Hooker*'s carronades were no longer bellowing, Roger could hear the crackle of small arms fire as the K'Vaernian boarders stormed up and over them. *Prince John*'s plasma cannon had accounted for a fifth raider, but the sixth and final pirate vessel had somehow managed to come through the brutal melee with its rigging more or less intact, and it was making off downwind just as fast as its shredded canvas would allow.

"Do we let them go, or close with them?" the prince asked.

"Close," Pahner said. "We want to capture the ships, and I'm not a great believer in giving a fleeing enemy an even break. They either surrender, or they die."

"They're not letting us go," Vunet said.

"Would you?" Cies shot back with a grunt of bitter laughter as he looked around the deck.

The crew was hastily trying to repair some of the damage, but it was a futile task. There was just too much of it. Those damned bombards of theirs were hellishly accurate. Unbelievably accurate. They'd smashed *Rage of Lemmar* from stem to stern and cut away over half her running rigging, in the process. Coupled with the way they'd shredded the sails themselves, the damage to the ship's lines—and line-handlers—had slowed their escape to a crawl.

The bombards had done nearly as much damage to the crew, as well. The quarterdeck was awash in blood and bodies, and the crew had put a gang of slaves to work pitching the offal over the side. The enemy's round shot had been bad enough, but the splinters it had ripped from the hull had been even worse. Some of them had been almost two-thirds as long as Cies himself, and one of them had gutted his original helmsman like a filleted fish. Nor was that the only crewman who'd been shredded by bits and pieces of his own ship. Some of that always happened when the bombards got a clear shot, but Cies had never imagined anything like *this*. Normal bombard balls were much slower than the Hell-forged missiles that had savaged his vessel. Worse, he'd never seen any ship that could pour out fire like water from a pump, and the combination of high-velocity shot and its sheer volume had been devastating beyond his worst nightmares of carnage.

Now the *Rage* was trying to limp to the south and away from the vengeful demons behind her. He'd hoped that with one of their own crippled (by what, for all intents and purposes, had been a single lucky shot) the other four might have let his own ship go. But it appeared they had other plans.

"We could . . ." Vunet said, then paused.

"You were about to suggest that we surrender," Cies said harshly. "Never! No Lemmar ship has ever surrendered to anyone other than Lemmar. Ever. They may take our ship, but not one crewman, not one slave, will be theirs."

"They're not heaving to," Roger said with a grunt. "Captain Pahner?"

"Yes, Your Highness?" the Marine replied formally.

"If we really want that ship intact, this is about to become a boarding action. I think it's about time to let the ground commander take over."

"You intend to take them on one-on-one?"

"I think we have to, if we don't want them to get away," Roger replied. Pahner gazed at him, and the prince shrugged. "*Pentzikis, Tor Coll,* and *Sea Foam* already have their hands full. *Prince John* can probably take the fourth pirate—I doubt there's more than a couple dozen of these Lemmar still alive aboard her, and she sure as hell can't get away with no masts at all. But this guy in front of us isn't just lucky. He's smart . . . and good. If he weren't, he'd be drifting around back there with his buddies. So if you want him caught, we're the only one with a real shot at him."

"I see. And when we catch up with him, you'll be where, precisely, Your Highness?" Pahner asked politely.

"Like I say, Sir," Roger said, "it's time to let the ground commander take over."

"I see." Pahner gazed at him speculatively for several moments, considering what the prince *hadn't* said, then nodded with an unseen smile.

"Very well, Your Highness. Since boarding actions are *my* job, I'll just go and get the parties for this one assembled."

CHAPTER TEN

"Come off the guns and rig the mortars!" Despreaux ordered, pulling gunners off the carronades as she trotted down the line of the starboard battery. "We're going to be boarding from port!"

The *Ima Hooker* was slicing through the water once more, rapidly overhauling the fleeing pirate vessel. It would have been difficult to guess, looking at the sergeant's expression, just how unhappy about that she was. Not that she was any more eager than Captain Pahner to see the raiders escape, if not for exactly the same reasons. Nimashet Despreaux had a serious attitude problem where pirates—any pirates—were concerned, but she would have been much happier if at least one of the other schooners had been in position to support *Hooker*. There were still an awful lot of scummies aboard that ship, however badly shaken they must be from the effects of the carronades. And as good as the K'Vaernians and their Diaspran veterans were, hand-to-hand combat on a heaving deck was what the Lemmar did for a living. There were going to be casualties—probably quite a lot of them—if the raiders ever got within arms' reach, and a Mardukan's arms were very, very long.

And Despreaux was particularly concerned about one possible casualty which wouldn't have been a problem if any of the other schooners had been in *Hooker*'s place.

But at least if they had to do it, it looked as if Roger intended to do it as smartly as possible. He was steering almost directly along the Lemmaran ship's wake, safely outside the threat zone of any weapon the raider mounted. Given *Hooker*'s superior speed and maneuverability, Despreaux never doubted that Roger would succeed in laying her right across the other ship's stern. Nor did she doubt that he would succeed in raking the pirate's deck from end to end with grapeshot with relative impunity as he closed. After which, *Hooker*'s crew and Krindi Fain's Diasprans would swarm up and over the shattered stern and swiftly subdue whatever survived from the Lemmaran crew.

Sure they would.

And Roger wouldn't be anywhere *near* the fighting.

And the tooth fairy would click her heels together three times and return all of them to Old Earth instantly.

She skidded to a halt beside another device that was new to Marduk. The boarding mortar, one of three carried in each of *Hooker*'s broadsides, was a small, heavy tube designed for a heavily modified grapnel, affixed to a winch and line, to fit neatly into its muzzle. Charged with gunpowder, it should be able to throw the grapnel farther and more accurately than any human or Mardukan. Of course, that assumed it worked at all. The system had been tested before leaving K'Vaern's Cove, but that was different from trying to use it in combat for the very first time.

Despreaux pulled open the locker beside the mortar, dragged out the grapnel, and affixed the line to the snaphook on its head as one of the gun boys ran down to the magazine for the propelling charge. He was back in less than a minute with a bag of powder, and Despreaux watched one of the Mardukan gunners from the starboard battery slide the charge into the heavy iron tube. A wad of waxed felt followed, and then Despreaux personally inserted the grapnel shaft and used it as its own ramrod to shove the charge home. When she was certain it was fully seated, she stepped back. A hollow quill, made from the Mardukan equivalent of a feather and filled with fulminating powder, went into the touchhole, the firing hammer was cocked, and the mortar was ready.

All three of the portside weapons had been simultaneously loaded, and Despreaux spent a few seconds inspecting the other two, then activated her communicator.

"Portside mortars are up."

"Good," Roger replied. "We're coming up on our final turn."

Despreaux grabbed a stay and leaned outboard, careful to stay out of the carronade gunners' way as she peered ahead beyond the sails and the tapering bowsprit. *Hooker* was coming up astern of the Lemmaran ship rapidly, and she heard the rapidfire volley of orders as seamen scampered to the lines. One of the portside gunners rapped her "accidentally" on the knee with a handspike, and she looked up quickly. Mardukan faces might not be anywhere near as expressive as human ones, but she'd learned to read scummy body language in the past, endless months, and she recognized the equivalent of a broad grin in the way his false-hands held the handspike.

She gave him the human version of the same expression and got the hell out of his way as the gun captain squatted behind the carronade and peered along the stubby barrel. Then he cocked the firing hammer.

"Back all sails!"

Now that the battle had resolved itself into a series of ship-to-ship actions, Roger found himself an admiral with no commands to give. It was all up to the individual ship captains now, like T'Sool, and Roger decided that the best thing he could do was get out from underfoot.

And he was planning on sitting out the boarding, as well. Everyone's comments on the stupidity of his putting himself out on a limb were finally starting to hit home. If he took point, the Marines aboard *Ima Hooker* wouldn't be able to pay attention to taking the ship, or to keeping themselves alive, because they would be trying too hard to protect him. So he'd taken a position in the ratlines, where he could observe the fighting without participating.

Getting a good look required that elevated position, because the ships could hardly have been more unlike one another. The Lemmaran was a high-sided caravellike vessel, fairly round in relation to its length, whereas the schooner was long, low, and lean. The result was a difference of nearly three meters from the top of the schooner's bulwarks to the top of her opponent's.

The boarders from *Hooker* would be led by some of the Diaspran veterans, under the command of Krindi Fain, with the human Marines—led by Gunny Jin—as emergency backup. The Diasprans weren't exactly experienced at this sort of combat, but the K'Vaernian seamen had explained the rudiments of shipboard combat to them before they ever set sail, and they'd practiced for it almost as much as they'd practiced their marksmanship. Given the disparity in the height of the two ships' bulwarks, even the Mardukans were going to find it an awkward scramble to get across the raider's high stern, but at least the savage battering the carronades' grapeshot had delivered upon arrival gave them an opening to make the crossing.

On the other hand, not even the Mardukans had been able to actually see across to the other ship from deck level. That was one reason Cord had joined Roger, perching precariously in the ratlines, along with his nephew Denat. The other reason was to get them close enough to Roger to let them throw up their outsized shields in the event that the Lemmar decided to hurl their throwing axes at him.

Roger watched the Marines forming up behind the Mardukan boarders and was just as glad that Despreaux was in charge of the grapnel mortars. For better or worse, he worried more about her than about the other Marines. Managing the grapnels, and the fast winches they were attached to, she would be in no position to participate. Whether that was simply a happy coincidence or something Pahner and Kosutic had considered with malice aforethought when they detailed her to the job, he didn't know. Nor did he particularly care. Not as long as it kept her out of the firing line.

The final broadside roared, and Roger nodded in grim approval as the hurricane of grapeshot swept most of the pirate ship's afterdeck clear. It also did a splendid job of cutting away rigging and what was left of the ship's canvas. It looked like the spars themselves were still more or less intact, though. Rerigging this prize would be an all-day task, but one that would be nowhere near as difficult as repairing the ships that had lost entire masts.

He watched as Despreaux ordered the mortars to fire and the lines flicked out across the enemy ship. The grapnels flew straight and true, arcing over the Lemmar ship's stern rail, and the Mardukan sailors on the fast winches started reeling them back in. The mortars appeared to have been a successful experiment, he observed, and allowed himself a certain smugness as the author of the idea. Trying to do the same thing with hand-thrown grapnels would have been a chancy process, at best.

Pedi Karuse refused to give in to despair. The worst had happened the moment the Krath raiding party hit the village. From there, it was only a matter of how long it took her to die.

In a way, her capture by the Lemmar had actually stretched out her existence. They were probably going to sell her back to the Fire Priests, eventually. Or she might end up as a bond slave, or in the saltpeter mines. But at least she wasn't on a one-way ticket to Strem. Or already a Handmaiden of the God.

So she'd been prepared to look upon her current situation with a certain degree of detachment, biding her time and husbanding her strength against the vanishingly slim chance that she might actually find an opportunity to escape. That attitude had undergone a marked change in the past few hours, however.

The problem, of course, was the peculiarly Lemmaran method of dealing with boarding actions. The Lemmar had a simple answer to the possibility of capture: don't allow it. In part, their attitude stemmed from their dealings with Fire Priests; unlike the Shin, they flatly refused to let themselves be captured to face the Fire Priests' . . . religious practices. But an even larger part of their attitude was the terror factor; no Lemmar would ever surrender under any circumstances, and they made certain all of their enemies knew it.

Generally, that meant that the Fire Priest's guards didn't bother trying to capture Lemmaran ships. They might sink them, but fighting a suicidal enemy hand-to-hand was a casualty-heavy proposition which offered minimal profit even if it was successful. Nor did the Fire Priests raid the Lemmar islands. They might have taken Strem away from the Confederation, but the island itself was all they'd gotten. And if they wanted to keep it, they'd have to completely repopulate it, since the Lemmar had killed even their women and children, rather than have them captured.

What that meant for Pedi Karuse, and the half-dozen other captives chained on the deck of the *Rage of Lemmar,* was that having avoided the Fire Priests on Krath, having avoided being shipped to Strem, and having lived through the splinter-filled hell of the broadsides, they were about to be slaughtered by their captors.

Some days it just didn't pay to do your horns in the morning.

She flattened herself as close to the deck as her chains allowed, even though her brain recognized the futility of her instinctive reaction, as another enemy salvo hit. Most of this one was aimed high, something that whistled through the air with an evil sound and shredded the ship's rigging like a *greg* eating a *vern.* But some of it flew by lower, and a splinter the size of her horn took one of the other Shin slaves in the stomach. It was really a rather small splinter, compared to some of the others that had gone howling across the deck, but the slave seemed to explode under the impact, and his guts splashed across the red-stained deck . . . and Pedi.

Even over the screams and the thunder of the enemy guns, she could hear the prayers of the captured Guard next to her, and the sound finally pushed her over the brink as her fellow clansman's blood sprayed over her.

"Shut up!" she shouted. "I hope you burn in the Fires for the rest of eternity! It was your stupid Guard that got me into this!"

There wasn't much she could do, with her arms chained behind her and coupled to the rest of the slaves, but she did her best—which was to lean sideways and snap-kick the stupid Krath in the head. It wasn't her best kick ever, but it was enough to send him bouncing away from her, and she grunted in delighted satisfaction as the other side of his skull hit a deck stanchion . . . hard.

"Shin blasphemer!" He spat in her direction. "The Fire will purify your soul soon enough!"

"It will purify you both," one of the pirates said as he drew his sword. "Time to show these *vern* why you don't board the Lemmar."

"Piss on you, sailor!" the Shin female snarled. "Your mother was a *vern* and your father was a *kren*—with bad eyesight!"

"Piss on *you*, Shin witch," the Lemmar retorted, and raised his sword. "Time to meet your Fire."

"That's what you think," Pedi said. She flipped her legs forward and both feet slammed home as she snap-kicked the pirate in the crotch. He bent explosively forward in sudden agony, and she wrenched herself as far upward as the chains allowed. It was just far enough. Their horns locked, and then, in a maneuver she knew would have left her bruised and sore for a week if she'd been going to live that long, she let herself fall backward and hurled the much larger male over her head and onto his back. Another wrench unlocked her horns just before he crashed down on the planking, and she flipped herself upward onto the back of her head, spun in place on the pivot of her manacles, and drove both heels down onto the winded pirate's throat.

The entire attack was over in a single heartbeat, along with the pirate's life, and she bounced back up into a kneeling position on the deck to survey the remaining pirates, clustered to repel borders.

"Next?" she spat.

Several of the Lemmar swore, and two of them started towards her to complete the imperative task of killing their captives. But before they could take more than a single stride, a grapnel came flying through the air. It was only one of three, but this particular grapnel landed two meters in front of Pedi, with the line running between her and the Krath guards.

"Oh, Fire Priest shit," she whispered as the four-pronged hook began skittering rapidly back along the deck. It was headed for the after rail, gouging splinters out of the planking as it went . . . and aiming directly for the chain binding all the slaves together.

It caught the chain and barely even slowed as it ripped away the forward of the two heavy iron rings that had anchored it—and the slaves—to the deck.

"This is gonna *hurt!*"

Pedi leaned forward and tightened her muscles against what was coming, but it was still incredibly painful when all four of her chained-together arms were wrenched backwards. Only one of the rings had come out of the planking, which made it even worse. Instead of dragging them all straight aft, the rampaging grapnel cracked the chain like a whip. Sparks flew as the grapnel's tines raked furiously down the heavy links, and someone's scream ended in a hideous, gurgling groan as the grapnel disemboweled him. She could hear the other slaves screaming as the whole group was snatched along the deck until the grapnel finally yanked entirely free of the chain. But not before it had slammed all of them brutally into the ship's starboard bulwark.

She felt as if her arms had been pulled out of their sockets, and when she looked sideways, she saw that that had literally happened to one of the other Shin. But she refused to let that stop her as she rolled over on her head again and slipped her legs between her arms.

That contortion would have been difficult enough for a human; most Mardukans would have found it virtually impossible, but the same training which had saved Pedi's life against the first pirate came to the fore once more. She folded practically in half and slipped first one, then the other leg out until she could lie with her arms bound in front of her. Of course, they were now flipped around, false-hands above true-hands, but her wrists slid in the manacles to let her relieve the pressure on her elbows and shoulders, and even with false-hands high, she was happier this way. Besides, it was also an insulting hand gesture, which suited her frame of mind perfectly.

Roger had been paying strict attention to the preparations for the attack. Despite his concentration on other things, he'd been vaguely aware of the low-voiced conversation between D'Nal Cord and Denat, but he hadn't paid it very much attention. Not until Cord suddenly snapped an angry retort at his nephew. The deep, sharp-edged sentence was short, pungent, and spectacularly obscene.

"What?" Roger's head whipped around at the highly atypical outburst from his *asi*.

"They appear to be trying to kill their prisoners," Denat said with a gesture towards the other ship.

Roger followed the waving true-hand and saw half a dozen

Mardukans chained to the deck near the center line. One of them was only too obviously dead, clearly a victim of *Hooker*'s broadsides. A chain, stretched between two raised iron rings, joined them all together, running up through a complex four-point restraint behind each Mardukan to hold his arms behind him. As Roger watched, one of the grapnels caught the chain, and he winced in sympathetic pain as it ripped one of the chain's anchoring rings out of the planking and yanked the prisoners across the deck. It also killed another of them, and then the rest of the captives were slammed into the ship's bulwarks with more than enough force to kill anyone who hit awkwardly. Indeed, it looked to Roger as if all but one of them had been injured, possibly severely. But that didn't prevent several more of the Lemmar from advancing on them with swords ready just as *Hooker*'s boarders started over the side of their own ship.

Pedi Karuse rose on her knees once more, examined her situation, and allowed herself one vicious curse. The grapnel had only managed to rip out one ring; the other one remained firmly fixed to the deck, still holding her prisoner. Worse, the other slaves chained to her had fared far worse than she had as they were hurled against the side of the ship and lay about like so many more inert anchors. Aside from having her arms in front of her again, she was as helplessly chained as before, and she looked aft, where the first of the boarders were coming over the stern. At first, she thought they might be Shin, for they wore bright blue harnesses, like those common to the Fardar clan. But in the next instant, she realized that it couldn't be her people. The boarders were using weapons she had never seen before, and their tactics were unlike any Shin.

The first wave over the transom formed a shield wall, more like the sort of thing Krath heavy infantry would do, which held off the pirates while reinforcements swarmed aboard behind them. The second rank bore something like long-barreled arquebuses. Unlike any arquebus Pedi had ever heard of, however, these had no problem with water or weather—as they demonstrated with the very first volley. At least some of that many normal arquebus would have had their priming soaked during the crossing, but *all* of these weapons fired successfully into the mass of pirates hammering at the shield wall.

The long-barreled arquebuses also had knives on the ends, and after the first volley the entire group charged forward. They wielded the guns more like spears than firearms, but they did so with a discipline and purpose that was decidedly un-Shin-like. They strode forward in step and struck in unison, while the shield bearers stabbed forward with short spears, sliding the thrusts upward from below their shields.

Unfortunately, she didn't have long to contemplate this new mode of warfare before some of the pirates recalled their duty as Lemmar and decided that killing bound captives was a better use of their time than fighting the boarders. She finally knew despair as four of the pirates approached, one of them slicing down to kill the mostly unconscious Guardsman while two more approached her warily.

"Lemmar slime! I'll eat your tongues for my breakfast!" she shouted, bouncing up to spin a kick into the nearest one's belly. He flew backwards, but so did she, and as she slammed down on her back, the one she hadn't kicked sprang forward, sword upraised.

Roger lost track of the prisoners as he watched the boarding party foam across onto the other ship's deck's under Krindi Fain's direction. Once again, the young Mardukan was proving his stuff, first sending over a small team of assegai-and-shield troops, then following it up with a double line of rifles. A command rang out, the assegai troops squatted instantly and simultaneously, with their shields angled, and the riflemen fired a double volley over their heads. The massive bullets smashed into the tight-packed Lemmar, and the Diasprans followed up immediately with a bayonet charge that was a beautiful thing to see. The combination scattered the remaining Lemmar defenders on the pirate ship's afterdeck, and the boarders stormed ahead towards the surviving clumps of raiders further forward.

"Yes!"

Even as Roger yelled in triumph, he felt rather than saw Cord leave his side. His head snapped around, and his eyes widened in a moment of pure shock as the shaman bounded down the ratlines. The huge Mardukan moved with unbelievable speed and agility, and then he flung himself through the air, onto the enemy deck.

He landed, absolutely unsupported, half-way up the ship from *Hooker*'s boarders. And as if that hadn't been enough, he'd thrown himself in front of what must have been the largest single remaining group of Lemmar still on their feet—a cluster of about twelve, with four in the lead and six or eight more following.

Roger couldn't believe it. In every battle, from the day he had first saved Cord's life, his *asi* had always been at his side, guarding his back. The only time he hadn't been, it was because he'd been too seriously wounded in the *previous* battle to stay on his feet. It was an unheard of violation of his *asi*'s responsibilities for him to desert his "master" at such a time!

The prince didn't even curse. Cord had backed him too often for him to waste precious seconds swearing. He just checked to ensure that his revolvers were secure in their holsters and his sword was sheathed across his back.

Then he leapt outward in Cord's wake.

The Lemmar with the sword snarled at Pedi and brought his weapon flashing down . . . only to be flung violently backwards by the enormous, leaf-bladed spear which suddenly split his chest.

Pedi didn't know where the fellow, frankly dangling, above her came from, but he was the best sight she'd ever seen in her life. Even from this angle.

The guy was old and naked as a *slith*, without even a harness, much less a bardouche, but he wielded his huge spear with a deft touch that reminded her of her father's personal armsman back home. That old armsman had seen more battles than she'd seen breakfasts, and could whip any three young bucks while simultaneously drinking a cup of wine. And it looked like this fellow was cut from the same cloth.

Nor was he by himself, although she'd never seen anything weirder than the creature beside him. It looked like a two-*sren*-tall *vern*. It had only two arms, long yellowish head tendrils, similar in color to her own horns, dangling down its back and gathered together with a leather band, and a most peculiar pistol in either hand. Right behind the two of them came another odd creature that looked like a cross between a *sorn* and an *atul*. It was longer than she was tall, about knee-high on the old guy with the spear, equipped with a *most* impressive set of fangs, and striped in red and black. The . . . striped thing hit the deck, took one look around, and charged into the pirates with a keening snarl.

Definitely the oddest threesome she'd ever seen, she thought with an oddly detached calm.

The older fellow took out two more of the pirates with his spear—another thrust to the chest, and the second with a really economical throat slash that was a pleasure to watch—and the striped creature dragged another down with jaws that took the pirate's head neatly off. But the rest of the Lemmar had formed up to charge, and they'd attracted at least another dozen of their fellows to assist them. The fresh cluster of assailants caught the attention of the red-and-black whatever-it-was, and the creature looked up from its initial victim to lunge forward in a counter-charge . . . just as the maybe-*vern* cocked his pistols.

Pedi considered pointing out that there was no way two pistols, especially pistols as puny as those, were going to stop two dozen pirates. Fortunately, he opened fire before she could. Her father had told her often enough to observe before she opened her mouth, and he turned out to have been right once more as the pistols spat shot after shot. They were accurate, too, as was the shooter. Each round hit one of the pirates just below the armoring horn prominence in a thundering cascade of explosions. After a few moments, all that was left was a drifting pall of gunsmoke and dead pirates with shattered, brain-leaking skulls.

Beauty.

Captain Pahner nodded in approval as the Diaspran infantry swept across to the enemy ship. Fain was no officer to let the enemy get the upper hand, and the young captain had thrown his assegai troops across the instant the vessels touched, even before Pahner could pass the order, then followed up with his rifles in an evolution so smooth it was like silk. Effective subordinates were a treasure, and Krindi Fain was as good as any the Marine had met since Bistem Kar.

Everything rikky-tik, he thought.

In days to come, Armand Pahner would reflect upon the premature nature of that thought. He would ponder it, as a sinner pondered the inexplicable actions of an irritated deity. He would wonder if perhaps, by allowing himself to think it, he had angered the God of Perversity, and Murphy, who is His Prophet. It was the only offense he could think of that might have explained what happened next.

Even as he allowed himself to enjoy Fain's success, something flickered at the corner of his eye, and he turned his head just in time to see Roger take a flying leap off of the ratlines, catch the hanging end of a severed Lemmar shroud, and go swinging through the air like some golden-haired ape to land square-footed on the enemy deck.

Pahner just . . . looked for a moment. He was that shocked. The prince, with Dogzard right on his heels, had landed next to his *asi* . . . in exactly the right spot to draw the last remaining formed group of pirates like a magnet. There was no way in hell for Pahner to support them, either. Even if he told the sharpshooters to cover the noble *idiot,* the Lemmar would be on the pair before the snipers could understand the order and redirect their fire.

Cord took down one of the group, which appeared to be intent on slaughtering the captives who'd been chained to the deck. Dogzard dragged down a second pirate, and the shaman dispatched another pair with ruthless efficiency as Roger drew both pistols, and then the prince opened fire. The revolvers—considerably smaller than the monsters Rastar favored, but still firing a twelve-millimeter round with a recoil sufficient to dislocate many humans' wrists—were double-action. Roger's rate of fire was far slower than he could have managed with his off-world bead pistol, but it was impressive, nonetheless. Especially to pirates from a culture that had never been exposed to the concept of repeating firearms at all. The deck of the Lemmar ship was already heavily obscured by the gunsmoke from the Diaspran rifles and *Hooker*'s final broadside, but visibility abruptly deteriorated still further under the clouds of smoke pouring from His Highness's pistols.

It was fortunate that, once again, good subordinates were coming to Pahner's rescue, as at least two of the sharpshooters began engaging the group attacking the prince on their own. The captain could hardly see what was going on aboard the other ship, but it was also obvious that Fain had spotted the action and ordered his assegai troops to advance. The Diasprans were going to have to be somewhat cautious, though, since they were advancing more or less directly into Roger's fire.

The deck of the Lemmar ship had been cleared, but there seemed to still be plenty of the pirates below decks. Some of them were attempting to fight their way up through the hatches, while others were defending still other hatches Diasprans were trying to fight their way *down* through. With, of course, Roger squarely in the middle of it all.

Whatever had happened to the now fully obscured prince, Pahner somehow doubted that Roger was dead. Whatever severely overworked deity had dedicated his full time and effort to keeping the young blockhead alive would undoubtedly have seen to that. On the other hand, what might happen to Roger when one Armand Pahner got his hands on him was a different matter.

He'd *promised* he wasn't going to do this sort of . . . shit anymore.

A sudden, ringing silence filled Pedi's ears, and she realized she was on a deck clear of (living) pirates, still chained, lying on her back, and looking up at this old fellow . . . dangling . . . above her. And while the sight had been welcome, in one way, the angle could have been better. Not to mention the fact that her neck and shoulders hurt like hell.

"Ahem," she said as sweetly as she possibly could under the circumstances. "I don't suppose you could be convinced to take these chains off me?"

CHAPTER ELEVEN

"Roooggger!"

The prince closed one reloaded revolver cylinder and turned around as Despreaux came clambering over the side of the ship.

"God *dammit*, Roger! When are you going to *learn*?"

"Your Highness," Captain Fain said, striding across the deck. "That was most thoughtless of you. We were well on our way to clearing the ship, and you jumped directly into our line of fire."

"I know, Captain Fain," Roger said, switching his toot to Diaspran. "But—"

"*ROOOGGGER!*" Armand Pahner strode out of the clearing gunsmoke. "What in the hell was *that*, Your Highness? We had the damned battle well in hand!"

A babble of Mardukan broke out behind Roger as he turned towards the Marine captain with a harassed expression. Denat had made his own, slower way to the deck and was engaged in a full throated harangue of his uncle. From the tone of the shaman's attempted responses—not to mention the irate set of his lower arms—Cord was about to start hollering back like a howler monkey.

Which was remarkably similar to the way *he* felt, the prince thought. Then he drew a deep breath and keyed the amplifier on his helmet.

"Everyone shut the hell up!"

The sudden silence was as abrupt as it was total, and Roger snorted in satisfaction. Then he turned the amplifier off and continued in a more normal tone.

"I will answer everyone's questions as soon as I have *mine* answered."

He turned to Cord and fixed the old shaman with a baleful look.

"Cord, what in the hell were you thinking?"

"They were killing the prisoners," the shaman answered in his best Imperial. His accent did . . . interesting things to it, but he'd spent many a long evening during the endless journey working on mastering the Empire of Man's universal tongue. He'd needed to, so that he could debate the way the Empire *ought* to be organized in long, evening discussions with Eleanora O'Casey. As a result, his basic grasp of the language was actually very good, despite his accent, considering that he lacked the advantage the humans' toots conferred upon them. It was also *much* better than his Diaspran, and Cord knew Fain would be able to follow at least some of the conversation if they all used that language.

"That's it? The whole explanation?" Roger asked, propping his hands on his hips. "We were clearing the whole ship, Cord. Most of those pirates were going to be overrun by Krindi's troops in no more than a few minutes. The usual pattern is, first, kill the enemy; *then* save the prisoners. Not the other way around!"

"They were killing them at that time, Your Highness," the *asi* pointed out in a tone of massive restraint. "The deaths would have been accomplished before even Captain Fain's soldiers could have stopped it. I could not, in good conscience, permit that to happen."

Pahner drew a deep breath and turned to stare up at the towering Mardukan.

"Hold on. You mean, *you* went first?"

"Yes, he did," Roger said with immense, overstrained patience. "I just followed him. And that's another thing," he continued, turning back to Cord. "What about me? Huh? You're supposed to cover my back. I *depend* on you to cover my back, for God's sake!"

"You were safe on the other ship," Cord said. "How was I to know you would follow me?"

"Of *course* I was going to follow you, you old idiot!" Roger shouted. "Cord— *Arrrgh!*"

"They were killing the prisoners," Cord repeated, gesturing at the one chained at his feet. "I. Could. Not. Let. That. Happen. As I am bonded to you for saving my life, so I am bound to save others. It is the only honorable thing to do."

"So, you were following Cord?" Despreaux asked. "I want to be clear about this."

"Yes," Roger said distinctly. "I was following Cord. It was not Prince Roger being a suicidal idiot. Or, rather, it was not Prince Roger *on his own* being a suicidal idiot."

"I was not being suicidal," Cord interjected. "As you yourself just pointed out, Captain Fain's group would have soon cleared the deck. All I needed to do was to hold off the pirates for a short time."

Roger grabbed his ponytail and yanked at it in frustration.

"Captain Pahner, do *you* want to handle this?"

"Shaman Cord," the captain said, very formally, "this was not a good decision on your part. It's not our job to endanger Roger unnecessarily."

"Captain Pahner," the shaman replied, just as formally, "I am Prince Roger's *asi*. He is not mine. It is not his duty to preserve my life, and he was in no danger of direct attack when I left his side. Moreover, the fact that I am *asi* does not absolve me from the responsibilities of every Warrior of the Way. Indeed, as one who is *asi*—whose own life was saved by one under no obligation to do so— I am bound by the Way to extend that same generosity to others. Symmetry demands it . . . which means that it was clearly my responsibility to prevent the slaughter of innocents. But it was *not* Prince Roger's responsibility to join me when I acted."

Pahner opened his mouth. Then he closed it again while he thought about it for a moment and, finally, shrugged.

"You know, Your Highness, he's got a point. Several of them, in fact." He thought about it a bit longer, and as he did, a faintly evil smile creased his face.

"What?" Roger asked angrily.

"Ah, well, Your Highness," the captain sounded suspiciously like a man who was trying not to chuckle, "I was just wondering how you feel with the shoe on the other foot for once."

Roger began a hot retort, then stopped abruptly. He glowered at the captain, then looked around as Despreaux began to laugh. Finally, he smiled.

"Ahhh, pock you all," he said with a chuckle of his own. "Yeah, okay. I get the point." He shook his head, then took a look around the deck. "So, now that that's out of the way, does anyone know what the situation is?"

"It appears to be mostly under control," Captain Fain said . . . just as two Mardukans—a Diaspran infantry private and one of the pirates—burst upward out of one of the hatches. They fell to the deck, rolling over and over, with the Lemmar using all four arms to push a knife at the private's neck while the private tried to push it back with his true-hands and flailed at the heavier pirate with both false-hands.

Roger and his companions watched the two of them roll across the deck, too surprised by their sudden eruption to do anything else. But Erkum Pol, as always following Fain like an oversized shadow, reacted with all of his wonted efficiency. He reached down with two enormously long arms, jerked the pirate up by his horns, head-butted him, and then let him go.

The pirate dropped like a rock, and the private waved a hand at Pol in thanks.

"As I was saying," Fain continued. "More or less under control. The Lemmar are fighting . . . very hard. None have surrendered, although a few—" he gestured behind him at Pol's victim "—have been rendered unconscious."

"I'm not sure that one's going to survive," Roger observed. "Maybe Erkum should have used a plank."

"Be that as it may," Fain said. "We have the ship."

"And these three surviving prisoners," Roger mused. He hooked one thumb into his gunbelt and drummed on the leather with his fingers while his free hand gestured at the female at Cord's feet. "Watch this one. She's a tough little thing."

Then he pulled out his clasp knife and stepped closer to her.

"So," he said, switching his toot to the local dialect. "What's your story?"

These new maybe-*vern* were very noisy, and the one with the pistols had a really incredible voice. It was so loud Pedi's ears were still ringing. More importantly at the moment however, and whatever language they were using, it was clear there was some disagreement, and she just hoped it wasn't over whether or not to throw everyone over the side, or burn the ships with them still on board. Finally, the one she'd tentatively pegged as the leader—although everyone seemed at first to be angry with him—turned to her.

"What you bard's tale?" he asked in a hash of Krath and High Krath.

Pedi knew enough Krath to figure out what he'd said, but the question didn't make very much sense. And she had to wonder what would happen if she told the truth. They knew Krath, so they were in contact with the Fire Priests. That meant that they would know what a Server of God was. But if she tried to tell them she and her fellow captives weren't Prepareds and they found out, it would only make things worse. Lie, or not lie? Some of them were dressed like Shin, though, and the old one had fought to save them from the Lemmar. Maybe they were allied to the Shin, and she'd just never heard of them?

Not lie.

"I am Pedi Karuse, daughter of the King of Mudh Hemh. I was captured by a raiding party to be a Slave of God. We were being sent to Strem, to be Servants there, but we were taken by the Lemmar in turn, and now by you. Who are you, anyway?"

One of the other Shin prisoners had recovered from the dragging and now looked over at her with wide eyes.

"What happened that the Vale of Mudh Hemh could be raided?" she asked Pedi in Shin.

"I guess the Shadem found a way through the Fire Lands," Pedi said, flicking her false-hands in the most expressive shrug her manacles allowed. "With the Battle Lands so picked over, they must have decided to strike deep. In our sloth and false security, we allowed them to come upon us unaware, but I was outside the walls and raised the cry. And was taken anyway, if not unawares," she snorted.

"What is the language you are using?" the leader asked. Or, she thought that was what he'd asked, anyway. It was difficult to be certain, given the mishmash of Krath and Shin he was speaking.

"It is called Shin," she told him, and decided to be diplomatic about his . . . accent. "How do you know it?"

"I know it from you," the leader said. Then he leaned over her, and a knife blade suddenly appeared on the . . . thing in his hand.

The one nearest him, another *vern,* caught her snap-kick in midair.

"Whoa, there," the *vern* said, with an even thicker accent. "He's just cutting the chain."

The leader had jerked back so quickly, despite being off center, that she probably would have missed anyway. She filed his—probably "his," although all of the *vern* wore coverings which made it hard to tell—extraordinary reflexes away for future consideration. But he seemed remarkably unbothered by her effort to separate his head from his shoulders and gestured at the chain with the knife.

"Do you want that cut off, or would you rather keep it on?"

"Sorry," Pedi said, holding out of her arms. "Off."

Now that she could see it clearly, the knife looked remarkably like a simple clasp knife, albeit made of unfamiliar materials. But whatever it might *look* like, its blade cut through the heavy chain—and her manacles—effortlessly. The *vern* seemed to exert no strength at all, but her bonds parted with a metallic twang, as easily as if they had been made of cloth, not steel.

"That's a nice knife," she said. "I don't suppose I could convince you to part with it?"

"No," the leader said. "Not that I don't appreciate your chutzpah." The last word was in an unknown language, but the context made it plain, and her false-hands shrugged again.

"I am a Mudh Hemh Shin. It is our way."

"Pleased to meet you," the leader said. His face moved in a weird muscle twitch which showed small, white teeth. "I am Prince Roger Ramius Sergei Alexander Chiang McClintock, Heir Tertiary to the

Empire of Man, and currently in charge of this band of cutthroats."
His face twitched again. "I saw you kick that one guard to death; you
look like you'll fit right in."

Only three of the six captives were still alive. One, the Fire Guard,
had been killed by the Lemmar, and the other two by the weapons of
the boarders or when the chain wrenched them across the deck.

Although both of those casualties had been Shin, Pedi didn't hold
them against the newcomers, these . . . "humans" or their guard. War
was a way of life to the Shin; from the lowliest serf to the highest of
kings. To die in battle was considered a high honor, and many a serf,
as the other captives had been, had won his or her freedom by heroic
defense against the Krath raiding columns.

Pedi wondered what to do next. Although the serfs came from
other clans, it was clearly her responsibility to take charge of them
and insure their welfare until they could be returned to their
fiefdoms. Should return prove impossible, she would be required to
maintain them to the best of her own ability. And at the moment,
that ability was rather low.

The female serf who had spoken so abruptly came forward, her
arms crossed, and knelt on the deck, head bowed in ritual
obeisance.

"Light of the Mudh Hemh, do you see me?"

"You must be from Sran Vale," Pedi said with a gesture of
humorous acceptance.

"I am, Your Light," the serf said in obvious surprise. "How did
you know?"

"If my armsman saw someone from Mudh Hemh bobbing and
scraping like that to me, he would die of laughter," Pedi said. "Get
up. Who are you?"

"I am Slee, serf to the Vassal Trom Sucisp, Your Light."

"And you?" Pedi asked the other serf.

"I am also of the lands of Vassal Trom Sucisp, Your Light," he
said, kneeling beside Slee. "Long may you shine. Pin is my name."

"Well, in Mudh Hemh, we don't put much stock in all this
bowing and scraping," Pedi said sharply. "Stand up and act like you

know what your horns are for. We're better off than we were, but we're not home yet."

"Yes, Your Light," Slee said. "But, begging your pardon, are we to return to our lands?"

"If I can arrange it," she said. "It is our duty."

"Your Light, I agree that it is *our* duty," Slee said in a tone of slight regret. "But surely it is the duty of a *benan* to follow her master?"

Pedi felt her slime go dry as she replayed the memory of that tremendous leap on the part of the old man. She would surely have died without his intervention—the intervention of a stranger, with no obligation to aid her.

"Oh, Krim," she whispered. "Oh, Krim."

"You had not realized, Your Light?" Slee asked. Pedi just looked at her, and the serf inhaled sharply. "Oh, Krim."

"By the Fire, the Smoke, and the Ash!" Pedi cursed. "I had not *thought*. My father will kill me!"

"Your Light," Pin said, "anyone can find themselves *benan*. It . . . happens."

"Not for that," Pedi said, cursing even more vilely. "For *forgetting*."

Roger watched the freed prisoners as the discussion of how to crew the vessels wrangled on. Usually, when a ship was captured, a small prize crew was put aboard by the victors. Its purpose was more to ensure that the survivors of the original crew took the captured vessel to the capturing ship's home port than to actually "crew" the prize itself.

But the Lemmar, almost to a Mardukan, had fought to the death. The reason for that ferocious, last-man defense had yet to be determined, but so far, the reaction to the pirates' efforts on the part of the Bronze Barbarians and their auxiliaries was fairly negative. The Lemmar had fought viciously and without quarter, but not particularly *well*. In the opinion of The *Basik*'s Own, that changed them from heroic defenders to suicidal idiots.

Whatever the Lemmar's reasons, there were too few left to man this ship, and much the same story was coming from all of the others. Coupled with the anticipated recapture of the convoy's merchantships to the north, it meant that most of the flotilla's present and prospective prizes would be severely undermanned by the time they reached their destination.

It was with that consideration in mind that Roger was examining the freed captives. Depending on their background, it might or might not be possible to press them into service as sailors. Thus far, though, they were looking fairly . . . odd.

For one thing, it was clear that the female Cord had "rescued" (to the extent that she'd needed rescuing) was in charge. That was strange enough, since there'd been only two places in their entire journey where women were considered anything but chattels. Even in those two places, a woman would not automatically be assumed to be the boss, but in this case, she most definitely was.

There was also the question of her age. Her horns were rather short and very light in color. That smooth, honey-yellow look was generally only found in very young Mardukans, but there was a darker, rougher rim at the base, so it was possible that their coloration and condition were manufactured rather than natural. The other female captive, who had been doing most of the talking thus far, also had horns that were smoother and somewhat lighter than normal. He wondered if the coloration and smoothness was a societal symbol? If that were the case, perhaps the warrior-female's companions were deferring to her because the condition of her horns marked her as belonging to a higher caste.

Whatever they'd been talking about seemed to have been wrapped up, though, because the leader—Pedi Karuse, if he recalled correctly—was striding over to the command group with a very determined set to her four shoulders.

"Your girlfriend's on her way over, Cord," Roger said.

"She is not my 'girlfriend.'" D'Nal Cord looked down at the prince and made an eloquent, four-armed gesture of combined resignation and disgust. "I do not play with children."

"Just save 'em, huh?" Roger joked. "Besides, I don't think she's all *that* young."

"It was my duty," the shaman answered loftily. "And, no, she is not 'that young'; she is simply *too* young."

"Then I don't see what the problem is," Roger continued. "Unless you're just feeling picky, of course."

He was enjoying the shaman's discomfiture. After all the months of having Cord follow him around, dropping proverbs and aphorisms at every turn (not to mention thumping him on the head to emphasize the points of his moral homilies on a ruler's responsibilities), it was good to see him off balance for once. And for all of his rejection of the local female as "just a child," it was clear that the shaman was . . . attracted to her.

Cord glowered at him, and Roger decided to let his mentor off the hook. Instead, he turned his attention to the Mardukan female as she arrived.

"Pedi Karuse? What can we help you with?"

Pedi was unsure how to broach the subject, so she fell back upon ceremony.

"I must speak to you of the Way of Honor, of the Way of the Warrior."

Roger recognized the formal phrasing as distinctly ceremonial, and his toot confirmed that the terms were in a separate dialect, probably archaic.

"I will be pleased to speak to you of the Way. However, most ways of the warrior recognize the primacy of current needs, and we are currently in a crisis. Could this discussion not wait?"

"I grieve that it cannot," the Mardukan female answered definitively. "Yet the full discussion should be short. I have failed in honor, through my failure to acknowledge a debt. The debt and other points of honor are, perhaps, somewhat in conflict, yet the debt itself remains, and I must address it."

"Captain," Roger called to Pahner. "I need Eleanora over here, please!" He turned back to the Mardukan and raised a hand. "I need one of my advisers in on this. I suspect it's going to involve societal differences, and we're going to need better translation and analysis than I can provide."

Although the *vern*'s accent was getting steadily and almost unbelievably quickly better, a great deal of what he had just said remained so much gibberish to Pedi. And whatever *he'd* just said couldn't change her obligations. Nor could the arrival of this "adviser" he mentioned.

"This cannot, on my honor, wait," she said, and turned to D'Nal Cord.

"I am Pedi Dorson Acos Lefan Karuse, daughter of Pedi Agol Ropar Sheta Gastan, King of the Mudh Hemh Vale, Lord of the Mudh Hemh. I bring to this place only my self, my training, my life, and my honor. I formally recognize the *benan* bond under the Way, and I thus pledge my service in all things, from here until we reach the end of the Way, through the Fire and through the Ash. Long may we travel."

"Oh, shit," Roger muttered in Imperial. He glanced at Cord, whose incomprehension of Pedi's language was only too apparent, and hastily consulted the cultural influence database of his toot. Then he consulted it again, cross indexing her words against the original language kernel and every other cultural matrix they'd passed through on their long trek. Unfortunately, it came out the same way both times.

"What?" Cord snapped. "What did she say?"

"Oh, man," Roger said, and shook his head bemusedly. "And you guys don't even have a language in common!"

"What?" Pahner asked, stepping over to the three of them.

"Hey, Cord," Roger said with an evil smile. "You remember all those times I warned you to think before you leap?"

"What did she say?" the shaman repeated dangerously. "And, no, that was usually myself or Captain Pahner speaking to *you*."

"Well, maybe you should have listened to yourself," Roger told him, beginning to chuckle. He waved a sweeping gesture of his arm and Pedi. "She says she's *asi*."

"Oh . . . drat," Pahner said. He gazed at Pedi for a moment, then swiveled his eyes to Cord. "Oh . . . pock."

"But . . . But only my people recognize the bond of *asi*," Cord protested. "I have had long discussions with Eleanora about the culture of the People and the cultures of others we have met on our travels. And only the People recognize the bond of *asi*!"

Roger shook his head, trying—although not very hard—to keep his chuckle from turning into full-throated laughter. The attempt became even more difficult when he looked back at Pedi and recognized her frustration at finding herself just as incapable of understanding Cord as he was of understanding her. Their complete inability to communicate struck the prince as Murphy's perfect revenge upon the cosmopolitan shaman who had appointed himself Roger's "slave," mentor, moral preceptor, and relentless taskmaster. Especially since it looked very much to him as if Pedi was going to be at least as stubborn about this *benan* bond as Cord had been about the bond of *asi*.

"Well," he observed with a seraphic smile, "at least you guys will have *that* much in common."

CHAPTER TWELVE

"Oh, they have more than that in common," Eleanora O'Casey told the people gathered in *Hooker*'s once again crowded wardroom just over three hours later. "*Much* more, in fact."

The problem of prize crews had been partially solved. The five surviving pirate ships had been provided with skeleton crews drawn from all six of the flotilla's schooners, along with a few of the K'Vaernian infantry who knew the difference between a bow and a stern. Then *Hooker, Pentzikis, Sea Foam,* and *Tor Coll* had headed northwest, closehauled and throwing up foam, while *Snarleyow* and *Prince John* (busy stepping a new foremast) kept company with Tob Kerr's *Rain Daughter* and the captured Lemmaran vessels. It was fortunate that the flotilla had brought along replacement spars as deck cargo aboard *Snarleyow*. Replacing *Prince John*'s mast wouldn't be a problem, but Roger wasn't at all sure that they'd be able to replace the rigging of both dismasted pirates, as well. Whether repairs could be made or not, however, he felt confident leaving *Snarleyow* and *Prince John* to look after things while the rest of the flotilla tried to run down the rest of the convoy the pirates had captured.

The current meeting had been called to try to resolve some of the problems that they would face taking or "recapturing" the remaining ships. In addition, Roger and Pahner were in agreement that it was also time to consider what problems might be anticipated following landfall. As part of that second objective, the meeting would also serve to bring most of the core of the command staff up to date—as far as possible, at least—with the mainland political situation.

"Go ahead," Pahner said now, pulling out a *bisti* root and cutting off a slice. "I've gotten bits and pieces of what we're sailing into, but you might as well tell everybody else."

"Of course." Roger's chief of staff pulled out her pad and keyed it on line. "First—"

"A moment, please," Cord interrupted. "While all of us—" a waving true-hand indicated the humans, Diasprans, and Northerners crowding the compartment "—will understand you well enough, my . . . *benan* will not. She must be aware of this as well."

"Oh, that's okay, Cord." O'Casey smiled with more than a hint of mischief. "We girls already hashed all this out. She's up to date."

"Ah," Cord replied stoically. "Good."

O'Casey waited a moment to see if she could get any more of a rise out of the shaman, but he only sat impassively. After several seconds, she smiled again—a bit more broadly—and continued.

"The pirates in the area, as Captain Kerr already informed us, are called the 'Lemmar.' Actually, I suspect that the term as he uses it isn't exactly accurate. Or perhaps it would be better to say that it isn't completely accurate. He seems to be using it as a generic ethnic term, but as nearly as I can tell, 'The Lemmar' appears to be a political unit, as well—similar to the Barbary Sultanate on Earth or the Shotokan Confederacy. It's based on raiding, high-seas piracy, and forced tribute. As for our particular lot of Lemmar, we captured charts and logs from two of their ships, and we've got a good fix on our position, the position of the raid, and the probable route the prize ships will be taking on their way home. So we should be able to find most of them and chase them down. The little local fillip is that, as I'm sure everyone noticed, the Lemmar don't care to be taken prisoner."

A fairly harsh chuckle ran through the compartment at her last sentence. The fighters in the wardroom had been through too much—Diaspran, Vashin, and human, alike—in the last year to really care if someone wanted to be suicidal. If that was their society's choice, so be it; the group that had taken to referring to itself as The *Basik*'s Own would be happy to oblige local custom.

Which didn't mean that they were blind to the tactical implications of the situation, of course.

"That's going to cause some problems retaking the ships," Kosutic pointed out after a moment, "considering the fact that they apparently don't care to allow any of their prisoners to be liberated, either. Should we even try to retake the prizes if the Lemmar are going to slaughter any captured crewmen before we get aboard? Will the mainland culture prefer to have their ships and no crews? Can we navigate them to the mainland with no crews? And is there any political payoff to retaking the ships if we get all of their crews killed in the process?"

"From what I've gleaned from Pedi, there should be both a political and financial payoff," O'Casey assured her. "The ships are, technically, the property of the Temple, but if they're taken on the high seas, fairly 'universal' salvage rules apply. If we return them, we'll be in for at worst a percentage of their value. And the supplies they have on board were apparently very important to establishing the Temple's presence on one of the formerly Lemmaran islands. The local priestdom has put a lot of political capital into that project, so helping save it from utter disaster should be viewed well, unless there's some odd secondary reaction."

"So retaking the ships would be a politically positive action?" Pahner said. "I want to be clear on that."

"Yes, Captain," O'Casey said. "I won't go so far as to say it would be 'vital.' But failure to act could be construed as being less friendly—and certainly less 'brave'—than taking action would be. In my professional opinion, barring clear military negative factors, it should be considered highly useful in making *positive* first contact with the mainland culture."

"Okay," Pahner said. "We'll discuss means later. But getting most of the ships and getting them intact may be hard."

"They'll have scattered," Roger mused aloud. "We'll have to *find* them first. Then figure out how to take them without getting all of the original crews killed."

"What about the Lemmar?" O'Casey asked.

"What *about* the Lemmar?" Roger asked in return. His response evoked another general chuckle, and the chief of staff nodded and turned to the next item on her list.

"In that case, I'd like to talk about what we'll call 'The People of the Vales'—the Shin, that is—versus the valley culture, or the Krath. I'll also offer some speculation as to where the cultures come from. Julian will discuss the purely military aspects later.

"The Shin are a fairly typical upland barbarian culture. They're centered around small, fertile valleys—the Vales—each of which has a clan chief, or 'king.' All of them are nominally independent, with a few of them allied to each other—or involved in blood feuds—at all times. There's a 'great king' or war leader, in theory, at least, but his authority is strictly limited.

"We do have a contact with the Shin," the chief of staff pointed out, nodding at the female Mardukan who'd taken a position beside Cord. The Shin would have sat behind the shaman, but with him already sitting behind Roger, there simply wasn't room. It had occasioned a certain amount of negotiation when they first entered the cabin.

"And the straight-line distance from the valley entrance to the spaceport is shorter through the vales," the chief of staff continued. "On the other hand, given the information thus far developed, we're more likely to encounter difficulties passing through the vales than if we stay in the valley."

"Those blood feuds," Pahner said.

"Precisely." O'Casey nodded. "The clans are constantly feuding. We would—could—presumably make contact with and get help and passage from the Mudh Hemh clan, but if we did, we'd automatically find ourselves at war with the Sey Dor clan. There's also a 'cross-valley' dichotomy that Julian will discuss. But it shouldn't affect us."

"Great," Roger said. "What about the valley? And what about the similarities between these . . . Shin and Cord's people?"

"The similarities can be inferred from the linguistic and cultural matrix," O'Casey replied. "The Shin language is *remarkably* similar to the language of The People. Same basic grammatical rules, similar phonemic structure, even the same words in many cases, and only mildly modified in others. There's no question that they come from the same root society, and that the separation is historically recent."

"Which, presumably, explains the cultural similarity between the *benan* and the *asi* bonds," Roger murmured, then cocked an eyebrow at his ex-tutor. "Any idea what's going on there?"

"Best guess is that the Shin are an aboriginal race of this continent which, like the Diasprans, survived the ice age by centering their culture on volcanic secondary features. That is, they stayed around hot springs and naturally warmed caves that should be fairly common on this continent. If I were to hazard a guess, I'd say that some of them then somehow moved over to Cord's continent, on the eastern verge. That would be a heck of a sailing journey, but it's possible that there's a shallow zone between here and there that was partially or mostly exposed by the ice age. We'd have to do a lot of surveying and research to confirm that, though."

"So the divergence is relatively recent, and you think the ancestral group is from this continent?"

"Yes, and a good example is language divergence," O'Casey pointed out. "*Benan* is clearly derived from '*banan*,' which is the Krath word for 'bride.' But compare that to The People's '*benah*,' which is their word for 'marriage.'" She shrugged. "Obviously, all three words are descended from a common ancestor."

"Obviously," Roger agreed, then grinned, leaned over, and punched Cord on the arm. "Feeling married yet, buddy?"

"Oh, shut up," Cord grumped. "It was for my honor."

"I know," Roger said, somewhat repentantly. "It was for mine, too. Sometimes, honor is a curse."

"Often," Pedi said, suddenly. "I . . . assure what . . . Light O'Casey understand. Word make sense. Some." She twitched one false-hand in a grimace of frustration. "Almost."

"Sort of," Roger agreed, switching to Shin. "But even if the languages are related, that was a real hash of a sentence."

"Yes, but I can learn People," Pedi said.

"No. I learn Shin," Cord said. "Here Shin. People not here."

"Good, it sounds like we can get over the language divide,"

Pahner interjected, then cocked his head at O'Casey and pulled the conversation back on track. "What about the Krath?"

"Looking at the map, the Shin vales probably make up the majority of the continent, which is mostly volcanic 'badlands,'" O'Casey said. "But the continent's bisected by a larger valley that curls like a tadpole, or a paisley mark, from the south in a big bend north and to the west. And that valley is where the majority of the population and real power of the continent lives.

"The valley of the Krath has a contiguous river that stretches, through some falls, all the way from a large upland vale to the sea. And, from Pedi's description, it's very heavily populated. The valley is one more or less continuous political unit, as well. I say 'more or less' because from the description of the scheming that goes on, the emperor, who is also the Highest of the High Priests and who rules from a capital near the spaceport, has only limited control over the lower valley.

"The society is a highly regimented theocracy, with the chief political officers of each region also being the high priests. And, unlike Diaspra, it is *not* a benevolent one. The society is similar to the latter medieval society of the Adanthi or the Chinese Manchu Dynasty. And it's also heavily slavery-based, as Julian will now discuss."

The NCO nodded at his cue and stood.

"We've got a bit of a problem. One of the reasons the Krath and the Shin don't get along is that the Krath see the Shin as a ready source of slaves for their theocracy—what are called 'The Slaves of God.' In addition, the base barbarian society is bisected by the valley. On the generally western and northern side are the Shin, but on the eastern and southern sides, the vales belong to the Shadem. And the Shin and the Shadem don't get along at all. In fact, the Krath use the Shadem for advance scouts for their raiding parties against the Shin. As a consequence, the Shin *really* hate the Shadem.

"As for the raiding parties themselves, they seem to be carried out by one of the three branches of the Krath military complex. In fact, the Krath military appears to be divided into these raiders, which are closely controlled by the Temple, and into an inner security military/police apparatus that maintains control of the civilian population, and a field army."

"The reason for having an 'army' in the first place is complex," O'Casey interjected. "With all due respect for Pedi's people, the Shin are at best a minor nuisance for the Krath. In fact, the valley has no effective external enemy, so there should be no need for a significant field army. But the satraps apparently engage in a certain amount of somewhat ritualistic warfare to settle disputes. The raiders and the internal security forces are controlled by the priesthood, but the priests in charge of them are almost a separate sect. The field army, in contrast, is closely controlled by the high priests, some of whom have even been officers. It's as if the internal security apparatus and these slave raiders are a 'subclass' of the military hierarchy. A necessary evil, but not particularly well regarded by the 'regulars.'"

"Just how big and how 'good' is this army of theirs?" Pahner asked. "We may need to use it against the spaceport."

"I'd guess they're pretty good in a set-piece battle, Sir," Julian replied. "All of our intel, presently, is from a single, biased source. Even allowing for that, though, my feeling is that they're not terribly flexible. I'm sure we could use them in a charge, or in a fixed defensive position, but I'm not sure how useful they'd actually be in taking the spaceport. Much as I despise the concept behind them, their slave raiders might actually be better."

"Justification?" Pahner asked. "And how numerous are they?"

"I don't have any firm estimates on their numbers at this time," Julian admitted. "From the fact that they appear to be the most . . . heavily utilized branch of the military, though, my guess is that they represent an at least potentially worthwhile auxiliary force. As for why they'd probably be more useful to us than the Krath field army, the raiders are the ones who regularly go in against the Shin, and the Shin are clearly no slouches on their own ground. The raiders have to be fast and nimble to handle them, and fast and nimble will probably be the way to go with the spaceport. So as . . . repugnant as they are, it would probably behoove us to try to . . ."

"Insinuate ourselves with them?" O'Casey asked. "Grand."

"I still don't get the whole thing with the slave raiders," Roger said. "They should have a surplus of labor in the valley, based on what Eleanora's just told us. So why go slave raiding?"

"Apparently, their slaves don't . . . have much of a lifespan, Your Highness," Julian said in a carefully uninflected voice. "That creates a constant need for fresh supplies of them. So the Krath raid the Shin lands for these 'servants.' Such as our own most recent recruits."

"Uh-oh." Roger grimaced. "Cord always wants to be at my back. And now Pedi has to follow him around—"

"And it will be evident that she's Shin, yes, Your Highness."

"That's going to cause problems in negotiations," O'Casey pointed out. "But we have another problem in that regard, as well. The Krath consider themselves the center of the universe, with all other polities subject to them. And their obeisance rituals are extensive."

"So they consider the Empress, as one more 'foreign barbarian,' to be their subject," Roger said. "That's . . . not an uncommon attitude in first-contact situations. Especially not with stagnant, satisfied planet-bound civilizations."

"Not for *first*-contact situations, no," Despreaux put in just a bit grimly.

"I understand where you're going, Nimashet," O'Casey said after moment. "And you're right. The Empire's policy is to refuse to recognize the insistence of such governments on their primacy, especially over the Empress herself. But usually an ambassador has a drop battalion available to *pointedly* refuse to make obeisance on the Empress' part."

"And the person doing the refusing is usually just that—an ambassador," Pahner pointed out. "Not a member of the Imperial family itself. So what do we do?"

"Well, I'll take point in the negotiations," O'Casey replied. "The first officials we encounter probably won't require a formal obeisance, so I'll politely tap dance for as long as I can, pointing out that while the Son of the Fire is, undoubtedly, a great sort, having our leaders do a full prostration is simply out of the question. We'll probably be able to avoid it by showing our personal might and only dealing with lower-level functionaries."

"What about the possibility of their informing the port?" Pahner asked.

"We may actually be in luck there," the chief of staff said cautiously. "Although the Son of the Fire is undoubtedly a god, it appears that some of his ministers are very secular in their desires. In addition, the valley is broken into five satrapies which are fairly independent of the central government. The local satrap may or may not contact the imperial capital at all, and even if he does, it wouldn't necessarily get noticed by the imperial bureaucracy. Or sent on to the spaceport even if it was. I get the feeling that the port authorities are avoiding contact with the natives to a great degree."

"Basis?" Pahner asked sharply.

"Pedi had never heard of anyone like us," Julian replied for O'Casey. "But she's otherwise very knowledgeable about local customs and politics. That suggests the humans are keeping a fairly low-profile. For that matter, she'd never even heard of 'ships that fly.' If there were any sort of regular aerial traffic between the port and the Krath, one would expect rumors about it to be fairly widespread, but neither she nor any of the Shin ever heard a thing about it. On the other hand, she knows what was served at the emperor's latest feast."

"Okay, that brings me to the second point that's throwing me," Roger said. "In just about every other culture we've dealt with, females were considered less than nothing. What's with the Shin?"

"Pedi?" O'Casey asked, switching her toot to Shin. "Why are you a warrior? We humans have no problem with that; some of our best warriors are women." She waved at Kosutic and Despreaux. "But we find it strange on your world. Unusual. We have seen nothing like it elsewhere in our travels since coming here. Explain this to us, please. In Shin or Krath, as you prefer."

"I am not a warrior," the female answered in Shin. "I am a *begai*—a war-child. My father is a warrior, a King of Warriors, and I am expected to mate with warriors. That our union may be stronger, I am trained in the small arts—the arts of Hand, Foot, and Horn, and also in the small arts of the Spear and Sword. If you want to see someone who is truly good at the arts, you must see my father."

"Do the Krath treat their women as equals?" Roger asked. "Or, at least, near equals, as you've described?"

"No, they do not," the Shin practically spat. "Their women are *vern,* no offense."

"None taken," Roger told her with a grin. "I've heard it before— although they prefer '*basik*' on the other continent. But if the Krath don't, what about the Shadem?"

"The Shadem women are even worse—slaves, nothing else. They go around swathed in *sumei,* heavy robes that keep even their countenances covered. The same with the Lemmar, the beasts!" She paused suddenly, cocking her head speculatively, as if something about Roger's tone had suddenly toggled some inner suspicion.

"Why?" she asked.

"Well," Roger said with another grin, "I think we've just found our disguise for the Shin."

"No, we have not!" Pedi said angrily. "I am no Shadem or Lemmar *vern* to go around covered in their stinking *sumei!*"

"Would you rather be a Servant of God?" Cord asked tonelessly in his native tongue. The shaman had clearly been following the conversation, in general terms, at least, and he turned a gaze as expressionless as his voice upon his new *benan.* "Or forsworn in your duty? The path of duty is not a matter of 'I will not.' Choose."

Roger doubted that Pedi understood Cord's words completely, either, but it was obvious that the gist had come through. Her mouth worked for a moment, then she hissed a one-word reply to him.

"Robes."

"There, all settled," the prince said brightly. "But what *kind* of robes? And where do we get them?"

"The *sumei* weighs at least five *latha*—that's 'what kind of robes,'" Pedi said bitterly. "And we can get them at Kirsti. That's one of the main weaving centers for all of Krath." After a moment she brightened up. "On the other hand, it's also one of the main producers of cosmetics." She made a complicated gesture of annoyance. "And on that subject, Light O'Casey has something else she needs to say."

"I'm not sure what we'll do about that, Pedi," the chief of staff said, with an odd, sidelong glance at Cord.

"What's the problem?" Pahner asked.

"Well," Julian began, heroically grasping the dilemma's horns for O'Casey, "you'll notice that most of the Mardukans we've run into on this side of the pond are clothed."

"Not Pedi," Roger objected, gesturing at the *benan* with his chin.

"Ah, yes, but she was a *slave*," O'Casey replied carefully. "It turns out that the Krath and the Shin—even the Shadem—have strong body modesty taboos."

"Oh, dear," Kosutic said. "I think maybe we should get the young lady some clothes then, eh?"

"That would be good," Julian agreed. "Cord feels perfectly normal the way he is. He's just . . . undressed. Pedi, on the other hand—"

"Feels nekkid," the sergeant major finished. "Gotcha. We'll deal with that in just a moment. But how does it affect the rest of us?"

"Well, the Vashin are generally in their armor," Julian pointed out. "Same with the Diasprans and K'Vaernians. If we just explain that the local custom is to wear clothing, and staying in armor is the easy way to do that, they'll stay in armor most of the time."

"We need to get them some clothes, anyway," Pahner observed. "Armor all the time is bad hygiene."

"Yes, Sir," Julian acknowledged. "But they're *used* to the concept. Cord and Denat, on the other hand . . ."

"What about us?" Cord asked.

"If we go wandering around with naked 'savages' we'll be violating various local taboos," O'Casey explained delicately. "It might have a certain 'kick' to it politically, but it would be much more likely to be destabilizing."

"Since the local custom is to wear clothes like humans do, Cord," Roger translated, "we'll all have to do the same thing or these snooty locals will think we're uncivilized."

"What? Cover myself in cloth?" Cord sounded incredulous. "Ridiculous! What reasonable person would do such a thing?!"

"*Pedi* would," Roger reminded him with unwonted delicacy. "The Lemmar didn't take her clothes away to be *nice* when they captured her, Cord."

"You mean . . . Oh." The shaman made a complex gesture of frustration. "I'm too old to have an *asi—benan*! Especially one I can't even understand!"

"Hey, don't blame that on the *language*, buddy!" Roger retorted. "*Nobody* understands women!"

"You'll pay for that, Your Highness," Despreaux warned him with a smile. Roger nodded in acknowledgment of her threat, but his expression had suddenly taken on an abstracted air. He tugged at a strand of hair for a second, then looked around the table.

"People wear clothes around here," he observed, and his eyes moved to Cord's new *benan*. "How many did the Lemmar assign to each of their prize crews when they took the convoy, Pedi?"

"It looked like five to ten—possibly as many as fifteen for the larger vessels. Why?"

"Rastar?"

The Vashin former prince looked up when Roger called his name. He'd been silent through most of the discussion, since it was related to seagoing matters, where he'd had little to add. Now he cocked his head, alerted by Roger's tone.

"You called, O Light of the East?"

Roger chuckled and shook his head.

"How many of these Lemmar do you think you can take. Seriously?"

"By surprise, I take it?" the Vashin asked. He let one hand rest on each of his revolvers' butts. "At least six, I believe. More if the range is great enough for additional shots before they can close. It all depends."

"And there, I think, is the answer to the question of how we capture the other ships," Roger said with a nod.

"And just who, if I may ask, backs him up?" Pahner asked darkly.

"Well," Roger replied with a smile of total innocence, "I suppose that depends on who—after Rastar, of course—is fastest with a pistol."

CHAPTER THIRTEEN

Tras Sofu had no intention of becoming a Servant of God.

Again.

He had escaped from the slave pens of the High Temple once. Only a handful of Servants could make that claim, and even fewer of those who had escaped had evaded recapture. That was a point which had been forcibly borne in upon Sofu when he realized that Agents of Justice were everywhere in Kirsti. That was also when he'd decided that the sailor's life was for him. Trade among the Lemmar Islands was dangerous—there were not only the pirates to consider, but many shoals and other hazards to navigation. But given the choice between sailing the shoals and risking the Agents, he'd take shipwreck any day.

Now, though, his bet had backfired, and he was probably headed right back to the pens. It was rumored, however, that the Lemmar would sometimes keep particularly good workers around. There were always plenty of Lemmar who wanted to work their ships—the greatest problem with the Islands was a lack of shipping, not lack of labor for the boats—but a good crewman, as Tras was, might be better than an untrained landsman. So whenever there was any little thing that needed doing, it was always Tras Sofu who was right on it. Any line that needed coiling was coiled immediately, and when the crew went aloft, it was always Tras Sofu in the lead.

His Lemmar captors—and his fellow crewmen, for that matter—knew what he was doing. Whether the Lemmar approved or were just sizing him up for the ax was another matter, though. He knew that the pirates could give slime whether any Krath lived or died. The way they'd casually chopped the heads off of the captain and the mate had made that point crystal clear. And, truth to tell, he wasn't all that much fonder of the pirates than he was of the Fire Priests themselves. But while a part of him hated acting as an accomplice in his own enslavement, being indispensable to his new masters was the only way he knew to avoid his old ones . . . and the pens.

None of the other crewmen seemed to share his attitude. They were sunk into apathy, never taking initiative at anything. The Lemmar literally had to whip them into position, and they acted as if they were already Servants, beyond redemption. Certainly none of them seemed to have any interest in emulating Tras's ingratiating eagerness.

Which was why it was Tras, always head-up and looking out for any change he might turn to advantage, who first spotted the strange, triangular sails on the horizon. The single ship closing fast on an impossible tack, practically straight into the wind, was the most outlandish thing Tras had ever seen—and he paused for a moment, staring at the sleek, low-slung craft as the slower Krath merchantman dipped into a swell. He wondered briefly what worm had devoured the brains of anyone stupid enough to sail *towards* a Lemmaran ship. Of course, the merchant ship didn't look very much like a raiding vessel, so perhaps these lunatics didn't realize what they were dealing with. If that were the case, was it his responsibility to try to warn them off before they sailed into such danger?

He considered the proposition from all angles for several breaths, then decided that other people's sanity wasn't his problem. Staying alive was, so he cupped his true-hands into a trumpet and turned towards the prize crew's captain.

"Sail *ho!*"

Roger refused to look across at Kosutic.

He knew that whatever emotion the sergeant major might be

feeling wasn't going to be evident. Which didn't mean what she was feeling was happy.

The prince's blistering argument with Pahner had been as private as possible on a ship as small as the *Hooker*. But the fact that the argument had taken place—and that the captain hadn't won—was obvious to the entire command. It was one of the very few times since their first arrival on this planet that Roger and the commander of his bodyguard, the man who had kept him alive through the entire nightmare trek, had had a clear and cold difference of opinion. And it was the very first time since landing on Marduk that Roger had pushed it to the wall.

He was aware that that sort of rift was a serious problem in any command, but he also felt that there'd been two positive aspects to it. The first was that even Pahner had been forced to concede that he really *was* the best close quarters fighter in their entire force, better even than Kosutic or Pahner himself. Both of those senior warriors had started the trip with far more experience than the prince. But this odyssey had involved more combat than any Marine usually saw in three lifetimes, and along the way Roger had proven that there was *no one* in the company as fast or as dangerous in a close encounter as the prince the company was supposed to protect. That meant that, argument or no argument, from any tactical viewpoint, he was the right person to have exactly where he was.

And the second positive aspect was that what he and Pahner had had was an *argument*. For all its ferocity, there had been no shouting, no screaming. The disagreement had been deep and fundamental, and in the end, Roger knew that his rank as a member of the Imperial family had played a major role in Pahner's concession of his point. But he also knew that Armand Pahner would never have conceded it anyway, whatever the potential future consequences for himself or his career might have been, if he hadn't learned to respect Roger's judgment. He might not share it, and at the moment the captain might not be particularly aware that he "respected," it either. But Roger knew. The spoiled prince it was Captain Armand Pahner's task to protect would never have won an argument with the Bronze Barbarians' company commander. The Colonel Roger MacClintock, the official commander of Pahner's regiment, who had emerged from the crucible of Marduk, could win one . . . if he argued long enough.

On the other hand, nothing Roger could say or do could change the fact that, from Pahner's perspective, this entire operation was completely insane. However great the political advantages of recapturing the Temple's merchant ships might be, the loss of Roger's life would make everything all too many of Pahner's Marines had died to accomplish on this planet totally meaningless. Roger knew it, and he knew Pahner did, too. Just as he knew that the commander of his bodyguard was capable of applying ruthless logic to the command decisions that faced him. Which left Roger just a bit puzzled. He supposed that some officers in Pahner's position might have looked at the shifting structure of interwoven loyalties and military discipline in The *Basik*'s Own and decided that it was time to apply that age-old aphorism, "Never give an order you *know* won't be obeyed." Especially not when the Marines' erstwhile object of contempt had metamorphosed into their warrior leader . . . and into *the* primary authority figure in the eyes of the "native levies" supporting them.

But that wasn't Pahner's style. If the captain had sensed that he was losing control—and, with it, the ability to discharge his sworn responsibilities—to a very junior officer (whatever that junior officer's birth-rank might happen to be), he would have taken steps to prevent it from happening. And Roger had come to know Pahner well enough to be certain that any steps the captain took would have been effective ones.

So there had to be another factor in the equation, one Roger hadn't quite identified yet. Something which had caused Armand Pahner to be willing to allow the prince he was oath bound to keep alive, even at the cost of pouring out the blood of every one of his own men and women like water, to risk his neck on what was essentially an operation of secondary importance.

Not knowing what that factor was . . . bothered Roger. It seemed to underscore some deep, fundamental change in his relationship with the man who had become even more of a father figure for him than Kostas had been. And though he would never have admitted it to Pahner in so many words, that relationship had become one of the most precious relationships in his entire life.

But at least things had gone smoothly enough so far to suggest that Colonel MacClintock's plan was an effective one. This was the fifth ship they'd approached, and each of the others had fallen like clockwork. The Lemmar couldn't seem to conceive of the possibility that two people could be so dangerous. Kosutic and Honal were the only ones with obvious weapons, so they tended to focus the pirates' attention upon themselves . . . and away from Rastar and Roger himself. Which was unfortunate for the Lemmar.

Rastar wore a robe, similar to a djellabah, open on both sides, that concealed the four pistols he had holstered across the front of his body without slowing him down when he reached for them. The ancient Terran fable about the wolf in sheep's clothing came forcibly to mind every time Roger glanced at the big Northern cavalryman. Not that he was any less dangerous himself. Pahner might have lost the argument about just who was going on this little expedition, but he'd flatly refused to let Roger take the human-sized revolvers he'd been carrying ever since they left K'Vaern's Cove. Conserving irreplaceable ammunition for the Marines' bead pistols was all very well, but as he'd rather icily pointed out, there was no point saving ammunition if the person they were all responsible for protecting managed to get his idiotic self killed. Which was why Roger wore a cloak of Marshadan *dianda* to help conceal the pair of bead pistols holstered under his uniform tunic.

Now, as the sailing dinghy came alongside its fifth target, Roger stood behind Rastar, looking as innocuous as possible, while Honal and Kosutic handled their own weapons with a certain deliberate ostentation designed to make *certain* all eyes were on them.

"Hullo the deck!" Rastar bellowed in a voice trained to cut through the bedlam and carnage of a cavalry battle.

"Stand clear!" one of the pirates bellowed back almost as loudly. The caller was amidships, on the starboard side, shading his eyes to pick out the small craft. Most of the rest of his fellow pirates seemed to be concentrating on the *Hooker,* which had taken up station a tactful three hundred meters off the prize ship's starboard quarter.

On the other hand, Captain T'Sool had his gun ports open and the carronades run out. These Lemmar wouldn't have any more clue about the deadliness of those weapons than the first pirates the flotilla had encountered, but they'd recognize them as a deliberate warning that their visitors had teeth of their own.

"We want none of you!" the pirate spokesman added harshly. "Stand clear, I say!"

"We're just here to buy!" Roger shouted up at him, taking over with the toot-given fluency in the local languages Rastar couldn't hope to match. "We've crossed the eastern ocean, and it was a longer voyage than we expected! We're short on supplies—especially food!"

He gazed upward, watching the Mardukans silhouetted against the gray-clouded sky, and glad that both Pedi Karuse and Tob Kerr had been able to confirm that it was fairly common practice to barter with chance-met ships when one's own supplies ran short. Of course, one normally avoided dealing with people like Lemmar raiders in the process, but there was—as far as these raiders knew—no way for the people in the small boat sailing up beside them to realize they weren't honest merchant traders.

"We'll send two people aboard—no more!" Roger added, his tone as wheedling as he could manage. "And we'll transfer anything we buy to small boats, like this one. Don't worry! We're not pirates— and our ship will stay will clear of you! We're willing to pay in gold or trade goods!"

There was a short consultation among the members of the prize crew, but in the end, as all of their fellows had done, they finally acquiesced.

"Keep your hands out from your sides—even you, *vern*-looking fellow! And only two! The leaders, not their guards."

"Agreed!" Roger called back. "But be warned! Our ship is faster than yours, and more heavily armed. And we aren't 'leaders'—just pursers and good swimmers! Try to take us prisoner, and we'll be over the side so fast your head swims. After which our crew will swarm over you like *greg,* and we'll take what we need and feed you to the fish!"

"Fair enough!" the Lemmar captain shouted back with an

undergrunt of half-genuine laughter. He wasn't entirely happy about the situation, of course. After all, he'd seen how rapidly *Hooker* had overhauled his own lumbering command, so he knew perfectly well that he could never hope to outrun her. And however undersized those bombards looked, the strange ship obviously mounted a lot of them, whereas his captured merchantship mounted no more than four pathetic swivels. Nor was he unaware of the ancient law of the sea: big fish ate little fish, and at the moment this clumsy tub of a merchant ship might turn out to be a very small fish indeed if it came to that. So if he could get through this encounter by simply selling some of the cargo—especially for a good price—so much the better. After all, *he* hadn't paid for any of it!

And if the negotiations went badly, these two peculiar 'pursers' could become Servants, for all he cared.

Roger caught the thrown line and went up the side of the ship hand-over-hand. Like the other merchantmen they'd taken, this one was nearly as round as it was long. The design made for plenty of cargo space, and with enough ballast, it was seaworthy—after a fashion, at least. But the ships were *slow,* terribly slow. If this thing could break six knots in a hurricane, he would be surprised.

It was also the largest they had so far encountered, which probably meant the prize crew was going to be larger, as well.

He reached the top and nodded at the staring Lemmar who'd thrown the rope, keeping his hands well away from his sides and the one knife he openly carried on his belt as he swung over the rail. Two of the pirates greeting him held arquebuses lightly in their true-hands, not pointed exactly at him, but close. There was a third pirate by the helmsman, and another directing a work party up forward. There'd been five pirates aboard three of the four ships they'd already taken, and seven aboard the fourth, so there was at least one still unaccounted for here. Given the size of the ship, though, Roger's guess was that there were at least three more somewhere below-decks. Possibly as many as five or six.

Rastar climbed over the side behind him and made a complex, multi-armed gesture of greeting.

"I greet you in the name of K'Vaern's Cove," he said in the language of the Vashin. "I am Rastar Komas, formerly Prince of Therdan. We are, as we said, in need of provisions. We need ten thousand sedant of grain, at least fourteen hundred sedant of fruit, four thousand sedant of salted meat, and at least seven hogsheads of fresh water."

Roger nodded solemnly to Rastar and turned to the obviously totally uncomprehending pirates.

"This is Rastar Komas, formerly Prince of Therdan," he announced through his toot. "I am his interpreter. Prince Rastar is now the supply officer for our trading party. He has listed our needs, but to translate them properly, I require better knowledge of your weights and measures, which must obviously be different from our own."

He paused. The prize crews of the other four ships had all reacted in one of two ways at this point in his little spiel, and he and Rastar had a small side bet as to which of those responses this group would select.

"You said something about gold?" the larger of the arquebus-armed pirates asked.

Ah, a type two. Rastar owes me money.

"Yes. We can pay in gold by balance measure, or we have trade goods, such as the cloth from which this cloak is made."

Roger spread the drape of the silken cape to the sides, then spun on his toes to show how well it flowed. When he turned back around, his hands were full of bead pistols.

The inquisitive pirate never had time to realize what had happened. He and his companion were already flying backwards, heads messily removed by the hypervelocity beads, before he even had time to wonder what the strange objects in the outsized *vern*'s hands were.

"By the Gods of Thunder, Roger!" Rastar complained as he took two shots to drop the Lemmar by the helmsman. "Leave some for the rest of us!"

"Whatever," the prince snapped. A third shot dispatched the pirate who had been supervising the work party up forward, and he kicked the arquebus out of the hands of a twitching body at his feet. Then he turned to examine the hatches as Kosutic swarmed over the side. The work party forward had taken cover behind the body of their erstwhile supervisor and showed no inclination to move out from behind it, so he couldn't form any idea of where the other pirates might be hiding.

"Take the stern. We'll start from the bow," he said, stepping forward. "Be careful."

"As always," Honal answered for his cousin. The Vashin noble jerked the slide on his new shotgun, which had a six-gauge bore and brass-based, paper cartridges. Then he tossed off a salute. "And this time, watch your head," he added. "No ramming it into the undersides of decks!"

"Speaking of which," Kosutic said, clapping the prince's helmet onto his head. "Now be a good boy and flip down the visor, Your Highness."

"Yes, Mother," Roger said, still looking at the forward-most hatch. It was lashed securely down from the outside, but it could just as well be secured from the inside, as well. He flipped down the helmet visor and sent out a pulse of ultrasound, but the region under the deck seemed to be a cargo hold, filled with indecipherable shapes.

"What do you think?" he asked the sergeant major.

"Well, I hate going through where they expect, but I don't want the damned thing to flood, either." Kosutic replied.

"At least they didn't have any bombards before they were captured," Roger pointed out. "Which means there's no powder magazine, either."

"Point taken," Kosutic acknowledged. "Swimming beats the hell out of being blown up, I suppose. But that wasn't exactly what I meant."

"I know it wasn't," Roger replied, and took the breaching charge the sergeant major had extracted from her rucksack. He laid out the coil of explosive on the foredeck and stood back from the circle.

"Shouldn't be any flooding problem coming down from above," he pointed out. "And I'm sure we can convince the original crew to fix any little holes in the deck for us later."

A deep "boom" sounded from the after portion of the ship as Honal broke in his new shotgun, and Roger reached for the detonator.

"Fire in the hole!"

Honal once again acknowledged how much the humans had taught the Vashin. The human techniques of "close combat," for example, were a novel approach. The traditional Vashin technique for fighting inside a city, for example, was simply to throw groups at the problem and let them work it out. But the humans had raised the art of fighting inside buildings, or in this case ships, to a high art.

He jacked another of the paper-and-brass cartridges into the reloading chute and nodded at his prince. Rastar had finally finished reloading one of his revolvers and nodded back. They were more than halfway through the ship, and so far they'd encountered four more of the Lemmar. None of the pirates had survived the meeting, and given that only one of the Krath seamen had been killed along the way, the "breakage," as the humans termed it, had been minimal.

Rastar closed the cylinder and eased cautiously forward towards the bulkhead door in front of them, then paused as he heard the distinctive "*Crack!*" of one of Roger's bead pistols. Then both Vashin heard a second shot. And a third.

"Careful," Rastar said. "We're getting close. One more compartment, maybe."

"Agreed," Honal replied, barely above a whisper, as he lined up on the latch of the door. "Ready."

"Go!"

Honal triggered a round into the latch and kicked the door wide, then stood to the side as Rastar went through it. The space beyond was apparently the ship's galley, and the only occupant was one of the Krath seaman—the cook, or a cook's mate, presumably—crouching in the corner with a cleaver in his hand. There were, however, two more doors: one in the far bulkhead, and one to starboard.

The sound of Roger's fire had come more from starboard, so Rastar kept one eye on that door in case the prince came barreling through it.

"Clear," Rastar called . . . just as the far door opened.

The Lemmar who came through it (a senior commander, from the quality of his armor and weapons) was tall as a mountain, and clearly infuriated. He'd turned to his left, towards the starboard door, as he entered, so he'd probably intended to intercept Roger and Kosutic on their way aft. Unfortunately, he'd run into the Prince of Therdan first.

Rastar's first shot took him high on the left side. It wasn't in a vital spot, which made it a poor shot indeed for Rastar, so he was able to raise his short sword and charge forward. Worse, two more Lemmar came through the door right behind him, both with arquebuses.

Rastar fired a second double-action shot at the leader from his upper left revolver, then followed up with his upper right true-hand. Both rounds hit his target's chest, barely a handspan apart, and the pirate officer's charge came to an abrupt end.

Rastar's lower left pistol was out of bullets, and only a single round remained in the lower right, but he used that one to hit the starboard arquebusman as he stepped around his now-falling commander. But that still left the *port* arquebusman, and Rastar's normally lightning reactions had never seemed so slow. His pistol hands seemed to be in slow motion as they swung towards the Lemmar, and his brain noted every detail as the Lemmar carefully raised his weapon, sighted, and lowered its burning slow match towards the touchhole—

Only to fly back in a welter of gore as Honal leaned around his cousin and triggered a single round.

"*Told* you to get a shotgun," Honal said as he stepped past the former prince.

"Oh, sure," Rastar grumped. "Just because they made you *real* cartridges, and I still have these flashplant things!"

The starboard door swung open, and Kosutic's head came slowly into view. She looked around the galley and shook her head.

"You're a fine one to talk about 'leave some for the rest of us,'" she observed dryly.

* * *

Roger watched the galley easing alongside *Ima Hooker* and shook his head.

"Why do I have this worm crawling up my spine?" he asked softly.

"Because we're about to lose a measure of our control," Pahner replied calmly. "Uncomfortable feeling, isn't it? Especially since it's pretty clear that if we upset these people, they can squash us like bugs."

Kirsti was huge. The harbor was a collapsed caldera, at least twenty kilometers across, that was cut by a massive river. The entire caldera, from the waterline to its highest ridge, was covered in a mixture of terrace cultivation and buildings. Most of the buildings were one- and two-story structures of wood frame, with whitewashed adobe filling the voids, and they were packed in cheek by jowl.

Nearer water level, the majority of the buildings were finer and larger. According to Pedi, they were residences for the hierarchy of the city, and they were constructed of well-fitted basalt blocks. On each of the caldera's landward flanks, where it was bisected by the river, there was also a vast temple complex. The westerly complex was larger and ran from the base of the slope up the massive ridge to the very crest.

Northwest of that temple were three obviously active volcanoes whose faintly smoking crests rose even over the massive caldera walls. And beyond the caldera a large valley—presumably the famous Valley of the Krath—faded into blue mystery.

The river was at least three kilometers across where it entered the harbor. The flooded portion of the caldera was close to twelve kilometers across, and the outer break was at least six kilometers wide, so the harbor enjoyed two massive natural breakwaters to either side of the entrance. Strangely, given the quality of the harborage, most of the boats in sight were local craft—small fishing caiques and dories, many of them pulled up on the basalt and tufa of the shore. There were a few larger merchant ships, like *Rain Daughter* and the other members of her ill-fated convoy, but most of the boatyards looked to be capable only of building smaller vessels.

The majority of the merchant and fishing vessels were in the eastern harbor, while the majority of the military vessels—a collection of galleys and small sailing vessels—were on the western side, close to the larger temple. Massive forts with gigantic hooped bombards flanked the outer opening, and a pile of wood and rusting chains on the western shore indicated that the harbor could be closed with a chain boom at need, despite the immensity of its entrance.

The river's current was strong where it entered the caldera, and the harbor's outflow had been evident for the last two days of the flotilla's approach to the city. With that sort of current, and the river's obvious silt load, any normal harbor would have filled up and become a delta in very short order. In Kirsti's case, though, all the silt seemed to be washing on out to sea, which Roger thought probably said some interesting things about the subsurface topography. On a more immediate level, the effects from the river's current must make things even more "interesting" for the local navy.

The flotilla had acquired its escort very early the day before, when two Krath galleys had appeared over the horizon and headed rapidly towards them. They'd slowed down quite a bit when they realized just how large—and peculiar-looking—the flotilla actually was. But the minor priest in command of them had also quickly recognized the recaptured merchantmen for what they were and continued onward to make contact. After looking the situation over and taking testimony from Tob Kerr and some of the other crewmen aboard the retaken ships, he had determined that any decision making needed to be done at a higher level.

The convoy had been ordered to proceed to Kirsti, accompanied by the junior galley, while the CO took his own ship ahead. The schooners had continued to laze along behind the slower Krath ships until they finally reached port, still accompanied by the junior galley, which was obviously trying to decide whether it was an honor guard or a captor.

Now the other ship had returned, and a group of clearly senior functionaries was prominently visible on its afterdeck. Actual first contact was about to be made with a group that was also in contact with the spaceport.

No wonder it was an . . . uncomfortable moment, Roger thought. They'd come a long way to reach this point, and it had felt at times that, given all they'd already overcome, nothing could possibly stop them now. But the reality, as demonstrated by this massive city, was that the hardest part of the journey was yet to come.

"There's no good way to do this part, Your Highness," Pahner continued. "We don't even know if this end of the valley is aware of the Imperial presence, and we have no feel for what the upper valley's attitude might be. If Kirsti's rulers *are* aware of the Imperial presence, and happy with it, then we can't exactly come right out and say we're going to evict the current residents. If they're *not* aware of the Imperial presence, then trying to explain our purpose would require a lot more explaining than any of us want to get into. So we'll just tell them we're shipwrecked traders, traveling with other traders and envoys from 'lands beyond the sea' to their capital to establish commercial and diplomatic relations with their High Priest. Trying to talk our little army past them should be interesting, though."

Roger looked over at the captain, then back at the galley. The fact that Pahner had said that much, at this point, didn't strike him as a good sign. It was as clear an indication of nervousness as he had ever seen out of the normally sanguine Marine.

"We're not going to be stopped at this point, Captain," the prince said. "We're going to the port. We're going to take the port, commandeer the first tramp freighter to come along, and go home to Mother. And that's all there is to it."

Pahner shook his head and chuckled.

"Yes, Sir, Your Highness," he said. "As you command."

Roger took a deep breath as the first of the local guards swarmed up the boarding ladder, then nodded sharply to his bodyguard's commander. They *were* going home, he thought . . . or his name wasn't Roger Ramius Sergei Alexander Chiang MacClintock.

Sor Teb tried to simultaneously control his shock and wriggle gracefully out of the silly rope and wood contraption that had lifted him aboard. The returning galley commander's description had taken nearly a day to filter up the chain of priests and high priests until it hit someone who knew of the human presence on the Plateau. When it did, of course, everyone had panicked. Given the political and personal friction between Gimoz Kushu and the Mouth of Fire, it had been immediately assumed that the humans had come as messengers from the Plateau, and that was the basis upon which Teb had been sent to greet them.

But one look at these visitors told him all of the hierarchy's elaborate calculations had been wrong. These people were clearly different from the ones on the Plateau.

First of all, there weren't very many of the humans. In fact, he saw no more than seven or eight of them currently in sight, which was a severe shock to the system. He'd never seen a senior human with so few guards! But apparently *these* senior humans had different priorities. Indeed, they actually seemed to be using the Mardukans in their group as *personal* guards, whereas none of the Plateau humans would have dreamed of trusting locals that deeply.

Second, although these humans' travel-worn uniforms were similar to the equipment of the guards of the Imperial port on the Plateau, their weapons were not. Those weapons weren't arquebuses, either, though. They fell into some middle ground, with that undeniable look of lethality which seemed to characterize all human weapons, but also with the look of something that had been manufactured locally, not brought in aboard one of their marvelous vessels from beyond the clouds. But what was most astonishing of all was that their native guards and attendants carried what were clearly versions of the same weapons which had been modified for their greater size. No human from the Plateau would *ever* have considered something like that!

At least one of the humans wore a holstered pistol of obvious Imperial manufacture, but Sor Teb saw none of the fire weapons—the "plasma guns"—that the Plateau guards carried. He didn't even see any of the "bead guns." There might be some on board this remarkable vessel, but if there were, why weren't any of the humans carrying them?

He wondered for a moment what their story was. And he also wondered what they would say. And, last, he wondered how he would determine the difference between the two.

It would be interesting.

★ ★ ★

Eleanora O'Casey nodded and smiled, her mouth closed, then backed away from the cluster of priests.

"Curiouser and curiouser," she said as she turned to Roger and Pahner.

"Pretty cagey, aren't they?" Roger replied. "I'm not getting anything."

"They're in contact with the port," O'Casey said. "No question about that. And at least two of them have met humans. Notice how they don't seem as goggle-eyed as the others?"

"Yep," Pahner said. "But they're not being real forthcoming, are they?"

"No, they're not. I think there are two things going on. This satrap isn't in contact with the port, but one of the 'minor' members of the party, that Sor Teb, has been to the capital and had dealings with humans recently. That's probably why he's part of this whole party. I'm guessing that he's the closest they've got to a 'human specialist,' so he's here as something like an ambassador from the court."

"Or a spy," Pahner pointed out.

"Or a spy," O'Casey agreed. "I also think he's really the one in control of the entire group, too. Nothing that they've done, but whenever he says something, the entire conversation shifts."

"Can we land?" the Marine asked, getting back to the point of the conversation.

"Yes, although they're obviously not real happy about having a small army come right through their city."

"We have to have the guards," the captain said firmly.

"It's more a matter of how many," the chief of staff replied. "They're not willing to permit more than three hundred at a time off the ships. And all of them have to carry their edged weapons peace bonded and their firearms unloaded, though they can carry ammunition with them. Everyone's going to be issued 'identification' showing what they're permitted to carry and where. All very civilized, frankly. Oh! And officers can carry loaded pistols."

"Well, that's the first company of attackers," Roger laughed. "Between Rastar and me."

"Okay," Pahner said unhappily. "I don't see any option but to accept their terms. But we've got gear to get to wherever we're barracking. And that's another thing—we have to be located together in a defensible spot."

"I covered that," O'Casey assured him. "I pointed out that Roger was a high noble of the human empire, although I called him Baron Chang. It wasn't even a lie, since it's one of his minor titles. But as a human baron, he's required to be secure at all times. And I also told them that we have quite a lot of bags and baggage. They're okay with that."

"And they don't have a problem with the official reason for our visit?" Pahner asked.

"Not yet, at any rate," O'Casey said. "I explained that 'Baron Chang' was shipwrecked on the other continent, and that the locals there aided him and his party. As a reward, and to discharge his honor obligations to those who helped him, the baron has guided representatives of the local merchants and princes to this continent to establish relations with the Krath, as well as to accompany him as guards to his 'friends' at the spaceport. They seem to accept all of that as reasonable enough, but they want us to barrack down here in the port area. I don't think they've dealt with large contingents from other civilizations before, but they're reacting a bit like Meiji Japan did. They're establishing an acceptable zone for the foreigners and making the rest of the city off limits to general movement.

"You'll need to approve the quarters when we get there, but they should be adequate. Also, we won't be able to just let the troops roam at will. They're going to get upset if there's a noticeable presence of foreigners wandering around, so our people will need to stay mainly in quarters,"

"Remember Marshad," Roger said quietly.

"Oh, yes," Pahner agreed with a frown. "We'll deep sweep the walls this time."

He looked back at O'Casey.

"What about the *civan*? And how do we resupply? People will have to go to the markets. And I'm not sure about keeping all the troops cooped up until they decide what to do with us."

"These people aren't used to foreigners," O'Casey said with a shrug. "The leadership is going to try to quarantine us as much as possible, and the populace is probably going to be a bit hostile, so keeping the troops close would probably be a good idea, anyway. And whatever else happens, the *civan* will have to stay down here with us by the docks. The Temple doesn't seem to have any stables. For that matter, there don't seem to be any *civan* on this continent at all, although they do have *turom*. Anyway, there's no proper stabling to be had further up in the city, but there are stock holding areas down here by the docks which should work for them, and we can get fodder and forage from the local merchants."

"Can we trade directly with the merchants?" Roger asked. "Or do we have to trade through the Temple?"

"We have to turn over a portion of the trade goods to the Temple as a tax. Actually, the toots translate that as a 'tithe.' Other than that, we can deal direct with the local merchants."

"I'm sure T'Sool will get right to work setting up contacts for Wes Til," Roger said, laughing.

"There are some additional restrictions," O'Casey went on, her expression thoughtful as she accessed her toot. "Lots of them. We'll each be issued plaques that define where we can go and under what circumstances. None of us can enter a temple, cross to the eastern city, or enter any private residence without specific, official permission. Officers and specified guards—no more than five—may enter Temple offices which are more or less secular property. And there's a pretty strict curfew: no being out of our compound after dark or during religious observances. I've got a list of ceremonies for the next couple of weeks, so we should be able to schedule around them without too much trouble."

"Jeez," Roger said. "Real friendly folks. Now I wish we'd let their damned ships go!"

"Arguably, their response could have been worse," O'Casey pointed out. "The problem is that this is an '*alles verboten*' society. If it's not specifically permitted, it's forbidden. They also tax everything but breathing, apparently. And I'd bet they're working on that!"

"Well, if you're in agreement, Captain, I'd still say let's do it,"

Roger said with a frown. "We'll take a company of the Carnan Battalion, with Fain in command, and leave the rest on the ships. They can land to stretch their legs, and we'll rotate the units. Same with the cavalry, but we'll take Rastar and Honal with us and leave the ship side with Chim."

Pahner looked around the massive city, then nodded his head slowly.

"Concur, Your Highness. But we'd better keep our heads down and be really patient. Any alternative to getting along with these people just doesn't bear thinking on."

CHAPTER FOURTEEN

"Whoooeee, now *this* is what I call civilization!" Julian laughed as the column of troops wound its way inland from the docks. The area where they were to be sequestered was about halfway between the wharves proper and the beginning of the temple zone.

The local population had been systematically evacuated from their path, but it was clear that the roads normally swarmed with buyers and sellers. Both sides of the route were lined with temporary stalls and carts which had been hastily abandoned, probably at the behest of the staff-wielding guards who "escorted" the humans. This area seemed to be primarily a fishmarket, but the slope gave a fair view of other boulevards, and all of them were packed with crowds.

"Still sheep to be fleece'," Poertena grunted as he shifted his pack for a better fit.

That pack was something of a legend. Its base was a standard Marine field ruck, but it had been "expanded" by a specially formatted multi-tool into about four times its normal volume. No one was quite sure what all it contained. They knew that it did *not* have a table-top tester for plasma rifles, although it now contained a field expedient replacement for one. And it did *not* have a sink; several of the Marines had asked. Other than that, it seemed to contain anything and everything normally found in a first-class armory, including—but not limited to—plasma welders, micrometers, parts, field lathes, and even a "tool about town" christened the "pick pocking wrench" that was stuffed sideways through the top flap. The "pick pocking wrench" was Poertena's tool of last resort—a meter-long Stilson adjustable. If a recalcitrant weapon failed to function to specification, or, God forbid, a suit of armor locked up, it was exposed to the "pick pocking wrench." Usually the piece of equipment shaped up immediately. If not, its exposure was increased until it shaped up or shipped out.

"We gonna teach 'em acey-deucy?" Denat asked. Cord's nephew had followed the company across half the world, more out of curiosity than for any other reason. Along the way, he'd proven invaluable as a natural born "intelligence agent"—only impolite people called him a spy. And he'd proven equally valuable, of course, as Poertena's right hand man when it came to introducing people to the new concept of "cards."

"Nah." The Pinopan spat. "For t'ese pockers? We teach them canasta."

"Oooooooo," Julian laughed. "That's nasty!"

"Canasta what I teach people I don' like," Poertena said. "Next to bridge, t'ere's nothin' worse. An' even t'ese bastards don' deserve to have bridge inflic' on t'em. I don't t'ink I like t'em much, but bridge be too nasty."

"I don't like this, Krindi." Erkum Pol turned the embossed plaque hung around his neck upside down and tried to read it. "I feel like a *civan* in the market."

"Get used to it," Fain replied, watching the line of Diaspran infantry being issued the amuletlike identification badges. "If we don't have them, we'll get arrested by the local guards for carrying illegal weapons."

"That's another thing—I don't like all these pocking guards." Pol peered suspiciously at the ranks of local Mardukans. The issuing ceremony was taking place in a large warehouse by the waterfront, part of a complex of four, and two walls of the warehouse were lined with Krath guardsmen.

Once everyone had been issued credentials and the area was considered secured, this warehouse and the other three would be turned over to the humans and their allies for their quarters and storage. The facility had very little going for it, but at least it was a roof, and it wasn't rocking. There was a public latrine just outside, and the locals assured them that it was capable of handling all the waste from the K'Vaernian contingent. Other than that, it would be not much better than camping out. All and all, it was in keeping with the unfriendly nature of their reception so far.

Krindi contemplated the ranks of guards for a moment, then made a gesture of negation.

"They're not anything to worry about," he grunted. Among other things, the guards were armed only with long clubs. It was obvious that they spent most of their "fighting" time dealing with robbers and rioters. His Diaspran infantry, by contrast, were armed with their breechloaders and still carried their bayonets. The guns were unloaded, and the bayonets were tied into their sheaths with cords, but that would take only a moment to fix.

Yet weaponry was only a part of it—and not the largest one. The veterans of The *Basik*'s Own were survivors of the titanic clashes around Sindi, where thirty thousand Diaspran, K'Vaernian, and Vashin soldiers had smashed over three times their own number of Boman warriors. Individually, caught in a bar fight by these Krath guards, their experience might not be of any particular consequence. But in a unit, under discipline, it was questionable whether there was another fighting force on all of Marduk that was their equal.

And if there *were* one, these pocking Krath pussies sure weren't it.

"Not a problem," Fain said with a quiet chuckle. "*Basik* to the *atul*."

"This isn't going well," O'Casey said as she slipped down onto one of the pillows and stretched out. Julian followed her into the room, and the intel NCO looked as if he'd bitten a lemon.

"More runaround?" Roger quirked an eyebrow.

"More runaround," O'Casey confirmed.

The meeting was small, composed of just the central command group: O'Casey, Roger, Kosutic, and Pahner, along with Julian for his intel information and Poertena to discuss supply. Even Cord and Pedi Karuse had wandered off somewhere. The difficulties O'Casey had already encountered suggested that they would have to meet again, with a larger group, if they were going to work out plans to deal with those same difficulties. But for now, it seemed wiser to discuss the bad news only with the commanders.

The bottom line was that they needed the Krath. On the K'Vaernian continent, there'd always been "handles" they could use—differing factions they could ally with or manipulate, or alternate routes they could use to go around obstacles. Here, though, the only way to get to their objective was through the Krath, and the Krath were turning out to be not only insular and hostile, but also remarkably lacking in handles.

"There are several things going on on the surface," she said with a sigh, "and who knows how many in the background! Sor Teb, our low-rank greeter, is actually the head of the slave-raiding forces. Technically, that's all he is, but the reality seems to be that he's something between a grand vizier and head of the external intelligence service. He's very much playing his own game, and my guess is that he's angling to succeed the local high priest. Everyone else in the local power structure seems to think he is, as well, and there seem to me to be two camps: one against him, and one neutral."

"No allies at all?" Roger's eyebrow quirked. "And what does this have to do with us?"

"No obvious allies, anyway," O'Casey replied with a headshake. "And what it has to do with us is that he not only has some of the best forces, but he's also the most probable danger to our plans. There's also the fact that, in general, nobody else on the council is willing to make a decision unless he's present, so it might be that what's actually happening is that his plotting is so far along everybody else is just staying out of his way."

"Guards like his troopers would probably make decent assassins," Julian pointed out. "And they are very feared—the Scourge, that is. Far more than the Flail."

"What's the Scourge? Or, for that matter, the Flail?" Pahner asked. "Those are new terms to me."

"We just picked up on them," Julian admitted. "The names of the three paramilitary groups associated with the Temple are the Sere, the Scourge, and the Flail. The Scourge is Sor Teb's group of slave-catchers, but the Sere is the external guard force, while the Flail is the internal police force. Together, that triumvirate's COs make up a military high council."

"I would surmise that the high priests use these groups to counterbalance each other," O'Casey interrupted. She looked out the window at the trio of volcanoes looming over the city and shrugged. "There is resistance to Sor Teb, mostly from the Sere, the conventional forces whose function is to skirmish with the other satraps. The Sere's leader is Lorak Tral. Of all the High Council, Tral acts the most like a true believer, so he's well liked by the general population, and his appears to be the next most powerful faction. The local satrap, however, is beginning to fail. The jockeying for his position is coming to a boil, and it looks like it may be happening a bit too soon for Tral's plans or prospects. The fact that the last two high priests have been from the Sere is fanning the fire under the pot, too. Apparently, the other interest groups think it would be a Bad Idea to let the Sere build up any more of a 'dynasty' by putting its third CO in a row into the satrap's throne, which is making it very difficult for Tral to rally much support amongst his fellow councilors. It looks like, whatever the general public thinks about it, the Scourge's leader is going to be the next high priest."

"Can't be a popular pick," Roger observed. He scratched Dogzard's spine and shook his head. "A slave trader as a high priest?"

"It's not popular, Your Highness," Julian agreed immediately. "People don't say it outright, but he's not well liked at all. He's feared, but it's not even a respectful fear. Just . . . fear."

"So what does this succession struggle have to do with us?" Roger asked again, then stiffened as the floor shuddered slightly under them. "Uh oh!"

The shuddering continued for a moment or two, then stopped, and Julian shook his head.

"You know, Your Highness, if you're going to turn on that earthquake-generator whenever you speak . . ."

"Damn," Kosutic said. "At least it was light. I hope it wasn't a pre-shock, though."

"Without a good sensor net, it's impossible to know," Roger said, leaning over and patting the hissing beast on her legs. "But I don't think Dogzard likes them."

"She's not the only one, Your Highness," Pahner said. "It would be a hell of a thing to get you this far and lose you to an earthquake!"

"Likewise, Captain." Roger smiled. "But where were we? Ah, yes. This Sor Teb and why he's important to our plans."

"It's starting to look like we're not going anywhere without his okay," O'Casey pointed out. "We haven't even gotten a solid yes or no on permission to leave the city, much less to head into the other satraps. The official position is that the local authorities have to get the permission of the other satraps in advance before letting us enter their territories, but that doesn't hold water."

"No, it doesn't," Julian agreed. "Denat's been talking with Pedi Karuse. It's funny, in a way. Cord is probably the best scholar we have, after Eleanora, of course, but Denat has a much better ear for languages."

Actually, Roger thought, Julian was considerably understating the case. He'd never met anyone, Mardukan or human, who had an ear for language that matched Denat's. Cord's nephew's natural affinity for languages was almost scary. The only native Mardukan who came close to matching it was Rastar, and even he had a much more pronounced accent, however good his grasp of grammar and syntax might be.

"He's picked up enough of the local dialect from her for a decent start," Julian continued, "and he went out doing his 'dumb barb' routine.

"According to what he's managed to overhear, a fairly large portion of the valley to the immediate north is controlled by Kirsti. The next satrap to the north is Wio, and Wio isn't well regarded by the locals. All of the satraps upriver from here—starting with Wio—charge extortionate tolls for goods to move through them, and Kirsti resents hell out of the way that subsidizes the other satrapies' merchant classes. In Wio's case, for example, the Kirsti merchants can either deal exclusively with Wio's . . . or lose half their value to Wio's tolls before they even get to another market on its other side."

"And, of course, trade can't pass through the tribal vales at all," O'Casey pointed out. "There's not much point trying to pass through the Shadem. Even if they wouldn't raid the caravans blind, they're on the 'outside' of the curve of the river, so there's nobody on their other side to trade with, anyway. And trying to pass through the Shin lands would be . . . really a bad idea."

"But there's a fair distance between Kirsti and the Wio border," Julian said. "They divide the satraps into districts called 'watches,' and it looks as if each watch is about fifty kilometers across. There are four of them between here and Wio, so we're looking at about two hundred kilometers of travel. And there's another entire major city between here and Wio, as well. They seem to have a pretty good internal transportation system. In fact, it looks to be far and away the best of any we've encountered so far. So there's no real physical bar to our making the trip. They just want to keep us in place."

"How far to the Imperial capital itself?" Roger asked. "And to the spaceport."

"Twenty marches," Julian promptly replied. "And three more satrapies."

"Could they have already sent a message?" the prince asked. "To the capital, or even the port? I know they're independent of the capital, but 'what if'? For that matter, 'what if' the entire reason they're keeping us from leaving Kirsti is to keep us penned up here until a message comes back down the chain to tell them what to do with us?"

"Well," Pahner said. He leaned back, gazed thoughtfully up at the ceiling, pulled out a *bisti* root, and carefully cut off a sliver. Then he slowly and deliberately inserted the sliver into his mouth. So far as they'd been able to discover, the root was unknown on this continent, and his supply was dwindling fast.

"We've been here for ten days," he said finally. "If it's twenty marches to the capital, that means another ten days for any messenger to get there, or to the port. If a message got to the capital, I'd think that there'd be some discussion before it was sent on to the port. So, figure another twelve days or so before it gets to the governor . . . or whoever is running the port."

"And we could see an assault shuttle here within a day or two afterwards," Roger said with a grimace.

"Yes, Your Highness," the captain agreed evenly. "We could."

"And what do we do about that?"

"One thing is to try to get a better feel for the intentions of this Sor fellow," Pahner replied. "If he's ambitious enough to want to head up the local satrap, he'd probably be even more interested in knocking off the entire valley."

"Try to recruit him?" O'Casey asked dubiously, and grimaced. "He's a slippery little snake, Armand. Reminds me of Grath Chain in Diaspra . . . only competent."

"I don't like him either," Pahner said. "But he's the most likely to be willing to take a chance. If we back his coup, we use our better position and his raiding forces to move up through the other satraps and take the port."

"And if he balks?" Roger asked.

"Well, if Eleanora's negotiations aren't completed by the end of the week, I suggest we come up with a Plan B and implement it," Pahner said. "At that point, we can assume that the port is aware of our presence."

"And what do we do about *that*?" Roger asked again.

Pahner let a flash of annoyance cross his face, but the question wasn't really off-point. In fact, it was bang on-point.

"Then we cut our way out of the city, head for the hills, and hope like hell we can disappear in the Shin mountains before the port localizes us."

"I thought you said there was no alternative to being patient," Roger said with a smile, and almost despite himself, Pahner smiled back, ever so slightly.

"And the Shin?" the prince continued after a moment.

"We'll cross that bridge when we come to it," Pahner said, his smile fading into a frown. "Getting out of town will be hard enough," he went on, and turned to the intelligence NCO.

"Julian, we need to work up a full order of battle on the local forces. In addition, I want routes from here to the gates, alternate routes, and alternate gates. I want to know where all the guard houses are, what the forces at each guardhouse consist of, probable reaction times, and how they're equipped. I want to know as much as you can find out about the forces *outside* the city, as well. And we need a better feel for the relative capabilities of the three different forces here in Kirsti. Last, I want to know where the main units of this slaving force are. It's beginning to look like they're both the most effective force, and the one with the most effective commander. I want to know, if we make a move to break out of town, where the majority of them are, and when we can expect their reaction."

"Tall order, Captain," Julian said as he marked up his pad. "But I'll try. We've still got some of our remotes left. I'll get them deployed and then get Poertena and Denat to spread around a little silver, see what sort of HumInt they can shake free."

"Shanghai Despreaux and anyone else you need," the captain said. "You know what to do."

"Yes, Sir," Julian replied. "That I do."

"Poertena," Pahner continued. "Supplies."

"Bad, Cap'n," the Pinopan growled. "T'e price of grain is ou'rageous—worse t'an anyt'ing since Ran Tai! An' t'ese pockers gots no barbarian armies to drive t'em up, either. Food has to be nearly half an annual income. Jus' feeding t'e *civan* is gettin' expensive. I been laying in supplies for t'e trip, but t'ey low, Sir. Low."

"Julian, figure out what's stored in the area around us. Get with Poertena on that. Make up a list of targets."

"These guys really have you exercised, Captain," Roger said carefully. "You don't normally think in terms of looting."

"They have me nervous, Your Highness," the Marine replied. "Their invariable response has been at least passively hostile. They're very closed, in ways I don't care for, and we're looking at the possibility that they may be in contact with the port. All of those things tend to trip my professional paranoia circuit."

"Mine, too," Kosutic said. "And that's not the only thing making me nervous. Or, rather, one of the ways they're 'closed' . . . bothers me. I've been trying to keep from stepping on any toes by avoiding the subject of religion, and it's been remarkably easy."

"I can tell from your tone that that does a lot more than just 'bother' you, Smaj," Roger said. "But why does it?"

"You've been to a theocracy, Your Highness," the sergeant major replied. "Think about Diaspra. Or about the Diaspran infantry. They're constantly discussing religion; it's their main topic of conversation. But these people don't talk about their religion *at all*. That isn't normal by any theocracy's viewpoint. In fact, it's frankly weird. They say that in Armagh, if you ask the price of a loaf of bread, the baker will tell you that His Wickedness proceeds from God. But if you ask the butcher for a steak, *he'll* tell you that God proceeds from His Wickedness. The best I can determine, these guys worship a fire god. That's *it*, Sir. The whole enchilada. The sum total of all I've been able to learn about a theocracy's doctrine and dogma, and I got most of that from discussions with Pedi."

She shook her head.

"I don't trust theocrats who won't discuss theology, Your Highness. I have to wonder what they're hiding."

"We'd still be better off with their support," Pahner said. "But in the event that it drops in the pot, that they inform the port of our presence and we have to deal with that, we should have plans in place for how to exit the town and how to obtain the supplies we need. Fortunately, we have a week or two to figure all of that out."

"There's just one thing," O'Casey said, her expression pensive. Pahner looked at her, and she shrugged. "What if they're quicker than that? Quicker than twenty days up?"

"What do you mean?" Roger asked uncomfortably. "They don't have *civan*, so I don't see how they can move much faster than a *turom* caravan."

"I'm thinking about the Incas," his chief of staff said with an unhappy grimace. "They used to use teams of runners. You'd be surprised how much distance you can cover when each person is running, oh, twenty kilometers as fast as he can go. Or, rather, how much distance a *message* can cover in how little time if each relay is by someone who has to run *only* twenty kilometers as quickly as he can."

"No, I wouldn't be surprised at all," Pahner said with an even unhappier grimace. "That's a lovely thought."

"Yep," Julian agreed. "On that note, I guess I'd better get started on that order of battle," he added. Then he laughed.

"What?" Pahner asked.

"Well, what's the worst case, Sir?" Julian asked with a decidedly manic grin. "I mean, that's what we've got to think about, right?"

"Yes, it is, Sergeant," Pahner agreed tightly. He cut the NCO a certain amount of slack, because pressure brought out two things in Julian: brilliance, and humor. "The worst case? The worst case would be that the starport is fully under the control of the Saints, and that they're able to determine that the humans reported to them are being led by His Highness."

"Yes, Sir. That *is* the worst case from our perspective," Julian agreed. "But now think about their *reaction* to the news."

It was the worst tradecraft that Temu Jin had seen in all the thirty-plus years since he'd first left Pinopa.

The small gap in the security wall at the back side of the spaceport required the governor's "secret contact" to cross the entire compound just to meet the native runner. And since the hike required the receiver to break his normal routine—usually with no advance warning to let him build a believable reason for him to be here—anyone investigating the governor's (many) illegal activities would have found it ludicrously easy to identify, analyze, and break the communications chain. All they'd have had to do would be to watch for the idiot marching back and forth at the most ridiculous time of day for the least logical reason.

Short of wearing an illuminated holo-placard saying "Secret Courier!" in meter-high letters, Jin couldn't think of anything else he might have done to make the hypothetical analyst's job any easier.

There were only two saving graces to the incredibly stupid set up. The first was that it had been set up by a previous communications technician, so Jin didn't have to take responsibility for it. The other was that the person on the base responsible for trying to *find* the link was Jin.

It was also a "hard contact." That was, the people at both ends knew if there was a message to be exchanged. By way of comparison, his own tenuous communications with his control had been a soft-connect, and almost entirely "one-way." His outbound communications method—message chips passed via a dead-drop to well-paid tramp freighter pursers—had been cut out when all three of his contacts became victims of "piracy" in the sector.

Inbound, it was easier. The local garrison received a variety of e-zines and carefully crafted personal ads passed all the information he needed to receive. He occasionally wondered, as he perused them, how many of the other messages were code. He especially did that after the last missive—the message for "Irene" that told her it was over. That she should go on with her life.

The one that told him he was out in the cold.

It had been interesting, from a professional perspective, that there'd been at least twice as many personals as normal in that particular month's e-zines. The memory still brought a certain grim chuckle, and he wondered how many other people there'd been on how many other planets, looking at those messages and going "What the . . . ?"

The code had been the ultimate disaster message, telling him that "the World" was gone, and he was to sever all contacts, trust no one, respond to nothing but personal contacts. For him, it had simply been one more nail in the coffin. Heck, bad news on Marduk was as expected as rain, right?

He took the leather satchel from the Mardukan and walked back into the bushes at the edge of the field. The entire set-up was just *too* asinine. So imbecilic. So *amateurish* he was embarrassed every time he went through the charade. The Mardukan, some unknown "agent" of the Kirsti satrap, would now go back through a cleared passage in the minefields, through a portion of the mono-wire that had been changed out in favor of less lethal materials, and through an area where the sensors had been bypassed. The governor, whose life and limb, in the event of attack, *depended* on all those defenses, had ordered the changes so that these "secret communiques" could slip through. *Ordered* it!

Jin shook his head and cracked the seal on the pouch. The governor could not, of course, read Krath, despite having been here for over fifteen years, and despite the fact that "learning" it would require only an upload to his toot and a few minutes of his time. No, the governor had better things to do than learn enough of the language so that the minor messages—like, oh, *secret communiques,* for an example that just *popped* to mind—could be read by someone other than his *communications technicians.* Such as the *governor.*

Jin shook his head again. Could it be possible that the Empire was truly so short on functional genetic material that they'd had no choice but to send this . . . this . . . *idiot* out to be governor?

No. No, he told himself. The Empire couldn't possibly be that hard up for talent. No, this was a brilliant ploy of the Imperial bureaucracy. They'd found themselves stuck with someone so stupid, so dazzlingly incompetent, that the only possible defense had been to send him someplace so utterly unimportant that even *he* could do no damage there.

Jin took a deep breath, clearing his mind of the governor and the asininity of whoever had assigned him to Marduk. It actually helped, and he felt marginally more cheerful as he unfolded the message. Then he read the first few words . . . and closed his eyes.

For just a moment, a remembered whiff of corruption seemed to fill his nostrils and he almost fell out of character. He knew—*knew*—that if anyone saw him in that moment, his life wouldn't be worth a Mardukan raindrop. He knew he had to get his composure together, that far more than just his life depended upon it, but for a moment it was all he could do not to cry. He *wanted* to cry. To scream. He wanted to shout for joy and terror. To announce the arrival of the moment he'd spent hours dreaming of as he stared up at the bunk above his. Although, he admitted, his dreamy imagination had never included the possibility that he'd want to throw up when the moment came.

He had a real problem, though. Not one that he hadn't planned for, but a problem nonetheless. Since returning from the aborted "rescue mission," he'd slowly and carefully worked himself into a position where he picked up most of these communications. It was generally shoved off on the low man on the totem pole—not only was it a long way across the port in the heat, but the messages rarely had any significance for the humans. They were generally about the shifting politics of the inter-satrap "wars," and how much was that going to affect the port? Other satraps sent messages to other locations, and he picked up most of those, as well. But this was the one communique that it was absolutely essential the governor never see . . . and the one he had set up the entire system to ensure that he *did* see.

Or would have, if Temu Jin had had any intention of ever allowing him to.

Unfortunately, the guv wasn't a *complete* idiot. He always had at least two people translate any missive from his local contacts, and he would be aware that Jin had gone out to collect this one. Which meant that Jin couldn't simply make this one disappear. There had to be a different one.

He reached into his tunic and pulled out a small package, then flipped through the various messages contained in it until he got to one that he liked. He read over it once more, and smiled thinly. It appeared that the Shin barbarians were contemplating allying with the Wio in return for the Wio's halting their raids. This was, in fact, bullshit. But since it was "unconfirmed" information from the Im Enensu satrap, when it turned out to be incorrect, it would simply be assumed that the Im Enensu satrap, or his intel chief, couldn't find his ass with all four hands.

Somebody might notice that the pickup signal had been the one for Kirsti, not Im Enensu, but that was unlikely. Temu had been the one to receive that as well . . . exactly as planned.

He heard a voice in his head, as if it were yesterday: "Plan! Prior Planning Prevents Piss Poor Performance! Plan for every contingency. And be ready when your plans fail!"

Come to think of it, he really wished someone had told his control that.

He put the new message into the satchel, closed it, and pocketed the original. He could analyze it later. It would be interesting reading.

He looked up at the eternal Mardukan clouds, flared his nostrils wide, and smiled into the first drops of rain.

"What a beautiful pocking day!"

CHAPTER FIFTEEN

Denat picked up the poorly baked clay cup and hunched his shoulders. A fine rain had started, and the denizens of the port bazaar had mostly sought the shelter of awnings. Personally, Denat was rather enjoying the gentle drizzle, and sitting out in the middle of it should make him look even more like an ignorant barbarian, too stupid to come in out of the rain. Certainly not the sort of eavesdropper a civilized city dweller would concern himself over—after all, the ignorant lout wouldn't be able to understand a *civilized* dialect, anyway!

But Denat understood enough to get along, and even from his place in the open, he could hear various conversations under the awnings. He grimaced as he sipped the thin, sour wine—just the sort of stuff any city barkeep would offer a dumb barbarian—and subconsciously sorted the discussions around him.

Denat's natural flair for espionage, like his gift for languages, had never been noticeable among the People as the nephew of the village shaman. His skill and expertise as a hunter, one who actually preferred to hunt the far more dangerous night than during the day, had been well-known. And even before the arrival of the Marines, he'd had an affinity for picking up information in Q'Nkok, which was one of the reasons Cord had asked him to accompany the humans as they made their way to that first city. But no one had ever seriously considered him for the role of a spy.

It had originally been assumed that he and the other village warriors would return after Cord and his *asi*'s companions had passed through Q'Nkok to begin their monumental, probably suicidal, trek halfway around the planet. Instead, he and a few others had stuck around, as much to play cards with Poertena as anything else, and the journey which had so noticeably changed the prince, had changed Denat almost as greatly.

He'd discovered his natural ability for languages, and a flair for the dramatic that permitted him to either blend into societies or to put on an excellent "dumb barbarian" routine. And he'd also discovered how much he enjoyed putting those talents to work.

It was in the dumb barb role that he had been wandering the city for the last few days, and the impressions he was picking up made him uneasy. He still had only a rudimentary grasp of Krath, and an even more rudimentary one of the society which spoke it, but nothing he had learned so far seemed to add up.

This city was filled with temples. In fact, it seemed that there was one on every third street corner, and they were all more or less identical, barring size. They had a square front that connected to a conical back. The cone was clearly meant to represent a volcano, and on the one holy day which had been observed since their arrival, smoke had issued from all the temples. And the smoke had been filled with the bitter-sweet scent of burning meat, which had to have been immensely expensive. Denat knew how much forage for the *civan* was costing Poertena, so he also knew that the cost of feeding meat animals had to be extremely high. So if the worshipers were prepared to tithe sufficient donations for the priesthood to fatten up sufficient sacrificial animals to scent that much smoke, then they must be *really* devout.

The *quantity* of smoke was explained readily enough. It had come from the endless loads of coal and wood that had been brought in through the previous few days by the many slaves of the Temple. What didn't add up was that there were no holding pens around the temples. The Diasprans hadn't practiced animal sacrifice, but other religions on Denat's home continent had, and behind all of those temples had been pens for the sacrificial animals. But there hadn't been so much as a single *turom* penned up around *these* temples.

In addition, as Sergeant Major Kosutic had pointed out, nobody *argued* religion. This city was clearly a theocracy, even more totally under the control of the local priesthood than Diaspra had been. But whereas, in Diaspra, everyone discussed the nature of Water, here no one discussed the nature of their god at all. It wasn't even clear what the god was, although Denat had been told it was a god of Fire.

The conversations around him were of no use. They were all complaining about the lack of trade, which was a pretty constant theme. Something had dried it up, and fairly recently, apparently. The immediate consequences were readily apparent, particularly in the dock areas, where many of the wharves were unused. Exactly what had happened to it was unclear, to say the least, though. The almost total lack of a long-range merchant fleet seemed to have had something to do with it, but the reason for the shipping shortage itself was, again, unclear.

Kirsti was turning out to be a mystery wrapped in a conundrum. And that was making him irritated.

Cord pushed his way through the bustling streets with his lower arms set in an expression of disapproval.

"A fine city, indeed," he growled, "but this covering of the body is barbarous." He pulled at the kiltlike affair, then snarled as one of the locals ran into him. "And the manners are atrocious."

"Krath, what to say?" Pedi looked around nervously. She was trying to simulate a Shadem accent while speaking in Imperial. Since she was far from eloquent in Shadem and even further from fluent in Imperial, it was tough. But the alternative was to let her Shin accent be noticeable, and she was trying very hard to avoid that. She also knew that there were habits to maintaining and managing a *sumei* which she simply didn't have. Hopefully, the fact that so few of the Krath's Shadem allies made it as far as Kirsti would mean that no one was familiar enough with the proper way to wear a *sumei* to recognize her own lapses. She told herself that as long as she didn't have to remove the robes, she should be fine.

In fact, she told herself that at least once every four or five of the humans' "minutes."

So far, this combined shopping trip and intelligence mission had gone well enough to indicate that she was probably right. On the other hand, one item she intended to purchase before returning to the quarters the city council had assigned to them might be looked at askance. She wasn't sure if Shadem females knew its use or not. Some Krath did, but it was not looked upon with wide favor. So be it. She wasn't going another day without some *wasen.*

Cord paused at the mouth of an alley and consulted a map Poertena had drawn. The sawed-off Marine had already "scoped out" much of the shopping in the western city, and his chart indicated that this would be one of the better places to look for the items Pedi had listed. Now that they were here, though, the opening was a dark cavern, a set of steps downward into a brick-lined tunnel which Cord found particularly unappealing.

"Go," Pedi whispered. "People look."

"I hate cities," Cord muttered, and stepped into the darkness.

From the bottom of the short set of steps, it was apparent that the tunnel was lit, after a fashion, by high skylights which threw occasional, bright circles on its floor at irregular intervals down its length. It continued with a faint, mildly organic curve to the right, then turned sharply left about fifty meters in. There were doorways to either side, many of them low, and in front of each doorway were groups of Mardukans, most of them sitting on cloth covers. In several of the doorways, one or more of the locals were working on some item—here a metalworker was hammering designs on a pot, there a knife-maker was riveting grips to a tang, and about halfway down the aisle a jeweler under one of the skylights was meticulously setting a teardrop of Fire into a horn bangle.

The atmosphere was thick with a mixture of smoke from coal fires, drifting like wisps of fog through the light from the skylights, and the heady scent of spices. Several of the doorways sheltered Krath, some of them female, cooking over small grills. Most of the food being prepared was seafood, ranging from boiling seaweed to grilled *coll* fish, along with small pots of the ubiquitous barleyrice.

Cord strode forward, ignoring the looks his outlandish dress and peace-bonded spear drew, until he reached an alcove on the left, decorated with a variety of dried items and bottles of mysterious liquids.

The Krath who ran the apothecary's shop was short, even by local standards. He peered up at the towering shaman suspiciously and babbled a quick, liquid sentence in the local trade patois.

Cord caught only a bit of the meaning, but the question was fairly clear. He settled into a squat as Pedi obediently settled in behind him.

"I need to buy," he said. "Need stuff for me. Stuff for wife. Need *wasen*."

The merchant made a gesture and grunted another fast sentence. Hand signs were closer to universal on Marduk, where so much was expressed by body language and gesture, than on many other planets. So while Cord had never seen this particular one, he'd seen one very much like it in K'Vaern's Cove.

His motioning true-hand stopped Pedi even as he felt her start to move forward. He waited for a breath or two to be certain she stayed stopped, then leaned forward until his ancient, dry face was centimeters from the merchant's.

"Don't think leather on spear save your life. Keep comments to self, or eat horn through asshole."

The shaman was beginning to distinctly regret this trip. He wasn't sure what *wasen* was, but he'd already decided it wasn't worth the trouble.

Pedi was beginning to wonder if it had been worthwhile herself. It might have made more sense just to forget about the *wasen*. It wasn't as if she were really going to need it anytime soon, after all. Or, failing that, it might have made more sense to come by herself, or in the company of one of the female Marines. Despreaux perhaps. But it was not permitted for a *benan* to leave her master, even for a moment.

Not when there was the possibility of danger . . . which happened to be the case anywhere in this Ashes-damned city.

She wondered suddenly if Cord lived under those strictures, as well. And, if he did, how he reconciled being away from Prince Roger. Or had her own insistence finally driven him to bend his honor? And, if it had, to what extent was her own honor tarnished by the action into which she had manipulated him?

Wasen was beginning to look less and less like a good idea.

She leaned forward and, keeping her hands draped in the *sumei,* gestured at one of the dried items. It was a type of sea creature that clung to rocks in the surf zone. Fairly rare on the continent, *wasen* was one of the major trade goods of the Lemmar Alliance, and one of the reasons for the recent successful effort to take Strem away from the Lemmar. Besides the use for which she intended it, it was employed in various industries, including textiles.

In a place like this, however, it would be bought only for less acceptable uses. Less acceptable, at least, to the Krath.

Cord looked at the dried bit of what looked like meat and pointed in turn.

"How much?"

He had learned as a boy traveling to far Voitan that along with "Where water?" and "Where food?" that was one of the three most important phrases any venturer could learn in the local dialect.

The merchant held up fingers indicating a number that certainly sounded outlandish to the shaman. But that was what bargaining was all about, and he automatically quoted a return price one-third the suggested one.

The merchant screamed like a stuck *atul* and grabbed his horns. The offer must have been just about right.

As Cord, with obvious reluctance, pulled out a pouch and started measuring silver against the merchant's weights, Pedi leaned forward and picked up the hand-sized mass of *wasen.* She noticed immediately that it was unusually hard, and after she brought it under her robes and broke it, she wanted to scream in anger. Instead, she leaned forward and pulled urgently at Cord's arm.

"Not good," she hissed in the little People she knew. "Bad quality. Old. Not good."

Cord turned around and fixed her with a glare.

"You use?" he asked.

"Too much," she insisted furiously. "Bad quality. Too old."

Cord turned back to the merchant.

"She say stuff too old," he snarled. "No can use."

"First quality *wasen*," the apothecary spat back. The rest of the sentence was too fast for the shaman to catch, but one word sounded particularly bad.

The apothecary didn't speak too rapidly for Pedi, though. She managed not to break into Shin, but after a moment's spluttering, she launched over the seated Cord and grabbed the merchant by the horns.

"Kick your ass, modderpocker!" she screamed, using the only Imperial curses she knew—so far. "*Kick your ass!*"

"Barbarian whore!" the merchant shouted back. "Let go of me, you bitch!"

Cord grabbed one of his erstwhile bodyguard's arms and disengaged it from the merchant, then pushed the Krath to the ground.

"Here's your silver," he said with a growl. "I'll keep the copper as a charge for calling my wife a whore."

"Barbarian *sathrek*," the merchant snarled.

Cord looked around at the other merchants. Some of them had started to come to the apothecary's aid, and he pulled the still cursing Pedi down the way until they were out of sight of the scene of the confrontation.

"Listen to me," he grated in a mixture of Imperial and People. "Do you want to kill us all? You want to kill your *asi*?" He could tell from the drape of her *sumei* that she had crossed all four arms under the muffling folds.

"Bad quality," she hissed. "Too much. And . . ." She stopped and stamped a foot. "Modderpocker," she muttered.

"What did he say?" Cord asked. "That was what really set you off, wasn't it?"

"He say . . . he say . . ." She stopped. "Don't know Imperial. Don't know People. Don't want say, anyway. Bad."

"What was it?" Cord asked. "I've been called some pretty bad things and survived."

"Was . . . was having season with slimer. With baby."

Cord thought about what she meant for a second, then fingered the peacebonds on his spear while he did a *dinshon* exercise to control anger.

"The Imperial term is pedophile," he said after a moment, once he was certain of his own composure. "And 'modderpocker' means having season with your own birther. If you should happen to be interested."

Pedi thought about that for a moment, then grunted a faint laugh.

"Wish pocking merchant speak Imperial," she said much more cheerfully, and Cord shook his head and sighed.

"Pedi Karuse, you are a lot of trouble."

Poertena flipped over the hole card and scooped in the pot.

"That was a a a lot of trouble for a measly few coppers," Denat growled, as he scooped up the cards to begin shuffling.

"Wha'ever it take," the Pinopan replied, leaning back with a shrug. "You not out looking por trouble?"

"You don't have to look with this lot," the barbarian said. "Most obnoxious group I've ever dealt with."

"You sure it's just one way?" Julian asked carefully. He usually sat out Poertena's card games—the Pinopan was deadly with a deck—but the waiting was getting on his nerves. And, apparently, on Denat's. "You've been pretty . . . touchy lately."

"What do you mean?" Denat shot back sharply. "I'm fine."

"Okay, you fine," Poertena agreed. "But you have to admit, you been pretty short temper lately."

"I am *not* short tempered," he insisted hotly. "What in nine hells are you talking about? When have *I* been short tempered?"

"Ummm . . . now?" the Pinopan replied easily. "And you nearly kill t'at Diaspran yesterday."

"He shouldn't have snuck up behind me! It's not my fault people go *creeping* around all the time!" Denat threw the cards down on their crate-card table and jerked to his feet. "I don't have to put up with this. You can just find somebody else to insult!"

"So," Julian asked as the Mardukan stalked away. "Did we start that, or were we right?"

"I t'ink you right," Poertena replied uneasily. "He didn' even insult me when he lef'. I t'ink we gots a problem."

"Should we talk to Cord about it?"

"Maybe." The Pinopan rubbed his head. "Cord pretty wrap up wit' his girlfrien', though. Maybe I ask Denat later. He might cool down, decide to talk. It could work."

"Better not let Cord hear you call her his 'girlfriend,' or Denat will be the least of your worries."

They had managed to secure better clothing at a small textile shop without even a single additional disaster. And at an herbalist, they had found some mysterious emollients. Not far from the herbalist's, Pedi had surreptitiously directed Cord's attention to two small swords, which he'd also purchased. These transactions had been relatively simple, although the locals were notably hostile towards both of them.

With those minimal supplies collected, Cord had unilaterally headed back to their assigned quarters, forcing Pedi to follow. The Shin clearly would have liked to have spent more time in the massive, dusky market, but the shaman was sure that something else would set her off if he allowed her to. She was the most difficult female it had ever been his misfortune to encounter. Smart, yes, but very headstrong, and unable or unwilling to rein in her temper. She'd shown some capacity to back up that temper, on the Lemmar ship, and the swords—which she had indicated she had some knowledge of—were to test whether or not she was all talk.

Back at their quarters, she snatched the packages—including the dual swords and the mysterious *wasen*—and disappeared into her private room. They had been scheduled to test their martial skills against one another after their shopping trip, but Cord found himself cooling his heels for some time while the sun glow moved across the clouds. In fact, the bright, pewter-gray light had swept low in the west before Pedi reemerged.

Her appearance had . . . changed.

The rough, dark rims at the bases of her horns were gone, and the overall color of the horns had faded slightly, to an even yellower honey with just a touch of rust. The mystery of the emollients' purpose was also revealed, for her skin had developed an even finer coating of slime. The clothing turned out to be a set of baggy pants and a vest that draped to her midsection, connecting at the base, but leaving all four arms free. The overall color was a light scarlet, with yellow embroidery along the edges of the vest and at the cuffs and waistline of the pantaloons.

"Do you like it?" Pedi stepped through the door and twirled lightly on one foot.

Cord looked at her for a moment and thought about saying what he thought. But only for a moment. Instead, he controlled his initial reaction and cleared his throat.

"You are my *asi,* my *benan,* not my bond-mate. Your appearance matters only in that it does not bring disfavor upon me or my clan. Your skill with those puny swords matters far more."

Pedi stopped in mid-pirouette with her back turned to him. A moment passed, then she leaned through the door and picked up her "puny swords." She turned back to Cord and took a guard position.

"Are you ready?" she asked with a certain, dangerous levelness of tone.

"Would you care to warm up or stretch first?" Cord asked, still leaning on his spear.

"You don't get a chance before a battle," Pedi replied, and, without another word, charged him with one sword held in a port guard, and the other stretched out before.

Cord had been expecting it, but he'd forgotten how fast she was, so his first reaction was to put the spearhead in position to spit her. It would have been a formidable obstacle, even with its leather binding. But after a bare hesitation, he checked that and brought the base of the spear around in a tripping blow, instead.

Her reaction made him wonder if she'd been actively courting the spitting maneuver. As the spear shaft swung around, she leapt lightly into the air, brought the left sword down to barely make contact with the spear. The right-hand sword licked around to meet it, and then she twisted through a midair course correction that left her with both sword hafts locked onto the spear.

A wrist twisted, a foot kicked lightly, and the spear was very nearly wrenched out of his hands. But the shaman had experienced a similar technique, albeit years before, and twisted his body through the disengage. He felt every lengthy year of his age as creaky muscles responded unwillingly to the move, but it seemed that Pedi had never dealt with the disengage before.

The spear shaft snaked through three dimensions, one of which pressed painfully on her wrists and nearly forced her to drop one of the swords. At the end of the maneuver, she was left leaning sideways and badly off balance, while Cord flipped his spear around and went back to peacefully resting on it.

Looking as if he had never moved at all.

"That was interesting," he said brightly, trying very hard not to let his earlier momentary lack of composure show. "Why don't we try the next one a little slower, so we can see where we went wrong?"

Pedi rubbed her wrist and looked at the shaman very thoughtfully.

"I'm not sure who needs the *benan* more," she said after a moment, with a gesture of rueful astonishment.

"I have been studying weapons since long before you were born," Cord pointed out serenely. "When I was your age, before the fall of Voitan, I was sent to the finest schools in the land, and I have studied and sought new ways ever since. The way of the sword—or the spear—is one of constant study. It is rich every day in new insights. Learn that, and you will be dangerous. Forget it, and we'll both be dead."

"Aargh!" Pedi groaned. "It wasn't pleasant to be caught by the Fire Priests. It wasn't pleasant to be shipped off to Strem as a Servant. It wasn't even pleasant to be captured by the Lemmar on my way there. But at least, at my darkest moment, I was able to console myself with the thought that I was finally rid of armsmasters!"

Cord wheeled around and stared out the window towards the mountains. It was a rather silly and dramatic pose, and he knew it, but he didn't want her to see his amusement. Or the fact that . . . parts of him had just surged.

Not the Season, he thought. Please, not that. That would be . . . bad.

"Whatever your life and destiny before," he said finally, solemnly, careful to keep any humor—or anything else—out of his voice, "your life and destiny now are to *become* an armsmaster."

So, as Julian would say, put that in your pipe and smoke it.

"I know that," Pedi said, with a gesture of resignation. "But that doesn't mean I have to like it."

"Perhaps you don't, but . . ." Cord began, only to pause, looking more intently out of the window.

"But what?" she asked.

"But I have a question for you."

"Yes?" She looked down at her outfit. "Is something wrong?"

"I'd rather hoped you could tell *me* that," Cord said, gesturing out the window. "You are from here, after all. So tell me, do the mountains often smoke?"

It was nearly noon, yet the only light in the room came from oil lamps as the human and Mardukan staff and senior commanders trickled into the room. Pahner looked towards the window, listening to the slow, atonal chanting that echoed through the darkened streets, and shook his head.

"I have the funny feeling that this is not a good thing," he muttered.

"They must have these eruptions on a fairly regular basis," O'Casey pointed out as she flopped onto one of the pillows. She pulled a strand of hair away from her face and grimaced at the gritty ash that covered it. "At least we know now why they wear clothing here. Getting this stuff out of a Mardukan's mucous must be an almost impossible task."

Roger pulled up his own cushion without even glancing behind him as the various entities who had taken to following him jockeyed for position. It usually ended up with Cord to one side, Pedi stretched in the same general direction, and Dogzard curled up on top of Pedi.

But for the fact that every one of them was, in his or her own way, heavily armed, it would have been humorous.

"I wish we had a better handle on their religion," he said seriously, listening to the same chant. "I can't figure out if this is a celebration or a funeral."

"The Krath Fire Priests consider this a dark omen of their gods," Pedi said. "Many Servants will be ingathered."

"More slave raids, then," Pahner said.

"Yes. And a great gathering." The Shin made a gesture of absolute disgust. "The Fire-loving bastards."

"T'e merchants have clam up," Poertena said. "Even t'e stuff we already contract for not getting delivered."

"How are we fixed?" Kosutic asked. "Can we hang on until things clear up, or do we need to talk to the Powers That Be?"

"We got ten days or so supply," the Pinopan said without consulting any of his data devices. "And more on t'e ship. But if we have to cut out, we gots problem."

"We may be able to avoid that," O'Casey said. "I think that something's broken free in the council. Maybe it has something to do with the eruption—I don't know." She shrugged. "Whatever it is, we've received a message from the High Priest indicating that he's willing to meet with Roger under the conditions we prescribed. That is, that Roger will not have to recognize the High Priest's sovereignty."

"I thought the council was more or less in control," Pahner said. "If that's true, what's the point of meeting with the High priest?"

"The council *is* in day-to-day control," O'Casey admitted. "But if the High Priest pronounces that we're free to travel, the council will have to accede to that."

"When is this thing?" Fain asked. "And who's going to accompany Roger?"

"Me, for one, obviously," O'Casey said with a faint smile. "After that, the guest list will be up to Captain Pahner. Who, I trust, will pack it with suitably lethal individuals."

"Kosutic in charge," Pahner said. "Despreaux and a fire team from her squad. Turn in your smoke poles and draw bead rifles.

We've got enough ammo left for almost a full unit of fire for your team, and some of these people may recognize Imperial weapons when they see them. If they do, I want them to know we cared enough to send the very best. Fain, one squad from your infantry and one squad of cavalry. You, Rastar, and Honal stay back, though."

"I'll send Chim Pri," Rastar said. "It will get him off the boats."

"Where is this going to take place, Eleanora?" Kosutic asked.

"At the High Temple. That's the one all the way up at the crest of the ridge."

"I wish we knew whether or not this is a good sign," Roger said.

"I think it's a good one," O'Casey told him. "If there hadn't been some movement on their front, it wouldn't make sense to arrange a meeting with the High Priest."

"We'll see," Pahner said. "It could also be because they have such bad news to give us that the High Priest is the only appropriate spokesman to break it to us, you know. Rastar, how are the *civan*?"

"They don't like the ash," the Prince of Therdan said. "Neither do I, for that matter, and their hides are a lot more resistant to it than my slime is! Other than that, they're fine. They've recovered from their sea voyage, at least, and we're getting them back into training."

"Okay." Pahner nodded. "I don't know how this meeting is going to work out, but we're getting to the end of the time we can afford to spend here. I want everyone to quietly and not too obviously get ready to move out on a moment's notice. We'll have an inspection and get everything packaged for that. Eleanora, when is this meeting?"

"Tomorrow, just after the dawn service."

"Right. We'll schedule the inspection for the same time."

"Does all this martial ardor indicate that you think I'm going to have problems at the meeting?" Roger asked, unconsciously tapping the butt of one of his pistols.

"I hope not," Pahner said. "I'll go further—if I thought you were going to, I wouldn't let you go. Period. We haven't gotten this far taking things for granted, but I don't expect this to be the sort of problem you'll need a pistol for. Nobody's going to call a visiting

Imperial nobleman and his bodyguards together with the High Priest of the entire *satrap* for a shooting match, at any rate."

"Nah," O'Casey agreed with a smile. "Heads of state are too valuable to use for targets or get caught in cross fires. That's what lower-level functionaries are for."

CHAPTER SIXTEEN

The large meeting room was near the highest point of the entire High Temple complex, with a single broad balcony at one end that looked down and out over the city. A marginal amount of illumination came from there, but not much. The city was still shrouded in the darkness and ash from the ongoing, low-level eruption. The room was long and low (by Mardukan standards), stretching back in a series of low arches into absolute blackness, punctuated by dim lamps that barely penetrated the gloom.

The prince had forgone his helmet in the interests of diplomacy, and his hair—unbound due to the formal nature of the meeting—spilled down his back in a golden wave. In deference to his image, and the fact that the meeting, however formal, had been arranged suddenly and with no specific agenda, he wore his bead pistol and had his sword slung over his back. Formal was all well and good, but on Marduk, paranoia was a survival trait.

Roger's eyes had benefitted from as much genetic tinkering as the rest of him and managed to compensate for the dimness of the illumination as he entered the meeting chamber. He could pick out the guards, arrayed in two groups along the walls, almost as well as his Marine bodyguards with their helmet low-light systems. And he could also see the High Priest, standing and waiting to greet him at the far end, shrouded in shadow and flanked by Sor Teb. It seemed a fitting situation: dark places, inhabited by dark souls.

Roger stopped a measured ten paces from the priest and bowed. It had been determined that a certain amount of kowtowing was permissible, but the dose had to be properly balanced. Yes, he was a prince of a star-spanning empire. But the High Priest—they hoped—knew him only as "Baron Chang." And there was also the minor fact that he was fundamentally lacking in heavy backup.

The prelate, an extremely elderly Mardukan, certainly looked frail enough to justify the rumors of his impending demise. He beckoned his visitors forward, and Roger took a few more steps, followed by his own guards.

Ever since Marshad, whose ruler had taken advantage of a relatively small guard force to take the prince "captive," the rule of thumb had been that Roger never went anywhere "threatening" with less than a dozen guards.

As the humans had become fewer and fewer in number, with more and more missions to perform, the native Mardukans had assumed a steadily growing degree of responsibility for guarding his safety. Thus, more than half the guard force detailed for this meeting consisted of Mardukan cavalry and infantry. The block of guards following the prince was a mixture of bead rifle-toting humans, breechloader-toting Diasprans, revolver-toting Vashin, the *sumei*-swathed Pedi, and the still mostly naked Cord and his immense spear. It made for a motley but dangerous crew.

Roger stopped and bowed again, making a two-armed gesture that corresponded more or less to the local one for respectful greeting.

"I am pleased to meet you, Your Voice. I am Seran Chang, Baron of Washinghome, of the Empire of Man, at your service."

"I greet you, Baron Chang," the priest responded in an age-quavery voice. "May the God favor you. I speak as His Voice. It is time to speak of many things that have been long avoided." The Mardukan stepped backward, with Sor Teb supporting him, and settled onto a low stool. "Many things."

"Such matters are generally discussed at a lower level, first,"

Roger observed with a frown. "Unless you refer to our petition to travel upriver?"

"Travel is for others to discuss," the High Priest said with a cough. "I speak of the needs of the God. The God is angry. He sends His Darkness upon us. He has spoken, and must be answered. Too long have the humans avoided Service to the Fire Lord. It is of this we must speak. I speak as His Voice."

Roger tilted his head to the side and frowned again.

"Am I to understand that you are requiring a 'Servant of God' from among the humans of our party before we will be permitted to leave?"

"That is not *our* requirement," Sor Teb answered for the High Priest with what, in a human, would have been an oily smile. "It is the God's."

"Pardon me," Roger said, then turned to the side. "Huddle time, people."

His senior advisers closed in, and he looked at the cloth-swathed Pedi Karuse, who was practically jumping up and down.

"In a minute, Pedi. I know you don't think this is a good idea. Eleanora?"

"We don't know the parameters of being a Servant of God," she said simply. "I've tried to get some idea of the duties, but the locals are very reticent about it, and talking to Pedi has been circular. The duties are 'to Serve the God.' I don't know if that means as a glorified altar boy, as a drudge scrubbing stone floors, or what. You don't see any of the Servants in public at all, so I have no idea where they all *go*, much less what they all do."

"So you're saying that we might actually go for this?" Kosutic hissed. "I don't think that's a good idea. Not at all."

"Look," O'Casey said sharply, "if being a servant means participating in some harmless rituals, and the alternative is trying to fight our way out of the city, which would you rather do?"

Kosutic glanced over at Pedi and shook her head.

"People don't fight like wildcats to avoid some 'harmless rituals.' So far, she hasn't said anything about cleaning. And I don't like any religion that doesn't perform its rituals out in the open.

Call me old-fashioned, but the only decent place for a ritual is the open air. Anything else smacks of—"

"—Christianity?" O'Casey asked with an arched eyebrow. "We can probably get some concessions on the nature of their duties. Then, after we retake the spaceport, we'll come back and negotiate some more. With some real firepower behind us."

Despite the tension of the moment, Roger almost smiled. His chief of staff might not have become quite as bloodthirsty as Despreaux thought *he* was becoming, but she certainly had become a convert to the notion of peace through superior firepower.

"You're saying that whether or not we should agree depends on the duties, then?" he asked her after a moment, and cocked an eyebrow of his own at Kosutic.

"Okay, okay," the sergeant major said. "If they're treated well, we could leave a volunteer behind. Somebody will be willing."

"I will," Despreaux said. "If it's ringing some bells and pouring some water versus fighting our way out of the city, well, just hand me the goddamned bells!"

"You're not under consideration," Roger said crisply.

"Why not?" Despreaux asked angrily. "Because I'm a *guuuurl*?"

"No." Roger's tone was curt. "Because you're my fiancée. And because everybody knows you are, and that puts you in a special category. Get over it."

"He's right," Kosutic said before Despreaux could swell with outrage. "And you *do* need to get over it, Sergeant Despreaux. Technically, we should be guarding *you*. If we were back on Earth, you'd have a ring around you twenty-four/seven. Since we don't have the manpower, you don't. But you are *not* 'just another troop' anymore." The sergeant major shook her head. "Probably me or Gunny Lai would be the best choice—both 'guuuurls,' you might note."

Roger chuckled at Despreaux's expression, then again, harder, as he looked at the group around him. Of the humans, better than half of his guards and advisers were females.

"I hadn't noticed until just now, but this does seem to be an episode of *Warrior Amazons of Marduk*."

"Smile when you say that, Your Highness," Despreaux said. But at least *she* smiled when she said it.

"I *am* smiling," Roger replied, making a face. "Okay, if the duties aren't too onerous—and *we'll* determine what 'onerous' means—we'll agree on the condition that the rest of us are given free passage to the spaceport."

"Agreed," Eleanora said, and Roger looked over at Pedi, who was still making surreptitious negative gestures under her *sumei*.

"Okay, why not?"

"Not Servant," she whispered in broken Imperial. "Bad, bad. Not Servants."

"And what if duties okay?" Roger asked in Krath.

"Duty of Servant is to *Serve*," the Shin whispered back. "*Is* no other duty."

"And what's so bad about that?" Roger asked quietly.

"*What?!*" The Shin's voice came out in a squeak as she tried not to scream the question. "Duty is to be of Service! How much worse could it be? To be of Service and to Serve! What you want, to Serve *twice*?"

Roger glanced over at O'Casey and Kosutic, both of whom looked suddenly very thoughtful.

"We're missing something," he said.

"Agreed," Kosutic said. "I mean, she's sliming, and this is a 'guuuurl' who killed two armed guards with her bare hands. While chained to the deck." She shook her head. "Could the translation be bad?"

"This is the only language group for which we actually had a comprehensive kernel when we landed," O'Casey said thoughtfully. "It's *possible* that the kernel has a bias built in. I'm not sure what to do about that, though."

Roger considered the translation program for a moment. Throughout the trip, the burden of translation of new dialects had fallen upon him and Eleanora due to their superior implants. To aid in that, he'd read most of the manual for the software, but that had been a long time ago. There was a section on poor translations related to initial impressions and inaccurate kernels, but at the moment he couldn't find it on the help menu.

"The only thing I can think of to do is to dump the kernel," Roger said. "Dump the whole translation scheme, and start fresh."

"We need time to do that," O'Casey objected.

"Agreed," the prince replied, and turned back to the local leaders. They were showing signs of impatience, and he smiled much more calmly than he felt.

"We need to discuss this with the other members of our party, and we seem to be having a problem with our translation system. Could we perhaps call a recess, and resume the discussion tomorrow?"

"It is with regret that I must decline that suggestion," Sor Teb replied. "The God speaks to us now. He sends His darkness upon His people now. Now is when we must gather our Servant, and you are the leader, the decision maker, of your people. If you would prefer that the Servant come from one of your lesser minions at your headquarters rather than from those here with you, we can send a runner. But the decision must be made now."

"Pardon me for a moment longer, then," Roger said slowly, and turned back to the others.

"Oh, shit," Despreaux said quietly.

"Did he just say what I think he said?" Cord asked.

"So much for 'minor functionaries,'" Kosutic said with a snort. "Marshad time."

"Stop talking," Roger said, pointing a finger directly at Pedi. As soon as she froze, he sent a command to his toot, "dumping" the entire Krath language and everything they had determined of Shin. Then he locked out the "kernel" that had come with the system, as well. It was now as if he had never heard of Shin or Krath, and any biases would be erased, as long as he concentrated on ignoring them. He also locked out the low-level interplay between the systems, so that his own would not be corrupted by the Marines' and O'Casey's. Taking a guess, based upon O'Casey's idea of a migratory connection between the Shin and Cord's people, he loaded the language of "the People" as a potential kernel.

"Okay," he said, crooking the petrifying finger. "*Now* talk."

At first, what the *benan* was saying was only a low, unintelligible gabble. But after a moment, bits and pieces began to join together.

". . . temple . . . priests . . . death . . . serve . . . sacrifice . . . serve the worshipers . . . feast."

"Oh, shit."

Roger pulled up the two translations, and the difference was immediately apparent. In the kernel, the word "*sadak,*" when used in the context of the priests, was translated as "Servant." When the kernel was dumped, though, it translated as "sacrifice." In fact, there was an entire series of synonym and thematic biases built into the system, but changing a few words around and removing a syntactic bias made everything clear.

Including why the Lemmar refused to be captured.

He punched the changes into his toot with the flashing speed of direct neural interfacing, then reloaded the corrected kernel and turned slowly back to the Scourge and the High Priest.

"We have determined the problem with our translator. What you want is a human sacrifice. Which will then be shared as a feast among your worshipers. The body and blood, so to speak."

"Oh, shit," Kosutic whispered, and grimaced as she took another look at the guards. "I *knew* I didn't like these guys. They're Papists! Man, I *hate* fanatics!"

"We recognize that certain lesser peoples refuse to accept this rite," Sor Teb replied, with a gesture of contempt at Cord and the swathed Pedi. "But humans are, after all, civilized."

"Civilized," Despreaux whispered. She was too well-trained to actually check a weapon, and she could *feel* the stillness that had descended over the troopers behind her. Each of them was very carefully not reaching for a weapon. They were carefully *not* counting their rounds, or ensuring that their bayonets were loose in the sheaths. Not, at least, on the outside.

Roger reached slowly into a pouch and extracted a thin leather band. Then he tossed his hair behind him and bound it slowly into a ponytail.

"And if we politely decline this invitation?" he asked, pulling his locks into place one by one as he smoothed the hair on the top of his head. Behind him, O'Casey drew a surreptitious breath and made sure her weight was balanced on her toes.

Sor Teb glanced at the High Priest, now apparently asleep on his stool, then back at the humans.

"My guards in this room outnumber you, and I have over a hundred in the corridors. At a word, you are all Servants. And then I will take all of the rest of you at the docks, and the people will know that it was the Scourge which brought humans to the God at last."

His false-hands moved in a complicated shrug which signified total confidence.

"Or," he continued, "you may surrender a single sacrifice of your choice. That will suffice for my purposes . . . and the God's, of course. But either way, I will have the Servant I require, and the people will know it. Those are your only alternatives."

"Really?" Roger said quietly, calmly, as he tugged one last time on his ponytail to tighten it down. "Hmmm. A binary solution set. Just one problem with your plans."

"What?" Teb's eyes narrowed, and Roger smiled gently.

"You've never seen me move."

The prince and his bodyguards had blasted their way through half a dozen city-states on their bloody march across Marduk. Roger knew he could depend upon them to do their job and back him up. So as his hands descended to the pistols holstered at his side, he concentrated solely on what was in his own field of view.

The local arquebuses weren't particularly accurate, and the Marines' uniforms were designed to protect against high-velocity projectiles by hardening to spread the impact over a wide area. Neither Roger nor O'Casey, however, were wearing helmets, so an unlucky hit from one of the arquebuses would be fatal. And Cord and Pedi were completely unarmored.

The first target, therefore, was the arquebusier to the left of the throne. The High Priest was no threat, and hitting the target to the left would permit Roger to track right and take Sor Teb with the next shot.

But by the time Roger had shifted targets, before the headless body had even had time to start to fall, Sor Teb had just *moved*. Roger had heard the Marines comment on his own speed, often in hushed tones. Now he understood why. When you see someone who is *preternaturally* fast—Rastar was one such—it is awe-inspiring. and Sor Teb, it turned out, was preternaturally fast at surviving. The councilor was behind the throne and out a side door before anyone besides the prince could target him.

But that didn't mean people were sitting on their hands.

Kosutic dropped the muzzle of her bead rifle and took down the arquebusier to the right of the throne even as the Scourge guards along the walls flung themselves forward. Their primary weapon seemed to be double sticks. The long rods were nearly as thick as a human's forearm, and the guards wielded them with precision. One of them descended towards the sergeant major's forearm, obviously intending to disarm her, but it was abruptly blocked by a short sword.

"*Mudh Hemh!*" Pedi screamed like a damnbeast and spun in place, flinging off her *sumei* as both swords appeared. She chopped down, to take all of the fingers off one of the guard's hands, then swept upward to gut him like a fish.

"The vales!!"

The astonished guards recoiled at the sight of the blades and frosted horns. Humans were unknown bogeymen from beyond even the farthest reaches of the valley, but the Shin were *always* there. And *never* underestimated. Even the females.

"Shin!!!"

The Mardukan female spun again, blocking another blow directed at her from behind and back-kicking the guard in the groin. She turned towards the throne, where the majority of the surviving guards had clustered in defense of the High Priest, and spat.

"TIME TO MEET THE FIRE, BOYS!"

"Boots and saddles!"

Pahner shot to his feet, rubbing an ear as the shout over his helmet commo systems rocketed him upright.

"Your Highness?" he called, heading for the door of his office while the sudden icy calm of a man who's seen too many emergencies—and has just heard the unmistakable sound of rifle volleys in the background of a truncated radio call—flooded through him.

"To all units, Bravo Company relay! Terminate all Krath guards in view with extreme prejudice. Do this NOW!"

Pahner heard screams from the warehouse, and firing broke out as he hit the door. Two Krath guards were attacking one of the Diaspran infantry by the main doors, but two shots took them down before the captain could even draw his sidearm. All the others in sight had already been dealt with.

"Prince Roger, this is Captain Pahner," he said calmly as he strode towards the piles of gear that were half ready for loading. "What's happening?"

"Servants are human sacrifices," Kosutic cut in on the command circuit, panting. In the background, Pahner heard a knife-hitting-a-melon sound with which the entire company had become all too familiar. "We're trying to fight our way out of the Temple. For some reason, they're just a bit ticked with us."

"That might be because Pedi Karuse cut her way through to the High Priest on our way out of the room," Roger said with a grunt against the background of a fading scream. "Fortunately, all the guards have been unarmored so far. We're conserving ammo by quite literally *cutting* our way out. But Sor Teb got away, dammit! He set us up."

"We're on our way," Pahner said, gesturing for the teams to drop what they were doing. The most vital equipment had already been packed for a run, most of it loaded into large, hard-sided leather trunks with multiple carrying rings, so that they could be easily on-loaded and off-loaded from pack animals. The remainder was food and other similar nonvital items that could be seized on the way. It was cold, but if you had bullets, you could always get beans.

"Negative!" Roger snapped. "We're heading for the city's main gate. You know the drill—Vashin to take the gate, flying columns to secure the intersections and block response, tell the ships to head for K'Vaern's Cove, and the rest all run like hell for the gates. We're going to join up in that vicinity. If you try to cut your way into the Temple, we'll never make it. Follow the plan, Captain. That's an order."

"Tell me you can fight your way out, Your Highness," the captain grated. "Tell me that."

"Hold one," Roger responded. Behind his voice, someone else bellowed in rage. The bellow grew louder, as if the throat from whence it sprang was charging towards Roger, but then the sound was cut abruptly short, and Pahner heard a thump, and a spraying sound.

"Pthah! Just make sure you bring a pocking towel."

CHAPTER SEVENTEEN

Temu Jin strode up to the last few meters of path and nodded to the Mardukan waiting for him. The Shin chieftain was middle-aged for one of the locals, calm and closed faced. He propped himself on the long ax which was his symbol of office—the symbol which had permitted him to pass more or less unmolested through the intervening tribes.

Now the chieftain leaned forward and fixed the human with a glare.

"I have traveled two weeks from my home for you, Temu Jin," he growled. "I have done this while my people are in jeopardy, when the young warriors are questioning my utility. I have done this because you indicated that it was vital that we meet. All I can say is that it had better be important."

"Decide for yourself," Jin said. "Humans have landed in Kirsti."

"*That* is not important!" the chieftain snapped. "*Everything* passes through Kirsti sooner or later, as I know all too well."

"Ah, but what humans?" Jim replied. "These humans did not travel to Kirsti from our base here. They arrived aboard ships—ships built here on Marduk, which crossed the sea to reach this continent."

"And what of that?" the chieftain demanded. "Why should the fact that they floated across the water rather than flew through the air excite me?"

"As I've told you, the Empire is not going to look kindly upon the Krath when I finally get word to my superiors. But I don't know when that will be. These humans could help in getting the word out."

"Why? Why *these* humans and not the waifs you have already dumped upon us?"

"These humans are . . . important," Jin temporized. "But they'll need some support."

"Of course. Don't they always?" the chief grumped. "What now?"

"I'll send you some packages. Ammunition and some essential spare parts they could probably use. Also some modern weapons. If you can make contact with them, it will greatly benefit us. It would be even better if you could woo them away from the Krath and into the Shin lands."

"What? No blankets? No 'sleeping bags'? No insect repellent?" the chief gave a Mardukan snort. "I hope that your superiors come to your aid soon—all these visitors are becoming tiring. As to 'wooing them away from the Krath,' I can send out the word to the clan-Chiefs, but it will be up to them individually. And they don't think much of humans. Only if they come directly to my lands will it be possible for me to ensure their safety."

"I think you'll find these folk a bit different," Jin said grimly. "And I doubt they'll need much looking after. Among other things, at least some of them are Marines."

"Marines?" the chief scoffed. "These are your space warriors, yes? Warriors we have aplenty."

"You don't have Imperial Marines," Jin cautioned. "And if they're the Marines I think they are, you don't have anything close."

The chieftain regarded him balefully for moment, then rubbed his horns in thought.

"Anybody have any idea where we are?" Roger asked. His stripped-down command group stood at the intersection of five dome-roofed corridors. A single oil lamp gave miserly illumination, and the prince idly wiped blood from his sword blade as he looked about himself.

They had lost their pursuers, mostly by leaving field expedient booby traps behind. After the first few explosions, the Scourge guards had become remarkably circumspect in their chasing. But that didn't help the fugitives find their way out of the palace. Or to the gates. Their helmet systems could tell them where they were in reference to their starting point and the gates their bug-out plans specified as their way out of the city, as well as which direction they were headed, but that was of strictly limited utility. The temple had backed onto the outer wall of the city, so there was probably a connection between where they stood and the walls' defenses—like the gates they needed. But they couldn't tell which of the myriad corridors would get them there.

"We're about a hundred meters below the gates," Kosutic pointed out, looking at the various corridors with him. "And still to the south. I think we need to head northeast and up."

"Uh-huh. Unfortunately," Roger noted, "that still leaves two."

"Eenie-meenie-miney-moe," the sergeant major said. "Chim, take the left corridor."

"Yes, Sergeant Major," the Vashin replied. "It smells like the kitchens are ahead."

"It does," Roger agreed uneasily. "A bit." Chim was right, a distinct odor of cooking came down the passageway to them, but it was overlaid by a fetid, iron smell that was unpleasantly familiar.

The corridor was a five-meter high arch, leading into darkness. Unlike the intersection, it lacked even the dimness of an oil lamp. The Marines' helmet vision systems let them see clearly even under those conditions, but did nothing for the Mardukans in the party— or for Roger or O'Casey, neither of them had brought helmets to what was supposed to be a diplomatic conference—so the Marines turned on the lights mounted on their rifles. The lights' white spots seemed to reveal and conceal in equal measure, for the walls were of basalt blocks, which seemed to swallow the light. The complex interplay of lights and dark lent an additional air of unreality to their flight, but at least the natives (and Roger) could see something.

After perhaps a dozen meters, the corridor terminated in a heavy wooden door. Fortunately, it was bolted on their side, and Chim waved one of the Diasprans forward to pull the bolt. As soon as the door opened, the Vashin nobleman darted through the opening, his pistol held in a two-handed grip. The rest of the Vashin poured through behind him, and Roger heard the blast of arquebuses, answered by pistol cracks and a bellow of rage.

The prince followed before the echoes of the pistol shots could fade, and as he stepped through the door, the reason for the bellow was obvious. The large room beyond was filled with bone pits. He could see a group of Krath Servants escaping through the far door, leaving the baskets of ash and bone they'd been carrying spilled across the floor.

Chim was down as well, caught in a death grip with one of the four guards. The smell in the room was much stronger than it had been in the corridor—a mixture of rotting meat and charred bone that caused Roger to flash back to Voitan. He swallowed his gorge and checked to make sure everyone else was okay. When he glanced sideways at Pedi, she seemed strangely unaffected. She simply glanced at the charnel pits, then looked away.

"You don't seem too broken up," Roger said. "This is . . . foul."

"Sometimes you get the priests," Pedi replied. "Sometimes they get you. We don't eat them, but we don't let any we capture live, either."

Cord's *benan* headed for the far door, but Roger put a hand on her shoulder.

"Let the professionals go through first. Any idea what's on the other side?"

"Not many come out of the Fire," Pedi pointed out. "But with the pits here, the kitchens should be to the right, and the sanctuary up and to the left."

"Sergeant Major," Roger said, gesturing at the door. "Head for the sanctuary. It's got to have public access, and that means a primary point of entry . . . and exit. That makes it our best chance to find a way out of this damned maze quickly."

"Yes, Sir," Kosutic said. She put her hand on the closed door's bar and glanced at the other grim-faced warriors crowding around the prince. "Let's dance."

The corridors beyond were more of the same black basalt,

drinking the light from the Marines' lights. A few more meters brought them to a narrow staircase up and to the right. Kosutic flashed a light up it, then climbed its treads with quick, silent steps. At the top, she found another heavy wooden door, this one with red light coming under it, and she cocked her head as she listened to the loud, atonal chanting coming from above.

"Lord, I hate Papists," she muttered, checking her ammunition pouches and fixing her bayonet. Then she drew a belt knife as Roger arrived beside her. "We really should have brought shotguns for this, Your Highness."

"Needs must," Roger replied. He left his bead pistol holstered, conserving its ammunition against a more critical need, and balanced a black powder revolver in his left hand. "Do it."

The sergeant major slid her knife into the crevice where the bar should be, and moved it upwards. The monomolecular blade sliced effortlessly through the locking device, the door sprang loose on its hinges, and she pushed forward into Hell.

The nave of the temple was packed with worshipers, females on one side, males on the other. Worship in the High Temple was clearly only for the well-to-do of Kirsti's society—most of the worshipers were not only clad in elaborate gowns and robes, but wore heavy jewelry, as well.

A double line of "Servants" ran down the centerline of the temple, surrounded by guards. The line led up to the sacrificial area, where three teams of priests were involved in mass slaughter. The priests wore elaborate gowns, rich with gold thread, and caps of gold and black opal that simulated volcanoes, and the decorations of the temple were of the finest. The walls were shot through with semi-precious gems and gold foil, adorned again and again with the repeating motif of the sacred Fire. All in all, it was a barbaric and terrible sight, made all the worse by the heavy leather aprons that the priests *also* wore. Of course, if they hadn't worn them, the gore from their butchery would have ruined the pretty gold thread.

Like a machine—or like what it really was: an abattoir—each bound captive would be placed upon an altar, then quickly dispatched and butchered, the parts separated into manageable chunks. The offal was hurled by teams of lower priests into the maw of the furnaces at the rear, while others bore the edible materials away even as another "Servant" was brought forward. The worshipers' deep, rhythmic chanting was a bizarre counterpart for the frantic screams as the captives were dragged forward . . . until the screams were abruptly cut off by the priests' knives.

If anything was worse than the hideous efficiency of the sacrifices, with its clear implication of frequent and lengthy experience, it was the well-dressed worshipers, swaying back and forth in hysterical reaction to the slaughter and chanting their ecstatic counterpoint to the prayers of the priests.

When Kosutic opened the door, the priests' prayers stopped abruptly, and the chanting shuddered to a halt in broken chunks of sound. Roger looked out over the suddenly silent tableau and shook his head.

"I'm just not having this," he said in an almost conversational tone.

"We're low on ammo, Sir!" Kosutic pointed out. "We can retreat. The door will hold them for a bit."

"Hell with that." Roger reached over his shoulder with his right hand. "The best, shortest way out is through the temple, Sergeant Major. And I don't think they're going to just let us walk through, do you?"

"No, Your Highness," the Satanist replied.

"Well, there you are," Roger said reasonably. "And I suppose if we're low on ammo, it'll just have to be cold steel, won't it?"

Steel whispered in the near-total silence as he drew his sword once more, and Dogzard lashed her tail back and forth. The smell of blood had hit her, and her spikes were shivering.

"*Roger!*" Despreaux yelled from the press around the door, then—"Ow! Dammit, Dogzard—watch the tail!"

"You hang back, Nimashet," Roger snarled. "Let me and the Vashin handle this."

"Allow me to note that this is not a wise endeavor," Cord observed as he hefted his spear. "That being said, clear the door, Your Highness!"

"Let me at them!" Pedi called, waving both bloodstained swords over her head. "I'll give them 'lesser races'!"

"Oh, the hell with that!" Despreaux said, stepping forward as the ceremonial guards in the temple below raised their staves. "You're not going any place without me!"

"No," Kosutic interjected, never taking her eyes from the waiting guards. "Cover the back door. We don't want to get hit from behind."

"But . . ."

"That wasn't a request, *Sergeant!*" The sergeant major snapped. "Cover our damned *backs!*"

"Vashin!" Roger called. "One volley, and draw! Cold steel!"

"Cold steel!"

"The People!"

"SHIN!"

"Two of the main intersections are secure," Rastar called as his *civan* trotted down the broad boulevard past Pahner. "We took the main Flail headquarters for the sector on the way. They tried to fight, but these guard pukes are no use at all."

"*Basik* to the *atul,*" Fain agreed as another volley crashed out. The Diaspran had tucked his company tight around the retreating wagons, letting the Vashin clear the way ahead. "They just fight dumb. Almost as dumb as barbs. No style, no tactics—simple personal attacks, and they just advance into our fire. Dumb."

"Not dumb, just . . . stagnant," Pahner corrected. "They're so used to fighting one way they don't know any other. And they haven't figured out how to change. I suspect that they're as good as it gets against other satrap forces or when it comes to suppressing riots in the city. But they've never dealt with rifle volleys or snipers."

The latter—mostly Marines, but a few of the Diasprans as well— had been picking off any leaders who showed real imagination.

"Any word on Roger?" Rastar asked.

"Nothing since they called from the Temple," the captain said.

"They'll make it, Sir," Fain said. "It's Roger, isn't it?"

"Yeah, that's what they tell me." Pahner shook his head. "I almost wish he was still considered incompetent. Maybe then I'd have sent a decent sized force to look after him."

"You know," Roger parried a blow from a staff and slid his blade down the shaft to cut off the Mardukan wielder's fingers, "I could wish that Pahner didn't have so much confidence in me!"

"Why?" Kosutic punched her bayonet through the roof of the staff wielder's screaming mouth. Unlike the Diaspran riflemen, the Marine's bayonets were made of monomolecular memory plastic, not locally produced steel blades. The impossibly sharp bayonet sliced up and outwards in an effortless spray of blood, and she kicked the falling body out of her path with a grunt.

"Well, if the captain hadn't been so sure we could handle anything, he would have sent more troops with us!" Roger yelled as Dogzard, unnoticed, landed on the back of a guard about to strike Cord. The Mardukan might have been able to support the one hundred and twenty kilos from a standing start, but when it hit him at forty kilometers per hour, he went over on his face in the red mash of the floor. And down on his face, with an enraged Dogzard on his back, there wasn't much he'd be doing but dying.

"But more troops would mean fewer guards for each of us!" Pedi protested as she slashed the throat out of one attacker and wheeled to chop another's true-arm just below the shoulder. A staff clanged off her horns in response, and she kicked out at the wielder, slashing at him with the edge of her horns and following up with the thrust to the chest. A handspan of bloody steel protruded out of the Krath's back, and she twisted her wrist. "Fewer Krath to kill and bodies to loot! What fun would that be?"

She withdrew her blade in a flood of crimson, and Roger paused to survey the blood-soaked sacristy. The area—fortunately or unfortunately—had been designed for adequate drainage, and a nasty sizzling sound and a horrible burned-steak smell rose from the furnaces at the rear, where the gutters terminated. The ground was littered with the bodies of priests and guards left in the Vashin's and Marines' wake. The few worshipers who had joined the guards to attempt to stop them had fared no better, and the Vashin had been particularly brutal. Many of the corpses showed more hacks than were strictly necessary.

"I suppose when you look at it that way," Roger said as one of the Vashin pried an emerald the size of his thumb out of a statue. Between the ornamentation and the clothing of the priests and worshipers, there was probably a month's pay per Vashin in this room alone. The prince leaned down and picked up a more or less clean cloth from the . . . debris and wiped his sword. There was hardly a sound in the entire Temple, except for the sizzle from the rear and an occasional groan from their only serious casualty. The Vashin had been particularly efficient in ensuring that there were no Krath wounded.

The sacrifices had scattered. Whether they would be able to survive and blend into the population, Roger didn't know. All he knew was that the way out was clear, and that there were no living threats in view. On Marduk, that was good enough.

"Three minutes to loot, and then it's time to go, people!" he called, waving his sword at the door. Even after a quick wipe, the blade left a trail of crimson through the air. "Let's find a way out of this place!"

"Third Squad has closed up, Captain, but we're getting quite a bit of pressure from the rear," Fain said. A rifle volley crashed out from someplace downslope, answered by high-pitched screaming. "Nothing we can't deal with. Yet."

"Still haven't heard from Roger," Pahner said with a nod. He looked around in the gloom and shook his head. One of the "civilized" aspects of Kirsti was that many of the major boulevards had gaslights. Now he knew _why_ they had gaslights; it was so they could see during broad day.

"There's been the occasional explosion from his direction, so I take it he's on his way," the Marine continued. "Now, if we could just take the gate before he gets here."

"Sorry about that." Rastar shrugged. "It was closed when we arrived. They probably did it ahead of time."

"Why not use a plasma cannon, Sir?" Fain asked.

"Signature." Pahner pulled out a _bisti_ root and cut off a sliver; it was covered with a thin layer of bitter ash by the time he got it into his mouth. "If they're going to be watching for advanced weapons anywhere, it will be on this continent. And plasma cannons aren't the weapon of a lost hunter. Much the same reason why, after his first message, we've been out of contact with His Highness. No, we're going to have to take this thing the old-fashioned way."

"That will be expensive," Fain said, looking at the gate defenses. The central gatehouse was flanked by two defensive towers, both of them loopholed to sweep the exterior of the gatehouse with arquebus and light artillery fire. The fortifications were obviously meant to be equally defensible from either side, so that if an enemy made it over the wall, he would still have a hard fight for the gate tower.

"Boiling oil will be the least of it," the Diaspran added.

"Well, I'm not planning on stacking bodies to climb up and over it," Pahner said, and pointed to a stairway. It ran up the inner face of the gatehouse to a heavily timbered door at the third-story level. "We go up there, blow the door with a satchel charge, and take the interior. Somewhere in there will be the controls."

The doorway in question was on the top of the wall, in full view of the western tower. Firing slits along that tower's eastern side had a clear shot at the stairs and the area in front of the door. Rastar surveyed the slits, which probably concealed heavy swivel guns. They would undoubtedly be loaded with canister, like giant shotguns. He'd seen the same sort of weapon in Sindi, used on the Boman barbarians, and knew exactly what the effect would be.

"We'll still take quite a few casualties."

"I know, Rastar," Pahner said sadly. "And it will fall mostly on the Diasprans and the Vashin. I can't afford to lose many more Marines. Hell, most of the ones I still have left are already busy, anyway."

"What's to be done, must be done," Rastar said philosophically, drawing his pistols. "We'll need the satchel charge prepared."

"I got t'at," Poertena said, pulling out his pack. "Two satchel charge. One or t'e other gonna work."

"Not your specialty, Scrgeant," Pahner said. "Somebody will need to go into the gatehouse and find the gate controls. That won't be like working in an armory."

"I'm a po . . . a Marine, Sir," the Pinopan shot back. "Gots to die someplace."

Pahner gazed at him for perhaps one second, then shrugged.

"Very well. It appears that the Vashin will have the honor of taking the gate, supported by the unit armorer."

"What's next?" Julian asked with a smile. "Arming the pilots?"

"And the cooks, the clerks, and the sergeant major's band," Pahner told him. "Take it from here, Rastar."

"Right." Rastar had revolvers in all four hands now, checking to make sure the ash hadn't jammed the actions. "Honal?" he said to his cousin.

"Vashin!" Honal called in turn to the cavalry drawn up behind him. "Good news! We get to take the gates! Up the stairs, the shorty blows the door, and we're in!"

"Well, I suppose that's as close as they're getting to an operations order," Pahner murmured as he stepped back. He hoped they would at least dismount. The *civan* might possibly make it up the stairs—all the Vashin were superb riders, after all—but getting them through the doorway would be tough.

As Honal was waving the cavalry to the ground, the lower embrasure on the western tower suddenly gouted flame. A tremendous explosion rocked the fortification, smoke poured through the structure, and a racket of rifle fire sounded from the conflagration.

"I believe His Highness has made an appearance," Pahner observed. "Go! Get up there now, Rastar!"

"About bloody time, Roger!" the former Vashin prince yelled. Then he waved his pistols at the wall and looked at his own men.

"Therdan!"

"I think we may have overdone it there, Sergeant Major," Roger said with a cough as he scrabbled in his pouch for cartridges. He'd expended the last of his irreplaceable pistol beads on the way out of the Temple. Then he'd expended all of the rounds for his own, human-sized revolver on his way *into* the gate tower defensive complex. That was when he'd picked up the revolver and ammo pouch from a wounded Vashin. It was oversized, designed for

Mardukan hands, and fit to fracture even Roger's wrists each time he fired. But the one thing he really hated about it was that he was flat out of ammo for it, too.

"Oh, I dunno, Your Highness." Kosutic shook her head to clear the ringing. "I think a keg of gunpowder was about right."

"The door is stuck!" St. John (J) announced. Through the smoke, Roger could just barely make out Kileti, levering at the door with a piece of bent iron. The prince smothered a curse and squinted, but even with his superb natural vision, details were impossible to make out. All morning, he'd regretted leaving his helmet behind at the barracks, since the entire trip had been from gloom to deeper gloom. And smoke-filled deeper gloom, at that.

"Well, we'd best get it unstuck," he said calmly as another volley echoed from behind him. "Don't you think?"

"And they would do that how, exactly, Your Highness?" Cord asked, then looked up suddenly. "*Down!*"

The spear had somehow flown past the blockade of Diasprans and Vashin holding the rear guard. How his *asi* had even seen it under such conditions was more than the prince could say. Unfortunately, just seeing it wasn't quite enough.

Cord's arm sweep knocked Roger to the side, but the short, broad blade of the spear took the shaman just below the right, lower shoulder.

"Bloody hell!" Roger rebounded painfully off the stone wall. Then he saw Cord. "Bloody *pocking* hell!"

The spear was embedded deep in the shaman's lower chest. Cord lay on his back, breathing shallowly and holding the spear still, but Roger knew the pain had to be enormous.

"Ah, man, Cord," he said, dropping to his knees. His hands fluttered over the surface of the shaman's mostly naked body, but he wasn't sure what to do. The spear was in the shaman's gut up to the haft. "I gotta get you to Doc Dobrescu, buddy!"

"Get out," Cord spat. "Get out now!"

"None of that," Roger said, and looked across at Pedi. The shaman's *benan* had both blood-covered swords crossed across her knees. "I guess we both missed that one, huh?"

"Will my shame never end?" she asked bitterly. "I turn my back only for a moment, and this—!" She shook her head. "We must take it out, or it will fester."

"And if we do that, we'll increase the bleeding," Roger disagreed sharply. "We need to get him to the doc."

"Whatever we do, Your Highness, we'd better do it quick," Kosutic said. "We've got the door clear, but the rear guard isn't going to last forever."

"Take the Marines. Clear the tower," Roger snapped as he pulled out his knife. Even with the monomolecular blade, the spear shaft twisted as he secured a firm grip on it, then sliced through it. The shaman took shallow breaths and slimed at every vibration, but the only sound he actually made came with the last jerk, as the shaft parted—a quiet whine, like Dogzard when she wanted a snack.

"We'll carry him out," Roger said as he threw the truncated shaft viciously across the stinking, smoke-choked stone chamber.

"We who?" Kosutic asked, shaking her head as she imagined trying to lift the two hundred-kilo shaman. Then she drew a deep breath. "Yes, Sir."

"Ammo! Anybody got any?" Birkendal called from the door. "Most of the lower room is clear, but we're taking fire from the second story."

"I do." Despreaux threw him her ammo pouch. "St. John, take your team and clear the upper stories," she continued. "I'll take an arm, Pedi takes an arm, Roger takes a leg, and we let the other one dangle."

"Chim Pri's down," Roger said as he grabbed a leg. "Who in hell is in charge of the Mardukans?"

"Sergeant Knever," Despreaux said. "Knever! We are *leaving*!"

She saw a thumbs-up sign come out of the force packed around the doorway and grabbed Cord's arm.

"Let's *go*!"

Poertena stepped over the remains of one of the Vashin cavalry. He placed the satchel charge against the door, pulled the friction tab to start the fuse, and looked around in the gloom for some cover. His helmet adjusted everything to a light level of sixty percent standard daylight, but the rendering washed out shadows, which had a negative effect on depth perception. Despite that, he could clearly tell that there wasn't much cover on the wall, but at least ducking around to the right of the door put a slight protuberance between his body and the two kilos of blasting powder.

He set his helmet to "Seal," folded his body into the smallest possible space, and pushed against the tower wall, but the overpressure wave still shook him like a terrier shaking a rat. The oversized pack was no help at all, as the blast wave caught it where it protruded from cover, spun him away from shelter, and hammered him down on the wall's stonework. He picked himself up and shook his head, trying to clear the cobwebs, and took a mental inventory of the situation. The downside was that he couldn't hear a thing; the upside was that there was now a hole where the door used to be.

Not that he had a whole long time to evaluate things.

Poertena had never been much of a hand with a rifle. He realized that no true Marine would ever admit to such an ignoble failing, yet there it was. And he was an even worse shot with the chemical-powered rifles the company had improvised in K'Vaern's Cove. Which was why he'd built himself a pump-action shotgun at the same time he designed Honal's.

It was smaller bore than the Vashin's portable cannon, and shorter than normal, with a pistol grip carved from wood and a barrel barely thirty centimeters long. It held only five shells, and kicked like a mule, but it had one saving grace—as long as you held the trigger back, it would fire with each "pump."

Poertena demonstrated that capability to the Mardukans picking themselves up off of the floor in the room beyond the demolished door. There were clearly more of them than shells in the ammo tube, but he didn't let that stop him as he furiously pumped and pointed, filling the room with ricocheting balls of lead, smoke, and patterns of blood.

The hammer clicked on an empty breech, and he rolled out of the doorway and back into his original cover. He lay there, licking a slice on the back of his hand where one of the ricochets had come too close, then reloaded while the second wave of Vashin finally made it up the slippery stairs.

"I t'ink I leave it up to you line-dogs from here," he said to the Mardukan cavalrymen as the last round clicked into the magazine.

"What? You mean leave some for us?" Honal asked. He stopped by the hole and glanced in. "So, how many were there?"

"I dunno." Poertena glanced at the far tower as shots rang out from its top floor. "Not enough, apparen'ly."

He'd decided not to stare at the muzzle of the medium bombard pointed from the top of the other tower to sweep the wall. It had fired once—carrying away the entire first wave of Vashin who'd been supposed to cover his own approach with the demo charge—and he'd fully expected it to sweep him away, as well. But the bombard crew had apparently had more important things on their minds after firing that first shot. Now the gun shuddered for a moment, then rolled out of the way to reveal a human face.

"Birkendal, what t'e pock you doing up t'ere?" Poertena called. "Get you ass down here and do some real work!"

"Oh, sure!" the private called back. "Expecting gratitude from a Pinopan is like expecting exact change from a K'Vaernian!"

"What is t'is t'ing, 'exact change'?" Poertena asked with a shrug, and followed Honal through the hole.

Roger thrust the blade of his sword through the doorway, then moved forward. There was a hole in the base of the opposite tower, which was apparently the inner side of the main gatehouse, and he could hear shots from the upper stories. But the top of the wall was momentarily clear.

There was more fighting to the south, back into town. It looked like the Diasprans and Vashin were being used to hold off the Kirsti forces. From the looks of the locals, there were more of the city guards, armed only with staves, and a sprinkling of the formal "Army." They were distinguishable by their heavier armor and heavier spears. The weapons were something like the Roman *pilum,* and the soldiers wielded them well, holding a good shield wall and pressing hard against the human-trained infantry.

The Diasprans and Vashin had been pushed back by force of numbers, and now they were so compacted they could barely use their firearms. It was obvious, however, that neither group had forgotten its genesis as cold steel fighters, for the Diasprans had brought forward their assegai troops. That elite force had started as city guards, similar to the locals, and had since smashed two barbarian armies in its travels with humans. Side-by-side with the Vashin, who had drawn their long glittering swords, the Diasprans held the Kirsti forces at bay. More than that, they were probably killing at least three of the locals for each of their own who fell.

But the locals had the numbers to take that casualty rate, and Roger could see more moving up the roads to reinforce the attack. It was only a matter of time before the Vashin and the Diasprans were overwhelmed. Time to get the hell out of Dodge. Or Kirsti, or wherever this was.

"So many cities, so many skirmishes," he muttered as the remnants of his own party poured through the door behind him.

Sergeant Knever was the last through, and the Diaspran closed it behind him.

"We've sealed the doors on the other side and set a slow fuse on the gun powder store," the sergeant said with a salute. The nice thing about Mardukans was that they could salute and keep their weapons trained at the same time, and Knever was careful to cover his prince even while saluting. "Shaman Cord is being evacuated back to the company, and all live personnel are clear of the building. We had three more killed in action, and two wounded, besides Shaman Cord. Both of those have also been evacuated."

The sergeant paused for a moment, then coughed on the harsh, smoky air.

"What about the dead?" Roger asked.

"Per your instructions, we loaded them in the Marine disposal utilities and burned them, Sir," the sergeant replied.

"I'm really tired of this shit," Roger said, checking his toot. It was barely ten a.m., local time. In a day which lasted thirty-six hours, that made it barely two hours after sunrise. "Christ, this is going to be a long day. We need to didee, Sergeant."

"Yes, Sir," Knever agreed, and waved towards the far tower. "After you, Sir."

The sergeant took one more look to the north, into the mysterious darkness of the valley. As far as the eye could see, there were thousands, millions—billions—of scattered lights, lining the darkness of the valley floor. What created the lights was unclear, but it appeared that the city continued for kilometers and kilometers and kilometers. He gazed at the vista for a moment, then shook his head in a human gesture.

"This is not going to be good."

"Now, this is not good," Honal said sharply. The upper compartment of the tower was a mass of wheels, belts, and chains. "We need some Diasprans up here, or something."

"Nah, you gots me," Poertena panted as he made it up the last stairs. He grabbed the wall and his side. "Jesu Christo, I t'ink t'ose step kill me!"

"It wasn't the stairs; it was your pack," Honal said. "But now that you're here, we need to get the gate open. You have any idea what any of this stuff does?"

Poertena took a look around, then another. He frowned.

"I . . . t'ink t'at big wheel in front of you is t'e capstan."

"You think," Honal repeated. "And what is a capstan?"

"It what you turn to open t'e gate," Poertena replied. "Only one problem."

Honal looked at the wheel. It was, as far as he could tell, devoid of such minor things as handholds.

"Where do we grab?" he asked.

Poertena shoved himself off the wall and walked forward. There were embrasures on the northern side of the room, and he walked over and looked down through them. They were clearly for pouring stuff on attackers, but he felt quite certain that they functioned very well for disposing of unnecessary equipment, as well.

"Took you a little bit to get in here, huh?" he asked. He turned back to the great drumlike wheel.

"Yes, it did," the Vashin nobleman admitted.

"Looks like t'ey had time to strip out the actual capstan," the Pinopan said, gazing at the capstan thoughtfully. It was nearly four meters across, clearly impossible to turn without a massive lever. On the other hand, there was a very convenient nut right at the top. "I jus' need a lever. . . ."

"Big enough to move the world?" Roger asked, stepping through the door. "Time to get the gate up, Poertena. What are you waiting for? A metaphysical entity?"

"No, You Highness," the Pinopan said, stooping to pick up a long baulk of wood. "A physical notion."

The dowel was wide, nearly ten centimeters, and longer than Poertena—probably a replacement for an interrupting rod. The armorer contemplated it for a moment, then dropped his pack and dove in.

"Okay, first you get out the metaphysical entity extractor," Roger agreed, and glanced at Rastar's cousin. "Honal, is this room secure?"

"Well, we haven't been counterattacked," the cavalryman said. "Yet."

"Hell, on t'is pocking planet, t'at t'e *definition* of secure," Poertena said as he extracted a roll of tape from the pack. "And *of course* I wasn't going to get a metaphysical extractor!"

"Of course not," Roger said as he went down on one knee and picked up the dowel. "I should have known it would be space-tape. That, or drop cord. What else? And what, exactly, are we going to do with it?"

"Well," Poertena replied, reaching into the top of the pack. "You know when we first met."

Roger eyed the wrench warily, remembering a recalcitrant set of armor and the armorer who had gotten him out of it so quickly.

"You're *not* going to hit me with that, right?"

"Nope," Poertena said as he laid the haft of the wrench along the dowel and began to apply tape, "but we going to see if it can move t'e world!"

Doc Dobrescu shook his head as he ran the sterilizer over his hands. They had over two dozen wounded, but of the ones who might survive, Cord was by far the worst.

"All I wanted to be was a pilot," he muttered, kneeling down beside the shaman. He looked across at the local female, who had shed her enveloping disguise somewhere along the way. "I'm going to need six arms for this, so you're elected. Hold out your hands."

"What is this?" Pedi asked, holding out all four hands as the human ran a wand over them.

"It scares away the demons," Dobrescu snapped. "It will reduce the infection—the gut-fever, you'd call it. He's hit bad, so it won't stop it entirely. But it will stop us from increasing the infection."

"He'll die," Pedi said softly. "I can smell the gut. He will die. My *benan*. What can I say to my father?"

"Screw your father," Dobrescu snarled. He tapped the female, who seemed about to drift off into la-la land, on the forehead. "Hey! Blondie, look at me!"

Pedi snapped her head up to snarl at the medic, but froze at his expression.

"We are *not* going to lose him!" Dobrescu barked, and thumped her on the forehead again. Harder. "We. Are. Not. Going. To. Lose. Him. Get that into your head, and get ready to help. Understand?"

"What should I do?" Pedi asked.

"Exactly what I say," Dobrescu answered quietly. He looked at the mess in Cord's abdomen and shook his head. "I'm a goddammed medic, not a xeno-surgeon."

Cord was unconscious and breathing shallowly. Dobrescu had intubated the shaman and run in an oxygen line. He didn't have a decent anesthetic for the Mardukans, or a gas-passer, for that matter. But he'd given the shaman an injection of "sleepy juice," an extract of one of the most noxious of Marduk's fauna, the killerpillar. If he had the dosage right, Cord wouldn't feel a thing. And he *might* even wake up after the "operation."

"Here we go," the warrant muttered, taking the spear by the shaft.

He started by using a laser scalpel to elongate the opening in the abdominal wall. The shaman's muscles had bound around the spearhead, and it was necessary to open the hole outward to extract the weapon. He applied two auto-extractors that slowly spread the opening, pulling away each of the incised layers in turn.

He finally had a good look at the damage, and it was pretty bad. The spear was lodged on the edge of the Mardukan equivalent of a liver, which was just about where humans kept one. There was a massive blood vessel just anterior of where the spear seemed to stop, and Dobrescu shook his head again at the shaman's luck. Another millimeter, a bad drop on the way back, and Cord would have bled out in a minute.

The spearhead had also perforated the shaman's large, small, and middle-zone intestine—the latter a Mardukan feature without a human analog—and ruptured a secondary stomach. But the damage to each was minor, and it looked like he wouldn't have to resect anything.

The worst problem was that a lesser blood vessel, a vein, *had* been punctured. If they didn't get it sewn up soon, the shaman would bleed to death anyway. The only reason he hadn't already was that the spear was holding the puncture partly closed.

"I'm going to pull this out," Dobrescu said, pointing to the spearhead. "When I do, he's going to bleed like mad." He handed the Mardukan female two temp-clamps. "I'm going to point to where I want those while I'm working. You need to get them on *fast*, understand?"

"Understand," Pedi said, seriously. "On my honor."

"Honor," the medic snorted. "I just wanted to fly shuttles. Was that too much to ask?"

CHAPTER EIGHTEEN

For the first time in a career that had seen the term used more times than he cared to remember, Armand Pahner had just discovered what "having your back to the wall" really felt like.

It was a much more powerful metaphor, under the circumstances, than he had previously believed. But that was because it was unpleasant to literally stand with his back to a closed gate while more and more enemies closed in on the humans and their allies. The *Basik*'s Own was being pushed back into a broad "C" around the gate, and he knew that unless they got the gate opened—somehow—they were all going to be killed.

And eaten.

That was more than enough to convince any CO that he was in for a bad day. In Pahner's case, however, it was only one minor, additional item. Armand Pahner was widely known as a man who got steadily calmer as the situation got worse. Which was undoubtedly the reason his voice was very, very calm when Sergeant Major Kosutic turned up to report in.

"And where," he asked her, "is Roger?"

The same circumstances which produced monumental calmness in the captain produced a sort of manic humor in the sergeant major, and Kosutic swept off her helmet and cocked her head at him.

"Feeling a bit tense, Captain?" she inquired, and Pahner gave her a thin smile.

"Sergeant Major," he replied quietly, "I have known you for some years. And we need every gun we can muster. So I will *not* kill you. *If* . . . you tell me where Prince Roger is. Right Now."

"Up there." Kosutic pointed upward as a sound of releasing locks echoed through the gate tower. "Opening the gates."

"Great," Pahner said with the grumpiness reserved for the moments when he found himself with no option but to depend upon his rambunctious charge's talent for surviving one near-suicidal bit of mayhem or another without him. "Now if we can just break contact, we'll be home free."

Poertena winced as the breaching charge blew in another heavy wooden door. The tower's internal defenses required double charges, and the overpressure slapping at the Marine caused his suit to go momentarily rigid yet again.

There probably wasn't much of a threat left on the other side of the portal, given the hail of splinters the charge should have blasted into the room. But Momma Poertena's boy hadn't made it this far on the basis of "probably," and he wasn't about to take chances when they were this close to home. So he thumbed the tab on a concussion grenade, tossed it into the room beyond, and waited until the weapon had gone off before following it through the shattered doorway.

The room was filled with a haze of propellant residue, but two Krath were still partially functional on the far side of the room. One was hopping up and down, clutching a piece of shrapnel in his leg, and the other was just climbing back to his feet after the dual explosions. Two shotgun rounds sufficed to deal with them, then Poertena took a closer look at the room and grunted in satisfaction as he spotted the large barrels stacked against the wall.

"About pocking time. CLEAR!"

"That what we came for?" Neteri asked as he entered behind the Pinopan and swept his rifle from side to side.

"Yeah," Poertena replied. "Get some of t'em Vashin up here; we gonna need some muscle." The armorer pulled the wrench he'd reclaimed once the gate was raised out of his pack and looked at the chocks holding the barrels in place. "I hope I don' bury myself doing t'is."

Pahner stepped through the second set of gates, looked around, and nodded. At least there wasn't an immediate threat on the far side of the walls.

The area beyond the gate was open for about a hundred meters— an obvious cleared defensive zone. Beyond that, however, a solid bank of buildings stretched as far as could be seen in the gloom. Obviously, the city continued well beyond the walls.

The heavy ash-fall seemed to be easing, and a little light was starting to peek through. Both of those changes were—probably— good signs. The ash was a misery for everyone, and some additional light on the battle would be helpful.

"Okay," the captain said to Kosutic. "We're through the gates. Now all we have to do is collect our charge and get him safely back under *our* protection, instead of the other way around. Oh, and somehow break contact with several thousand screaming religious fanatics. Any suggestions?"

"Well," a disembodied voice said from the darkness overhead, "I think using the plasma cannon is right out." Roger hit the release on his descender harness to flip out of his head-down position and dropped the last few meters to the ground. "Morning, Captain."

"And good morning to you, Your Highness," the Marine said tightly. "Having fun?"

"Not really," the prince replied. "I seem to have gotten my *asi* the next best thing to killed, I lost a Marine and four Vashin, and I seem to have really pissed off the Krath. Other than that, everything is peachy."

"Yeah, well," Pahner said, after a moment. "We'll talk about it later. I doubt from the brief bit Eleanora told me that you could've done much different."

"I'm of the same opinion," Roger admitted. "But that doesn't make me any happier about it. And the fact that I keep having to shoot my way out of these situations is becoming . . . annoying."

"I'd say that it was 'annoying' for your enemies as well, Your Highness," Kosutic observed with a bark of laughter. "Except that they don't usually survive long enough to *be* annoyed."

"Sor Teb did," Roger admitted. "That pocker is fast. I took out the arquebusier first, and by the time I'd shifted target, Teb was behind the throne and then *gone*."

"It happens." Pahner shrugged. "The important point is that we've got you back, along with most of your party. We're into the gatehouse, and we've closed up our forces, too. Now all we have to do is break contact."

"Poertena's working on that," Roger said. "We need to get everyone to this side of the gate, though. And we need to do it fast."

Pahner looked at the traffic jam of *turom,* Mardukan mercenaries, porters, and hangers-on in the gateway and sighed.

"I don't know about 'fast,' Your Highness. But we'll get to work on it."

"As long as the gate is cleared by . . ." Roger consulted his toot, "fifteen minutes from now."

"Got it," Kosutic said. "I'll extricate some of the Vashin and get them out here as security, then get the noncombatants moving."

"Do it," Pahner agreed. "In the meantime, we need to start planning what disaster we're going to have next."

Poertena took another peek through the hole in the floor and shook his head.

"Come on, You' Highness," he muttered. "Time's a'wastin'."

"We've got company," Kileti said from the demolished doorway. "There are Krath in the gate control room."

"Good t'ing we smashed t'e control, t'en, huh? T'ese gates ain't closing until somebody get a whole new set built. T'ey can drop t'e portcullis, but even t'at won't be easy, not wit' t'e way we jam it!"

"Yeah, but if they get into the second defense room, we're cut off," the rifleman pointed out.

"Yes," one of the Vashin cavalrymen standing by the barrels of oil said. "And then we go kill some more of these Krath bastards."

"Timing on t'is is tricky," Poertena said, with another glance through the hole as the sound of axes biting into wood came from the far room. "I t'ink you Vashin better get in t'e other room and keep it clear, huh?"

"Right," the Vashin NCO said, and nodded to his fellows. "Let's go collect some horns, boys."

Poertena shook his head as the four cavalrymen left the room.

"I swear, t'ose guys *enjoy* t'is shit." There was movement below, and he saw the Diaspran infantry reforming and beginning a slow back march into the gut of the gate tunnel, all the while keeping up a steady crackle of rifle fire. "Almost time to start t'e ball."

"Back one step, and *fire!*" Fain barked. His throat was raw from the combination of gun smoke, ash, and shouting, but the company was maintaining a good fire, and at least half of their steadiness was because of their confidence in the voice behind them. He wasn't about to stop now. He did turn at the polite tap on a shoulder, though.

"Good morning, Captain Fain," Roger said. "I need to adjust your orders slightly, if you don't mind."

Fain looked at the prince, then shook his head. He could tell by now when Roger was being tricky.

"Of course, Your Highness. How can the Carnan Battalion— what's left of it—be of service?"

Roger winced at the qualification.

"Has it been bad?" he asked.

"Now that we have the Krath on a limited front, it's much better," Fain said, gesturing to the gate opening his men filled. "But the street fighting was quite bloody."

"I'm sorry to hear that," Roger said quietly. "I'm getting tired of losing friends." He gazed into the smoke and ash for a heartbeat or two, then drew a sharp breath.

"We need to break contact sharpish," he said more briskly. "Sergeant Major Kosutic has gotten everyone out of the way behind you, with the exception of one rank of Vashin. I need you to coordinate a high-firepower retreat to the rear of the gate area. It's imperative that the city half of the gate tunnel be absolutely clear of all our people, including the wounded. Understood?"

Fain looked upward at the murderholes above him. He been half waiting for them to open up on his company at any moment, and he hadn't enjoyed the mental image of that eventuality which his imagination had conjured up. Now, however, the thought of descending slaughter was downright comforting.

"Understood, Your Highness," he replied, with a false-hand flick of grim amusement. "Will do."

Poertena waved in an ineffectual attempt to disperse the smoke drifting up through the hole as the Diasprans went to a higher rate of fire. That wall of lead couldn't be sustained for very long—individuals would quickly run out of ammunition, for one thing—but while it lasted, it permitted them to begin retreating, opening up the gap between them and the pressing Krath.

"I t'ink it's time to get to work," he said, as another volley of pistol shots sounded from the far room. He pulled out his wrench one last time and waited until the first Krath came into view through the hole.

"Say hello to my leetle priend!" he shouted, then swung over and down at the head of the barrel like a golfer.

Fain nodded as the first gush of fish oil fell through the holes. The Krath, who'd expected it to be hot or even boiling, were pleasantly surprised that it was neither. The slippery substance made it even harder for them to move forward over the bodies piling up in the tunnel, but as far as they were concerned, that was a more than equitable trade-off. Fain doubted they'd feel that way much longer.

"That's right," he whispered. "Just a little further. . . ."

Poertena rolled the third, massive barrel aside as the last of the oil gushed from it, then nodded at Neteri and pulled out a grenade.

"One, two, t'ree—"

He thumbed the tab on the grenade and dropped it through the hole. Neteri dropped his own grenade simultaneously through the hole beside it, then both of them moved on to the next pair of holes and repeated the process.

"Time to get t'e pock out of here," Poertena said, headed for the door and accelerating steadily. "T'is t'e next best t'ing to teaching t'em bridge!"

The incendiary grenades were ancient technology—a small bursting charge, surrounded by layers of white phosphorus. Simple, but effective.

The burning metal engulfed the interior of the gate, and some of it spread as far as the front rank of the Diaspran infantry. Despite the weight of their rifle fire, they had been unable to keep the fanatic Krath from staying closer to them than Roger had hoped. Unfortunately, in the words of that most ancient of inter-species military aphorisms, "Shit happens," and so a few of the humans' allies learned the hard way that the most terrible thing about white phosphorus is that there is no way to extinguish it. You have to get it off, or simply let it burn out. Water doesn't quench it; it only makes it burn hotter.

Yet what happened to the Diasprans was only very bad; what happened to the *Krath* was indescribable. The blazing phosphorus raised the temperature in the gate tunnel to over a thousand degrees Kelvin in a bare instant. The dozens of Mardukans who were covered in Poertena's fish oil never had a chance as it flashed into vapor and flame. The only mercy—if such a noun could possibly be applied to a moment of such transcendent horror—was that death came very swiftly, indeed.

It came less swiftly for the forces gathered around the interior side of the gate as the ravening flames licked outward. Some of those at least fifteen or twenty meters back actually survived.

The flame gouted up through the murderholes, as well, narrowly missing the last Vashin cavalryman as he scrambled down the scaling rope on the outer wall. The inside of the gate tower was like a chimney, channeling the explosion of heat and fury that set fire to all the woodwork and oil-drenched barrels in the tower's interior. Force fed from the conflagration underneath, which now included burning bodies, the flame and heat swept through the upper sections of the tower as if it were a blast furnace.

In seconds, the entire gatehouse was fully involved.

* * *

"Cut it out, you stupid beast!"

Roger jerked on the reins of his *civan* as it stamped nervously. He understood why the flames and the smell of burning flesh made all of the cavalry mounts uneasy, but understanding didn't make his own mount any easier to control, and he felt a sudden longing for Patty.

For virtually the entire march across the far continent, his primary mount had been a *flar-ta* pack beast—an elephant-sized monstrosity that resembled nothing so much as an omnivorous triceratops. His particular mount had had more than a touch of the much more dangerous wild strain that the Marines had taken to calling "capetoads." Patty had been five tons of ravening, unstoppable mean in a fight, and at times like this, when it looked like a hard slog all the way to the mountains and possible battles with barbarian tribes beyond, he missed her badly.

But there'd been No Way to fit a *flar-ta* onto a schooner, so for the time being, he'd just have to put up with these damned two-legged idiots, instead.

Pahner walked over and glanced up at the prince as Roger attempted to soothe the nervous *civan*.

"I think your plan worked, Your Highness."

"Better than I'd hoped, actually," Roger admitted, listening to the steady roar of the flames consuming the gate tower's interior. "They'll have to wait for it to cool before they can pursue us on this side of the river. Either that, or climb down the walls."

"But they'll have sent out runners on the far side," Pahner pointed out, gesturing across the barely glimpsed river. "You know there's a bridge upstream somewhere and garrisons are already being turned out."

"Then I suppose we should get headed out," Roger said, kneeing the beast around to face north, away from the inferno at the gate. He lowered his helmet visor and tightened his gauntlets.

"Time to show these religious gentlemen why you don't pock with House MacClintock."

CHAPTER NINETEEN

"You are an absolute *idiot,* Sor Teb," Lorak Tral snarled.

The general fingered his sword as he glared at the Scourge while smoke from the fires wafted even into the small interior meeting room. It hadn't taken long for the fire from the gate to spread throughout the upper temple district, especially with oil- and fire-covered soldiers running screaming in every direction. A brief, fortuitous deluge had helped control the worst of the flames, but the damage was extensive. And that didn't even count the damage to the gatehouse itself . . . or the loss of the High Priest. The jockeying for that position always led to social unrest, and in the wake of the chaos left by the retreating humans, the city balanced precariously on the brink of civil war.

"You may not speak to me that way, Lorak," the Scourge's reply made an insult of the naked name. "Whatever has happened, I am still the Scourge of God. I am the Chooser. Beware who you call an idiot."

"I'll call you anything I want, you idiot," the general told him in a voice of ice. "You may be the Scourge, but until this is settled, you are to refrain from *any* further action. Is that perfectly clear?"

"And who made you High Priest?" Teb snapped. He refused to show it, but a tiny trickle of fear had crept into his heart. Lorak was normally a rather self-effacing type; there must have been notable changes in the last hour or so for him to take this high a hand.

"He is not the High Priest," Werd Ras said quietly. The Flail, the head of the internal police, had kept out of most of the maneuvering for the succession, but he had eyes and ears everywhere.

"However," Ras continued, "a quorum of the full council *has* determined that he will have plenipotentiary authority to deal with this situation. And he is specifically ordered to bring the humans to ground. The council was . . . not impressed by your actions, Sor Teb. Endangering the Voice was idiotic. Doing so with too few guards simply compounded your idiocy. And deserting him when it was clear your plan had failed was inexcusable."

"You're going to try to stop the humans with your Sere *vern*?" Teb said to Lorak scornfully. "All you know is how to make pretty formations. The humans are headed for the *Shin*. They had one with them, disguised as a Shadem female. You do know what that means, don't you?"

"You make too much of the Shin," the general replied with equal scorn. "It is high time to teach those barbarians a lesson."

Teb's eyes widened.

"You *are* joking, right?" He turned to Werd Ras. "Tell me he's joking."

"The fact that there was a Shin in the group that killed the Voice was reported to us. In fact, there are some indications that it was the Shin who actually did the deed. Be that as it may, if the Shin aid the humans, they will be pursued to destruction. Messages have been forwarded to Queicuf and Thirlot and will be passed to the Shin. If the Vales aid the humans, they will be put to the torch, and all of them will be taken as Servants."

"So now you're Choosing, as well," Sor Teb said with a gesture of humor. "I suppose the Shin are just going to take this lying down?"

"I don't care *how* they take it," Lorak said. "It is high time that those barbarians learned who their masters are."

"'Masters,'" Sor Teb repeated thoughtfully. "'Masters.' You know that the last three times Kirsti tried to mount punitive expeditions against the Shin, they were cut off and slaughtered."

"That's because none of them insured their line of supply," Lorak replied with a gesture of contempt. "We'll set up Thirlot and Queicuf as fortified supply depots and maintain heavily guarded convoys into the mountains. Like the Scourge, the only thing the Shin know is raid and ambush. They won't be able to cut that line of supply, because— like your precious Scourge—they don't even know what 'line of supply' means."

"Ah, yes, that's us," Teb said, tossing a false-hand in a gesture of mock agreement. "Not much more than barbarians ourselves. Just one last question; you say you informed Queicuf and Thirlot. Does that mean you're just going to let them scurry all the way to the hills before you go after them?"

"It's impossible to mount a prepared assault in the time it will take them to travel that far," Werd said. "And what's happened here today is sufficient proof that a prepared assault will be necessary to overcome the humans alone, far less crush the Shin, if they should be stupid enough to offer them aid. So, yes, we're going to let them 'scurry to the hills.' If the garrison in Thirlot or Queicuf is able to stop them, all the better. If not, we'll inform the Shin that they can turn the humans over to us or face the consequences."

Sor Teb fingered his horns for a moment. He hadn't come from within the social hierarchy like Werd or Lorak. He'd gotten his start as a junior Scourge raider, and he knew the true fire of the mountain tribes far better than this idiot, who'd only seen Shin after they had been "gentled" by the Scourge. The plan might even work, because the Sere had a point about the Shin's inability to organize a large action. But as for the tribes' simply rolling over and baring their bellies . . . that was about as likely as the mountains suddenly going flat.

"I see," was all he said. "It's apparent I don't have anything to do here. I'll go to my quarters and remain there until summoned."

"We'll need a few of your personnel for guides," Werd Ras said. "You'll be sent the list of requirements. With the exception of that group, you are to keep your forces in barracks. Any movement on their part will be considered hostile by the council, and will be met with all due force."

Teb considered that for a moment, then shrugged. "Very well. Am I free to go?"

"For now," Lorak replied. "For now."

Roger slid off the *civan* and slapped its muzzle as it turned to take a bite out of him.

"Cut that out, you son-of-a-bitch, or I'll shoot you for dinner!"

Pahner shook his head at the prince's mount while the rest of their caravan continued steadily past them.

"I never did like having to worry about whether or not my transport was going to try to take chunks out of me," he observed. "I think I'll just go on walking, thank you very much."

"No decent way to keep up on foot. You're pretty much stuck to one part of the caravan if all you have is your own feet," the prince opined. He glanced at the pack ambulances swaying by, and his face tightened. "Any word on Cord?"

"I don't know, but I do know that it's time to pick his *benan*'s brain," the Marine replied.

"Agreed." Roger strode over to his *asi*'s stretcher and shook his head. The contraption was swung between two *turom* and had to be incredibly uncomfortable, even for someone who was unwounded, he thought, just as Doc Dobrescu appeared out of the column as if summoned by magic.

"How are you doing, Your Highness?"

"Fine, I suppose. Taking my cod liver oil, and all that. How are the casualties?"

"Most of them are either gone, or out of the woods, Your Highness," Dobrescu admitted. "St. John—Mark, that is—lost his *right* arm this time. An arquebus round, I think. He lost the left in Voitan, of course, just like the sergeant major. This one was low on the forearm, more lost his hand, really, and it should grow back fairly quickly. He'll be fully functional in a month or so. And we had one of the wounded Vashin expire—general systemic failure, I think."

"And Cord?" Roger asked, gesturing at the *asi*. Pedi was walking beside his stretcher, straight backed and stony faced. She looked the very dictionary image of the stoic tribesman, totally disinterested in asking quarter for herself or anyone else, yet she glanced occasionally at the shaman.

"Tough to tell," the medic admitted. "He took a solid hit, and the surgery was very rough and ready. Then there's the dosage on the anesthetic, and any secondary effects it might have, like increased bleeding. He's a tough old bird, but the emphasis on that could be on 'old.' If you know what I mean."

"Maybe, maybe not," Roger said with a sigh. "Do whatever you can, Doc."

"I won't ask if we could stop someplace, Sir," Dobrescu said to Pahner as the captain walked up. "I don't want to end up as somebody's lunch."

"You heard, I see," Pahner observed. "Yeah. Great guys, huh?"

"Gotta love civilization," Roger said, and gestured around. The ash had finally stopped falling, and the true expanse of the Valley of the Krath could be seen, opening out in a vast panorama before them.

The valley itself was at least a hundred kilometers wide, a broad U-shaped cut through the midst of rugged mountains, some of them rearing to well over five thousand meters. The Krath ran down its middle, a broad, silt-laden stream that fed and watered the valley via the repeated canals that ran up towards the flanking mountains.

The valley's floor and walls, though, were what caught the eye. As far as the eye could see, the valley was a patchwork of irrigation canals and tended fields. It was so intensively cultivated that not one square meter of land appeared to be unused. The majority of the houses, and all of the towns, were on the steep slopes of the mountains to leave every flat patch for cultivation, and each and every one was surrounded by growing greenery, most of it clearly edible.

The road itself followed the line where the flatter base of the valley started to climb up the mountain slopes. All of the towns they had passed had been evacuated before they arrived, leaving an eerie, unnatural feeling of ghost towns and mysterious disappearances. There was a sense of thousands, millions, of eyes watching from the distance, and there were actually a handful of visible Mardukans working in some of the more distant fields, plowing with *turom* or weeding rows of barleyrice and legumes.

Other than that, there wasn't a soul in sight.

The management of the valley—the regular roads, the neat villages, and the well tended canals—was arguably more frightening than the city of cannibals behind them, Roger thought. It was the visible sign of an entire country, a *massive* country of *well-organized* cannibals. After all the battles they'd fought against endless tides of barbarians on K'Vaern's Cove's continent, the thought of what "civilization" meant on *this* continent was horrifying.

"Civilization is either great, or truly terrible," he said, putting his thoughts at least partially into words. "Mediocre doesn't enter into it." He gazed out over the valley for a moment longer, then shook his head and looked over at Pedi. "Now on to the next battle," he said.

Pahner nodded and walked around the line of *turom* to touch Pedi on the arm.

"Ms. Karuse, could you join us for a moment?"

Pedi looked around at the Marine, then at the medic, who shrugged.

"I'll keep an eye on him," Dobrescu told her. "Right now, the best thing for him would be for us to stop. But that's not going to happen anytime soon."

"Very well," she said. She patted the covering over the shaman, then turned to Pahner and Roger as the ambulance moved on. "What can I do to help?"

"You know we're heading for the hills," Roger said. "What can you tell us about the route?"

Pedi obviously had to stop and think about that.

"What I know is all from traders and raiders. I've never traveled the hills myself." She paused until the prince nodded understanding of the qualification, then continued. "There's supposed to be a broad road to the town of Thirlot, where the Shin River drops through the Seisut Falls from the Vales to the valley of the Krath. There is a road up along the Shin, but it is closed by the citadel of Queicuf, and the town of Thirlot itself is walled, very heavily defended. You would have to take the gates, at least, and I don't think that's possible."

"You might be surprised," Roger told her. "We could probably take out the gates, but then we'd still have to fight our way through the city."

"And we probably don't have enough forces to do that," Pahner said. "We took the Krath in Kirsti by surprise, but fighting our way through a fully prepared town is something else."

"You could call upon them to surrender," the Shin said, rubbing her horns in thought. "If they refused, and you took them by storm, they would be liable for total destruction. If you created even a small breach, they would almost automatically have to surrender."

"That's a recognized law of war?" Pahner asked. "It sounds like it."

"Yes," the Shin answered. "The satraps fight all the time, and they don't want to destroy the cities. So they have elaborate rules about what is and isn't permissible, and what cities should and must do. Fortifications, also, but those are considered much harder to take. But even if Thirlot surrendered, you'd also have to fight your way through the stronghold of Queicuf, and that would be much harder."

"Two fortifications." Pahner pulled out a piece of *bisti* root and cut off a slice. He slipped it into his mouth and chewed thoughtfully, then shook his head. "If this were a purely military party I could see it. But we've got a swarm of hangers-on and the human noncombatants to worry about, too. I'd really rather not risk it, under these circumstances."

"What kind of alternative do we have?" Roger asked.

"Up the mountains," Pedi replied, with a gesture to the east. "There's a small track that leads to the south side of the Mudh Hemh lands; it comes out near Nesru. The Krath have a curtain wall there to prevent Shin parties from taking the Shesul Pass, but the position is only lightly defended from this side."

"So you think we could punch them out of our way?" Pahner asked.

"Having witnessed your warriors in action, I feel sure of it," she replied. "But there are Shin raider parties on the other side of the wall, from Mudh Hemh and elsewhere. Those from Mudh Hemh, I can talk out of attacking us, if they announce their presence in advance. Those from other Vales might or might not recognize my authority, and there are other hazards. The route is lightly used, so it hasn't been cleared of *nashul* and *ralthak*."

"And what," Roger asked, "are *nashul* and *ralthak*?"

"*Nashul* are . . . burrower-beasts. They look like rock and attack by surprise. Very large, very hard to kill. *Ralthak* are fliers, very large. They both eat the high-*turom*, the *tar*."

"And if we take the route by the Shin?" Pahner asked.

"We will be headed directly to the Vale of Mudh Hemh," Pedi said with a gesture equivalent to a human shrug. "We will have to pass through the Battle Lands, and I have no idea what the traders in Nesru will think of that, but they're all under the control of Mudh Hemh, more or less. We shouldn't have trouble on that route. Not from Shin, at any rate. Thirlot and Queicuf are considered impregnable, though."

"I'm sure we could take them," Pahner said. "If we used plasma cannon to take down the gates."

"Not," Roger said. "Overhead."

"Precisely, Your Highness," Pahner said dryly. "That was in the nature of sarcasm."

"Oh," the prince replied with a smile. "And there I was thinking it was a test." He shrugged. "Whichever, the mountain route it is."

CHAPTER TWENTY

Semmar Reg stepped out of the Place of Justice and looked up at the monster towering over him. It was a two-legged beast, with vicious talons and an obviously wicked disposition. The rider on its back, however, was even more terrifying. His weapons and accouterments were different from those of the Valley Guards—armor of leather and fine-linked mail, a lance, and a long weapon like a thin arquebus. Reg bowed low as the apparition drew up at the head of a column of similarly equipped riders and dismounted. Whatever else the stranger might be, Reg noted, he carried more pistols than anyone the mayor had ever seen.

Reg had hurried to the town hall as soon as he heard the sound of a firefight from the south. From Sran's bell-tower, he could easily see the Guard checkpoint on the Kirsti Road on a clear day. Of course, today was far from clear, despite the recent rainstorm which had washed much of the ash out of the air, and the current visibility conditions had made it difficult to make out details. But when he reached the tower's top, he saw a small amount of smoke from arquebuses and bombards still drifting around the fortification. He'd also seen this column of riders, well on its way to the town, and if they'd taken many casualties from the Guard, it wasn't apparent.

What *was* apparent was that a formed military unit was just about to descend upon Sran. And that hadn't happened in two hundred years.

Rastar looked around at the town and felt a distinct glow of pleasure. It climbed up the mountains at its back, with one house piled practically on top of another. On the south side, a mountain stream tumbled out of a knife-edged gorge and was gathered for use by several mills that seemed to be the main source of local income.

It was evident that at least some of the place's citizenry had once been more prosperous than they were today, for several large one-time manors had been converted into housing for workers. But if the manor houses' previous owners had fallen upon hard times, the workmen living in their homes today appeared to be doing well enough. For that matter, the entire town seemed relatively prosperous, which was good. Prosperity mattered to the humans, since they felt so very kindly towards town-living *turom*. Rastar, on the other hand, was Vashin. The Vashin had settled into their northern fortresses barely three generations before the Boman overran them, and the long tradition of raiding was bred into their bone and blood. It might have become somewhat muted in the last generation or so, but they certainly weren't "townies."

Thus it was that Rastar saw the town from the uncomplicated perspective of a cavalry leader on a long march. Which was to say, as a chicken waiting to be plucked. Of course, there was no need to be impolite about it.

"Good day to you, kind Sir," the former Prince of Therdan said in truly vilely accented Krath with a gesture of greeting. "It's lucky for you I got here first!"

Reg bowed again, nervously.

"It is a great honor to meet you . . . ?" he said.

"Rastar Komas," the armored stranger supplied. Or, at least, that was what Reg *thought* he said. Between the outlandish name and the even worse accent, it was very difficult to be certain. "Prince of Therdan," the stranger went on, with a false-hand gesture of expansive goodwill. "It would seem that a caravan, of which I am a member, is about to pass through your town and into the Shin Hills. Unfortunately, we're just a tad short on supplies."

"I believe you are the party from over the seas?" Reg said delicately. "I was informed of your presence. However, the High One has decreed that you are not permitted to leave Kirsti. I . . . wonder at your presence here. Also, the Shesul Road is closed to all but military traffic. I'm afraid that you're not authorized access."

"Oh, trifles, my good man. Trifles, I'm sure!" Rastar said with a human grin. It was not a normal Mardukan expression, since Mardukans, like any sensible species, regarded the baring of teeth as a sign of hostility. Not even Eleanora O'Casey could fault him for smiling so cheerfully at the local mayor, but Rastar was pleased to observe that the expression had exercised the proper effect upon him.

"I'll admit that there was some minor unpleasantness when we left Kirsti," he continued. "But surely no rational government would hold you responsible for our presence when half the Kirsti Guard is dead at the *Atul* Gate."

"Oh." Foreign accent or no, Reg had no problem understanding that last sentence. He tried not to flinch as he absorbed its dire implications, but he was fairly sure where the rest of the conversation was going. "I agree with your assessment," he said, after a moment. "What can the town of Sran do for you?"

"Well, as I mentioned, we're terribly short of supplies," Rastar said with another smile which just coincidentally happened to show a bit more tooth than the last one. "But you're in luck, because I got here before those barbarians from Diaspra or . . . even the worse, the *humans*. So I'm thinking that we can get clear with, oh, say one measure in five of your storehouses. And, of course, some little trinkets. Purely to satisfy the wanton lusts of those Diaspran infantry barbarians. We'll *try* to keep the humans from burning the town down, but you know how they are. Perhaps if everything was assembled, on carts, ready to go, when they arrived it would be easier to restrain them. And now that I think about it, if we could distract them with a feast outside town, we might actually be able to keep them in check.

"Now, I suppose we *could* pay for some of it," he added with a gesture expressive of anxious consideration. "But then we'd be here all day negotiating, and they'd probably arrive before we were ready for them. What do you think would be best?"

"I'll go get the head of supply," the mayor said.

"God, I love good subordinates!" Roger said as he looked around with a sigh of pleasure.

"They are a treasure, aren't they?" Pahner agreed with a laugh.

A long column of *turom* carts was lined up beside the road. Some of them were still being loaded, but most were already piled high with sacks of barleyrice and other less identifiable merchandise. On the other side of the road there was a large tree-park, apparently a source of firewood for the town, and scattered amongst the trees was a mess line. Several cauldrons of barleyrice steamed over fires, and two *turom* were turning on a spit just beyond several long tables covered with fruit and fresh vegetables. The meat was going to be a little rare, but . . .

"Tremendous, Rastar," Roger said as he trotted his *civan* up to the Vashin prince, who was gnawing on a *basik* leg. "I'm surprised you were able to do all this so easily."

"Oh, it was tough," Rastar assured him, then belched and tossed the leg bone over his shoulder. "The local mayor was a tough negotiator."

"What's it going to cost us?" Pahner asked as he walked up to them, still pointedly refusing to ride one of the *civan*.

"Oh, as to that," Rastar said airily, "it seems the locals were so impressed with our riding form that—"

"Rastar," Roger growled, "you were supposed to *pay* for the supplies."

"I *tried* to press payment upon them," the Therdan said. "But they absolutely refused. It was truly amazing."

"What did you threaten them with?" Pahner asked.

"Me? *Threaten?*" Rastar demanded with a Mardukan hand gesture eloquent of shock. "I can't believe you could accuse me of such a thing, when we Vashin are so universally known for our humility and boundless respect for life!"

"Hah!" Roger laughed.

"Well, I *will* admit that the reputation of humans for boundless cruelty and wanton slaughter had, unfortunately, preceded you."

"Oh, you bastard," Roger said with another laugh. "I'm going to have to govern these people some day, you know."

"As well they sense the iron hand inside the glove, then, Your Highness," Pahner said. "Until their society is stable and they themselves are educated enough for democracy to take hold, a certain rational degree of fear is a vital necessity."

"I know that, Captain," Roger said sadly. "I don't have to like it."

"As long as you *follow* it," Pahner said. "The difference between the MacClintock Doctrine and the fall of the ISU was a lack of respect for the ISU and its thinking that it could 'nation-build' on the cheap, which left the cupboard bare when it came up short on credit and couldn't pay cash with its military."

"I'm aware of that, Captain," Roger sighed. "Have you ever noticed me trying to use 'minimal force'?"

The Marine looked at him thoughtfully for a moment, then shook his head. "No, I haven't. Point taken."

"I've become more comfortable than I ever wanted to be with calling for a bigger hammer," Roger said. "I don't have to like it, but the past few months have provided all the object lessons anyone could ever want about what happens when you're afraid to use force at need."

He started to say something more, then closed his mouth, and Pahner saw him look across to where Nimashet Despreaux rode her own civan beside the line of ambulances. For just a moment, the prince's eyes were very dark, but then he gave himself a shake and returned his attention to the Bronze Barbarians' commander.

"Since you—and Rastar—seem to have everything thoroughly under control, I'm going to go check on Cord and the other casualties. Ask somebody to bring me a plate, would you?"

Roger dipped his head under the leather awning and looked across the litter at Pedi.

"How is he?"

Most of the wounded were being transported in the leather-covered *turom* carts that looked not much different from Conestoga wagons. Roger had spent some time in similar conditions on the march, so he knew what it was like to be bounced and bumped over the poorly maintained roads while regrowing an arm or a hand. Unpleasant didn't begin to describe it. But until they got back to "civilization," and convinced civilization that there was the hard way, and then there was Roger's way, there wasn't a great deal of option.

What option there was, though, had been extended to Cord. His litter was suspended between two *turom,* which had to be at least marginally better. At least he wasn't being shaken by every bump in the road, although whether or not the side-to-side motion was actually all that superior was probably a matter of opinion. At the moment, however, it was the best Roger could offer his *asi.*

He had seldom felt so inadequate when he offered someone his "best."

"He still won't wake up," Pedi said softly. "And he's hot; his skin is dry."

"Afternoon, Your Highness," Dobrescu said. The medic climbed down from one of the carts to stand beside the litter and gestured at Cord. "I heard you were checking on the wounded and figured I'd find you here."

"How is he?" Roger repeated.

"He's not coming out of the anesthesia," the medic admitted. "Which isn't good. And as Blondie here noted, he's running a fever. That isn't anything I've run into before; they're cold-blooded by nature, so a fever isn't normal with them. It's not all that *high* a fever, but he's about three degrees above where I think he should be, based on the ambient temperature."

"He's . . ." Roger paused, trying to decide how to put it. "He's sort of a . . . warrior monk. Is it possible that he's unconsciously . . . ?"

"Using *dinshon* to increase his body temperature?" Dobrescu finished for him. "Possible. I've seen him use *dinshon* a couple of times to control his metabolism. And the fever might be whatever metabolic remnant lets him do it reacting to the infection. There's a reason people develop fevers; the higher temperature improves the immune response. So fever, under certain circumstances, might be normal in Mardukans. But he's still in a bad way."

"Is there anything else to be done?" Roger asked. "I hate seeing him like this."

"Well, as far as I know, I'm *the* expert on Mardukan physiology," the medic said dryly, "and I'm afraid I can't think of a thing. I'm sorry to put it this way, Sir, but he's either going to pull through, or he isn't. I've given him the one antibiotic I know is usable in Mardukans, and we're pumping him with fluids. Other than that, there's not much we can do."

"Got it," Roger said. "I'll get out of your hair. Pedi?"

"Yes, Your Highness?" the Shin said miserably.

"Wearing yourself down caring for him isn't going to bring him back any sooner," the prince said pointedly. "I want you to rotate with those other slaves we 'rescued' and get some rest when you can. I'm going to need you up and ready to deal with the tribes as we're moving. If we get overrun because you're too tired to wrap your tongue around the words to get us through, it's going to kill him deader than dead. Understand?"

"Yes, Your Highness. I'll make sure I'm available. And capable."

"Good," Roger said, then sighed. "This is going to be a long trip."

"What?" Dobrescu said darkly. "On Marduk? Really?"

"Rastar, we also need intelligence on what we're heading into," Pahner said, after the prince had left. "Pedi has never used this route herself."

"I've talked with the locals," Rastar replied. "The language problem is pretty bad, but I got Macek to use his toot to check the translation for me. According to the locals, the road to the pass is steep and apparently of poor quality. It's maintained for *turom* carts from here to the pass itself, but past the keep, it's nothing more than a track. I don't think we can use the carts after that. Or, at least not very far after that."

"Well, if your Vashin are rested, head up the road, slowly." The captain shook his head. "I never thought I'd be back to the days when my idea of good intel was some vague descriptions of the road and cavalry a couple of hours out ahead of me."

Roger's *civan* balked at what passed for a crossroads. The road through Sran had been steep enough, but just the other side of the town, it went nearly vertical. It was paved with flat stones and had obviously been maintained, but a fresh Mardukan gullywasher had just opened up, and the roadbed had turned instantly into a shallow river of racing brown water laced with yellow foam.

"This is insane, Captain! You know that, right?" Roger practically had to scream over the thunder of the rain and the bellowing of panicky *turom*. After the caravan had passed, the roadbed would be awash with more than rain.

"It is, indeed, Your Highness!" Pahner shouted back. He'd been in conversation with the Vashin cavalry scout who'd been left at the intersection, but now he turned and crossed the road to look over the far side. There was a sheer drop to the white water fifty meters below. "Unfortunately, it's the only route. If you have any other suggestions, I'd be happy to hear them!"

"How about we click our heels together three times and say 'there's no place like home, there's no place like home'?" Roger suggested, and the captain laughed.

> There's a wheel on the Horns 'o the Morning,
> An' a wheel on the edge of the pit,
> An' a drop into nothing beneath you,
> As straight as a beggar can spit . . .

"Kipling again?" Roger said with a lift of an eyebrow.
" 'Screw Guns,' " Pahner informed him.

Roger grinned through the pounding rain, then kneed his mount back into motion once more, ascending into the storm. After another hundred meters or so, the road flattened out a little, going from a twelve- or fifteen-degree slope to one of a mere six or seven. The prince began to relax just a bit . . . only to have the *civan*'s foot slip. Roger threw his weight against the saddle as the *civan* skittered on the slick paving stones, searching for footing. After a moment, it recovered, and he kicked it in the side.

"Come on, you bastard! Onward and upward!"

Krindi Fain grunted and heaved at the wheel of the *turom* cart. For a moment, nothing happened, and then someone else shouldered in beside him. Erkum Pol's massive muscles flexed, and the cart lurched upward, lifting out of the crevice hiding under the knee-deep water roaring down the roadbed. Fain straightened his aching back and watched the cart move farther up the hill, then turned as someone tapped him on the shoulder.

"Captains don't, by and large, push carts up mountains, Captain," Armand Pahner observed.

The line of carts was barely moving—not too surprising, perhaps, given the steep slopes they'd encountered since leaving Sran. The first three had been bad enough, but the fourth was the worst so far, nearly two hundred meters long, and climbing at a constant fifteen-degree angle. Virtually everyone, human and Mardukan, had a shoulder into the carts, and the *turom* had been unhitched from the rearmost carts and doubled up on the lead ones to make the ascent.

As Fain turned towards the human, a ripple of lightning struck, jumping from one side of the gorge to the other with a sound like an artillery barrage. It started a small landslide, and the *turom* went berserk—or tried to, straining at their harnesses and slipping on the stones of the road as boulders careened about their feet.

"Well, I'm not a commander at the moment, Sir!" Fain shouted over the tumult, jumping forward to throw his shoulder back into the cart beside Erkum's as it started to slide backwards. "And I don't have any significant duties. So it seemed to be the best use of my time."

Pahner grabbed a chock and threw it under the right wheel as one of the *turom* slipped to its knees.

"Just don't get yourself killed, okay?"

"Not a problem," the former quarryman panted. "What is it you humans say? 'Caution is my middle name.'"

"To the winds," the Marine laughed. " 'Captain Krindi Caution-to-the-Winds Fain.'"

"Maybe so," the Mardukan captain grunted as the cart slipped again. "But at least 'caution' is in there somewhere!"

"This isn't going well," Roger said, "but at least we don't have company."

The reason the road was so little used had become only too evident. The column had made less than twenty kilometers since leaving Sran, and the long Mardukan day was well into its equally lengthy afternoon. It was hard to estimate how fast the Kirsti forces could react, but all of them were surprised that nothing had come up the road after them already.

"It's possible that the High Priest's death has kicked off an outright civil war," O'Casey pointed out. "Unlikely, but possible. In which case the lack of reaction is because everyone is consolidating their positions and they don't have any forces to spare for something as unimportant as chasing *us* down."

"It's more likely that they're simply taking their time," Pahner said. "I'd guess that the raiders really are out of it, though. They probably could've reacted before this, unless there was some specific reason not to. Like, for example, if Sor Teb was in enough trouble to possibly get a personal introduction to the Fire."

"We can always hope," Roger said sourly.

"But hope is all," O'Casey pointed out. "And even if he *is* dead— or, at least, in serious disfavor—*someone* should be chasing after us by now, unless something is distracting them closer to home."

"Don't rely too much on the delay," Pahner cautioned. "I'm sure the Scourge could move quickly enough to have overtaken us by now, but a conventional unit is going to want all its logistics in place before it moves. And speaking of logistics—"

"—we've got too much, for once," Roger finished.

"Not precisely, Your Highness. What we have is too few carts, or too few *turom*, for the stuff we've got. We need to reduce the load. Probably to about half of what we're pulling now."

"If we do t'at we won't have 'nough to make it to t'e port," Poertena pointed out.

"And if we try to drag it all with us, we won't live to get there, anyway," Pahner said. "If we can't trade with the tribes for what we need, we'll never make it through, period. Dump it."

"Aye, aye."

"The Vashin say that there's another forty or fifty kilometers of this," Pahner continued. "They're at the pass, though, or close enough to see it. We need to be to their position by tomorrow evening, or we're going to be in deep trouble."

"Of course, if we can't take the pass after we get there . . ." Roger pointed out.

"Oh, thank you so very much for reminding me of that, Your Highness."

"Good gods," Honal said. "That's not a curtain wall—that's a bloody fortress."

He and Rastar were perched on a ridgeline with a good view of the pass. The opening was narrow, not much more than a wide canyon with nearly vertical sides. A stone wall and gatehouse had been thrown across it, and a series of structures were under construction or complete along the nearer side of the wall. On the southeast side of the pass, a wooden palisade and keep were being converted to stone, and on the western side a bastion was being laid out. The keep had been tied into the curtain wall, and it was apparent that in the long run the Krath intended to fill the pass with fortifications.

"I'm not going to underestimate the humans," Rastar said. "Maybe they can do this. Send a messenger. We're not going to take this place with cavalry."

"We might as well get dug in and get some fires going," Honal commented, looking at the angle of the sun. "It's going to be a long day."

Roger reined in his *civan* and slid to the ground, handing the reins to one of the waiting Vashin. He started to turn away, but he caught Dogzard's warning growl just in time, and backhanded the *civan* as it tried—again—to take a chunk out of his arm.

"It's not time for dinner yet, you beast," he said. "And you'd better be glad, or I'd shoot you and have you spitted."

"They just have to know who the boss is, Your Highness," Honal said with a gesture of humor.

"That's usually not a problem," Roger said. "Where's your position? I take it you're not standing out in the open so they can all watch you checking out their little fort."

"Up on the ridge," Rastar said, gesturing over his shoulder. "We're pretty sure we've been spotted, but we're not making our presence, or numbers, known."

"Have they sent out a patrol?" Roger asked as he started to climb the hill.

"Two of them," Honal said with a grunt of laughter.

"And?"

"We captured both groups," Rastar said. "We're holding them in a side valley. It looks like the garrison is composed almost entirely of lowland peasants, too. They certainly aren't mountain boys, anyway! They didn't even see our ambush until we'd sprung it, and they gave up almost immediately. The second patrol had ten in it, and we took it with only two Vashin."

Roger chuckled as he topped out on the ridgeline and increased the magnification on his helmet visor.

"What's so funny?" Rastar asked.

"What you just said is the punchline to a very old human joke. It's in a lot of cultures, but the punchline is always the same: 'It's a trap! There were two of them!'"

"I'd like to hear it sometime," Honal said. "You humans have good jokes."

"Yes, it's surprising how many points of congruence there are between humans and Mardukans," Roger said. "More than between us and the Phaenurs, that's for sure! Those people are *weird*. Of course, humor is one of the qualities that has the hardest time translating across species lines. That's what I meant about points of congruence."

"We laugh at the same stuff? That's a big thing?" Honal asked.

"Bigger than you can probably guess, yet," Roger assured him as he peered out across the valley. Then he zoomed his helmet back and removed it so he could run his fingers through his hair.

"Not a problem," he announced.

"Really?" Honal grunted a laugh. "If you think *this* isn't a problem, maybe we have fewer 'points of congruence' than you thought!"

"No, I'm serious," Roger assured him with a grin.

"Oh, I don't doubt we can take it," Honal said. "But we're going to lose a lot of people doing it."

"No," Roger said. "Or, rather, we probably would lose them if the garrison knew we were coming. Or where we're coming from."

He regarded the fortress for a few more moments, then shook his head.

"Send a messenger back. Ask Captain Pahner to expedite getting a team from Julian's squad up the road. I've got a little project for them."

Roger wiped his hands as Julian rode into the encampment. The sun was barely down, but the Vashin had already broken up into squads across the ridgeline, lighting fires against the mountain cold and settling in for the night. The cold-blooded Mardukans found it nearly impossible to move when the temperature dropped below what humans considered sweltering. The humans, on the other hand, including the small guard detachment with Roger, thought the nighttime temperatures were balmy.

"Cold enough for you, Julian?" Roger asked, as the Marine climbed off the *civan*. With the sunset, the temperatures had dropped to what could be considered a pleasantly warm fall day in Imperial City.

"Just great, Sir," the sergeant said sourly. "Except for the saddle sores, that is. I can't believe you made us ride these things!"

"I suspect it's just going to get cooler," Roger said, looking to the north. "And as for the saddle sores, I'm afraid I didn't have much choice. We're going to be on a tight timetable, and as the temperature drops, it's going to get even harder to move for the Mardukans."

"On that, I've got a message for you," the squad leader said uncomfortably. "Captain Pahner dropped half the carts and doubled up the *turom* on the rest. So they're moving better."

"Good! Will they be here in time?"

"Probably, but they had some problems. They ran into something like a 'mountain *atul*.' Some of the *turom* panicked, and one of the carts ran back over . . . Despreaux."

"What?!"

"She's fine! Just a broken arm," Julian said, raising a hand as Roger shot to his feet and turned towards the picketed *civan*. "And the captain asked me to point out that you've got a job here."

"Yes, but—" Roger began in a semi-frantic tone.

"And Despreaux said for me to tell you that if you come rushing back to see 'your poor hurt girlfriend' *you'll* have a broken arm, too."

"Yes, but—"

"And you called me all the way up this frigging road on one of those ass-busting *civan*," Julian finished. "So you can damned well tell me why, Sir."

Roger thought about that for several moments, then drew a deep breath and turned back around.

"Ah, hell," he sighed.

"Let's just get on with the job, Sir." Julian patted him on the shoulder. "Life's a bitch, and then you die. Right?"

"Right." Roger sighed again, then gestured into the darkness. "All right, then. I've got a job for you. And, I have to admit, not one that could wait while I went back to check on Nimashet. Take a look at the target."

They walked to the crest of the ridge, and Julian jacked up his helmet's light-gathering and zoom.

"Big pocker," he remarked, gazing at the wall. "Any idea on the garrison?"

"About two hundred," Roger said calmly.

"Be a bitch to take by frontal assault, even against swords and arquebuses," Julian observed. He looked up both flanking ridges, and grimaced. "Are you thinking what I think you're thinking?"

"You and Gronningen are our high-country experts," Roger said, with a smile in his voice.

"Sure," the sergeant grumped. He didn't mention that that position had previously been occupied by Dokkum. The native of the planet Nepal had been an expert at everything involving "elevation." Unfortunately, "had been" was the operative term. He'd died just before Ran Tai.

"This isn't going to be a short movement," the NCO went on after a moment. The carpeting Mardukan jungle had given way to a more open, deciduous forest, but even that stopped well short of the tops of the ridges. There was a faint track, a trail left by the local equivalent of goats, along the ridgeline, but getting to it would be difficult. The ridge was at least five hundred meters above their present position, and those meters were damned near vertical.

"We'll get the Vashin moving by just before dawn, one way or the other," Roger said. "I need you in position by then."

The Mardukan night was eighteen hours long, which would give the squad at least fifteen hours to effect the move. Julian thought about it for a few seconds, then nodded.

"Can do, Boss." He shook his head in mock sorrow. "I need to get less competent, or something."

Roger chuckled and clapped him on the back.

"Just imagine the stories you'll be able to tell in the NCO club. You'll never have to buy a beer again."

Julian looked back up at the trackless mountain and nodded.

"Now there's a motivator. Free beer. Free beer. I'll just keep repeating that."

CHAPTER TWENTY-ONE

Macek spat over the edge of the ridge and shook his head.

"You look into the abyss, and the abyss looks back," he muttered.

"Less philosophy, more climb," Gronningen growled back from where he'd paused on a wide spot at the base of the second peak.

The squad was strung out along a knife-edged ridge, the top of the saddle between two mountains. The "flat" surface was no more than a meter wide, with sheer drops on both sides. And the assault team would have to cross a nearly vertical shoulder of the second peak to get into position above the citadel.

"There was a shelf," Julian said, puffing slightly. The ridge was nearly five thousand meters above Mardukan sea level, which meant that even with the slightly thicker atmosphere, oxygen was in short supply. More than that, Julian had let Gronningen set the pace, knowing the indomitable Asgardian would push them to the limits . . . and he had. "About another hundred meters up and to the northwest," the NCO added with another pant.

"I think I see it," Gronningen agreed. He dialed up the zoom on his helmet and studied the terrain feature. "Narrow," he opined, then removed his helmet and wiped at the sweat on his forehead. The night had gotten downright cool, and there was a strong wind blowing up from the valley, but the pace had everyone sweating as if they were still in Marduk's jungles. "Really narrow."

"Best His Nibs could spot before sundown," Julian replied, checking his toot for the time. "Four more hours until we need to be on the walls."

"We can make that easily," Gronningen said, replacing his helmet and picking up his pack. "If we keep going, that is."

"Lead on, Mule," Julian said. "Onward and upward."

Julian leaned out from the narrow ledge and sent a laser sweep across the top of the fortress far below.

"Two thousand meters."

"Right at The Book's outside drop limit," Macek said with a dubious headshake. "Long way to fall."

"It is that," Julian agreed unhappily.

The ledge was, indeed, narrow—a thin shelf of slightly harder granite intruded into the surrounding matrix. Some latter-day earth movement had shifted and folded the mountain, thrusting the horizontal dike outwards, exposing it to erosion. Over time, the remnants had become a half-meter wide section of granite, suspended over a two thousand-meter drop.

"It's the only choice we have, though," the squad leader added. "I want everyone to spread out. It looks like we're right over the inner battlements. Watch your distribution, and for God's sake, don't get entangled—this damned spider-wire'll slit you in half if you give it a chance."

"Yeah, but it works," Gronningen said as he surreptitiously attached a clip to the sergeant's descent harness. The combination of his voice and the night wind concealed the tiny sound it made as it clicked home . . . and then he pushed Julian off the cliff.

There wasn't a thing Julian could do—the blow to his back was too unexpected. He was thrown well out from the cliff, and found himself almost automatically shifting into a delta-track, a sky-diving position for maneuvering. His brain ran frantically through a list of ways to survive the drop, but nothing came to mind, nor could he understand why one of his best friends had just succeeded in killing him.

★ ★ ★

Macek spun in place, his bead rifle level, but Gronningen held up one hand with a screaming spider reel in it. It was obvious that the other end of the wire was attached to Julian.

"What the pock are you *doing*, Gron?" the corporal snarled. "You've got about two seconds to explain!"

"Just this," Gronningen said, with a rare smile. He attached the reel to the wall with a mag-clamp and laid on the tension. "I mean, now we know it works, right?"

Julian gazed down at the battlements, a hundred meters below him. He'd been observing them fairly carefully for the last several minutes, since the spider-line had slowed him to a halt. There wasn't much else he could do; the line had him suspended almost head-down.

He heard a faint rattle of rock, and then Gronningen appeared next to him, fully inverted.

"Gronningen, what are you dicking around at?" Julian asked with deadly menace.

"'I love you, too, man,'" the Asgardian quoted. "You remember in Voitan, I said 'You gonna pay'?"

"Oh, you son-of-a—"

"Ah-ah!" The Asgardian grinned. "I pull this clamp, and it's really gonna smart when you hit the top of that thing."

"Oh, you son-of-a . . ." Julian stopped and sighed. "Okay. You got me. Jesus, did you get me. I promise, no more jokes. Just . . . don't do something like that again, okay?"

"You should have seen Geno," Gronningen said with another grin, as he handed a fresh spider-spool across to the squad leader. "I think he nearly burst a blood vessel."

"Well, I'm proof positive that you don't die of fright on the way down," Julian said. "Jesus. This isn't a truce, though. I'm gonna get you. Just you wait."

"I tingle with anticipation," the Asgardian told him with a chuckle. "You got a good grip on that reel?"

"Yeah. Why?"

"Good," Gronningen said, and flicked off the clamp that was holding the sergeant suspended.

Julian tried not to scream as he dropped into empty air again.

Macek looked around the top of the battlements with an expression of disbelief. Except for the eternal sighing of the wind, there wasn't a sound to be heard, and there was no one in sight.

"Okay, I'll bite," he whispered. "Where's the guards?"

"I don't know," Julian said. "Not here."

The top of the gatehouse was about thirty meters across, with a trap door at either end. The gate filled the pass from side to side. On the southeast side, a narrower walkway led to the top of the secondary keep, apparently a barracks or headquarters. Gronningen walked back from there, shaking his head, while Macek grimaced.

"Don't tell me they don't post sentries," he said. "That's . . . insane."

"It's freezing," Julian pointed out. "I mean, it's only about ten degrees out here. If they were out in this, they'd be catatonic, maybe dead."

Gronningen consulted his toot, then nodded with a remote expression.

"Fifty or so, Fahrenheit, yes?" he said. "Not cold, but brisk."

"More than just brisk for scummies, man," Julian said.

"So they just don't guard at all?" Macek asked. "Still not too smart."

"They're used to fighting Shin," the squad leader replied, "and I don't think they can move in this, either. Look at the Vashin. They're all huddled around fires being torpid. This kind of cold can *kill* Mardukans."

"So they're all inside waiting to hit us on the heads as soon as we stick 'em in there?" Macek asked. "It's a clever plot to lure us to our deaths?"

"No, that was the recruiter who got us to join the Marines," Gronningen said. He walked over to the nearer trap door and pulled at the handle. The door was outsized, designed for Mardukans, and Gronningen was probably the only man in the company who could have lifted it. It didn't even quiver, though, and he knelt down to examine it more closely. Light seeped up around the edges, and he grunted as he found the darker shadow where a latching bar cut across the light.

"Not a problem," Julian said, kneeling beside him. The sergeant slipped a device from his belt and slid the incredibly sharp, flexible ribbon-blade into the crack. It sliced through the half-meter ironwood bar as if it hadn't even been there.

Gronningen was ready, and air hissed in his nostrils as he heaved upward. The door rose a few centimeters, and Julian got under it and threw his own weight against it. Between them, they raised it shoulder high, and Macek propped it up with a piece of wood.

There was no ladder, but it was a simple enough proposition—after climbing the mountain—to lower themselves into the room below. The chamber was about fifteen meters on a side, with a high, domed ceiling, and a stairway in the west corner. It, too, was deserted, with a dead coal fire in a hibachilike affair in the middle of the room.

"That's a quick way to asphyxiate," Macek observed in a whisper.

"Out?" Gronningen murmured, pointing to a door on the east side. "Or down?"

"Down," Julian whispered back promptly, although his expression was puzzled.

The spiral stairs led to a passageway—high for the humans, but low and narrow for Mardukans—that went both right and left, towards the gates and the barracks, respectively.

"Right," Julian said, and led the way.

The passageway turned, apparently following the shoulder of the hill, and opened onto a large room with barred windows through which a cold wind blew. The room was at the base of the gates, and stairs disappeared upward into the gloom where the gate controls were presumably located.

Other than some litter in one corner, the room was empty.

"This is getting silly." This time, Macek didn't bother to whisper.

"We'll try the barracks," Julian said. "There has to be *somebody* around here."

They followed the same passage back in the opposite direction, towards the barracks. They had to deal with two more barred doors along the way, but finally they entered the main hall of the keep. It was a vaulted monstrosity, with a huge fire pit in the middle and the ubiquitous cushions that served Mardukans for chairs scattered around the pit.

No one was using any of the cushions, however. Instead, the middle of the pit was filled by a group of Mardukans, arranged in a fairly neat pile. Half-burned logs and ash had been dragged out of the center and pushed to the side. Obviously, the Mardukans had set a fire in the pit during the day so that they could sleep on the warmed rock underneath at night.

And every one of them was in the semi-hibernation torpidity that extreme cold induced in their species.

"Oh, puhleeease!" Macek exclaimed in disgust. "This is *it*? I rode all the way up here, played mountain goat, and then jumped off a damned cliff for *this*?"

"I think these guys must've taken the short airbus to school," Julian said. "The Vashin at least try to keep *one* guy per squad awake. This is idiotic. Geno, get up to the roof and signal the prince. Tell him we've taken the 'fortress.'"

"Will do," Macek said with a sigh. "But this really bites."

"What? You wanted a fight?" Gronningen asked, looking at the heaped Mardukans. The entire garrison's weapons were stacked neatly along one wall, and all of their armor was laid out in ranks. Obviously, they were ready to get up in a few hours, when things warmed up, and start banging horn with the best of them. "*I* think this is great," the Asgardian announced.

"Whatever," Macek grumped. "It just offends my sense of professionalism."

"And Gomer here pushing me off the cliff didn't?" Julian asked.

"Nah," the corporal replied with a grin. "In fact, that was about the most professional payback I've ever seen!"

The column rounded the last corner of the interminable track just after dawn. It had started to rain again, but with the increased elevation, it was a cold, miserable rain that ate into the Marines' uniforms like acid. The chameleon uniform was, technically, all-environment—capable of handling anything from jungle to arctic.

But the Marines had been slogging across a hostile world for nearly six months, and it showed.

The uniforms were a tattered patchwork of different cloths. There were whole sleeves and legs of *dianda*—the silklike flax of distant Marshad—as mute testimony to the terrible battle at Voitan. The *dianda,* in turn, was patched with the fine sedgelike cloth of K'Vaern's Cove and Diaspra. All of the patches were of faded dark cloth, which had the virtue of low visibility but blended poorly with the changeable chameleon cloth.

The Marines looked as faded as their uniforms. Their faces were drawn and pale, from the ascent into the mountains, from the cold, from the ongoing low-level vitamin deficiencies of their *coll*-oil supplements substitute, and from the omnipresence of war. All in all, Roger thought, the company looked on its last legs.

He walked to the front of the column and waved an ironic salute at Captain Pahner.

"I make you a gift of the Fortress of Shesul Pass, with fifty *turom*, one hundred and twenty rather questionable soldiers, and a rich booty of small arms," he announced, and Pahner chuckled.

"I think you're getting too into this, Your Highness."

"Just trying to make like a Roman, Captain," Roger replied with a grin. "Seriously, we should probably rest up for a day or two before we move on."

"We can't discount pursuit," Pahner pointed out.

"No," the prince agreed. "But when you get a good look at this place, I think you'll agree we can also leave a nonexpendable rearguard to hold any pursuit off." He waved to O'Casey as she joined them.

"Ms. O'Casey." He greeted her with a nod. "The mountain air appears to agree with you," he said, and it was true. In many ways, the academic looked better than the Marines about her.

"That's a long walk to force on an old woman," his chief of staff replied.

"Well, the captain has almost convinced me to let you take a break," Roger joked. "The Krath must've had plans for this pass; the facility's area is far larger than necessary for the garrison. There are sufficient quarters to house all of us in relative comfort, although they don't appear to have discovered the chimney, so the fires fill the rooms with smoke."

"If you don't mind, Captain," Doc Dobrescu said, dropping down from one of the passing carts, "I have to agree. We've got a lot of wounded and injured, and these carts are pure hell on them. Give them a couple of days under a roof and warm, and they'll be able to heal much faster."

"All right," Pahner said. "We'll stay. Two days. Your Highness, I assume the Vashin are down from the cold as well?"

"They're not doing well," Roger agreed. "Actually, they're more used to it than I expected, probably from being from the northern plains, but the most they can do is to maintain sentries."

"We'll let them rest as well," Pahner decided. "We should be able to go down to about ten percent security. I'd really prefer to put out a sentry group down the valley, but we'll settle for putting them up on the walls. Sergeant Major!"

"Yes, Sir," Kosutic replied. The carts had reached the open bailey of the fortress and were now stopped in a line. Roger noticed that most of them were being driven by Marines, and the handful of native teamsters driving the rest had small charcoal braziers burning under their seats.

"We're stopping here for a day or two," Pahner told Kosutic. "Leave the carts mostly packed; there should be stores in the castle, and we'll live off of them. Ten percent security, Marines only. Get everybody bunked down and working on gear."

"Yes, Sir," Kosutic repeated, making no effort to conceal her obvious relief. The sergeant major was like iron, but she knew when a unit was on its last legs. Now she looked up and shook her head.

"Speak of the devil," she said, and grinned as Julian walked towards the command group. But the intelligence sergeant didn't grin back, and her own smile faded as she absorbed his expression.

"Sirs," he said, nodding at the officers, then held up a small device. "I found this in the commander's quarters."

Pahner accepted it, turned it over in his hands, and frowned at the maker's mark.

"A Zuiko tri-cam?" he mused.

"I think they must have been in contact with the port," Julian said darkly. "We may have a real problem, Sir."

"Maybe," Roger said. "And maybe not. We need to find out where it came from. Get some of the locals functional and find out."

"Yes, Sir," the sergeant said. He turned towards the fortress' main entrance, then stopped. "Or, maybe not."

One of Rastar's Vashin was walking slowly towards them, trailing a plume of smoke. One of the ways the cavalry coped with the cold was by toting small braziers of charcoal around with them like incense censors.

"Captain Pahner," the cavalryman said slowly when he finally reached the group, and saluted. "Marine. Gronningen. Has. Found. A human." The sentence seemed to have taken everything he had, and he dropped his salute and stood like a statue.

"We have *got* to get lower. Soon," Kosutic said to fill the gap in the conversation.

They'd all known that this moment would come, but this was the first "new" human they'd had contact with since crashing on the planet. And while the Mardukans *might* have stopped them from getting off-planet at any time, the humans *could* stop them if they realized what they faced. How to handle the local humans had been considered and debated at vast and exhausting length, but it had been impossible to make any clear plans without more information than they had. Now the moment of reckoning was upon them.

"Well, I guess we'd better go meet him," Pahner said finally.

Harvard Mansul wished he had his camera. Of course, he might as well have wished he were back at Society headquarters on Old Earth, while he was at it. As a matter of fact, he *did* wish that, too, but he was a realist. He would have settled for getting the tri-cam back intact. The Zuiko was tough—it had to be, to survive around him—but it wasn't invulnerable, and sooner or later they would open it up to find out how it worked.

At which point, it would stop. Working, that was.

When he wasn't worrying about his tri-cam, he passed the time in his rather dank cell by wondering how long it would take the Society to mount a rescue. If they ever bothered. He'd reached the point of regretting his habit of disappearing for years at a time. Considering his stint on Scheherazade, the Society might not start looking for *decades*.

He sighed and banged on the door again. Usually the horned-ones roused before now, and he looked forward to the morning exercise time. But so far, there'd been virtually no sound filtering down to his little stone cube today.

"Hellooo! It's *morning*! Would you kind gentlemen mind letting me out?"

"I felt it was best to let you handle it, Sir," the private said. "I didn't know how you wanted to play it, or even if you wanted him to know we were here, so I sent one of the Vashin down to check on him. He's been . . . kind of loud."

"Okay, come on," Roger said. "Let's find out what they caught."

"I wonder if they were keeping him tucked away in the larder for munchies later?" Kosutic mused.

"I doubt it," O'Casey said. "I haven't seen a trace of any religious items here in the fortress. I think they probably just picked him up somewhere and stashed him until they were told what to do with him."

"Given our own experience, I can guess what that would have been," Roger snorted, leading the way down the flight of stone steps and along the narrow—for a Mardukan—passageway. They reached the cell door, and he threw back the bolt and pulled it open.

"And who might you be, Sir?" he asked cheerfully.

Mansul looked up at the human confronting him and frowned in puzzlement. Judging by the remains of the uniform, the person was an Imperial Marine. Given the rest of his appearance, he was probably also a deserter, because no Marine of Mansul's acquaintance who *wasn't* a deserter would ever have allowed his uniform to get into such a state.

The man in the cell door was not just a full head taller than

Mansul. He was also either very clean-shaven, or had almost no facial hair. Good bone structure, a hint of pre-Diaspora Asian around the eyes, but otherwise very classically Northern European. Great hair falling in a golden mass, too. He'd make a wonderful picture all around, the photographer decided. Then there was the odd rifle—chemical propellant, by the look of it—and the long sword tossed over his back. Quite the neobarb. Absolutely perfect. Even the lighting was good.

It really made him wish those horned barbarians hadn't taken his camera.

Mansul took another look, and it was actually the family resemblance that caught him first. One of his last assignments before Marduk had been to cover the Imperial Family when Her Majesty had celebrated the Heir's birthday. Mansul couldn't remember having seen a shaggy, broad-shouldered, sword-toting barbarian standing around to help cut the cake or pour the punch, yet the young man before him had the distinctive MacClintock brow. So who—?

"Good God!" he heard himself exclaim. "I thought you were *dead*!"

Roger couldn't help himself. The astonishment in the prisoner's expression and voice was simply too great, and a trace of his own recent classical reading came to mind. Despite the response he *knew* it would elicit from O'Casey, he simply couldn't resist.

"I am happy to say that the news of my demise was exceedingly exaggerated." He waited for the groans to stop behind him, then held out his hand. "I'm His Highness Prince Roger Ramius Alexander Chiang MacClintock. And you are?"

"Harvard Mansul," the man replied in a voice which was still half stunned. "Imperial Astrographic Society. You've been *here* the whole time?"

"I've been on Marduk, yes," Roger said. "The rest is a somewhat long story. And I believe we've gotten hold of some of your property." He held out a hand to Pahner for the tri-cam, then passed it over.

Mansul gave the item for which he had so passionately longed for more than a week barely a glance, then flicked the lenses open.

"Smile."

Roger knocked on the door, waited for the quiet voice from the other side to respond, then opened it, looked around, and grinned.

"Private room, I see," he observed. "Very nice."

"Quite the little love nest," Despreaux replied. She was propped up on a pile of cushions on the floor, her arm immobilized in the force-cast. Her face was slightly gray, she was still covered in mud from the trek, and bits of leaf and dirt were caught in her hair and on her pants. Any other woman would've looked like hell, Roger thought, but Nimashet Despreaux managed to come across like a tridee star made up to look like a maiden in distress.

"I'm really upset with you," Roger said, sitting down and taking her good hand. "You're supposed to take care of yourself better than this."

"I tried," she said, and leaned against him. "God, I'm tired of this."

"Me, too," Roger said as he wrapped an arm carefully around her.

"Liar. You're dreading getting back to court, aren't you?"

Roger paused for a moment, then shrugged.

"Yes," he admitted. "Marduk is . . . uncomplicated. We make friends, or we don't. We negotiate, or we kick ass. It's black and white, most of the time. Court is . . . all negotiation. It's all gray. It's all who you pissed off last, and people jockeying for position. There's nobody to . . ."

"To watch your back?" she finished for him, leaning into him. "I will."

"You've never had to deal with the court ladies as a 'person,'" he replied. "You were just a Marine; you didn't count." He shook his head, eyes troubled. "It'll be different now, and their knives go right through armor."

"So do mine, love," she said, twisting carefully around until she could look him in the eye. "And, Roger, the Marines see *everything*, they *hear* everything. And you're going to be supported in a way that I doubt even another MacClintock ever was. *We're* going to be at your back."

He picked a bit of leaf gently out of her hair.

"I love you," he said.

"I look like hell," she snorted. "You're just trying to make me feel better."

"You look great," he said huskily. "Absolutely beautiful."

She looked at him for a moment, then pulled his head down to hers. The kiss lasted a long time, while Roger ran his fingers up and down her back. But finally she drew back with a snort.

"So that's it," she said. "You just like me when I'm immobilized!"

"I *always* like you. I was in love the first time I saw you out of armor, although I'll admit I was a bit . . ."

"Intimidated?" Despreaux supplied.

"Yes," he admitted. "Intimidated is probably the right word. You're a bit overpowering, and I really didn't want to get into a relationship. But . . . you're as good as it gets."

"Your mother is going to go spastic," Despreaux said. "I mean, completely ballistic."

"I don't really care about Mother's reaction," he replied. "Frankly, after what we've gone through, Mother is going to owe me, big time. And it's not as if I were the heir, so I'm not exactly a great dynastic match. Mother can kiss my ass before I'll give you up."

"I love it when you talk dirty," she said, and pulled him down for another kiss.

Roger ran his hands up her sides, leaving a trail of goosebumps in their wake. After a moment, the hands migrated around to the front, as if by their own accord, and ran across her midriff in subtle fingertip touches. She writhed to the side, pushing up her T-shirt, and—

There was a discreet knock on the door.

"*Shit*," Roger muttered with intense feeling. Then he sighed, sat up, and raised his voice. "Yes?"

"Your Highness," Corporal Bebi said from the far side of the door, "Captain Pahner wants a command conference in seven minutes in the fortress commander's office. Sergeant Despreaux is excused on account of her injury."

Roger didn't have to see the private's face. His tone alone made it eloquently clear that butter would never melt in his mouth.

"I told you the Marines know everything," Despreaux whispered, pulling her top down with a moue of disappointment.

"*Seven* minutes?" Roger asked.

"It . . . took a few minutes to find you, Your Highness," Bebi explained, and Despreaux took the opportunity to run her hands up Roger's back.

"I'll—" Roger cleared his throat. "I'll be right there."

"Yes, Your Highness."

"Two minutes to run from here to the commander's office," Despreaux said. "Now, where were we?"

"If I turn up out of breath and rearranging my clothes, everyone will know where I was," Roger said.

"Rogerrr," Despreaux said dangerously.

"On the other hand," he said, leaning back down towards her, "they can kiss my ass, too."

She smiled in delight as he ran his hands up her back once more. He leaned even closer, her lips parted, and—

There was a discreet knock on the door.

"Bloody . . . *what?*"

"Your Highness," Dobrescu said diplomatically, "I know you have a conference in a minute, but I'd like to talk to you about Cord."

Roger shoved himself to his feet, shaking his head and breathing heavily, as Despreaux rearranged her clothes again.

"Come!" the Heir Tertiary to the Throne of Man said grimly.

"What now?" Sergeant Despreaux whispered.

Most of the supplies the Krath had laid in were stored in boxes of boiled *turom* leather. At first, going over the collection in the citadel's storerooms had been a bit like a very leathery Christmas. But after a few hours of opening boxes and cataloging contents, Poertena and Denat were getting worn out.

"Dried and salted fish." Denat slammed the top of the box closed and resealed it. "More damned dried and salted fish! I'm surprised these Krath didn't grow gills."

"T'ey needed to grow some damned brains," Poertena said. The company was still chuckling about Julian's find. "You scummies are frigging weird when it gets cold."

"Well, at least we don't go around bitching about a decently warm day," Denat snapped back. "How many times have I seen one of you Marines writhing on the ground over a little heat?!"

"Hey, I t'ink t'at was Pentzikis, and heatstroke's no joke!" Poertena protested. "I was only kidding! Get a pocking grip—we're almost done here."

"Well, pock you, you shrimp!" the Mardukan snarled. "I'm done. *You* finish. If you can even lift the boxes!"

"Denat, what's eating you?" Poertena asked, and there was genuine alarm in his tone. The Mardukan was trembling, as if he were having a fit. "We can quit t'is if we need to. You don' look so good."

"I'm *fine!*" Denat bellowed. He grasped his horns and yanked furiously at them. "I'm *fine*. I'll . . . *aaaarh!*"

Poertena thought very hard about keeping his mouth shut, but he'd just noticed something, and it was really bothering him.

"Uh, Denat?" the armor asked carefully. "Did you know t'at t'e bases of your horns were swelling?"

Roger smiled and accepted the candied apsimon from O'Casey. "Ah, for the days of kate fruit!" he sighed.

The main command group had gathered, and he turned to the newest member of their party.

"So, Harvard. What in hell are you doing here?"

The IAS journalist set down his *basik* leg and wiped his hands fastidiously.

"It was a routine assignment, Your Highness. Not much has been done on Marduk, since there's not a regular passenger line that stops here. There was an IAS piece back in your grandfather's time, when they were first planning on opening the planet to colonization, but since then, nothing. And that piece just covered the Krath capital. At the time, the Shin were more or less at peace with the Krath, and a sidebar about the Shin in the article caught my editor's eye. He sent me out to get a story about the 'mountain tribes.'"

He took a sip of wine and shook his head.

"I knew as soon as I landed that things had changed. The only information on the planet available was the earlier IAS article and two studies of Mardukan sociology and planetography. They didn't say much, but there were obvious sociological changes in the Krath capital. Among other things, when I tried to get updated photos of their religious celebrations, I was barred from their temples."

"Updated?" O'Casey asked. "The previous IAS team had gotten pictures? And *included* them in its article?"

"Yes, the Krath were very open about their ceremonies," Mansul said. "It was a highly ascetic religion, similar in some ways to Buddhism, stressing personal restraint and meditation. The ceremonies involved small sacrifices of grain and meat to the God of Fire. Most of the contributions actually went to the priests, who were also the primary researchers and archivists, to pay for their upkeep. I don't know what they're doing now, but the rate of sacrifices has certainly gone up, if the smoke from the fires is any indication."

"You might say there have been a few . . . liturgical changes," Roger said darkly. "I wonder what bright person introduced them to the concept of human sacrifice?"

Mansul choked on his wine.

"Human sacrifice?"

"Well, Mardukan, mostly," Roger said. "Cannibalism, too." He took another bite of apsimon and grimaced at the taste.

"I take it you find their transition . . . unusual?" O'Casey asked Mansul.

"To put it mildly." The IAS photographer wiped daintily at the spilled wine. "All of the source material on the Krath religion insists that it's an ascetic faith, similar in some respects to Taoism in ancient China. Or, at least, that was the case when the original IAS team came through. Its sacrificial aspects were personal: meditation, and acts of generosity. They didn't even sacrifice *turom!*"

"Well, they sacrifice their slaves, now," the chief of staff said flatly. "And then they eat them. We saw the inside of the temples. And the kitchens and the bone pits."

"Are all the slaves from the Shin?" the journalist asked.

"I don't know," O'Casey admitted, "and our local Shin guide seems to be missing."

"She's tending to Cord," Roger said. He glanced at Mansul. "It's a long story."

"I like long stories," Mansul admitted. "Once they're boiled down, they make excellent articles. Why don't you tell it to me?"

"Where to start?" Roger asked.

"Start at the beginning," Pahner advised. "Go to the end—"

"—and fill in all the stuff in the middle." Roger nodded. "Okay."

"But maybe later," the Marine added. "We need to determine what happens next. Mr. Mansul, you came from the port?"

"Yes, and there are problems there, too."

"Saints," Roger said.

"Really? That I hadn't noticed. What I did notice was that the governor did *not* want any humans drifting out of the compound. He hadn't been apprised of my visit, and he acted like I was an Imperial spy. Frankly, I was starting to wonder if I was going to be an 'accidental death' when one of the locals offered to smuggle me out. I fell in with the Shin, and I was with a village south of Mudh Hemh when a Krath raiding party fell on the group I was filming. They took the Shin with them to Kirsti, but left me here, presumably for repatriation. Or maybe to wait for the governor to recover me. And then you happened along."

"How were you 'smuggled out'?" Pahner asked.

"There are breaks in the defenses," Mansul replied. "Contraband moves in and out." He shrugged. "I was just one more package."

"Now that's interesting," Roger said.

"Isn't it, just?" the captain agreed.

"Oh, there's more," Mansul said. "There's a small . . . colony, might be the right word . . . of humans living among the Shin. Others who have run afoul of the governor's bully boys. There's about fifteen or twenty of them, and supplies are funneled to them from somewhere."

"From where?" Julian asked.

"That I don't know, although I think the local chieftain does. These people aren't given to charity. He'd only be supporting the refugees if there was a reason."

"Satan," Kosutic sighed. "Complicateder and complicateder."

"Yeah," Roger said. "And no. The basics are the same, maybe even easier, if their security is so lax smugglers can move in and out at will. We need to get to Mudh Hemh and make contact with this Shin leader."

"Pedi Gastan," Mansul inserted.

"Pedi Gastan?" Pahner repeated sharply.

"Why, yes." Mansul looked surprised. "You've heard of him?"

"You might say that." Roger's expression was a cross between a grimace and a smile. "Truth being stranger than fiction, we rescued his daughter from pirates." Mansul blinked, and the prince chuckled. "But what I don't quite understand," he went on, "is why we didn't hear anything about this 'colony' of humans from *her*." He gazed at the photographer with just an edge of suspicion. "She's been very open with us, as far as we can tell, and she's never even *heard* of humans, much less anything about any refugees her father might be shielding."

"I don't know why she wouldn't have," Mansul said slowly. "I only met the Gastan briefly, and my understanding is that the refugees' existence is kept very secret. In fact, none of us are allowed in Mudh Hemh at all. Instead, he keeps the 'colony' hidden away in one of the really remote vales under the eye of a very small clan. I was on my way there when my escorts and I ran into the Krath. I suppose it's possible that even his daughter might not know what he was up to."

"I guess *anything* is possible," Roger allowed slowly. Then he snorted. "Of course, some things are more possible than others, and keeping a secret from Pedi strikes me as one of life's more difficult endeavors!"

"But it *is* possible," O'Casey said. "And if the Krath are in contact with the port, and if the Gastan knows it, then he'd have every imaginable reason to keep the Krath from finding out that *he* was, too."

"But could he really keep it so secret that Pedi hadn't even heard about humans at all?" Roger asked a bit skeptically.

"Probably he could," O'Casey replied. "Don't forget that this is a pre-technic society, Roger. I know there's a trading interface between the Krath and the Shin, but every bit of information has to be passed by word-of-mouth, and I doubt very much the there's anything like a true information flow between the Shin and the people who keep slaughtering them as religious sacrifices. So even if the Krath know about the human presence here on Marduk, they probably don't discuss it with the Shin. Anyway, it's obvious from the way most of the Kirsti population have reacted to us that the existence of humans isn't general knowledge even among them."

She shook her head.

"I'd say that it's entirely possible that the very existence of humans is restricted to the uppermost levels of Krath society this far from the port itself. In which case, it's probably entirely possible that the Gastan could keep the secret even from his own people. Of course," she frowned thoughtfully, "I'd *love* to know how this human managed to contact him in the first place."

"You may have a point," Roger conceded, and nodded to Mansul. "You were saying before we interrupted?" he invited.

"Well, if you've rescued the Gastan's daughter, that should work out well," the reporter said, trying not to show his relief as the hard light of suspicion dimmed just a bit in the prince's dangerous green eyes. "I think he's on our side, anyway, but—"

There was a knock at the door, and then Poertena stuck his head in without waiting for permission.

"Beggin' you pardon, You Highness, but I need Doc Dobrescu right pocking now! Somet'ing's wrong with Denat. I t'ink he going nuts!"

"Go," Pahner and Roger said simultaneously. Then they looked at each other for a moment before Roger gestured at Pahner.

"I think we're about done here," the captain continued smoothly. "Doc, you go. Julian, wring everything you can out of the prisoners about the rest of the route to the Shin lands. Sergeant Major, everyone else is on full rest and refit. I want us to be in good condition when we leave. Let's get to it."

"And I'll go find out what's wrong with Denat," Dobrescu said.

"Any ideas?" Roger asked.

"I haven't even looked at him yet, Your Highness," the medic protested. "And I'm a shuttle pilot, not a psychologist. I'll keep you posted, though."

Warrant Dobrescu followed Poertena into the small supply office that the Pinopan and Denat had taken over and shook his head at the Mardukan.

"What have you been sniffing, Denat?"

"I'm fine," the Mardukan said. He was shivering, his body sliming heavily, and a reddish bulge had appeared around the base of each of his horns. "I'm sorry I snapped at you, Poertena. But I'll be fine. This will pass."

"What is it?" Dobrescu asked, setting down and laying out his med-scanner. The scanner could pick up a lot even from a distance, and it showed Denat's heart and metabolic rate off the scale. The Mardukan was actually at an elevated temperature compared to ambient, which was very unusual. "Poertena said you'd been grouchy lately, and he told me about what just happened. I need to know what's going on."

"It's . . . a Mardukan thing," Denat said. A shudder ran through his massive body.

"I kind of need to know a little more than that," the medic persisted. "I have to tell Captain Pahner something. That's a human thing."

"It's nothing!" Denat shouted, banging all four fists on the massive, ironwood desk so furiously that the eight-hundred-kilo piece of furniture leapt into the air.

"Denat, according to my instruments, you're coming apart at the seams," Dobrescu said mildly. "Why not tell me what's wrong?"

"Because nothing's *wrong*," the Mardukan ground out. "This is perfectly *normal*."

"Then what is it?" the warrant officer asked reasonably.

Denat looked at him, rubbing his hands together in distress. Then he sighed, and told him.

Pedi removed the rags from around the injury and dropped them into the solution the healer had given her, then reached for fresh dressings. She and the two other released slaves had been caring for Cord ever since the injury. The wound itself was mostly healed, but he still wouldn't awaken, and he was getting even more restless and warmer. Lately, though, she'd at least been able to get him to take a little food, and he'd been muttering under his breath. She'd picked up a few words of his home language before he was wounded, but not enough to recognize much of what he was saying, although the word "*banan*" was close to "*benan*," so perhaps he was talking to her.

She opened a jar of lotion and began smoothing it on the dry patches in his skin. She'd picked up some of his background, more from talking to the humans and Denat than from him, and she realized what a valued person he must have been in his home country. To come to such knowledge as he had developed was hard for the sort of backcountry village from which he'd sprung, and men—warriors especially—who gathered that much training and understanding were extremely valuable to any tribe. She suspected that the human prince, surrounded as he was by a plethora of warriors and scholars, didn't know what a wrench it must have been for both Cord and his people to lose him.

And she had to admit that it would be a wrench for the human to lose him. And for her. The old shaman was one of the finest men she'd ever met; strong, yet gentle and wise. Knowledgeable, but physically brave, and often humble to a fault. It was hard to find such qualities anywhere, and she had to admit that they were even harder to find amongst the Shin than most places.

Because the medic didn't know if the increased body heat might cause mental damage—surely a horrible thought!—they had been wrapping the shaman's head in cool cloths. She started to replace the current cloths, then stopped with a gasp.

She laid her hands on the swellings at the base of the shaman's horns and felt a shudder pass through her body. She had to fight conflicting emotions, but finally she drew a deep breath, pulled back the light sheet that covered him, and took a peek before she quickly dropped it back again.

She sat back, thinking hard, and many things fell abruptly into place. She remembered what Light O'Casey had said about the language similarity, and she thought about the ramifications of the situation. She thought about them very carefully, and then, last of all, she thought of the sight of Cord coming over the railing of the pirate ship.

"Oh, Pedi, this is *such* a bad idea," she whispered as she pulled the sheet all the way back.

"What we have here is a failure to communicate," Dobrescu said with a chuckle.

He'd asked Captain Pahner, the sergeant major, and the prince to meet him in the stores office. They had—and they'd also reacted predictably to the sight of Denat's trembling body and bulging forehead.

"What the hell does that mean?" Roger demanded. "Denat, are you okay?"

"Aside from wanting to kill you, I'm fine," the Mardukan grated. "And that has nothing to do with your being a prince. You just spoke to me, is all."

"Is it a good idea to do this here?" Pahner asked.

"He should be fine," Dobrescu said soothingly. "And we'll leave in just a second. But the actual problem is fairly simple: he's in heat."

"In what?" Kosutic asked. "That's a . . . Oh, yeah."

"That's right. Mardukan 'males' are functionally and technically females, by our standards," Dobrescu said. "And vice versa. Denat's sex produces the eggs, the other sex produces the sperm. When the time comes, and the two, ahem, 'get together,' Denat's sex use their . . . notable organs to implant their eggs in the other sex.

"He's currently ovulating. Which means, evolutionarily speaking, that he should be battling other 'males' for a chance to mate. Thus the horn prominences and other signs. Unfortunately . . ."

"I have no mate here," Denat growled. "And I won't simply wander around, howling into the wilderness while I look for anything to couple with."

"In a way, he ought to," Dobrescu said. "Mate, that is. From a population standpoint, it's a bad idea to take one of these guys out of the equation."

"The problem of conservation you were talking about a while back," Kosutic said.

"Yes, because the sex that produces the eggs only does so twice per year. If they don't implant the other sex, they lose the chance for a long period, statistically speaking," Dobrescu said. "The reason the Kranolta took such a beating *after* they overwhelmed Voitan was that their egg-producers were scattered all over hell and gone."

"Can the—I have to think of them as females," Pahner said. "Can the *females* accept the eggs at any time?"

"Yes. They maintain a sort of 'sperm sac,' equivalent to the *vans* in humans," Dobrescu said with a slight smile for the captain's obvious discomfort. "The eggs are implanted by . . . well, we've all seen the ovipositors. Once implanted, they're joined by the sperm in the region, and become fetuses. I've been looking forward to watching the development, but we've always missed that stage. There were some in development in Marshad, but I didn't get much of a look at them."

"I didn't see them at all," Kosutic said. "Pregnant Mardukan females?"

"Yeah," the medic said. "The fetus sacs form what look like blisters on their backs."

"So . . ." Pahner began, then paused. "I just discovered that I don't want to know the details. Or, at least, while I'll be interested in reading your report, I don't want to discuss it at the moment. Is this important to the mission?"

"Just from a medical perspective," Dobrescu said. "The only military consideration I see is that I wouldn't expect them to be much use from a military point of view during their heat."

"Are *all* of them going to start acting like this?" Kosutic asked. "Denat is a fairly controlled fellow, but if the Vashin and Diasprans get hit, we're going to have some big-time fights. I don't want to even try to imagine what Erkum Pol would be like, for example."

"I don't know what their season is," Dobrescu admitted. "The Vashin and Diasprans, I mean. It could happen, and when it does, it will probably happen all at once. Denat's from a different area, and it seems to be seasonally affiliated. Which is probably all to the good at the moment. He's the only Mardukan from that area with us."

"Wrong, Doc," Roger said. "Cord and Denat come from the same village."

"Ouch!" Dobrescu grimaced and shook his head. "Good point, Your Highness. I need to check him out and find out if he's got the same condition. If he does, it might explain some of the strange stuff that's been going on with him since he was hurt."

"Please do," Roger said, and stood up. "Denat, sorry, man. Wish there was something we could do."

"It's all right," the Mardukan said. "Now that I know what's going on, I can focus on controlling it." He gave a gesture of rueful humor. "I wish that I were in Marshad, though."

"What was her name?" Roger asked. "The spy girl in Marshad?"

"Sena," Denat whispered.

"Well, if you're still . . ." the prince paused, looking for the right term.

" 'In season,' is probably the easiest way to refer to it," Dobrescu said with a grin.

"If you're still 'in season' when we take the port, we'll see what we can do," Roger said with a sigh. "Otherwise, I guess you'll just have to grit your teeth."

"I've always recommended cold showers, myself," Kosutic said with a grin. "But that's probably contraindicated for a Mardukan, huh?"

"We need to consider the ramifications of this long-term," Pahner said. "Doc, as soon as you check Shaman Cord out, I want you to try to determine how soon the rest will go . . . into 'season.' We need to be able to plan around that."

"Yes, Sir," the warrant officer said. "Personally, though, I plan on taking that week off. These guys can be downright touchy."

CHAPTER TWENTY-TWO

"Tell me again what you heard," the Gastan said. He peered at the fortress through the device, the *binoculars,* the humans had given him.

"The merchants all quit Nesru at once," the Shin guardsman said. "All at once. A messenger arrived from Queicuf with word that Shesul Pass was under attack from the rear, or that it had fallen. He said at first that a small force had arrived and taken it with demons. But no one believes him."

Of course no one believed him, the Gastan thought wryly. After all, only a tiny handful of the Shin knew about the humans. Most of his tribesmen believed that his binoculars had been produced by Krath craftsmen from far up the great valley, and none of them recognized the enormous difference between the artisans who could produce them and the most skilled craftsman the Krath had ever produced. But any Shin who ever saw human weapons used would have every right to believe he looked upon demons.

"And now Queicuf heats its oil," he mused aloud, trying to get more detail out of the image the binoculars showed him. He and the guardsman stood on the edge of an ash cone to the north of Mudh Hemh. It gave an excellent view of the Krath stronghold without going to the trouble and danger of crossing the river. Of course, a view was all it gave him, and the way things were going, the time might come when he would have to carry his banner to Nopet Nujam. Which would be . . . inconvenient.

The danger which might impel him to do that was that the Krath seemed to have found a way through the Fire Lands. It was obvious that whatever path they had found was difficult and not suited to the movement of large numbers, but the Scourge raiding parties which had used it had inflicted painful losses. Very painful ones.

The problem was that the discovery seemed to have convinced the Krath that it was time to take Mudh Hemh at last, while the Vales were distracted by the knowledge that the Scourge had found a way into their rear. If they were determined to make a fresh attempt, the main thrust would come—as always—through the Battle Lands, and he would have no choice but to oppose that attack.

Yet if he took his banner to Nopet Nujam, he would face two problems. The first was that the motley mass of raiding parties that always gathered around Mudh Hemh would feel constrained to follow him, which would make the trip a logistic nightmare. But in many ways, that would be better than the alternative, because if they indicated a willingness to stay behind, he would have to assume it would be to do some casual raiding and looting in his own lands during his absence.

Unfortunately, if they chose to follow his banner, he would face his *second* problem. He would have to leave the Vale too lightly covered against the Krath who might creep through the Fire Lands along their new, secret path, because he would need his clan to control the hangers-on among his own "allies." And that didn't even consider the possibility that the clan would get into a feud with one of the Shin raiding groups, resulting in who knew how much bloodshed and who knew what political headaches with other clan-chiefs.

Being the "king" of the Shin was like juggling live coals.

Not for the first time, he felt sorrow for the loss of his daughter Pedi, and not just the natural grief of a father whose daughter had gone to the Fire. She'd been headstrong and stubborn as the mountains, but if he'd sent her to Nopet Nujam to be his eyes and ears, she would have returned with a concise and correct report. He really didn't have anyone else he could trust to do that; they all "embellished." And not one in a hundred of them could read. It was like pulling teeth to get them to study anything but raiding and hunting.

He felt a stronger pang of grief—and guilt—as another thought crossed his mind. Grief that he had lost her . . . and guilt that he wished he had lost Thertik instead.

He raised the binoculars once more, using them to hide his eyes from Nygard lest they reveal too much, but he could not hide the truth from himself. Much as the Gastan loved all of his children, it was . . . unfortunate that only Thertik and Pedi survived out of their litter and that Thertik was male. Perhaps even worse, his eldest son was the perfect model of a Shin warrior. Fearless in battle. Skilled with every weapon. Able to drink the most hardheaded of his fellow tribesmen under the table.

And utterly devoid of any trace of imagination. If only Pedi had been his heir! Or if only Thertik had been a weakling he could have convinced the clan to set aside in favor of Pedi or a consort carefully chosen for her. But she hadn't been, and Thertik wasn't. And so at a time when the very existence of the Shin hung from a thread, he dared not trust his own heir's discretion sufficiently to tell him about the clans' one, slim chance for survival.

But he could have told Pedi. If she'd been his heir. Or if he had been willing to betray Thertik by trusting his daughter with information he dared not entrust to his son.

I should have told her anyway, he thought. Not that it would have made any difference in the end.

"So Shesul Pass might be under attack," he said aloud, letting no trace of his thoughts shadow his voice. "Or may be fallen. Any word who the enemy was? Aside from 'demons,' of course!" he added with a grunt of laughter.

"No, Gastan," Nygard said. "The messenger from Queicuf didn't know."

"Who could have penetrated to the Shesul?" the chieftain mused. "None of the raiders that I know of could scratch those walls." He thought about that statement for a moment. It was true enough, as far as it went, because he *didn't* know of any 'raiders' who might have taken the pass. And if he could think of anyone else who it might have been, this was not the time or the place to share that thought with Nygard.

"Enough," he said instead, with a gesture of resignation, "I have too many other problems to worry about to consider this one in depth."

He straightened and took a sniff of the air, heavy with the scent of brimstone, wafting down from the Fire Lands to the north. It was one of the Vales' many products. Brimstone for gunpowder, ores, hides, gems, and raw nuggets of gold—all of them flowed out of the Vales and through Mudh Hemh. And everyone wanted it. The other Shin, yes, but especially the Krath. Mudh Hemh was the most populous Vale, since the fall of Uthomof, and it was also the richest, acting as a conduit for trade with the entire eastern half of the Shin Range. Which was why it was the Vale above all Vales the Krath wished to seize.

They had tried at least a dozen times, from as many directions, to invade the Shin Range and wipe out the Shin once and for all. The destruction of Uthomof had been the result of one such war, and he could smell a change in the air, a danger as faint and sharp as the hint of sulfur on the wind, but just as real . . . and growing stronger. War was coming; he could feel it in his bones.

But until it did, he had heads to crack and disputes to settle. It generally came down to the same thing.

Roger swung up onto the *turom* cart and waved at the valley spread out before them.

"Tell me what I'm seeing, Pedi."

It was obvious that the Vale of Mudh Hemh was a pretty complicated place, geologically, as well as politically. The valley was at least partially an upland glacial cirque, with some evidence of blown volcanic caldera. The various geological catastrophes had created a sort of paisley shape, broken by regular hills and surrounded by rearing volcanic mountains. The Shin River cut across the valley almost due east and west, and its course was flanked on both sides by a mixture of fields and fortifications.

To the east, on the nearer side of the river, two massive fortresses faced each other across a large, torn sward. Each was easily as large as the main temple in Kirsti, and each sealed off the entire width of its respective vale from mountain to river. The fields in between them were large—it was at least ten kilometers from the nearer fortress to the further one—and they'd clearly been cultivated until fairly recently. At the moment, however, they were occupied by an army.

The nearer fortress had a new, raw look to it, as if it had been thrown up in haste, but it was holding its own against the force spread out before its walls. The army (it could only be the Krath regular forces) spread across the fields, filling the vale from side to side. A tent city to the rear was laid out in widely spaced blocks, while massive squares of infantry closer to the fortress awaited their orders to assault the Shin walls. They were moving forward against the nearer fortress in regular waves, but reinforcements for what Roger assumed were Shin defenders could be seen crossing a covered causeway behind the fighting and moving down side roads in the protected lee of the fortress.

Both fortresses had companion forts on the far side of the river, or perhaps they could more accurately have been considered overly large outer works, protecting the farther shore. There was no open ground on that side, just a broken mass of rubble, fallen basalt, and flood ravaged shore. But neither side seemed to consider it uncrossable.

To the west, behind the fighting but on the nearer side of the river, lay the ruins of what had once been a fair sized city. It might not have been much compared to Kirsti or K'Vaern's Cove, but it had been larger than Voitan. Now it was a tumbled ruin, clearly being mined for the stone of its buildings.

On the far side of the river there was a large embayment, or secondary valley, with a walled town built into the side of an ash cone. The ash cone, in turn, was the outrider of a large area of geothermal activity. A small stream, tinged bright blue with minerals, flowed down from the ash cones, geysers, and fumaroles.

A massive bridge, wide enough for four *turom* carts abreast, crossed from the town to the ruined city. Obviously, it was the conduit for the majority of supplies and reinforcements for the newer fortress.

"The two main forts are Nopet Nujam and Queicuf," Pedi told him. "The area between them is usually a trade city, Nesru, full of Krath and Shin traders. The far forts are Nopet Vusof and Muphjiv."

Roger nodded. He still didn't know why her father might have concealed any contact he had with the human at port from her. Which was fair enough, since she hadn't been able to think of any reason, either. Although it was probable that O'Casey was right about the reasons the Gastan felt impelled to keep it a secret, but why conceal it even from Pedi? She might be stubborn, impulsive, and personally reckless, but Roger and the rest of the *Basik*'s Own had seen more than enough of her to realize that she was also highly intelligent and possessed of an iron sense of honor. Her father should have trusted her with his secret.

Then again, Mother should have trusted me instead of finding trumped-up excuses to send me away from court, he thought. *Not that I'd ever given her the sort of proof that she could trust me that Pedi must have given her father.*

He shook the thought aside and returned his attention to Pedi.

A part of him wished that she'd conducted this briefing sooner than this, but she'd been very little in evidence since the sojourn at Shesul Pass. Part of that was because of how much of her time had been devoted to nursing the now clearly recovering Cord, but she'd been nearly invisible even when she wasn't attending to the shaman's needs. In fact, she'd spent much of her time sleeping in the back of a *turom* cart, which Roger put down to recovery from all the time she'd spent with the ailing Cord. She'd certainly earned the downtime, at any rate, and she appeared to be on the mend as well. Her energy levels seemed to be up today, anyway, and at the moment, happiness at being home was written in every line of her body language.

"The city across the way is Mudh Hemh, and the closer one, the ruined one, is Uthomof. It fell to the Krath in the time of my great-grandfather, and they passed on to besiege the walls of Mudh Hemh itself. But in my grandfather's time, we drove them back to Queicuf and built Nopet Nujam. They lost heavily in that battle, and they've rarely sent great forces against us since."

She looked down at the attacking army and shook her head in one of the human gestures she had absorbed.

"I fear we have, as you humans would say, 'ticked them off,'" she added. "May I borrow your binoculars, please?"

Roger handed them over. They were clumsier than his helmet systems, but they were also more powerful, and Pedi observed the nearer fortress through them for several moments. Then she nodded.

"My father's emblem is on the walls, along with those of virtually all the clan-chiefs. I wonder who defends Mudh Hemh?"

"I imagine we should go find out," the prince said, updating his map to reflect her information and dumping it into the network. Pahner had decided that the humans could make use of the low-powered, low probability of intercept, inter-toot network. It was unlikely that the standard communications and recon satellite that was parked over the port would be able to pick it up.

"Father is not going to be happy about any of this," Pedi warned him.

"Not even about having you back?" Roger asked lightly. Then he smiled. "Well, in that case, we'll just have to see if we can't persuade him to be happier."

It took nearly three hours to arrange the meeting. The sun was on its way down by the time Roger, Pahner, and a cluster of Marines and Mardukans—including Pedi and an adamant, if barely ambulatory, Cord—were brought into the presence of the Gastan.

Pedi's father was short for Mardukan, not much taller than an average Mardukan female, but broad as a wall. The double swords which were the customary armament of a Shin warrior were slung across his back, and between those and the gaggle of trophy-covered chieftains at his back, he was quite the picture of a barbarian war chief.

Roger waved Pedi forward, and she stepped in front of her father, a leather bag in one hand, and bowed her head.

"Father, I have returned."

"So I was told." The Gastan spoke quietly, sparing the humans barely a glance. "*Benan*," he added.

"*Benan*, Father," she agreed. "And allied to the *humans*."

No one could have missed the emphasis she'd placed upon that final noun, or the ever so slight edge of challenge in her body language. But if the Gastan noticed either, he gave absolutely no sign of it.

"I suspect you have something for me in the bag?"

Pedi bowed again, slightly. Then she reached into the bag and removed the head of the Kirsti high priest. She held it out by its horns, and a whisper ran through the mass of chiefs like a wind in the pass. The Gastan contemplated it for a moment, then reached out and took it from her.

"Taken by you?"

"Yes, Father."

"I have an army at the gates, I'm holding the reason, and I have a daughter who confesses to the crime. You know that we are— were—at peace with the Krath. The penalty for such an offense is to be given to the Fire Priests."

"And what of their offense against us, Father?" she snarled. "What of the taking of my party, of the attack upon Mudh Hemh?"

"A price we accept to prevent . . . that," he said, gesturing with one false-hand in the direction of the surflike sounds of combat. Roger suddenly realized that they were very near the top of the wall, probably in the upper levels of one of the bastions flanking the main gate.

"What do you think I should do, Daughter?" the Gastan asked after moment.

"I suppose . . ." She hesitated for a moment, then inhaled and raised her head proudly. "I suppose I should be turned over to the priests. If it will end the war."

"Over my dead body," Roger said conversationally, and smiled.

"Perhaps, human," the Gastan said. "And we have yet to deal with you. In fact, it is not my daughter towards whom the Fire Priests bend their malice, but one 'Baron Chang.' Would that be you, human?"

"It would," Roger replied. "And you won't be handing me over like a lamb to the slaughter, either."

"Baron," the Gastan mused. "That is a noble of your human lands, yes?"

"Yes," Roger agreed.

"You are responsible for the good of others, 'Baron'? You hold their lives in your hand and feel the weight of that?"

"Yes," Roger replied soberly.

"I have lost over four hundred Shin warriors since this war started, 'Baron.' Including Thertik, my son and heir." Roger heard Pedi inhale sharply, but the Gastan's attention never wavered from the human. "That is the price my people and I have already paid. And you think that I would quail at the thought of turning you over to the Krath if it ends this slaughter?"

"I don't know," Roger said. "I would ask you this one thing, though. If they came up to you and pointed to one of your warriors and said 'Give *him* to me. We will sacrifice him to the God and devour him, and that will end this war,' would you?"

The Gastan regarded him levelly for a long moment, then made a gesture of ambiguity.

"Would you?" he responded.

"No," Roger said. "That was the choice put to us, and I rejected it. Pointedly."

"Hmmm. But just who are you responsible for, 'Baron'? This group? These ragged mercenaries? Humans seem to have such in plenitude. Why not give one, if it saves others?"

"Because humans, and Mardukans, aren't pawns," Roger said, then sighed. "I can stand here debating this all day if you like, I suppose, but it's really not my forte. So are you going to try to kill us, or not?"

"So quick to the battle," the Gastan said with a gesture of humor. "Do you think you would win?"

"That depends on your definition of 'win,'" Roger said. "We'll make it out of this citadel alive, some of us, and we'll collect our group and leave. You'll get overrun by the Krath while you're trying—and failing—to kill us, and while that happens, we'll keep right on heading for the spaceport. It's nothing that we haven't done before. It will, however, tick off my *asi's benan*. I have to consider that."

"Hmmm," the Gastan said again. "You're just going to walk to the spaceport, 'Baron'?"

"Of course," Roger said. "We're humans, after all. They'll accept us."

"I see that you've fallen into evil company," Pedi's father said. One of Roger's eyebrows arched at the apparent *non sequitur,* and the Gastan gestured at the IAS journalist who had been quietly recording the entire meeting. "We have warning from the Office of the Governor that this man is a wanted criminal, a dangerous traitor and thief who should be returned to the port for trial," he said.

"I'm *what*?" Mansul lowered the Zuiko and glared at the Gastan.

"I have other such messages, as well," the Shin continued as if the journalist had never spoken. "One of them mentions a group of humans, ragged mercenaries who may attempt to pass themselves off as Imperial Marines. They are to be considered very dangerous and should be killed on sight and without warning. There is a reward—a very attractive one, in fact—for their heads. What do you think of *that,* 'Baron'?"

"Gastan, you know that's a lie about me, at least!" Mansul protested. "So you must realize the rest of it is lies, as well!"

"Must I?" the Gastan asked easily. "Softly, Harvard Mansul. I want to hear the answer of this human noble. This 'Baron Chang.'"

Roger regarded the Gastan for a long slow moment, then nodded.

"My name," he said, clearly and distinctly, "is Prince Roger Ramius Sergei Alexander Chiang MacClintock. And I am going to wipe the floor with the governor. And with anyone else who gets in my way."

"Roger," Pahner growled, and his hand dropped to the butt of his bead pistol.

"Softly, protector," the Gastan said, raising his own hands in placation of both the Marine commander and of his own chieftains, who had shifted at the human's movement. "Softly, Armand Pahner. Softly, humans, Shin. Friends. Friends I think, oh yes."

He hefted the head of the High Priest. The climate of Marduk had not been kind to it, and he regarded the loathsome object coldly for a moment, then looked over his shoulder at one of his guardsmen.

"Bring me my sigil."

He waited until the trophy staff was brought forward, then strode to the outer door. The humans followed at his gesture, and as they stepped onto the walls, the bull-throated roar of the Shin and the howling of the Krath forces arrayed against them pressed against their faces like the overpressure waves of distant explosions.

A large horn, longer than Roger was tall, had been laid upon the walls, obviously in preparation for this moment, and the Gastan first blew into a side valve. A mournful hum cut through the sound of the battle noise, and faces turned towards him from below. He gave them a few moments, then opened a speaking tube built into it.

"*Krath!*" he bellowed, and the megaphone effect sent his voice echoing across the valley like thunder. "Here is the head of your High Priest! We have the humans who took it within our walls! And here is the answer of the Vale of Mudh Hemh to your demands!"

He raised the head high in both true-hands and spat upon it, his motions broad enough to the observable across the entire battlefield. Then he attached it to the highest point of the staff, raising it for all to see, and set the iron shod foot of the staff into a socket atop the battlements.

He left it there and strode back into the conference room without so much as another backward glance, his shoulders set, while the ear-splitting shouts of the Shin on the walls bayed jubilant defiance at the Krath. Roger and his companions followed, and the Gastan turned to them grimly.

"And so my daughter's allies are mine, as well, it seems," he said. "But, Prince Roger Ramius Sergei Alexander Chiang MacClintock and Captain Armand Pahner of the Bronze Battalion, if you think you are scurrying off to Marduk Port without helping us out of this mess my daughter has gotten us into, you are sorely mistaken."

"There is a human group, the Imperial Bureau of Investigation," the Gastan said as he passed over a flagon of wine. "You know it, yes?"

"Yes," Roger agreed, pouring a glass of the wine. The meeting had been narrowed down to the main staff and a few of the tribal leaders. The IAS photographer had managed to shoehorn himself into the group and was discreetly recording in the background, and Roger was—inevitably—accompanied by Dogzard. But for once, the size of Roger's entourage wasn't completely out of hand.

As their commanders settled down to talk things over, both groups of subordinates were weighing each other and wondering who was bringing the most to the table.

There were certainly more of the Shin. At the first sign of the Krath attack, the Gastan had gathered the tribes, and every segment of the Shin Mountains was represented. There were at least three distinctly separate groups, distinguishable by their armor and weapons, as well as their features.

The most numerous group seemed to be the one associated closely with Pedi's father. They were of about normal height for Mardukans, armed with a motley of weapons—mostly swords and battle axes—and wearing armor that ranged from light boiled leather to heavy plate. Their horns, like Cord's, were high and rounded, with prominent ridges along the sides. Many of them had elaborate decorations on their horns, and helmets designed to display them to best advantage.

The second group appeared to be displaced Krath officers. They were equipped almost exactly like Flail commanders, armored in heavy plate with mail undershirts, and armed with long swords and square shields. They also had the haughty bearing that Roger had come to expect from the Krath.

As it turned out, they were clan leaders from "lowland" vales, where the influence—and money—of the Krath was strongest. They were heavily raided, so they tended to be unflinching in battle, but they were also ready to negotiate if battle could be avoided.

The last group seemed to be the poorest, and was armed with spears and not much else. Physically, they were shorter than the average Mardukan, and their horns were strange—very dark in color, and curving sharply back along the skull. Their senior clan leader wore light chain armor over boiled leather and bore a huge and obviously ancient battle ax. From a combination of Pedi's previous briefings and overheard comments, Roger knew that these were clans from the very back of the high country; Shin that were seen only once in a generation—so seldom that many of the *Shin* considered them to be little more than a legend.

"There is an agent of the IBI in the port," the Gastan continued. "He is presently out of communication with his superiors, but he has been acting against the governor, waiting for one of his contacts to turn up. It was he who contacted me and began sneaking humans he believed to be at risk out of the port. He was asking for some rather extraordinary help in your regard, so I forced him to tell me why. He told me much—not all, I'm sure, but much—and gave me this." The Gastan handed over a data chip. "Your 'Empire' is in sore straits, Prince. I fear I have very bad news."

"What?" Roger asked. He shrugged and took a sip of wine. "As bad as it's been on this planet, how much worse can it be at home?"

"The port is closed to you. The governor has sold his soul to your enemies, the 'Saints.' They aren't always in the system, but they often are, and no Imperial spaceship has come to here in nearly a year. As far as anyone can tell, everyone here has been forgotten by the Empire. Without a ship, even after taking the port, there is no way off the planet, and if the Saints detect that their bought governor has been overthrown, your lives will be worth nothing."

"We've gotten that far in our own assessments," Roger told him. "On the other hand, *your* analysis of just exactly how piss-poor our chances are brings a question rather forcefully to mind. If our odds are so bad, and if the Saints are going to rain down so much grief when they swat us, why should you risk helping us?"

"The governor has allied himself with the Krath. He has not yet used your human weapons against us, but if the Krath do not overwhelm us with this attack, it will be only a matter of time until he does. He has already done so in support of the Son of the Fire closer to your port. Sooner or later he will do so here, as well, and when he does, we will be unable to resist. The IBI agent promised me that if we aided him, he would ensure that we were supported when the planet was retaken. It is a slim hope to cling to, but better than none."

"Well, in that case, let me fatten it up for you," Roger said. "We don't begin to have time for me to explain to you exactly how many of our laws the governor and his cronies have broken here on Marduk. Let's just say that the conditions he's created, alone, would force the Empire to step in to repair the damage. But in addition to that, I personally guarantee that the gratitude of House MacClintock will follow, as well. If it's the last thing I do, the Krath and their depredations *will* be stopped."

"But for that to happen, one must assume that Her Majesty can be bothered to find Marduk on a map," the Gastan sighed. Roger stiffened slightly, and the Mardukan made a quick gesture of negation. "I question neither your laws, your word, nor your honor, Prince Roger, but at times even the most honorable of leaders must look first to problems closer to home, and there is worse news than I have already given you."

Roger sat very upright on his cushion, gazing at the Mardukan war leader narrowly, and the Gastan raised both false-hands in a complex gesture of sympathy.

"There was an attempt to overthrow your mother, the Empress," he said levelly. "Units of your Marine Raiders attacked the palace. They were repulsed, but not without heavy loss of life and much damage to the palace."

"Mother?" Roger was stone-faced, all expression locked down in almost instant reaction, but the cold of interstellar space swirled suddenly through his heart and belly, and for all his formidable self-control he knew his voice was flat with shock . . . and fear. He felt the sudden, frigid silence of the other humans behind him, but he never looked away from the Gastan. "My mother is alive?" he asked in that same, flat, level voice.

"She is," the Gastan said, "although she was injured in the fighting. But there is worse, Prince. Much worse. I grieve to tell you that your brother and sister are dead. So also are your brother's children. He and they were killed in the attack upon the palace; your sister's ship was destroyed in an ambush in space."

"Bloody *hell*," Julian whispered into the stunned stillness. "Does that mean what I think it means?"

"I think not," the Gastan said. "Not, if you mean what I believe you do, at any rate. Because the word of the Empress is that the plotter who was central to the attempt is none other than her youngest son, Prince Roger MacClintock. And for his crimes, he and all with him have been outlawed for treason."

"The general outline is the same as the one the Gastan gave us," Julian said as he transferred the data from his pad to the others' systems. The Marine meeting had really been narrowed down for this one; everyone but the core command staff had been excluded. Decisions had to be made based on the information on the chip, and the nature of those decisions would determine the actions of what remained of Bravo Company for the foreseeable future.

"If anything," the intelligence sergeant continued, "the details are worse."

"The coup appears to have been an attempt by the Fleet to take control. That's the official analysis, anyway, but the reasoning is really nebulous, and no one has actively taken responsibility for any of the actions. All of the Raiders were killed, either in the assault, or in a response drop by Line Marines. As nearly as I can tell, virtually the entire Empress' Own was wiped out holding the attackers until the line beasts could take them from behind." He looked up from his pad, grim eyes meeting those of the other Marines. "It looks like we're effectively all that's left of the Regiment, Skipper," he told Pahner.

"I'd already assumed as much," the captain said quietly. Silence hovered for a moment as he and his subordinates thought of all the men and women they would never see again. The men and women they had assumed were safe at home while they battled their own way across the steaming hell of Marduk.

"Go on, Sergeant," Pahner said finally, his voice still quiet but unwavering.

"Yes, Sir." Julian glanced back at his notes, then resumed. "This IBI agent—Temu Jin—included a group of articles from various e-news outlets, as well as analysis articles from *Jane's*, *Torth*, and *AstroStrategy*, as well as full e-news loads from the top outlets. They're all indexed, and he highlighted some of them. I've only skimmed those.

"Apparently, the coup caught the IBI flat. A flier bomb was set loose in IBI headquarters—it's a pile of rubble, now. The head of the IBI was at Home Fleet headquarters at the time. It was also struck, but it managed to survive and launch a counterattack, including calling down a drop by the Marines of Home Fleet. Nefermaat, the IBI's second-in-command was off-planet at the time, and he's now wanted for questioning. There's a note on that from Jin. He thinks Nefermaat's disappearance is probably an indication that he's dead rather than linked to the coup in any way."

"Reason?" Pahner asked flatly.

"It turns out that Nefermaat was in Jin's line of control. Jin's orders to lie low came in about two days after the coup, along with a note that said basically that the real legal situation was unclear, and that all agents were to ignore orders from *any* higher authority, unless they could verify that they were valid."

"That could just be Nefermaat cutting out a section of the IBI," O'Casey mused. "Or this could be disinformation directed at Roger."

"What in the world makes you think that?" Roger asked. "How would anyone even know we're here—that *I'm* here—to be disinformed in the first place?"

"I don't know," O'Casey said. "But when you start getting into these labyrinthine games of empire, you have to be aware that some of them are very deep and very odd. And that some are just odd, but look deep and mysterious because the people running them are so confused."

"For now, until something else presents itself, we'll take Jin's data as valid," Roger decided. "Just keep in mind that it could be wrong."

"Very well, Your Highness," Julian agreed. "We'll get to Jin's speculation in a moment, but for right now, I'll just say that I agree with it. And if he's right, that means Nefermaat is a scapegoat. A dead one. Or, at least, on the run and in hiding."

He referred back to his pad once more and nodded.

"Your mother is alive, Your Highness, but according to the reports, she was injured. It's only the last article in the queue which has her back in public at all . . . accompanied by Prince Jackson and the Earl of New Madrid."

"My *father*?" Roger stared at him in stark disbelief.

"Yes, Your Highness," Julian confirmed. "He's now established as a pro-consort, engaged to your mother."

"Holy shit," Roger said very, very quietly. "I can see why you think there's something fishy in Denmark."

"According to the news accounts, we were all reported dead, along with Roger, when the *DeGlopper* failed to arrive at Leviathan on schedule," Julian continued. "It looks like our 'demise' made quite an impression on the news services . . . until the coup attempt came along and pushed us to the back of the queue."

"I thought the story was that I'm behind everything," Roger said.

"Yes, Sir, but that's a recent development. A *very* recent one, in fact. It's only turned up in the last news from Sol, and it represents an entirely new twist on the original story.

"In the immediate aftermath of the coup, our disappearance was linked with Alexandra's death, as part of the general attack on the Imperial Family, but that didn't last. I can't tell from the data where the suggestion first came from, but eventually someone pointed out that we'd disappeared well *before* the rest of the Family was attacked. The new theory is that what really happened was that we dropped out of sight as the first step in a deep, complicated plan on Roger's part to kill off everyone between him and the Throne." He grinned tightly at his silent audience. "At least we're no longer dead; now they want all of us for treason."

"Standard protocol," Pahner said. "How much?"

"Lots," Julian told him with an even tighter grin. "There's a forty-million-credit reward on your head, Captain."

"I hope I'm around to collect it." Pahner grinned back, but then his expression sobered once more. "You're right, though. This doesn't add up. What are the fleets doing?"

"Prince Jackson ordered all fleets, with the exception of Home Fleet, away from the Sol System. In fact, he ordered most of them into his sector of control, but that's also along the Saint border, so it makes some sense. Sixth Fleet hasn't been able to move yet, though. According to reports, they're having trouble scaring up the logistic train they need to shift stations so radically. Especially with every other Fleet command moving at the same time and scrambling to meet its own logistical requirements. For now, they're still in the Quarnos Sector."

"Admiral *Helmut* can't find the lift capacity he needs?" Roger stared at Julian for a moment, then snorted harshly. "Oh, yeah. *Right!*" He shook his head. "And what are the Saints doing while all this is going on?"

"As far as I can tell, nothing. And that has me worried."

"Why would they sit this out?" Roger wondered aloud. "I'd expect them to pick off a few systems, at least. Like, well, Marduk."

"From what Julian's saying about Prince Jackson's redeployments, plenty of Fleet units are headed this way," Pahner pointed out. "Presumably, they know that, too. So maybe they're lying low, figuring that now is a bad time to attack."

"And maybe they were told that if they lie back now, they can have a concession later," Roger said harshly.

"And maybe that, too," Pahner admitted.

"Okay." Roger drew a deep breath. "We won't make any assumptions about their motivations for the moment, simply note that they haven't moved—yet—and hope it stays that way." He looked back at Julian. "That still leaves a few dozen other burning questions, though. Like who's in charge of the Fleet? What happened with Home Fleet? And what the hell happened with the IBI to let them blindside Mother this way?"

"General Gianetto has been given the position of High Commander for Fleet Forces," Julian said.

"Ah," Pahner said with his first real smile of the meeting. "Excellent!"

"Uh," O'Casey cut in. "Maybe not so excellent."

"Why is it excellent?" Roger asked. "And why maybe not? Armand first."

"I've known Guy Gianetto on and off for nearly half a century," Pahner said, frowning at O'Casey. "He's ambitious, but he's also solidly in favor of a strong Empire, a strong imperium. He would never betray the Empire." He started to say something more, then made himself visibly change his mind. "What does Eleanora have to say?" he asked instead, his tone half-challenging.

"That you're entirely correct," she replied. "General Gianetto would never betray the Empire. As he sees it."

"You're saying he might feel that some action is necessary to save the Empire from itself?" Roger asked. Pahner opened his mouth, but the prince raised a hand gently. "Let her speak."

"He and Prince Jackson have gotten closer and closer over the last decade," O'Casey said. "Both of them favor a strong defense, although Jackson's interest in such questions is . . . complex. For one thing, his family fortune is closely tied to defense industries. For another, he's the most prominent noble of the Sagittarius Sector, so he's constantly aware of the threat from the Saints. That gives him two reasons to favor a strong defense, which is why he's so consistently found on defense-related committees."

"What's wrong with wanting a strong defense?" Pahner asked. "It's a big, ugly galaxy out there, Councilor."

"Preaching to the choir here, Captain," O'Casey said seriously. "But there are inevitable questions. There's a *lot* of corruption in the procurement process—you know that even better than I do—and Jackson and his family have fingers in all the pies. He's also cultivated very friendly relationships with the majority of the senior officer corps. *Very* friendly relations. He not only hosts them to parties and junkets, but he's even gone so far as to countersign loans for some of them. Even covered some of them when they defaulted."

"That's against Fleet Regulations," Pahner said. "If it's true—I'm not saying it isn't, mind—but *if* it's true, where the hell has the IG been? And why didn't *I* get invited?"

"At a guess, you didn't get invited because you were too junior until you took this command," O'Casey said. "And, yes, where *was* the Inspector General?" She looked Pahner straight in the eye. "What was Gianetto for the last seven years?"

"Oh," the captain said in a flattened tone of voice, and his mouth twisted bitterly.

"Gianetto is considered a paragon of virtue," the chief of staff went on. "That's why he was made IG in the first place. And, okay, he's a much . . . smoother guy than Admiral Helmut. And Her Majesty initially trusted him. But over the last couple of years, she's been getting more and more indications that—Well, let's just say that I'm not surprised to see him in this. Saddened, but not surprised."

"So what do we think is happening?" Roger asked. "Julian."

"I think the coup succeeded, Your Highness," the sergeant said flatly. "I think Jackson is either directly or indirectly controlling the Empress. I think Gianetto and your father, at least, are in on it."

"Who's got Home Fleet?"

"That's still Admiral Greenberg, Sir," Julian said after a quick reference to his notes. "Commodore Chan, his chief of staff, was fingered as the local planner of the coup. He was 'killed resisting arrest'. . . ."

"And you can believe as much or as little of that as you like," Roger added bitterly.

"At any rate, Greenberg managed to retain command and acted as his own chief of staff for at least a few days, maybe a week or two. It's hard to tell. Eventually, though, Chan was replaced by Captain Kjerulf, the fleet Operations officer," Julian added.

"Greenberg is a snake," Pahner said. "Unless you have something countervailing to add, Ms. O'Casey?"

"I concur entirely," the chief of staff said. "Snake. I recall that Chan was well thought of, on the other hand."

"He might have fallen in with bad companions," Pahner said with a grimace of distaste. It was clear he was still unhappy and unsure about Gianetto. "But it's more likely he was a convenient scapegoat. But Kjerulf, now. That's an interesting datum."

"You know him?" Roger asked.

"Oh, I know just about everyone, Your Highness," Pahner told him with a bleak smile. "Maybe not all of them as well as I *thought* I did, I suppose. But Kjerulf is Gronningen with five years of college, then Staff School and Command College, plus thirty years of experience."

"Hmmm," Roger said. "So what does that tell us?"

"He was probably a ready pick," O'Casey replied. "They couldn't justify letting Greenberg operate permanently without proper staff backup, and he was the first person logically available, whether the real conspirators wanted to use him or not. If that's the case, it tells us the coup isn't fully spread through the Fleet. And that not everyone may be quite as convinced by the 'party line' as they'd like. Not if they need to worry so much about window dressing and allaying suspicion that they've put a man like Kjerulf into such a sensitive position."

"Everyone agree with that?" Roger asked, looking around his advisers' faces. "There was a successful coup. Its control may not be entirely solid yet, but it's heading that way. And Mother's under duress." Heads nodded around the table, and he grimaced. "Wonderful. Because if it was, there's just one problem."

"It can't last," O'Casey supplied for him. "Eventually she'll either break their control, or—if it's a direct drug or toot control—it will get found out."

"So what does that tell us?" Roger said again. "Assume they think I really am dead."

"I think it's obvious that that's exactly what they think, Your Highness," Kosutic put in. "*DeGlopper* was the first bead in the magazine, and they obviously think they got us. What I don't know was whether they intended to make you the fall guy all along, or if this was some sort of *ex post facto* brainstorm." The sergeant major snorted a bitter laugh. "You know, from a purely tactical viewpoint, you gotta love it. Look at it—they've got the perfect Overlord of Evil! They can keep right on chasing you for decades as a way to maintain the 'threat' that justifies whatever 'emergency measures' they decide to take, and they know they can never catch you, because you're *dead*!"

"The sergeant major is right," O'Casey agreed. "And if they think you're dead, and they're worried about the Empress slipping out of their control, they have to be angling for an Heir. Probably another one by New Madrid."

"And if they don't get an Heir and mother suffers a tragic accident anyway?" Roger asked. "Uncle Thorry, right?"

"The Duke of San Cristobal, yes," O'Casey agreed. "But—"

"But he's damned near senile, and never bothered to have children," Roger completed. "And after him?"

"At least a dozen claimants," O'Casey said. "All with more or less equal claims."

"Jackson's not in that group," Roger amused. "But he's close. And given his position of advantage . . ."

"It's probable that the Throne would fall to him," O'Casey said. "But whether or not he could hang onto it would be another matter. Given all of the other competing heirs, it's almost as likely that the Empire would simply dissolve into warring factions. The rival cliques are still out there, you know, Your Highness."

"Arrrgh." Roger closed his eyes and rubbed his face. "Julian, what's the dateline on the first news story that said Mother was something like 'alive and recovering'?"

The sergeant did a quick scan and pulled up an article.

"Nice word choice, Sir. 'Alive and should fully recover from her wounds.' Two months ago. *Three days* after the attack."

"Now those must've been some tense days," Roger said with a lightness which fooled none of them. "And I thought being on Marduk was a *bad* thing. We have seven months."

"Aye," Pahner agreed. "The child must be born of her body."

"Which means she at least has to be alive when the can is cracked," Roger said.

"Well, technically, yes," O'Casey said. "But, it's possible—"

"Under other circumstances, maybe," Roger cut her off. "But not these. If she dies before they have an acknowledged Heir to the Throne, then—like you just said—odds are the entire Empire could fall apart on them." He shook his head. "No, Eleanora. For right now, she's their trump card. With the child born and well, proven to be of her genetics, while she's still alive to confer legitimacy on their regime, they're covered. *Then* Mother dies, Jackson becomes Regent, and from there he can do as he wishes. But she has until the child is born to be relatively safe. Which means we only have seven months until my mother's life probably isn't worth spit."

"Agreed," Pahner said. "At the same time, Your Highness, we have to get through our other problems before we can do anything about that one. We'll just have to cross that bridge when we come to it."

"Indeed, Captain. Indeed." Roger sighed sadly. "Well, if it were easy, they wouldn't pay us the big bucks."

CHAPTER TWENTY-THREE

Harvard Mansul was lurking just outside the conference chamber when the meeting broke up.

The journalist rarely asked the prince any questions, preferring to pump the junior Marines and the Mardukan mercenaries, who were more than willing to share their stories. And, of course, he had *not* been invited to attend the command staff meeting, itself. But he was getting hours of video of the prince, and it was beginning to bother O'Casey.

She stepped out of the meeting room just as Mansul started to dart off after Roger, and she stuck out an arm and grabbed him before he could get away. He looked at her in some surprise, but the chief of staff had developed remarkably sinewy arms during the trek across Marduk, and he was wise enough not to resist as she dragged him back into the now empty room.

"We need to talk," she said pleasantly.

"Yes, Ma'am," the photographer said. "I'm trying to stay out of the way."

"And you're succeeding," she noted. "And I know that this is a heck of a story. But it's not necessarily one the IAS can publish when we get back."

Mansul sighed and nodded.

"I understand that. But do you know what the prince intends to do? Is he going to contact the Empress when we return? How are we *going* to return?"

"That's . . . not settled yet," O'Casey temporized. "But . . . You do understand why we've got to start excluding you from some meetings?"

"I understand," Mansul repeated. "But this isn't just a good story, you realize. This is history unfolding. And *what* history! I mean, this is the best story in a thousand years! He could play his own leading man!"

"What do you mean?" the chief of staff asked.

"Come with me," Mansul said, and took her arm. "I want to show you something."

He led her out of the door and towed her down the corridor, asking the occasional guard for directions to the prince.

They finally found him out on the battlements, conferring with the local Shin leadership. The skies, as always, were gray, but the brilliant pewter cloud glare of Marduk's powerful sun was near zenith and the day was bright—hot, and almost dry at this altitude. The prevailing wind in this area came down from the glaciers up-valley, and on some days it built up to a near-gale. Today it was running about thirty kilometers per hour, and the prince's hair had come unbound. It streamed sideways in the wind as he and the native leaders conferred, gesturing at the distant battle lines.

"There," Mansul said.

"What?"

"That's what I brought you to see," he replied. "*Nobody* sees it. I want you to look at the prince and tell me what you *see*. Take your time."

"I'm very busy, Mr. Mansul," the chief of staff said. "I don't have time for games. It's Prince Roger."

"This isn't a game, Ms. O'Casey," he said seriously. "Now look."

O'Casey looked at Roger. He was talking with the Gastan and one of the other Shin warlords, accompanied by Pahner and Kosutic, the still barely mobile Cord, a group of Vashin and Diaspran bodyguards, and Dogzard.

"I see Roger and company," she snapped. "What about it?"

"Describe him," Mansul said quietly. "As if *you* were writing the article."

"A tall man . . ." she began, and then, suddenly, stopped.

A tall man, darkly tanned by alien suns, a sword on his back and a pistol at his side, his unbound blond hair streaming in the wind. He was surrounded by a group of powerful, intelligent, capable followers who were not just willing to follow him anywhere, but already had—and would again, at a moment's notice, even knowing the impossible tasks they faced. His face was young, but with almost ancient green eyes. The eyes of a man who had already strode through a dozen hells. . . .

"Oh . . . my . . . God," she muttered.

"Now you understand." The journalist's whisper was an odd mix of delight and something very like awe. "This isn't just the story of a lifetime. This is the story of a *century*—possibly a millennium. You couldn't pry me off with a grav-jack."

"That's . . ." She shook her head, trying to clear the vision. "It's just *Roger*."

"No. It's not," the journalist said. "And, trust me, you aren't the Ms. Eleanora O'Casey I had a passing view of at the palace. You've *survived*, Ms. O'Casey. Sure, you were protected, but are you ready to tell me you're the same person you were before this tremendous trek?"

"No, I'm not." She sighed at last, and took one more look before she turned away. "But it's still silly. I don't care what he's become, he's still *Roger*."

"This is silly," Roger muttered. "I take it back. There *is* such a thing as too much overkill."

They were observing the Krath siege lines from the top of the western wall, trying to determine if there was anything Roger's force could add to the defense. Pahner had dragged all the senior commanders, along with the main "battle staff," up to the battlements with them for a good hard look. And it didn't look good.

"Yes," the Gastan said with a gesture of amusement. "It is a bit overwhelming, isn't it?"

It looked very much as if Kirsti had moved its entire army in toto up to the plain. From the mountains, standing beside Pedi's *turom* cart, that army had looked like a large ant mound; from the walls, it looked like . . . an *immense* ant mound.

The tent city at the rear measured nearly four kilometers on a side, broken into three distinct camps with regular roads and well laid out garbage and personal waste management. The latter seemed to be primarily trucked out, rather than simply dumped into the river, which struck the humans as the best field hygiene they'd come across yet. On the other hand, it was apparent that the majority of the forces weren't spending much time under canvas.

A regular siege had been laid on in front of the Shin citadel. Dozens of separate zig-zagging communications trenches led forward from the area of the Krath encampment to a much larger trench parallel to the walls. The parallel trench was covered by stout wooden palisades, and bombards fired occasionally from emplacements along the parallel. But the bombards in use were on the small side; they were still far enough from the fortress that they were barely in range; and there weren't very many of them. Coupled with their low rate of fire, their impact on the defenses was marginal . . . so far.

Despite the indications that the Krath were here for the long haul, they seemed quite prepared to settle things more quickly if the opportunity offered. And they obviously considered that they had the manpower to explore . . . more direct and straightforward alternatives to battering a way through stonework with artillery. A frontal assault—or, more precisely, *another* frontal assault—had obviously been tried earlier in the day, and the dead hadn't been cleared away from the base of the walls yet.

The forces arrayed against the Shin were enormous. Between the rear of the siege works and the tent city, there were blocks and blocks and blocks of infantry. So many that all most of them could do was sit on the ground, awaiting their next orders. There literally wasn't *room* to use more than a fraction of them against the fortress at any given time.

"There are at least two hundred thousand troops *in view*," Julian said, consulting his toot. "It looks like that could be another sixty thousand in Queicuf and the wing forts, and an unknown number in the tents."

"Worse than the Boman," Rastar muttered. "These bastards are *organized.*"

"The majority of them return to the tents at night," the Gastan said. "They're as much for warmth as for cover, and they have to clean their pretty armor, don't they?"

"I suspect that they wait until they return to do their business, as well," Honal commented. "Otherwise, they'd be up to their knees in shit by now."

"If they just charged all at once, they'd overwhelm you," Pahner said, ignoring the side conversations.

"Possibly," the Gastan replied with a gesture of resignation. "And possibly not. Moving them all forward at once is . . . a bit of a challenge. It takes a lot of tricky coordination. And they'd have to stack themselves on top of each other to get to the top of the wall. We're the Krath's prime source for any number of raw materials, including wood, so they're having a bit of trouble finding sufficient materials for enough ladders. Then, even if they took the fortress, they'd have to manage the groups that were in it. They've taken *sections* of the wall before, but those Krath who seize them just mill around on top, wondering what do next until we counterattack and kill them or drive them off. They're perfectly willing to keep trying assaults on the off-chance that one may work—they've certainly got the manpower for it!—but they've also fallen back on more complicated means."

He waved at the palisaded parallel . . . and at the trenches zig-zagging forward from it. It was obvious that the smaller trenches had perhaps another fifty to seventy-five meters to go to reach the point at which the next parallel would be cut, that much closer to the walls.

"They've been moving the siege lines forward steadily," the Gastan said. "They won't have to get a lot closer to bring their bombards into effective range. When they do, they can pound us hard enough to cause a breach. Then they'll pour their troops through, and it will all be over."

"Not much I can add," Fain said. He'd been doing a few

calculations on the back of the wall, and now he dropped his piece of charcoal and dusted his true-hands, body language distinctly disgruntled as he contemplated the figures he'd scrawled across the stone. "Each of my fellows would have to kill fourteen hundred of them. I can't guarantee anything over a thousand, unless we get more ammunition."

Pahner had been rubbing his chin in thought. Now he pulled out a piece of *bisti* root and cut off a sliver.

"I'll tell you the truth," he told Pedi's father. "We need to take the spaceport, and from what you've said, it's not all that long a trek from here. If we took it, we could come back with all the firepower we need to clear out the Krath."

"It's a point," Roger agreed. "A couple of cluster bombs would be a treat on these guys."

"That would be . . . difficult," the Gastan said coldly. "I have a hard enough time convincing my people that it's worth fighting the Krath at all, especially given the reason that they sit on our doorstep. If you were to go, for whatever reason, I doubt I could continue to ensure your safety. Or that of my other human guests."

Pahner sighed, nodded, and slipped the slice of root into his mouth. He chewed thoughtfully for a few seconds, then shrugged.

"I suspected it would be something like that. Okay, let's try a few 'old-fashioned' remedies first. If those don't work, we'll think about alternatives."

"I guess that's about our only option," Roger agreed. "On the other hand, sooner or later, we're going to have to move on the port, anyway. I truly hope taking it won't be as tough as it could turn out to be when we do get around to it, and I think we need to think about that simultaneously. Armand, you and I need to concentrate on ways to deal with the Krath. But while we get fully up to speed on the local situation and the balance of forces, Julian, you need to start massaging the data Jin gave us. We need a way into the port."

"Yes, Your Highness," the NCO said doubtfully. "If there are any of us left to take it."

Roger tried not to let his amusement show as he watched Pedi and the still limping, very slowly moving Cord jockey for precedence through the door. The Marines had already swept the other side, and even including Despreaux and Pedi, Roger was probably the most dangerous person present. But the precedence of security was everything.

"I'm sure we're all friends here, Pedi," he said, placing a hand on her back as she passed him. Then he drew his hand back and looked at it oddly. Her back had felt . . . lumpy. If she'd been a human, and if it had been her front, instead of her back, he would have thought he'd accidentally put his hand on a breast. But the feel had been firmer, like a large blister. Or a tumor.

Whatever it had been, Pedi shied away from the touch. Then she seemed to recover her customary poise.

"And we were sure the High Priest would never have your party attacked in his presence, Your Highness," she said. "My duty to my *benan* is clear. It is *my* responsibility to ensure the room is safe. Not the Marines'."

"And it is mine to ensure that it is safe for you, Roger." Cord's voice still wheezed alarmingly, and Roger shook his head.

"You need rest, old friend," he said. "You can't guard me if you're as weak as a day-old *basik*."

"Nonetheless, it is my duty," Cord said, trying unsuccessfully to conceal how heavily he was forced to lean upon his spear for support.

Roger paused in the doorway and turned to his *asi*. He looked up into the face that now seemed familiar, rather than alien.

"Cord, I need you for your advice more than your guarding. And I need you *well*. Respect my opinion in this; you need to rest still. Get your strength back. I hate to mention it, but you're not as young as you used to be, and you need more time to recover. That was a bad wound, so rest. Go to Mudh Hemh. Have a mud bath. Get some sleep. I have the Marines to cover me, and I'll come to Mudh Hemh myself, as soon as the last of these negotiations are complete."

Cord regarded him impassively for a long moment, but then made a gesture of resignation.

"It is as you say. I cannot perform my duties as I should in this condition. I'll go."

"Good!" Roger clapped him on the arm. "Recover. Build up your strength. You'll need it soon enough."

"Good morning. My name is Sergeant Adib Julian, and I will be giving the first briefing on suggested tactics for relieving the Krath problem," Julian said, looking around the room. The hall was near the center of the Shin citadel and was large enough to accommodate all of the prince's commanders and the senior Shin warlords.

The latter were an extremely mixed bag. Some of them were from groups that were in long-term close contact with the Krath, and those were fairly "civilized." They'd turned up wearing well polished armor and seemed to be following the briefing with interest. They seemed especially fascinated by the hologram of the force structure the NCO had thrown up. However, many of the other chieftains were obviously from "the back of beyond." The latter were notable for their lighter and less well maintained armor, and the wide separation the Gastan had instituted between the groups—and between some of the clans *within* each group, for that matter—suggested that some of them would rather beat on each other than on the Krath.

"A short analysis of relative combat strengths of the Krath and the Shin/Marine alliance indicates that direct assault is unlikely to be effective," Julian continued, bringing up a representative animation of a Shin/human assault. "The inability of the human forces to use their plasma weapons, coupled with a lack of powered armor, means that any direct assault, even with human, Diaspran, and Vashin support, is liable to be swallowed without a burp."

As he finished speaking, the short, holographic animation ended with the "good guys" dead on the field and the Krath flag flying over Nopet Nujam.

"Alternatives to this may be viable, however," he continued, and brought up a new animation. "The Krath have had only very limited experience with a *civan* charge, and have no equivalent at all of the pike wall."

In the animation, a unit of *civan* quickly ran down one flank of the Krath forces, causing the rest to redeploy. As they did, the animation drew back, showing a hazily outlined "blue" unit of pikemen and assegai troops, supported by conventional Shin forces, on the slopes above the Krath tent city.

"If this attack is simultaneous with an attack on the tent city by a stealthed armor unit, sufficient chaos may be created to permit a major sortie, supported by Diaspran and Marine infantry, to retake the siege lines and destroy the palisades and the majority of their bombards before they ever get them into effective action."

The "blue" troops on the slopes swept downward, butchering the surprised Krath in their path, and the animation ended with the wooden palisades of the siege lines, the tent city, and the bombard emplacements all sending up pillars of black smoke as they blazed merrily away.

"And then what?" one of the more barbaric chieftains asked, looking up from the design he'd been carving into a tabletop with a dagger. "You think they'll turn and run after a single defeat? We need to take Thirlot! We'll cut them off from food and retreat as we always have, and it's good loot, besides!"

"Thirlot is well defended," one of the lowland chieftains said, buffing his polished breastplate. "They left a good portion of their force there on the way up, and another is in Queicuf. If your scruffy band thinks it can take Thirlot, more power to it."

"Scruffy?! I'll give you *scruffy!*"

"Enough!" the Gastan barked, and his guards banged the floor with their ceremonial spears. "Shem Cothal, Shem Sul. Taking Thirlot was considered and rejected. Sergeant Julian?"

"We might be able to take Thirlot," Julian said, looking pointedly at the chieftain in the breastplate. His toot, taking its cue from the Gastan, flashed the name Shem Sul across his vision. "Certainly we could enter the city. With our aid, you could probably destroy the forces that the Gastan's spies indicate are in the city. Our non-plasma heavy weapons could smash the doors, our armor could open up any hole necessary to get you inside the walls, and a force of Shin and Marines could enter the city and roam almost at will."

He held the eye of the more polished barbarian until the latter made a gesture of agreement.

"What we could not do is *hold* it," he said then, turning to the other chieftain, Shem Cothal. "And if we can't hold it, we can't cut their supply lines. The Krath would turn their army to the rear and assault Thirlot by swarming the walls. Those walls are barely ten meters high; they could stand on each other's shoulders and come right over them. And they can march back down the road on the rations they have right here in camp—it's barely two days to Thirlot. When they got there, our force in the city would be overrun. It would certainly be forced out with severe casualties, possibly cut off and destroyed. Other plans involving putting a blocking force on the Queicuf-Thirlot road have also been rejected for the same reason. We simply don't have sufficient forces to hold anything other than Nopet Nujam against the Krath army."

"All of that is no doubt true," Shem Sul said. "But I have to agree with my colleague." He gestured at the hologram. "You're discussing a spoiling attack, nothing more."

"It's the best we can do at this time," Julian said. "And it's a spoiling attack we can replicate almost at will."

"They're not so stupid," the other chieftain said. "They'll change their dispositions. 'Tis but a tithe of them that attack at any time. All they have to do is pull some of their other troops back, and your raiders are going to be useless."

"Then we'll change tactics," Roger said. "The point is to wear them down."

"As opposed to us being frittered away," Sul replied. "You'll take casualties on each raid, and they will *win* a battle of attrition. I have to agree with Shem Cothal; we have to cut their supply lines. Cut those, and their army withers on the vine. Nothing else, short of a human superweapon, will work."

"We can't use our superweapons until we've taken the port," Pahner said. "And you're correct, this is an attrition battle, with the addition of trying to break their will. At some point, we might take Thirlot, if only to burn it to the ground, but only if it helps with our objective, which isn't to *beat* them so much as to convince them to go away. We don't have the numbers to kill them all—our arms would fall off before we were done—so we're looking at ways to convince them victory would simply be too expensive. We'll look at other options, as well, but for the time being, we need to discuss the briefed plan."

Roger had been listening carefully, but now he sat up straight, picked up his pad, and started rotating the hologram, zooming in and out on the region around Queicuf. He zoomed in on the road just to the east of the fortress, where the valley narrowed down to the gorge of the Shin River, pinching the road bed between the valley walls and the deep, broad river.

"Julian, is this map to scale?"

"No, Your Highness. The vertical exaggeration is at one to three."

"Hmmm . . . fascinating . . ."

"What, Your Highness?" Pahner asked. He eyed the prince thoughtfully, wondering what the youngster was up to now. Whether it was *practical* or not, it should at least be interesting as hell, the Marine thought, because at some levels, Roger was a much more devious tactician than he himself was.

"There might just be an exploitable weakness here," the prince said, rotating the image again so that he was looking at the battlefield from ground level. "Captain Pahner, Lords of the Shin, we probably should try the briefed plan, if for no other reason than to put them a bit more on the defensive. But there might just be another way. Oh my, yes. Quite a weakness."

Cord turned back down the corridor, still leaning heavily on his spear for support, as the door closed on the prince. Pedi started to take his arm, then snatched her hand back as he jerked away.

"I am not so weak that I need your support, *benan*," he said harshly.

"I ask pardon, *benai*," she said. "I had not realized that contact with your *benan* was so beneath you."

"Not beneath me," Cord sighed. "Perhaps I should not snap, but . . ."

"But?" Pedi opened the door and checked the hallway beyond. The Gastan had placed guards along the corridor, and they nodded to her as she passed. She had known some of them for years, grown up with them. But she could feel the distance that now separated them, a gulf that was hard to define, yet as real as death itself. All that she knew was that either she had grown away from Mudh Hemh, or it was somehow rejecting her.

"But . . ." Cord began, then inhaled deeply, and not just from the pain of moving with his partially healed wound. "I know that I'm your *benai,* not your father," he growled. "But in the *asi* bond, the master has certain responsibilities. Although in my culture, females cannot become *asi,* if they had . . . problems, it would be the . . . responsibility of the master to deal with them."

"Problems?" Pedi asked archly as they came to their shared chamber. "What problems?" she asked as she opened the door and swept the room.

"Don't play with me, Pedi Karuse," Cord said firmly as he lowered himself onto the pile of cushions within. The fact that he barely managed to stifle a groan as he settled into them said a great deal about how far from recovered he truly was. "I'm in too much pain to play games. I can see your condition clearly, as can anyone with eyes. It is only the humans who are confused. I would have expected your father to be fuming by now."

"It is not my father's place to 'fume,'" she said sharply. "As *benan*, I am beyond the strictures of my family."

"Then it *is* my responsibility to investigate the situation," Cord said. "I am furious about this, you know. No true male would do this and then leave you to bear the burden."

Pedi opened her mouth, then shut it.

"It is my burden to bear," she said, after a moment. "It was my choice."

"It takes two to make such a choice," Cord pointed out, grimacing as he tried to find a comfortable position. "There is a male, somewhere, who has much explaining to do. A male who would impregnate you and then refuse to acknowledge that fact—such a male is without honor."

"It's not his fault," Pedi said. "I cannot—I *will* not—say more. But this is my responsibility to bear."

Cord sighed in exasperation, but made a gesture of resignation.

"As you will. I cannot imagine you lying with a male without honor. But let it be your secret, your 'cross,' as the humans would say. I shall raise any of the brood as if they were my own."

"I wouldn't hold you to that," Pedi said, getting the balm the human physician had made. "It is . . . It isn't your fault."

"I, however, am a male of honor," Cord said, then sighed in relief as she rubbed the salve into the inflamed wound. "I thank you for that," he told her, then shook himself and looked at her sternly. "But to return to what truly matters, I will not let your children be raised as bastards, Pedi. I will not. It will be as if they were mine."

"I understand, *benai,* but I can handle it," she said woodenly. "And the situation with the father is . . . complex. I wish that you would let me manage it in my own way."

"As you wish," he said with another sigh. "As you wish."

"I wish this didn't look so easy," Julian muttered.

"What?" O'Casey asked. "Something about this god-forsaken mess strikes you as 'easy'?"

She sat up straight on the camp stool, rubbing her back, and grinned at the sergeant. It was a very crooked grin, because both of them had been perusing their separate "slices" of the intelligence data from the IBI agent for the last couple of hours. While Julian concentrated on Marduk itself, she had been wading through the data about the coup, and she was coming to the conclusion that Julian was right about that information's reliability. And about the implications of that reliability.

There was too much data on the disk, and it was too consistent, and from too many known sources, to have been entirely generated locally. But if it had been generated by a central authority, if either the Empire or the Saints knew that Roger was alive on Marduk, the planet would have been crawling with searchers. Since it wasn't, the data was probably genuine, and the IBI agent was probably on the level. In which case, whatever happened here on Marduk, "just going home" was no longer an option.

"If you have good news, I could use some," she went on, leaning back from her own pad.

"That's just it—I don't know if it *is* good news," Julian said. "The problem is that this governor is either a complete and total idiot . . . or else subtly brilliant. And I've been working on the premise of subtly brilliant, looking for the dastardly plan."

"I haven't even looked," O'Casey admitted. "Who is the governor?"

"Ymyr Brown, Earl of Mountmarch," Julian said, then looked up sharply as O'Casey let out a rippling peal of laughter before she slapped her hand over her mouth to restrain the follow-on giggles.

"You know him?" Julian asked. She nodded, both hands over her mouth, and the sergeant's eyes glinted wickedly. "Okay, I can see from your reaction that you *do* know him, and that he's probably not all that great. But you have to give him a break—growing up with a name like 'Ymyr' couldn't have been all that much fun."

"You're being much too kind to him," O'Casey assured him. Another giggle slipped out, and she shook her head. "And take my word for it, whatever you're looking at is *not* a deeply laid plan. However stupid it seems."

"I almost wish it was," the sergeant said. "I just *hate* relying on the bad guys' stupidity. Even idiots have a bad habit of slipping up and doing something reasonably intelligent every so often, if only so Murphy can screw with your mind. Besides, *nobody* could really be this dumb."

"What did he do?" O'Casey asked, looking over his shoulder at an indecipherable schematic. After a moment, it resolved itself into a map of the port.

"Well, he set up an intelligence network in all the satraps of Krath," Julian said. He touched a control and brought up a picture of the continent, with data scrolling along the sides and political boundaries mapped in. "That much isn't dumb. But he has all these reports coming in, and he didn't want the spies just walking through his front gates. So he set up *cleared lanes* in the *defenses*!"

O'Casey grinned again, this time at his expression. Disbelief mingled with professional outrage on the sergeant's face, until he ended up looking just plain disgusted.

"That's Mountmarch all over," she said. "He's a brilliant media manipulator, and thinks his brilliance at that extends to everything.

There's nothing in the world for which he doesn't have a better, and much more brilliant, plan. Of course, the reality is that the vast majority of them backfire—often badly."

"Who is he?" Julian asked. "Other than the governor of the colony, that is?"

"He used to be a power at court," O'Casey said as she leaned back. She hadn't bothered to store her files on the Earl of Mountmarch in her toot, so they'd been lost along with most of her reference works and papers when *DeGlopper* was destroyed. Now she delved deep into plain old, biochemical memory for as much as she could recall about the earl and frowned thoughtfully.

"That was back in Roger's grandfather's later days," she went on. "There's not much question that he really was a brilliant example of a 'spin merchant,' and the old Emperor was very fixated on public opinion. Even though he wasn't elected, he felt that the will of the people should be observed. Which is all well and good, but ruling based on opinion polls, especially ones pushed by narrow agendas, is never a great idea. It's one of the reasons that the Empress is still having so many problems. Or was, before the coup, at any rate."

Their eyes met grimly for a moment. Then she gave herself a shake and resumed once more.

"The approach of the Imperial bureaucracy—that it's either completely untouchable, or that its function is solely to act in accordance with the will of opinion polls (which actually means at the will of skilled manipulators like Mountmarch who *shape* those polls)—is a tremendous drag on getting anything fixed," she said. "It's that holdover of bureaucratic and senior policy officer inertia, coupled with the iron triangle of senatorial interests, the interests of the bureaucracies, and the special interest groups and polls that combine to drive the senatorial agenda, that have made it nearly impossible for the Empress to get any real change enacted or to replace the worst of the bureaucrats with more proactive people.

"But I digress," she said, pausing to inhale, then cocked her head as Julian broke out in laughter. "What?"

"Well, to tell you the truth, I don't think I've heard you say that much about the situation back home this entire trip."

O'Casey sighed and shook her head.

"I'm *familiar* with preindustrial societies, and plots and plotters seem to be the same on Earth as on Marduk. But it's modern Imperial politics that are my real forte."

"I can tell," Julian said with another chuckle. "But you were saying about Mountmarch?"

"Mountmarch," she repeated. "Well, he excelled at taking the interests that were brought to him—whatever they were, but they tended to be on the 'Saints' end of the political spectrum—and turning molehills into mountains. He knew just about everyone in the media, and no matter who paid him, or for what, before you could say 'it's for the children,' whatever was going to end the universe this time would be the number one headline on all the e-casts and mags. And suddenly, with remarkable speed, there'd be committees, and blue ribbon panels, and legislation, and opinion polls, and nongovernmental charity organizations—all of them with lists of contacts and almost identical talking points, sprouting up like mushrooms. It really was quite an industry.

"And the leaks! He had access to everyone in the upper echelons of His Majesty's Government, either because they were afraid of him, or else because they wanted him to do the same thing for them. And whenever there was a tidbit of information that worked for the interest he was pushing at the moment, it would be major news the day he got it. Then along came Alexandra.

"Roger's mother had been watching him basically push her father around for years, and she didn't care for it one bit. In general, Alexandra tends towards the socialistic and environmentalist side of the political spectrum herself, but she's also aware of the dangers to society of going too far. So when the newest item Mountmarch was pushing was over the Lorthan Cluster, she pushed back—hard."

"Lorthan?" Julian asked. "You mean the Lorthan Incident?"

"The very same," she said. "Mountmarch was given the information that a task force had been sent out to lie doggo and try to catch the Saints red-handed raiding the Lorthan colonies. They'd been insisting that it was nothing but pirates, and offering 'military assistance in our need,' but all the indications were that it was a Saint force or forces that were trying to drive humans, and their 'contamination,' off of the Lorthan habitables."

"So was it Saints, or pirates?"

"Well, officially, no one knows," O'Casey said. "The task force was the ambushee rather than the ambusher, and officially, there was no information one way or the other on whether it was Saints or pirates. Of course, a pirate fleet that could take on an Imperial task force is pretty unlikely. And then there were the two *Muir*-class cruisers that were captured nearly intact."

"I hadn't heard that," Julian said.

"And you still haven't. But when we get back and I get situated, I'll take you out to Charon Base and you can see them. The point is that the leak cost nearly fourteen *hundred* Fleet lives, and Alexandra was *not* pleased."

"So she pinned it on Mountmarch?"

"He was the most common facilitator of such things. Whether he did it, or someone else, she really didn't care. She used administrative actions to remove most of his titles, but as a sop she must have posted him to Marduk. The most out of the way, barren, forsaken, and useless post in the Empire. And he's under Imperial law, so if he so much as sneezed, he'd be dealing with IO and the IBI, instead of local officers and the IC Authority. He can manipulate those; he still has people who, for some godforsaken reason, think he has a clue. But the Inspectorate and the IBI are another thing entirely."

"Remind me not to get on her bad side," Julian said. "Of course, I think that with a little training, Roger's going to be nearly as nasty. Maybe nastier. The tough part will be keeping him from killing anyone who pisses him off. But for right now, at least I can give him some good news—the local commander is an idiot, if a good manipulator of the media, and it looks like the port is going to be a cakewalk."

"Let's not get cocky," she said warningly.

"Oh, we won't," Julian said. "Two of the plasma cannon are listed as off line, but Item Number One will be to take them out anyway, just to be on the safe side. We'll send the armor in first to remove the wire, in case it's really there, then the mines. There's other bits. We'll get it right."

"And then grab a ship and go home," she said.

"To what?" Julian asked. "That's not going to be so easy."

"No," she admitted. "Everything in this download is hanging together, so I think Temu Jin is on the up and up. All the usual suspects in something like the 'attempted coup' are saying all the usual things. In fact, they're being so 'normal' that I've got the very definite feeling of either excellent information management, or pressure from behind the scenes. Although the *Imperial Telegraph* has called for a 'full and independent medical review of Her Majesty' with 'all due deference to the Throne.' On the other hand, they're being castigated by most of the major news outlets for 'pressuring her in her grief.'"

"As if that matters when the safety of the Empire is on the line?" Julian asked.

"Well, it does to some, or at least the polls will say so," O'Casey said with a thin smile. "Only the Commons can call for a vote of confidence on Her Majesty, and that's what it would take to force an independent medical exam, if our suspicions are correct. And we're not the only ones voicing them; there's a broad rumor that the Empress is being mind-controlled by Roger's father, with Jackson barely even mentioned. The problem is, that its being spun into a 'conspiracy theory' tying back to the death of the Emperor John and everything up to an invasion by implacable alien bugs from the Andromeda Galaxy."

"Thank goodness for the Andromeda Galaxy!" Julian laughed. "Without it, there'd be no science-fiction at all!"

"Indeed," she smiled. "Well, one wag does have it as the Andromeda *System,* but he's probably talking about Rigel."

"Probably," Julian agreed. "Another favorite."

"But if—w*hen* it turns out that she *is* being controlled, we're going to have an uphill climb to convince people that she was. In this case, something which happens to be the absolute truth is being successfully tied to every silly, paranoid fantasy floating around loose. Which means that it's undoubtedly in the process of being dismissed by every 'serious-minded' person in the Empire."

She shook her head.

"I wish I could be convinced that it was just happening to work out this way, but I don't think it is. *I* think what we're looking at is a carefully organized defense in depth. First, the people really behind the coup are counting on 'sensible people' to reject such crazy rumors out of hand. That will undercut any effort to force an independent exam of the Empress which might prove that she's being controlled, which is bad enough. But even worse, if Roger turns back up and claims he's been framed and that his mother's being mind-controlled, it's going to be really, really hard to convince anyone that he's telling the truth.

"But at the same time, I think Jackson is deliberately setting New Madrid up as the fall guy—the 'evil manipulator' the 'good Regent' can discover and pin all the blame on if the wheels start to come off. He can hammer New Madrid under any time he has to, and look at the other advantage it gives him. New Madrid is Roger's *father*, whether Roger can stand him or not. So who would be a more natural 'evil manipulator' than the father of that arch traitor, Roger MacClintock? Obviously, father and son thought the whole thing up together!"

She sighed, and shook her head again.

"I'm sure he believes Roger really is dead, so the whole thing is designed to use New Madrid as a scapegoat and a diversion if he needs one. I suppose I could even argue that the fact that he thinks he may need a diversion badly enough to concoct this new story blaming it all on Roger is a sign that his control is a lot shakier than it looks from here. But even though he's setting it up for an entirely different set of reasons, it's only going to make things look even worse for Roger if Jackson 'suddenly discovers' that New Madrid has been controlling the Empress all along. And it's going to be a lot tougher for us to deal with *that* than it's going to be to get through Mountmarch's defenses here on Marduk."

"Oh, I'm sure you'll figure something out," Julian said. "And the good news is that if you can't, it's just as likely we'll all be dead long before the problem crops up."

CHAPTER TWENTY-FOUR

"I wish we could use the pocking radios."

Roger peered through the battlefield smoke and cursed. The Krath army used about one arquebus for every ten soldiers, and between those, the Marines on the right, the Diaspran infantry on the left, and the occasional bombard firing from either side, the fields were covered in a veritable smokescreen. His helmet visor's systems gave him far better vision than any unaided eye could have provided, but that wasn't saying a lot. Worse, the billowing waves of smoke made it impossible to use visual signals in place of the radios. He could punch the occasional communications laser through, but enough gun smoke deprived him even of that.

"Tough, isn't it, Your Highness?" Pahner asked. "The fact is, up until we hit the Krath, you were spoiled as far as emissions discipline is concerned. When you don't have a complete monopoly on it, there are plenty of times when you don't have the luxury of using radio. Doesn't do to let the other side hear you, whether they can understand you or not. Then there's direction-finding. Or the battle could be taking place across lag distances where the turnaround time on transmissions just makes it impractical." He looked out across the smoke-covered fields between the two citadels and nodded. "At least this time you can *almost* see what's happening. That gives you at least a chance of judging what's going on."

Feet pounded on the stone steps behind them, and Roger turned to the runner who'd just arrived from the left wall. The sound in that direction had switched back to regular platoon volleys, he noted.

"How goes it, Orol?"

"Captain Fain says the enemy is off the wall and in retreat," the runner replied, rubbing blood from a cut at the base of his horns out of his eye.

"Bad?" Roger asked.

"Not really, Your Highness," the Mardukan said with a grunt of laughter. "They're not much as individual fighters; not a patch on the Boman. They barely got to the top of the wall, and we counterattacked with steel. We had a good killing."

Roger laughed and slapped him on the shoulder.

"Go get your head looked to, you old coot," he said. "There's more where those came from."

"Aye, and they'll be back tomorrow," the Mardukan replied. Then he saluted and headed back down the stairs, and Roger turned to Pahner.

"It sounds like the action on that side is pretty much the same as what's happening on the right. Time to sally?"

"I think so," Pahner replied. "Gastan?"

"If you think it wise," the Shin king said. "They could get bogged down and trapped, though," he added, looking just a bit dubious.

"Time to find out," Roger said, and walked to the rear of the wall. His position overlooked the courtyard directly behind the gates, which was currently packed with *civan*. The aggressive, bipedal omnivores were stamping their great three-toed feet and snapping at each other restlessly. The older of them recognized the conditions and were ready for action; it often led to a really good feed.

"Time for you to earn your damned pay, Rastar!" he shouted.

"Just make sure you're around to cover it!" the last Prince of Therdan shouted back, then looked at the commander of the gate tower. "Open the gates!"

The cavalry unit headed out in column of fours, crossing the double moat system and bypassing a bit of ruined siege tower from the Krath's farthest advance until they reached the outer works. Then they shook out into a single column, riding down the road and away from the castle at a walk. As the last rider cleared the outermost fortifications, the entire column began to pivot until it had turned into a line faced at right angles away from the roadway.

The instant the maneuver was completed, the *civan* broke into a long, bounding canter towards the left flank . . . and disappeared almost immediately into a fog bank of smoke.

"Blast!" Roger glared in disgust as the smoke overloaded his helmet's thermal sight capability—easier to do with the cold-blooded Mardukans than with most species. "The hell with this, I'm heading down to Fain's position. Maybe I can see something from there!"

"Very well, Your Highness," Pahner said, and gestured with his head to the collection of Marines and Diasprans, headed by Julian, who had remained behind to guard the prince's back. "But please keep firmly in mind that you are now Heir Primus."

"I will," Roger sighed. "I will."

Captain Fain looked up from a brief conversation with Erkum Pol and nodded as Roger loomed out of the smoke billowing up from the Diasprans' rifle fire.

"Good afternoon, Your Highness. How is it going with the rest of the wall?"

"They seem to have come in most heavily over here," Roger said, peering through the smoke towards the enemy trenches. "Is it just me, or do they seem to still be up and about?"

"As a matter of fact, they appear to be contemplating another attack, Your Highness," Fain replied. "I would consider that unwise, were I their commander, particularly given how disordered they are. But . . . nonetheless."

"They won't be contemplating it for long," Roger told the captain with an evil chuckle. "I'd hoped that they wouldn't have regained their trenches; it was too much to hope that they'd actually be getting ready to try again."

"Ah, are we going to witness a *civan* charge?" Fain asked, then gave a grunting Mardukan laugh when Roger nodded. "I'm sure Honal is just *hating* that!"

★ ★ ★

"I can't see a blasted thing!" Honal cursed.

"Well, if we stay on this heading, we should find something to attack . . . eventually. Even if we can't see it," Rastar said calmly, consulting the tactical map on the human pad Julian had programmed for him. "According to this, we're about two-thirds of the way to the forces opposite Fain."

"If that bloody Diaspran even knows where he is," Honal said as his *civan* stumbled in a hole. A Krath who appeared to be lost stumbled out of the fog of smoke within the sweep of Honal's sword and promptly died. "Come on, Valan!" Honal snarled as he flipped blood from his blade. "Give us a *breeze!*"

"Rain coming," Roger said as the sky darkened slightly. "That should finish off any visibility."

"Breaks of the game, Your Highness," Fain replied. "Of course, rain could lay some of the smoke, too, which wouldn't hurt." The native captain shrugged, never taking his eyes from the field before him. "I do believe that the Krath have dressed their lines. Perhaps you should consider moving back to the central keep."

"Hell with it," Roger said, leaning out and peering into the smoke himself. "I'm safe enough here."

Fain sighed and looked over his shoulder for Erkum Pol.

"You're safe enough *for the time being,* Your Highness. But if I ask you to retire, I must insist that you accept my judgment. I will not explain to Captain Pahner why I got you killed."

Roger looked at him with an expression very like surprise, then burst into laughter and nodded.

"All right, Krindi!" he said, wiping his eyes. "I'm sorry, but you sounded *exactly* like Pahner there."

"That wasn't my intention, Your Highness," the officer said, looking towards the Krath lines again. "But I don't consider it an insult. And, I have to add, that time might be soon."

The Krath used human-sized signs, held on long poles, as their unit guidons. The signs were marked with complex color patterns that designated unit and rank. In a culture without radio or any of the other adjuncts of high-tech civilization, such extremely simple visual signals were the only way for units to maintain cohesion in the smoke and confusion of a battlefield. The Krath had no option but to use them—or something very like them—if they wanted to hang on to any sort of organization, but the system also made it easier for the Diasprans to estimate when they had really reconsolidated. And they seemed to have gotten their act back together in record time.

"Just a bit more," Roger said. "Then I'll leave." He looked towards the Krath citadel, which had just disappeared behind a wall of silver. "Rain's almost here anyway. Won't be able to see a thing in a few minutes."

Even as he spoke, the blast of wind that precedes a storm tore aside the smoke, revealing the battlefield in all its detail.

"Oh, my," Roger said.

"Ho! My prayers are answered!" Honal said, as a breeze caressed his cheek. Then, as the smoke cleared, he grimaced. "Maybe it was better the other way."

The Krath hadn't simply reconsolidated the units which had just assaulted; they'd brought up reinforcements, as well. The new units had been deployed in blocks to either side of the original assault group, and the last few were moving into position as the smoke blew aside. Which left the Vashin barely two hundred meters from the nearest Krath battalion . . . which was just starting to dress its lines.

"Too late to worry about that!" Rastar snapped as he glanced in both directions. For a wonder, the cavalry had more or less kept its dress. "Now, for Shul's sake, don't get so carried away you get cut off or something; I'm tired of having to come to your rescue. Bugler, sound the charge!"

"'The kazoos, the kazoos of the North,'" Roger muttered. The Vashin used a short metal and bone horn that sounded remarkably like a kazoo, to a human.

"Now that is pretty," Pahner commented over Roger's shoulder.

"I thought you were staying by the gates," Roger said, glancing back at the Marine. Then he returned his attention to the field. "And, yes it is."

The pennon-fluttering Vashin lances had come down as one, and the *civan* had burst into a gallop, heads down and legs pumping. The species was similar in appearance to the extinct Terran velociraptor, and nearly as dangerous. At the moment, laid flat-out, tails whipping to maintain their balance, they looked like the most dangerous thing in the galaxy. Coupled with the Vashin on their backs, they were certainly the most deadly shock melee force ever evolved on Marduk.

"What's that quote?" Roger asked softly. "Something about it's good that war is so terrible?"

" 'It is good that war is so terrible, else we might grow too fond of it.' An American general named Lee in the early industrial period. He had a point."

"It's beautiful," Roger said. "But the Krath are going to swallow them without a burp."

The battalion the Vashin were charging contained at least three times as many men as they had. And it was but one of at least twenty drawn up in front of the walls.

"After fighting the Boman, the one thing Rastar knows is when to disengage," Pahner pointed out.

"Let's hope," Roger replied.

Rastar tried to withdraw the lance which had just transfixed the Krath infantryman, but it was stuck fast. He hated to give up the weapon's reach advantage, but he also knew better than to make himself a stationary target trying to recover it. And so he kept right on moving while he drew his sword and slashed at one of the swarming locals just as his *civan* stamped at another. The wicked, iron-shod claws shredded their target's torso even as the sword bit into flesh, but it was obvious they were getting bogged.

It wasn't that the locals were trained to receive cavalry. Indeed, the battalion that they'd struck at first was gone, shattered and scattered to the winds. But there'd been another behind it, and still more forces pouring out of the trenches. At this point, the Vashin were almost surrounded simply because of the sheer inertia of the

Krath forces on either flank of their penetration. The terrified infantry *wanted* to get out of the way, but there was nowhere for them to go.

He looked around for the bugler and realized he was almost all alone.

"Bloody hell," he muttered. It was a curse Honal had picked up from the human healer, and it was appropriate for the moment. The ground in every direction was covered with bodies. "I really need to get us out of this."

He began waving at nearby units, gathering them about him as he headed to the rear and the rain began to fall. At first, the drops were scattered, but in moments the storm had become a real Mardukan gullywasher. Water pounded down like a hammer—or a waterfall—and quickly formed puddles nearly knee deep to a human.

Rastar slashed down a few of the locals on the way out, especially when they were delaying his forces, but his main objective now was to withdraw his men intact, not to run up his body count. He'd only drawn his pistols once, but when he saw a cluster around a group of dismounted Vashin, all four came out. The Vashin, including Honal, were hunkered down behind their dropped *civan,* slashing and firing at a group of about twenty Krath who obviously wanted their weapons and harnesses.

Rastar pressed the *civan* into a gallop, and it responded wearily. He could tell the beast was badly fatigued, but its feet spurned the bodies of the fallen and it leapt over the occasional *civan* body until it finally bounded into the midst of the Krath attackers. Rastar laid down a curtain of revolver fire all around himself, while the *civan* kicked and bit in every direction, until a dozen of the other troopers he'd rallied came charging in to finish the enemy off .

"Rastar!" Honal protested as he drove his sword into one of the wounded Krath. "You're not leaving any for me!"

Rastar leaned over and offered his cousin an arm up as one of the other troopers dismounted to retrieve the bugler and the flag of Therdan.

"And what the hell was the colors group doing following you, and not me?" he demanded.

"You bloody idiot! You ran ahead of us. And you complain about *me* being headstrong! We got bogged down, and there you were, charging into the distance like some kid!"

"Oh, sure, blame it on me," Rastar said. He took the bugle from the bugler, who was clearly too cut up to wield it, and put it to his lips.

"Sounds like they're withdrawing," Pahner said, stepping back under an awning as the skies opened up.

"I wonder if the Krath will advance in this?" Roger asked.

"Probably, Your Highness," the Gastan said.

"What is this, 'Follow Roger Week'?" Roger asked with a smile he hoped the Gastan interpreted correctly.

"The buildup on this flank was easy to note," the Gastan said. "I'm not sure the sally was worth the loss of your riding beasts."

"I don't think it was," Roger agreed. "And even if the raiding party in the rear started any fires, they've been put out by the rain."

"Time for Plan B," Pahner mused. "If we had one. But the only one I can think of is to take the spaceport first. Gastan, I won't argue for that plan, but how long would it take for a force to make it to the port from here?"

"No more than twenty days," the Gastan replied. "Less for runners. I can have a message to Temu Jin in less than nine, and a reply in twice that."

The brief, intense rain squall was already clearing, and Roger gazed at the distant fortress.

"It's slightly lower than us, but we don't have any effective artillery to destroy it," he mused.

"They were starting to cast real siege cannon in K'Vaern's Cove," Julian said. Then he grimaced apologetically. "Sorry, just brainstorming. Too far, too long."

"And what would we do if we destroyed the walls?" Roger asked, gesturing at the Krath. The good news was that it seemed the combination of rain and the sally had caused the enemy to withdraw for the day, but—"They still outnumber us forty-to-one," he observed.

"We broke up their formations when they came at us by targeting the leadership," Fain said. The concept of brainstorming had been explained to him, and he found it a valid idea. "It was a technique I'd considered against the Boman, but I was never able to implement it at the time; my men weren't good enough shots. All the target practice since made the difference."

"The French introduced that technique during the Napoleonic wars," Pahner commented. "Congratulations on rediscovering it. I should have suggested it."

"But we can't snipe them to death," Roger said, looking up at the mountains looming above the citadel. The mountains to the north and south had relatively shallow slopes, and the Krath fortress had been cut into them. But beyond that, the valley necked down to the gorge of the Shin River. From there, it dropped over a thousand meters to the town of Thirlot. "We could drop teams on them, but even with armor, that would be pinpricks."

"Assassinate the leadership?" Julian suggested.

"They're relatively civilized," Pahner pointed out. "They're fighting by policy, not personality, and they have a solid chain of command. If we kill the current leaders, their replacements will step into their positions with hardly a ripple. Otherwise, that would work."

"We could roll rocks down the hill on them," Julian said. "Gronningen can handle the boulders."

"Pinpricks again," Pahner objected. "Even a large landslide onto the citadel or the army wouldn't do enough damage. Even if we did it several times, they'd just give up the slopes. And we *still* couldn't move them."

"Do it enough, and it might break their will," Julian argued mulishly. " 'The objective is to break the will of the enemy.' "

"A combination of all of them?" Fain mused. "Marines and my fellows sniping, the Shin to take to the heights and start rockslides, the occasional sally and raid . . . over time, we might be able to wear them down to the point they'd quit the field?"

"No." Roger shook his head, still looking at the distant ranges. "Not a battle of attrition; we need a battle of checkmate. Gastan, how long, again, to get a message to Jin?"

"Nine days." The Shin king gave Roger a sidelong glance. "What are you considering?"

"I'm going to make them wish they'd never pissed me off," Roger said. "I'm going to get them to surrender, without the need for a single battle. I'm going to send them home without their arms, their food, their bedding, or their pretty little tents. And with virtually no loss of life. I'm going to humiliate them."

"And how, exactly, are you going to do all that, Your Highness?" Pahner asked.

"I'm going to introduce them to geology," Roger said with a feral smile.

Pahner looked at him, then up at the mountains, and then up at the end of the valley. The intensity of his speculation was obvious, but, finally, he shrugged with a puzzled expression.

"The salient point to the plan is that this entire valley was once a lake," Roger said, looking around the steam-filled room.

The conference had been moved to the town of Mudh Hemh for a multitude of reasons, but the main one was that Roger wanted input from Despreaux. Since all the wounded had been moved to Mudh Hemh, the conference had to be moved to follow them.

The shift was beneficial on another level, as well. Although the town was filled with the sharp smell of rotten eggs from the nearby geothermal area, it was also surprisingly pleasant for the humans—which, of course, meant unpleasantly chilly for Mardukans. The Shin of Mudh Hemh maintained their movement ability by bathing in the warm waters from the Fire Lands, and the town was half-barbarian village, half-sybaritic spa.

Indeed, since the conference had been pushed into evening, it ended up being held in the primary bathhouse of the Gastan; and most of the Mardukans were submerged up to their necks in the steaming hot water. In any other circumstances, the thought of a major war-planning session being held in a spa would've been ludicrous. But to the Bronze Barbarians, who had held them in pouring thunderstorms, swamps, mountains, and flooded plains over the last half-year, this was infinitely better than many alternatives.

The sight of Dogzard, paddling from person to person to mooch treats, and of the IAS journalist, discreetly filming the entire conference, simply added an amusing counterpoint.

But the prince had to admit that the sight of Nimashet, half-undressed to submerge in the water, was a tad distracting.

"The geology of this region indicates that during the last glacial period, the valley was first carved by a glacier, and then the glacier was slowly replaced by a deep upland lake," he continued, and threw up the first picture, a representation of the valley with the lake sketched in. He hoped that it was clear enough that the Shin, unaccustomed as they were to representations, would understand what they were seeing.

"Somewhere around the vicinity of Queicuf, there was once a massive dam—probably half volcanic debris, and half ice; you can still see some of the traces of it in the slight prominence that Queicuf is established upon.

"It's the sediment from that upland lake and the ash from the volcanoes that gives you the rich soil you till. But the most important point for us right this minute is that it's possible to create the lake again."

"You're not going to flood the valley!" one of the chieftains protested.

Roger had sketched out the plan for the Gastan before the conference, and he more than suspected that the wily Shin monarch had planted that particular question. The chieftain who'd "spontaneously" blurted out the protest was one of the Gastan's personal retainers, and Pedi's father had very carefully gone over the points which might be expected to create concerns among his followers when he and Roger first discussed the possibilities. The human prince was beginning to appreciate how skillfully the Gastan manipulated his meetings. It was an important point to retain for his own later use, and also one to keep in the forefront of his mind now. If the Gastan decided that he didn't like a human plan, he was going to be a dangerously capable opponent.

"No," Roger said now, with a grin and a wave of his arms that replicated, as well as the under-equipped, two-armed humans could, the Mardukan gesture for intense amusement. "No, not the entire valley—just the bit the Krath are standing on."

A wave of ripples spread out from the chieftains gathered in the steaming water, and by the way some peered at the hologram and rubbed their horns, he could see that they understood the representation just fine.

"Even if we wanted to flood the entire valley, we don't have the materials," Roger told them. "What we propose to do is to drop a portion of the mountainside above the Shin River where it exits the valley. Please send messages to our contacts in the spaceport requesting that they send us as much octocellulose as possible. That's a very strong conventional explosive, and we'll use it first to drill holes in the slopes above the exit, and then to blow out a large chunk of the mountain.

"This chunk will create a temporary dam. We should be able to drop enough material into the river to raise the level to a point which will force the Krath to move out into the open, under our walls. The alternative will be drowning, or at least standing in cold water up to their groins. Their army will have no choice but to surrender."

"Or to charge the walls," one of the other chieftains said darkly.

"The water is going to rise *fast*," Pahner interjected. "They'll have, at most, two hours to decide what to do and to do it, and all the indications are that they're pretty incapable of reacting to surprise. I'd be astonished if they could even get a decision *made* in two hours, much less implement it."

"But if they realize what we're planning," Roger said, "and the preparations will of necessity take place in plain sight, they'll have ample time to plan a response. So we'll have to have a deception plan. We'll make it look as if the forces emplacing the charges are actually building a fortress to threaten their logistics line."

"What if we can't get the explosives?" Despreaux prompted.

"In that case, we'll use gunpowder," Roger said. "There's a powder mill here; Mudh Hemh is a primary supplier. It will take longer, and more materials, but it'll still work."

"I could make some nitro," she mused. "They have everything I need."

"I'd prefer you in one piece," Roger told her with a grin. "Nitroglycerin is far too volatile. If we can get the octocellulose, let's go with that."

"You said a temporary dam," the Gastan said. "How 'temporary'?"

"It will last at least two days," Roger said confidently. "It may last for years, depending on how the material falls."

"It could be made semi-permanent, if you wish," Fain interjected. "We Diasprans are quite familiar with such structures; with a few days' work, we could insure that it stays up for weeks. With a few weeks, we could make it permanent. That assumes that the subgrade is good—I'd need to look at that. But I concur on the couple of days, minimum. The material of the mountain appears to be a mixture of this black rock—"

"Basalt," Roger said.

"This 'basalt,' and the fine ash. The basalt will create the structure, and the ash—which is notably nonporous—will fill the gaps. I suspect that it will make an excellent dam all by itself."

"I have seen dams like this," one of the highland chiefs offered. "They're scattered throughout the mountains. This . . . this could work. If you can 'drop' enough of the mountain."

"If we can get the octocellulose, that's not a problem," Roger said with a shrug. "A piece of octocellulose the size of your thumb has the explosive power of a keg of gunpowder. The material is hard to describe, but it's a very tight packing of eight carbon molecules associated with nitrates, such as your saltpeter that goes in gunpowder. It's a common explosive among my people."

"We can't just lay it on the surface, Your Highness," Doc Dobrescu interjected. "We'll have to dig the charges in. Dig 'em in deep, if you want the sort of material movement you're talking about."

"That will be a challenge," Roger said. "I spoke with Krindi about it, and we can either blow out a sort of mining cavity by hammering in a spike and then blasting out the cavity, or we can try to produce very long steel drills that can be hammered in over time."

"Nah," Julian said. "Despreaux, can you make a shaped charge?"

"Sure," the sergeant replied, then grimaced. "Well, supervise," she amended, shrugging her arm. "There are field expedient shaped charges you can make out of hammered iron. Why?"

"I had a buddy who was an engineer," Julian said with a thoughtful expression. "He said that when they were in school, they made craters by first blowing a hole with shaped charges, then filling the cavity with explosives. I don't know the size of the shaped charges, though, or how much to put in."

"Well, if we blow a series of holes, then pack them with a combination of octocellulose and gunpowder, not having the materials for a decent ANFO slurry, it should work," Despreaux said, her face lighting up.

"I think that your paramour likes explosives more than you, Prince Roger," the Gastan commented dryly, and Roger shrugged as grunting Mardukan laughter filled the room. His relationship with Despreaux had become widely known.

"She likes it hot, what can I say?"

"We still have to assume that the Krath will become aware of our plans," the Gastan said.

"Even if they do, they'll find it difficult to attack the workings," Roger responded. "Your forces—and ours—fight better on the heights."

"Still, I think they'll try," the Gastan said. "And when they fail to take them, they'll come here, instead."

"They've come before!" one of the chieftains protested, dipping into the sulfurous water and coming back up blowing bubbles. "We'll stop them as we have before!"

"If they all come at once?" the Gastan asked. "Desperate in their fear of the rising waters?"

"You'll have to be prepared to offer them a truce, you realize," Roger said. This, too, was something he and the Gastan—and O'Casey—had discussed, and so he was prepared to look around mildly as the bellows of protest arose. One serendipitous advantage of having the conference in the bath chamber was that the chieftains were unarmed. Of course, it still looked as if they were willing to tear him limb from limb with their bare hands.

"No quarter for the Burners of the Shin!" "Death to the Krath!" "Blood! *Blood!*"

"What?" Roger shouted back, waving his hands at them. O'Casey had helped the Gastan set this part up, and the prince could see her trying not to smile.

"You can't kill them all!" he continued. "I don't mean 'you shall not'; I mean you *can*not! You'd have to cut throats until your arms fell off! And that assumes they lined up to have them cut! No, you're going to have to *feed* them, instead, which means bringing in food from the upper Krath and across the Shesul Pass, so the first thing to do is put them to work repairing that road. You *do* realize that you're going to be disarming them all, right? And that all their weapons and armor are going to be spoils?"

He looked around at the suddenly silent chieftains and saw the credit signs dancing in their eyes.

"Yep. For that matter, you can probably squeeze the Krath for tribute. This is Kirsti's primary field army. If they don't have it, the next satrap up the line can take all the territory he wants—they're probably holding him back by an agreement to refrain while they crush you. If you crush them, instead, they're going to be between a rock and a hard place. Tributes galore. Control of Queicuf again, control of all the trade routes, tribute—hell, an end to the slave raids and sacrifices. 'When you have them by the balls, their hearts and minds will follow.'"

"You make it sound so easy," one of the chieftains complained.

"Ah, well, that's my job," Roger said with a grin. They laughed again, but then he allowed his grin to fade. "Easy? No. They'll probably hit Nopet Nujam hard. They might hit Nopet Vusof. But they won't have much time to do anything, unless someone goes tattling from this meeting. If we use cratering charges—and that sounds like the best plan—we can drop the mountainside the day after we reach the heights. Two hours after it goes down, the water will be up to their tents."

"We must be ready to face a heavy attack, though," the Gastan said. "We will need every warrior ready, either on the walls or resting for their time. With the aid of our human allies, we may yet win the day—win it fully, and for all time. But there is hard battle ahead of us still, and we must steel ourselves for it. The Shin! Death to the Krath!"

"DEATH TO THE KRATH!"

CHAPTER TWENTY-FIVE

Roger sank into the water and sighed as the chieftains filed out.

"That went well," he said, hooking an arm around Despreaux.

"Perhaps," the Gastan said. "Perhaps."

"What's wrong?" Roger asked. "I think the plan will work. Things will go wrong, but we should be able to implement the basics, no matter what."

"My father fears for our people," Pedi said. She and Cord had remained silent throughout the meeting, but they'd been a presence nonetheless—the adviser to the prince and the Light of Mudh Hemh, who was now his *benan*. There was something else going on there, as well, but Roger was unsure what it was.

"We'll take fierce casualties in the final attack, if it comes," the Gastan said finally. "The deaths of warriors. That is what concerns me, because it is only through warriors that the people can continue, that . . . new life comes into the world."

He glanced over at his daughter, then away.

"I'm missing something here," Roger said.

"I think I've got it," Dr. Dobrescu said. "It's like the Kranolta, Your Highness. Gaston, pardon me if I'm blunt. What you're afraid of is that whereas females, like Pedi, can carry many children, it's only through the warriors—the males—that children can be made. Is that correct?"

The Gastan sighed and gestured.

"Yes. When a male lies with a female, only a few pups are produced. But if two males lie with the female, more are produced. A female can carry . . . oh, maybe six or eight, with difficulty. But a male can never . . . give more than three or four. So if the males fall in battle, from whence comes the next generation?"

"You have to remember, Your Highness," Dobrescu said, after carefully deactivating his toot's translator program, "that Mardukan 'males' are technically females."

"And they implant eggs rather than injecting sperm," Roger said, also in Imperial. "Got it. And since they only come into season twice a year . . ."

"We have lost more warriors than females to the raids," the Gastan said, "and we already feel the effects of this long war. If we lose as many as half of our warriors—and in a great attack, that is possible—we may be doomed even if your plan succeeds. The Krath will just *outbreed* us."

"Co-opt them," Eleanora suggested. "Let them 'immigrate.' The Krath are overcrowded. Let them trickle up into the mountains. Have them rebuild Uthomof."

"Perhaps," the Gastan said with an edge of doubt. "It's been suggested before. There are outer villages that have been so stripped by the raiders that they're empty. We don't want the Krath Fire Priests, though."

"Priests can be . . . adjusted," Fain said. "You may be faced in the near future with more prisoners than you have population. Before they leave, ask the best of them if they want to move up here. Make them Shin, not Krath. If they keep their religion, make sure it renounces sacrifice. You should make that a condition of the peace treaty, anyway."

"I'm still confused about that," Kosutic said. "According to Harvard, it's a recent innovation, and it doesn't fit his data on their religion at all. I'm guessing that it's human cultural contamination, but from where and why is the question."

"It started in the time of my father's father," the Gastan told her. "Initially, it was solely among the Krath, but in my father's time, they started raiding us for Servants of the Fire. Part of that may have been because the warriors of Uthomof had raided all the way to the outskirts of Kirsti. The first of the Shin Servants were taken in punitive raids, but it has grown steadily ever since."

"It was among the Krath, at first?" Kosutic asked. "They didn't start by raiding you?"

"No, not at first. Later . . . it's more from us than from them, now."

"Eleanora?" The sergeant major looked at O'Casey. "Human sacrifice and cannibalism?"

"In civilizations? As opposed to, say, tribal headhunters?"

"Yeah," the Armaghan said, slipping deeper into the water. "Aztecs. Kali . . ."

"Baal, if you count ritual infanticide," the chief of staff said with a quizzical expression.

"Baal!" Kosutic sat upright and slapped her forehead. "How could I forget Baal? I bet that's it!"

"What's 'it'?" Roger demanded.

"Where to start?" sergeant major asked.

"Start at the beginning . . ." Pahner suggested with a slight smile.

"Gee, thanks a lot, Sir!"

The priestess settled back in the water once more, frowning thoughtfully.

"Okay," she said finally. "The worship of Baal is *old*. Baal is an only slightly 'mixed' god; he's mostly a cattle god, and he only added a human form later. The Minotaur is probably related to his worship, and there are some very significant pre-Baal religious motifs in pre-Egyptian culture.

"One of the major aspects of the worship of Baal is ritual infanticide. Children, infants younger than eight weeks, are wrapped in swaddling clothes and put in fires that burn within a huge figure, usually that of a bull but sometimes of a minotaur-looking human. These are frequently children of high-caste couples.

"Prior to the development of civilization in the Turanian and Terrane regions, the area was a hunter-gatherer paradise. But a tectonic shift—a change in Terra's axial inclination, actually—in about 6000 b.c.e., caused a severe climate change. The Sahara was created, which was a desert where the Libyan Plains are now. Civilization developed rapidly in response, as the hunter-gatherers were forced to change their lifestyles to adjust to the climate changes.

"Now, the first evidence of the cult of Baal arose practically in tandem with civilization. Aspects of it were found in very early Egyptian society, although the sacrificial aspects are ambiguous. But it was definitely found in the proto-Phoenician cattle herders and fishermen in the Levant. The Phoenicians, of course, carried it far and wide, and it might have influenced the shift from Tolmec self-sacrifice to Aztec human sacrifice. Certainly they were in contact with the Tolmecs, as well as the proto-Incans and the Maya; the Phoenician logs that were, ahem, 'recovered' from Professor Van Dorn in 2805 proved that conclusively."

"One of the classics of ideological bias," O'Casey said with a laugh. " 'Analyzing them for authenticity' indeed! If his research assistant hadn't called the authorities, he would've destroyed *all* the tablets."

"Exactly," the sergeant major agreed. "But at least it finally ended the two hundred-year reign of the Land-Bridge Fanatics in anthropology. Now, the rationale for infanticide is still occasionally debated. Infanticide is practiced by every society, and it's often supported more by women than by men . . ."

"Excuse me, Sergeant Major," Despreaux said with a frown. "*Every* society? I don't think so!"

"Ever heard of abortion, girl?" the Armaghan snapped back. "What in hell do you think *that* is? I'm not arguing for or against infanticide, but it's the same thing. The point being that there's a widespread human drive towards it. But that doesn't explain the ritualization, which is only found in certain cultures, and most notably in the cult of Baal. In 2384, Dr. Elmkhan, at the University of Teheran completed the definitive study of the rise of Baalism. He analyzed results from over four thousand digs throughout Terrane and Turania and came to the conclusion, which to this day is hotly debated, that it was a direct response to population problems in the immediate aftermath of the climatic change."

"Ah, bingo," Roger said. "The Krath population problem!"

"The Krath population problem" Kosutic agreed. "My guess is that it *was* cultural contamination—and not accidentally, either. There was a satirical piece by an early industrial writer about the Irish. . . . What was his name? Fast? Quick?"

"Swift?" Pahner asked. " 'An Elegant Solution' or something like that. 'Let them eat their young.'"

"Yes," O'Casey agreed. "But what Swift didn't realize was that there were societies where, for all practical purposes, that was what *happened*. In fact, one of the major factors influencing the rise of Christianity in Roman culture was its proscription against infanticide. There *is* a drive towards it, but it is *not* widely supported. Roman matrons, given the choice of saying 'My God forbids it' jumped on board by the thousands. It was that proscription, along with the acceptance of the Rituals of Mithras as the standard Mass, that *created* the Catholic church."

"The Rituals of *what*?" Despreaux asked plaintively. "You're going too fast."

"I'm just sort of sitting here with my jaw on the table," Roger told her with a snort. "I'm not even trying to understand half of it."

"The Rituals of Mithras," Fain put in, lifting up so that more than just his ears and horns were out of the steaming water. "One of the conversations the Priestess and I had. As a political ploy to gain the support of the Roman Army, the early Christians took the entire series of rituals from a religion called the Mithraists and turned it into their Mass."

"If imitation is the sincerest form of flattery, the early Christian church was very impressed with the Mithraists," Kosutic said sourly. "But at that point the Christians had two of the major political forces in Rome on their side: the Army, which switched to Christianity in droves as soon as they saw that it was just Mithras in another guise; and the matrons who no longer had to throttle their excess children. The rest is known history—the Emperor converted, and it was all over but the shouting. And let me tell you, that was ferociously argued— and occasionally warred over—for nearly two thousand years *after* it could be debated in public. But in the end, the preponderance of evidence pointed to that being the pattern, rather than his mother telling him he had to do it.

"On the other hand," she noted, "it has little or nothing to do with the Krath, other than as an example of the intersection of religion and politics."

"Can I ask one thing that's bothering me?" Roger said.

"Ask away, Your Highness," the sergeant major replied.

"You used the *present* tense a *lot* when discussing the cult of Baal and its sacrifices," Roger said carefully. "And I recall you saying something about 'the Brotherhood of Baal' among the Armaghans . . ."

"The Brotherhood does not practice human sacrifice," Kosutic said, then waggled her hands. "As far as I know. Although they do have the occasional death under the 'enhancement' rituals, which might count. They certainly do *not* practice ritual infanticide. The Church of Ryback, on the other hand, has a variety of Baalian influences."

"The Saints," Pahner said. "I wondered when you'd get to the point."

"The Saints," the sergeant major said with a nod. "There are various . . . word choices and phrases in the Church of Ryback that indicate to comparative theologians that it was influenced by the New Cult of Baal, which was formed—and died—during the Dagger Years. Also, the Rybackians have various sub-cults, which are, ahem, more 'fundamental' than others."

"I notice that you say 'ahem' when you're trying not to say something," Roger observed. "What was *that* 'ahem'?"

Kosutic sighed and shook her head.

"There are . . . rumors that are generally discounted about some of the sub-cults of Ryback eating their young. Personally, I don't put much faith in them. You hear that sort of thing about all sorts of hated sub-groups. But . . . I also wouldn't put it past them, either. Anyway, you can imagine *their* reaction to the overcrowding of the Krath. Never prove it, though."

"And we could be wrong," O'Casey pointed out. "There's the whole influence of the spaceport, the original survey team, the previous group of archeologists . . . It could have been any of them, or spontaneous serial development, for that matter."

"Oooo, like pyramids?" Kosutic asked with one eyebrow arched.

"Well . . ." O'Casey blushed faintly and actually wiggled in the water. "In this case, it's at least possible. I know that archeologists still have a bad reputation from that, but in this case it's *possible*. Cannibalism is endemic in every culture except the Phaenurs."

"Who don't even have *wars*," Despreaux whispered to Julian.

"Oh, they have them," the intelligence sergeant replied. "They just don't get noticed."

"They're empaths," she protested quietly. "How could *empaths* have a war?"

"You've obviously never had a Jewish mother-in-law," Julian told her under his breath.

"Sergeant Major, you're clearly having fun," Pahner interjected. "But I'm not sure that knowing where the Krath got the idea for sacrifices gets us. I think we need to concentrate on the tactics for a little bit, here."

"I think that's straightforward," Roger said. "We'll write a message to Jin. The Gastan sends it via his runners. When we get the explosives, Nimashet builds the shaped charges, we blow the mountain, and then we call for the Krath's surrender."

"And in the meantime, Your Highness?"

"Well, in about five or six days, we start assembling teams and training," Roger said. "And until then, I intend to drink some wine and sit in a hot tub with my girlfriend. I suggest you do the same. Well, except the girlfriend part. You can abstain from that."

"Thanks so very much, Your Highness," Pahner said.

"No problem," the prince replied. He held out a flask and cup. "Wine?"

Temu Jin looked at the message, then at the messenger.

"Do you know what they're going to do with it?" he asked.

"I don't even know what 'it' is, human," the Shin runner replied curtly. The runner appeared to be almost a different species from the Gastan. He was as tall as any Mardukan Jin had ever dealt with, and had weirdly long fingers and shortened horns. Combined with the four arms and widely spaced eyes, it made him look like a mucous-covered insect. "All I know is that there are four more of us waiting. And we are to take packages from you. We wait until the packages are prepared."

"Come on, then," Jin said, with a gesture.

The meeting was taking place at the back of the spaceport, as usual. Now Jin descended the slight slope from the edge and headed to the nearest Krath hamlet, a tiny burg called Tul by the locals. The majority of the few off-planet visitors stayed on the port reservation. The few who didn't usually exited by the main gates, and thence down the road to the Krath imperial city, called, with surprising imagination, "Krath." Very few humans, or any other visitors, for that matter, came to Tul.

On one level, that made it a bad place to hide purloined materials. The sight of a human face there was a dead giveaway that something was going down. On the other hand, the bribes were lower, and the local farmers and craftsmen reminded him of home. As long as he kept up the payments, they were unlikely to go squealing to the taxmen, who were their only contact with the central government.

And it was convenient for the purpose—which was to build up a cache against the day he needed it.

Originally, the caches had started as insurance against the possibility that Governor Mountmarch might decide he could dispense with the services of one Temu Jin. Jin was well aware that he was deep into the "knows too much; not close enough to the inner circle to be trusted" category. Life on the frontier was cheap, and the only law was the governor. If Mountmarch wanted him dead, it was a matter of a nod. Against that almost inevitable day, he'd started smuggling the odd weapon or ammo pack out of the port. And when he'd realized how easy it was, he'd upped his depredations to using whole pack teams of Mardukans to smuggle material out.

As far as anyone would be able to tell, it was just a regular black-market operation. He sold Imperial materials to the Mardukans, and in return he had a nice Mardukan servant and trade goods, which he used to purchase materials from docking spacers. In reality, the majority of materials weren't being sold, but stored in bunkers. Each time he sent stuff down, he also sent along payments to the mayor—either human goods, or Krath coin. And each time he pulled stuff out, he paid more. He had backup caches in the hills, including a full set of armor, for which he had the codes, and a heavy plasma gun. If he had to fight to get the rest, he could. But he'd never had any trouble with Tul. He thought of it as his little war-bank.

And now it was time to make a withdrawal.

They came into the village the back way, through the *turom* fields, stepping carefully around the round balls of horselike dung. Like much of the continent's architecture, the mayor's house was a squat construction of heavy basalt rocks. It was built more like a fortress than most, and its back door was constructed of half-meter thick planks that didn't respond well to a standard knock. Which was why Jin drew his bead pistol and pounded on the door with its handgrip, swinging the gun like a hammer.

After a few moments, the door swung open to reveal a wizened old Mardukan female. Jin had never been sure if she was the cook, or a mother-in-law, or what. It probably didn't matter, but it nagged at his sense of curiosity. She was *always* the one to answer the door, no matter if he was early or late.

She looked at him, looked at the Mardukans with him, made a motion to wait, then closed the door. After a few moments more, it was opened by the local Krath leader.

"Temu Jin, I see you," he said. "You bring Shin to my door?"

"I need to get a few things."

"Of course," the mayor said with a gesture of resignation. "I fear that the authorities are becoming too interested in this affair."

"I'll do my best not to let you get caught up in it," and Jin said. "I treasure your security as much as you treasure my gold."

"Perhaps," the mayor muttered, then beckoned for Jin to follow him and led the way through the darkened town.

The route took them to an abandoned basement which had been hollowed out and reinforced on one side. The hollow, in turn, had been packed with boxes, and Temu Jin started checking packing lists.

"Cataclysmite," he muttered, shaking his head. "What in *hell* does he want two hundred kilos of cataclysmite for?"

★ ★ ★

Despreaux waved the cup of wine away as Julian filed out of the door.

"Not for me, either."

"Don't make me drink it all alone," Roger said. "Besides, it's good for healing bones. It's got calcium in it."

"That's *milk*, you goof," Despreaux said. She chuckled, but then she sobered. "Roger, we have to talk."

"Uh, oh. What have I done now?"

"I think . . ." She stopped and shook her head. "I think we should stop seeing each other."

"Look, you're my bodyguard," Roger said. "I have to see you."

"You know what I mean."

"If it's the fraternization thing, we'll handle it," he said with a frown. He was beginning to realize that she was serious. "I mean, we've been . . . well . . . friends for this long. If it was going to go wrong, it would have before now."

"It's not that," she said, shaking her head. "Let's just leave it, okay? Say 'thanks,' and shake hands and be friends."

"You're *joking*," he spat. "Tell me you're joking! What ever happened to 'eternal love' and all that?"

"Some things . . . change. I don't think we're right."

"Nimashet, right up until we got to Mudh Hemh, you thought we were as right as— Well, I can't think of a metaphor. *Very* right. So what's changed?"

"Nothing," she said, turning away and getting out of the water.

"Is it one of the Marines?"

"No!" she said. "Please don't play twenty questions, all right?"

"No, not all right. I want to know what's changed."

"You did, *Your Highness*," she said, sitting back down on the edge of the water and wringing out her hair. "Before, you were prince Roger, Heir Tertiary to the Throne of Man. Now, you're either a wanted outlaw, or the next Emperor. And you're not willing to settle for wanted outlaw, are you?"

"No," Roger said balefully. "Are you?"

"I don't know," she sighed. "There's been so much death, I'm afraid it's never going to end. Not even get better."

"Hey, yo, Sergeant Despreaux," he smiled. "You're the one who carried me out of the battle in Voitan. Remember?"

"Roger, I haven't fired a shot in combat since . . . Sindi. Yeah, I think that's it. That little 'holding action' of yours before the main battle."

"What?"

"Remember when we were coming out of the temple in Kirsti? Who was the only person with ammo?"

"You were," Roger replied. "But . . . I thought you'd just been very conservative with your fire."

"I hadn't fired *at all*!" she snapped. "Not even when that bastard almost took your head off on the back stair!"

"But—" Roger stared at her, stunned by the revelation. Then he shook himself. "Kosutic had me covered," he said. "Besides, what does *that* have to do with never seeing me again?"

"Nothing," she admitted. "Except that you're not going to just let bygones be bygones. You're going to go charging back to Imperial City with blood in your eye. And you'll either overthrow Jackson, or die trying. Right?"

"Damned right!"

"So, you're either going to be dead, or the Emperor, right?"

"Well, Mother is probably competent—"

"But when *she* dies, or abdicates, you're the Emperor, right?"

"Oh."

"And do you think that the Emperor can just marry any old rube farm girl from the back of beyond?" she asked. "Sure, when you were just Prince Roger, it was like a dream come true. I figured I'd be a nine-day celebrity, and then we'd find some out of the way place to . . . be Roger and Nimashet. But now you're going to be Emperor, and Emperors have *dynastic* marriages, not marriages to girls from the out-planets."

"Oh," he repeated. "Oh, Nimashet—"

"You know I'm right," she said, wiping at her eyes. "I saw the way O'Casey was looking at me. I'm willing to be your wife. I'm even willing to be your girlfriend. I'm not willing to be your mistress, or your concubine. And those are the choices available to Emperor Roger and Sergeant Nimashet Despreaux."

"No," he said, wrapping his arms around her knees. "Nimashet, I'll *need* you. Even if we succeed, and that's not a given, I'll need you to be there. I . . . you're always at my back. Maybe you're not shooting anymore, but you're still there. Even when Cord isn't, *you're* there. You're like my right arm. I can't make it without you."

"Hah," she snorted through the tears. "You'd still be cursing your enemies with both arms and legs hacked off. And drown them in blood to kill them. *You* don't know when to quit. Me? I do. I quit. When we get back and everything is done, I'm turning in the uniform. And until then, I'm going to see Sergeant Major Kosutic about putting me on noncombat duties. It's beyond combat fatigue, Roger. I just can't focus anymore. I may be at your back, but that's because you're wiping everything out in front of you, and at your back is the safest place to be. The only problem is that I'm supposed to be *your* bodyguard, not the other way around."

"You've saved my life . . ." He thought about it. "Three times, I think."

"And you've saved mine as many," she replied. "It's not a matter of keeping score. Just, let it go, okay? I can't marry the Emperor, I can't guard you worth a damn, and I'm not much good for anything else. I'll head back to Midgard, buy a farm, find a nice stolid husband, and . . . try not to think about you. Okay?"

"No, it's not 'okay'! I can see your logic, sort of. But if you think I'm going to release you to go hide on a farm, you've got another think coming. And unless there's a clear reason for a dynastic marriage, I'm still going to marry you, come hell or high water. Even if I have to drag you into the church, kicking and screaming!"

"You and what army, Mister?" she asked dangerously. "If I say no, I mean no."

"Look, none of this is settled until we get to Terra," Roger said. "Let's just . . . bank it right now. We'll pull it out and look at it again when things settle down. But I don't care if you're not one hundred percent in close combat. Who's making the shaped charges?"

"Me," she sighed.

"And who's going to be managing the demolitions?"

"Me."

"And when we get back to Terra, can I trust you to hang in there and do whatever needs to be done to the best of your ability, as long as you don't have to kill anyone?"

"Yes," she admitted.

"Can I go get any old joker off the street that I can trust? Or any of the Marines on Terra? No. I'll need every single body I can trust. And you're a body that I can both trust and admire," he finished with a leer.

"Gee, thanks." She smiled.

"You told me a long time ago that we might not get to retire to Marduk. That Mother might have other plans for us. Well, the same goes for you. Unless we're all killed, I'm going to have things I need you to do. Only one of them involves marrying me, and we'll discuss that when the time comes. Okay?"

"Okay."

"Does this mean I can't wrestle with you in the water?" he asked, running his hand up her side.

"If you get this cast wet and short it out, Dobrescu will kill you," she pointed out.

"It's okay. I'm a faster draw than he is."

"Well, since you put it that way," she replied, and slid down into the water and leaned forward to kiss him.

"Your Highness," Bebi said, leaning in the door. "Captain Pahner's compliments, and he'd like to see you in his quarters."

"I think I'm beginning to detect a pattern here," Roger snarled under his breath.

"Once is happenstance, twice is coincidence, and three times is enemy action," Despreaux replied huskily. "So far, it's just coincidence."

"So far," Roger replied. "But I have to wonder."

CHAPTER TWENTY-SIX

"You are a cruel human, Adib Julian," Kosutic said.

"It's an art," he replied, tapping the pad. "Despreaux's blood pressure and heart beat both increase, they're having an argument. Heart beat increases, and blood pressure drops, and they're . . . not."

"What about Roger?" the sergeant major asked.

"To tell you the truth, he's scary," Julian said. "The whole time, his heartbeat never changed within any sort of standard of variation. Steady fifty-two beats per minute. That's the lowest in the company, by the way. And his blood pressure barely flickered. You can't tell *anything* about what he's thinking or feeling from biometrics. Spooky."

"He gets angry," Kosutic said. "I've *seen* it."

"Sure," the sergeant agreed, flipping the pad closed. "And when he does, he's *still* got ice water running in his veins."

"Hmmm. You know, I think we're just starting to understand why you *don't* want to pock with a MacClintock."

Thousands of years before the coming of the race called Man, the mountain had been fire. Molten rock and ash spewed from the bosom of the world, laying down interleaving layers of each as the mountain grew higher and higher. Side openings occurred, and the red rock

383

flowed from them like a steaming avalanche, occasionally breaking loose whole sides of the mountain in a semiliquid, fiery hot gel called pyroclastic flow.

Eventually, the fierce nuclear fire that was at the core of the local hotspot passed on, and the mountains began to cool. Water brought its beneficence of cooling to the steaming mountain, scouring its flanks and bringing growth where there had been molten rock. In time, the black, smoking wasteland became a fertile slope of trees and flowers.

Time passed, and the sun of the planet called Marduk flickered. For a time that was short for a sun, or a planet, the sun became cooler. To the sun itself, the effect was barely noticeable. But on the sole life-hugging planet that orbited it, the effect was devastating.

The rains stopped. Where there had been steaming jungles, there were sunbaked plains. Ice came. Where there had been liquid-drenched mountains, the water fell as snow and compressed, and compacted, and stayed and stayed, until it became mountains—walls of glacial ice.

Species died, and the nascent civilizations of the higher latitudes fell. Survivors huddled around hot springs while the white walls drew ever closer.

Along the side of the mountain, the white ice grew and grew. The hot spots to one side kept a continual melt in place, and the runoff water—dammed up behind the terminal moraine of the glacier—filled the valley from end to end. Regular floods laid down layers of lighter and darker materials on the valley floor, improving the already excellent soil. The glacier brought with it loess, the fine dust that was left when ice crushed its enemy rock. The glacier also brought massive boulders that it laid down in complex, swirling patterns that later residents would often use as roadbeds and quarry for building stone. And everywhere, it crushed the sides of the valley, hammering at the walls of the mountain and tearing at its stone and ash foundations.

Finally, in a short time for a star, the sun restarted and turned its thermostat all the way back to high. The rains came. Jungles regrew. And the ice . . . melted.

It started slowly, with more floods each spring than there'd been the spring before. Then the glacier started to break up, and the terminal moraine, the dam at the head of the valley, became intermingled with chunks and blocks of the ice. For a time, the dam grew higher, as the floods carried the silt and debris of four thousand years of glaciation to it. But finally, inevitably, the dam at the head of the valley burst. First came a trickle, then a flood, then a cascade, and finally, a veritable tsunami of water, crashing down the gorge in a flash flood to end all flash floods. It scoured the gorge wider than a hundred thousand years of lesser floods. It wiped out the small village that had been recently founded at the base of the gorge. And it drained the Vale of the Shin, leaving a fertile pastureland that simply begged for colonization.

And the mountain slept.

Erkum Pol wielded the machete like a machine, hacking away at the undergrowth while holding on to the rope to prevent himself from sliding back down the slope. It was also wrapped around his waist; it was a very steep slope.

" 'Set a few charges,' he said," Julian muttered as he slid sideways and stopped himself by grabbing a tree. Unfortunately, its bark was well provided with long spines, one of which jammed itself into his hand. "Aarrrgh! 'Blow up the side of the mountain,' he said. 'No problem,' he said."

"We have the explosives," Fain said, sliding down the rope beside him. "We have the 'shaped charges.' What's the difficulty?"

"Maybe emplacing them on a sixty-degree slope? We're going to have to dig out pits for the charges and hold them down with pins hammered into the rock. They have to have a bit of something holding them down. Usually, it's just the charge's case and the weight of the material, but in this case, we're going to have to anchor the cases, since they're pointing sideways. And I'm not sure any weight of cataclysmite is going to be enough to cut *out* from the bores."

"A trench," Roger said, coming hand-over-hand along the slope through the undergrowth. "We'll dig a shallow trench and fire them directly down. From this height, we should get plenty enough material to seal the river."

"We can do that," Fain said. "Like starting a new quarry."

"Exactly. In fact, if you can scratch out a trench in the loam, we can put in a line of det-cord which will practically make it for us."

"That will give away our position, Sir," Julian pointed out. The top of the Krath citadel was vaguely visible from their position, or, its northern bastion was, at least.

"They'll spot us up here before long anyway," Roger pointed out in return. "And they'll definitely notice when we blow the shaped charges."

The latter were waiting up the slope on the narrow track a local guide had "found" over the mountain. It was obvious that despite the best efforts of both the Gastan and the local Krath to restrict all commerce between them to Trade Town, and thereby tax it, plenty of smugglers moved through the hills around it.

"Captain Fain, put out some security teams and let's get to work," Roger said.

"Yes, Your Highness. It will be like old home week."

"What in the Fire do they think they're doing up there?" Lorak Tral wondered aloud.

The Sere's commander had envisioned the entire plan in a single instant when word of the High Priest's death reached him. For too long, the Shin, and the Scourge which pursued them, had been a thorn in the side of the Krath. But with the High Priest's death at the hands of humans (humans presumably allied with the Shin, judging from their actions), the stage had been set at last for the elimination of the Scourge. For two generations, the Scourge—most of them little more than jumped up Shadem and Shin themselves—had been on the upsurge. If they were permitted to continue to grow, the Krath would fall under the sway of slave-raiders. Better to use this opportunity to cut their legs off. By crushing Mudh Hemh, the Sere would show its importance to the council and the utility of the Scourge would be cut in half.

And it didn't hurt that it would leave *him* as High Priest.

"Perhaps they're planning to cut the supply line," Vos Ton said. The fortress' commander rubbed his horns nervously. "Even a slight stoppage in resupply will make our position difficult. I could wish you'd brought fewer troops."

Tral gazed up at the position and shook his head.

"Even with their rifles, they'll have a hard time stopping us from using the road. And they cannot stop us from taking Mudh Hemh."

"If we ever do," Ton groused. "Nopet Nujam is not a simple proposition. I warned you of that when you came up with this scheme."

"It's important to show that no one can simply walk in and kill our High Priest," Tral replied. "We must show them the error of their ways."

"Each day we laboriously besiege them gives them another day to try something new," Ton pointed out. "That's all I'm saying."

"No matter what they do, they are too few to truly affect us," the Sere replied. "Unless you think they can call the God of Fire down upon us?"

"No," Vos Ton replied, looking up at the figures, mostly hidden by trees. Even if they rolled rocks down, they wouldn't fall on his castle. "No, but I wonder what they *are* going to call down on us."

A moment later, a tremendous boom bellowed down the mountainside. A towering cloud of dust and smoke reared up, and then, as quickly as it had arisen, it rained down rocks and severed trees. They bounced and tumbled, battering downwards, and although most were captured by the trees below the cut, many made it all the way to the base, leapt off the last ledge, arced across the road, and ended up in the Shin River.

The roadbed at the narrows was cut into a shallow natural ledge that wended its way about ten meters above the river, higher than almost any reported flood. The few rocks and trees that made it to the river raised the water slightly, but the increase was only a fraction of the difference between its normal surface and the roadway.

"Are they trying to block the road?" Ton asked in a puzzled voice. "Or raise the river to block it?"

"Whichever it is, if they get enough into the river to become a problem, we'll send out a working party," Tral replied. Then he grunted in laughter. "Look," he added as the deep, rushing water broke up the shallow dam and carried it away. "The river does our work for us."

"Perhaps," the fortress commander agreed dubiously. "But I wish we had some reports from our spies. I would like to know what their conference was about. I want to know what they think they're doing up there."

"Hmmm . . ." Tral said. "We're almost ready for the great attack. We can move it up by a few hours; then, whatever it is, we'll have taken their fortress before they're able to use it."

"What about the Scourge force?"

"They were to attack as we did," the Sere leader said. "And, really, they were never to be anything more than a distraction. Whatever happens, it will be the Sere that breaks the back of Mudh Hemh for all time. It is *that* which will be remembered."

"From your mouth to the Fire God's ears," the fortress commander said.

"You know," Roger said, stepping into the narrow trench, "I bet they really are wondering what we're doing up here."

"Well, in about six more hours, it won't matter what they think," Despreaux said. She'd gotten out of her force cast that very morning, and she waved her newly liberated arm enthusiastically, pointing to spots along the trench even as she elbowed Roger out of the way with the other arm. "Here, here, here . . ."

"Hmmm," the prince murmured. After a moment's thought, he threw his rifle to his shoulder and zoomed up the gain on the telescopic sight. "Interesting."

"What?" Julian asked. His rifle had no scope at all.

"Just . . . some of the groups down there," Roger muttered. He walked to the end of the trench, where a tree had been uprooted, sat down behind it, and laid the rifle across the trunk. "Most of them are just scurrying around. But there's a couple of groups that are clearly watching us. And one of them looks like a batch of commanders . . ."

"We discussed this, Your Highness," Julian said repressively. "We're not supposed to shoot."

"I know," Roger sighed. "But I'm still pissed at them over the thing in Kirsti."

"Let me worry about that," Despreaux said. "And the demo. We've only got about fifteen minutes until the shaped charges are in place; you need to be heading for the crest."

Roger gathered up his rifle and stood with manifest regret.

"I think one of them is that senior war leader, Lorak Tral. One shot wouldn't hurt anything, would it?" he sounded so much like a little boy trying to wheedle a special treat out of his tutor that Julian smiled. But the sergeant also shook his head firmly.

"Go with the plan, Your Highness. You promised."

"Okay, okay." Roger looked up the hill and grimaced. "That's a long damned climb."

"And when you get there, you might as well keep going," Despreaux said. "I'll be pouring the slurry fifteen minutes after the shot. By the time you climb back down here, it'll be time to retreat, and if you're in my way then, I'll leave boot prints all over you. I, for one, don't intend to be on the mountain *at all* when we shoot this one."

"I get the point," Roger sighed. "And you're to come directly to Mudh Hemh, understand? You're in no condition to be in Nopet if they assault."

"I will," she said with a smile. "Now get going, Your Highness."

Roger slid off the *civan* and gave Pahner a casual salute.

"It's hard to consider a group that can build something like this 'barbarians,'" he said, waving at the massive walls above them. The back gates to Nopet Nujam weren't as large as the front gates, but their protective towers and bastions still made an imposing edifice.

"Local craftsmen, sure," Pahner said. "But it was Krath engineering. Your Highness, you're not supposed to be here."

"Anything going on?" Roger asked.

"No," the captain said stolidly. "The Krath got some small forces up on the mountain after you left, but the Diasprans beat them off. No injuries on our side. The emplacement team is on the way back, and the security team has retired to the back of the mountain. We're going to fire the shot anytime now, and it would really please me an immense amount to have you back in Mudh Hemh when that happens."

"I've got the picture," Roger laughed. Then he sobered. "Remember to send Despreaux back, as well. With that bum arm, she's not in shape for combat ops yet."

"Nor will she be even after the cast comes off," Pahner observed, looking him straight in the eye. "As I believe you're aware."

"When did you find out?" Roger asked after a long moment of silence. "I . . . She told me the other night."

"Oh, I started to suspect back around Sindi," Pahner said. "It was to be anticipated in most of the Marines—that's one of the reasons I've been trying to shift them to leadership positions, rather than shooting. Despreaux's not the only one. About the only squad I have full confidence in any more is the Third; Julian's maniacs are relentless."

"That . . . makes things difficult," the prince said quietly. "What about me? Or the Mardukans?"

"I think you're one of those guys who doesn't really peak, Your Highness." Pahner shook his head. "Dobrescu's been pointing out your vitals to me lately. Your heartbeat and respiration hardly changed the whole time you were in the Temple; that's unusual, in case you hadn't been aware of it."

"Oh, I'm getting that feeling," Roger said. "But what are we going to do at the spaceport?"

"If we can get this one licked, I think the rest will be a walkover," Pahner told him. "From Jin's data, the way Mountmarch has compromised his own security should make taking the port itself easy. And taking an arriving ship with modern equipment, which just happens to be stockpiled at the port where we can get at it, shouldn't be too hard. If we can just deal with this little problem. Which, I might add, brings us back to you. Specifically, to your presence at this particular locus of space-time."

"Okay, already," the prince said, pulling himself back onto the *civan* and kicking it on the snout as it turned to take a piece out of his leg. "I'm sure we'll muddle through somehow. See you after the surrender."

"Yep," Pahner agreed, with a waved salute as casual as Roger's own. He waited until the prince and his Mardukan guards were well down the road before he shook his head.

"Whose, Your Highness?" He murmured then. "Whose?"

Roger tapped on the door and entered at the grunted reply.

He'd returned to Mudh Hemh accompanied by a bare minimum security detail, but when he reached the town and found only two guards on the entire front wall, he'd realized the extent to which it had been stripped of defenders to reinforce Nopet Nujam. So he left his three Diasprans at the gatehouse to reinforce the Shin guards, and he was accompanied only by two Vashin. Those he left outside as he entered the dwelling the Gastan had turned over to Cord.

The interior was dark, but high for a human. Stone benches along two of the sides were covered in pillows, and the back side of the chamber was occupied by a cooking hearth and a large, low bath.

Cord was dangling his feet in the latter with his back to the door, while Pedi and the two serfs they'd liberated from the Lemmar rubbed his back.

"It looks like you've fallen into a good pond, Old Frog," Roger observed with a chuckle.

"I'm glad you've returned safely," the shaman said, and Roger carefully hid his concern as Cord clambered laboriously to his feet. Officially, his wound was well on its way to healing, but the old warrior wasn't snapping back the way he had after he'd been wounded at Voitan. Indeed, Roger was beginning to worry, very privately, that his *asi* might *never* snap back. Not all the way, at least.

"And I'm ashamed of my weakness," Cord went on, almost as if he'd read Roger's thoughts. "An *asi* should have been at your side."

"I have plenty of bodyguards," Roger remarked. "I have far fewer counselors I trust. Although, come to think of it, I'm running low on bodyguards, as well. It doesn't really matter, though. You need to get healed up; worry about the rest later."

"So why are you here?" Cord asked, limping over to one of the benches.

"Despreaux's on her way here from Nopet, which means they

must be about to put off the shots. It should be spectacular, even from here. I thought you'd like to watch."

"Oh, that *would* be fun to watch," Pedi said. "You're taking off the whole face of Karcrag, yes?"

"Pedi should not be exerting herself," Cord said, lying back on the bench. "We will stay here."

"*Pedi* should not be exerting herself?" Roger repeated. "What in hell does that mean?"

"Nothing," Pedi answered angrily. "Nothing that he has any right to make a decision about."

"You are my *benan*," Cord said coldly. "It is my responsibility to ensure your welfare as it is yours to ensure my safety."

"*Welfare,* perhaps" she spat back. "But not *safety*. I will be fine, thank you!"

"Whoa," Roger said. He glanced at the other two former slaves, who were huddled in the corner, clearly unhappy about the argument. "I don't want to cross this whole planet just to die in a domestic disturbance. Cord, you need to get out in the fresh air . . . well, as fresh as it gets around here. We'll head up to the walls, watch the shot, and come back. And while we're walking, both of you can be thinking about what you want to tell me about what's going on."

"It is none of your responsibility, Prince Roger," Cord said.

"As you've pointed out to me before, Old Frog, I'm responsible for the success or failure of everything in this band. And we *will* have that talk. After we watch the shots."

"They're getting nervous," Pahner said. The Krath had sent another group up the mountain, using a different path from the one their own people had used. Since the security team had pulled back, it was just as well that the Krath would be too late arriving. They'd also pulled most of their forces out of the tent city, however, and seemed to be preparing for a large-scale assault.

"Yes," the Gastan said silkily. "Isn't it lovely?"

"You have your daughter's approach to handling enemies," Pahner said with a laugh.

"Fortunately, I don't have her approach to handling friends," the Shin king replied in a tone which was so suddenly exasperated that Pahner looked at him in genuine surprise.

"And I thought we were welcome," he said. "Or is there something I'm missing?"

"No, you're welcome, even chased by an army," the Gastan said. "It should be obvious to your Light O'Casey that this war has permitted me to consolidate my power as no Gastan has in three decades. And your support has been invaluable in that. But I could wish that my daughter had made better personal choices."

"Okay, now you've really got me confused," Pahner said as the Krath began filing into the assault trenches. The Gastan looked down at him and made a gesture of confused resignation.

"I wish that I understood your human body language better. Are you jesting? Or do you really not see the signs?"

"Signs of what?" Pahner asked. In the distance, the Krath assembly horns began to sound as the entire host started to move forward. The troops in the assault trenches would seek to pin the defenders in order to clear the way for the mass assault of the walls.

"You really don't see them, do you?" the Gastan said. Pahner gazed back up at the Shin's ruler and shook his head.

"She's pregnant," the Gastan said as the explosives on the hillside detonated and the mountain came apart.

By luck, more than knowledge, the amount and spacing of the explosives was almost perfect—not too hard, and not too soft. At first, the only sign of the impending disaster was a series of muffled thuds and a dust-jet mushroom shape above each of the boreholes. Despreaux had set them to detonate sequentially, instead of simultaneously, and the series went off like a very large machine gun as the sixteen charges exploded in under three seconds.

For a moment afterwards, there was stillness, and Pahner feared that all the planning had been for nothing. Then, slowly, the face of the mountain started to slide. The giant faux-teak trees were the first to show the movement, swaying back and forth as if tossed by a heavy wind before they began to slide. Then dust began to rise, and finally the whole mass began sliding towards the valley floor to impact in a gigantic crash that was felt as far away as Mudh Hemh.

At which point, the blocked waters started looking for an outlet. And looking and looking . . . and rising and rising.

"Cool," Roger said, gazing at the neat divot that had been taken out of the side of the mountain. He and Despreaux had moved to the wall of the Shin town, and now they stood watching the battle from the safety of the southern parapet.

The town's walls weren't very much compared to the mighty ramparts of Nopet Nujam. In fact, they were simply double wooden palisades with a stamped earth fill, and the works flanking the gates were open on top, with small guard rooms underneath. The walls of the town were designed to stop the occasional Scourge or hostile Shin raiding party, not to beat off the sort of serious attack that was directed at Nopet Nujam. And for the former purpose, they had worked just fine. They also made a dandy viewing platform.

From a distance, it looked as if some giant had taken an ice cream spoon and scooped out a serving of basalt and ash. The massive Krath fortress obscured anything but the column of dust rising into the air behind it, but it was clear that most of what they'd intended to do had worked.

"Now to see if it blocks the water," Despreaux said.

"You did good, Nimashet," he replied, slipping his arm around her waist.

"We'll see."

"Pessimist," he chuckled.

"I always keep in mind what can go wrong."

CHAPTER TWENTY-SEVEN

"This isn't going well," Pahner said.

"Tell me something I don't know!" the Gastan yelled back as he stuck one of the short Shin swords through a spear slit and drew it back red.

The Krath had started a full-court press, and unless something changed drastically very soon, it was going to work. The assault groups had come hollering out of the trenches, piling up bodies on the already blood-soaked ground. They'd barely made it to the walls before dying, but in doing so, they'd absorbed enough of the defenders' fire to permit the main Krath force to come in behind them in successive waves. The frenzied assault had concentrated on the main gates and the walls to either side, and the third wave had managed to smash the Shin defenders on the battlements and take three sections.

The humans' contribution had mostly been to remove the leadership, and they'd done a good job. Krath companies that had made it to the wall with any officers still on their feet were rare, but even that hadn't stopped the assault. The pressure from behind each wave had driven even the most cowardly into the defenses and up the walls. Now the gates' defenders were down to holding the gate-flanking bastions and doing their best to keep any battering rams away.

"Poertena, what do you have on your side?" the captain called.

"Krat', Krat', and more Krat', Sir," the Pinopan called back even as he took aim and fired through a slit. "T'e other bastion is holding out, though."

"Captain!" Beckley shouted from one of the front slits. "You can see water coming up out of the river! On this side of the fortress!"

"Where?" the captain demanded as he stepped across to a slit beside Beckley and zoomed up the magnification on his helmet. "Never mind." After a moment, he chuckled. "Now if we can only point it out to *them*."

"Look behind you, you stupid bastards!" the Gastan yelled out his slit. "The river rises! *The river fights for the Shin!*"

"Get it unplugged!" Tral shouted. "Break that dam! *Now!*"

"How?" the fortress commander asked. He'd already considered the problem, and he was preparing rafts loaded with gunpowder. He had his doubts about their efficacy, yet they were the only possibility he saw. Unfortunately, even if they had any chance of success of all, they would have to be guided into place, and in another hour—less— the water would be up over the work area. It was rising faster than the boatbuilders could finish their craft.

"I don't know!" the Sere commander snarled. "Figure it out!" He glared at the distant Shin fortress and waved both false-hands in a gesture of furious anger. "We have forces on the wall. All they have to do is take Nujam and we can move in there. That's *all* they have to do!"

"Tallow!" the Gastan ordered, never looking away from the slit. "*Look behind you! The river rises!*" he bellowed as the boiling fat was poured onto the Krath troops swarming atop the battlements outside the bastion. "*Go cool off there!*"

"They are," Pahner panted over the rising chorus of screams that greeted the splashing fat. The Marine had just returned to the slit beside the Shin king after dealing with another threat. A Krath assault group had forced the bastion's lower doors, and it had been hot work stopping them and then throwing up a barricade. The long climb back to the top hadn't done anything for his breathing, but he could clearly see the enemy army starting to stream from the walls. It was unraveling from the rear, where the remaining forces could see the river rising to overwhelm all their worldly goods. But those on the walls could see it as well, and they were scrambling down faster than they had come up. Already the water was halfway into the tent city; by the time those on the walls reached it, the entire area would be underwater.

"All we do now is wait for them to come to the inevitable conclusion," Pahner continued. "And conserve our own people in the meantime."

"That's it." Roger dialed back the magnification of his helmet. "There are no Krath on the walls. It's all over but the negotiating."

"That should be complicated enough to go on with." Despreaux shook her head. "That army is going to come apart when it realizes its predicament."

"I'm sure the captain can handle it," Roger replied, and turned as Cord and Pedi climbed up into the small, wooden bastion, followed by the two freed serfs.

"You sat this one out," Cord observed with a grunt. "Good."

"Are you up to this, Cord?" Roger asked. The shaman still had a pronounced limp and hunched to one side when he moved, and Roger didn't much care for the sound of his breathing.

"The healer Dobrescu tells me I need to start to move around," Cord replied. "I am moving around. The ladder, I admit, was unpleasant."

"Old fool," Pedi muttered under her breath.

"And you're looking better, as well, Pedi," Roger noted. The Shin female's step had a spring that he hadn't seen in quite some time.

"Thank you, Your Highness," Pedi replied. "It's amazing what a little sleep and some *wasen* can do for a female's outlook."

Despreaux snorted and shook her head.

"I could never get into the whole cosmetics thing. I'm totally challenged that way."

"It's like any other weapon or armor," Pedi said with a gesture of humor. "You must practice, practice, practice."

"Oh, like sex," Despreaux observed brightly, then grinned at Roger's stifled gasp.

"That is . . . different with us," Pedi said somewhat primly. "We do not engage in it as . . . entertainment."

"Too bad." Despreaux grinned again. "You don't know what you're missing."

"Well, isn't it a nice day out?" Roger waved to the north, where a darker patch of clouds indicated approaching rain. "Volcanoes smoking, smell of sulfur on the wind, Krath army surrendering . . ."

"They've surrendered?" Pedi demanded excitedly.

"We haven't received a message yet," Roger admitted. "But they're off the walls. The war appears to be over."

"I look forward to slaughtering *them* for a change," the Shin female said darkly.

"Ah, we were intending to offer them terms," Roger pointed out. "I think it would be . . . difficult to kill them *all*. And we can probably get more for them if they're alive."

"You humans are so silly that way." Pedi's gesture bordered on contempt. "I say chop off all their heads and float the bodies down the river. They'll get the message that way."

"Well, there are alternatives," Roger said. "We could simply blind and castrate them all and then have them walk back. All except one in twenty or so that we can leave with one eye to lead the rest. Or we could fire them out of cannon; you could load them all the way to the hips in the bombards. Or we could lay planks over them, then put tables and chairs on top of the planks, sit down, and eat our dinner while they were all crushed to death. Or, best of all, we could go retake the spaceport, come back with assault shuttles, and drop jellied fuel weapons on them. They want fire, we'll give them fire."

"Roger," Despreaux said.

"Those would do," Pedi agreed. "But I can tell you're joking."

"The point is that humans quit doing that sort of thing because we're too damned good at it," Roger said. "We can do it efficiently or baroquely, using a million different methods, culled from our entire history. I doubt that Mardukans can exceed our inventiveness, although they might equal it. But taking that route never gets you anywhere; you get trapped in an eternal round of massacres and counter massacres. It's only after you break the cycle and create strong groups—nations—that enforce the laws and demand some sort of international standard of acceptable behavior, that things start to improve."

"Fine, but we're here. And it's now," the Shin protested. "And when you humans leave, the Krath will still be there. And their soldiers will still be there, and the Scourge will still be there."

"All part of the negotiations," Roger replied. "They've lost their field army. If they don't get it back, they're dead meat for the other satraps. We'll strip them of their treasure, make them pay tribute, and have them sign binding treaties against slave-raiding. We won't take the tribute to 'punish' them, but to weaken them so that they're not death threats to you. The conditions might hold, and they might not. But humans who are friendly to the *Shin* will also be in control of the spaceport, Pedi. If the Krath get out of hand, we *can* send an assault shuttle. And we will."

"What about the Scourge?" Slee asked.

"What about them?" It was the first time Roger had heard one of the released serfs ask a question, so it caught him a bit off guard.

"I don't care about the Sere, My Lord," the serf replied. "But it's the Scourge that has burned our homes and taken our children. Do they go free?"

"I doubt we'll be able to specifically target them," Roger said, after a moment. "But they'll be out of a job."

"Which means they'll go back to being bandits," Pedi said. "So be it. The Shin are better bandits than the Scourge any day."

"Not exactly something that I'd aspire to," Roger sighed. "But if that's what floats your boat."

"Your Light!" the sole Shin guard called. "There's a message from the north tower. A group has been spotted on the edge of the Fire Lands!"

"How large?" Pedi asked. She moved to the bastion's parapet and craned her neck, trying to get a glimpse beyond the northern defenses of the town.

"I don't know," the guard replied. "The message was simply 'a group.'" He pointed to the northern bastion, where a red flag with a complex design had been raised.

"Time to switch positions, people," Roger said. He turned and headed for the ladder. "I don't like this timing."

"Shit." Roger dialed back the magnification on his helmet. "Unless I'm much mistaken, that's a Scourge raiding party. How the hell did they get around our backside that way?"

"We knew that the Scourge had found a way through the Fire Lands," Pedi told him almost absently, straining her own eyes as she stared out over the wall. "We should have remembered that. *I* should have remembered, since it was how I came to be in their hands before the Lemmar captured me. But all of their captives were hooded on the way through the lava fields, so I was unable to tell Father where their route lies." She snorted bitterly. "It would seem they have chosen to use it again."

"Roger, we're . . . way outnumbered." Despreaux put in. She'd been doing her own count, and she didn't like her total. "We've got about fifteen guards in the town, and there are over a hundred Krath."

"It's not good," Pedi agreed. "But it's not quite as bad as it seems, either. Many of the clan leaders brought their families, and many of them are trained as I am. And we have the walls. I will go organize them, get them up here. Can you send a message to Nopet Nujam?"

"I can," Roger said. "But it's an hour's ride from there. Even if they sent the Vashin *now,* they'd be here too late. Get your battle-ladies. I'm going to find my armor."

"What are you going to do, Roger?" Despreaux asked nervously.

"Try to politely dissuade them," the prince replied.

"Sor Teb, as I live and breathe."

"Good afternoon, Prince Roger Ramius MacClintock," the head of the Scourge replied, walking up until he was within arm's length.

The Scourge raiding party had stopped and deployed just out of dart range from the walls. There were perhaps a hundred and fifty of them—a mixture of Krath and Shadem raiders. They were lightly armed and armored, but given what they were up against, that probably wouldn't matter.

Except for Roger.

The prince had donned his battle armor and packed along a heavy bead cannon. They hadn't gotten much in the way of ammunition from the spaceport yet, because they'd used most of their carriage for the explosives required to demolish the mountain. But they'd gotten a few rounds for the bead cannons, and his magazine was loaded first with shot rounds, then with solid. If he opened fire, he was going to cover the field in bits and pieces of Krath and Shadem.

"Well, if you know who I am, you ought to know that I don't bluff or negotiate very well," Roger told Teb calmly, and felt a trickle of amusement as the Scourge commander stiffened ever so slightly. Obviously, the Mardukan had hoped that the shock of knowing he'd been identified would throw Roger at least a little off stride.

"You're here on a fool's errand, Sor Teb," the prince continued. "The Sere have been stopped butt cold, and our reinforcements will be here in no time at all. Your army's trapped between our walls and a rising river, and it's surrendering *en masse*. Any captives you take will be returned, or you won't get your field army back. And if you don't turn around right now, as part of the negotiations we'll add your head to our demands."

"Very brave, Your Highness," the Scourge said with a grunting laugh. "But there are three things you're unaware of. First, given the situation that you and your people created in Kirsti, my head isn't worth spit in the Fire, anyway. Second, we're not here to take captives; we're here to kill everyone we can and loot the town to the ground, then return to the Shadem. I'm not *going* back to the Krath."

"Well, in that case my last point is that if you don't turn around, I'm going to turn you into paste," Roger said, hefting the bead gun. "I can kill at least half of you before you can make it to the walls. And then I can track down the rest and tear your arms out of their sockets. Oh, and you can't count—that was only two points."

"But I can, Your Highness." The Krath brought his hand around. "My third point is that I have a surprise for you."

Roger had never actually seen an example of the device in the Scourge commander's left true-hand—not in the flesh, as it were. But he recognized it instantly. It was no larger than an old, prespace flashlight, and the principle upon which it worked was almost as ancient as its appearance. Very few things could actually penetrate ChromSten armor, but there were ways around that. Essentially, Sor Teb's "surprise" was a last-ditch, contact-range weapon specifically designed to knock out battle armor or lightly armored combat vehicles. Known as a "one-shot," it consisted of a superconductor capacitor, a powerful miniaturized tractor beam, and a hundred-gram charge of plasticized cataclysmite in a ChromSten-lined channel.

If a one-shot could be brought into physical contact with its target and activated, the capacitor-powered tractor locked it there like an immovable limpet. Then the cataclysmite was driven at high speed down the weapon's hollow shaft in a wad with the consistency of modeling clay. When it hit the armor's outer surface, it spread over it, then detonated. The contact explosion couldn't blow a hole *through* the ChromSten . . . but it could transmit a shock wave through it, and the inner surface of the armor wasn't made of ChromSten. It was made of plasteel, far tougher and stronger than any prespace alloy, but far less damage resistant than ChromSten. It supported the ChromSten matrix, on one side, and the host of biofeedback monitors and servo activators which lined every square millimeter of the armor's insides, on the other. And the detonation of that much cataclysmite was perfectly adequate to blow a "scab" of plasteel no more than a centimeter or so across off the armor's inner backing.

With more than sufficient power to blast the scab right through whoever was wearing the armor it came from.

It was, in many ways, a suicide weapon. The maximum range at which the tractor could be activated with any chance of a successful lock-on was no more than five or six meters, and the odds against a successful attack rose sharply as the range rose. That meant that just getting it close enough to hurt someone in powered armor was problematical, but there were more than enough other drawbacks to it.

The one-shot's grip was specifically designed to contain the late cataclysmite's explosion, but it often failed. And even if it didn't, if the tractor failed to lock tightly to the target, back blast from the face of the target's armor would normally kill any unarmored human in the vicinity. Not to mention the fact that when the tractor lock *completely* failed, the one-shot became an old-fashioned chemical-fueled rocket with all the thrust it would ever need to blast right through a human body, or at least rip off the odd hand or arm. But when it worked, it let someone without armor take out an armored opponent.

Sor Teb had proven how fast he was in Kirsti. Whether or not he was actually faster than Roger was no doubt an interesting point, but not really relevant at the moment. He had the advantage of surprise, and unlike him, Roger was trying to do two things at once. He'd already begun to raise the bead cannon when he recognized the one-shot, and his own weapon's movement distracted him ever so slightly as the Mardukan brought the one-shot flashing towards him. Even if it hadn't, the physics were against him.

CHAPTER TWENTY-EIGHT

"*Fuck!*" Despreaux threw her rifle to her shoulder. "*ROGER!*"

She tried to find Sor Teb, but as soon as he'd fired, the entire Scourge party had started sprinting for the walls. And Teb was no fool. He'd disappeared into the mass, vanishing beyond her ability to pick him out of it. So she chose one at random in frustration and put a round through his chest.

"Modderpockers!"

"What happened?" Cord shouted. "What happened?!"

All he'd been able to see was that there'd been a bright flash, and that Roger was on the ground. His armor appeared intact from this distance, but he wasn't moving.

"One-shot!" she snarled. "It's a short range anti-armor weapon. No good above a few meters' range, and a bitch to use, but if you hit, it can take out armor." She scanned the oncoming Scourge, this time looking for someone who seemed to be in charge. She found someone who was waving, which was good enough for her, and punched out another round. Her target went down and disappeared under the charging feet of his fellows, and she took an instant to fix her bayonet as the attackers reached the palisade.

"Is he alive?" Cord demanded, then shook his head and raised his spear. "We should have gone to negotiate, not him!"

"Too late for that," Despreaux shot back, and lunged across the palisade. The Shadem had leapt onto the shoulders of two other Scourge, but he tumbled backwards as the half-meter of steel punched through his throat. She spun in place as another head came over the wall. This one let go and grasped at his face as her slash opened it up from side to side, but it was the butt-stroke that got rid of his ugly mug.

She worked the bolt and fired from the hip, blowing a third raider back from the top of the palisade.

"Too late for that," she repeated, "but if he lives, I'll kill him!"

"Worry about whether or not we'll be here *to* kill him," Pedi advised as she took off the head of a Shadem who'd been pinned against the inner face of the parapet by Dogzard. Cord might not be able to move with his wonted speed and power, but at least he was wise enough to admit it to himself, and he moved behind his *benan*, covering her back without getting into her way.

"Good point," the Marine muttered, as she sought out a target further down the wall. "Damned if we're not going to have to kill them all."

"I'd heard you were having problems with that," Cord said through a grunt of self-inflicted pain as he drove his spear into the throat of a veiled Shadem who'd tried to sneak around Pedi's flank.

"I just got over it!"

"Mudh Hemh is under attack," the Gastan told Pahner evenly.

The two commanders had moved to the battlements to observe events. For a time, the battlefield had been absolute chaos as the Krath army mutinied *en masse*. Now its commanders were restoring some order, and a formal parley had started. The initial negotiations had been unspoken; groups that were armed and came within weapons' distance of the walls were engaged. Those who threw down their arms were allowed to huddle near the walls, still at a distance, but well away from the rising floodwaters.

Other groups, more foolhardy or desperate to retrieve their belongings, had been caught by the rising water. A few of them huddled on scattered outcrops of higher ground, but most had been swept away by the flood. The total who'd been lost in that fashion was small, but it had been intensely demoralizing, and it was after the first groups disappeared into the hungry waters that the Krath had actively started to surrender.

With the first recognized heralds on their way, and the Krath throwing down their arms, it seemed the war was over. Before the walls of Nopet Nujam, at least.

"Talk about snatching victory," Pahner said, looking to the rear. The red distress flags above the town were evident . . . as were the struggling figures on the walls. "Damn it."

"We can't get word to them to surrender," the Gastan said. "That will take too long."

"Roger will be fine," Pahner replied. "Despreaux will make him put on his armor, and nothing the Krath have will get through that. But the rest . . ."

He leaned over the edge of the battlements and looked around until he spotted a human.

"Turner! Find Rastar. Tell him to take *all* the Vashin to Mudh Hemh; it's under attack! Spread the word!"

"This is most unpleasant." The Gastan lowered his binoculars. "They're burning my town. If they think this is going to improve negotiations, they are sorely mistaken."

"Worry about that after we find out who's alive and who's dead," Pahner muttered.

"Erraah!" Despreaux butt-stroked the Krath so hard in the face that it smashed her rifle, but it didn't really matter. She was flat out of ammo . . . and just about out of time.

"Son of a *vern!*" Pedi yelled as she blocked a strike from a Shadem staff. She drove forward in a windmill of steel that ended in a kick which sent the Shadem stumbling back over the edge of the wall. His intestines slithered after him.

"*Pedi!*" Despreaux gasped, and threw her broken rifle past the Shin like a spear.

Sor Teb blocked the missile with one of his swords and snarled.

"I'm going to enjoy sending you to the Fire, you Shin witch!" the Scourge commander told the Gastan's daughter. He was just about the last Krath on the battlements. But, then again, they were pretty much alone, as well.

"You'll have to manage it first," Pedi said, and darted forward.

From Despreaux's perspective, the engagement was nothing but a vortex of steel. The sound of the swords grating on each other sounded like so many sharpening steels in action, and neither combatant was paying attention to any of the other battles going on around them. They were in a focused, private world of steel and fury, and as Despreaux watched the deadly, flashing blades, she realized to her amazement that Pedi's reflexes were just as extraordinary as Roger's or Sor Teb's.

They broke apart for moment, as if by mutual consent, just as Cord limped up to them, and the shaman shook his head.

"Wrist! Keep your wrist straight!"

"Thanks," Pedi panted. "I'll keep that in mind."

"No, I was talking to him," Cord said. "His technique is awful. *Your* wrist is perfect, darling."

"Darling?" Pedi looked over her shoulder at him.

"I'm sorry," he said. "It just slipped out."

"I'm going to feed you, your boyfriend, *and* your get to the Fire," the Scourge panted.

"You talk big," Pedi replied, focusing once more on the task at hand. "We'll see who's going to the Fire today."

"Yes, we will."

Sor Teb gestured with his left false-hand. Pedi's eyes flicked towards it for just an instant, and that was when his *right* false-hand moved. It threw a handful of dust into her face, and he drove forward right behind.

Pedi flung up a false-arm. She managed to stop most of the powder, but some of it still took her in the eyes and mouth, and she buckled as instantaneous pain and nausea ripped through her. But she still managed to drop to one knee, and she drove upward with both swords as the Scourge's downward cut sliced into her shoulder.

Sor Teb looked at the two swords buried to their quillons in his stomach and coughed out a gush of blood.

"No," he muttered, raising his off-hand sword.

Cord raised his spear, but before he could drive it forward, Dogzard—who'd had enough of this stupid single-combat and fairness stuff—crashed into the dying Krath's chest and settled matters by ripping out his throat.

Despreaux darted forward and caught Pedi as blood from her shoulder poured out.

"Damn it, why is Dobrescu *never* around when you need him?" she demanded of the universe.

"Pedi?" Cord went to his knees beside her, ripping at his hated clothing until he tore off a strip and wadded it into an impromptu bandage. "Pedi, don't go away from me."

"I . . ." She shuddered. "It hurts."

"The healer Dobrescu will be here soon," Cord said. "He's a miracle worker—look at me. Just hold on. Don't . . . don't leave me. I don't want to lose you, too."

"You won't . . . darling," she grimaced a smile. "I have too much to live for. You . . . and your children."

"Mine?" he repeated, almost absently. Then grabbed his horns in frustration. "*Mine?* How?"

"I . . . I'm sorry," she said with a sigh. "You were so hurt, so needing. You came into your season while you were injured. I couldn't stand to watch you in such agony, and you were calling for your . . . for your wife. I—Ahhh!" She panted in pain. "I love you. . . ."

"Look, this is touching and everything, but are you going to let me work on her shoulder, or not?" Dobrescu demanded.

"What?" Cord looked up as the medic tapped him with a foot, then stood. "Where did you come from?"

"I said I don't have much use for *civan*," the warrant officer replied. "Never said I didn't know how to use one," he added as the first of the Vashin appeared on the walls.

"Oh," he added. "The cavalry's here."

Roger opened his eyes and groaned.

"Crap," he muttered. His ribs hurt like hell.

"Water?" Dobrescu inquired sweetly. The medic had dark rings around his eyes, but he looked as mischievous as ever.

"Well, since I'm alive, I take it we won." Roger took a sip from the proffered camelback, then grimaced. "What was the egg breakage?"

"Pretty hefty, Your Highness," a new voice said, and Roger turned his head just as Pahner sat down beside his bed. The captain looked as if he hadn't slept in far too long, either.

"Tell me I look better than you two," the prince said, and winced as he levered himself very gingerly into a sitting position.

"Actually, you probably do," Pahner replied. "Doc?"

"Four broken ribs and contusions, mainly," the medic said. "Which is no big deal with His Highness." He grinned tiredly at Roger. "I kept you under for a day just to keep you out of the way and give your nannies a chance to begin the repairs," he added. "You can start moving around whenever you like."

"It hurts like . . . heck," Roger noted.

"That's good," Dobrescu told him, and stood. "It might keep you from doing stupid things."

He tapped the prince lightly on the shoulder and walked out, leaving him with Pahner.

"You're alive," Roger said, returning his attention to the Marine. "That's good. How are we doing otherwise?"

"Just fine," Pahner replied. "The breakage was bad for the Shin, both in Nopet and Mudh Hemh. But they'll survive. The Gastan is talking about letting some of the Krath settle in the valley, since the Shin own both citadels again."

"The company? Diasprans? Vashin?"

"Low losses," Pahner reassured him. "We didn't lose any Marines, not even Despreaux—who, I note, you *haven't* asked about. We lost two Vashin, and a Diaspran. That's it."

"Good," Roger sighed. "I was going to ask about Nimashet as soon as I'd asked about business."

"I won't tell her about your priorities," the captain said with a rare smile. "But I'll note that I approve. And at least we've solved the whole problem with Cord and Pedi."

"What problem? I knew something was going on, but I couldn't tell what."

"Ah, you were asleep for that." Pahner's smile segued into a grin, and he shook his head as he pulled out a *bisti* root and cut off a slice. "The Gastan wasn't all that happy, either, although he wasn't showing it. It turns out she's pregnant."

"Pedi?" Roger asked. "When? How?" He paused a moment, then shook his head, an almost awed expression on his face. "*Cord?*"

"Cord," Pahner confirmed. "While he was recovering. He didn't have any memory of it."

"Ouch. Oh, and the whole 'I cannot use my *asi* that way' thing . . . Oh, man!"

"Yes," the captain said. "Which was why she couldn't tell him whose child—children—they were. He assumed she'd had . . . a fling, for want of a better term. Add to that that she was considerably less than half his age but that he was . . . interested in her anyway, and—"

Roger laughed, then clutched at his chest in pain.

"Oh, my. May-December romance, indeed!" he got out, almost crying between the laughter and the pain.

"So now the Gastan has a new son-in-law, who's older than he is," Pahner acknowledged. "And from what Eleanora and I can figure out, it's even more complicated than that. Since the Gastan's oldest son, Thertik, managed to get himself killed, Pedi is his legal heir. But a *benan* can't inherit his position. There have been a handful of female Gastans in the history of the Shin, although they're very rare. It's more common for a female heir's consort to inherit the title. But a *benan* is required to follow his—or her—*benai* wherever that leads, so he can hardly stay home to rule the tribes. Unfortunately, a *benan's* children *can* inherit. So Cord's children—the Gastan's *grand*children—are the legal heirs to the overlordship of the Vales."

"And since Cord insists on following me off-planet . . ."

"Precisely," the captain agreed with a thin smile. "I hope you'll pardon me for pointing this out, Your Highness, but the three of you have a positive talent for leaving chaos in your wake. Well, to be fair, I suppose I shouldn't include Cord in that. Not, at least, until we met the Lemmar and his sense of honor got him into all of this!"

"I think you're being too hard on him," Roger said with a laugh. "As far as I can tell, he fought the good fight to resist his attraction to

Pedi. It's not his fault that he lost in the end—especially not with her taking such unscrupulous advantage of him when he was unconscious and unable to resist her advances!"

"You *would* come up with something like that," Pahner told him, shaking his head in resignation. "And I suppose it actually is sort of funny, in a way. But don't you dare laugh when you see them. They're like a couple of teenagers. It's worse than you and Despreaux."

"Oh, thank you very much, *Captain*," Roger said, and chuckled. Then grimaced as the chuckle claimed its own stab of pain.

"Or Julian and Kosutic. Or Berent and Stickles. Or, God forbid, Geno Macek and Gunny Jin, for that matter." The Marine sighed, rubbing his head.

"I'm sorry, Armand." Roger reached out to his bodyguards' commander. "I know we've laid burdens on you that were unnecessary, and for that, I apologize."

The captain looked down at the hand on his arm, then patted it and shook his head.

"Command challenges just make life more interesting," he said with a faint smile. "Although, after a certain point, they do tend to drag you down." He shook his head again. "For example, I would really appreciate it if you could stay out of one-shot range for the foreseeable future."

"Sounds like a good idea to me," Roger acknowledged, settling back against his pillows and feeling very carefully of his chest. "Of course, it never occurred to me that the bastard might *have* one."

"It wouldn't have occurred to me, either," Pahner admitted. "And I can't say that the fact that he did makes me very happy. But at least he didn't drill you clean."

"I don't understand why he didn't," Roger said thoughtfully. "I thought once one of those things locked onto your breastplate, you were pretty much screwed."

"Pretty much," Pahner agreed. "But from the looks of your armor, you managed to twist sideways just as he hit the tractor-lock. It didn't lock squarely. Instead of depositing the explosive charge at right angles, it hit you obliquely and a lot of the force of the explosion leaked sideways across the face of the plate. It was still enough for the shock damage to break your ribs, disable about sixty percent of your armor systems, and knock you unconscious. But it never managed to blow a scab loose, and you were lucky, Your Highness. Your anti-kinetic systems lasted long enough to keep it from doing anything worse than pounding your ribs—hard. Doc Dobrescu wouldn't have been quite so cheerful about the state they were in if you didn't have an even better nanny pack than the Corps gets issued. I know they still hurt like hell, but they're rebuilding fast."

"I know I was lucky," Roger agreed, still exploring his chest gently. "It just doesn't *feel* that way."

"Maybe not," Pahner said somberly. "But if he'd manage to blast that scab loose, all the anti-k systems in the galaxy wouldn't have helped you. And if *they'd* failed, the concussion alone should have turned every bone in your torso into paste." He shook his head. "No, Your Highness. You definitely *were* lucky. That's all that saved you—well, that and those souped-up reflexes of yours. I don't know if anyone else could have turned enough to take it at a survivable angle."

"And what about Sor Teb?"

"He was lucky, too . . . for a while," Pahner said. "The tractor must have gotten a good enough lock to at least stay put, instead of blasting right back through him. And the angle must have been oblique enough to direct the back blast away from him. I'm sure he figured you really were dead, since he had a *second* one-shot on him and he didn't use it on you to make certain. Unfortunately for him, he encountered Pedi on the parapet and suffered a mischief."

"God, I bet she enjoyed that!"

"You could put it that way. Especially since it was what pushed Cord into declaring his feelings for her," Pahner agreed with an evil chuckle.

"But to return to you and Sor Teb's little surprise," the Marine continued, "he may not have managed to kill *you*, but he certainly did manage to kill your armor."

"Which isn't good," Roger said with a grimace. "It's not like we had all that many operable suits to begin with."

"Oh, it isn't all that bad," Pahner reassured him. "In fact, Poertena ought to be able to take care of the problem without too much difficulty. Assuming, of course, that we take the spaceport before he implodes."

"Poertena?" Roger quirked an eyebrow. "What's his problem?"

"He just found out that Mountmarch has a complete Class One manufactory at the port," Pahner said, standing up. "Can you imagine Poertena with a full-scale manufacturing plant at his mercy?"

CHAPTER TWENTY-NINE

Temu Jin picked up his cup and sipped. His attention—obviously—was entirely focused on the coffee, and he kept it that way as the timer clicked over to just past Mardukan noon.

There were normally two com techs on duty in the communications control center, but at lunchtime, they went off duty, one at a time, to get something to eat. There were still the two guards, of course, but they were stationed in the vestibule just inside the blast door that was the only possible way in, not in the center itself. On this particular day, it was the other tech's turn to go to lunch first, which left Jin as the only person actually in the room. Which worked out just fine for him. Especially since the com center also doubled as the control room for the security perimeter.

He watched the schematic from the corner of one eye and nodded internally as the first notation of a possible perimeter breach popped up on his screen. Right on time. It was nice to deal with professionals for a change.

The com center guards were supposed to be cycled off together just before noon, instead of one of them at a time going to get something to eat, but their relief was late. That wasn't particularly unusual—the relief was *usually* late on Marduk, and they would be late in their turn. But it meant they were suffering just a tad from low blood sugar, which made them more surly than usual with the Mardukan messenger.

"What do *you* want, scummy?"

"I have a message from the governor," Rastar said, in carefully badly accented Imperial as he held his message up in front of the security cameras. He stood there in the poncholike garment the peasants in the area around the spaceport habitually wore, and made himself look as much like one of the local rubes as he could.

It must have worked.

"Okay, we'll give it to the geek," one of the guards said, and keyed in the code to open the door.

"Thank you," Rastar said in his horrible Imperial, and stepped inside to hand over the folded message as the door finished opening. Then he reached under the "poncho" once more.

"And if you'll be good enough to take me to the communications center," he continued in suddenly flawless Imperial, as four polymer-bladed knives closed like scissors on the guards' necks, "I'll let you live."

"Rastar and Jin have the communications center," Julian said. "Fain's team has taken down the guards on the main gate. The Shin are through the wire on the spaceport, and they've seized the vehicle park. I've got the code that the plasma towers are off-line."

"I'll believe it when we're in," Pahner growled, and wiggled his body, writhing up through the chunks of ore in the back of the *turom* cart.

The main difficulty in taking the spaceport was that the sensor net extended well beyond its perimeter. Besides increased radar sweeps from the geosynchronous satellite, there were micrite sensors scattered all over the surroundings. Those tiny sensors sent back readings on power emissions, nitrite traces, metal forms, and a variety of other indicators that could mean a potential attack by either low-tech or high-tech foes. Defeating them wasn't really hard, but it was time-consuming and complex.

One of the things the sensors looked for was evidence of ChromSten or high-density power packs. To cloak both of those, the armored personnel had been secreted in piles of metallic ores after tests had shown that the ores were sufficient to hide them from the Marines' own sensors.

The facility routinely purchased bulk materials from the Krath and the Shin, and, once again, the IBI agent had been invaluable. He'd spent his time and limited resources suborning various persons in the facility, which gave him all sorts of interesting handles when he needed them. In this case, he'd not only convinced the chief of supply that he needed to order "a little early," but had even given him a list of what to order. If the chief hadn't chosen to comply, certain pictures that he had on his personal system would have been turned over to the governor. Amazingly, an order for six carts of iron ore and ten of mixed foodstuffs had been placed within a day.

Now, with the sensor net and—hopefully—the plasma towers under the control of "friendly" forces, the time had come to knock on the front door.

"Well, let's find out what's going to go wrong," Kosutic said as she dropped out of the bottom of a *turom* cart into a spider-crouch. She looked up at the open gates and shook her head. "Look out for one-shots; we know there are some around."

There was virtually no other conversation as the Marines poured out of the carts and through the gates. They broke up into teams of three and four, and spread out through the facility.

"Commo secure," Julian chanted, trotting after Pahner as they both headed for the governor's quarters. "Armory: a Diaspran took a hit there, but the Marine team has it secured." A burst of firing sounded from the left, and he checked his pad. "Barracks are holding out, but the situation is secure."

"Send the second wave of Vashin there," Pahner said. "Diasprans to remain on call. Shin to the spaceport."

"Secondary control tower secured," Julian continued. "Nobody there. Maintenance and repair: no resistance."

They rounded the Armory and pounded across the manicured lawn of the governor's quarters. Two humans by the front doors were being securely trussed up by Diasprans dressed as lawn maintenance "boys."

"Servants are secure, Sir," Sergeant Sri said as he yanked one of the human guards back to his feet. "The governor's in his quarters."

Pahner followed the schematic, helpfully forwarded from Temu Jin, to the rooms marked on the map, and stopped outside the main doors.

Julian stepped forward and swept the interior with deep radar. Since Roger's unpleasant interaction with the one-shot, they'd all started getting back into "stuff can hurt us even in armor" mode. It took some adjustment—the armor had been the absolute trump card in so many previous encounters—but they were getting there.

"No high-density weapons," Julian reported as he swept the sensor wand back and forth. "A twelve-millimeter bead pistol. That's it."

Pahner considered the door's controls for a moment, then shrugged and kicked at the memory plastic until he'd inflicted sufficient damage to encourage it to dilate. He stepped through it, then cursed as a bead round bounced off his armor.

"Oh, *this* is lovely," he snarled.

Julian followed him through and shook his head as he saw the naked, trembling boy in the middle of the bed. The boy—he couldn't have been much more than ten—had grave difficulty just holding up the heavy bead pistol, but his expression was almost as determined as it was terrified.

"Put that thing down, you little idiot," Pahner told him severely over his armor's external speakers. "Even if you manage to hit me again, it'll only bounce off and hurt somebody. Where's the governor?"

"I'm not telling you!" the boy yelled. "Ymyr told me not to tell you anything!"

"Bathroom," Julian said, and crossed to the bed. He reached out and thumbed the bead pistol to "safe," then yanked it out of the kid's hands. "Just stay there for a second," he told him.

Pahner strode across the bedroom. This time, he didn't bother kicking; he just put a bead cannon round through the upper part of the bathroom door after ensuring that his armored body was between the bed and any blow back that might occur.

The bead went through the door, through the wall beyond, through a section of barracks wall, and then headed for the mountains in the distance as Pahner stepped through the door and picked up the naked fat man inside the bathroom by what was left of his hair.

"Governor Mountmarch," he growled, tilting the official's chin up with the muzzle of the cannon, "it gives me distinct pleasure to place you under arrest for treason. We were going to add all sorts of additional items, but I think we'll just stop at pedophilia. You can only execute someone once."

"Damn." Julian grimaced at the sudden yellow puddle on the floor. "Cleanup on Aisle Ten."

"That's it?" Roger leaned back in the chair at the head of the conference table. "That's the big fight for the spaceport we've been sweating for the last six months?" He shivered and looked over by the door. "Speaking of sweating, or, rather not, somebody turn the thermostat up."

Pahner smiled. Then he tapped a control on the surface of the faux-teak table and an image of the planet blossomed above it.

"Well, Your Highness, we had two hundred Vashin and Diasprans," he said, nodding at Fain and Rastar, who were looking notably lethargic. Julian had set the thermometer at about thirty-five degrees, which was on the low side for Mardukans. "We also had inside help from Agent Jin and almost a thousand Shin."

"Who expect to be paid," the Gastan said. "I'll need various gee-gaws to placate the hill clans, but for me, I need weapons. Bead rifles, for preference."

"Not a problem," Roger assured him. "We'll get a shipment set up as soon as possible."

"We've got other needs, as well, Your Highness," Pahner pointed out. "The troops need to be refitted. We've got base stores on most of the materials, but they'll need to be set and the electronics fitted. That takes the manufactory."

"We'll set up a schedule," Roger said. "I hope no one minds if outfitting the troops takes precedence?" He looked around at the shaking heads and gestures of negation. "Good. I want the Vashin and Diasprans outfitted as well."

"Why?" Pahner asked. "I thought we'd agreed they were going to secure the port, not come with us?"

"Well, they still need uniforms," Roger replied. "Proper, antiballistic uniforms—I want them running around in better armor than those steel breastplates. And the temperature control will keep them from going into hibernation every evening, too."

"And there's the taking of this ship to consider," Rastar commented. "I know you think we can be of no use in that, but I have to differ. Our place is in battle with the prince and his Marines."

"Rastar," Roger said uncomfortably, "again, I thank you for the offer. But ships are . . . They're not good places for the untrained to be running around."

"None the less," Rastar said, "it is our duty."

"Well," Roger said after a moment's thought, "how about if you're backup? We're going to recover the assault shuttles, anyway. We can pack about sixty Mardukans into them, once we pull out all the extraneous gear. If we need you in the assault, we'll call you in. If we don't need you, sorry, you'd really just be in the way. Once we have a ship and you've had a chance to examine it, you'll understand."

"That's a good point, Your Highness," Pahner put in. "Actually, they could get a little off-planet training by lofting the shuttles; there's plenty of fuel on the base. And the manufactory can be programmed to fit them with chameleon suits and standard helmets. They won't have all the features of our stuff, but enough. Coms at least, and basic tactical readouts. And thermostats.

"Furthermore," he smiled thinly, "they can act as bodyguards for *you,* Your Highness. You realize, of course, that you're not going to be in on the ship assault."

"Oh?" Roger said dangerously.

"Oh," the captain replied. "You're Heir Primus now, Your Highness . . . and there is no Heir Secondary or Tertiary. You can't be risked. And, frankly, many of the points you brought up about the Mardukans hold for you. You're not *trained* in shipboard combat. I'll freely admit that—leaving aside such minor matters as the imperial succession, a little matter of a coup, the need to rescue your Lady Mother, and my personal oath to protect your life at all costs— I'd take you in a Mardukan jungle over a squad of Marines any day. But not in a ship. Different circumstances, different weapons—and you're not trained for either. And it's not a time to let 'natural ability' take its course."

"So the Mardukans and I sit it out on the planet? While you and the Marines take the ship?"

"That's the right plan, Your Highness," the sergeant major interjected.

"But—"

"If you decide to overrule me, Your Highness," the captain said stoically, "I will resign before I'll attempt the action. I will not risk you at this point."

"Pock," Roger said bitterly. "You're serious."

"As a heart attack, Your Highness. You're no longer in a category that can be even vaguely threatened. You are *the* Heir. I can't stress that enough."

"Okay," Roger said, shaking his head. "I'll stay on the ground with the Mardukans."

"I want your word on that. And no weaseling."

"I'll stay on the ground . . . unless you call for reinforcements. And take note; if you *don't* call for reinforcements when you need them, you'll be endangering me. And if *you* are rendered *hors de combat,* all bets are off."

"Agreed," Pahner said sourly.

"So you'd better take the ship quick," Roger pointed out.

"That shouldn't be a big deal," the sergeant major said. "Most tramp freighters are pretty coy about being jacked, for obvious reasons. But we'll have a shielded shuttle, and once we're through the airlock, there's not much they can do with a platoon of Marines on board."

"You're taking everybody?" Roger asked.

"There are enough suits in the Morgue to outfit all our survivors," Kosutic pointed out. "It's another thing to toss on Poertena's pile, but it's not like he's busy."

★ ★ ★

Julian strode down the hallway, twisting his shoulders from side to side. The issue uniforms were made of a soft, pleasant cloth, and should have been very comfortable. But the uniform he'd just carefully folded and put away had been on his body for almost eight months. The various cloths of which it was comprised had been worn in. No matter how well-made, or how basically comfortable its fabric, a new uniform always took a certain amount of breaking in.

He forgot his minor discomforts as he rounded a corner on the final approach to the Armory. Besides new uniforms, they were drawing new weapons and turning in the ones they'd wielded for the last half year. Given that most of the bead rifles and grenade launchers with which they'd arrived were suitable only for salvaging as spare parts, he'd simply packed the weapon up and headed for the Armory. Like the uniforms, it made more sense to throw the guns away than store them.

Which was why he stopped with an expression of surprise. Half the remaining Marines were lined up on the floor in the corridor outside the Armory, laboriously cleaning their weapons.

"Don't even bother, man," Gronningen growled. "Poertena's being a pocking bastard."

"You're joking."

"Go ahead," Macek said tiredly. "See for yourself."

Julian stepped through the blast doors and shook his head. The new weapons, many of them freshly manufactured, and all of them gleaming with lethal purpose, were arrayed on racks in the back of the Armory, with a mesh security screen between them and the main administrative area. In the front of the large vault was a counter, with a swinging gate on one end and a repair area on the opposite end. Poertena had settled himself behind the counter and was minutely inspecting each weapon that was turned into him.

"Pocking pilthy," he said, and tossed the grenade launcher back to Bebi. "Bring it back when it clean."

"Come on, Poertena!" the grenadier snarled. "I've cleaned it twice! And you're just going to DX it anyway!"

"I'm not explaining to Captain Pahner why t'e pocking

Inspectorate downcheck my pocking Armory," the sergeant growled. "Bring it back when it clean."

"We're planning on *overthrowing* the Inspectorate!" the grenadier protested, but he left anyway. With the launcher.

"Poertena," Julian said, "you've got too much to do to be picking over guns with micro-tools!"

"Says you," the Pinopan replied, and snatched the bead rifle out of Julian's hands. "Barrel dirty!" he said, as he broke the weapon open and checked it. "Silica buildup in t'e pocking discharge tube! Julian, you know better t'an t'at! Nobody gets a pass in t'is Armory!"

"Goddamn it, Poertena, you've got thirty suits to get online!" Julian snapped. "There's a week of solid day-in-day-out work right there. More, probably! Not to mention reconfiguring the manufactory to outfit all the Vashin and Diasprans!"

"I guess I'm going to be too busy," the armorer replied with a grin. "I hear t'at t'e sergean' major is looking for you, though . . ."

"Ah, there you are, Adib!" Kosutic strode into the Armory. "Poertena, take the sergeant's rifle and find somebody else to clean it. He's going to be rather busy."

"Oh, no," Julian groaned. "Come *on,* Eva."

"Don't you 'Eva' me, Sergeant," she said with a grin. "You're fully qualified out on a Class One—I checked your records. And it's going to take a squad to get all the work done, anyway. Fortunately, you're a squad leader."

"Look," Julian said mulishly, "I can stand here and argue all day over whether you should pick me or somebody else. And do it well. To start with, I *am* a squad leader; I'm supposed to manage my squad. You're the one who told me that—"

"Hi, Poertena," Roger said, as he stepped through the blast door. "I need to turn in my bead pistol and—"

"I'm outta here," Julian announced, and darted for the exit. "I think you said something about setting up the manufactory, Sergeant Major?"

"What did I say?" Roger asked as Kosutic snickered her way out of the room in Julian's wake, and Poertena snatched the pistol from his hand.

"What? You call t'is po . . . You call t'is *clean?* You Highness."

"Okay, Captain Fain, welcome to Supply Central," Aburia said as she beckoned for the Mardukan to come through the door.

In deference to the locals' temperature sensitivity, the room had been set at nearly forty degrees. For most humans, it would have been sweltering, but after six months on Marduk, the Marines found it pleasantly cool. Which didn't prevent the corporal from wiping a drop of sweat from her forehead as she gestured to the platform.

"Sir, I'd like you to stand up here, please," she said. "We're going to measure you for your uniform."

"This is an odd way," the Diaspran said. The room was filled with sounds that the Mardukan classified as a triphammer, and also a peculiar rushing noise. The most prominent feature, though, was a low vibration through the floor that Fain found very unpleasant.

"Well, we do it a bit differently, Sir," the corporal replied. "Please, on the platform."

The captain complied, and the Marine triggered a code with her toot.

"The lights are harmless, Sir," she said, as lasers patterned the Mardukan's body in blue. "They're measuring you for your uniform."

After a moment, they winked off.

"And if you'll step down," the corporal continued as she removed a piece of plastscrip from the console, "this is your number. Stickles is in the other room, and he'll show you where to pick up your gear."

"That's it?" Fain asked, waving for Erkum to climb up onto the platform.

"Yep," the Marine said. "Back there, there's a big machine that's going to turn everything out. It's got imported material for the base on the uniform, and various imported and local materials will be used to make the helmet. It's just like the machines in K'Vaern's Cove," she finished, "only—"

"Much more sophisticated," Fain finished as Pol stepped down from the platform and accepted his own piece of plastscrip.

"Yes, Sir," the human said with a grin. "We've got a few thousand years of technology on you, Sir. Don't take it badly."

"I don't," the captain said as he left. "I'm just glad you're on our side."

"Well, it's not always perfect," Aburia admitted. "And just being able to make stuff doesn't always mean it works the way you planned."

"Oh?"

"Look, you stupid beast. If you want to go with me on the ship, I have to get this on you."

Roger appreciated the time it must've taken Julian to design and build the custom-made suit for Dogzard. He considered that the sergeant's efforts were a nice compliment, especially considering all the other duties he'd fitted it in around. Dogzard, however, failed to share his appreciation for the final product.

The Mardukan beast hissed as Roger tried to force one talon into the suit. Then she jerked suddenly backwards, twisted away, and darted into a corner.

"It's state-of-the-art," Roger panted as he leapt across the compartment in an effort to pin the monster down. "It's even got little thrusters, so you can maneuver in zero-g, and . . ."

Dogzard writhed in his grip until she managed to twist loose, then raced for the door. Showing a startling level of sophistication, she hit the door release and dashed out.

"Well," Roger said, sucking a cut on his hand. "I think that went well."

CHAPTER THIRTY

"I think this is going pretty well," Pahner said as he watched a Vashin cavalryman try out his new plasma cannon. For any human not in powered armor, the heavy weapon was a crew-served mount, but the Mardukan stood on the range, holding the cannon and firing it "off-hand." Not only that, he was putting a round a second down range. Then he stopped for a moment, flipped the selector to "auto," and began putting out bursts of plasma that ate into the cliff being used as a backstop until the power magazine discharged itself and automatically popped out. At which point, the cavalryman used a false-hand to pop a new one into place . . . and resumed fire in under a second.

"We still can't use them inside the ship," Kosutic said, grinning as the hillside started to smoke from the target practice. "They do too much damage."

"Agreed," Pahner said, and cut himself a fresh slice of *bisti* root. It had struck him that Murphy was working overtime when it turned out that there wasn't a single stick of gum left in the entire compound. He'd nearly shot one person who was chewing his last stick when Mountmarch's personnel were rounded up.

"We can't use them on shipboard if we want it intact, at any rate," he continued as he began to chew. "Although . . . when we load them, we'll outfit most of them with bead cannons. Maybe one plasma cannon in three. And instead of loading with beads, we'll load flechette packs. That way they won't be a cataclysm just waiting to happen."

"You're thinking you might actually use them?" the sergeant major asked with a frown.

"I'm thinking that if you're going to have a backup, it might as well be a backup you can use," the captain replied with a sigh. "And it's the little details that are crucial."

He was right about that, the sergeant major reflected. And it had been a fortnight for details. Besides refitting and rearming all the Marines and their Allies, there'd been a billion other "details" to handle, all of them as quickly as possible.

The first order of business had been to determine just how deeply the Saints actually had their hooks into the planet. As it turned out, the governor had partially covered himself by getting permission for "occasional welfare and socialization visits" from passing Saint warships. His request had pointed out that he was on the backend of nowhere, with no naval backup, and that refusing requests might be a good way to start a war.

But his personal files, helpfully cracked by the ever-useful Temu Jin, had revealed the other side of the story. The steadily growing accounts in New Rochelle banks would have been hard enough for Mountmarch to explain, but the electronic communications records were damning. It was clear that he'd been in the Saints' pocket almost from the day he arrived on Marduk. Indeed, some references in the correspondence raised the very real possibility that he'd been a Saint operative even while he was a centerpiece of court intrigue. One reply from his Saint handler—identified in the messages only as "Muir"— indicated that the Saints had used a combination of money and blackmail, probably about his illegal predilection for young boys, as a means of control. When the Bronze Barbarians returned to Old Earth (and assuming they managed to both survive the trip and then get the various warrants against them dropped) the database would make interesting reading at IBI.

For the moment, however, what was more important was that

the data gave them a good read on Saint visits, and the next warship wasn't scheduled for over two months. Furthermore, it indicated that activity overall would be cut back for the foreseeable future. Prince Jackson's coup had all the other star nations surrounding the Empire on high alert, and the majority of the Saint fleet had been pulled to more important systems.

While Julian and Jin had been tickling the electronic files, a team made up of Third Squad and augmented by Eleanora O'Casey for political interaction had been sent out to cover their back trail and pick up the shuttles. Harvard Mansul had requested and been granted permission to accompany them, and they'd visited most of the Company's waypoints. They'd retraced their entire six-month journey in less than a week, and insured that the various societies they'd passed through had survived. Mansul, in the meantime, recorded interviews with many of the Mardukans who'd experienced the Company's passage. Besides laying the groundwork for a series of fascinating articles and one heck of a docudrama, his records were intended as evidence for Roger's defense when the time came, since they made it clear he and Bravo Company had been far too busy surviving to be involved in any plots against the Throne.

K'Vaern's Cove's was well on its way to a major industrial revolution, and dragging Diaspra kicking and screaming along behind it. The flotilla's ships' captains had returned, and the Cove had been very much in two minds about precisely what to do about Kirsti. Public attitude had been hardening towards sending a follow-up military expedition, but O'Casey had been able to inform them that by the time a fleet could make it back to Kirsti, the Fire Priests would have had their attitudes adjusted and be waiting for a *friendly* visit.

Marshad was experiencing some political instability, and had been mauled in two minor wars. The team "counseled" everyone involved, but O'Casey recognized that it would take a full soc-civ team to get the city-states cooperating, rather than competing for territory. Marshad did still have control of the lucrative *dianda* trade routes to Voitan, however, and the revenues from that were helping it recover from its near demise at the hands of its former overlord.

Denat had accompanied the team, but rather than return to his home tribe, he had decided to remain in Marshad until their return trip.

Voitan was in a renaissance, as well. It had developed a lively merchant class that traded wootz steel ingots and finished weapons to Marshad for *dianda,* then shipped the *dianda* south to the city-states. New trade routes had been opened all the way to the Southern oceans, and the market in the south was hungry for both Voitan steel and Marshad cloth. Voitan was having some trouble with an influx of workers fleeing the war in the south, which sounded something like the worst of the city-state wars in ancient Italy, but given the shortage of labor with which the reborn city had started, the influx was mostly to the good.

Q'Nkok was flourishing as a side benefit of the rebirth of Voitan. In many ways, the first town the Marines had visited was the least changed by their passage. It supplied raw materials from the mountains and jungles to its west and north to Voitan and the other, larger city-states, and the only real change seemed to be the increased clearing on both sides of the river. With the shift of the People to materials suppliers, rather than hunter/gathers, their need for extensive forests had dwindled, and a new treaty for extended lands had been signed, ending for the time being any rationale for conflict between the two groups.

The shuttles were virtually untouched. All they needed for liftoff was fuel, and on the way back the team stopped to pick up Denat, along with T'Leen Sena, who had accepted his proposal of marriage.

The shuttles, and the port's other aircraft, had also sufficed to pick up the Vashin and Diaspran dependents, along with spare *civan* and even a few *flar-ta,* including Patty. They'd found that they could just fit one *flar-ta* to a shuttle, and as long as they kept the beasts sedated, the trip was a piece of cake.

In addition to all that, the Mardukan members of The *Basik*'s Own had been put through a brief course in shipboard combat. They'd been taken into orbit aboard the assault shuttles and shown how to move in free-fall. After a brief period of total disorientation, most of them had taken to it well, and it turned out that the locals' four arms were incredibly helpful in zero-gravity combat.

After their initial exposure to micro-gravity, they were put through a few maneuvers and finally exposed to vacuum in their new uniforms. After that, there wasn't much more to do. The best the humans could do with the materials at hand was to familiarize the locals with space combat in its most basic sense. If it came down to it, the Mardukans would have to learn the ins and outs as they went, which was rarely a path to long-term survival.

Cord had not joined them in their training. Despite the old Shaman's sulfurous protests, Roger had decided that his *asi* had no business in any potential boarding actions. It looked more and more as if Cord would be at least partly disabled permanently from his wound, despite all Dobrescu could do. Even if he'd been in perfect health, Roger had pointed out ruthlessly, nothing Cord could have done in battle would make much difference one way or the other to the protection of someone already in powered armor. But he *wasn't* in perfect health, and that was that.

What Roger very carefully had not mentioned was his conviction that his *asi* had no business in combat under any circumstances when he stood on the brink of finally becoming a parent. Pedi had been equally careful to stay out of the entire discussion, but Roger had recognized her gratitude when Cord finally grumpily accepted that his "master's" decision was final.

With the Mardukans' training as close to complete as it was going to get, they'd hidden the assault shuttles away, reloaded with fuel and ammunition, in the jungle on the edge of the Shin lands and settled down to wait for the right ship. When the time came, the main force would loft in one of the port shuttles, suitably stealthed, while the Mardukan "backup" waited on the ground in the much more threatening assault shuttles.

One ship had come and gone already, but since it was a tramp freighter flagged by Raiden-Winterhowe, they'd passed it up. Hijacking ships under the protection of one of the other major interstellar empires wasn't a good idea. What they were looking for was a ship flagged by the Empire, or even better, one that was *owned* by an Imperial company but under a flag of convenience. They might be returning to attempt a counter-coup, but they didn't want to start an interstellar war in the process.

It had been a hectic two weeks, but now, with all the preparations in place, all they had to do was wait and train. And if a ship didn't come soon, they'd either have to cut back on the Vashin ammunition allotment—which might lead to a mutiny—or else find a new hill for them to shoot up.

Pahner chuckled at the thought, then keyed his helmet com in response to a call from the com center. He listened for a moment, then nodded, and turned to Kosutic.

"All right, Sergeant Major. Tell the troops to quit their fun and suit up."

"Ship?"

"Yep. A tramp freighter owned by Georgescu Lines. Due in thirty-six hours. I doubt they can detect plasma bursts from more than twenty hours out, but I think we should start shutting down the ranges and getting our war faces on."

"Georgescu? That's a New Liberia Company, isn't it, Sir?" Kosutic asked, and Pahner frowned. He understood the point she was making, because New Liberia definitely wasn't a part of the Empire of Man.

"Yes," he said, "but the company's owners appear to be Imperial. Or maybe a shell corporation. And it's not like New L is going to go to war with the Empire, even if we do cop one of their ships."

"No, I don't guess so," Kosutic agreed.

New Liberia belonged to the Confederation of Worlds, which was a holdover from the treaties which had ended the Dagger Wars. The Confederation was a rag-picker's bag of systems none of the major powers had wanted badly enough to fight each other for, and the treaties had set it up primarily as a buffer zone. Despite the centuries which had passed since, however, it had never progressed much beyond subsistence-level neobarb worlds, most of them despotisms, of which New Liberia was by far the most advanced. Which wasn't saying much. Even that planet wasn't much more than a convenient place to dump an off-planet shell corporation, or register a ship at a minimum yearly cost. As for New Liberia itself, the planet had a population under six million—most of them dirt poor—and a few in-system frigates that were play-toys for whatever slope-brow bully-boy had come out on top in the most recent coup. They were unlikely to charge the Empire with piracy, especially of a freighter which was owned by an Imperial corporation skating around the tax laws.

"We'll call on them to surrender, try to keep casualties to a minimum, and pay Georgescu off when we get back," the captain said. "I suppose we *could* simply say that we're commandeering the ship and ask the captain to come down to the surface to surrender, but then there's the little issue of there being a price on our heads.

"If I thought there was a chance in hell that we'd do anything but get ourselves disappeared when we returned, I'd turn us over to the first authorities we found," he continued with a frown. "But there isn't one. Jackson couldn't afford *not* to make us disappear."

"Do you think he was the one who put the toombie on *DeGlopper*?" Kosutic asked. They'd lost so many Marines on the trip that she had a hard time even coming up with all the names, but she remembered shooting Ensign Guha as if it had happened yesterday. Killing a person who was acting under his own volition was one thing. Shooting that toombie—a good junior officer who'd desperately wanted to do anything but what the chip in her head was telling her to do—still made her sick to her stomach. Even if the shot *had* saved the ship.

"Probably," Pahner sighed. "As the head of the Military Committee in the Lords, he had the contacts and the knowledge. And he was no friend of the Empress."

"Which means he also killed the rest of the Family," the sergeant major said. "I'd like some confirmation, but I think that he's one person I'll take active pleasure in terminating with as much prejudice as humanly possible."

"We *will* require confirmation that the Empress isn't in full and knowing agreement with his handling of the situation," Pahner said. "I don't think there's any doubt that she isn't, but getting hard proof of that will be . . . interesting. I have a few ideas on the subject—where to begin, at least—but before we can do anything about it one way or the other, we need a ship." He waved to Honal, who'd been overseeing the training. "Round them up, Honal. We're expecting company."

"Good!" the Vashin said. "I'm looking forward to ship combat. And I like the thought of seeing all those other worlds you keep talking about."

"So do I," Pahner said quietly. "And especially to seeing one that's not Marduk."

"Captain." Roger nodded in greeting as the Marines walked into the command center. "It looks like everything is prepared to receive visitors."

"It had better be," Pahner growled. "We've only been getting ready for the last two weeks."

"I was thinking. You have any major plans between now and when we launch the shuttles?"

"Nothing I'd classify as *major*," the Marine said. "Why?"

"In that case, I was thinking it would be a good idea to have a party," Roger said with a smile. "I've done up a few suitable awards. . . ."

Roger had been a bit put out to discover that he hadn't originated the concept of the dining-in. But after he watched Pahner and Kosutic put together the plan for the evening in less than five minutes, he was less upset.

The sun was setting over the mountains in the west as the majority of the group that had fought its way to the spaceport gathered around tables arranged under awnings. The spaceport's mountain plateau was much higher and drier than most of Marduk, which gave a rare clear sky and a view of both of the moons. It was also much cooler, but the Mardukans' new uniforms finally made them immune to the torpor which set in with the evening's chill.

Supper was a seven-course dinner. It started with fruits gathered from their entire trip, and everyone agreed that the winner was either the K'Vaernian sea-plum or Marshad's kate fruit. The wine was a light white from a vineyard in the Marshad plain that came highly recommended by T'Leen Targ. The second course was wine-basted *coll* fish flown in from K'Vaern's Cove—small, tender ones, not steaks from giant *coll*—accompanied by nearpotatoes skillet fried with slivered Ran Tai peppers. The wine for the second course, a light, sweet sea-plum vintage which had been recommended by T'Seela of Sindi, was perfect for cooling the palette after the peppers.

The third course was a fruit-basted *basik* on a bed of barleyrice. Roger's table was presented with a very large platter. Several normal *basik* had been clustered around a sculpture of a very large, very pointy-toothed *basik* made out of barleyrice. The wine for that course was a kate-fruit vintage from the new vineyards around Voitan.

The fourth course was the *piece de resistance*. Julian had gone out and single-handedly downed a damnbeast, using nothing more than a squad of backup and a bead cannon, and his prize was served roasted as whole as possible. A certain amount of careful rearrangement had been required to cover up the enormous hole in its neck, and it was delivered on a giant platter carried in by six of the local Krath servants. Julian personally officiated over the carving of the steaks, which were served along with *peruz*-spiced barleyrice and steamed vegetables. The wine was a vintage from Ran Tai that the company had come to like during its sojourn there.

The remaining courses were desserts and niblets, and the feast culminated with everyone sitting around on the ground, picking bits of damnbeast out of their teeth while they tried to decide how much wine they could drink.

Finally, as the last course was cleared, Roger stood and raised his wine glass.

"Siddown!" Julian called.

"Yes, sit, Roger," Pahner said. "Let's see . . . I think . . . Yes, Niederberger! You're to give the toast."

The designated private took a hasty gulp of wine, then stood while Gunny Jin whispered in his ear. He cleared his throat and raised his glass.

"Ladies and Gentlemen, Her Majesty, Alexandra the Seventh, Empress of Man! Long may she reign!"

"The Empress!" The response rumbled back at him, and he tried not to scurry as he settled back into his chair in obvious relief.

"*Now* you stand up, Roger," Pahner said.

"Shouldn't it be you?" Roger asked.

"Nah. You're the senior officer, *Colonel*," the captain said with a grin.

"No rank in the mess!" Julian called.

"I was just pointing it out," Pahner said. "Your turn, Roger."

"Okay." Roger got to his feet again. "Ladies and Gentlemen, absent companions!"

"Absent companions!"

"Before we get into any more toasts," Roger continued, waving Julian back down, "I have a few words I'd like to say."

"Speech! Speech!" Poertena yelled, and most of the Vashin joined in. The armorer had taken a table with them, even though they'd made it clear that they didn't want to play cards.

"Not a speech," Roger disagreed, and held out his hand to Despreaux. She handed over a sizable sack, then sat back down with a smile.

"On the auspicious occasion of us almost getting off this mudball," Roger said. "Sorry to all you people who were born here, by the way. But on this occasion, I think it's fitting that we distribute a few mementos. Things to remember our trip by."

"Uh-oh," Kosutic whispered. "Did you know about this?"

"Yep." Pahner grinned. "Or, rather, I found out just in time."

"Lessee," Roger said, pulling out a piece of plastscrip and a small medallion. "Ah, yes. To St. John (J), and St. John (M). A silver 'M' and a silver 'J,' so that we can frigging tell you apart!"

Roger beamed as the twin brothers made their way up to accept their gifts, then shook their hands (Mark's had regenerated quite nicely since Kirsti) as he handed over the mementos.

"Wear 'em in good health. Now, what else do we have? Ah, yes." He reached into the sack and pulled out a wrench no more than three centimeters long. "To Poertena, a little pocking wrench, for beating up on little pocking bits of armor!"

He continued in the same vein through the entire remaining unit of Marines and many of the Vashin and Diasprans, showing that he recognized their individual quirks and personality traits. It took almost an hour of mingled laughter and groans before he started wrapping up.

"To PFC Gronningen," he said, holding up a silver badge. "The unsleeping silver eye. Because you *know* Julian is going to get you, sooner or later."

He handed the badge to the grinning Asgardian and punched him on the shoulder.

"You're doomed. You know that, right?"

"Oh, yeah."

"Lessee. We're getting near the bottom of the bag. . . . Oh, yes. To Adib Julian, a marksman's badge with a 'no' symbol over it. The marksman's bolo badge for always being second in any shooting match!"

Julian accepted it with good grace, and the prince turned to the sergeant major, Pahner, and the senior Mardukans.

"I'd considered the unsleeping eye for Rastar, as well," Roger said, and the wave of human chuckles was swamped in grunting Mardukan laughter as the Marines and the Vashin alike recalled their first meeting and Roger's ambush of the sleeping Rastar. "But in the end, I decided on this." He reached into the bag and withdrew an elaborately chased set of Mardukan-sized bead pistols. "May you never run out of ammo."

"Thank you, Your Highness." Rastar accepted the gift with a flourishing bow.

"No rank in the mess," Roger reminded him, and turned to his next victim. "For Krindi, a set of Zuiko binoculars. It seems you're never able to fight at long range, but what the heck."

"Thank you, Y—Roger," the Diaspran said, and took the imaging system with a slight bow of his own.

"To Eva Kosutic, our own personal Satanist," Roger said, with another grin, and handed her a small silver pitchfork. "The silver pitchfork medal. She was always there to prod buttock; now she has something to prod with. You can feel free to put it anywhere you like."

"And yours was always a nice buttock to prod, Roger," she told him with a grin as she accepted the award. Roger laughed with everyone else, then turned to Cord.

"Cord, what can I say? You've stuck with me through thick and thin, mainly thin."

"You can say nothing and sit back down," the shaman replied.

"Nah, not after I went to all this trouble," the prince said, and winked at Pedi. "Okay, we have: a package of baby formula Dobrescu promises me will work for Mardukan kids just fine. A package of disposable diapers—I know you guys stick your kids in your slime, but when we get among humans, that might not always be an option. A set of four baby blankets—what can I say, do you *always* have to have quartets? And last, but most certainly not least, a set of earplugs. Just for Cord, though. He's going to need them."

"Oh, thank you very much, Roger," Cord said, accepting the items and sitting down.

"Don't think of it as a roast," Roger told him. "Think of it as a baby shower."

"What is that?" Pedi asked Despreaux quietly.

"Normally," the Marine whispered back, "it's when you give gifts that can help with an expected baby. In this case, though, Roger is twitting Cord."

"And here comes Dogzard," Roger said, looking under the table.

The beast raised her head as she heard her name, then she leapt to her feet when she saw her master's body posture.

"Dat's a good Dogzard," Roger told her, and pulled a huge leg of damnbeast off the table. "Who's a good beastie, then?"

The semi-lizard snatched the bone out of Roger's hand and retreated back under the table. Her meter-and-a-half-long tail stuck well out from under it, lashing happily from side to side, and Roger waved his hand.

"Ow, ow!" He counted his fingers ostentatiously, then sighed in relief while everyone laughed. But then the prince lowered his hands, and turned to the last person on his list.

"And so we come to Armand Pahner," he said seriously, and the laughter stilled. "What do you present to the officer who held you together for eight horrible months? Who never wavered? Who never faltered? Who never for one instant let us think that we might fail?

What do you give to the man who took a sniveling brat and made a man of him?"

"Nothing, for preference," Pahner said. "It really *was* my job."

"Still," Roger said, and reached into the now all but empty bag to pull out a small badge. "I present you the Order of the Bronze Shield. If I can, I'm going to have Mother turn it into an order of knighthood; we need at least one more. For service above and beyond the call of duty to the Crown. Thank you, Armand. You've been more than you've needed to be at every turn. I know we still have a long way to go, but I'm confident that we can get there, together."

"Thanks, Roger." The captain stood to accept the gift. "And I have a little present for you, as well."

"Oh?"

"Yes." The Marine cleared his throat formally. "Long before the ISU, before the Empire of Man, in the dawn of the space age, there was a mighty nation called the United States. As Rome before it, it rose in a pillar of flame and eventually fell. But during its heyday, it had a few medals to reckon with.

"There were many awards and ribbons, but one, while common, perhaps surpassed them all. It was a simple rifle on a field of blue, surrounded by a wreath. What it meant was that the wearer had been where the bullets flew, and probably shot at people himself, and had returned from the fire. It meant, simply, that the wearer had seen infantry combat, and survived. All the other medals, really, were simply icing on that cake, and like the ISU before it, the Empire has maintained that same award . . . and for the same reasons.

"Prince Roger Ramius Sergei Alexander Chiang MacClintock," the captain said, as he took the newly minted badge from Sergeant Major Kosutic and pinned it onto the prince's uniform, "I award you the Combat Infantryman's Badge. You have walked into the fire again and again, and come out not unscathed, but at least, thank God, alive. If your mother gives you all the medals you deserve, you're going to look like a neobarb world dictator. But I hope that you think of this one, sometimes, because, really, it says it all."

"Thank you, Armand," Roger said quietly.

"No, thank you," Pahner replied, putting his hand on the prince's shoulder. "For making the transition. For surviving. Hell, for saving all of *our* asses. Thank you from all of us."

The party had descended to the point at which Erkum Pol had to be dragged down before he hit someone with a plank, and Roger had gotten Despreaux off to one side. She'd been quiet all night, and he thought he knew why.

"You're still insisting that you can't marry me, aren't you?" he asked.

"Yes, and I wish you'd quit asking," she replied, looking down the hills to the Krath city in the valley. "I'm short, Roger. I'll stick along to Earth, and I'll do what I can to get your mother out of danger. But I won't marry you. When we're settled, and things are safe, I'm putting in my discharge papers. And then I'll take my severance bonus and go find me a nice, safe, placid farmer to marry."

"Court is just another environment," Roger protested. "You've been through a hundred on this planet, alone. You can adjust!"

"I probably could," she said, shaking her head. "But not well enough. What you need is someone like Eleanora, someone who knows the rocks and shoals. Part of the problem is that we're too alike. We both have a very direct approach, and you need someone who can complement you, not enhance your negative qualities."

"You'll stay until Earth, right?" he asked. "Promise you'll stay until then."

"I promise," she said. "And now, I'm turning in, Roger." She stopped and looked at him with a cocked head. "I'll make an offer one last time. Come with me?"

"Not if you won't marry me," he said.

"Okay," she sighed. "God, we're both stubborn."

"Yeah," Roger said, as she walked away. "Stubborn's one word."

CHAPTER THIRTY-ONE

"We've never had a 'health and welfare' inspection *before,*" the voice said suspiciously.

"Yeah, tell me something I don't know." Jin controlled his voice carefully, sliding just the right hint of exasperation into it. "We've got a task force with an IBI inspection team coming out, and we need to make a big show. Personally, I think they're operating on the theory that everyone needs a good shaking up after the coup attempt, but what do I know? According to The Book, we're *supposed* to do these things on every ship, not that anybody ever did it! But now we're under the gun, so we're trying to get a paper trail going."

There was a long pause, and Jin wished that he could see the other's face, but the freighter had supplied only a voice channel.

Emerald Dawn was a known ship. She'd passed through the system at least twice before, once since Jin had been inserted. She generally traded minor technological trinkets like fire-starters for local gems and artwork. In addition, she got a small fee for dropping electronic transfers in the system, which was the real reason for her visits. As a matter of fact, he'd talked with the ship on her previous run, and he hoped the familiarity of his voice would lull them to some extent.

"Okay," a new voice said finally. "This is Captain Dennis. One person can come aboard for your 'health and welfare' check. But this is the *last* time I'm coming to this port. I don't need this aggravation for a handful of cheap-ass gems, a mail chit that barely covers our air loss, and a cargo of scummy art-shit."

"Whatever." Jin let a bit of the peevish bureaucrat into his tone. "I'm just doing my job."

The shuttle was on autopilot, so he slid out of the pilot's chair with a nod at Poertena, and pulled his way aft. This was made somewhat difficult by the fact that the small craft was crammed with Marines in battle armor. Most of them had clamped onto the walls and floors, but a few were drifting, more or less at random.

He stopped opposite Captain Pahner, whose feet were stuck to the ceiling as he stood "head-down," perusing the schematics for the target.

"They're not real happy," the IBI agent said.

"I don't care if they're happy," Pahner said. "Just as long as they open their doors."

"One shot, and we're all vapor," Jin noted.

"And as far as they know, they're suddenly the most wanted ship in the Empire," Pahner pointed out. "It would be very bad form for a tramp freighter to shoot up an official Imperial inspection craft. They'll let us dock. After that, you just hit the deck."

"Why does this make my butt pucker?" Fiorello Giovannuci— known to the dirt-side com station as "Captain Dennis"—asked as he gazed at the viewscreen image of the approaching small craft.

"Because your butt always puckers when we get boarded." Amanda Beach, his first officer, shook her head in mock gravity. "Relax. It's got all the codes for an Imperial customs ship. Really, it's because your conscience isn't pure. You need to spend some time on the planets, reacquiring your oneness with Gaia."

Giovannuci glanced at her, then shook his own head and sighed.

"Your sense of humor is the reason you're out here, you know. Just keep it up." He leaned forward, as if the viewscreen could tell him more if he only stared hard enough, and rubbed his cheek. "And you're wrong. There's something very much not right here."

"You want me to go down to the airlock?" Beach asked as the CO fell silent, watching the shuttle make its final approach. He continued to say nothing for several more seconds, but, finally, he nodded.

"Yes. And take Longo and Ucelli."

"My," she said, pursing her lips as she got to her feet, "you *are* nervous. Isn't that sort of overkill?"

"Better over than under," Giovannuci said. "Go. Fast."

Jin waited until all the telltales turned green, then opened the airlock door and swung forward through it cautiously. The three people waiting for him represented a fair percentage of the total crew for a tramp like this, and their presence in such numbers indicated just how uncomfortable they must be.

He'd have been just as nervous in their shoes. The profit which could be made from "jacking" ships like this were enough to make them high-priority targets. Even a tramp as old and beat up as *Emerald Dawn* was worth nearly a billion credits. So anytime one was parked anywhere but at a fully secured port—which did not, by any stretch, describe Marduk—its crew was always on the lookout for pirates. And it wasn't impossible to imagine the entire port being captured, or even that one Temu Jin would be in on it. Stranger things had transpired in the borderlands.

Besides, now that he thought about it, that was actually a pretty fair description, in a slightly skewed way, of what was actually going to happen.

The threesome had obviously been chosen with some care. According to her collar tabs, the woman was senior, a merchant lieutenant, so probably she was *Emerald Dawn*'s second-in-command. She looked a bit long in the tooth for that, and fairly beat up. Regen healed *almost* perfectly, but scars were inevitable—at least when a limb hadn't had to be completely regrown—and this one, for all her striking looks, had plenty. She'd been in more than one fight, and a couple of them must have been with knives.

The second most notable was the largest of the group, a hulking figure which outmassed even the redoubtable Gronningen. But something about him told Jin that he was one of those big, fast men people tended to underestimate on the theory that anyone that big had to be too slow to be dangerous. He would bear watching.

For that matter, so would the little guy. He was the calmest seeming of the lot as he leaned nonchalantly against a bulkhead, but the low-slung double pistols sort of said it all.

And all three of them wore light body armor.

Jin stepped forward carefully, keeping his hands in view at all times, and extended the pad.

"Pax, okay?" He tabbed the controls and gestured around. "All I want is a thumbprint saying that the 'inspection' was complete, and that you have no complaints. I'll put in all sorts of stuff checked, basically half the stuff on your manifest. And we're all happy. I'm happy, *you're* happy, the IBI asshole is happy, and everybody can go back to business as usual."

Beach took the pad and glanced at the document on its display. As the bullet-sweating geek had suggested, it showed a detailed inspection of an imaginary ship conforming to their class, with a list of cargo opened and checked. It was quite an artistic forgery, a masterpiece of the genre.

"Why, thank you," she said, giving him a thin smile as she annotated and thumbprinted the pad. "What's wrong? You look nervous."

"Yeah? Well, Mr. Gun-Happy over there looks like he's remembering the last baby he ate, and I ain't even gonna comment on Mr. Troll," Jin said with a nervous laugh.

"I don't eat babies," the gunman whispered. "They stick in your teeth."

"Ha. Ha," the IBI agent said.

"Done," Beach said, and handed him the pad.

"Thanks," Jin replied with a relieved sigh. His hand was unaccountably clumsy as he accepted the pad, and it slipped out of his fingers. He swore, grabbed for it, then followed it to the deck, and as he did, he noted with the cool, professional detachment available only to the truly frightened that the threesome had reacted to the little ruse as if such things happened to them every day.

The fabric of his suit hardened under the kinetic impact of the first round just as the shuttle doors exploded open behind him.

"Shit," Giovannuci said, and hit the alarm button with a fist as he erupted from his seat. "*Jackers!*"

They couldn't simply announce that they were Marines who were commandeering the vessel in the name of the Empire. First, no one would have believed them, and, second, they were all wanted for treason. Somehow, they were pretty sure that "No, really. It was all a big mistake," wouldn't fly. So the plan was to secure the "welcome party" and try to keep casualties to a minimum in the assault.

The "plan," clearly, was a bust even before Gronningen did a flying leap out of the airlock. The undersized gun-boy was pumping rounds into Jin as the IBI agent rolled across the deck to spread the hits across the protective surface of his uniform. The big guy, on the other hand, had produced a cut-down flechette cannon—from where was a mystery—and was filling the airlock with flechettes, while the leader type had produced a heavy bead pistol and had Gronningen perfectly targeted.

"Don't fire until fired upon" obviously wasn't going to work under these circumstances.

Gronningen hit the deck sliding, and targeted the little gunner first, but the gunman had taken one look at the Marine battle armor and decided the odds were against the home team. The heavy bead round clove through the bulkhead, but the gunner was already gone. Gronningen's next round, however, flipped the heavy gunner over backwards in a spray of red.

The woman was *fast*. Before he could reacquire her, she'd hit the deck exit button and was *out* of there. The inner airlock door slammed shut behind her, and Gronningen levered himself to his feet as Macek slid by and hit the door button.

"Sealed," Geno said. "Oh, well." He rolled out a slab of claylike substance and slapped it onto the hatch. "Fire in the hole!"

"Who in Muir's Name *are* these guys?" Giovannuci demanded.

A security team was on the way to the command deck, but he wanted to be forward. The last thing he'd seen was a wave of heavy Imperial armor coming out of the shuttle, and that was not good news.

"I don't know," Beach replied over her communicator. "What kind of jackers wear battle armor? Or even know how to *use* it, for that matter? But if they're Empies, why don't they have a warship? And if there *is* a warship, where in hell is it?"

"I don't know," the CO replied, looking at his schematic. "But whoever they are, they're already through the lock. And moving down Deck C. It looks like they know where the morgue is."

"Do they want to *capture* us?" the second officer demanded. "I'm falling back to the Morgue, but I've only got a limited group. So far, only eight and the two commandos at the Morgue door."

"Well, I've got bodies, but *you've* got all the weapons," Giovannuci snapped. "Sidearms are useless against that armor."

"I know," Beach said. "I'm into the Armory. Now, if we can just match bodies to bullets!"

"I'll send groups through the side passages," Giovannuci said. "For once, the way they butchered this thing when they converted her will work in our favor."

"Oh, yeah? Well, next time, tell them to put the Pollution-bedamned Armory further away from the main hatch!"

"Will do. Giovannuci, out."

"Lai, go with First Squad to Engineering," Pahner snapped. "Gunny Jin, you're with Second." As the teams headed out, the sergeant major snagged Jin and Despreaux. She peered into the squad leader's helmet visor, but its swirling mirrored surface made it impossible to see the younger woman's expression.

"Despreaux, I know you're not tracking too well . . ." Kosutic said.

"I'm *fine*, Sergeant Major," the sergeant replied.

"No, you're not," Kosutic contradicted calmly. "You're a basket case. So's Bebi and Niederberger. And Gelert and Mutabi, for that matter."

"Shit," Jin said. "Mutabi went?"

"Yes," Kosutic replied. "I've been trying to hold all of you out of combat as much as possible. This time, I don't have any choice."

"I'll be fine," Despreaux said desperately. "Really. I was fine in Mudh Hemh."

"Nevertheless, Jin's going along," Kosutic told her. "Let him run your squad; you just cover everyone's back."

"I can *handle* it, Sergeant Major," the sergeant said. "I *can.*"

"Despreaux, just do what I say, okay?" the NCO snapped.

"Yes, Sergeant Major," she replied bitterly. "I'll go ahead and give up my squad to the Gunny."

"Trust the Gunny," Jin told her quietly, tapping her on the shoulder.

"It'll be okay," Kosutic said, as the deck shook with a distant detonation. "Somehow or another, it'll be okay."

"Who the pock *are* these guys?" Julian snapped. He'd narrowly missed being smeared by the hypervelocity missile that had just torn the bulkhead into so much confetti. For a "tramp freighter," *Emerald Dawn*'s crew had some heavy-duty hardware. And a lot of personnel.

"Captain Pahner, this is Julian. Third Squad is stuck on the approach to the Bridge. I'd estimate the defenders are in at least squad strength, with heavy weapons, and they're fighting hard. We tried to cut through bulkheads, but several of them are made of reinforced blast steel. We're having a hard time cutting that. We've eliminated two defense points, but we've also lost two suits to get here." He looked around at the four members of the squad behind him. "Frankly, Sir, I don't think we're going to get through without some reinforcements."

"Julian, hold what you've got. I'll see what I can scrounge up."

Pahner looked over at Temu Jin and raised an eyebrow. The IBI agent had been attempting to hack the ship's infonet for almost two minutes. It was clear that whatever they'd run into—smugglers, pirates, or whatever—this was no "tramp freighter."

"So, what did we just walk into Agent Jin?"

"Well, if it's a tramp freighter, I'm an Armaghan High Priest. No offense, Sergeant Major."

"None taken," Kosutic rasped. "We need to do something here, Captain."

"Yes, we do, Sergeant Major." Pahner looked over at her. "But we really, really need some information to decide what, don't you think?"

"Personnel, personnel . . ." Gunny Jin muttered, looking at the faded signs stenciled on the bulkheads. "Where's the crew quarters?"

"Kyrou, cover your sector," Despreaux snapped. The private had been glancing over at Jin as the gunny tried to navigate the unfamiliar maze.

"Yes, Sergeant," the plasma gunner replied, turning back to the right.

"Ah, crew quarters," the gunny muttered finally, then took a few steps and turned left into a cross-passage. "Oh . . . shit."

Despreaux froze as the gunny and Kyrou vanished in a ball of silver and the bulkheads to either side began to melt.

"Nimashet?" Beckley called. "*Sergeant?!*"

Despreaux felt her hands begin to shake. For just a moment, Beckley seemed kilometers away, and she closed her eyes. But then she drew a deep breath and opened them once more.

"Alpha Team, lay down a base of fire. Bravo, *move!*"

The sergeant major glanced at her schematic and grimaced.

"Lamasara's gone," she said bitterly. "We're losing people by the minute, Captain."

"Yes, we are," Pahner replied calmly. "But until I know to *whom*, we're just going to hold where we are. With one exception." He flipped to a different frequency. "St. John. Go, go, go."

St. John (J) looked over at his brother and smiled.

"Oh, goody. Time to take a little walk."

"I hate freefall," St. John (M) grumped, but he also tapped the controls of the Class A Extra-Vehicular Unit. The round EVU pack, more of a small spaceship than a suit, accepted the previously set up commands and released carefully timed puffs of gas that sent the two Marines on a course that hugged the surface of the globular starship. A course that would eventually intersect the first of two weapons hard points.

"Ah, just think of it as a stroll down to the bagel shop," St. John (J) said. He cycled his bead cannon to ensure that it was working in vacuum. "Or the Muffin Man."

"Them was the days, wasn't they, Bro?" Mark sighed. "Do you know the muffin man . . ."

"The muffin man, the muffin man," John replied.

"Do you know the muffin man," they chorused as the EVU packs picked up speed, rocketing them towards an anti-ship missile platform. A platform that probably would be heavily defended. "Do you know the muffin man, he lives in Drury Lane!"

"Got it," Jin called. He watched the data streaming out of the ship-sys and blanched. "Oh, no."

"Sergeant Julian, this is Pahner."

Julian leaned forward and sent a stream of heavy beads down the passage to cover Gronningen. The big Asgardian darted across the opening and dove through a hatchway, barely avoiding a stream of plasma fire.

"Go ahead, Sir," the sergeant gasped.

"There's bad news and worse news. The bad news is that this isn't a tramp freighter. It's a Saint Special Operations insertion ship under the command of one Colonel Fiorello Giovannuci."

"Oh . . . pock. Commandos?"

"Greenpeace Division," Pahner confirmed. "And in case you didn't recognize the name, Giovannuci was the bastard in command of the Leonides operation a few years back. He's as good as they come . . . and a true believer."

"Oh . . . I—" Julian paused, unable to think, then shook himself. "Go ahead, Sir."

"This is where we get to the worse news," Pahner's voice said calmly. "Gunny Jin is down, probably gone, at what turned out to be the Armory, and not the crew quarters, ship's plans notwithstanding. Where Despreaux's squad is apparently blocking the majority of the commando *company* from making it into the Morgue."

"Oh. A *full* company?"

"Yes. They are, therefore, the current priority. If the Peacers get to the Armory, we are well and truly screwed, so we're just going to have to take care of them before we can reinforce *you*."

"Yes, Sir."

"Cover your back. Do not let reinforcements into the Bridge. By the same token, do not let the Bridge guards, who are almost the only ones with heavy weapons, out. Understood?"

"Hold what we've got. Nobody goes in, nobody comes out. Engineering?"

"Gunny Lai bought it there, so did Sergeant Angell. But Georgiadas has the situation under control; there's a security point there that they took, and they're covered in both directions. You're not, so hold on hard. Got it?"

"Got that in one, Sir. What's to stop them from taking off, Sir?"

"Nothing." Julian could hear the grim humor behind that single word. "Georgiadas reports that the drive is warming up under remote from the Bridge even as we speak."

"Yes, Sir." Julian licked his lips and cursed quietly. "Sir, I'll be asked. What in the hell are we going to do? I think I'd rather face the Kranolta again."

"I'm going to do the one thing that I swore to myself I would not, under any circumstances whatsoever, especially if things were bad, stoop to."

"Go! Go! Go!"

"Your Highness, just wait!" Dobrescu snapped. "Thirty more seconds to lift. That's the optimal window. So just sit the hell down and shut the hell up."

"God*damn* it!" Roger almost punched the display, but he remembered all those centuries ago, the last time he'd been in a cramped little compartment like this one in powered battle armor and gently tapped a control panel. Yet it was hard to restrain himself. Hard. The display showed that the thirty Marines who'd lifted off to the "tramp freighter" had been reduced to twenty-four already. At this rate, there wouldn't be anyone to rescue.

"Prepare for lift," Dobrescu called over the all-hands circuit. "Helmets on! You sc—Mardukans get ready. You're going to feel *realll* heavy. Three, two, one . . ."

"Just hang on, Nimashet," Roger whispered. "Just hang on. . . ."

Four Marine assault shuttles, containing the Mardukan contingent of the *Basik*'s Own, lifted skyward on pillars of flame.

"All units, hold what you've got," Pahner called. "The cavalry is on the way."

"Satan, protect us," Kosutic snapped as a team of commandos rolled across the corridor. She winged one, but the other three got away. "We're getting outmaneuvered and outshot, Captain."

"I've noticed," Pahner said calmly. "Suggestions?"

"Let Poertena and me take it to them," Kosutic said. "Having a mobile force will force them to react."

"I'll have a mobile force here in—" He consulted his suit. "Seven minutes."

"Seven minutes is a lonnng time, Armand."

Pahner sighed and nodded.

"That it is."

"Aaaahhh!"

"Oh, calm down, Rastar," Roger grunted. The shuttles still had the extra hydrogen tanks installed, and the plotted intercept had been calculated based upon that almost limitless fuel supply. So they'd lifted at three gravities and would hit a DV-Max of almost seven. For Roger and the pilots, that was simply very unpleasant. For the Mardukans, who had never experienced more than a couple of gravities during their limited micro-gravity familiarization flights, it was a nightmare.

They'd put all of them through at least one lift, but nothing like this. The humans had managed to convince themselves that there was no conceivable situation in which the Mardukans would actually be used for a combat assault, so they hadn't subjected them to the real stresses of such a launch. And now the Mardukans, and their allies, were paying the price for that complacent gentleness.

"All hands, remember, *crunch!*" Roger gasped. "Squeeze your stomach like you're taking a dump, but plug your butt." He glanced over at the telltales. "There's only another . . . three minutes."

"I *hate* freefall," St. John (M) said as he hugged the hull of the ship.

Their EVU packs were gone, and the two Marines were now flat on their faces behind a tiny exterior catwalk. The first emplacement, a missile launcher, had been undefended. But by the time they made it to the second and last, a heavy plasma cannon, the Saints had suffered a rush of common sense and sent one of their few "free" heavy weapons to protect it. The ship-to-ship cannon itself couldn't depress far enough to engage the Marines, or they'd already have been reduced to constituent atoms, but the heavy bead gun that had popped out of the firing port had them well and truly pinned. Because of the angle it had, they couldn't even back up and swing around.

"Mom always said we'd come to a bad end," St. John (J) said.

"Don't go all heroic on me, Bro," Mark said. "There's got to be a smart way out of this."

"In about thirty seconds, the prince is going to come over the horizon, Mark." John readied his plasma cannon. "So you've got exactly twenty seconds to figure something out."

"Oh, that's not hard," Mark said . . . and stood up.

The first bead took him in the left arm. The heavy projectile smashed the ChromSten armor like tissue paper, severing the limb just above the elbow in a spray of gas and body liquids.

"Pock, not again," he gasped as he aimed his cannon one-handed at the base of the defensive platform and locked the trigger back.

"Pollution," Giovannuci whispered as he turned away from the display. The armored form had taken three bead rounds before the plasma platform went up, but it was still firing. Whoever it was *had* to be dead. But he kept firing until *Emerald Dawn*'s last space defenses turned into floating bits of wreckage.

"What does it take to *kill* these people? *Who the fuck are they?*"

"Sir," his com tech said, "you have *got* to hear this."

CHAPTER THIRTY-TWO

"Saint ship, this is His Highness Prince Roger MacClintock. Cease resistance to this legal boarding, and you will be detained for eventual repatriation as prisoners of war. Continue your resistance, and you'll be considered unlawful combatants under the laws of war. In two minutes, I will be performing a forced boarding with the remainder of Prince Roger's Own. You have until then to comply."

"Is there any indication which shuttle that's coming from?"

"Negative, Colonel Giovannuci. It's being rebroadcast from all four."

"Pity," *Emerald Dawn*'s commander murmured, then shrugged. "Put me on."

"Approaching shuttles, be aware that the prince is dead. He was killed in a shipwreck. So you're not him."

Roger looked at the communicator and shrugged.

"Believe what you will, but the report of my demise was exceedingly exaggerated. One minute, twenty seconds."

"If we surrender, they'll probably do what they say," Beach said over the discrete command channel. "These can't be jackers. Only Imperial Marines are this precise. Its Empies, all right."

"And that means it might *be* the prince," Colonel Giovannuci mused. "But it doesn't really matter. If we surrender and they repatriate us, the clerics will send us to the wall. The only real choice is to win."

He considered the situation, regarding the monitors covering the three main fights. He knew that Beach, like most naval officers assigned to SpecOps, resented the tradition which put Army officers in command of the ships assigned to them. He was even prepared to admit—privately—that the Navy's arguments against the practice might have a point when it came to naval actions. But this was *his* sort of fight, not Beach's, and he thought about his options for a moment longer, then looked up at the commando lieutenant at his elbow.

"I don't like them holding the Bridge passage. I want some freedom of movement. Take some of the Bridge guards and work around to the other side of them. Then we'll try to nutcracker them between us—clear them out and get ourselves some room to maneuver. While you get into position, I'll be dealing with this pompous oaf."

"Prince Roger, or whoever you are, thanks for the offer. But, no. I think we'll take our chances."

Roger shrugged again and flipped the schematic to show the approach vectors.

"Have it your way. See you in a few minutes." He changed frequencies and nodded at the image of Fain that appeared on the monitor. "Captain, when we dock, send one platoon to the Bridge, one to the Armory, and one to Engineering."

"As you command, Your Highness," the Diaspran said.

"I'll be going to the Bridge. I recommend that you take one of the other locations." Roger turned to the Vashin who shared the compartment and waved a hand. "Rastar, I want your guys to head for the boat bays, but other than that, just spread out and slow down these Saints that are trying to sneak their way to the Armory. Send one unit to Captain Pahner, though, for him to use as a reserve."

"Okay," Rastar said as the acceleration finally came off. "That's a relief," he added with a sigh of bliss as the shuttle changed to freefall.

"Don't get used to it," Roger advised . . . just as the deceleration hit.

"Aaaaaaahhhh . . ."

"Colonel, we're getting killed down here," Beach said. "I've slipped a few people through to the Armory, but they're just making up for our losses. We're stalemated."

She looked at her schematic and shook her head with an unheard snarl.

"And we've got somebody moving around. I just lost a team by Hold Three."

"I know," Giovannuci replied, watching his own displays. The internal systems hadn't been designed to handle a pitched battle, but he'd been able to use the monitors to follow at least some of the action. Not that very many of them were left; the invaders had been systematically shooting them out. He could more or less tell where they'd *been* from the breadcrumb trail of smashed pickups in their wake, but not, generally, where they currently were.

"The bad news is that they're about to receive reinforcements," he told his executive officer. "We need to break the stalemate before that happens, or at least to get some mobility going for us."

"Suggestions are welcome," Beach said tartly.

"About the only thing that might work is hitting one of the defense points and breaking out," the colonel said. "It will only take a couple of minutes to get set. We'll hit them simultaneously in five minutes."

"Works for me," Beach agreed laconically. "And I hope to hell it works for all of us. If the Empies don't kill us, the clerics will."

Eva Kosutic slid along the passage, using her turned-up audio and movement sensors to search for hostiles . . . and trying very, very hard not to let anyone on the other side know where *she* was. The majority of the Saints were in light body armor and skin suits, so fairly light weaponry was capable of penetrating it with carefully aimed fire. In her case, she'd loaded one of her dual magazines with low-velocity penetrator rounds. Designed to avoid damage to important systems in shipboard actions, they left a very small hole in their victim and didn't tumble or expand upon entry. But they were capable of defeating light armor points and portions of helmets. And for Eva Kosutic, that was all that was required.

Her sensors told her there was another group moving along the same passage, trying to infiltrate past the various Marine groups to the Armory. She looked around, and then lifted herself into an overhead position, holding herself in place against the deckhead with one hand and both legs planted.

"I'm going to send all these Pollution-damned Empies straight to Hell," Sergeant Leustean said. The commando NCO twisted his hand on the foregrip of his bead rifle and snarled. "Straight to Hell."

"Well, don't get us all kilt doin' it," Corporal Muravyov replied.

"We'll be doing the killing!" the sergeant snapped . . . just as the sergeant major opened fire.

The first three shots entered just below their targets' helmets, penetrating the light armor on the relatively undefended patch at the top of the neck and severing the cervical vertebrae. But by the third shot, the team was reacting, the highly trained commandos spinning and diving for cover. But good as they were, they didn't stand much of a chance up against a suit of combat armor, and an even more highly trained Imperial bodyguard who'd just gone through an advanced course in combat survival.

Kosutic dropped to the deck and walked over to prod the bodies.

"Not today, Sergeant." She sighed, then glanced at her telltales. More movement. "Not today."

Roger double-checked the seal, then hit the hatch release, letting Rastar and two other Vashin precede him through the still-smoking hole in the ship's side.

Even freighters used ChromSten for their hulls. The material was expensive, making up a sizable fraction of the total cost of the ship. But given that it was proof against almost all varieties of space radiation, and an excellent system to protect against micro-meteor impacts, it was worth every credit.

Freighters did not, however, have warship-thickness ChromSten. The material on the outside of a freighter was generally less than two microns thick, whereas a warship's might be up to a centimeter. And it was that difference which had permitted the thermal lances on the assault shuttles to eat through the hull in less than three seconds.

The point Roger had chosen for his hull breaching was one of the vessel's innumerable holds, and its interior was filled with shipping canisters of every conceivable size and shape. Roger took a look around, shrugged, and waved the Vashin forward. Somewhere, there was a battle to be joined.

Rastar tapped the controls of the sealed portal, but it was clear that the hatch out of the hold was locked.

"I'll fix that, Your Highness," one of his Vashin said, lifting his plasma gun.

Rastar backpedaled furiously, but he still caught the fringes of the blast as the door shattered outwards.

"Watch those things!" he shouted, then keyed the radio to transmit as the luckless cavalryman flew back from the doorway, most of his mass converted to charcoal. "Watch those things. They're not carbines, for Valan's sake!" He looked around and then down at his suit. "Why is the suit hardening?"

"Damned scummies," Dobrescu growled as he clambered past the prince. Roger could barely hear him over the shrill wail of escaping atmosphere. The blast from the plasma cannon and the resulting overpressure had popped part of the temporary seals between the shuttle's hull and the hole blasted through *Emerald Dawn*'s skin.

"Watch your fire!" the warrant officer shouted over the Vashin frequency.

"Can we do anything about it?" Roger asked.

"Not unless I pull away and reseal," Dobrescu replied sourly. "We might as well wait until we repair the hole."

"Which brings up an interesting point. Do we have anyone who knows how to weld ChromSten?"

"Fine time to ask now, Your Highness," Dobrescu said with a harsh laugh.

"We weren't supposed to have been facing this much resistance," the prince pointed out.

"Begging your pardon, Prince Roger," one of the Vashin said as he trotted over through the increasing vacuum. "Prince Rastar's compliments, and we have no idea which way to go."

Roger chuckled and gestured at Dobrescu.

"Get going, Doc. Raise as much hell as you can while doing the minimum damage. Keep them from reinforcing the Bridge, Engineering, and the Armory. Pay attention to the shuttle bays, especially."

"Got it," Dobrescu acknowledged, adjusting his carbine sling. "Where are you going?"

"Bridge," Roger replied as four Vashin fell in with him. He arranged them so that the sole plasma gunner was in *front* of him. The others' bead cannons were loaded with shot rounds and couldn't penetrate his armor.

"Now we find out if I'm a genius, or an idiot."

Giovannuci flipped through screens, trying to get a handle on the battle. He was sure all four of the shuttles had managed to breach and board, and one was visible on an exterior monitor. Unfortunately, the holds were poorly covered at the best of times, and so far he hadn't been able to find out how many of the Marine reinforcements had come aboard.

He touched another control, then looked up as he heard Lieutenant Anders Cellini, his tactical officer, gasp.

"Sir," the tac officer said in a strangled voice. "Screen four-one-four."

Giovannuci keyed the monitor for Hold Three and froze in shock.

"Are those what I think they are, Sir?" Cellini asked with a pronounced edge of disbelief.

"They're scummies," Giovannuci replied in a voice of deadly calm. "With plasma and bead cannons. That resource-sucking, inbred cretin gave *scummies* plasma cannon. And he brought them aboard *my* ship!"

"Well, at least it's not more Empie Marines." The tac officer sounded as if he were trying very hard to find a bright side to look upon, and Giovannuci barked a harsh, humorless almost-laugh.

"You're joking, right?" he snapped. "Empie Marines would at least know not to blow holes in the side of the *ship*; that hold is *depressurized*."

When Harvard saw the yellow light above the hatch, he knew that volunteering to "help out" had been a bad idea. Not that he'd had a lot of choice. There were so few Marines left that, in the end, the prince had shanghaied every human he thought he could trust to assist the Mardukans. Now technicians from the port, and even complete civilians like Mansul, were running around the interior of a Saint Q-ship, trying to keep the scummies from killing themselves.

It was turning out to be a difficult assignment.

"The button won't open the door," Honal snarled, hitting the circuit again.

"Uh . . ."

For entirely understandable safety considerations, Harvard had wedged himself into the middle of the scummies' formation. Unfortunately, this meant he couldn't reach the Vashin nobleman before the light dawned.

"Aha!" Honal said. "The emergency release."

"Honaaalll!"

It was too late. Before the human could get the Vashin's attention, Honal had flipped out the emergency unlock lever and thrown it over.

As Honal would have realized, had he been able actually to read the information displayed on the lock-assembly, the far compartment wasn't totally depressurized. It was, however, at a much lower atmospheric pressure than the near side of the hatch. The result was a rather strong suction.

Honal was unable to let go of the hatch before it flew backwards, dragging him with it. However, the physics of its opening, rather than spinning him to slam into the bulkhead, combined with the blast of wind at his back to pick him up and pitch him violently down the passage.

All that Mansul could hear was a short, cut-off cry, the clang of the hatch hitting the stops, and a crunching sound. Then he was carried along by the stampede as the Therdan contingent rushed to the aid of its commander.

Harvard found him lying against a piece of radiometric monitoring gear, crumpled and twisted like a pretzel. His head was tucked under one armpit, and one of his legs was thrown over backwards, touching the deck.

"So, Harvard Mansul," he croaked. "What *does* a yellow light mean?"

"You're joking, right?" Beach had lost contact with Ucelli and was trying to round up more stragglers to feed into the cauldron around the Armory. She was also hunting Empies. A team had been ambushed somewhere around here, and she was determined to track down the Marines responsible. She'd sent Ucelli to block the passage leading up from Cargo Main, but now she wished she'd kept him around. The little gunslinger would've been good backup for facing down scummies. Although . . . maybe not scummies armed with plasma cannon.

"No, we're down to the wire, here," the colonel said. "If we can't get more people armed up and armored, I'm going to have to punch the ship."

"I'd really appreciate it if you didn't do that," Beach said. "I know we've had our differences over the One Faith, but you have to admit that suicide generally isn't a good thing. Think of the resource waste."

Giovannuci smiled thinly at her over the monitor.

"No, Beach, we *are* different. You see, I *believe,* and you don't. That's why I'm in command, and you're not. If you can't break the deadlock at the Armory, I'll have to set the scuttling charges."

"Oh, grand," she whispered, after she'd cut the circuit. She thought furiously for a moment, but she couldn't really see a way out. The tactical officer had a second key for the self-destruct mechanism, so she was unnecessary; her absence from the Bridge wouldn't keep Giovannuci from doing exactly what he'd just said he would.

"Oh, Pollution," she whispered again . . . then slammed into the bulkhead as her uniform hardened under a savage kinetic impact.

She bounced back and spun in place, raising her bead rifle, but a whirl of silver smashed into the breech, crushed her left hand, and pitched the weapon from her grasp. She started to drop into a crouch, but the backswing caught her on the side of the helmet, and she rebounded off the bulkhead again, then slumped to the deck.

Poertena used the wrench to smash out the monitor, then dragged the unconscious officer into a nearby supply cabinet. Assuming they survived this goat-pock, they might need her, so he pulled off her communicator and weapons, then welded the door shut. The door had an air seal and was marked as an emergency life-support shelter, so as long as the ship didn't explode, she should be fine.

Rastar looked down the seemingly endless passageway, and then glanced at the human pilot.

"You're sure it's this way?"

"That's what the schematic said," Dobrescu replied shortly. "It's a ways yet."

"Very well." The Vashin prince lifted his arm into the air in a broad and a dramatic gesture. "To the shuttle bays!"

He continued down the high, wide passage. It was the first thing they'd found on the ship that wasn't made for midgets, and it was a vast relief. He and Honal had divided their forces in order to approach the shuttle bays from different directions in the hope that one of them might get through unintercepted. So far, neither of them had encountered any actual resistance, and that made Rastar very, very nervous. It was also one reason he was so glad to see this spacious corridor. All the Mardukans found the normal short, narrow passages, and the strangely close "horizon" caused by the curvature of the ship, very odd and alien, but his concern was much more basic. The farther ahead he could see, the less likely he was to walk into an ambush.

After about five minutes, they reached a "T" intersection, with signs leading to the Bridge and the shuttle bays. The Vashin noble waved to the left, then watched as the plasma gunner on point flew backwards with the entire back of his head blown out.

Rastar didn't even think about his response. He simply drew all four bead pistols and leapt across the relatively narrow intersection, guns blazing. He was surprised, however, to see only a single human figure in the passage. The human was standing with pistols in each hand, and they flashed upward like lightning as Rastar leapt. Despite the fact that the human couldn't possibly have known exactly where and when Rastar would appear, four rounds cracked into the Vashin's suit before he landed on the far side of the intersection.

Fortunately, none of them penetrated, and Rastar slammed to the deck. He raised his hands to the group on the far side, motioning for them to stay put. Then he popped his head out and back, quickly, followed by a hand in a "wait a moment" gesture that was nearly as universal among Mardukans as it was among humans.

When that didn't draw any fire, he poked his head out into the corridor, as close to the deck as he could get it. This time the response was immediate and vigorous, and Rastar swore as he jerked back. One of the incoming rounds had missed completely, but the other had plowed a groove in the side of his helmet. Another half-centimeter to the side, and it would have plowed a hole clear *through* the helmet, which would have been most unpleasant.

The Prince of Therdan sat back, considering what he'd seen in his single, brief glance. The Saint was short, even for a *basik*—not much taller than Poertena. But the speed and lethal accuracy he'd already demonstrated told the prince that here was an opponent worthy of him. It wasn't as good as swords or knives, but it would have to do.

He thought for a few more moments, then grinned in the human fashion as he saw the sign on the bulkhead beside him. He didn't know where the passage the human was in actually led, but it *didn't* lead to the shuttle bays, assuming the bulkhead sign was correct. The little gunman must have chosen his position to take anyone headed for the shuttle bays in the flank as they passed.

"Dobrescu?" he said over the radio.

"Yes?"

"Go back the way we came. Link up with Honal."

"What about you?"

"I think this fellow is good enough that we'd all like him kept right where he is," Rastar replied.

As he spoke, he eased a bit closer to the intersection, then leaned out, spotted the human—half-concealed now behind what looked like a ripped-out hatch—and fired four rounds rapid-fire. His opponent ducked, but only for an instant, and then it was Rastar's turn to roll hastily further into cover as beads screamed lethally past.

"You go find Honal," he told the human healer cheerfully. "I'll stay here and play for a while."

"We've got to go," Giovannuci said, and sealed his uniform jacket. The material wouldn't be proof against the plasma and bead cannon of the Empie Marines, but it would at least give some protection from flashback and spalling.

"What about Beach, Sir?" Cellini asked.

Giovannuci only shrugged and gestured at the hatch, but as the armored commando keyed the opening, he wondered himself. The first officer was one of only four people who could disarm the scuttling charges, after all.

"Captain Pahner, we've got a counterattack going!" Despreaux called. "They're attempting to break out from the Armory!"

"How are you doing?" Pahner asked. Captain Fain had been held up by a small group of wandering commandos, but he was nearly to the sergeant's position—no more than a minute out. Of course, in combat, a minute was a *long* time.

"Kyrou and Birkendal are dead, Sir," the sergeant replied. Pahner could hear the thump of fire in the background over her voice. Given that she was inside armor, that meant some heavy impacts. "Clarke's hit, but still fighting, and the St. Johns are out on the hull. I'm down to four people, Sir."

"Just hold out for another minute, Sergeant," the captain replied calmly. "Just one minute. Fain's nearly there."

"We'll try, Sir," she said. "I'm—"

Pahner shook his head as the communications system automatically dumped a feedback squeal. Something had filled the frequency with static. He knew what the sound meant, but that didn't mean he had to like it.

"Sergeant Despreaux?" He asked. Silence answered. "Computer, switch: Beckley?"

"Sir!" The Alpha Team leader was panting. "Despreaux's down! We're in bug-out boogie mode, Sir. The Armory is open!"

"Hold tight, Beckley," Pahner replied. "You just have to hold on!"

"I'd like to, Sir, but it's just me and Kileti functional. Kane bought it, Chio has Clarke, and I have Nimashet. We're going to try to pull back through the Diasprans and hand over the fight. We don't have a choice, Sir."

"Computer, switch: Fain!"

Gronningen ducked as a burst of plasma filled the passage with steam. A previous burst had penetrated the inboard bulkhead and cracked a gray-water pipe. Now the blast turned the gray-water to vapor and fecal plasma.

"Julian!" he called, lifting his own plasma cannon over the security station and blasting away in return. "They're trying to break out!"

"All units," Pahner announced over the general frequency. "General counterattack underway. Hold what you've got; the Diasprans are nearly there!"

"Pocking hell," the squad leader snarled, sliding on his belly towards the plasma gunner's position. "Why couldn't they just wait for our reinforcements?"

"Because they don't want to die?" the Asgardian suggested. "You know—"

The second blast of plasma had been more carefully coordinated, with two plasma cannons and a bead cannon all aimed at the base of the security point. Although the security point was a "hard patch," a

ChromSten plate which was not only secured to the bulkhead but anchored into the next deck, the concentrated blast from multiple sources first weakened the armored patch, then ripped it out of its frame.

The ChromSten plate, its backing of hardened steel melted in the intense heat, flew down the passage, catching Moseyev unawares and slamming him into the outboard bulkhead.

And all the coordinated fire the plate was no longer intercepting tore into Gronningen.

Julian ducked under the last blast of plasma fire, reached the stricken Asgardian, and rolled him over. The final blast had caught him just below the waist, and shredded the heavy body armor with effortless viciousness. Gronningen's eyes were screwed shut, but he opened them for just a moment, raising a hand to his squad leader. His mouth worked soundlessly, and the hand clamped on the sergeant's armored shoulder.

Then it dropped, and Adib Julian let out a scream of pure primal rage.

"Stay down!" Macek bellowed as he grabbed Julian from behind and fought to wrestle him to the deck, but Julian wasn't interested in staying down.

"*Dead!* They're all *dead!*" he yelled, and swatted Macek away like a toy.

"Sergeant Julian," Pahner called. "What is your situation?"

"*I'm sending them all to hell, Sir!*" the sergeant yelled back, and picked up the plasma gunner's weapon.

Julian's toot, courtesy of Temu Jin, had been reloaded with all the hacking protocols available to military and civilian intelligence, alike. He used them now, diving deep into the central circuits of his own armor, ripping out security protocols until the system was down to bare bones. Although personal armor was designed to be partially mobile in zero-gravity, the jump system had never been designed for full-gravity combat. But by taking all the control systems off of what was, effectively, a small plasma cannon, the sergeant could create a jump capability that was actually worth the name.

Of course, there were drawbacks.

"Don't try this at home, boys and girls," he hissed, and hit the power circuit.

His leap carried him over the barricade and into the deckhead, and the howling plasma stream melted the bulkheads behind him.

Macek let out a yowl as the stream passed across his lower legs, heating the nearly invulnerable armor of his suit and jumping the internal temperature nearly a hundred degrees. The automatic systems dumped the heat nearly as fast as it went up, but for just a moment, the armor made Marduk seem cool.

Julian's armor smashed into the overhead, taking him partially into the upper deck, throwing him from side to side in an erratic pattern that was impossible for the Saint battle armor to track. Somehow, he managed to turn a bounce into a spin, bringing himself around as the last of the power was expended, and as the jump gear's last, spiteful bit of plasma bit into the overhead, he caromed from one side of the passage to the other until he landed on his feet *behind* the Saint defenders.

The four Saints were still trying to track in on him as his first blast hit them. He swept the weapon from side to side, low, ripping their legs out from under them. As the commandos fell, he continued to sweep the weapon back and forth, ignoring the screaming emergency overload indicator as he melted not only their fallen battle armor, but the deck underneath and the bulkheads to either side. He expended the cannon's power like a drunkard, but before the capacitor completely discharged, the overloaded control circuits let go.

The ball of undirected plasma picked the sergeant up and slammed him backwards into the armored command deck hatch. Since the door was made of ChromSten, like the armor, but much thicker, he hit and bounced.

Hard.

Krindi Fain shook his head as the human suits fell backward into the intersecting side passage and then rolled around the corner for shelter. The air in the other passage was silver and red with plasma bolts, and the bulkhead on the opposite edge of the corridor disappeared as the fire from the Saints punched through it into one of the innumerable holds before dissipating itself on the cargo.

His unit—twenty Diasprans, the captain himself, Erkum Pol, and the drummer—was approaching from the ship's west. The Armory ought to be about twenty meters up the passageway the humans had just tumbled out of. And, obviously, it was heavily defended.

"Ah, me," he muttered as he fumbled with the human radio controls. "SNAPU: Situation Normal, All Pocked Up. First Platoon will prepare to engage," he said, continuing to trot towards the intersection as he finally got the radio to work properly. The fire had slackened off to what the defenders obviously believed was enough to keep the Marines from reentering the passage. "Platoon will face right into the corridor, in column of threes, proceeding to the Armory by volley fire at a march. Platoon, quick time . . . *march*."

"Sergeant, what's that?"

Private Kapila Ammann would have been just as happy to crawl back into his bunk. He'd long ago quit trying to figure out why he'd ever joined the commandos. It was days like this that made him count the number of hours until his ETS date, but the way things were going, he wasn't going to make it for another one hundred and twenty-six days, fourteen hours, and—he glanced at his chrono—twenty-three minutes.

"What's what?" Sergeant Gao snapped, then looked up in surprise from the casualty he was treating. "A unit . . . marching?"

"Holy Pollution," Ammann whispered as the Diasprans rounded the corner. "*They gave scummies plasma guns!*"

In the last few months, the Diasprans had gone through revolutions in weaponry that humans had taken millennia to achieve. They'd started off as untrained conscripts who had been turned into pikemen. Then they'd progressed to musketeers, then to rifle skirmishers, and now they were plasma and bead gunners. But much of their drill from the early days remained. And they used it now.

The first rank turned the corner, pivoting on the interior Mardukan, leveled their plasma cannon, and opened fire, stepping forward at a walk.

CHAPTER THIRTY-THREE

"Aaaaahh!"

Kapila hugged the deck as the air literally disappeared around him. The Mardukan fire mostly went over his head, but its intensity first superheated the atmosphere in the corridor, then expanded it to the very fringe of vacuum. He supposed he could return the fire, but there didn't seem to be much point. If he killed one or two of the scummies with a shot, the rest would turn him into drifting atoms for his efforts. Even if they didn't, a near miss would be sufficient to kill him. Flying fragments could easily punch holes in his standard ship suit, which would permit the intense heat to fry him to a crisp . . . which would at least save him from asphyxiation when his suit depressurized.

But so far, they seemed to be missing. He liked that, and he had no intention of doing anything to change it.

He rolled his head to look back up the passage behind him and saw that the entire unit was gone. One or two of them might have gotten back into the Armory, but he saw at least four carbon statues that indicated casualties. Graubart was still alive, though. He might even stay that way, if he got some prompt medical attention. Sergeant Gao, on the other hand, was just a pair of legs, attached to some cooked meat.

Kapila slid his bead rifle carefully to the side and spreadeagled himself on the deck, hoping that the scummies would settle for just capturing him.

Of course, he'd heard that scummies tortured their prisoners to death. But if it was a question of the possibility of torture, or absolutely buying it from a plasma blast, he'd go for the possibility any day.

"Cease fire," Fain ordered as he stepped around a gaping hole in the deck. His troopers' fire had opened the bulkheads on either side of the passage to the surrounding compartments, and the wrecked corridor sparked with electricity and finely divided steam. The ChromSten reinforced Armory had shrugged off most of the damage, and now most of one of its walls and its support structure—which had taken a beating—could be seen through the gaps in the bulkheads. All in all, they'd done quite a bit of damage, he reflected. But as long as they were in their suits, the environmental conditions were survivable. Actually, things were looking good; the Armory hatch was shut, and the passage was secure.

"Sergeant Sern, take four men and secure the far end of the hall." He fumbled with his radio some more until he managed to shift frequencies. "Captain Pahner, we have the corridor outside the Armory. The doors are shut, though."

There was a human—presumably one of the "Saint Commandos"—lying face-down on the deck. He didn't appear to be injured, but he had his fingers interlaced on the back of his helmet, and he wasn't moving. Fain gestured to Pol, who picked the wretch up by the back of his uniform and dangled him in the air.

"And it seems that we have a prisoner, too."

Roger rounded the corner to the bridge entrance and stopped, shaking his head in awe. The ship was trashed. Indeed, never in his worst nightmares had he ever imagined that a ship *could* be so trashed and still hang together.

More or less.

The deck looked as if it had been carved by a giant kindergartner who had somehow gotten his hands on an absentmindedly mislaid blowtorch. The heavy-duty plastic of the decksole had melted and splashed, leaving jagged splatters, like impressionistic stalagmites, on the bulkheads and huge dripping holes in the deck itself. The bulkheads had sustained major damage of their own, as well. Many of the holes blasted through them were large enough for battle armor to crawl through into the surrounding compartments. One of the larger ones led to what had once been the captain's day cabin, which was as thoroughly trashed as the passageway itself.

And the Bridge hatch was, once again, firmly shut.

Roger sighed as the drifting smoke and steam suddenly moved sideways and disappeared. He didn't have to look at the red vacuum morning light on his helmet HUD to figure out what had just happened.

"Memo to self," he muttered. "Giving Mardukans—or Marines, for that matter—plasma cannon on a ship assault is contraindicated."

Honal followed the first entry team into the shuttle bay, then dove sideways as a blast of bead-fire tore the three Vashin apart. Fire seemed to be coming from everywhere in the open bay, but the majority of the human defenders were on the far side, near the bay's huge outer hatches. It was easy enough to tell where they were, but doing anything about it was another matter, because they'd taken shelter behind a massive raised plate which undoubtedly did something significant when shuttles were parked in the vast, cavernous space.

Honal favored bead rifles over cannons, since the full-sized rifles—after suitable reshaping by Poertena—made a short, handy carbine for someone the size of a Mardukan. Now he used his to return fire, walking the beads along the top of the plate. Each hit tore a chunk out of the top of the device—whatever it was—but didn't seem to faze any of the humans crouched behind it.

The rest of the Vashin entered behind him, but the fire which greeted them was murderous. Besides the Saints by the main airlocks, there were more scattered on catwalks around the bay, and some sheltering by a second set of hatches. The combined crossfire had the

Vashin pinned down in the open, without any cover of their own, and the defenders were methodically massacring them.

"The hell with this!" Honal snarled. He and the human Mansul were partially sheltered by a control panel. It had taken a few hits, but it was still functional, judging by the red and green flashing symbols above the buttons at its center. He contemplated the device for a moment, and then smiled.

"Mansul, can you work this thing?"

Harvard Mansul had been in a few tight situations in his life. He'd dealt with bandits on more than one occasion, and even done a small piece on them at one point. Then there'd been the pirates. He'd been on a ship once when it was boarded by pirates, but the head of the group had been an IAS reader and let him go. In fact, he'd been sent on his way with an autographed photo of the suitably masked pirate leader. He'd been shot at by inner city gangs, stabbed doing a shoot in Imperial City, and nearly died that time his team got lost in the desert. Then there'd been being picked up by the Krath and imprisoned by a batch of ritualistic cannibals. That had been unpleasant.

But being pinned down by a Saint Special Operations team raised "unpleasant" to a new high. Nothing else on the list of his previous life experiences even came close. So sticking his head up to look at the control panel was not high on his list of priorities.

But he took a quick peek, anyway.

"Hatches, grav, cargo handling, environmental!" he shouted, pointing to the appropriate sections of the panel in turn. "What are you going to do?"

"Play a practical joke."

"Here goes nothing," Honal muttered to himself, and hit a green button.

Nothing happened. He waited a heartbeat or two to be certain of that, then grimaced. Time for Phase Two, he thought, and lifted the clear, protective plastic box over the red button beside the green.

He depressed it.

The blast of wind from the half-melted hatch behind him shoved him into the control panel hard, but that was about all. The Saints on the far side of the bay, with their backs to the opening shuttle bay doors, were less fortunate. More than half of them were picked up and sucked out the opening portal before they could react. The rest, unfortunately, managed to find handholds and hung on until the extremely brief blast of pressure change stopped. Then they opened fire again.

"Well, *that* didn't work," Honal grumbled irritably. The brief delight he'd felt when the first humans vanished out the opening only made his irritation when the others didn't even more intense, and he contemplated the controls again. Mansul's description of their functions was considerably less than bare bones, he reflected. And he, after all, was only an ignorant Vashin *civan*-rider. It was unreasonable to expect him to actually understand what any of them did, so perhaps he should simply do what came naturally.

He started hitting buttons at random.

Lights went on and off. Panels appeared out of the deck and rose, and other panels disappeared, while cranes and pulleys and less readily identifiable pieces of equipment dashed back and forth on overhead rails. Honal had no idea what any of the fascinating, confusing movements and energy were supposed to achieve under normal conditions. But he didn't much care, either, when one of the buttons lowered the platform the Saints had been sheltering behind into the deck. And then, finally, the gravity itself disappeared.

Honal watched an astonished Saint commando spin over in mid-air—well, mid-vacuum, the Vashin noble corrected himself—when he fired his bead rifle just as someone snatched the shuttle bay's gravity away from him. The Saint sailed helplessly out into the open, propelled by the unexpected reaction engine his rifle had just become, and then exploded in a grisly profusion of crimson blood beads as a burst of someone's fire tore him almost in half.

"Now this is more like it!" Honal said with a huge, human-style grin as he drew his sword and gripped the top of the control center with his false-hands as if it were a vaulting horse. "Vashin! Up and at 'em! *Cold steel!*"

★ ★ ★

"Roger, what's your position?" Pahner asked.

For a wonder, it looked as if things might be stabilizing. Georgiadas had managed to kill enough of the Saints counter-attacking his position to hold on until the Diasprans arrived. Now he had Engineering intact, and while there might (or might not) still be a few of the enemy inside the Armory, Krindi Fain's troops had it isolated and fully contained. The counterattack by *Emerald Dawn*'s bridge personnel had also been stopped, and the Vashin were running rampant. Pahner's own area was still pressurized, but two-thirds of the ship had lost pressure, and large portions of the internal gravity net had been shut down. The Northern cavalry had developed a positive liking for zero-g combat. Which was just . . . sick.

He didn't want to think about the hideous price his people and their Mardukan allies had paid, but the Saints were clearly on the defensive and well on the way to completely losing their ship. Now if they could only talk *Emerald Dawn*'s surviving officers out of the Bridge before they did irreparable harm.

"I'm at the Bridge security point. Gronningen's dead, and Julian is injured. About the only ones standing are Moseyev, Aburia, and Macek, and even they aren't in very good shape; I'd put their armor at no more than thirty percent of base capability. Max. I'm getting ready to negotiate with the Saint commander."

"Understood." Pahner waved for Temu Jin to stay where he was, monitoring the hacked infonet, then headed up the passageway at a trot. "Wait until I get there. I've seen the results of your negotiations too many times."

"Saint commander, this is Prince Roger."

Giovannuci looked over at the sweating tactical officer. Sergeant Major Iovan, who'd been with the colonel since Giovannuci was a shavetail, stood with a bead pistol screwed into Cellini's ear. Having a gun in one's ear could make just about anyone sweat, but the tactical officer was looking particularly wan. It had taken a while to get him to give up his release codes, and even longer for the computer to accept them. Probably because of his stammering. But now he seemed more or less resigned to his fate.

"Well, Prince Roger, or whoever you are. This is Colonel Fiorello Giovannuci, Imperial Cavazan Special Operations Branch. What can I do for you?"

"You can surrender your ship. I gave you one chance, and now most of your crew, and commandos, are dead. Last chance. Surrender, and we'll spare the rest. Resist, and I'll give you all to the Krath. They're ritualistic cannibals, but they don't get squeamish about humans."

"Well, I'll give *you* a couple of choices, buddy," the Saint snarled furiously. "Get off my ship, or I'll blow it up!"

"Talk to me, Armand," Roger said, looking at the sealed hatch.

"I'm on my way to the Bridge. Engineering and the Armory are secured. Captain Fain just took the Armory. But we've got to figure out what to do about this scuttling threat."

"Do think he's serious?" Roger asked. "He sounds that way."

"*Most* Saints aren't true-believers," Pahner said. "Unfortunately, I've heard of Giovannuci, and he *is*. Hold one, Your Highness. Computer: patch Kosutic."

"Kosutic," the sergeant major acknowledged, peering over her bead rifle's sights at the Saints she'd captured. "I think we've got most of the actual ship's crew, Armand. They seem a lot less interested in dying gloriously than the commandos."

"Good, but we have a situation," Pahner told her. "Tell me what you know about Saint scuttling charges."

"I take it this isn't an academic exercise," she said with a grimace. "They're always timer-delayed. They require a code and a key to activate—two of them, actually; they can't be set by just one person. They require at least one key and code to deactivate, but any key and code will work. They work on the basis of positive action locks; if you don't have the code and key, you're not going to turn them off. Authorized code/key holders are usually the CO, the exec, the tactical officer, and the chief engineer."

"Okay," Pahner replied. "That's what I recalled, too. Computer:

all hands. All Imperial personnel, begin evacuation of the ship. Computer: command group. Captain Fain? Rastar?"

"Here," Fain called.

"This is Honal," Rastar's cousin said a moment later. "Rastar is . . . occupied, but we've secured the shuttle bays. They're damaged, but secure."

"You need to start evacuating the ship," Pahner said. "Pull off as many of the Saint prisoners as seems practical."

"Armand," Roger said on a discrete frequency. "We can't let them go. If we do, my life isn't worth spit."

"No, but if we get our forces off, we might have a shot at the next ship," Pahner replied.

"Imperial commander," Giovannuci called. "You have thirty seconds to begin evacuation. After that, I'll start the detonation sequence, and there's no way to stop it."

Roger had automatically shifted back to the command group frequency, which meant that the Saint colonel's voice had gone out to everyone else patched into it with him. He grimaced, but then he shrugged. Maybe it was for the best.

"That's the situation, guys," he said.

"Not good," Honal said. "We're loading on the shuttles, but our assault did a certain amount of damage."

"Honal," Kosutic said. "Send a team of Vashin down to the southwest quadrant. I've got a group of crew that needs evacuating."

"Colonel Giovannuci," Roger called, this time making certain that he wasn't putting it out over the command frequency, as well. "We're evacuating as we speak, but both sides have casualties, and there are depressurized zones all over the ship. It's going to take a little time."

"I'll give you two minutes," Giovannuci replied. "But that's it."

"Armand, I am *not* giving up this ship," Roger snarled over the discrete frequency. "If they're stupid enough to go ahead and blow themselves up after we evacuate, well and good. But if they just fly away, we're pocked."

"I know, Your Highness," the captain sighed.

"Captain Pahner," Poertena's voice interrupted. "Are we suppose' to evacuate t'e Saints?"

"Yes," Pahner replied calmly. So far, only the command group knew they were looking at a self-destruct situation, and he intended to keep it that way as long as possible. "The ship is in bad shape. We need to get the Saints off for their own safety, and as prisoners of war."

"Okay. I t'ink I gots t'e ship's exec tied up in a closet. I'll go get her."

"Wait one, Poertena," Roger interrupted. "Where are you?"

"In t'e southeas' quadrant," the armorer replied. "Deck Four."

"Sergeant Major," Roger instructed. "Head to the southeast quadrant and link up with Poertena. Do it now."

"Don't go off half-cocked, Roger," Pahner warned. He was nearly to the Bridge tunnel.

"Not a problem," Roger replied. "I'm cool as cold."

Kosutic took the proffered crowbar and inserted it into a crack between the door and its frame. Then she threw her weight on it, and the metal seal popped loose with an explosive "Crack!" The closet door sprang open, and she looked in at the female officer in a combat crouch and shook her head.

"I could probably take you *out* of the armor," the sergeant major warned her. "And we don't have time for games."

"I know we don't. We need to get out of here," Beach replied. "That Pollution-crazed idiot is getting ready to blow up the whole ship."

"What happens if we take the Bridge?" Kosutic asked. "For general information, we already have Engineering and the Armory."

"Well, if you take the Bridge, it's *possible* that I could shut down the scuttling charges," Beach admitted. "It all depends."

"We don't have a lot of time to debate here," Kosutic said.

"Look, we're technically illegal combatants," Beach said. "You know it, I know it. What's your law in that regard?"

"Generally, you're repatriated," Kosutic told her. "Especially if we can trade you for one of our groups."

"And then, most of the time, we replace *your* group on a recovery planet," Beach said. "So I can die fast, here, when the charges go off. Or I can die slow, being worked and starved to death."

"Or?"

"Or, I can get asylum."

"We can't grant asylum," Kosutic said. "We can *try*, but we can't guarantee it. We don't have the authority."

"Is the guy leading you *really* Prince Roger? Because, according to our intelligence, he's dead, and has been for months."

"Yeah, it's really him," Kosutic replied. "You want his word on it or something?"

"Yes. If a member of your Imperial Family promises, at least it's going to be a big political stink if the Empies don't comply."

"You have no idea how complicated you're making this," the sergeant major muttered.

"Imperial commander, you have fifteen seconds to exit the ship," Giovannuci called. "I don't think you're gone yet."

"We're working on it," Roger said, just as his helmet flashed a priority signal from the sergeant major. "Hold one, Colonel Giovannuci. This may be from my people in the shuttle bay. Computer: switch Kosutic."

"It's the Saint second, all right," the sergeant major confirmed over the secure channel. "She's willing to give us the codes in exchange for asylum. She wants Roger's personal word."

"If she thinks that's going to help, she obviously doesn't know there's a price on my head, does she?" Roger said with a grim chuckle.

"I think we're dealing with intelligence lag," Kosutic replied. "She knows you're dead; she hasn't heard Jackson's latest version yet. Either way, what do I do? We're on our way, by the way."

"Tell her she has my personal word as a MacClintock that I will do all in my power to ensure that she gets asylum from the Empire," Roger replied. "But I want to be there when she finds out I'm an outlaw."

"Will do," the sergeant major said with a grin that could be heard over the radio. "About a minute until we're there."

"And I'm here already," Pahner said as he strode up behind Roger. "You need to get the hell off the ship, Your Highness. Sergeant Despreaux is already on the shuttle, and so are most of the wounded."

"Somebody needs to take this bridge, Armand," Roger said tightly. "And we need it more or less intact. Who's the best close-quarters person we have?"

"You're *not* assaulting the bridge," Pahner said. "Lose you, and it's all for *nothing*."

"Lose the *ship*, and it's all for nothing," Roger replied.

"There'll be other ships," Pahner said, putting his hand on the prince's shoulder.

"Yeah, but if this one leaves, they'll be Saint carriers!"

"Yes, but—"

"What's the mission, Captain?" Roger interrupted harshly, and Pahner hesitated for just a moment. But then he shook his head.

"To safeguard you, Your Highness," he said.

"No," Roger replied. "The mission is to safeguard the *Empire*, Captain. Safeguarding *me* is only part of that. If just Temu Jin makes it back and saves my mother, fine. If you make it back and do the same, fine. If *Julian* makes it back and performs the mission, fine. She can make a new heir. If she wants to, she can use DNA from John and Alexandra's dad. The *mission*, Captain, is 'Save the Empire.' And to do that, we have to take this ship. And to take this ship, we have to use the personnel who can do that most effectively and who can physically get here in *time* to do it. And that makes taking this bridge Colonel Roger MacClintock's best possible role. Am I *wrong*?"

Armand Pahner looked at the man he'd spent eight endless months keeping alive on a nightmare planet for a long, silent moment. Then he shook his head again.

"No, you're not. Sir," he said.

"Thought not," Roger said, and pointed his plasma cannon at the hatch.

Giovannuci looked at the tactical officer and nodded as the first blast shook the bridge.

"On three," he said, inserting his key into the console.

Lieutenant Cellini reached out slowly to insert his own key, but then he stopped. His hand dropped away from the board, and he shook his head.

"No. It's not worth it, Sir." He turned to face Iovan, pivoting in place until the noncom's pistol was pointed squarely between his eyes. "Two hundred crew left, Sergeant Major. Two hundred. You're going to kill them all for what? A corrupt leadership that preaches environmentalism and builds itself castles in the most beautiful parts of the wilderness? Kill me, and you kill yourself, and you kill the colonel. *Think* about what we're doing here!"

Giovannuci looked over at the sergeant major and tipped his chin up in a questioning gesture.

"Iovan?"

"Everybody dies someplace, Lieutenant," the sergeant major said, and pulled the trigger. Cellini's head splashed away from the impact, and the sergeant major sighed. "What a senseless waste of human life," he said, as he wiped the key clear of brains and looked at the colonel. "On three, you said, Sir?"

ChromSten was almost impervious to plasma fire, but "almost" was a relative term. Even ChromSten transmitted energy to its underlying matrix, which meant, in the case of the command deck, to a high stress cero-plastic. And as the heat buildup from the repeated plasma discharges bled into it, that underlying matrix began to melt, and then burn. . . .

"Breach!" Roger shouted, as the center of the hatch buckled, and then cracked open. For just a moment, white light from the bridge illuminated the smoke and steam from the blazing matrix before it was sucked greedily away by the vacuum.

The approach corridor was just *gone*. The intense heat from the plasma discharges had melted the material of the surrounding bulkheads and decks, creating a large opening that revealed the bridge as a ChromSten cylinder, thirty meters across, and fifty high, attached to the armored engineering core.

Getting across the yawning, five-meter gulf between his present position and the breach was going to be Roger's first problem.

"No time like the present," he muttered, and triggered his armor's jump gear with a considerably gentler touch than Julian had used.

He sailed across the chasm, one hand supporting the plasma cannon while the other stretched out for the hole, and slammed into the outer face of the cylinder. The outstretched arm slipped through the breach, but his reaching fingers found nothing to grip. His arm slithered backwards, and for just a moment he felt a stab of panic. But then his fingers hooked into the ragged edge of the hole and locked.

"Piece of cake," he panted, and exoskeletal "muscles" whined as he lifted himself up onto the slight lip which was all that remained of the outer door frame. He braced himself and ripped at the hole, widening it. The matrix of the ChromSten itself had begun to fail under the plasma fire, and the material sparked against his armored hand, returning to its original chrome and selenium atomic structure.

Giovannuci and Iovan stood with their hands behind their heads, with the rest of the command deck crew lined up at their stations behind them, as Roger entered the compartment behind his plasma cannon. All of them were in skin-suits against the soft vacuum that now filled most of the ship.

Roger looked around the bridge, then at the gore splattered over the self-destruct console, and shook his head.

"Was that strictly necessary?" he asked, as he walked over to the tactical officer's body and turned it over. "Who?"

"Me," Iovan said.

"Short range," Roger said contemptuously. "I guess you couldn't hit him from any farther away."

"Take off that fucking armor and we'll see how far away I can shoot," Iovan said, and spat on the floor.

Pahner clambered through the hole, widening it further in the process, and crossed to the prince.

"You should've waited for us to secure it, Your Highness," he said over the command frequency.

"And give them a chance to destroy the controls?" Roger replied over the same circuit. "No way. Besides," he chuckled tightly, "I figured they were probably down to bead guns after Julian's crazy stunt. If they hadn't been, they'd still be shooting at us in the passageway."

He switched back to the external amplifier, cranked up to maximum in the near-vacuum that passed for "air" on *Emerald Dawn*'s bridge at that particular moment, and looked at Giovannuci and Iovan.

"I can't read 'merchant marine' rank tabs. Which of you is Giovannuci?"

"I am," the colonel told him.

"Turn off the self-destruct," Roger said.

"No."

"Okay," Roger said, with an unseen shrug inside his armor, and turned to Iovan. "Who are you?"

"I don't have to tell you that," Iovan said.

"Senior NCO," Pahner said.

"Yeah, he's got that look," Roger said. "Not a bridge officer, so you can't turn it off, can you?"

"Nobody in here can," Giovannuci said. "Except me."

Roger started to replied, then half-turned as Kosutic crawled into the bridge.

"I've got that second officer out here," the sergeant major said over the command frequency. "She's ready to turn off the self-destruct, just as soon as we clear all these guys off the Bridge. She said to watch the CO. He's a real true-believer."

"So which one of you is Prince Roger?" Giovannuci asked.

"I am," the prince replied. "And I'm going to see to it that you hang, if it's the last thing I do."

"I don't think so," the Saint colonel said, calmly, and pulled the one-shot from behind his neck.

Time seemed to crawl as Roger started to lift his plasma cannon, then dropped it. If he fired it, the blast would take out half the ship controls . . . including the self-destruct console. So instead, he sprang forward, his hand continuing upward to the hilt of his sword even as the plasma cannon fell.

The prince was almost supernally fast, but whether he could have killed the colonel before he fired would remain forever unknown, since Pahner slammed into his suit, arms spread.

The impact threw the prince's armor to the side, sending it smashing into the tactical display and out of the Saint's' line of fire just as Giovannuci swung the weapon forward, catching Pahner dead center, and squeezed the button.

Roger lunged back upright with a shriek of pure rage and spun in place as Iovan produced another of the weapons and came at him. But this time there was no mistake, and the flashing Voitan-forged blade took off the sergeant major's head and hand in a steaming fan of blood.

The shot from the anti-armor device had spun Giovannuci backwards and on to the deck. Now he climbed back to his feet and raised his hands.

"I'm sorry I missed," he said tightly. "But we're all going to die anyway. Pollution take you."

"I don't think so," Roger grated. "We have your second-in-command, and she's more than willing to turn it off. *You* are going to, though, I promise you," he continued in a voice of frozen helium, and looked at Kosutic. "Sergeant Major, take the colonel to the shuttle bays. Make sure he doesn't do any more damage, but don't let anything happen to him on the way, either. We'll deal with him later, and I want him in perfect shape when he faces the hangman."

The sergeant major said something in reply, but Roger didn't hear her as he dropped to his knees beside Pahner. He turned the captain over as gently as possible, but there wasn't really much point. This time, the placement had been accurate. The one-shot had struck the Marine squarely on the his armor's carapace, and the ricocheting scab of armor had done precisely what it was supposed to do.

Roger bent close, trying to see through the flickering distortion of the captain's helmet. The readouts indicated that there was still brain function, but as the blood drained from the head into the shattered body, it was fading fast.

"I promise," Roger said, lifting the captain and holding him. "I promise I won't die. I promise I'll save my mother. You can depend on me, Armand. You can, I promise. Rest now. Rest, my champion."

He sat there, rocking the body, until the last display flickered out.

EPILOGUE

Roger tapped his display as the former Saint officer left the captain's office. All things considered, Beach had taken the news rather well. On the other hand, since she'd thrown her lot in rather definitively with the group around Roger, there wasn't much she could do but help. As it was, she was an outlaw under both Saint and Imperial law. If Roger succeeded, she'd be sitting pretty. If he didn't, she wouldn't be any worse off. Once they got near civilization, of course, he wouldn't be able to trust her. But until they got to wherever they were going to start the process of infiltrating the Empire, she really had only two choices: help them, or die. It wasn't much of a choice.

He looked up from the display and stood as the next person on his calendar entered.

"Sergeant Despreaux," he said. "I'd like to speak to you about near-future plans."

He sat back down and returned his attention to his display, then looked back up with an irritated expression as Despreaux came to a position of parade rest.

"Oh, hell, Nimashet. Would you *please* sit down?" he demanded in exasperation, and waited until she'd obeyed before he glanced back at the display and shook his head.

"I hadn't realized how short you really were when we left Old Earth. You should have ended your term while we were still in Sindi."

"I thought about that at the time," she replied. "Captain Pahner spoke to me about it, as well. Obviously, I couldn't just leave."

"I could probably find a way for you to leave now," Roger sighed. "Along with the four other people who are alive and over their terms. But there'd be the little problem of the price on your heads."

"I'll stay with you for the time being, Sir," Despreaux said.

"Thank you," Roger said formally, then drew a deep breath. "I . . . I have to ask a . . . I'd like to make a request, however."

"Yes?"

He rubbed his face and looked around the cabin.

"I—Nimashet, I don't know if I can do this . . . ." He stopped and shook his head. "I—Damn it, I know I can't do this *alone*. Please, *please* promise me that you won't leave at the first opportunity. Please promise that you won't just go. I *need* you. I don't need your gun; I can find plenty of gunners. I need your strength. I need your sense of humor. I need your . . . balance. Don't leave me, Nimashet Despreaux. Please. Just . . . stay with me."

"I won't marry you," she said. "Or, rather, I'll marry 'Prince Roger,' but I refuse to marry 'Emperor Roger.'"

"I understand," Roger said with a sigh. "Just don't leave me. Okay?"

"Okay," she said, and stood. "Will that be all, Sir?"

Roger looked at her for a moment, then nodded.

"Yes, thank you, Sergeant," he said formally.

"Then goodnight, Sir."

WE FEW

Publisher's Note:
We Few is not divided into separate chapters,
but simply is separated into the prologue and main text.
"Chapter 1" is the only chapter.

PROLOGUE

Of Alexandra VII's three children, the youngest, Roger Ramius Sergei Alexander Chiang MacClintock—known variously to political writers of his own time as "Roger the Terrible," "Roger the Mad," "the Tyrant," "the Restorer," and even "the Kin-Slayer"—did not begin his career as the most promising material the famed MacClintock Dynasty had ever produced. Alexandra's child by Lazar Fillipo, the sixth Earl of New Madrid, whom she never married, the then-Prince Roger was widely regarded prior to the Adoula Coup as an overly handsome, self-centered, clothes-conscious fop. It was widely known within court circles that his mother nursed serious reservations about his reliability and was actively disappointed by his indolent, self-centered neglect of those duties and responsibilities which attached to his position as Heir Tertiary to the Throne of Man. Less widely known, although scarcely a secret, was her lingering distrust of his loyalty.

As such, it was perhaps not unreasonable, when the "Playboy Prince" and his bodyguard (Bravo Company, Bronze Battalion, of the Empress' Own Regiment) disappeared *en route* to a routine flag-showing ceremony only months before an attack upon the Imperial Palace, that suspicion should turn to him. The assassination of his older brother, Crown Prince John, and of his sister, Princess Alexandra, and of all of John's children, combined with the apparent attempt to assassinate his Empress Mother, would have left Roger the only surviving heir to the throne.

What was unknown at the time was that those truly behind the coup were, in fact, convinced that Roger and his Marine bodyguard were all dead, as his assassination had been the first step in their plans to overthrow Empress Alexandra. By hacking into the personal computer implant of a junior officer aboard the Prince's transport vessel, they were able, through their unwilling, programmed agent, to plant demolition charges at critical points within the vessel's engineering sections. Unfortunately for their plans, the saboteur was discovered before she could quite complete her mission, and the ship, although badly crippled, was not destroyed outright.

Instead of dying almost instantly in space, the "Playboy Prince" found himself marooned on the planet of Marduk . . . a fate some might not have considered preferable. Although legally claimed by the Empire and the site of an Imperial starport, it was obvious to the commander of his bodyguard, Captain Armand Pahner, that the system was actually under the *de facto* control of the Caravazan Empire, the ruthless rivals of the Empire of Man. The "Saints'" fanatical attachment to the principle that humanity's polluting, ecology-destroying presence should be excised from as many planets as physically possible was matched only by their burning desire to replace the Empire of Man as the dominant political and military power of the explored galaxy. Their interest in Marduk was easily explainable by the star system's strategic location on the somewhat amorphous boundary between the two rival star nations, although precisely what at least two of their sublight cruisers were doing there was rather more problematical. But whatever the exact details of their presence in the Marduk System might be, it was imperative that the Heir Tertiary not fall into their hands.

To prevent that from happening, the entire crew of Roger's transport vessel, HMS *Charles DeGlopper*, sacrificed their lives in a desperate, close-range action which destroyed both Saint cruisers in the system without ever revealing *DeGlopper*'s identity or the fact that Roger had been aboard. Just before the transport's final battle, the Prince and his Marine bodyguards, along with his valet and his chief of staff and one-time tutor, escaped undetected aboard *DeGlopper's* assault shuttles to the planet. There, they faced the formidable task of marching halfway around one of the most hostile, technically habitable planets ever claimed by the Empire so that they might assault the spaceport and seize control of it.

It was, in fact, as virtually all of them realized, an impossible mission, but the "Bronze Barbarians" were not simply Imperial Marines. They were the Empress' Own, and impossible or not, they did it.

For eight endless months, they fought their way across half a world of vicious carnivores, sweltering jungle, swamp, mountains, seas, and murderous barbarian armies. When their advanced weapons failed in the face of Marduk's voracious climate and ecology, they improvised new ones—swords, javelins, black powder rifles, and muzzle-loading artillery. They learned to build ships. They destroyed the most terrible nomadic army Marduk had ever seen, and then did the same thing to the cannibalistic empire of the Krath. At first, the horned, four-armed, cold-blooded, mucus-covered, three-meter-tall natives of Marduk seriously underestimated the small, bipedal visitors to their planet. Physically, humans closely resembled oversized *basiks*, small, stupid, rabbitlike creatures routinely hunted by small children armed only with sticks. Those Mardukans unfortunate enough to get in the Empress' Own's way, however, soon discovered that *these basiks* were far more deadly than any predator their own world had ever produced.

And along the way, the "Playboy Prince" discovered that he was, indeed, the heir of Miranda MacClintock, the first Empress of Man. At the beginning of that epic march across the face of Marduk, the one hundred and ninety Marines of Bravo Company felt nothing but contempt for the worthless princeling whose protection was their responsibility; by its end, Bravo Company's twelve survivors would have fixed bayonets to charge Hell itself at his back. And the same was true of the Mardukans recruited into his service as The *Basik's* Own.

But having, against all odds, captured the spaceport and a Saint special operations ship which called upon it, the surviving Bronze

Barbarians and The *Basik*'s Own faced a more daunting challenge still, for they discovered that the coup launched by Jackson Adoula, Prince of Kellerman, had obviously succeeded. Unfortunately, no one else seemed to realize Empress Alexandra was being controlled by the same people who had murdered her children and her grandchildren. And, still worse, was the discovery that the notorious traitor Prince Roger Ramius Sergei Alexander Chiang MacClintock was being hunted by every member of the Imperial military and police establishments as the perpetrator of the attack on his own family.

Despite that . . .

—Arnold Liu-Hamner, PhD,
from "Chapter 27:The Chaos Years Begin,"
The MacClintock Legacy, Volume 17, 7th edition, © 3517,
Souchon, Fitzhugh, & Porter Publishing,
Old Earth

Imprimis, they nuked the spaceport.

The one-kiloton kinetic energy weapon was a chunk of iron the size of a small aircar. He watched it burn on the viewscreens of the captured Saint special operations ship as it entered the upper atmosphere of the planet Marduk and tracked in perfectly. It exploded in a flash of light and plasma, and the mushroom cloud reached up into the atmosphere, spreading a cloud of dust over the nearer Krath villages.

The spaceport was deserted at the moment it turned into plasma. Everything movable, which had turned out to be everything but the buildings and fixed installations, had been stripped from it. The Class One manufacturing facility, capable of making clothes and tools and small weapons, had been secreted at Voitan, along with most of the untrustworthy humans, including all of the surviving Saint Greenpeace commandos who had been captured with the ship. They could work in the Voitan mines, help rebuild the city, or, if they liked nature so much, they could feel free to escape into the jungles of Marduk, teeming with carnivores who would be more than happy to ingest them.

Prince Roger Ramius Sergei Alexander Chiang MacClintock watched the explosion with a stony face, then turned to the small group gathered in the ship's control room, and nodded.

"Okay, let's go."

The prince was a shade under two meters tall, slim but muscular, with some of the compact strength usually associated with professional zero-G ball players. His long blond hair, pulled back in a ponytail, was almost white from sun bleaching, and his handsome, almost beautiful, classic European face was heavily tanned. It was also lined and hard, seeming far older than his twenty-two standard years. He had neither laughed nor smiled in two weeks, and as his long, mobile hand scratched at the neck of the two-meter black and red lizard standing pony-high by his side, Prince Roger's jade-green eyes were harder than his face.

There were many reasons for the lines, for the early aging, for the hardness about his eyes and shoulders. Roger MacClintock—Master Roger, behind his back, or simply The Prince—had not been so lined and hard nine months before. When he, his chief of staff and valet, and a company of Marine bodyguards had been hustled out of Imperial City, thrust into a battered old assault ship, and sent packing on a totally nonessential political mission, he had taken it as just another sign of his mother's disapproval of her youngest son. He'd shown none of the diplomatic and bureaucratic expertise of his older brother, Prince John, the Heir Primus, nor of the military ability of his older sister the admiral, Princess Alexandra, Heir Secondary. Unlike them, Roger spent his time playing zero-G ball, hunting big game, and generally being the playboy, and he'd assumed that Mother had simply decided it was time for him to steady down and begin doing the Heir Tertiary's job.

What he hadn't known at the time, hadn't known until months later, was that he was being hustled out of town in advance of a firestorm. The Empress had gotten wind, somehow, that the internal enemies of House MacClintock were preparing to move. He knew that now. What he still didn't know was whether she'd wanted him out of the way to protect him . . . or to keep the child whose loyalty she distrusted out of both the battle and temptation's way.

What he did know was that the cabal behind the crisis his mother had foreseen had planned long and carefully for it. The sabotage of *Charles DeGlopper*, his transport, had been but the first step, although neither he nor any of the people responsible for keeping him alive had realized it at the time.

What Roger *had* realized was that the entire crew of the *DeGlopper* had sacrificed their lives in hopeless battle against the Saint sublight cruisers they had discovered in the Marduk System when the crippled ship finally managed to limp into it. They'd taken those ships on, rather than even considering surrender, solely to cover Roger's own escape in *DeGlopper*'s assault shuttles, and they'd succeeded.

Roger had always known the Marines assigned to protect him regarded him with the same contempt as everyone else at Court, nor had *DeGlopper*'s crew had any reason to regard him differently. Yet they'd died to protect him. They'd given up their lives in exchange for his, and they would not be the last to do it. As the men and women of Bravo Company, Bronze Battalion, The Empress' Own, had marched and fought their way across the planet they'd reached against such overwhelming odds, the young prince had seen far too many of them die. And as they died, the young fop learned, in the hardest possible school, to defend not simply himself, but the soldiers around him. Soldiers who had become more than guards, more than family, more than brothers and sisters.

In the eight brutal months it had taken to cross the planet, making alliances, fighting battles, and at last, capturing the spaceport and the ship aboard which he stood at this very moment, that young fop had become a man. More than a man—a hardened killer. A diplomat trained in a school where diplomacy and a bead pistol worked hand-in-hand. A leader who could command from the rear, or fight in the line, and keep his head when all about him was chaos.

But that transformation had not come cheaply. It had cost the lives of over ninety percent of Bravo Company. It had cost the life of Kostas Matsugae, his valet and the only person who had ever seemed to give a single good goddamn for Roger MacClintock. Not Prince Roger. Not the Heir Tertiary to the Throne of Man. Just Roger MacClintock.

And it had cost the life of Bravo Company's commanding officer, Captain Armand Pahner.

Pahner had treated his nominal commander first as a useless appendage to be protected, then as a decent junior officer, and, finally, as a warrior scion of House MacClintock. As a young man worthy to be Emperor, and to command Bronze Battalion, Pahner had become more than a friend. He'd become the father Roger had never had, a mentor, almost a god. And in the end, Pahner had saved the mission and Roger's life by giving his own.

Roger MacClintock couldn't remember the names of all his dead. At first, they'd been faceless nonentities. Too many had been killed taking and holding Voitan, dying under the spears of the Kranolta, before he even learned their names. Too many had been killed by the *atul*, the low-slung hunting lizards of Marduk. Too many had been killed by the *flar-ke*, the wild dinosauroids related to the elephant-like *flar-ta* packbeasts. By vampire moths and their poisonous larva, the killerpillars. By the nomadic Boman, by sea monsters out of darkest nightmares, and by the swords and spears of the cannibalistic "civilized" Krath.

But if he couldn't remember all of them, he remembered many. The young plasma gunner, Nassina Bosum, killed by her own malfunctioning rifle in one of the first attacks. Corporal Ima Hooker and Dokkum, the happy mountaineer from Sherpa, killed by *flar-ke* almost within sight of Ran Tai. Kostas, the single human being who'd ever cared for him in those cold, old days before this nightmare, killed by an accursed damncroc while fetching water for his prince. Gronningen, the massive cannoneer, killed taking the bridge of this very ship.

So many dead, and so far yet to go.

The Saint ship for which they'd fought so hard showed how brutal the struggle to capture it had been. No one had suspected that the innocent tramp freighter was a covert, special operations ship, crewed by elite Saint commandos. The risk in capturing it had seemed minor, but since losing Roger would have made their entire epic march and all of their sacrifices in vain, he'd been left behind with their half-trained Mardukan allies when the surviving members of Bravo Company went up to take possession of the "freighter."

The three-meter-tall, horned, four-armed, mucus-skinned

natives of The *Basik*'s Own had come from every conceivable preindustrial level of technology. D'Nal Cord, his *asi*—technically, his "slave," since Roger had saved his life without any obligation to do so, though anyone who made the mistake of treating the old shaman as a menial would never live long enough to recognize the enormity of his mistake—and Cord's nephew Denat had come from the X'Intai, the first, literally Stone Age tribe they had encountered. The Vasin, riders of the fierce, carnivorous *civan*, were former feudal lords whose city-state had been utterly destroyed by the rampaging Boman barbarians and who had provided The *Basik*'s Own's cavalry. The core of its infantry had come from the city of Diaspra—worshipers of the God of Waters, builders and laborers who had been trained into a disciplined force first of pikemen, and then of riflemen.

The *Basik*'s Own had followed Roger through the battles that destroyed the "invincible" Boman, then across demon-haunted waters to totally unknown lands. Under the banner of a *basik*, rampant, long teeth bared in a vicious grin, they'd battled the Krath cannibals and taken the spaceport. And in the end, when the Marines were unable to overcome the unexpected presence of Saint commandos on the ship, they'd been hurled into the fray again.

Rearmed with modern weaponry—hypervelocity bead and plasma cannon normally used as crew-served weapons or as weapons for powered armor—the big Mardukans had been thrown into the ship in a second wave and immediately charged into the battle. The Vasin cavalry had rushed from position to position, ambushing the bewildered commandos, who could not believe that "scummies" using cannon as personal weapons were really roaming all over their ship, opening shuttle bay doors to vacuum and generally causing as much havoc as they could. And while the . . . individualistic Vasin had been doing that, the Diaspran infantry had taken one hard point after another, all of them heavily defended positions, by laying down plasma fire as if it were the rank-upon-rank musketry which was their specialty.

And they'd paid a heavy price for their victory. In the end, the ship had been taken, but only at the cost of far too many more dead and horribly injured. And the ship itself had been largely gutted by the savage firefights. Modern tunnel ships were remarkably robust, but they weren't designed to survive the effect of five Mardukans abreast, packed bulkhead-to-bulkhead in a passage and volley-firing blast after blast of plasma.

What was left of the ship was a job for a professional space dock, but that was out of question. Jackson Adoula, Prince of Kellerman, and Roger's despised father, the Earl of New Madrid, had made that impossible when they murdered his brother and sister and all of his brother's children, massacred the Empress' Own, and somehow gained total control of the Empress herself. Never in her wildest dreams would Alexandra MacClintock have closely associated herself with Jackson Adoula, whom she despised and distrusted. And far less would she ever have married New Madrid, whose treasonous tendencies she'd proven to her own satisfaction before Roger was ever born. Indeed, New Madrid's treason was the reason she'd never married him . . . and a large part of the explanation for her distrust of Roger himself. Yet according to the official news services, Adoula had become her trusted Navy Minister and closest Cabinet confidant, and this time she had announced she *did* intend to wed New Madrid. Which seemed only reasonable, the newsies pointed out, since they were the men responsible for somehow thwarting the coup attempt which had so nearly succeeded.

The coup which, according to those same official news services, had been instigated by none other than Prince Roger . . . at the very instant that he'd been fighting for his life against ax-wielding Boman barbarians on sunny Marduk.

Something, to say the least, was rotten in Imperial City. And whatever it was, it meant that instead of simply taking the spaceport and sending home a message "Mommy, come pick me up," the battered warriors at Roger's back now had the unenviable task of retaking the entire Empire from the traitors who were somehow controlling the Empress. The survivors of Bravo Company—all twelve of them—and the remaining two hundred and ninety members of The *Basik*'s Own, pitted against one hundred and twenty star systems, with a population right at three-quarters of a trillion humans, and uncountable soldiers and ships. And just to make their task a bit more daunting, they had a time problem. Alexandra was "pregnant"—a new scion had been popped into the uterine replicator, a full brother of Roger's, from his mother's and father's genetic material—and under Imperial law, now that Roger had been officially attainted for treason, that fetus became the new Heir Primus as soon as he was born.

Roger's advisers concurred that his mother's life would last about as long as spit on a hot griddle when that uterine replicator was opened.

Which explained the still dwindling mushroom cloud. When the Saints came looking for their missing ship, or an Imperial carrier finally showed up to wonder why Old Earth hadn't heard from Marduk in so long, it would appear a pirate vessel had pillaged the facility and then vanished into the depths of space. What it would *not* look like was the first step in a counter coup intended to regain the Throne for House MacClintock.

He took one last look at the viewscreens, then turned and led his staff off the bridge towards the ship's wardroom. Although the wardroom itself had escaped damage during the fighting, the route there was somewhat hazardous. The approaches to the bridge had taken tremendous punishment—indeed, the decks and bulkheads of the short security corridor outside the command deckhead been sublimed into gas by plasma fire from both sides. A narrow, flexing, carbon-fiber catwalk had been built as a temporary walkway, and they crossed it carefully, one at a time. The passageway beyond wasn't much better. Many of the holes in the deck had been repaired, but others were simply outlined in bright yellow paint, and in many places, the bulkheads reminded Roger forcibly of Old Earth Swiss cheese.

He and his staffers picked their way around the unrepaired holes in the deck and finally reached the wardroom's dilating hatch, and Roger seated himself at the head of the table. He leaned back, apparently entirely at ease, as the lizard curled into a ball by his side. His calm demeanor fooled no one. He'd worked very hard on creating an image of complete *sang-froid* in any encounter. It was copied from the late Captain Pahner, but Roger lacked that soldier's years of experience. The tension, the energy, the anger, radiated off him in waves.

He watched the others assume their places.

D'Nal Cord squatted to the side of the lizard, behind Roger, silent as the shadow which in many ways he was, holding himself up with the long spear that doubled as a walking stick. Theirs was an interesting bonding. Although the laws of his people made him Roger's slave, the old shaman had quickly come to understand that Roger was a young nobleman, and a bratty one at that. Despite his official "slave" status, he'd taken it as his duty to chivvy the young brat into manhood, not to mention teaching him a bit more of the sword, a weapon Cord had studied as a young man in more civilized areas of Marduk.

Cord's only clothing was a long skirt of locally made *dianda*. His people, the X'Intai, like most Mardukans the humans had met, had little use for clothing. But he'd donned the simple garment in Krath, where it was customary to be clothed, and continued to wear it, despite the barbarism of the custom, because humans set such store by it.

Pedi Karuse, the young female Mardukan to his left (since there was no room for her behind him), was short by Mardukan standards, even for a woman. Her horns were polished and colored a light honey-gold, she wore a light robe of blue *dianda*, and two swords were crossed behind her back. The daughter of a Shin chieftain, *her* relationship with Cord was, if anything, even more "interesting" than Roger's.

Her people shared many common societal customs with the X'Intai, and when Cord saved her from Krath slavers, those customs had made her the shaman's *asi*, just as he was Roger's. And since Roger had been squared away by that time, Cord had taken up the training of his new "slave," only to discover an entirely new set of headaches.

Pedi was at least as headstrong as the prince, and a bit wilder, if that were possible. Worse, the very old shaman, whose wife and children were long dead, had found himself far more attracted to his "*asi*" than was proper in a society where relations between *asi* and master were absolutely forbidden. Unfortunately for Cord's honorable intentions, he'd taken a near-mortal wound battling the Krath at about the same time he entered his annual "heat," and Pedi had been in charge of nursing him. She'd recognized the signs and decided, on her own, that it was vital he be relieved of at least that pressure on his abused body.

Cord, semiconscious and delirious at the time, had remembered nothing about it. It had taken him some time to recognize what was changing about his *asi*, and he'd only been aware that he was going to be a father again for a handful of weeks.

He was still adjusting to the knowledge, but in the meantime, Pedi's father had become one of Roger's strongest allies on the planet. After a futile protest on the shaman's part that he was far too old to be a suitable husband for Pedi, the two had been married in a Shin ceremony. If the other Shin had noticed that Pedi was showing signs of pregnancy—developing "blisters" on her back to hold the growing fetuses—they had politely ignored it.

Despite the marriage, however, Pedi's honor as Cord's *asi* still required her to guard the shaman's back (pregnant or no), just as he was required to guard Roger. So Roger found the two almost constantly following him around in a trail. He shook them off whenever he could, these days, but it wasn't easy.

Eleanora O'Casey, Roger's chief of staff and the only surviving "civilian" from *DeGlopper*'s passengers, settled into the seat to his right. Eleanora was a slight woman, with brown hair and a pleasant face, who'd had no staff to chief when they landed on Marduk. She'd been given the job by the Empress in hopes that some of her noted academic skills—she was a multidegree historian and specialist in political theory—would rub off on the wastrel son. She was a city girl, with the flat, nasal accent of Imperial City, and at the beginning of the march across the planet, Roger and everyone else had wondered how long she would last. As it had turned out, there was a good bit of steel under that mousy cover, and her knowledge of good old-fashioned city-state politics had proven absolutely vital on more than one occasion.

Eva Kosutic, Bravo Company's Sergeant Major and High

Priestess of the Satanist Church of Armagh, took the chair across from Eleanora. She had a flat, chiseled face and dark brown, almost black hair. A deadly close-in warrior and a fine sergeant major, she now commanded Bravo Company's remnants—about a squad in size—and functioned as Roger's military aide.

Sergeant Adib Julian, her lover and friend, sat next to her. The onetime armorer had always been the definitive "happy warrior," a humorist and practical joker who got funnier and funnier as things looked worse and worse. But his laughing black eyes had been shadowed since the loss of his best friend and constant straight man, Gronningen.

Across from Julian sat Sergeant Nimashet Despreaux. Taller than Kosutic or Julian, she had long brown hair and a face beautiful enough for a high-class fashion model. But where most models had submitted to extensive body-sculpting, Despreaux was all natural, from her high forehead to her long legs. She was as good a warrior as anyone at the table, but she never laughed these days. Every death, friend or enemy, weighed upon her soul, and the thousands of corpses they'd left behind showed in her shadowed eyes. So did her relationship with Roger. Despite her own stalwart resistance and more than a few "stumbles," she and Roger could no longer pretend—even to themselves—that they hadn't fallen hard for each other. But Despreaux was a country girl, as lower-class as it was possible to be in the generally egalitarian Empire, and she'd flatly refused to marry an emperor. Which was what Roger was inevitably going to be one day, if they won.

She glanced at him once, then crossed her arms and leaned back, her eyes narrowed and wary.

Next to her, in one of the oversized station chairs manufactured to fit the Mardukans, sat Captain Krindi Fain. Despreaux was tall for human, but the Mardukan dwarfed her. The former quarryman wore a Diaspran infantryman's blue leather harness and the kilt the infantry had adopted in Krath. He, too, crossed his arms, all four of them, and leaned back at ease.

Behind Fain, looming so high he had to squat so his horns didn't brush the overhead, was Erkum Pol, Krindi's bodyguard, senior

NCO, batman, and constant shadow. Not particularly overburdened intellectually, Erkum was huge, even by Mardukan standards, and "a good man with his hands" as long as the target was in reach of a hand weapon. Give him a gun, and the safest place to be was between him and the enemy.

Rastar Komas Ta'Norton, once Prince of Therdan, sat across from Krindi, wearing the leathers of the Vasin cavalry. His horns were elaborately carved and bejeweled, as befitted a Prince of Therdan, and his harness bore four Mardukan-scaled bead pistols, as also befitted a Prince of Therdan who happened to be an ally of the Empire. He'd fought Roger once, and lost, then joined him and fought at his side any number of other times. He'd won all of those battles, and the bead pistols he wore were for more than show. He was probably the only person in the ship who was faster than Roger, despite the prince's cobralike reflexes.

The outsized chair next to Rastar was occupied by his cousin, Honal, who'd escaped with him, cutting a path to safety for the only women and children to have survived when Therdan and the rest of the border states fell to the Boman. It was Honal who had christened their patched-together mixed force of humans and Mardukans "The Basik's Own." He'd chosen the name as a joke, a play on "The Empress' Own" to which the Bronze Battalion belonged. But Roger's troopers had made the name far more than a joke on a dozen battlefields and in innumerable small skirmishes. Short for a Mardukan, Honal was a fine rider, a deadly shot, and even better with a sword. He was also insane enough to win one of the battles for the ship by simply turning off the local gravity plates and venting the compartment—and its defenders—to vacuum. He was particularly fond of human aphorisms and proverbs, especially the ancient military maxim that "If it's stupid and it works, it ain't stupid." Honal was crazy, not stupid.

At the foot of the table, completing Roger's staff and command group, sat Special Agent Temu Jin of the Imperial Bureau of Investigation. One of the countless agents sent out to keep an eye on the far-flung bureaucracy of the Empire, he had been cut off from contact by the coup. His last message from his "control" in the IBI had warned that all was not as it appeared on Old Earth and that he was to consider himself "in the cold." He'd been the one who'd had to tell Roger what had happened to his family. After that, he'd been of enormous assistance to the prince when it came time to take the spaceport and the ship, and now he might well prove equally vital to regaining the Throne.

Which was what this meeting was all about.

"All right, Eleanora. Go," Roger said, and sat back to listen. He'd been so busy for the last month handling post-battle cleanup chores and the *maskirova* at the spaceport that he'd been unable to devote any time to planning what came next. That had been the job of his staff, and it was time to see what they'd come up with.

"Okay, we're dealing with a number of problems here," Eleanora said, keying her pad and preparing to tick off points on it.

"The first one is intelligence, or lack thereof. All we have in the way of information from Imperial City is the news bulletins and directives that came in on the last Imperial resupply ship. Those are nearly two months old, so we're dealing with an information vacuum on anything that's happened in the interim. We also have no data on conditions in the Navy, except for the announced command changes in Home Fleet and the fact that Sixth Fleet, which is normally pretty efficient, was last seen apparently unable to get itself organized for a simple change of station move and hanging out in deep space. We have no hard reads on who we might be able to trust. Effectively, we're unable to trust anyone in the Navy, especially the various commanders who've been put in place post-coup.

"The second problem is the security situation. We're all wanted in the Empire for helping you with this supposed coup. If any *one* of the *DeGlopper*'s survivors goes through Imperial customs, or even a casual scan at a spaceport, alarm bells are going to ring from there to Imperial City. Adoula's faction has to believe you're long dead, which makes you the perfect bogeyman. Who better to be wanted for something he didn't do, covering up the fact that they were the real perps, than someone who's dead? But the point remains that without *significant* disguise mod, none of us can step foot on any Imperial planet, and we're going to have real problems going anywhere *else* that's friendly with the Empire. Which means everywhere. Even the Saints would grab us, for any number of reasons we wouldn't like.

"The third problem is, of course, the actual mission. We're going to have to overthrow the current sitting government and capture your mother *and* the uterine replicator, without the bad guys making off with either. We're also going to have to prevent the Navy from interfering."

"'Who holds the orbitals, holds the planet,'" Roger said.

"Chiang O'Brien." Eleanora nodded. "You remembered that one."

"Great Gran's former Dagger Lord daddy had a way with words," Roger said, then frowned. "He also said 'One death is a tragedy; a million is a statistic.'"

"He cribbed that one from a much older source," Eleanora said. "But the point is valid. If Home Fleet comes in on Adoula's side—and with its current commander, that's a given—we're not going to win, no matter who or what we hold. And that completely ignores the insane difficulty of actually *capturing* the Empress. The Palace isn't just a collection of buildings; it's the most heavily fortified collection of buildings outside Moonbase or Terran Defense Headquarters itself. It might *look* easy to penetrate, but it's not. And you can be sure Adoula's beefed up the Empress' Own with his own bully boys."

"They won't be as good," Julian said.

"Don't bet on it," Eleanora replied grimly. "The Empress may hate and detest Adoula, but her father didn't, and this isn't the first time Adoula's been Navy Minister. He knows good soldiers from bad—or damned well ought to—and either he or someone else on his team managed to take out the rest of the Empress' Own when they seized the Palace in the first place. He'll rely on that same expertise when he brings in his replacements, and just because they work for a bad man, doesn't mean they'll be bad soldiers."

"Cross that bridge when we come to it," Roger said. "I take it you're not just going to give me a litany of bad news I already know?"

"No. But I want the bad to be absolutely clear. This isn't going to be easy, and it's not going to be guaranteed. But we do have some assets. And, more than that, our enemies do have problems. Nearly as many problems as we have, in fact, and nearly as large.

"The news we have here is that there are already questions in Parliament about the Empress' continuing seclusion. The Prime Minister is still David Yang, and while Prince Jackson's Conservatives are part of his coalition, he and Adoula are anything but friends. I'd guess that a lot of the reason they seem to be hunting so frantically for you, Roger, is that Adoula is using the 'military threat' you represent as the leverage he needs as Navy Minister to balance Yang's power as Prime Minister within the Cabinet."

"Maybe so," Roger said, with more than a trace of anger in his voice, "but Yang's also a lot closer to the Palace than we are, and *we* can tell what's going on. Yang may actually believe I'm dead, but he knows *damned* well who actually pulled off the coup. And who's controlling my mother. And he hasn't done one pocking thing about it."

"Not that we know of, at any rate," Eleanora observed in a neutral tone. Roger's eyes flashed at her, but he grimaced and made a little gesture. It was clear his anger hadn't abated—Prince Roger was angry a lot, these days—but it was equally clear he was willing to accept his chief of staff's qualification.

For the moment, at least.

"On the purely military side," O'Casey continued after a moment, "it seems clear Adoula, despite his current position at the head of the Empire's military establishment, hasn't been able to replace all of the Navy's officers with safe cronies, either. Captain Kjerulf, for example, is in a very interesting position as Chief of Staff for Home Fleet. I'd bet he's not exactly a yes-man for what's going on, but he's still there. And then there's Sixth Fleet, Admiral Helmut."

"He's not going to take what's happening lying down," Julian predicted confidently. "We used to joke that Helmut got up every morning and prayed to the picture of the Empress over his bed. And he's, like, prescient or something. If there's any smell of a fish, he'll be digging his nose in; you can be sure of that. Sixth Fleet's going to be behind *him*, too. He's headed it for years. Way longer than he should have. It's like his personal fiefdom. Even if they send someone out to replace him, five gets you ten that the replacement has an 'accident' somewhere along the line."

"Admiral Helmut was noted for some of those tendencies in reports I've seen," Temu Jin interjected. "Negatively, I might add. Also for, shall we say, zealous actions in ensuring that only officers who met his personal standards—and not just in terms of military capability—were appointed to his staff, the command of his carrier and cruiser squadrons, and even to senior ship commands. Personal fiefdoms are a constant concern for the IBI and the Inspectorate. It was only his clear loyalty to the Empress, and the Empire, that prevented his removal. But I concur in Sergeant Julian's estimate of him, based on IBI investigations."

"And there's one last possibility," Eleanora continued. Her voice was thoughtful, and her eyes were half-slitted in a calculating expression. "It's the most . . . interesting of all, in a lot of ways. But it also depends on things we know the least about at this point."

She paused, and Roger snorted.

"You don't need the 'cryptic seer' look to impress me with your competence, Eleanora," he said dryly. "So suppose you go ahead and spill this possibility for us?"

"Um?" Eleanora blinked, then flashed him a grin. "Sorry. It's just that a fair percentage of the Empress' Own tends to retire to Old Earth. Of course, a lot take colonization credits to distant systems, but a large core of them stays on-planet. After tours in the Empress' Own, I suppose backwaters look a bit less thrilling than they might to a regular Marine retiree. And the Empress' Own, active-duty or retired, are loyal beyond reason to the Empress. And they're also, well . . ." She gestured at Julian and Despreaux. "They're smart, and they have a worm's eye view of the politics in Imperial City. They're going to be making their own estimations. Even absent what we know, that Roger was on Marduk when he was supposedly carrying out this attempted coup, they're going to be suspicious."

"Prove I was out here, not anywhere near Sol . . ." Roger said.

"And they're going to be livid," Eleanora said, nodding her head.

"How many?" Roger asked.

"The Empress' Own Association lists thirty-five hundred former members living on Old Earth," Julian replied. "The Association's directory lists them by age, rank on retirement or termination of service, and specialty. It also gives their mailing addresses and electronic contact information. Some are active members, some inactive, but they're all listed. And a lot of them are . . . pretty old for wet-work. But, then again, a lot ain't."

"Anybody that anyone *knows*?" Roger asked.

"A couple of former commanders and sergeants," Despreaux answered. "The Association's Regimental Sergeant Major is Thomas Catrone. No one in the company really knew him when he was in. Some of us crossed paths, but that doesn't begin to count for something like this. But . . . Captain Pahner did. Tomcat was one of the Captain's basic training instructors."

"Catrone's going to remember Pahner as some snot-nosed basic training enlistee, if he remembers him at all." Roger thought about that for a moment, then shrugged. "Okay, I doubt he was a snot-nose even then. It's hard to imagine, anyway. Any other assets?"

"This," Eleanora said, gesturing at the overhead and, by extension, the entire ship. "It's a Saint insertion ship, and it's got some facilities that are, frankly, a bit unreal. Including some for bod-mods for spy missions. We can do the extensive bod-mods we're going to require for cover with those facilities."

"I'm going to have to cut my hair, aren't I?" Roger's mouth made a brief one-sided twitch that might have been construed as a grin.

"There were some suggestions that went a bit beyond that." Eleanora made a moue and glanced at Julian. "It was suggested that to ensure nobody began to suspect it was you, and so you could keep your hair, you could change sex."

"*What?*" Roger said in chorus with Despreaux.

"Hey, I also suggested Nimashet change at the same time," Julian protested. "That way—*oomph!*"

He stopped as Kosutic elbowed him in the gut. Roger coughed and avoided Despreaux's eye, while she simply rolled a tongue in her cheek and glared at Julian.

"We've come to an agreement, however," the chief of staff continued, also looking pointedly at Julian, "that that extreme level of change won't be necessary. The facilities are extensive, however, and we'll *all* be retroed with a nearly complete DNA mod. Skin, lungs, digestive tract, salivaries—anything that can shed DNA or be tested in a casual scan. We can't do anything about height, but everything else will change. So there's no reason you can't keep the hair. Different coloration, but just as long."

"The hair's not important," Roger said frowningly. "I'd considered cutting it, anyway. As a . . . gift. But the time was never right."

Armand Pahner had cordially detested Roger's hair from first meeting. But the funeral had been a hurried affair in the midst of the chaos of trying to keep the ship spaceworthy and simultaneously clear the planet of any sign the Bronze Barbarians had ever been there.

"But this way you can keep it." Eleanora kept her own tone light. "And if you didn't, how would we know it was you? At any rate, the body-mod problem is solved. And the ship has other assets. It's too bad we can't take it deep into Imperial space."

"No way," Kosutic said, shaking her head sharply. "One good look at it by any reasonably competent customs officer, even if we could get it patched up, and he's going to know it's not just some tramp freighter."

"So we'll have to dump it—trade it, rather—with someone we can be sure won't be telling the Empire what they traded for."

"Pirates?" Roger grimaced and glanced quickly at Despreaux. "I'd hate to support those scum in any way. And I wouldn't trust them a centimeter."

"Again, considered and rejected," Eleanora replied. "For both of those reasons. And also because we're going to need a considerable amount of help pirates simply aren't going to be able to provide."

"So who?"

"Special Agent Jin now has the floor," the chief of staff said, rather than responding directly herself.

"I've completed an analysis of the information that wasn't wiped from the ship's computers," Jin said, tapping his own pad. "We're not the only group the Saints have been messing with."

"I'd think not," Roger snorted. "They're a pest."

"This ship, in particular," Jin continued, "has been inserting agents, and some covert action teams, into Alphane territory."

"Aha." Roger's eyes narrowed.

"Into whose territory?" Krindi asked in Mardukan. Because the humans' personal computer implants could automatically translate, the meeting had been speaking the Diaspran dialect of Mardukan with which all the locals were familiar. "Sorry," the infantryman continued, "but I've been getting up to speed on most of your human terms, and this is a new one."

"The Alphanes are the only nonhuman interstellar polity with which we have contact," Eleanora said, descending into lecture mode. "Or, rather, the only one which isn't *predominately* human. The Alphane Alliance consists of twelve planets, with the population about evenly split between humans, Altharis, and Phaenurs.

"The Phaenurs are lizardlike creatures—they look something like *atul*, but with only four legs and two arms, and they're scaly, like the *flar-ta*. They're also empaths—which means they can read emotions—and, among themselves, they're functional telepaths. Very shrewd bargainers, since it's virtually impossible to lie to them.

"The Altharis are a warrior race that looks somewhat like large . . . Well, you don't have the referent, but they look like big koala bears. Very stoic and honorable. Females make up the bulk of their warriors, while males tend to be their engineers and workers. I've dealt with the Alphanes before, and the combination is . . . difficult. You have to lay all your cards on the table, because the Phaenurs can tell if you're lying, and the Altharis lose all respect for you if you do."

"But the critical point, for our purposes, is that we have information the Alphanes need," Jin continued, picking up the thread once more. "They need to know both the extent of Saint penetration—which they're going to be somewhat surprised about, I suspect—and the true nature of what's going on in the Empire."

"Even if they do need to know that, and even if we tell them, that doesn't necessarily mean they're going to help us," Roger pointed out.

"No," Eleanora agreed with a frown. "But they can, and there are reasons they may. I won't say they *will*, but it's our best hope."

"And do you have any suggestions about how we're going to

penetrate the Empire?" Roger asked. "Assuming we can convince the Alphanes to help us, that is?"

"Yes," Eleanora said, then shrugged. "It's not my idea, but I think it's a good one. I didn't at first, but it makes more sense than anything else we've come up with. Julian?"

Roger looked at the noncom, and Julian grinned.

"Restaurants," he said.

"What?" Roger frowned blankly.

"Kostas, may he rest in peace, gave me the idea."

"What does Kostas have to do with it?" Roger demanded, almost angrily. The bitter wound of the valet's death had yet to fully heal.

"It was those incredible meals he'd summon up out of nothing but swamp water and day-old *atul*," Julian replied with another smile, this one of sad fondness and memory. "Man, I still can't *believe* some of those recipes he came up with! I was thinking about them, and it suddenly occurred to me that Old Earth is always looking for the 'new' thing. Restaurants spring up with some new, out-of-this-world—literally!—food all the time. It's going to require one helluva lot of funding, but that's going to be a problem for anything we do. So, what we do, is we come to Imperial City with a chain of the newest, most you've-got-to-try-this-new-place, most brassy possible restaurants serving 'authentic Mardukan food.'"

"You've wanted to do this your whole life," Roger said, wonderingly. "Haven't you?"

"No, listen," Julian said earnestly. "We don't just bring Mardukans and Mardukan food. We bring the whole schmeer. *Atul* in cages. *Flar-ta*. *Basik*. Tanks of *coll* fish. Hell, bring Patty! We throw a grand opening for the new restaurant in Imperial City that's the talk of the whole planet. A parade of *civan* riders and the Diasprans bearing platters of *atul* and *basik* on beds of barleyrice. Rastar chopping the meat off the bone right there in the restaurant for everyone to watch. Impossible to miss."

"The purloined letter approach," Kosutic said. "Don't hide it, flaunt it. They're looking for Prince Roger to come sneaking in? Heaven with that! We'll come in blowing trumpets."

"And do you know how good a restaurant is for having

meetings?" Julian asked. "Who thinks about a group of former Empress' Own having one of their get-togethers in the newest, hottest restaurant on the face of the planet?"

"And we've got the whole *Basik*'s Own right there in the heart of the capital," Roger said, almost wonderingly.

"Bingo," Julian agreed with a chuckle.

"Just one problem," Roger noted, with another of those quick, one-side-of-the-face smiles. "They're all lousy cooks."

"It's *haute cuisine*," Julian said. "Who can tell the difference? Besides, we can scrounge up cooks on the planet. Ones that are either loyal to us, or don't know what's going on. Just that they were hired to go to another planet and cook. That place in K'Vaern's Cove, the one down by the water—you know, the one Tor Flain's parents own. That's a whole *family* of expert cooks. Ones we can trust, come to think of it. And how many humans *speak* Mardukan? It was only your toot and Eleanora's that let us get by at first. Then there's Harvard."

"Harvard?" Roger asked.

"Yeah, Harvard. If you trust him," Julian said seriously.

Roger thought about that for a long time. They'd discovered Harvard Mansul, a reporter for the Imperial Astrographic Society in a cell in a Krath fortress the Marines had captured. He'd been almost pathetically grateful to be rescued, and to have his prized Zuiko tri-cam returned more or less unharmed. Since then, he'd been attached to Roger like a limpet. Not for safety, but because, as he'd frankly admitted, it was the story of all time. Marooned prince battles neobarbarians and saves the Empire . . . assuming, of course, that any of them survived.

But Mansul wasn't in it solely for the story. Roger felt confident about that. He was not, by any means, scatterbrained, and he was loyal to the Empire. And furious at what was happening at home.

"I think I trust him," the prince said finally. "Why?"

"Because if we send Harvard back early, he thinks he can get a pretty good piece—maybe a lead piece—into the *IAS Monthly*. He's got good video, and Marduk is one of those 'I can't believe worlds like that still exist' places the IAS loves. If we hit right after the IAS piece, it'd make for that much better publicity, and he's willing, more than willing, to help. Obviously, he'll hold off on the *big* scoop. And he can do some other groundwork for us in advance. We're going to need that."

"Why do I have the feeling Captain Pahner is watching us," Roger said with a crooked smile, "and clasping his head and shaking it. 'You're all insane. This isn't a plan; this is a catastrophe,'" he added in a slightly deeper voice.

"Because it isn't a plan," Kosutic replied simply. "It's the germ of a plan, and it *is* insane, because the whole idea is insane. Twelve Marines, a couple of hundred Mardukans, and one scion of House MacClintock taking on the Empire? No plan that *isn't* insane will save your mother and the Empire."

"Not quite," Eleanora said, carefully. "Well, there's one other approach that *might* do either of those. Government-in-exile."

"Eleanora, we talked about this." Julian shook his head stubbornly. "It won't work."

"Maybe not, but it still needs to be laid on the table," Roger said. "A staff's job is to give its boss options. So let me hear this option."

"We go to the Alphanes and lay out everything we know," Eleanora said, licking her lips. "Then we make a full spectacle of it. Tell the whole story to anyone who'll listen, especially the representatives of other polities. On the side, we dump them the data we got from the ship, by the way. There are already questions in Parliament about your mother's condition—we all know that. This would make it *much* harder for her to conveniently die of 'remnant trauma from her ordeal.' We've got Harvard, who's a known member of the Imperial press, to start the ball rolling, and others. will come to us to follow it up. That much I can absolutely guarantee; the story's a natural."

"And what we'll have is a civil war," Julian said. "Adoula's faction's in too deep to back out, and they're not going to go down smiling. They also control a substantial fraction of the Navy and the Corps, and they *own* the current Empress' Own. We do this, and Adoula either sits tight on Imperial City, declaring a state of martial law in the Sol System while the various fleets have internal squabbles and duke it out in space. Or, maybe even worse, he runs back to his sector with the baby, your mother being dead, and we end up in a civil war between two pretenders to the Throne."

"He's going to get some portion of the Navy, no matter *what* we do," Eleanora argued.

"Not if we capture the king," Julian countered.

"This isn't a chess game," Eleanora said mulishly.

"Wait." Roger held up his hand. "Jin?"

The agent raised an eyebrow and then shrugged.

"I agree with both," he said simply. "All of it. Civil war and all the rest. Which will mean, of course, the Saints will be busy snapping up as many planetary systems as they can manage. The flip side, which, curiously, neither of them mentioned, is that it means all of us will be relatively safe. Adoula wouldn't be able to touch us if we were under the Alphanes' protection. And if they offer it, it will be full force. They're very serious about such things. You can live a full life, whether Adoula is pushed out or not."

"They didn't mention it because it's not part of the equation," Roger said, his face hard. "Sure, it's tempting. But there are too many lives on the trail for any of us to ever think about turning aside because it's 'safer.' The only question that matters here is where our duty lies? So how do you evaluate *that* question?"

"As one with too many imponderables for a definite answer," Jin replied. "We don't have enough information to know if the insertion and countercoup plan is even remotely feasible." He paused and shrugged. "If we find that it's impossible to checkmate Adoula, and we're still undetected, we can back out. Go back to the Alphanes— this all assumes their support—and go for Plan B. And if we're caught, which is highly likely given that the IBI is *not* stupid, the Alphanes will be authorized to release the entire story. It won't help us, or your mother, most likely, but it will severely damage Adoula."

"No," Roger said. "One condition we'll have to have on their help will be that if we fail, we *fail*."

"Why?" Julian asked.

"Getting Adoula out of power, rescuing Mother—those are both important things," Roger said. "I'll even admit I'd like to live through accomplishing them. But what's the most important part of this mission?"

He looked around at them, and shook his head as all of them looked back in greater or lesser degrees of confusion.

"I'm surprised at you," he said. "Captain Pahner would have been able to answer that in a second."

"The safety of the Empire," Julian said then, nodding his head. "Sorry."

"I've contemplated not trying to retake the Throne *at all*," Roger said, looking at all of them intently. "The *only* reason I intend to try is because I agree with Mother that Adoula's long-term policies will be more detrimental to the Empire than another coup or even a minor civil war. Give Adoula enough time, and he'll break the Constitution for personal power. *That's* what we're fighting to prevent. But the long-term good of the Empire is the *preeminent* mission. Much, *much* more important than just making sure there's a MacClintock on the Throne. If we fail, there will be no one except Adoula who can possibly safeguard the Empire. He won't do a good job, but that's better than the Empire breaking up into small pieces, ripe for plucking by the Saints or Raiden-Winterhowe, or whoever else moves into the power vacuum. We're talking about the good of three-quarters of a *trillion* lives. A major civil war, with the half-dozen factions that will fall out, would make the Dagger Years look like a pocking *picnic*. No. If we fail, then we fail, and our deaths will be as unremarked as any in history. It's not heroic, it's not pretty, but it *is* the best thing for the Empire . . . and it *will* be done. Clear?"

"Clear," Julian said, swallowing.

Roger leaned his elbow on the station chair's arm and rubbed his forehead furiously, his eyes closed.

"So we go to the Alphanes, get them to switch out the ship for one that's less conspicuous—"

"And a bunch of money," Julian interjected. "There's some technology on here I don't think they have yet."

"And a bunch of money," Roger agreed, still rubbing. "Then we take the *Basik*'s Own, and Patty, and a bunch of *atul* and *basiks* and what have you—"

"And several tons of barleyrice," Julian said.

"And we go start a chain of restaurants, or at least a couple," Roger said.

"A chain would be better," Julian pointed out. "But at least one in Imperial City. Maybe near the old river; they were gentrifying that area when we left."

"And then we *somehow* parlay that into taking the Palace, checkmating Home Fleet, and preventing Adoula from killing my mother," Roger finished, looking up and gesturing with an open palm. "Is *that* what we have as a plan?"

"Yes," Eleanora said in an uncharacteristically small voice, looking down at the tabletop.

Roger gazed up at the overhead, as if seeking guidance. Then he shrugged, reached back to straighten his ponytail, pulled each hair carefully into place, and looked around the compartment.

"Okay," he said. "Let's go."

"Hello, Beach," Roger said.

"I cannot *believe* what your guys did to my ship!" the former Saint officer said angrily. She had soot all over her hands and face and was just withdrawing her head and shoulders from a hole in a portside bulkhead.

Amanda Beach had never been a Saint true-believer. Far too much of the Saint philosophy, especially as practiced by the current leadership, was, in her opinion, so much bullshit.

The Caravazan Empire had been a vigorous, growing political unit, shortly after the Dagger Years, when Pierpaelo Cavaza succeeded to its throne. And Pierpaelo, unfortunately, had been a devotee of the Church of Ryback, an organization dedicated to removing "humanocentric" damage from the universe. Its creed called for the return of all humans to the Sol System, and the rebuilding—in original form—of all "damaged" worlds.

Pierpaelo had recognized this to be an impossibility, but he believed it was possible to reduce the damage humans did, and to prevent them from continuing to seek new frontiers and damaging still more "unspoiled" worlds. He had, therefore, started his "New Program" soon after ascending to the throne. The New Program had called for a sharp curtailment of "unnecessary" resource use via ruthless rationing and restrictions, and a simultaneous aggressively expansionist foreign policy to prevent the "unholy" from further damaging the worlds they held by taking those worlds away from them and transferring them to the hands of more responsible stewards.

For some peculiar reason, a substantial number of his subjects had felt this was a less than ideal policy initiative. Their disagreement with his platform had led to a short, but unpleasant, civil war. Which Pierpaelo won, proving along the way that his particular form of lunacy didn't keep him from being just as ruthless as any of his ancestors.

From that time on, the Saints, as they were called by everyone else in the galaxy, had been a scourge, constantly preaching "universal harmony" and "ecological enlightenment" while attacking any and all of their neighbors at the slightest opportunity.

Beach, in her rise through the ranks of the Saint Navy, had had more than enough opportunities to see the other side of the Saint philosophy. What it amounted to was: "The little people deserve nothing, but the leaders can live as kings." The higher-ups in the Saint military and government lived in virtual palaces, while their subjects were regulated in every mundane need or pleasure of life. While extravagant parties went on in the "holy centers," the people outside those centers had their power turned off promptly at 9 p.m., or whatever local equivalent. While the people subsisted on "minimum necessity" rationing, the powers-that-were had feasts. The people lived in uniform blocks of concrete and steel towers, living their lives day in and day out at the very edge of survival; the leaders lived in mansions and had pleasant little houses for "study and observation" in the wilderness. Always in the most charming possible locations in the wilderness.

For that matter, she'd long ago decided, the whole philosophy was cockeyed. "Minimum resource use." All well and good, but who belled the cat? Who decided that this man, who needed a new heart, deserved one or did not? That this child—one too many—had to die? Who decided that this person could or could not have a house?

The answer was the bureaucracy of the Caravazan Empire. The bureaucracy which insured that *its* leadership had heart transplants. That *its* leadership had as many children as they liked, and houses on pristine streams, while everyone else could go suck eggs.

And she'd poked around the peripheries of enough other societies to see the real black side of Rybak. The Saints had the highest population growth of any human society of the Six Polities, despite a supposedly strictly enforced "one child only" program. Another of what she thought of as the "real" reasons they were so expansionist. They also had the lowest standard of living and—not too surprisingly; it usually went hand-in-hand—the lowest individual productivity. If there was nothing to work towards, there was no reason to put out more work than the bare minimum. If all you saw at the end of a long life was a couple of children who were doomed to slave away their lives, as well, what was the point? For that matter, Caravazan cities were notorious for their pollution problems. Most of them were running at the bare minimum for survival, mainly due to their shitty productivity, and at that level, no one who could do anything about it cared about pollution or the inherent inefficiency of pollution controls.

She'd visited Old Earth during an assignment in the naval service, and been amazed at the planet. Everyone seemed so *rosy*. So well fed, so happy—so smugly complacent, really. The streets were remarkably clean, and there were hardly any bums on them. *No* bums who'd lost hands or arms because of industrial accidents and been left out to die. A chemical spill was *major* news, and nobody seemed to be working very hard. They just *did*, beavering away and getting tons of work done in practically no time.

And Imperial *ships*! Efficiently designed to the point of insanity. When she'd asked one of their shipbuilders why, he'd simply explained—slowly, in small words, as if to a child or a halfwit—that if they were less efficient than their competitors, if their ships didn't get the maximum cargo moved for the minimum cost, both in power usage and in on/off loading speeds, then their customers would go to those competitors.

Lovely rounded bulkheads and control panels, for safety

reasons . . . which were considered part of overhead. Control runs that took the shortest possible route with the maximum possible functionality. Engines that were at least ten percent more efficient in energy use than any Saint design. Much less likely to simply blow up when you engaged the tunnel drive or got to max charge on the capacitors, for that matter. And *cheap*. Comparatively speaking, of course; no tunnel drive ship was anything but expensive.

Saint ships, on the other hand, were built in government yards by workers who were half drunk, most of the time, on rotgut bootleg, that being the only liquor available. Or stoned on any number of drugs. The ships took three times as long to build, with horrible quality control and lousy efficiency.

The *Emerald Dawn* was, in fact, a converted Imperial freighter. And it had been converted by a quiet little *Imperial* yard that was happy for the work and more than willing to avoid unnecessary questions, given the money it was being paid. If the work had been done in one of the ham-handed Saint yards, the quality loss would have been noticeable.

In fact, if the *Dawn* had been a Saint ship, those idiot Mardukans would probably have blown it all the way to kingdom come, instead of only halfway.

Amanda sometimes wondered how much of it was intentional. The official purpose of the Church of Ryback was to ensure the best possible environmental conditions. But if they actually *succeeded* in being as "clean" as the Imperials against whom they inveighed so savagely, would people see that level of "contamination" as that great a threat? Would the workers even care about the environment? Could the Church of Ryback sustain itself in conditions where the environment was clean *and* people went to bed hungry every night?

Her commander in the *Dawn*, Fiorello Giovannuci, on the other hand, had been a real, honest, true-believer. Giovannuci wasn't stupid; he'd seen the hypocrisy of the system, but he ignored it. Humans weren't perfect, and the "hypocritical" conditions didn't shake his belief in the core fundamentals of the Church. He'd been in command specifically because he was a true-believer despite his lack of stupidity; no one *but* a true-believer ever got to be in command of a ship. Certainly not of one that spent as much time poking around doing odd missions as the *Dawn*. And when the *Basik*'s Own's assault was clearly going to succeed, he'd engaged the auto-destruct sequence.

Unfortunately for his readiness to embrace martyrdom, there'd been a slight flaw in the system. Only true-believers became ship commanders, true, but the CO wasn't the only person who could *shut off* the auto-destruct. So when Giovannuci had been . . . removed by the ever-helpful Imperials, Beach had been in nowise unwilling to turn it off.

Giovannuci himself was no longer a factor in anyone's equations, except perhaps God's. He and his senior noncommissioned officer had tried to murder Roger with "one-shots"—specialized, contact-range anti-armor weapons—after surrendering. The sergeant had died then, but only Armand Pahner's sacrifice of his own life had saved Roger from Giovannuci's one-shot. Unfortunately for Fiorello Giovannuci, the *Dawn*'s entire cruise had been an illegal act—piracy, actually, since the Saints and the Empire were officially at peace—and that was a capital offense. Then, too, the accepted rules of war made his attempt to assassinate Roger after surrendering a capital offense, as well. So after a scrupulously honest summary court-martial, Giovannuci had attained the martyrdom he'd sought after all.

As for Amanda Beach, she had no family in the Caravazan Empire. She'd been raised in a state creche and didn't even know who her *mother* was, much less her father. So when the only real choice became dying or burning her bridges with a vengeance, she'd burned them with a certain degree of glee.

Only to discover what a hash the damned Empies and their scummy allies had made of her ship.

"Six more centimeters," she said angrily, rounding on the prince and holding up her thumb and forefinger in emphasis of the distance. "Six. And one of your idiot Mardukans would have blown open a tunnel radius. As it is, the magnets are fried."

"But he didn't blow it open," Roger noted. "So when are we going to have power?"

"You want *power*!? This is a job for a major dockyard, damn it! All I've got is the few spaceport techs who were willing to sign on to this venture, some of your ham-handed soldiers, and *me*! And I'm an *astrogator*, not an engineer!"

"So when are we going to have power?" Roger repeated calmly.

"A week." She shrugged. "Maybe ten days. Maybe sooner, but I doubt it. We'll have to reinstall about eighty percent of the control runs, and we're replacing all the damaged magnets. Well, the worst damaged ones. We're way too short on spares to replace all of them, so we're having to repair some of the ones that only got scorched, and I'm not happy about that, to say the least. You understand that if this had been a *real* freighter that wouldn't even be possible? Their control run molycircs are installed right into the ship's basic structure. We're at least modded to be able to rip 'em out to repair combat damage, but even in our wildest dreams, we never anticipated *this* much of it."

"If it had been a real freighter," Roger said, somewhat less calmly, "we wouldn't have *done* this much damage. Or had our butcher's bill. So, a week. Is there anything we can do to speed that up?"

"Not unless you can whistle up a team from the New Rotterdam shipyards," she said tiredly. "We've got every trained person working on it, and as many untrained as we can handle. We've nearly had some bad accidents as it is. Working with these power levels is no joke. You can't smell, hear, or see electricity, and every time we activate a run to check integrity, I'm certain we're going to fry some unthinking schlub, human or Mardukan, who doesn't know what 'going hot' means."

"Okay, a week or ten days," Roger said. "Are you getting any rest?"

"*Rest?*" she said, cranking up for a fresh tirade.

"I'll take it that that means 'no.'" Roger quirked one side of his mouth again. "Rest. It's a simple concept. I want you to work no more than twelve hours per day. Figure out a way to do that, and the same for everyone else involved in the repairs. Over twelve hours a day, continuous, and people start making bad mistakes. Figure it out."

"That's going to push it to the high end on time," she pointed out.

"Fine," Roger replied. "We've got a new project we need to work out, anyway, and it's going to mean loading a lot of . . . specialized stores. Ten days is about right. And if you blow up the ship, we're going to have to start all over again. As you just noted, you're an astrogator, not an engineer. I don't want you making those sorts of mistakes just because you're too pocking tired to avoid them."

"I've worked engineering," she said with a shrug. "I can hum the tune, even if I can't sing it. And Vincenzo is probably a better engineer than the late chief. At least partly because he's more than willing to do something that's not by the Book but works. Since the Book was written by the idiots back on Rybak's World, it's generally wrong anyway. We'll get it done."

"Fine. But get it done *after* you get some rest. Figure out the schedule for the next day or so, and then tuck it in. Clear?"

"Clear," she said, then grinned. "I'll follow anybody that tells me to knock off work."

"I told you to cut back to twelve hours per day," Roger said with another cheek twitch, "not to knock off. But now, tonight, I want you to get some rest. Maybe even a beer. Don't make me send one of the guards."

"Okay, okay. I get the point," the former Saint said, then shook her head. "Six more damned centimeters."

"A miss is as good as a mile."

"And just what," Beach asked, "is a 'mile'?"

"No idea," Roger answered. "But whatever it is, it's as good as a miss."

Roger continued down the passageway, just generally looking around, talking to the occasional repair tech, until he noticed a cursing monotone which had become more of a continuous, blasphemous mutter.

"Pock. Modderpocking Saint modderpocking equipment . . ."

Two short legs extended into the passage, waving back and forth as a hand scrabbled after the toolbox floating just out of reach.

". . . get my pocking wrench, and *t'en* you gonna pocking work . . ."

Sergeant Julio Poertena, Bravo Company's unit armorer when the company dropped on Marduk, was from Pinopa, a semitropical planet of archipelagoes, with one small continent, that had been settled primarily from Southeast Asia, and he represented something of an anomaly. Or perhaps a necessary evil; Roger was never quite certain how the Regiment had actually seen Poertena.

While the Empress' Own took only the best possible soldiers, in terms of both fighting ability and decorum, the Regiment did allow some room in its mental framework for slightly less decorum among its support staff, who could be kept more or less out of sight on public occasions. Staff such as the unit armorer. Which had been fortunate for Poertena's pre-Marduk career, since a man who couldn't get three words out without one of them being the curse word "pock" would never have been allowed, otherwise.

Since their arrival on Marduk, however, Poertena had marched all the way across the world with the rest of them, conjuring miracles from his famed "big pocking pack" times beyond number. And, when miracles hadn't been in the offing, he'd produced serious changes of attitude with his equally infamous "big pocking wrench." More recently, as one of the Marines' few trained techs, he'd been assisting with the ship repairs . . . in, of course, his own, inimitable fashion.

Roger leaned over and tapped the toolbox, gently, so that it drifted under the scrabbling hand on its counter-grav cushion, apparently all on its own. The hand darted into it and emerged dragging a wrench that was as long as an arm. Then, the hand— with some difficulty, and accompanied by more monotone cursing—hauled the giant wrench into the hole, and there was a series of clangs.

"Get in *t'ere*, modderpocker! Gonna get you to pocking—"

There was a loud zapping sound, and a yowl, followed by more cursing.

"So, *t'at's* t'e way you gonna . . . !"

Roger shook his head and moved on.

"Get *up* there, you silly thing!" Roger shouted, and landed a solid kick behind the armored shield on the broad head.

Patty was a *flar-ta*, an elephant-sized, six-legged Mardukan packbeast, that looked something like a triceratops. *Flar-ta* had broad, armored shields on their heads and short horns, much shorter than those of the wild *flar-ke* from which they were clearly descended. Patty's horns, however, were just about twice normal *flar-ta* length, and she obviously had more than her share of "wild" genes. She was a handful for most mahouts, and the Bronze Barbarians had long ago decided that the only reason Roger could ride her was that he was just as bloody-minded as the big omnivore. Her sides were covered in scars, some of which she'd earned becoming "boss mare" of the herd of *flar-ta* the Marines had used for pack animals. But she'd attained most of those scars with Roger on her back, killing the things, Mardukan and animal, that put them there.

Now she gave a low, hoarse bellow and backed away from the heavy cargo shuttle's ramp. She'd had one ride in a shuttle already, and that was all she was willing to go for. The long, sturdy rope attached to the harness on her head prevented her from drawing too far away from the hatch, but the massive shuttle shuddered and scraped on its landing skids as she threw all six-legs into stubborn reverse.

"Look, Roger, try to keep her from dragging the shuttle back to Diaspra, okay?" Julian's request was just a little hard to understand, thanks to how hard he was laughing.

"Okay, beast! If that's how you're gonna be about it," Roger said, ignoring the NCO's unbecoming enjoyment.

The prince slid down the side of the creature, jumped nimbly to the ground via a bound on a foreleg, and walked around her, ignoring the fact that she could squash him like a bug at any moment. He hiked up the ramp until he was near the front of the cargo compartment, then turned and faced her, hands on hips.

"*I'm* going up to the ship in this thing," he told her. "*You* can either come along or not."

The *flar-ta* gave a low, high-pitched sound, like a giant cat in distress, and shook her head.

"Suit yourself."

Roger turned his back and crossed his arms.

Patty gazed at his back for a moment. Then she gave another squeal and set one massive forepaw on the shuttle ramp. She pressed down a couple of times, testing her footing, then slowly eased her way up.

Roger gathered in the slack in the head rope, pulling it steadily through the ring on the compartment's forward bulkhead. When she was fully in the shuttle, he secured the rope, anchoring her (hopefully) as close to the centerline as possible. Then he came over to give her a good scratching.

"I know I've got a kate fruit around here somewhere," he muttered, searching in a pocket until he came up with the astringent fruit. He held it up to her beak—carefully, she could take his hand off in one nip—and had it licked from his palm.

"We're just going to take a little ride," he told her. "No problem. Just a short voyage." You could tell a *flar-ta* anything; they only knew the tone.

While he was soothing her, Mardukan mahouts had gathered around, attaching chains to her legs and harness. She shifted a few times in irritation as the chains clicked tight against additional anchoring rings, but submitted to the indignity.

"I know I haven't been spending much time with you, lately," Roger crooned, still scratching. "But we'll have lots of time on the way to Althar Four."

"What the hell are you going to do with her aboard ship?" Julian asked as he entered the compartment through the forward personnel hatch and picked up a big wicker basketful of barleyrice. He set it under Patty's nose, and she dipped in, scooping up a mouthful of the grain and then spraying half of it on the cargo deck.

"Put her in hold two with Winston," Roger answered, using a stick to reach high enough to scratch the beast's neck behind the armored shield. The big, gelded *flar-ta* was even larger than Patty, but much more docile.

"Let's hope she doesn't kick open the pressure door," Julian grumbled, but that, at least, was a false issue. The cargo bay pressure doors were made out of ChromSten, the densest, strongest, *heaviest* alloy known to man . . . or any other sentient species. Even the latches and seals were shielded by too much metal for Patty to demolish.

"I don't think that will be a problem," Roger said. "*Feeding* her now. *That* might be."

"Not as much as feeding the *civans*," Julian muttered.

"Quit that!" Honal slapped the *civan* on its muzzle as it tried to take a chunk out of his shoulder. It was never wise to allow one of the ill-tempered, aggressive riding beasts to forget who was in charge, but he understood why it was uneasy. The entire ship was vibrating.

Cargo was being loaded—*lots* of cargo. There were flash-frozen *coll* fish from K'Vaern's Cove, kate fruit and *dianda* from Marshad, barleyrice from Diaspra and Q'Nkok, and *flar-ta, atul* and *basik*— both live examples and meat—from Ran Tai, Diaspra, and Voitan. There were artifacts, for decoration and trade, from Krath, along with gems and worked metals from the Shin. All of it had been traded for, except the material from the Krath. In the Krath's case, Roger had made an exception to his belief that it was generally not a good idea to exact tribute and simply landed with a shuttle and ordered them to fill it to the deckhead. He was still bitterly angry over their attempt to use Despreaux as one of their "Servants of the God"— sentient sacrifices to be butchered living and then eaten—and it showed. As far as he was concerned, if *all* of their blood-splattered temple/slaughterhouses were stripped of statuary and gilding, so much the better.

Honal couldn't have agreed more with his human prince, except, perhaps, for that bit about "not a good idea" where tribute was concerned. But he understood perfectly how the continuous rumble of the loading, not to mention the strange smells of the damaged ship and the odd light from the overheads, combined to make the *civan*, never the most docile of beasts at any time, nervous. And when *civan* got nervous, they tended to want to spread it around. Generally by making anyone around them afraid for their lives.

Civan were four-meter tall, bipedal riding beasts that looked something like small tyrannosaurs. Despite their appearance, they were omnivorous, but they did best with a diet that included some meat. And they were often more than willing to add a rider's leg or arm to that diet. On the other hand, they were *always* willing to add an *enemy's* face or arm to the menu, which made them preeminent cavalry mounts. If you could get them to distinguish friend from foe, that was.

The Vasin were experts at creating that distinction, which had made them the most feared cavalry on the Diaspran side of the main continent of Marduk. Up to the coming of the Boman, that was.

The Boman had been a problem for generations, but it was only in the last few years that they'd organized and increased in numbers to the point of becoming a real threat. The Vasin lords, descendents of barbarians who had themselves swept down from the north only a few generations ahead of the Boman, had been established as a check on the fresh barbarian invasion from the northern Plains. They'd been paid in tribute from the more civilized areas—city-states like Sindi, Diaspra, and K'Vaern's Cove—to prevent people like the Boman from causing mischief to the south.

But when the Boman had combined under their great chief, Kny Camsan, they'd swept the severely outnumbered Vasin cavalry from the field in waves of infantry attacks. The fact that the Vasin cities' food supplies had been systematically sabotaged (for reasons which had, presumably, made sense to his own warped thinking) by the particularly megalomaniacal ruler of Sindi, one of the cities they were supposed to be defending, had effectively neutralized the Vasin's traditional strategy for dealing with that sort of situation. With their starving garrisons unable to stand the sieges which usually outlasted the Boman's ability to maintain their cohesion, the Vasin castles and fortified cities had been overwhelmed, their garrisons and citizens slaughtered to the last babe in arms. And after that, the Boman had continued on to conquer Sindi and put its miscalculating ruler and his various cronies to death in the approved, lingering Boman style.

They undoubtedly would have destroyed K'Vaern's Cove and the ancient city of Diaspra, as well, but for the arrival of Roger's forces. The Marines' core of surviving high-tech gear and their thousands of years of military experience and "imported" technology—pike formations, at first, and then rifles, muskets, artillery, and even black powder bombardment rockets—had managed to hold together an alliance against the Boman and break them in the heart of their newly conquered citadel of Sindi.

The entire occupied area had been recovered, with the Boman forces scattered after hideous casualties and either forced to resettle under local leadership or driven back across the northern borders. Even the Vasin castles, what was left of them, had been retaken. The last Boman remnants had been driven out as soon as the humans took the spaceport and, reassured that there were no Saints around, could use their combat shuttles and heavy weapons against the barbarians.

Honal and Rastar could have returned to their homes. But one look at the ruined fortifications, the homes they'd grown up in and in which their parents, families, and friends had died, was enough. They'd returned to the spaceport with Roger and turned their backs upon the past. The Vasin—not only the force Honal and Rastar had led out of the ruins of Therdan to cover the evacuation of the only women and children to survive the city's fall, but all that had been gathered from all of their scattered people's cities—were now surrogates of Prince Roger MacClintock, heir apparent to the Throne of Man. Most of the survivors remained on Marduk, relocated to new homes near Voitan and provided with locally produced Imperial technology to ensure their survival and well being. But Rastar's personal troops were committed to the personal service of the human who had made their survival as a people possible. Where Roger went, they went. Which currently meant to another planet.

Honal had to admit that if it weren't for the circumstances which made leaving possible—his entire family was dead, as well as Rastar's—he would have felt only pleased anticipation at the prospect of following Roger. He'd always had a bit of the wanderlust, probably inherited from his nomadic forefathers, not to mention his Boman tribute-bride mother. And the chance to see another planet was one very few Mardukans had been given.

On the other hand, it meant getting the *civan* settled aboard a starship. It had been bad enough on those cockleshell boats they'd used to cross the Western Ocean, but starships were even worse, in a way.

For one thing, there was that constant background *thrum*. He was told it was from the fusion plants—whatever they were—that fed power to the ship, and that they'd been charging the "capacitors" for the "tunnel drive" (more odd words) for the last two days. And the gravity was different from Marduk's. It was lighter, if anything, which allowed for some interesting new variations on combat training. And, like most of the Mardukans, Honal had developed a positive passion for the game of "basketball." The humans, on the other hand, had insisted that the Mardukans had to use baskets which were mounted at two and a half times regulation height the instant they saw the Mardukan players soaring effortlessly through two-meter jump shots in the reduced gravity. But if the Mardukans enjoyed the lighter gravity, the *civan* didn't like it—not at all, at all. And they were taking out their dislike on their grooms and riders.

Honal looked around the big hold at the other riders settling the *civan* in their stalls. Those stalls had been custom-made by the "Class One Manufacturing Plant" which had been shipped from the spaceport to Voitan. They were large enough for the *civan* to pace around in, or lie down to sleep, and strongly made from something called "composite fibers." And there were attachment points on the floor—the *deck*—of the hold, to which the structures had been carefully secured.

The stalls were also roofed, and much of the material the *civan* were going to be eating on the voyage was stuffed into the vast area above them. Huge containers of barleyrice and beans had been hoisted into the area and stacked in tiers. There was water on tap in several spots, and arrangements had been made to dispose of the *civan's* waste. He'd been told that human ships occasionally had to move live cargo, and from the looks of things, they'd figured out how to do it with the normal infernal human ingenuity.

An open area on the inner side of the hold had been fenced off to provide space in which they could work the *civan*. It was big enough for only a few of the beasts to be exercised or trained at once, but it was better than they'd managed on the ships of the Crossing, where the only exercise choice had been to let them swim alongside the ships for short periods. Still, with only one working area available, the grooms and riders were going to be working around the clock to keep them in decent shape.

The clock. That was another thing that took getting used to. The Terran day, which the ship maintained, was only two-thirds as long as Marduk's day. So just about the time it felt like early afternoon, the ship lights dimmed to "nighttime" mode. He'd already noticed the way it affected his own sleep, and he was worried about how the *civan* would react.

Well, they'd make it, or they wouldn't. He loved *civan*, but he'd come to the conclusion that there were even more marvelous transportation options waiting beyond Marduk's eternal overcast. He'd lusted after the humans' shuttles from the instant he'd seen them in flight, and he'd been told about, and seen pictures of, the "light-flyers" and the "stingships" available on Old Earth. He wondered just how much they cost . . . and what he was going to be earning as a senior aide to the Prince. A lot, he hoped, because assuming they survived for him to collect his pay, he was bound and determined to get himself a light-flyer.

"How's it going?" a voice asked, and he looked up as Rastar appeared at his shoulder.

"Not bad," Honal replied, raising a warning hand to the *civan* as he sensed the lips drawing back from its fangs and its crest folding down. "About as well as can be expected, in fact."

"Good." Rastar nodded, a human gesture he'd picked up. "Good. They think they'll finish loading in a few hours. Then we'll find out if the engines really work."

"Won't that be fun?" Honal said dryly.

"Engaging phase drive—" Amanda Beach drew a deep breath and pressed a button "—now."

At first, the image of the planet below seemed unchanged on the bridge viewscreens. It was just the same slowly circling, blue-and-white ball it had always been. But then the ship began to accelerate, and the ball began to dwindle.

"All systems nominal," one of her few surviving engineering techs said. "Accel is about twenty percent below max, but that's right on the numbers, given our counter-grav field status. Runs one, four, and nine are still out. And charge rate on the tunnel capacitors is still nominal. Nine hours to full tunnel drive power."

"And eleven hours to the Tsukayama Limit," Beach said, with a sigh. "Looks like it's holding. We'll find out when we try to form a singularity."

"Eleven hours?" Roger asked. He'd been standing by in the control room. Not because he felt he could do anything, but because he thought his place was here, at this time.

"Yeah," Beach said. "If everything holds together."

"It will," Roger replied. "I'll be back then."

"Okay." Beach waved a hand almost absently as she concentrated on her control board. "See ya."

"I've just had a suspicion I don't much care for," Roger said to Julian. He'd called the sergeant into his office, the former captain's office, once the phase drive had turned out to work after all.

"What kind of suspicion?" Julian crinkled his brow.

"How in the hell do we *know* Beach is headed for Alphane space instead of Saint space? Yes, she seems to have burned her bridges. But if she pops out in a Saint system with the ship—and me—they're going to be somewhat forgiving of any minor lapses on her part. Especially given conditions on Old Earth."

"Ack." Julian shook his head. "You've picked a fine time to think about that, O My Lord and Master!"

"I'm serious, Ju," Roger said. "Do we have anyone left who knows *anything* about astrogation?"

"Maybe Doc Dobrescu," Julian suggested. "But if we put somebody on the bridge to watch Beach, she's going to know damn well what we suspect. And I submit that pissing her off would be the worst possible thing we could do right now. Without her, we're *really* up the creek and the damncrocs are closing in."

"Agreed, and it's something I've already considered. But beyond that, my mind is a blank. Suggestions?"

Julian thought about it for a moment, then shrugged.

"Jin," he said. "Temu Jin," he clarified. Gunnery Sergeant Jin, who'd made the entire crossing of the planet with them, had died in the assault on the ship.

"Why Jin?" Roger asked, then he nodded. "Oh. He's got the whole ship wired, doesn't he?"

"He's in the computers," Julian said, nodding in turn in agreement. "You don't have to be on the bridge to tell what the commands are, where the ship is pointed. If Dobrescu can figure out the stellar positions, and where we're supposed to be, then we'll know. And none the wiser."

"So now you want me to be a star-pilot?"

Chief Warrant Officer Mike Dobrescu glowered at the prince in exasperation. Dobrescu liked being a shuttle pilot. It was a damned sight better job than being a Raider medic, which was what he'd been before applying for flight school. And he'd also been damned good at the job. As a chief warrant with thousands of hours of no-accident time, despite surviving several occasions where accidents really had been called for, he'd been accepted as a shuttle pilot for the small fleet that served the Imperial Palace.

Not too shortly afterwards, he'd been loaded aboard the assault ship *Charles DeGlopper* and sent off to support one ne'er-do-well prince. Okay, he could adjust to being back on an assault ship. At least this time he was in officers' country, instead of four to a closet, like the rest of the Marines. And when they got to the planet they were headed to, he'd be flying shuttles again, which he loved.

Lo and behold, though, he'd flown exactly *once* more. One hairy damned ride, with internal hydrogen tanks and a long damned ballistic course, and then landed—damned nearly out of fuel—in a *deadstick* landing on that incomparable pleasure planet, Marduk.

But wait, things got worse! There being no functional shuttles left, and him being the only trained medic, he was stuck back in the Raider medic business, making bricks out of straw. Over the next eight months, he'd been called upon to be doctor, vet, science officer, xenobiologist, herbalist, pharmacologist, and anything *else* that smacked of having two brain cells to rub together. And after all *that*, he'd found out he was a wanted man back home.

It really sucked. But at least he was back to having shuttles under his fingertips, and he was damned if he was going to get shoved into another pigeonhole for which he had no training and less aptitude.

"I cannot astrogate a starship," he said, quietly but very, very definitely. "You don't have to do the equations for it—that's what the damned computers are for—but you do have to *understand* them. And I don't. We're talking high-level calculus, here. Do it wrong, and you end up in the middle of a star."

"I don't want you to *pilot* the ship," Roger said carefully. "I want you to figure out if *Beach* is piloting it to Alphane space. Just that."

"The ship determines its position in reference to a series of known stars every time it reenters normal-space between tunnel jumps," Jin said. "I can find the readouts, but it's a distance estimate to the stars based on something called magnitude—I'm not familiar with most of the terms—and it gives their angles and distance. From that, the astogrator determines where to go next. They tune the tunnel drive for a direction, charge it up, and they go. But without any better understanding of how they establish their starting position in the first place, I can't begin to figure out where we are, or which direction we're going. For that matter, I only vaguely know which direction Old Earth and the Alphane Alliance—or Saint space—*are* from here."

"Turn right at the first star, and straight on till morning," Dobrescu muttered, then shook his head. "I had a course in it—one one-hour course—in flight school, lo these many eons ago. I forgot it as fast as it was thrown at me. You just don't need it for shuttle piloting. We did a little of it on that ballistic to Marduk, but I was given the figures by *DeGlopper*'s astogrator before we punched the shuttles. I don't think I can figure it out. I'm sorry."

"You look sorry," Roger said, shaking his head, and gave another of those one-cheek grins. "Okay, go ask around. I know Julian and Kosutic don't know any of it. Ask the rest of the Marines if any of them even have a clue. Check with *all* of them, because we really, really need a crosscheck on her navigation. I want to trust her, but *how far* is the question."

"Well, until we get to the Alphanes, at least," Julian said.

"Oh?" Roger lifted one eyebrow at the sergeant. "And who, pray tell, is going to pilot the ship from Althar Four to Old Earth?"

"Come!" Roger called, looking up from a hologram of ship's stores with a pronounced sense of relief.

He hated paperwork, although he realized he had to get used to it. His "command" was now the size of a small regiment—or, at least, an outsized battalion—including shipboard personnel and noncombatants, and the administrative workload was one of some magnitude. Some of that, thankfully, could be handled by the computers. It was much easier now that they had all the automated systems up and running. But he still had to keep his finger on the pulse and make sure his subordinates were doing what *he* wanted them to do, not just what *they* wanted to do.

He hadn't realized how much of that Captain Pahner had handled before his death, and eventually, he knew, he'd shuffle much of it off onto someone else. But before he could deputize and delegate any of it, he had to figure out what was important right now, in addition to wracking his brain for every detail of the Imperial Palace he could recall. He knew exactly how essential all of that was, but that didn't make him enjoy it one bit more, and he tipped back his chair with alacrity as the cabin hatch opened.

Julian and Jin stepped through it, followed by Mark St. John, the surviving member of the St. John twins. Mark still shaved the left side of his head, Roger noted with a pang. By now, it was long-ingrained habit, but it had grown out of an early order from a first sergeant who'd been unable to tell the two of them apart.

The twins had been two of the more notable characters of the trek across the planet. They'd maintained a permanent, low-level sibling argument every step of the way—whether it was who Mom liked more, or who'd done what to whom in some bygone day, they'd always found something to argue about. They'd also covered each other's backs, and made sure they got through each encounter alive. Right up until the assault on the ship, that was.

The two of them had had more experience with zero-G combat than anyone else in the company, and they'd found themselves detailed to take out the ship's gun emplacements.

Mark St. John had come back, injured but alive. His brother John, had not.

John had been a sergeant, a hard-working, smart, capable, NCO. Mark had always been more than willing to let his brother do the thinking and mental heavy-lifting. He was a good fighter, and that, as far as he was concerned, was enough. Roger would take any of the surviving Marines at his back in any sort of firefight, or with swords or assegais, come to that. But he wasn't sure he'd trust Mark's brains on a bet. Which was why he was surprised to see him with the other two.

"Should I take it you found an astrogator?" Roger raised one eyebrow and waved at chairs.

"Sir, I'm not an astrogator, but I know stars," St. John said, remaining at a position of parade rest as Jin and Julian sat down.

"Tell me," Roger said, leaning further back.

"Me and John," St. John said, with a swallow. "We was raised on a mining platform. We were shuttling around near the time we started walking. Stars're all you got to go by when you're out in the beyond. And later, we had astrogation in school. Miners don't always have beacon references to go by. I can pilot and steer by stellar location. Give me the basic astro files, and I can figure out where we are, at least. And which way we went to get there. I know the basics of tunnel navigation, and I can read angles."

"We're entering the first jump in—" Roger consulted his computer implant "toot" and frowned. "About thirty minutes. Did Jin show you what he has?"

"Yes, Your Highness. But I only had time to glance at it. I'm not saying I can tell you off the top of my head. But by the time we're ready for the *next* jump, I'll know if we're headed in the right direction."

"And if we're not?" Roger asked.

"Well, I think then some of us should have a talk with Lieutenant Beach, Sir," Julian said. "Hopefully, that talk will be unnecessary."

"Preparing to engage tunnel drive," Beach said. Normally, that announcement would have come from the Astrogator. Since she didn't have one, she was conning the ship from the astrogation station so she could handle it herself.

"Engaging—now," she said, and pressed a button.

The background thrum of the engines rose in key, climbing higher and higher as a rumble sounded through the ship. Roger knew it had to be his imagination, given the meters upon meters of bulkheads and hatches between him and the cargo hold, but he was almost certain he could hear a distant trumpeting.

"Somehow, I'm willing to bet Patty doesn't much care for this bit," he said softly, and Beach gave him a smile that looked slightly strained.

The engine sound rose and entered a period of prolonged high-pitched vibration. Then it passed.

"We're in tunnel-space," Beach said. The external viewscreens had gone blank.

"That didn't sound right, though," Roger observed.

"No, it didn't," Beach sighed. "We'll just have to find out if we come out in the wrong spot. If we do, and if no major damage's been done, we'll be able to compensate on the next jump."

"How many jumps?" Roger asked lightly.

"Eight to the edge of Alphane space," Beach replied. "Two of them right on the edge of Saint territory."

She didn't look particularly happy about that, which didn't surprise Roger a bit. Each of the jumps, which lasted six hours and took the ship eighteen light-years along its projected course, required a standard day and a half of charting and calibration—not to mention charging the superconductor capacitors. In *Emerald Dawn*'s case, just charging the capacitors took a full forty-eight hours, although ships with better power generation, like the huge carriers of the Imperial Navy, could recharge in as little as thirty-six hours. But they all had to recalibrate and chart between jumps, and Beach was the only qualified bridge officer they had to see to it that it was all done properly.

"Fourteen?" Roger repeated with a sour chuckle. "Well, let's hope the drive holds together—especially through the ones close to the Saints. And that we're in *deep* space."

Ships, especially merchant ships on their lonely sojourns, tended to move directly from system to system, as much as possible. They couldn't hyper into any star system inside its Tsukayama Limit, but as long as they popped back into normal-space no more than a few light-days out from their destination, someone would come out and tow them home in no more than a week or so if their TD failed.

Warships, which more often than not traveled in squadrons and fleets, tended to move from deep space point to deep space point. In the *Dawn*'s case, deciding exactly how to plan their course was an unpleasant balancing act. Too far out, and the failure of the tunnel drive—a real possibility, given the cobbled-together nature of their repairs—would maroon them, probably for all time, in the deeps of space. But too close in to a Saint star system, and there was the chance of a Saint cruiser's wandering out to look over the unexpected, unscheduled, and—above all—*unauthorized* tunnel drive footprint which had suddenly appeared on its stellar doorstep.

"I'm in favor of deep space," Beach said with a grimace. "And, yes, let's hope it holds together."

Despreaux stepped onto the bridge and made a crooking gesture at Roger with one finger. Her smile, he noticed, had a definitely malicious edge.

"My advisers tell me it's time to get my game face on," he said to Beach. "So you won't have the pleasure of my company for a while."

"We'll try to manage," Beach said, with a grin of her own.

Roger worked his jaw muscles and stared into the mirror. The face that stared back at him was utterly unfamiliar.

The Saint mod-pods were liquid-filled capsules into which a patient was loaded for body sculpting. They doubled as autodocs, and two of the four *Dawn* carried were still filled with Marine casualties from the assault. Roger had slipped into one of the other two and been hooked to a breathing apparatus. Then, as far as he was concerned, he'd simply gone to sleep . . . until he'd been reawakened in recovery by an unhappy-looking Despreaux.

Her expression hadn't been because of anything wrong with the ship—they'd made the first two tunnel transfers while he was out, and everything was still functioning. It was because of his looks.

The face looking back at him was wider than his "real" face, with high, broad cheekbones and far more pronounced epicanthic folds around eyes which had been transformed into a dark brown. He also had long, black hair, and his hands seemed shorter. They weren't, but they'd become broader in proportion, and he was markedly heavier in the body than he ought to have been. It felt wrong, like in ill-fitting suit.

"Hello, Mr. Chung," he said in someone else's voice. "I see we're going to need a new tailor, as well."

Augustus Chung was a citizen of the United Outer Worlds. The UOW was even older than the Empire of Man, having been a brief competitor for stellar dominance against the old Solarian Union. It still maintained "ownership" of Mars, some of the more habitable of the Sol System's moons, and several outworlds in Sol's vicinity— enough to retain its independence from the Empire and be officially considered the sixth interstellar polity. Its territory, however, was entirely surrounded by Imperial star systems.

The UOW survived mainly because of its value as an area where deals which weren't strictly legal among Imperial worlds could be transacted. And citizens of the UOW did not fall under normal Imperial law. Furthermore, it would be difficult for the Imperials to look up much data on Augustus Chung, because UOW personal data was not readily available to Imperial investigators. In fact, it would take a formal finding of guilt in an Imperial court to pry any information about him out of the UOW. And if things got that far, it wouldn't matter.

Augustus Chung was a businessman. That was what his documents said, anyway—founder, president, and CEO of "Chung

Interstellar Exotic Imports Brokerage, LLC." He'd been a purser on various small merchant vessels before going into the "import/export brokerage" business. His sole fixed business address was a post office box on Mars, and Roger wondered what was in it. Probably stuffed with ads for herbal remedies.

Chung was, in other words, a covert agent identity which had been "stockpiled" by the Saints. In fact, over a hundred such identities were available on the ship, which must've taken considerable work to set up. Given the logistics involved, Chung probably had just enough "reality" to survive a light scrutiny. It was a very nice cover . . . and one the Imperial Bureau of Investigation would recognize as such the instant anything attracted its attention and it ran a real check.

"A *tailor*? Is that all you can say?" Despreaux demanded, looking into the mirror beside him.

"Well, that . . . and that I'm looking forward to seeing what Doc comes up with for *you*," he said. He smiled at her in the mirror, and, after a moment, she smiled back and shrugged.

"All he told me is that I'm going to be a blonde."

"Well, we'll make a pretty pair," Roger replied, turning and feeling his footing, carefully. Chung's body was just as muscular as his normal one and, if anything, a tad more powerful. Higher weight, mostly muscle. Broad chest, heavy pectorals, massive shoulders, flat abdominals. He looked like an underweight sumo wrestler. "Assuming I can find a good tent-maker," he added.

"It looks . . . good." Despreaux shrugged again. "Not you, but . . . good. I can get used to it. He's not as pretty as you are, but he's not exactly ugly."

"Darling, with all due respect, *you're* not the girl I'm worried about."

Roger smiled broadly. It felt strange these days, but Chung was a smiler.

"What?" Despreaux sounded confused.

"Patty is *not* going to like this."

Neither did Dogzard.

The Mardukan dog-lizard was defending the middle of Roger's stateroom, hissing and spitting at the intruder into her master's territory.

"Dogzard, it's me," Roger said, pitching his voice as close to normal as he could.

"Not to her, you're not," Julian said, watching carefully. He'd seen Dogzard rip a full-grown Mardukan to shreds in battle, and he was not at all happy about seeing Roger down on one knee with the dog-lizard in its present state. "You don't even *smell* the same, Boss; entirely different genetic basis on your skin."

"It's me," Roger said again, holding out his hand. "Shoo, *doma fleel*," he added in the language of the X'Intai. It meant something like "little dog," or "puppy." When Roger had picked up the stray in Cord's village, it had been less than a quarter of its current six hundred-kilo size, and the runt of the village.

He continued talking to the dog-lizard in low tones, half in Mardukan, half in Imperial, until he had a hand on her head and was scratching her behind the ears. Dogzard gave a low, hissing whine, then lapped at his arm.

"She is having a moment of existential uncertainty," Cord said, leaning on his spear. "You are acting as if you were her God, but you neither sound nor smell like her God."

"Well, she's going to have to get used to it," Roger replied. Patty had been, if anything, worse. But when he'd climbed onto her back, despite her hissing and spitting, and slapped her on the neck with his sword, she'd gotten the message.

"Okay, Dogzard. That's enough," he added sternly, standing up and waving at the door. "Come on. There's work to do."

The beast looked at him uncertainly, but followed him out of the room. She'd gotten used to life being strange. She didn't always like it, but the good news was that, sooner or later, whenever she followed her God, she eventually got to kill something.

"Despreaux?" Pedi Karuse said.

"Yes?" The tall, blonde sergeant walking down the passage stopped, her expression surprised. "How could you tell?"

"The way you walk," the Shin warrior-maid said, falling in beside her. "It's changed a little, but not much."

"Great," Despreaux said. "I thought all us humans looked alike to you?"

"Not friends," Pedi answered, working her back in discomfort, and eyed the sergeant thoughtfully. "You look as if you were four months pregnant, but on the wrong side. And you lost two of your litter. I'm sorry."

"They're not pregnancy blisters," Despreaux said tightly. "They're tits."

"You had them before, but they were . . . smaller."

"I know."

"And your hair's changed color. It's even lighter than my horns."

"I know."

"And it's longer."

"I know!"

"This is bad?" Pedi asked. "Is this ugly to humans?"

"No," Despreaux said, just a tad absently. She was busy staring hard at one of the passing civilian volunteers . . . who didn't notice for quite some time because he was *not* looking at her eyes. When he did notice, he had the decency to look either ashamed or worried.

"So what's the problem?" Pedi asked as the civilian scurried off a bit more rapidly than he'd appeared.

"Oh . . . damn." Despreaux's nostrils flared, and then she gave her head a brisk shake.

"Okay," she said then, pointing at her chest, "these are like baby *basik* to an *atul*. Men can *not* seem to get enough of them. I was . . . medium to small before. Probably a little too pretty, too, honestly, but I could *work* with that. These, however," her finger jabbed at her chest again, "are *not* medium to small, and the problems I've got now go way beyond 'a little too pretty.' Just getting a guy to look me in the eye is damned hard. And the hair color—! There are *jokes* about girls with this kind of hair. About how stupid they are. I've made them myself, God help me. I had a *fit* when Dobrescu showed me the body profile, but he swore this was the best personality available. The bastard. I look like. . . . God, it's too hard to explain."

Pedi considered this as they walked down the passage, then shrugged.

"Well, there's really only one thing that matters," she finally said.

"What?"

"What Roger thinks of it."

"Oh, good God."

Roger's eyes looked downwards—once—and then fixed resolutely on her face.

"What do you think?" Despreaux asked angrily.

She looked like she could have posed as a centerfold. Long legs were a given, too hard to change. Small hips and waist rising to . . . a really *broad* rib cage and shoulders. Slim neck, *gorgeous* face—if anything, even more beautiful than she had been. Bright, nearly purple eyes. Hair that was probably better than his had been. Nice ears. And—

"Christ, those are *huge*," was what he blurted out.

"They're already killing my back," Despreaux told him.

"It's . . . as good as you were before, just entirely different . . ." Roger said, then paused. "Christ, those are *huge*."

"And all this time I thought you were a leg man," Despreaux said bitingly.

"I'm sorry. I'm *trying* not to look." He shook his head. "They've *gotta* hurt. The whole package is fantastic, though."

"You don't want me to *stay* this way, do you?" Despreaux said desperately.

"Errrr . . ." Roger had grown up with an almost passionate inability to communicate with women, which more than once had landed him in very hot water. And whatever he felt at the moment, he realized this was one of those times when he should be very careful about what he said.

"No," he said finally and firmly. "No, definitely not. For one thing, the package doesn't matter. I fell in love with you for who you are, not what you look like."

"Right." Despreaux chuckled sarcastically. "But the package wasn't bad."

"Not bad," Roger admitted. "Not bad at all. I don't think I would have been nearly as attracted if you'd been severely overweight and out of shape. But I love you for *you*. Whatever package you come in."

"So, you're saying I *should* keep this package?"

Roger started to say no, wondered if he should say yes, and then stopped, shaking his head.

"Is this a 'does this dress make me look fat' thing?"

"No," Despreaux said. "It's an honest question."

"In that case, I like them both," he confessed. "They're totally different, and I like them both. I've always been partial to brunettes, especially leggy ones, so the hair is a wash. But I like a decent-sized chest as much as any straight guy. Those are, honestly, a bit too large." Okay, so it was a little white lie. "On the other hand, whether you marry me or not, your body is *your* body, and I'm not going to tell you—or ask you—to do anything with it. Which do you prefer?"

"Which do you think?" she asked sarcastically.

"It was an honest question," Roger replied calmly.

"My *real* body. Of course. The thing is . . . I guess the question I'd ask if I were trying to trap you is: Does this body make me look fat?"

"No," Roger said, and it was his turn to chuckle. "But you know the old joke, right?"

"No," Despreaux said dangerously. "I *don't* know the old joke."

"How do you get guys to find a kilo of fat attractive?" he said, risking her wrath. She glared at him, and he grinned. "Put a nipple on it. Trust me, you don't look fat. You do look damned good. I suppose I do, too, but I'll be glad to get my old body back. This one feels like I'm maneuvering a grav-tank."

"This one feels like I'm maneuvering two blimps in front of me," she said, and smiled at last. "Okay, when this is over, we go back to our own bodies."

"Agreed. And you marry me."

"No," she said. But she smiled when she said it.

"Mr. Chung," Beach said, nodding as Roger came onto the bridge.

"Captain Beach."

Roger looked at the repeater plot. They were in normal-space, building charge and recalibrating for the next jump. That one would be into the edge of Saint territory.

"So, have you found someone to crosscheck me?" Beach asked an offhand manner.

"Yes," Roger replied, just as offhandedly.

"Good." Beach laughed. "If you hadn't, I would've turned this damned ship around and dropped you back on your miserable mudball planet."

"I'm glad we see eye to eye," Roger said, smiling thinly.

"I don't know if we do or not." Beach gazed at him for a moment, then tossed her head at the hatch. "Let's go to my office."

Roger followed her to her office, which was down the passage from the bridge. It had taken some damage in the assault, but most of that had been repaired. He grabbed a station chair and sat, wondering why it had taken this long for the "conversation" to occur.

"We're fourteen light-years from the edge of what the Saints consider their space," Beach said, sitting down and propping her feet in an open drawer. "We're in deep space. There's exactly one astrogator on this ship: me. So let's be clear that I'm holding all the cards."

"You're holding *many* cards," Roger responded calmly. "But let me be clear, as well. In the last nine months, I've become somewhat less civilized than your standard Imperial nobleman. And I have a very great interest in this mission's success. Becoming totally intransigent at this time would be, at the very least, extraordinarily painful for you. I'd taken you for an ally, not a competitor, although I'm even willing to have a competitor, as long as we can negotiate in good faith. But failure of negotiations will leave you in a position you *really* don't want to occupy."

Beach had raised an eyebrow. Now she lowered it.

"You're serious," she said.

"As a heart attack." Roger's newly brown eyes gave a remarkable imitation of a basilisk's. "But as I said," he continued after a moment, "we can negotiate in good faith. I hope you're an ally, but that remains to be seen. What do you *want*, Captain Beach?"

"Most of what I want, you can't give me. And I was raised in a hard school. If it comes down to force, you're not going to like the results, either."

"Agreed. So what do you want that I *can* give you?"

"What are you going to get from the Alphanes?" Beach countered.

"We don't know," Roger admitted. "It's possible that we'll get a jail cell and a quick trip to Imperial custody. I don't think so, but it's possible. We'll be negotiating, otherwise. Do you want money? We can negotiate you a more than fair fee for your services, assuming all goes well. If we fully succeed, and I believe we will, we'll be freeing my mother, and I'll be Heir Primus to the Throne. The next Emperor of Man. In that case, Captain, the sky is the limit. We *owe* you—*I* owe you. Do you want your own planet?" he finished with a smile.

"You do know how to negotiate, don't you?" Beach smiled in turn.

"Well, I really should be letting Poertena handle it, but you wouldn't like that," Roger told her. "But, seriously, Captain, I do owe you. I fully intend to pay that debt, and since it's an open one, you can draw on it enormously. Right now, I have virtually nothing you could want. Even this ship is going to have to go away—you know that?"

"Oh, yeah. You can't get this thing anywhere *near* Sol. We could only hang around the fringes, where it was easy to bribe the customs officials."

"So we can't give you the ship; we're going to need it to trade to the Alphanes."

"But you're going on to Old Earth?"

"Yes."

"Well . . ." Beach pursed her lips, then shrugged. "What I want, as I said, you can't give me. Now. Maybe ever." She paused and made a wince. "How . . . Who are you going to use as a captain on the Old Earth trip?"

"I don't know. The Alphanes will undoubtedly have at least one . . . discreet captain we can use. But he or she will be one of *their* people. Are you volunteering to captain the ship to Sol? And if so, why?"

"I will want money," Beach said, temporizing. "If you fully succeed, a *lot* of money."

"Done." Roger shrugged. "A billion here, a billion there, and sooner or later, you're talking real money."

"Not *that* much." Beach blanched. "But . . . say . . . five million credits."

"Agreed."

"In a UOW numbered account."

"Agreed."

"And . . ." She made a face and shook her head. "If— What are you going to do about the Caravazans?"

"The Saints?" Roger leaned back in his chair with a tight smile. "Captain, right now we're wondering if we can make it to Alphane territory in one piece! After that, we have the little problem of springing someone from a fortified palace and somehow keeping the Navy from killing us. I'm in no position to discuss *anything* about the Saints, except how we're going to sneak by them."

"But in the long run," Beach said, half-desperately. "If you become Emperor."

"I'm not going to start a unilateral war against the Caravazan Empire, if that's what you mean," Roger replied after a moment. "I have . . . many reasons I don't care for them, but they pale beside the damage such a war would cause." Roger frowned. "What do you have against the Saints? You *were* one."

"*That's* what I have against them," Beach said bitterly. "And so, I will ask this of you. If you see the opportunity, the one thing that I'll ask—screw the money!—the *one* thing that I ask is for you to take them down. All the way. Conquer the whole damned thing and kill the leaders."

"Not all of them," Roger said. "That's not how it's done." He gazed at her for several seconds, his expression almost wondering, and she half-glared unwaveringly back at him.

"So that's the deal, is it?" he asked finally. "For captaining the ship, for turning off the self-destruct, you want me to invade the Caravazan Empire?"

"If the time comes," Beach said. "If the time is right. Please. Don't hesitate. Don't . . . do it by half measures. Take the whole thing. It's the *right* thing to do. That place is a cesspool, a pit. Nobody should have to live under the Saints. Please."

Roger leaned back and steepled his fingers for a moment, then nodded.

"If we succeed, if I become Emperor, *if* war comes with the Saints—and I won't go looking for it, mind you—then I will do everything in my power to ensure that it's a war to the knife. That not one member of the Saint leadership is left in power over so much as a single planet. That their entire empire is either transferred to a more rational form of government, or else absorbed by the Empire of Man or other less irrational polities. Something close to that anyway. As close as I can get it. Does that satisfy you, Captain?"

"Entirely." Beach's voice was hoarse, and her eyes glittered with unshed tears. "And I'll do whatever you need done to ensure that day comes. I swear."

"Good," Roger said, and smiled. "I'm glad I didn't have to break out the thumbscrews."

"Hey, 'Shara," Sergeant Major Kosutic said, sticking her head into Despreaux's stateroom. "Come on. We need to talk."

Kosutic was a blonde now, too, if not nearly as spectacularly so as Despreaux. She was also her regular height, with equally short hair, and a more modest bosom. She was stockier than she had been—she looked like a female weightlifter, which was more or less how she'd looked before, actually—but her stride was a little more . . . feminine, now. Something about the wider hips, Despreaux suspected. The transformation hadn't changed her pelvic bones, but it had added muscle to either side.

"What does Julian think of the new look?" Despreaux asked.

"You mean 'Tom?'" the sergeant major said in tones of minor disapproval. "Probably about what Roger thinks of yours. But 'Tom' didn't get the big bazoombas. I've detected just a hint of jealousy about that."

"What is it with men and blonde hair and boobs?" Despreaux demanded angrily.

"Satan, girl, you really want to know?" Kosutic laughed. "Seriously, the theories are divergent and bizarre enough to keep conspiracy theorists babbling happily away to themselves for decades. 'Mommy' fixation was an early one—that men want to go back to breast-feeding. It didn't last long, but it was popular in its time. My personal favorite has to do with the difference between chimps and humans."

"What do *chimps* have to do with anything?"

"Well, the DNA of chimps and humans is really close. Effectively, humans are just an offshoot of chimpanzee. Even after all the minor mutations that have crept in since going off-planet, humans still have less variability than chimps, and on a DNA chart we just fall in as a rather minor modification."

"I didn't know that," Despreaux said. "Why do you?"

"Face it, the Church of Armagh has to make it up as we go along." Kosutic shrugged. "Understanding the real *why* of people makes it much easier. Take boobs."

"Please!" Despreaux said.

"Agreed." Kosutic smiled. "Chimps don't have them. Humans are, in fact, the only terrestrial animal with truly pronounced mammary glands. Look at a cow—those impressive udders are almost all functional, milk producing plumbing. Tits? Ha! Their . . . visual cue aspect, shall we say, has nothing to do with milk production per se. That means there's some other reason for them in our evolutionary history, and one theory is that they developed purely to keep the male around. Human females don't show signs of their fertility, and human children take a long time, relatively speaking, to reach maturity. Having a male around all the time helped early human and prehuman females with raising the children. The males probably brought in some food, but their primary purpose was defending territory so that there was food to be brought in. In addition, human females are also one of the few species to orgasm—"

"If we're lucky," Despreaux observed.

"You want to hear this, or not?"

"Sorry. Go ahead."

"So, that was a reason for the female to not be too upset when the male was always having a good time with her. And it was another reason for men to stick around. Tits were a visual sign that said: 'Screw me and stick around and defend this territory.' Can't be proven, of course, but it fits with all the reactions males have to them."

"Yeah," Despreaux said sourly. "*All* the reactions. They're still a pain in the . . . back."

"Sure, and they're effectively as useful as a vermiform appendix these days," the sergeant major said. "On the other hand, they're still great for making guys stupid. And *that* is what we're going to talk about."

"Oh?" Despreaux's tone became decidedly wary. They'd reached the sergeant major's stateroom, and she was surprised to see Eleanora waiting for them. The chief of staff had been modded as well and was now a rather skinny redhead.

"Oh," Kosutic confirmed. She closed the hatch and waved Despreaux onto the folded-down bed next to Eleanora, who looked at her with an expression which mingled thoughtfulness and determination with something Despreaux wasn't at all sure she wanted to see.

"Nimashet, I'm going to be blunt," the chief of staff said after a moment. "You have to marry Roger."

"No." The sergeant stood back up quickly, eyes flashing. "If this is what you wanted to talk about, you can—"

"Sit down, Sergeant," Kosutic said sharply.

"You'd *better* not use my *rank* when talking about something like this, *Sergeant Major!*" Despreaux snapped back angrily.

"I will when it affects the security of the Empire," Kosutic replied icily. "Sit. Down. Now."

Despreaux sat, glaring at the senior NCO.

"I'm going to lay this out very carefully," Eleanora told her. "And you're going to listen. Then we'll discuss it. But hear me out, first."

Despreaux shifted her glower to the chief of staff. But she also crossed her arms—carefully, given certain recent changes—and sat back stiffly on the bed.

"Some of this only holds—or matters—if we succeed," Eleanora said. "And some of it is immediately pertinent to our hope of possibly pulling off the mission in the first place. The first point is for everything—current mission and long-term consideration, alike. And that point is that Roger literally has the weight of the Empire on his shoulders right now. And he loves you. And I think you love him. And he's eaten up by the thought of losing you, which raises all sorts of scary possibilities."

Desperaux's surprise must have shown, because the chief of staff grimaced and waved one hand in the air.

"If he *fails*," she said, "if we go with the government-in-exile program and he becomes just some guy who was *almost* Emperor, you'd marry him, wouldn't you?"

Desperaux looked at her stony-eyed for two or three heartbeats, then sighed.

"Yes," she admitted. "Shit. I'd do it in a second if he was 'just some guy.' And I'm setting him up *to* fail so I can do just that, aren't I?"

"You're setting him up to fail," Eleanora agreed with a nod. "Not to mention contributing to the mental anguish he's in right now. Not that I think for a moment that you've been doing either of those things intentionally, of course. You're not manipulative enough for your own good, sometimes, and you certainly don't think *that* way. But the effect is the same, whether it's intentional or not. Right now, he has to be wondering, in the deeps of the night, if being Emperor— which he knows he's going to loathe—is really worth losing *you*. I presented the alternate exile plan because I thought it was a good plan, one that should be looked at as an alternative. It was Julian and the sergeant major who pointed out, afterwards, the *consequences* of the plan. Do you *want* Prince Jackson on the throne? Or a six-way war, more likely?"

"No," Despreaux said in a low voice. "God, what that would do to Midgard!"

"Exactly," Kosutic said. "And to half a hundred other worlds. If Adoula takes the Throne, all the out-worlds are going to be nothing but sources of material and manpower—cannon fodder—he and his cronies will bleed dry. If they don't get nuked in passing during the wars."

"So he has the weight of the Empire on his shoulders," Eleanora repeated, "and he's losing you. And there's a bolt-hole that he can go to that gets both of those problems off his back. It happens that that bolt-hole would mean very bad things for the Empire, but men aren't rational about women."

"That's another thing I can lay out in black and white," Kosutic said. "Lots of studies about it. Long-term rational planning drops off the chart when men are thinking about women. It's how they're wired. Of course, *we're* not all that rational about *them* sometimes, either,"

"Now, let's talk about what happens if we succeed," Eleanora went on gently and calmly. "Roger is going to end up Emperor— probably sooner than he expects. I don't know how bad the residual effects of whatever drugs they're using on his mother are going to be, but I do know they're not going to be good. And after what's going on right now gets out, the public's confidence in her fitness to rule is bound to drop. If the drugs' effects are noticeable, it will drop even more. Nimashet, Roger could well find himself on the Throne within a year or less, if we pull this thing off."

"Oh, God," Despreaux said quietly. Her arms were no longer crossed, and her fingers twisted about one another in her lap. "God, he'll really hate that."

"Yes, he will. But there's much worse," Eleanora said. "People are neither fully products of their genetics, nor of their experiences, but . . . traumatic experiences can . . . adjust their personalities in various ways. And especially when they're still fairly young and unformed. Fairly young. Roger is *fairly* young, and, quite frankly, he was also fairly *unformed* when we landed on Marduk. I don't think anyone would be stupid enough to call him 'unformed' now, but the mold in which he's been shaped was our march halfway around Marduk. Effectively, Roger MacClintock's done virtually all of his 'growing up' in the course of *eight months* of constant, brutal combat ops without relief. Think about that.

"More than once, he's ended serious political negotiations by simply shooting the people he was negotiating with. Of course they were negotiating in bad faith when he did it. He never had a choice.

But it's become . . . something of a habit. So has destroying any obstacle that got in his path. Again, because he didn't have a choice. Because they were obstacles he couldn't deal with any other way, and because so much depended on their being dealt with effectively . . . and permanently. But what that means is that he has . . . very few experiential reasons to *not* use every available scrap of firepower to remove any problems that arise. And if we succeed, this young man is going to be Emperor.

"There will probably be a civil war, no matter what we do. In fact, I'll virtually guarantee that there'll be one. The pressures were right for one—building nicely to one, anyway—when we left Old Earth, and things obviously haven't gotten any better. What with the problems at home, I'd be surprised if a rather large war doesn't break out—soon—and if it does, a man who has vast experience in killing people to accomplish what he considers are necessary goals is going to be sitting on the Throne of Man. I want you to think about *that* for a moment, too."

"Not good," Despreaux said, licking her lips.

"Not good at all," Eleanora agreed. "His advisers," she added, touching her own chest, "can mitigate his tendency to violence, to a degree. But only if he's amenable. The bottom line is that the Emperor can usually get what he wants, one way or another. If he doesn't like our advice, for example, he could simply fire us."

"Roger . . . wouldn't do that," Despreaux said positively. "No one who was on the March is ever going to be anyone he would fire. Or not listen to. He might not take the advice, though."

"And the armed forces swear an oath to the Constitution *and* the Emperor. He's their commander-in-chief. He can do quite a bit of fighting even without any declaration of war, and if we manage to succeed in this . . . this—"

"This forlorn hope," Kosutic supplied.

"Yes." The chief of staff smiled thinly, recognizing the ancient military term for a small body of troops sent out with even smaller hope of success. "If we succeed in this *forlorn hope*, there's automatically going to be a state of emergency. If a civil war breaks out, the Constitution equally automatically restricts citizens' rights and increases the power of the sitting head of state. We could end up with . . . Roger, in his present mental incarnation, holding as much power as any other person in the history of the human race."

"You sound like he's some bloody-handed murderer!" Despreaux shook her head. "He's not. He's a *good* man. You make him sound like one of the Dagger Lords!"

"He's not that," Kosutic said. "But what he is is damned near a reincarnation of Miranda MacClintock. She happened to be a political philosopher with a strongly developed sense of responsibility and duty, which, I agree, Roger also has. But if you remember your history, she also took *down* the Dagger Lords by being a bloody-minded bitch at least as ruthless as *they* were."

"What he is, effectively," Eleanora continued in that same gentle voice, "is a neobarbarian tyrant. A 'good' tyrant, perhaps, and as charismatic as hell—maybe even on the order of an Alexander the Great—but still a tyrant. And if he can't break out of the mold, putting him on the Throne will be as bad for the Empire as disintegration."

"What's your point?" Despreaux demanded harshly.

"You," Kosutic said. "When you joined the Regiment, when I was interviewing you on in-process, I damned near blackballed you."

"You never told me that." Despreaux frowned at the sergeant major. "Why?"

"You'd passed all the psychological tests," Kosutic replied with a shrug. "You'd passed RIP, although not with flying colors. We knew you were loyal. We knew you were a good guard. But there was something missing, something I couldn't quite put a finger on. I called it 'hardness,' at the time, but that's not it. You're damned hard."

"No," Despreaux said. "I'm not. You were right."

"Maybe. But hardness was still the wrong word." Kosutic frowned. "You've always done your job. Even when you lost the edge and couldn't fight anymore, you contributed and sweated right along with the rest of us. You're just not . . ."

"Vicious," Despreaux said. "I'm not a killer."

"No." Kosutic nodded in acknowledgment. "And I sensed that.

That was what made me want to blackball you. But in the end, I didn't."

"Maybe you should have."

"Bullshit. You did your job—more than your job. You made it, and you're the key to what we need. So quit whining, soldier."

"Yes, Sergeant Major." Despreaux managed a fleeting smile, though it was plain her heart wasn't in it. "On the other hand, if you *had* blackballed me, I would have avoided our little pleasure stroll."

"And you could never be Empress," Eleanora said.

Despreaux's new indigo eyes snapped back to the chief of staff, dark with dread, and Eleanora put a hand on her knee.

"Listen to me, Nimashet. What you are is something the opposite of vicious. I'd call it 'nurturing,' but that's not really right, either. You're as tough-minded and obstinate—most ways—as anyone, even Roger. Or can you think of anyone else in our happy little band who could argue him to a standstill once he gets the bit truly between his teeth?"

Eleanora looked into her eyes until Despreaux's innate honesty forced her to shake her head, then continued.

"But whatever it is we ought to be calling you, the *point* is that with you by Roger's side, he's calmer. Less prone to simply lash out and much more prone to think things through. And that's *important*—important to the Empire."

"I don't *want* to be Empress," Despreaux said desperately.

"Satan, girl," Kosutic laughed. "I *understand*, but listen to what you just said!"

"I'm a country girl," Despreaux protested. "A sod-buster from Midgard! I'm no good, never have been, at the sort of petty, backbiting infighting that goes on at Court." She shook her head. "I don't have the right mindset for it."

"So? How many people do, to start with?" Kosutic demanded.

"A hell of a lot more of them at Court than there are of me!" Despreaux shot back, then shook her head again, almost convulsively. "I don't know how to be a noblewoman, much less a fucking *Empress*, and if I try, I'll fuck it up. Don't you understand?" She looked back and forth between them, her eyes darker than ever. "If I try to do the job, I'll blow it. I'll be out of my league. I'll do the wrong thing, *say* the wrong thing at the wrong time, give Roger the wrong piece of advice—something! And when I do, the entire Empire will get screwed because of *me!*"

"You think Roger isn't thinking exactly the same thing?" Kosutic challenged more gently. "Satan, Nimashet! He has to wake up every single morning with the piss scared out of him just *thinking* about the job in front of him."

"But at least he grew up knowing it was coming. He's got the background, the training for it. I don't!"

"Training?" Eleanora flicked one hand in a dismissive gesture. "To be *Emperor?*" She snorted. "Until Jin told us what's been happening on Old Earth, it never even crossed his mind once that *he* might ever be Emperor, Nimashet! And, frankly, his mother's distrust of him meant that everyone, myself included, was always very careful to never, ever suggest the possibility to him. To be honest, it's only recently occurred to me how much that may have contributed to his refusal—or failure—to recognize the fact that he truly did stand close to the succession."

She shook her head again, her eyes sad as she thought of how dreadfully her one-time charge's life had changed, then looked back at Despreaux.

"Admittedly, he grew up in Court circles, and he may have more training for that than you do, but trust me, he didn't begin to have enough of it before our little jaunt. I know; *I* was the one who was supposed to be giving him that training, and I wasn't having a lot of success.

"But he's been much more strongly . . . motivated in that regard recently, and you can be, too. You've seen how much he's grown in the last half-year, probably better than anyone else besides me and Armand Pahner. But nobody's *born* with that 'mindset'; they learn it, just like Roger has, and you've already pretty conclusively demonstrated your ability to master combat techniques. This is just one more set of combat skills. And, remember, if we succeed, you're going to be *Empress*. It's going to take either a very stupid individual, or a very dangerous one, to cross you."

"Our kids would be raised in a cage!"

"All children are," Eleanora countered. "It's why no sane adult would ever really want to be a child again. But your kids' cage would be the best protected one in the galaxy."

"Tell that to John's kids!" Despreaux exploded. "When I think about—"

"When you think about the kids who just up and disappear every year," Kosutic said. "Or end up a body in a ditch. Or raped by their uncle, or their dad's best friend. Think about that, instead. That's one thing you'll never have to worry about, not with three thousand hard bastards watching anyone that comes near them like rottweilers. Every parent worries about her child; that comes with the job. But *your* kids are going to have three thousand of the most dangerous baby-sitters—and you know that's what we are—in the known galaxy.

"Sure, they got to John and his kids. But they did it by killing the *entire* Empress' Own, Nimashet. Every mother-loving one of them. In case you hadn't noticed, there are exactly *twelve* of us left in the entire frigging Galaxy, because the *only* way they could get to the kids, or John, or the Empress was over *us*—over our dead bodies, stacked in front of the goddamned door! And there's been one—count 'em, *one*—successful attack on the Imperial Family in five hundred fucking years! Don't tell me your kids wouldn't be '*safe*'!"

The sergeant major glared at her, and, after a moment, Despreaux's gaze fell.

"I don't want to be Empress," she repeated, quietly but stubbornly. "I swore to him that I wouldn't marry him if he was going to be Emperor. What would I be if I took that back?"

"A woman." Kosutic grinned. "Didn't you know we're allowed to change our minds at random? It comes with the tits."

"Thanks very much," Despreaux said bitingly, and folded her arms again. Her shoulders hunched. "I don't want to be Empress."

"Maybe not," Eleanora said. "But you do want to marry Roger. You want to have his children. You want to keep a bloody-minded tyrant off the Throne, and he'll be far less bloody-minded if he wants to keep your approval in mind. The *only* thing you don't want is to be Empress."

"That's a pretty big 'only,'" Despreaux pointed out.

"What you want is really beside the point," Kosutic said. "The only thing that matters is what's good for the Empire. I don't care if you consider every day of the rest of your life a living sacrifice to the Empire. You swore the oath; you took the pay."

"And this was *never* part of the job specs!" Despreaux shot back angrily.

"Then consider it very unusual duties, if you have to!" Kosutic said, just as angrily.

"Calm down—both of you!" Eleanora said sharply. She looked back and forth between them, then focused on Despreaux. "Nimashet, just think about it. You don't have to say yes now. But for God's sake, think about what refusing to marry Roger will mean. To all of us. To the Empire. To your home planet. Hell, to every polity in the galaxy."

"A person's conscience is her own," Despreaux said stubbornly.

"Heaven's bells, if it is," Kosutic said caustically. "We spend most of our lives doing things because we know they're the right things to do in other people's eyes. Especially the eyes of people we care about. It's what makes us human. If he loses you, he'll do anything he pleases. He knows most of *us* won't give a damn. If he told us to round up every left-handed redhead and put them in ovens, I would, because he's Roger. If he told Julian to go nuke a planet, Julian would. Because he's *Roger*. And even if we wouldn't, he'd find someone else who would—for power, or because he has the legal authority to order them to, or because they *want* to do the deed. The only person who could have kept him under control was Pahner, and Pahner's dead, girl. The only one *left* that he's going to look to for . . . conscience is you.

"I'm not saying he's a *bad* man, Nimashet—we're all agreed on that. I'm just telling you that he's in one Heaven of a spot, with nothing anywhere he can look but more boots coming down on the people the Emperor is responsible for protecting. Just like he was responsible for *us* on Marduk. And do you think for one moment that he wouldn't have killed every other living thing on that planet to keep us alive?"

She half-glared into Despreaux's eyes, daring her to look away, and finally, after a small, tense eternity, the younger woman shook her head slowly.

"Eleanora's spelled it out," Kosutic continued in a softer voice. "He's learned a set of responses that *work*. And he's learned about responsibility, learned the hard way. He'll do *anything* to discharge that responsibility, and once he starts down the slope of expediency, each additional step will get easier and easier to take. Unless someone gets in the way. Someone who prevents him from taking those steps, because his responsibility to her—to be the person *she* demands he be—is as powerful a motivator as his responsibility to all the rest of the universe combined. And that person is you. You're it, girlie. You leave, and there's nothing between him and the universe but the mind of a wolf."

Despreaux bowed her head into her hands and shook it from side to side.

"I *really* don't want to be Empress," she said. "And what about dynastic marriages?" she added from behind her hands.

"On a scale of one to ten, with your stabilizing effect on him at ten, the importance of holding out for a dynastic marriage rates about a minus sixty," Eleanora said dryly. "Externally, it's a moot point. Most of the other human polities don't have our system, or else they're so minor that they're not going to get married to the Emperor, anyway. Internally, pretty much the same. There are a few members of the Court who might think otherwise, but most of them are going to be shuffled out along with Adoula. I have a list, and they never will be missed."

"But that does bring up another point you might want to consider," Kosutic said.

Despreaux raised her head to look at the sergeant major once more, eyes wary, and the Armaghan smiled crookedly.

"Let's grant that with the shit storm coming down on the galaxy, or at least the Empire, there might even be some advantages to having a wolf on the Throne. Somebody the historians will tag 'the Terrible.' At least we know damned well that he'll do whatever needs doing, and I think we're all pretty much agreed he'll do it for the right reasons, however terrible it is. But someday, one of his *children* is going to inherit the Throne. Just who's going to raise that kid, Sergeant? One of those backbiting, infighting Court bitches you don't want to tangle with? What's the *kid's* judgment going to be like, growing up with a daddy smashing anything that gets in his way and a mommy who's only interested in power and its perks?"

"A point," Eleanora seconded, "albeit a more long-ranged one." It was her turn to gaze into Despreaux's eyes for a moment, then she shrugged. "Still, it's one you want to add to the list when you start thinking about it."

"All right." Despreaux raised a hand to forestall anything more from Kosutic. "I'll think about it. I'll *think* about it," she repeated. "Just that."

"Fine," Eleanora said. "I'll add just one more thing."

"What now?" Despreaux asked tiredly.

"Do you love Roger?"

The soft question hovered in Kosutic's stateroom, and Despreaux looked down at the hands which had somehow clasped themselves back together in her lap.

"Yes," she replied, after a long moment. "Yes, I do."

"Then think about this. The pressure of being Emperor is *enormous*. It's driven more than one person mad, and if you leave, you'll be leaving a man you love to face that pressure, all alone. As his wife, you can help. Yes, he'll have counselors, but at the end of the day it will be *you* who'll keep that strain from becoming unbearable."

"And what about the pressure on the Empress?" Despreaux asked. "His prosthetic conscience?"

"Roger's sacrifice is his entire life." Kosutic told her softly. "And yours? Yours is watching the man you love *make* that sacrifice . . . and marching every meter of the way right alongside him. That's *your* true sacrifice, Nimashet Despreaux. Just as surely as you would have been sacrificed on that altar in Krath, if Roger hadn't prevented it."

"This takes some getting used to."

Julian fingered his chin. His hair was light brown, instead of black, and his chin was much more rounded. Other than that, he had generally European features, instead of the slightly Mediterranean ones he'd been born with.

"Every day," Roger agreed, looking over at Temu Jin, the only human aboard *Dawn* who hadn't been modified. The IBI agent had perfectly legitimate papers showing that he'd been discharged from his post on Marduk, with good references, and now was taking a somewhat roundabout route back to Old Earth.

"Where are we?" Roger asked.

"One more jump, and we'll be at Torallo," Jin said. "That's the waypoint the Saints normally use. The customs there have an understanding with them."

"That's pretty unusual for the Alphanes," Roger observed.

"One of the things we're going to point out to them," Julian replied. "It's not the only point where they've got some border security issues, either. Not nearly as bad as the Empire's problems, maybe, but they're going to be surprised to find out that they have *any*."

"Is the 'understanding' with humans?" Roger asked.

"Some humans, yes," Jin said. "But the post commander and others who have to be aware are Althari."

"I thought they were incorruptible," Roger said with a frown.

"So, apparently, do the Altharis," Jin replied. "They're not, and neither are Phaenurs. Trust me, I've seen the classified reports. I'm going to have to avoid that particular point, and thank Ghu I don't have any names of our agents. But we *have* agents among both the Altharis and the Phaenurs. Let's not go around making that obvious, though."

"I won't," Roger said. "But while we go around not making that obvious, what else happens?"

"Our initial cover is that we're entertainers, a traveling circus, to explain all the critters in the holds," Julian said. "We'll travel to Althar Four and then make contact. How we do that is going to have to wait until we arrive."

"Aren't the Phaenurs there going to . . . sense that we're lying?"

"Yes, they will," Jin said. "Which is going to be what has to wait. We have no contacts. We have to play this entirely by ear."

★ ★ ★

The Alphanes were everything they'd been described as being.

The Althari security officer at the transfer station—a male—wasn't as tall as a Mardukan, but he was at least twice as broad, not to mention being covered in long fur that was silky looking and striped along the sides. The Phaenur standing beside him was much smaller, so small it looked like some sort of pet that should be sitting on the Althari's shoulder. But it was the senior of the two.

The entry into Alphane space had been smooth. Although *Emerald Dawn* had visited Torallo several times, the Saint-friendly customs officials at Torallo had scarcely glanced at her papers, despite the fact that they now identified her as the Imperial freighter *Sheridan's Pride*. They'd simply taken their customary cut, and the ship had proceeded onward with nothing but a cursory inspection that didn't even note the obvious combat damage.

Two jumps later, at the capital system of the Alphane Alliance, the same could not be said. Docking had been smooth, and they'd presented their quarantine and entry passes to the official, a human, sent aboard to collect them. But after that, they'd been confined to the ship for two nerve-wracking hours until "Mr. Chung" was summoned to speak to some "senior customs officials."

They were meeting in the loading bay of the transfer station, a space station set out near the Tsukayama Limit of the G-class star of Althar. It looked like just about every other loading bay Roger had ever seen, scuffed along the sides and floor, marked with warning signs in multiple languages. The big difference was the reception committee which, besides the two "senior customs officials" included a group of Althari guards in combat armor.

"Mr. Chung," the Althari said. "You do not know much of the Althari, do you?"

"I know quite a lot, in fact," Roger replied.

"One of the things you apparently don't know is that we take our security very seriously," the Althari continued, ignoring his response. "And that we do not let people lie to us. Your name is not Augustus Chung."

"No, it's not. Nor is this ship the *Sheridan's Pride*."

"Who are you?" the Althari demanded dangerously.

"I can't tell you." Roger raised a hand to forestall any reply. "You don't have the need to know. But I need—*you* need—for me to speak to someone in your government on a policy level, and you need for that conversation to be very secure."

"Truth," the Phaenur said in a sibilant hiss. "Absolute belief."

"Why?" the Althari asked, attention still focused on Roger.

"Again, you don't have the need to know," Roger replied. "We shouldn't even be having this conversation in front of your troops, because one of the things I *can* tell you is that you have security penetrations. And time is very short. Well, it's important to me for us to get to the next level quickly, and it's of some importance to the Alphane Alliance. How much is up to someone well above your pay grade. Sorry."

The Althari looked at the Phaenur, who made an odd head jab.

"Truth again," the lizardlike alien said to its partner, then looked back at Roger. "We need to contact our supervisors," it said. "Please return to your ship for the time being. Do you have any immediate needs?"

"Not really," Roger said. "Except for some repairs. And they're not that important; we're not planning on leaving in this ship."

"Mr. Chung," Despreaux said, cutting her image into the hologram of the Imperial Palace Roger and Eleanora O'Casey had been studying. "Phaenur Srall wishes to speak to you."

The hologram dissolved into the face of a Phaenur. Roger wasn't certain if it was the same one he'd been speaking to. They hadn't been introduced, and they all looked the same to him.

"Mr. Chung," the Phaenur said, "your ship is cleared to move to Station Five. You will proceed there by the marked route. Any deviation from the prescribed course will cause your vessel to be fired upon by system defense units. You mentioned a need for repairs; is your vessel capable of making that trip without them?"

"Yes," Roger said, smiling. "We'd just have a hard time getting out of the system."

"Any attempt to approach the Tsukayama Limit will also cause your vessel to be fired upon," the Phaenur warned. "You will be met by senior representatives of my government."

The screen cut off.

"Not much given to pleasantries, are they?" Roger said.

"Not if they don't like you," Eleanora replied. "They know it ticks us off. They can be very unsubtle about things like that."

"Well, we'll just have to see how subtle we can convince them to be."

Roger stood at the head of the wardroom table as the Alphane delegation filed in. There was a Phaenur who, again, was in charge, two Altharis, and a human. One of the Altharis was a guard—a hulking brute in unpowered combat armor who took up a position against the rear bulkhead. The other wore an officer's undress harness with the four planetary clusters of a fleet admiral.

Roger's staff was gathered around the table, and as the visiting threesome sat, he waved the others to their chairs. This time Honal was missing; his out-sized seat was taken by the Althari admiral.

"I am Sreeetoth," the Phaenur said. "I am head of customs enforcement for the Alphane Alliance, which is just below a Cabinet position. As such, I am as close to a 'policymaker' as you are going to see without more information. My companions are Admiral Tchock Ral, commander of the Althari Home Fleet, and Mr. Mordas Dren, chief of engineering for the Althar System. Now, who are you? Truthfully."

"I am Prince Roger Ramius Sergei Alexander Chiang MacClintock," Roger answered formally. "For the last ten months, I have been on the planet Marduk or in transit to this star system, and I had nothing to do with any coup. My mother is being held captive, and I've come to you for help."

The human rocked back in his chair, staring around at the group in wild surmise. The Althari looked . . . unreadable. Sreeetoth cocked its head in an oddly insectlike fashion and looked around the compartment.

"Truth. All of it is truth," the Phaenur said after a moment.

"Apprehension, fear so thick you could cut it with a blade . . . except off the Mardukans and the Prince. And great need. Great need."

"And why, in your wildest dreams, do you believe we might put our necks on the block for you?" the Althari rumbled in a subterranean-deep voice.

"For several reasons," Roger said. "First, we have information you need. Second, if we succeed in throwing out the usurpers who are using my mother as a puppet, your Alliance will be owed a debt by my House that it can draw upon to the limit. And third, the Alphane require truth. We will give you the truth. You'll find it hard to get one gram of it from anyone associated with Adoula."

"Again, truth," the Phaenur said. "Some quibbling about the debt, but I expect that's a simple matter of recognizing that the needs of his empire may overrule his own desires. But I'm still not sure we'll choose to aid you, Prince Roger. You seek to overthrow your government?"

"No. To restore it; it's already been overthrown . . . to an extent. As things stand at this moment, Adoula is still constrained by our laws and Constitution. For the time being . . . but not for long. We believe we have until the birth of the child being gestated to save my mother; after that, she'll be an impediment to Adoula's plans. So she'll undoubtedly name him Prime Minister and he or the Earl of New Madrid—" Roger's voice never wavered, despite the hardness in his eyes as he spoke his father's title "—will be named Regent for the child. And then she'll die . . . and Adoula's coup will be complete."

"That is *all* surmise," Sreeetoth said.

"Yes," Roger acknowledged. "But it's valid surmise. Mother would never ally herself with Adoula, and I was *definitely* not involved in the coup. In fact, I was totally incommunicado when it occurred. She also hates and reviles my biological father . . . who's now at her side at all times, and who is the biological father of her unborn child, as well. Given all that, psychological control is the only reasonable answer. Agreed?"

"You believe it to be," the Phaenur said. "And I agree that the logic is internally valid. That doesn't prove it, but—"

"It is true," Tchock Ral rumbled. "We are aware of it."

"I'm in way over my head," Mordas Dren said fervently. "I know you guys thought you needed a human in the room, but this is so far out of my league I wish I could have a brain scrub and wash it out. Jesus!" His face worked for a moment, and he squeezed his eyes shut. "Adoula is a snake. His fingers are in every corporation that's trying to kick in our doors. Him as Emperor . . . That's what you're talking about, right?"

"Eventually," Roger said. "What's worse, we don't think it will work. More likely, the Empire will break up into competing factions. And without the Empress to stabilize it . . ."

"And this would be bad how?" the Althari admiral asked. Then she twitched her massive head in a human-style shake. "No. I agree, it would be bad. The Saints would snap up territory, increasing their already formidable resource base. If they managed to get some of your Navy, as well, we'd be looking at heavy defense commitments on *another* border. And it's my professional opinion that the Empire would indeed break up. In which case, chaos is too small a word."

"The effect on trade would be . . . suboptimal," Sreeetoth said. "But if you try to place your mother back upon the Throne and fail, the results will be the same. Or possibly even worse."

"Not . . . exactly." Roger looked back and forth between the three Alphane representatives. "If we try and fail, and are discovered to be who we are, then Adoula's tracks are fully covered. Obviously, it was me all along, in which case, he'd be much more likely to be able to hold things together. The reputation of House MacClintock would be severely damaged, and that reputation would have been one of the things that stood against him. If I'm formally saddled with responsibility for everything, he'll actually be in a better position to supplant my House in terms of legitimacy and public support."

"Only if no word of where you *really* were at the time of the initial coup attempt ever gets out," the Phaenur pointed out.

"Yes."

Tchock Ral leaned forward and looked at Roger for a long time.

"You are telling us that if you fail, you intend to cover up the fact that you are *not* guilty of staging the first coup?" the Althari said. "That you would stain the reputation of your House for all time, rather than let that information be exposed."

"Yes," Roger repeated. "Letting it out would shatter the Empire. I would rather that my House, with a thousand years of honorable service to mankind, be remembered only for my infamy, than allow that to happen. Furthermore, your Alliance—you three individuals, and whoever else is let in on the secret—will have to hold it, if not forever, then for a very long time. Otherwise . . ."

"Chaos on the border," Dren said. "Jesus Christ, Your Highness."

"I asked for senior policymakers," Roger said, shrugging at the engineer. "Welcome to the jungle."

"How will you conceal the truth?" Sreeetoth asked. "If you're captured? Some of you, no matter what happens, *will* be captured if you fail."

"It would require a concerted effort to get the information out in any form that would be believed, past the security screen Adoula will throw up if we fail," Roger captured. "We'll simply avoid the concerted effort."

"And your people?" the Althari asked, gesturing at the staff. "You actually trust them to follow this insane order?"

Roger flexed a jaw muscle, and was rewarded by a heel landing on either foot. Despreaux's came down quite a bit harder than O'Casey's, but they landed virtually simultaneously. He closed his eyes and breathed for a moment, then reached back and pulled every strand of hair into line.

"Admiral Tchock Ral," he said, looking the Althari in the eye. "You are a warrior, yes?"

Eleanora was too experienced a diplomat to wince; Despreaux and Julian weren't.

"Yes," the admiral growled. "Be aware, human, that even asking that question is an insult."

"Admiral," Roger said levelly, meeting her anger glare for glare, "compared to the lowest ranking Marine I've got, you don't know the meaning of the word."

The enormous Althari came up out of her chair with a snarl like crumbling granite boulders, and the guard in the corner straightened. But Roger just pointed a finger at Sreeetoth.

"Tell her!" he snapped, and the Phaenur jabbed one hand in an abrupt, imperative gesture that cut off the Althari's furious response like a guillotine.

"Truth," it hissed. "Truth, and a belief in that truth so strong it is like a fire in the room."

The lizardlike being turned fully to the bearlike Althari and waved the same small hand at its far larger companion.

"Sit, Tchock Ral. Sit. The Prince burns with the truth. His — soldiers—even the woman who hates to be one—all of them burn with the truth of that statement." It looked back at Roger. "You tread a dangerous path, human. Altharis have been known to go what you call berserk at that sort of insult."

"It wasn't an insult," Roger said. He looked at the trio of visitors steadily. "Would you like to know why it wasn't?"

"Yes," the Phaenur said. "And I think that Tchock Ral's desire to know burns even more strongly than my own."

"It's going to take a while."

In fact, it took a bit over four hours.

Roger had never really sat down and told the story, even to himself, until they'd worked out the presentation, and he'd been amazed when he truly realized for the first time all they'd done. He'd *known*, in an intellectual way, all along. But he'd been so submerged in the doing, so focused on every terrible step of the March as they actually took it, that he'd truly never considered its entirety. Not until they'd sat down to put it all together.

Even at four hours, it was the bare-bones, only the highlights— or low-lights, as Julian put it—of the entire trip.

There was data from the toombie attack on the *DeGlopper*; downloaded sensor data from the transport's ferocious, sacrificial battle with the Saint cruisers and her final self-destruction after she'd been boarded, to take the second cruiser with her. There were recorded helmet views of battles and screaming waves of barbarians, of Mardukan carnivores and swamps and mud and eternal, torrential rain until the delicate helmet systems succumbed to the rot of the jungle. There were maps of battles, descriptions of weapons, analyses of tactics, data on the battle for the *Emerald Dawn* from the Saints' tactical systems, enemy body counts . . . and the soul-crushing roll call of their own dead.

It was the after-action report from Hell.

And when it was done, they showed the Alphane delegation around the ship. The admiral and her guard noted the combat damage and fingered Patty's scars. The engineer clucked at the damage, stuck his head in holes which still hadn't been patched over, and exclaimed at the fact that the ship ran at all. The admiral nearly had a hand taken off by a *civan*—which she apparently thought was delightful—and they were shown the *atul* and the *basik* in cages. Afterward, Rastar, stony-faced as only a Mardukan could be, showed them the battle-stained flag of the *Basik*'s Own. The admiral and her guard thought it was a grand flag, and, having seen an actual *basik*, got the joke immediately.

Finally, they ended up back in the wardroom. Everyone in the command group had had a part in the presentation, just as every one of them had had a part in their survival. But there was one last recorded visual sequence to show.

The Althari admiral leaned back in the big station chair and made a clucking sound and a weird atonal croon that sent a shiver through every listener as Roger ran the file footage from the bridge's internal visual pickups and they watched the final actions of Armand Pahner. The Prince watched it with them, and his brown eyes were dark, like barriers guarding his soul, as the last embers of life flickered out of the shattered, armored body clasped in his arms.

And then it was done. All of it.

Silence hovered for endless seconds that felt like hours. And then Tchock Ral's face and palms were lifted upward.

"They will march beyond the Crystal Mountains," she said in low, almost musical tones. "They will be lifted up upon the shoulders of giants. Their songs will be sung in their homesteads, and they shall rest in peace, served by the tally of their slain. Tchrorr Kai Herself will stand beside them in battle for all eternity, for they have entered the realm of the Warrior, indeed."

She lowered her face and looked at Roger, swinging her head in a circle which was neither nod nor headshake, but something else, something purely Althari.

"I wipe the stain of insult from our relationship. You have been given a great honor to have known such warriors, and to have led them. They are most worthy. I would gladly have them as foes."

"Yes," Roger said, looking at the freeze-frame in the hologram. Himself, holding his father-mentor's body in his arms, the armored arms which, for all their strength, had been unable to hold life within that mangled flesh. "Yes, but I'd give it all for one more chewing out from the Old Man. I'd give it all for one more chance to watch Gronningen being used as a straight man. To see Dokkum grin in the morning light, with the air of the mountains around us. To hear Ima's weird laugh."

"Ima didn't laugh, much," Julian pointed out quietly. The retelling had put all the humans in a somber mood.

"She did that first time I fell off Patty," Roger reminded him.

"Yes. Yes, she did," Julian agreed.

"Prince, I do not know what the actions of my government will be," Tchock Ral said. "What you ask would place the Alphane Alliance in no little jeopardy, and the good of the clan must be balanced against that. But you and your soldiers may rest in my halls until such time as a decision is made. In my halls, we can hide you, even under your true-name, for my people are trustworthy. And if the decision goes against you, you may rest in them for all eternity, if you choose. To shelter the doers of such deeds would bring honor upon my House forever," she ended, placing both paws on her chest and bowing low across them.

"I thank you," Roger said. "Not for myself, but for the honor you do my dead."

"You'll probably have to make this presentation again," Sreeetoth said with another head bob. "I'll need copies of all your raw data. And if you stay at Tchock Ral's house, you'll be forced to tell your stories all day and night, so be warned."

"And whatever happens, you're not taking this ship to Sol," Mordas Dren put in. The engineer shook his head. "It won't make it through the Empire's scans, for sure and certain. And even if it would, I wouldn't want to trust that TD drive for *one* jump. For one thing, I saw a place where some feeble-minded primitive had been *beating* on one of the capacitors."

"No," Roger agreed. "For this to work, we're going to need another freighter—a clean one—some crew, and quite a bit of money. Also, access to current intelligence," he added. He'd been fascinated by the fact that the admiral *knew* his mother was being controlled.

"If we choose to support you, all of that can be arranged," the Phaenur hissed. "But for the time being, we must report this to our superiors. That is, to *some* of our superiors," he added, looking at the engineer.

"The Minister's going to want to know what it's all about," Dren said uncomfortably.

"This is now bound by security," the admiral replied. "Tell her that. And only that. No outside technicians in the ship until the determination is made, either! And any who finally do get aboard her will be from the Navy Design Bureau. I think, Mordas, that you're going to be left to idle speculation."

"No," the Phaenur said. "Other arrangements will be made. Such conditions are difficult for humans, and more so for one like Mordas. Mordas, would you go to the Navy?"

"I'm in charge of maintenance for the entire star system, Sreeetoth," Dren pointed out, "and I'm a bit too old to hold a wrench. I *enjoy* holding a wrench, you understand, but I'm sure not going to take the cut in pay."

"We'll arrange things," the admiral said, standing up. "Young Prince, *Mr. Chung*, I hope to see you soon in my House. I will send your chief of staff the invitation as soon as determinations are made."

"I look forward to it," Roger said, and realized it was the truth.

"And, by all means, bring your sword," Tchock Ral said, with the low hum Roger had learned was Althari laughter.

Humans are descended from an essentially arboreal species. As a consequence, human homes, whenever it's economically possible, tend to have trees near them, and growing plants. They also tend to rise up a bit, but not very far—just about the height of a tree.

The Altharis, for all that they looked like koala bears, were anything *but* arboreal-descended. That much became abundantly evident to Roger when he first saw the admiral's "halls."

Althari homes were almost entirely underground, and when economics permitted, they were grouped in quantities related to kinship. The admiral's "halls" were a series of low mounds, each about a kilometer across and topped with a small blockhouse of locally quarried limestone . . . and with clear fields of fire stretching out over a four-kilometer radius. There were paved roads for ground cars between them, and several landing areas, including one nearly two hundred meters long, for aircars and shuttles. But the big surprise came when they entered their first blockhouse.

Ramps sloped downward into high-ceilinged rooms. And then downward, and downward . . . and downward. Among Althari, rank was indicated by the depth of one's personal quarters, and Roger found himself ushered into a room about twenty meters across and six meters high, buried under nearly three hundred meters of earth.

He was glad he didn't have a trace of claustrophobia.

Below the surface, all of the standard homes were linked through a system of tunnels. There were stores in the warren, escape routes, weapons—it was a vast underground *fortress,* and the Altharis living in it were a highly trained militia. And it was only one of thousands on the planet. Altharis who didn't live in their own clan homes lived in similar local communities, some of which, from what the visiting Imperials had been told, were far more extensive, virtually underground cities. No wonder the Altharis were considered unconquerable.

The Imperials had arrived the night before, more or less surreptitiously, and been shown to their quarters. Those quarters had been modified to some extent for humans, so there were at least human lavatory facilities, built to human sizes. But the bed had been Althari, and Roger had been forced to actually *jump* to get into it. All in all, they weren't bad quarters—as long as you ignored the weight of rock, concrete, and dirt sitting overhead. Nonetheless, Roger still preferred being up on the surface, as they were now.

The sky above was a blue so deep it was right on the edge of violet. Althar IV's atmosphere was a bit thinner than Old Earth's, although its higher partial pressure of oxygen made for a slightly heady feeling, and the humidity was very low. At the moment, there were no clouds, and after the eternal cloud cover of Marduk, Roger found himself drinking in the clear sky greedily.

Tchock Ral's halls were placed in the approximate center of a long, wide valley on a bit of a plateau. To the east, north, and south, high mountains sparkled with snow; to the west, it opened out. The majority of the valley was given over to other warrens, farms, and a small, primarily Althari city. The city could be seen right on the western horizon, where a few slightly higher bumps marked low multistory buildings.

About a thousand Altharis, all the Marines, and half the Mardukans were either watching the competitions the admiral had decreed in honor of her visitors, preparing an outdoor feast, or just roaming around talking.

The day had started with a simple breakfast of prepared, dried human foods. Since then, for the last couple of hours, they'd been watching Althari sparring matches—mostly, Roger suspected, so that the humans and Mardukans could see the traditional Althari fighting methods. After the sparring matches were done, it had been time for the humans and Mardukans to show their stuff.

Rastar was sparring with a young Althari female. They were of about the same age, and similarly armed. Instead of whetted steel, each was armed with weighted training blades with blunted edges. The Althari held two, one in either bearlike paw, while Rastar held four of them. Rastar was the only Mardukan Roger had met who was truly quaddexterous. Whereas most Mardukans settled for fighting with two hands on only one side, if not a single hand, Rastar could fight with all four hands simultaneously. At the moment, each of his hands held a knife which would have been a short broadsword to a human, and they flickered in and out like lightning.

Each contestant wore a harness which noted strikes and managed scoring. In addition, Rastar wore an environmental suit that left only his face exposed, for Marduk was an intensely hot world, whereas Althar IV was on the cool side of the temperature range even humans would have found acceptable. It was the equivalent of an ice-planet for the cold-blooded Mardukans, and they found it necessary to wear the environment suits everywhere, except in the specially heated rooms set aside for them.

Climatological considerations didn't seem to be slowing him down, however, as all four arms licked in and out. The Althari was good, no question, but Rastar was able to block with both upper hands while his lower hands—the much more powerful pair—flicked in to strike, and he was outscoring her handily.

"Score!" Tchock Ral called as Rastar's lower left-hand blade tapped the Althari's midsection yet again. "*Adain!*"

Adain was the command to separate and prepare for the next round, but instead of lowering her weapons and stepping back, the Althari female let out a hoarse bellow and charged, just as Rastar *was* stepping back. Roger had seen the same Althari win two other fights hands down, so he could imagine why she was so chagrined, and as Sreeetoth has warned him aboard the *Dawn*, no Althari had ever been noted for her calm disposition.

Rastar was taken slightly off-balance, backing away from his opponent as the command required, but he spun nimbly to the side and let her charge past. All four of his blades flickered in and out in flashes of silver, painting the Althari's combat harness with purple holograms at each successful strike. The Althari roared in fury, wheeling and charging furiously after him. But Rastar faded away from her attack like smoke, his own blades flick, flick, flicking with a merciless precision that painted violet blotches across her sides, back, and neck.

"*Adain!*" Ral shouted, and at the second bellow, Rastar's opponent stopped, quivering.

"I apologize for that breach of protocol, Prince Rastar," the admiral said. "Toshok, go to the side and contemplate the dishonor you just brought upon our House!"

"Perhaps it would be better for her to contemplate what real blades would have meant," Rastar suggested. The Mardukan spoke excellent Imperial by now, and the Althari, with their own equivalents of the Empire's implanted toots, understood him perfectly. Not that it made things much better.

"If you wish to face me with live blades—" Toshok ground out in the same language.

"You would be a bleeding wreck on the ground," Ral said. "Look at the markers, you young fool!"

Toshok clamped her mouth shut and glanced angrily at the holographic scoreboard beside the sparring area. Her eyes widened as she saw the numbers under her name and Rastar's, and then she rolled her ursine head from side to side, looking down at the glaring swatches of purple decorating her scoring harness.

"These are nothing!" she snapped angrily. "He barely *touched* me!"

"That's because in a knife fight, the object is to bleed your opponent out, not to get your knife stuck in his meat," Rastar told her. "Would you care to go another round with padding and use these—" he twitched all four blades simultaneously "—as *swords*, instead?"

"I think not," Ral said before Toshok could reply. "I don't want bones broken." The admiral gave a hum of laughter, then beckoned to another Althari. "Tshar! You're up."

The Althari who rolled forward at Ral's summons was a massive juggernaut of muscle and fur, enormous even by Althari standards, and the admiral looked at Roger.

"This is the daughter of my sister's cousin by marriage, Lieutenant Tshar Krot. She is our champion at weaponless combat. Choose your champion, Prince Roger."

Roger shook his head as he contemplated the sheer size of the Althari, but he didn't hesitate. There was only one choice.

"Sergeant Pol," he said.

Erkum stepped forward at the sound of his name. Seeing that the Althari was naked, he removed his harness and kilt, but kept on his environment suit and stood waiting patiently.

"What are the rules?" Roger asked.

"There are *rules* in weaponless combat?" Ral replied with another hum of laughter.

"No gouging, at least?"

"Well, of course not," the admiral said.

"I think we need to make sure Erkum knows that," Roger commented dryly, looking up at Krindi Fain's towering shadow. "Erkum," he said sternly in Diaspran, "no gouging."

"No, Your Highness," the Diaspran said, pounding all four fists together as he sized up his opponent. The Althari was nearly as tall as he was, and even broader. "I'll try not to break any bones, either," Erkum promised.

"*Gatan!*" the admiral barked, beginning the match, and all the Marines and Mardukans started shouting encouragement.

"Break bones, Erkum! Break bones!"

"Turn her into bear paste!"

The two combatants circled each other for a moment, and then Tshar darted forward, grasping an upper wrist and rolling in for a hip-throw. But Erkum dropped his weight, and both of his lower hands grabbed the Althari by the thighs and picked her up. It was a massive lift, even for the big Mardukan, since the Althari must have weighed five hundred kilos, and she got one hand on the environment suit. But Erkum still managed to turn her upside down, then straightened explosively and sent her spinning through the air.

Tshar hit on her back, rolled lithely, and dodged aside as the Mardukan stamped down. Then she was back on her feet. She charged forward again, this time lifting *Erkum* into the air, and threw him down in turn. But he got one hand on one of her knees as he fell, and twisted her off her feet.

Both of them sprang back up, as if they were made of rubber, and, as if they'd planned it ahead of time, charged simultaneously. There was a strange, unpleasant sound as the Mardukan's horns met the Althari's forehead, and then Tshar was on her back, shaking her head dazedly. There was a trickle of blood from her muzzle.

"*Adain,*" the admiral said, just a bit unnecessarily, then moved her head in another complex gesture Roger's toot's analysis of Althari body language read as indicating wry amusement.

"Important safety lesson, there," she observed. "Never try to head-butt a Mardukan."

Erkum had a hand around the base of each horn, and was shaking his own head from side to side.

"She got a hard head," he muttered, and sat down with a thump.

"I suggest we call that a draw, then," Roger suggested as Doc Dobrescu and a male Althari darted forward.

The Althari ran a scanner over Tshar and gave her an injection, then came over to the admiral.

"Nothing broken, and no major hematoma," he said. "But she's got a slight concussion. No more fighting for at least two days."

"And the Mardukan?" Ral asked.

"He's got a headache, but that's about it," Doc Dobrescu said, and slapped the still-seated Pol on the upper shoulder as he stood. "They've got a spongy padding under the horns that absorbs blows like that. Still hurts, but he's fine."

"In that case, Your Highness, I don't think we can call that a draw in honor," the admiral pointed out.

"By all means, score it as you prefer," Roger replied.

The admiral waved her right hand at Pol, formally granting him the victory, then turned back to Roger.

"Your companions say you're deft with the sword," she noted.

"I'm okay. It's kept me alive a couple of times."

"Your Mardukans have been competing against my clan," the admiral said in an offhand manner. "Would you care to try?"

"I don't have a practice blade," Roger pointed out.

"Your sword was remotely measured," Ral said and gestured to one of the hovering Althari. The male brought forward a sword that looked very much like Roger's, except that the blade was blunted and seemed to be made of carbon fiber.

Roger stood up and weighed it in his hand. The balance was right, and so was the shape—about a meter and a half long, slightly curved with a thin but strong blade. The weight felt very close, as well, although it might be a tad heavier.

While he was examining the blade, a young Althari female appeared, bearing padding and a sword. The weapon she carried would have been a two-handed blade for a human, something like a claymore in design, but with a straight blade and broad cross guard. The Althari was a bit older than the two previous competitors, fully mature with a broad band of black running up and over her shoulders. She carried the sword with a measure of assurance Roger found somewhat intimidating. Most of his fighting had been in harum-scarum battles, where formal ability counted less than simply making sure the other guy died.

"This is Commander Tomohlk Sharl, my husband's sister's husband's cousin," the admiral said. The relationship was one word in Althari, but Roger's toot translated ably. "She has some knowledge of *tshoon*, our traditional sword art."

"I'll give it my best shot," Roger said, shaking his head when the padding was offered. "That won't help me much," he observed dryly, looking up at his outsized opponent. He did, however, take the helmet after a murderous glance from Despreaux. It was something like a zero-G ball helmet, carbon fiber, padded, with a slotted mask. And he donned the scoring harness, mentally noting that if the monstrous Althari *did* score, it was going to be pretty obvious.

There were two marks, about four meters apart, and Roger moved to one of them, taking the carbon fiber sword in a two-handed grip and settling his shoulders.

"*Gatan*," the admiral said, and sat back down in her chair.

Roger and the Althari approached one another cautiously, reaching out to touch blades, and then backing off. Then the Althari started the match by springing forward, striking quickly from *quarte* towards Roger's chest.

Roger parried on his foible and stepped to the side, measuring his opponent's speed. The Althari followed up quickly, pressing him, and he turned to the side again, rolling her blade off of his and springing to his left and back.

She spun again, bringing her blade down in a forehand strike. But this time he took it on his sword, rolling it off in a neat parry and moving inside the blade, driving past her with a snake-quick slice towards her unprotected stomach. He ended up behind her, and cut down at the hamstring. Both strikes scored in less than a second.

"*Adain*," the admiral said, and Roger returned smoothly to a guard position. The commander was rubbing her leg and shaking her head.

"That's not a legal blow in *tshoon*," she said.

"I'm sorry. I didn't know that," Roger admitted. "I haven't been in any encounters where the term 'legal blow' had meaning."

"I think you're lucky in that," the Althari said. "I've never had the opportunity to battle with the sword in truth. Or, for that matter, to battle more than the occasional pirate with any weapon. Wars are few these days." She made a sound Roger's toot interpreted as a sigh of envy, then produced an Althari chuckle. "You're quick. Very quick."

"I have to be." Roger grinned. "You're huge. But, then again, so are most Mardukans. I've had to learn to be quick."

They resumed their places, and the admiral gave the signal to reengage. This time, the Althari worked to keep Roger outside, using her superior reach against his speed. Time and time again Roger tried to break through the spinning blade, but he couldn't. Finally, the Althari scored on his arm. He partially blocked the blow, but she'd closed slightly, and the leverage was enough to break down his defense. The score was relatively light, but it hurt like hell.

"*Adain*," the admiral said. "One score apiece."

She beckoned them back to their marks.

"Gatan."

They closed again, with the Althari pushing Roger this time. He had to back away, spinning to stay inside the fighting circle. They worked back to the center, and then the commander feinted a stroke, stopped it in mid-blow, and sprang forward in a lunging strike with the point, instead.

The feint fooled Roger completely. He'd been set to block the stroke and found himself abruptly forced to fumble up a parry against the unanticipated thrust, instead. He fell backwards, then bounced back up like a spring, using the weight of his sword for balance. It was a desperation move, but it placed him inside the Althari's defense. He came up to one knee, then struck up and across. The move left a bold purple slash across the commander's stomach.

"*Adain*," the admiral said. "Very nice."

"Hell with nice," Roger responded, rubbing his back. He'd pulled something there. "On the battlefield, I'd have been dead if I didn't have someone at my back."

"You're quite fortunate in that regard," Ral noted, waving at the *Basik*'s Own.

"I've got a lot of friends, that's true," Roger admitted.

"Which is due to your leadership," the admiral pointed out. "Do not discount yourself."

"A good bit of it had to do with Captain Pahner," Roger replied sadly. Then he turned his head. Three groundcars were approaching from the far side of the warren. Roger had already noticed a large shuttle landing, but there'd been a fair amount of comings and goings during the morning, so he'd thought little of it. This caravan seemed pointed towards them, however.

"We seem to have company," he observed.

"Sreeetoth," the admiral agreed, standing up. "And others."

Roger just nodded his head and looked over at Eleanora. The chief of staff shrugged.

The party was still going on overhead, but the meeting had been moved to one of the underground conference rooms. It had the indefinable look of a secure room. Admittedly, getting a bug into any of the Althari rooms would have been difficult, but this one looked as if the walls were encased in a Faraday cage, and the door had sealed like an airlock.

The surface of the table within was adjustable to three different levels, and the chairs about it were also of different heights, with contours which reconfigured at the touch of a control, obviously designed to provide for humans, Althari, and Phaenurs. Another Althari, not the admiral, took the chair at its head, while a Phaenur Roger had not yet met took an elevated, padlike "chair" at the far end. Sreeetoth was seated beside the new Phaenur, with Tchock Ral to the left of the new Althari.

"I am Sroonday, Minister of External Security," the Phaenur at the foot of the table said. "Sreeetoth, Chief of Customs, you know. My coleader is Tsron Edock, Minister of War. We apologize for the . . . informal fashion in which you have been greeted, Your Highness, but . . ."

Roger held up a hand and shook his head.

"There can be nothing formal in my greeting, Minister, given the circumstances," he said. "And I thank you for the indulgence of this meeting."

"It is more than indulgence," Tsron Edock said, leaning forward. "The Empire of Man has been a competitor for the Alphane Alliance's entire existence. But it has been a *friendly* competitor. We do not have to station war fleets on its border with us, which makes it the *only* border we do not have to defend. We maintain fair and equitable trading relations with it. All of this will pass if it breaks up into internecine warfare, or if the Saints are able to establish large inroads into its territory. We have always looked to it as an ally against the Saints, but under current circumstances . . ."

She looked at the Phaenur, and made a head gesture.

"Everyone has sources of information," the Phaenur said sibilantly. "Yes?"

"Yes," Roger replied. "Although the Alphanes are notoriously hard to penetrate."

"This is so," Sroonday admitted. "And Imperial internal security is also quite good. But we do have sources of information . . . including sources in the Adoula faction."

"Ah." Eleanora nodded. "And you don't like what you're hearing from there."

"No," the External Security Minister said. "We do not. Our source is very good. We knew, long before you arrived, that the supposed coup was Prince Jackson's doing. And, yes, your mother is being held under duress, Your Highness. A combination of control of her implants and psychometric drugs. Other things as well . . ."

Sroonday's voice trailed off uncomfortably. Roger simply sat there, brown eyes like stones, and after a moment, the Phaenur continued.

"Opinion among the plotters over the long-term disposition of the Empress is divided. Most, yes, wish her to have a terminal event as soon as the Heir is born. New Madrid wishes to keep her alive, but our analysts believe that is because she is his only hold on power. Furthermore, our source tells us that Adoula intends to . . . change the relationship between the Empire and the Alphane Alliance. Specifically, he intends to invade the Alliance."

"Is he *nuts*?" Roger blurted.

"We have a fine fleet," the War Minister said, glancing at Admiral Ral. "The Empire, however, has *six* rather fine fleets, the smallest of which is the size of our *entire* fleet. We could go down fighting, but we will probably be offered some sort of local autonomy, as a separate satrapy of the Empire."

"And how will that sit with the Althari?" Roger asked.

"Not well," Tchock Ral said angrily. "I did not know this. My clan will not be slaves to the Empire. Not as long as one Tshrow remains alive."

"None of us will allow it," Edock said. "The Altharis can be destroyed, but not conquered."

"The Phaenurs have a somewhat more philosophical approach," Sroonday hissed. "But given that the bulk of our armed forces are Althari, and that we and our dwellings are intermingled with them, our philosophical approach will be of little use. Taking one of our worlds will require sufficient firepower to ensure that the survivors will be so few in number that—"

"Adoula has to understand that," Eleanora interjected. "I mean, that's a known fact in any intelligence estimate about the Alphane Alliance. You can destroy it, but you can't simply absorb it. All he'd get in a war is a bunch of battle casualties and twelve destroyed planets."

"Prince Jackson is fully aware of the estimates," the Phaenur said. "And disbelieves them."

"That's insane," Roger said flatly.

"Perhaps," Sroonday replied. "It is possible that his understanding of us suffers from his own lack of a multispecies outlook. Whereas all three of the Alliance's member species have been forced to come to comprehend the strengths, weaknesses, and fundamental differences which make all of us what we are, Prince Jackson has not. More importantly, he is a creature of the deal. He believes that after our orbitals are taken, he can 'cut a deal' with us, thereby adding our not inconsiderable economic base to the Empire, and placing the Caravazan Empire between two enemies. His long-term goal is to force the Caravazans to . . . retreat. To become less threatening. He believes he can accomplish this by creating a balance of force which is overwhelmingly weighted against them.

"But to accomplish this, he must conquer us, and that will not happen until the entire Alphane Alliance lies in smoking ruin. It brings one of your own folk tales—about a golden avian, I believe— rather forcibly to mind. Unfortunately, he would appear to be unfamiliar with that particular tale's moral. And thus, Prince Roger," the Phaenur concluded, "we have an immense vested interest in considering support for your endeavor. *If* you can convince us it is even remotely likely to succeed."

"We need access to current intelligence," Roger said. "As current as available. And we'll need a ship, and quite a bit of cash. We also need some read on the . . . reliability of Navy units. Our plan relies, perhaps too much, upon the . . . irregularity of the Sixth Fleet. Do you have any current information on it?"

"A replacement for Admiral Helmut was sent out a month ago," Edock said with an odd roll of her shoulders. "The carrier transporting him apparently had severe mechanical problems and had to pull into dock in the Sirtus System. It remains docked there, having twice had major faults detected in its tunnel drive. Absolutely valid faults, as it happens, which apparently appeared quite suddenly and unpleasantly. In one case, it would seem, due to a couple of kilos of well-placed explosives. Helmut's replacement, Admiral Garrity, unfortunately, is no longer concerned about the delays. According to our reports, the good admiral's shuttle suffered a major malfunction entering the atmosphere of Sirtus III shortly after the second tunnel drive malfunction. There were no survivors."

"You don't pock with the Dark Lord of the Sixth," Julian said.

"This has got to stop," Despreaux protested. "I mean, I know why it's going on, but killing fleet commanders—legally appointed fleet commanders . . ."

"Some question about the legality of the appointment," Kosutic replied grimly. "But I have to agree with the general sentiment."

"Unfortunately, it's part and parcel of the way the Empire has been trending for a long time," Eleanora said with a shrug. "The fact that Admiral Helmut probably doesn't think twice about going to these lengths—certainly not under the circumstances—and that other segments of the Navy are supporting Adoula in this coup, is a symptom, not the disease. The disease is called factionalism, and the level of internal strife is reaching the point of outright civil war. That disease is what your mother was trying to head off, Roger. Unsuccessfully, as it turns out."

"It's not *that* bad," Despreaux said. "There's a lot of political infighting, sure, but—"

"It *is* that bad," Eleanora replied firmly. "Largely due to Roger's grandfather, in fact.

"The Empire is going through a very rough period right now, Nimashet, and unfortunately, that's not sufficiently apparent for most people to be worried about doing something to prevent it.

"We've settled out fully from the psychological, economic, and physical results of the Dagger Wars. It's been five hundred and ninety years since Miranda the Great kicked their asses, and we haven't had a real *war* with anyone else since, despite our periodic bouts of . . . unpleasantness with the Saints. And even those have all been out among the out-worlds. So there's no one alive in the core-worlds who remembers a time of actual danger. We had our last serious economic crisis over a generation ago, too, and politics in the core-worlds have revolved around the strife between the industrialists and the socialists for over seventy years.

"The industrialists, by and large, are truly in it purely for the power. There've been times when corporations were unfairly held up as great, evil empires of greed by individuals who were simply deluded, or else intentionally using them as strawmen—as manufactured ogres, created for their own propaganda purposes. But Adoula's cadre truly *is* in the business of seeking personal power and wealth at any cost to anyone else. Oh, Adoula has the additional worry that his home sector is right on the Saint border. That's why he concentrates on what used to be called the 'military-industrial complex.' But while he might be trying to build military power, the way he goes about it is counterproductive in the extreme. The way the power packs blew up on your plasma guns, Your Highness, is a prime example, and he and his crowd are too far gone to realize that making money by cutting costs at every turn, even if it means a suicide bomb in the hands of a soldier, actually *decreases* their own security, right along with that of the rest of the Empire.

"The socialists are trying to counter the industrialists, but, again, their chosen methods are counterproductive. They're buying votes among the poor of the core-worlds by promising more and more social luxuries, but the tax base is never going to be there to support uniform social luxury. They get the taxes which have kept the system propped up so far by squeezing the outer worlds, because the industrialists have sufficient control in Parliament and the core-world economies to work tax breaks that allow them to avoid paying anything like the taxes they might incur if the lunatics weren't running the asylum. At the same time, if the socialists ever did manage to impose all the taxes *they* think the corporations should cough up in order to pay for their social benefits and all the other worker benefits—like increased paid holidays and decreased workweeks—it really would cripple the economy.

"The ones getting squeezed are the out-worlds, and they're also where most of the new economic and productive blood of the Empire is coming from. All the new devices and arts are coming from there. By the same token, they supply the bulk of the military forces, sites for all the newer military bases and research centers, and more and more manufacturing capability. That shift has been underway for decades now, and it's accelerated steadily as local marginal business taxes in the core-worlds build up and up.

"But the out-worlds still don't have the population base to elect sufficient members of Parliament to prevent themselves from being raped by the inner-worlds. Nor do they have the degree of educational infrastructure found in the core-worlds, which is why the core is still supplying the elite research and business brains. The out-worlds are growing—fast, but not fast enough—and to add to all of their other problems, they're the ones most at risk from surrounding empires, especially the Saints and Raiden-Winterhowe.

"It would be an unstable situation under the best of circumstances, and we don't have those. The members of Parliament elected from the core-worlds are, more and more, from the very rich or hereditary political families. By now, the Commons representation from the core is almost indistinguishable from the membership of the House of Lords. They have a lot of commonality of viewpoint, and as the out-worlds' representation in the Commons grows, the politicians of the inner-worlds see an ever-growing threat to the cozy little power arrangements they've worked out. To prevent that from happening, they use various devices, like the referendum on Contine's elevation to full member-world status, to prevent loss of their power. The politics have become more and more brutal, more and more parochial, and less and less focused on the good of the Empire. In fact, the only people you see walking the walk of the 'good of the Empire' are a few of the MPs from the out-worlds. Adoula *talks* about the good of the Empire, but what he's *saying* is all about the good of Adoula.

"And the real irony of it is that if any of them were capable of truly enlightened self-interest, they'd realize just how stupid their cutthroat tactics really are. The inner-worlds, the out-worlds, the socialists, the industrialists, and the traditionalists all *need* each other, but they're too busy ripping at one another's throats to see that. We're in a bit of a pickle, Your Highness, and, frankly, we're ripe for a really nasty civil war. Symptom, not disease."

"So what do we do about it?" Roger asked.

"You mean, if we rescue your mother and survive?" Eleanora smiled. "We work hard on getting all sides to see themselves as members of the Empire first, and political enemies as a distant second. Your grandfather decided that the problem was too many people in the inner-worlds with too little to gain. So, besides siding with the socialists and starting the trend toward heavy taxation of the out-worlds, he tried to set up colonization programs. It didn't work very well. For one thing, the conditions on the core worlds, even for the very poor, are too comfortable, and woe betide the politician who tries to dial back on any of the privileges that have already been enacted.

"Your grandfather was unwilling to cut back there, but he had this romantic notion that he could engender some kind of 'frontier spirit' if he just threw enough funding at the Bureau of Colonization and wasted enough of it on colonization incentives. But the way he paid for simultaneously maintaining the existing social support programs while pouring money into colonization schemes that didn't work was to cut all other spending—like for the Navy—and turn the screws on the out-worlds. And to get the support in Parliament that his colonization fantasies needed, he made deals with the industrialists and the aristocracy which only enhanced their power and made things even worse.

"He never seemed to realize that even if he'd been able to convince people to *want* to relocate from the core-worlds to howling wildernesses in the out-worlds, there simply aren't enough ships to move enough of them to make a significant dent in the population of the core-worlds. And then, when he had his moment of disillusionment with the Saints' promises to 'peacefully coexist' and started trying to build the Navy back up to something like its authorized strength, it made the Throne's fiscal position even worse. Which, of course, created even more tensions. To be perfectly honest, some of the people who're supporting Adoula right now probably wandered into treason's way in no small part because they could see what was coming. A lot of them, obviously, wanted to fish in troubled waters, but others were seeking any port in a storm. And at least some of them, before the Old Emperor's death, probably thought even someone like Adoula would have been an improvement.

"Your mother watched all that happening, Your Highness. I hope you'll forgive me for saying this, but one of the greater tragedies of your grandfather's reign was how long he lived. He had so much time to do damage that, by the time your mother took the Throne, the situation had snowballed pretty horrifically.

"She decided that the only solution was to break the stranglehold of *both* the industrialists *and* the vote-buyers. If you do that, you can start to make things 'bad' enough in the core-worlds that at least the most motivated will move out-system. And you can start reducing the taxation rape of the out-worlds and shifting some of the financial burden onto the core-world industries which haven't been paying their own share for so long. And once the out-world populations begin growing, you can bring in more member worlds as associate worlds, which will bring new blood into the entire political system at all levels. But with the socialists and the industrialists locked together in their determination to maintain the *existing* system while they duel to the death over who controls it, that's pretty hard."

"It won't be when I stand half of them up against the wall," Roger growled.

"That . . . could be counterproductive," Eleanora said cautiously.

"Anyone associated with this . . . damnable plot," Roger said flatly, "whether by omission or commission, is going to face rather *partial* justice. So is anyone I find decided that the best way to make a credit was to cut corners on military gear. Anyone. I owe that debt to too many Bronze Barbarians to ever forget it, Eleanora."

"We'll . . . discuss it," she said, looking over at the Phaenur.

"It's your Empire, but I agree with the Prince," Tchock Ral said. "The penalty for such things in our Alliance is death. To settle for any lesser penalty would be to betray the souls of our dead."

"But a reign of terror has its own unpleasant consequences," Eleanora pointed out. "Right now, the penalty for failure, at the highest level, is already so great that desperate chances are being taken. Or, what's worse, the best and the brightest simply avoid reaching that level. They . . . opt out rather than subject themselves and their families to the current virulent version of Imperial politics. Only the most unscrupulous strive for high office as it is; enact a reign of terror, and that trend will only be enhanced."

She shook her head, looking for an argument Roger might accept.

"Look, think of it as something like guerrilla warfare," she said.

"I think you're reaching," Roger replied. "It's not to *that* level yet."

"*Yet*," she said. "Not yet. But there's a saying about counterguerrilla operations; it's like eating soup with a knife. If you try to simply *break* the political alliances, by cutting up the obvious bits, then you're going to lose, and lose hard. You've got to not simply break the *old* alliances; you have to establish *new* ones, and for that you need an intact political template and people to make it work. You've got to convince the people running the system to make the changes you recognize are necessary, and you're not going to convince the people whose support you need that they should cooperate with you if they think you'll have them shot if they don't do exactly what you want. Not unless you're willing to enact a full reign of terror, turn the IBI into a secret police to watch everyone's actions and suppress *anyone* who disagrees with you. Turn us into the Saints."

"The IBI would be . . . resistant to that," Temu Jin said. "Most of it, anyway; I suppose you could always find a few people who always secretly hankered to play storm trooper," he added reluctantly.

"And if you did find them, and you could impose your reign of terror, the Empire you're fighting for—the Empire they *died* for—" she gestured at the Marines, "would be gone. There'd be something there with the same name, but it wouldn't be the Empire that Armand Pahner served."

"I see the point you're trying to make," Roger said with manifest reluctance. "And I'll bear it in mind. But I reiterate; *anyone* associated with this plot, by omission or commission, and *anyone* associated with accepting, creating, or supporting defective military gear—with knowledge, and for profit—is going up against the wall. Understand that, Eleanora. I will not enact a reign of terror, but the point will be made, and made hard. I *will* put paid to this . . . evil rot. We may have to do it by eating soup with a knife, but we *will* eat the entire bowl. To the dregs, Eleanora. To the *dregs*."

Those eyes of polished brown stone swept the beings seated around the conference table like targeting radar, and silence hovered for a handful of fragile seconds.

"We will if we win," Julian said after a moment, breaking the silence.

"*When* we win," Roger corrected flatly. "I haven't come this far to lose."

"So how, exactly, do you propose to go about not losing?" Sroonday asked.

The meeting had gone on well into the afternoon, with a brief break for food served at the table by members of the admiral's family. The "External Security Minister" was the Alphane equivalent of the head of their external intelligence operations, and it had brought a wealth of information with it. The most important, from Roger's perspective, was the nature of the newly reformed "Empress' Own."

"Household troops?" Roger asked, aghast.

"Well, that's what the Empress' Own always have been, after all," Eleanora said.

"But these are Adoula's paid bully-boys," Kosutic pointed out. "They're from his industrial security branches, or else outright hired mercenaries." She shook her head. "I expected a whole hell of a lot better than this out of someone in Adoula's position. Most of them have no real military training at all. For all intents and purposes, they're highly trained rent-a-cops—used to keeping workers in line, breaking up labor riots, and preventing break-ins. The Empress' Own *was* composed of the best fighters we could find from throughout the entire Marine Corps. Troops trained to fight pitched battles, and *then* trained to think in security force terms and given a bit of polish and a pretty uniform."

"Agreed," Admiral Ral said with the Althari equivalent of a nod.

"Either we've been overestimating his military judgment," Eleanora said, "or else his hold on the military is even weaker than we'd dared hope."

"Reasoning?" Roger asked. She looked at him, and he shrugged. "I don't say I disagree. I just want to see if we're thinking along the same lines."

"Probably." The chief of staff tipped her chair back slightly and swung it in a gentle side-to-side arc. "If Adoula actually thinks the force he's assembled is remotely as capable as the *real* Empress' Own, then he's a certifiable lunatic," she said succinctly. "Admittedly, *I* didn't really know the difference between a soldier and a rent-a-cop before we hit Marduk, but I certainly do now. And someone with his background ought to have that knowledge already. But if he does, and if he's chosen to build the force he has anyway, it strongly suggests to me that he doesn't believe he can turn up sufficient troops willing to be loyal to him—or to close their eyes to the irregularities of what's going on in the Palace—from the regular military. Which, in turn, means that his control of what you might call the grass roots of the military, at least, is decidedly weak."

"About what I was thinking," Roger agreed.

"And either way, the first *good* news we've had," Ral said.

"True. But the Palace is still a fortress," Eleanora pointed out. "The automated defenses alone could hold off a regiment."

"Then we don't let the automated defenses come on line," Roger said.

"And how do we stop them?" Eleanora challenged.

"I have no idea," Roger replied, then tapped the face of a hardcopy hologram from one of the data packets the minister had brought. "But I bet anything he does."

"Catrone?" Kosutic said, looking over his shoulder. "Yeah. If we can get him on our side. The thing to understand is that the Palace's defenses aren't one layer. There are sections of the security arrangements I never knew, because I was in Bronze Battalion. You're a senior member of Bronze, you learn the defenses Bronze needs to know. Steel knew more, Silver more than Steel. The core defenses were only authorized to Gold, and Catrone was the Gold sergeant major for over a decade. Not quite the longest run in history, but the longest in *recent* history. If anyone knows a way to penetrate the Palace, it's Catrone."

"Putting all your faith in one person, with whom you have no significant contact, is unwise," Sroonday pointed out. "One does not build a successful strategy around a plan in which *everything* must go right."

"If we can't get Catrone's help, we'll find another way," Roger said. "I don't care how paranoid the Palace's designers were, there'll be a way in. And we'll find it."

"And your Home Fleet?" Edock asked.

"Strike fast enough, and they'll be left with a *fait accompli*," Roger pointed out. "They're not going to want to escalate to the point of nuking the Palace with Mother inside, and if they don't act immediately, we'll have news media and reasonably honest politicians all over it before they can do anything else. Home Fleet doesn't *have* a sizable Marine contingent, and there's a reason for that. They *could* nuke the Palace—assuming they could get through the surface-to-space defenses—but I'd be interested to see the reactions among the officers who heard the order. And that assumes we can't checkmate them, somehow."

"Take out Greenberg, for starters," Julian said. "And Gianetto. We'll have to get control of the Defense Headquarters, anyway."

"And a base?" the Phaenur asked.

"We've got one," Kosutic replied. Sroonday looked at her, and her mouth twitched in a tight grin.

"We've been talking about the Palace's security systems, but security for the Imperial Family isn't about individual structures, no matter how intimidating they may be. It's an entire edifice, an incredibly baroque and compartmentalized infrastructure which, for all intents and purposes, was directly designed by Miranda the First."

"With all due respect, Sergeant Major," War Minister Edock said, "Miranda the First has been dead for five hundred and sixty of your years."

"I realize that, Minister," Kosutic said. "And I don't mean to say that anything she personally designed is still part of the system. Mind you, it wouldn't really surprise me if that were the case. Miranda MacClintock was a bloody dangerous woman to get pissed off, and the terms 'incredibly devious' and 'long-term thinking' could have been invented expressly for the way her mind worked. But what I meant was that she was the one who created the entire concept of the Empress' Own, and established the philosophy and basic planning parameters for the Imperial Family's security. That's why things are so compartmentalized."

"Compartmentalized in what sense, Sergeant Major?" Edock asked.

"The same way the Palace's security systems are," she said. "There are facilities—facilities outside the Palace, outside the entire normal chain of command—dedicated solely to the Imperial Family's security. Each battalion of the Empress's Own has its own set of secure facilities, known only to the battalion's senior members, to be used in case of an emergency. This is the first coup attempt to even come close to success in over half a millennium, Minister. There's a reason for that."

"Are you saying that no one from Steel, Silver, or Gold would know about these 'facilities,' Eva?" Temu Jin asked. "They're *that* secure?"

"Probably not," she conceded. "Most of the senior members of those battalions came up the ladder, starting with Bronze. So it's likely at least someone from the more senior outfits knows where just about everything assigned to Bronze is located. But they're not going to be talking about it, and even if they wanted to, our toots are equipped with security protocols which would make that an . . . unpleasant experience even after we retire. Which means there's no way anyone working for Adoula could have that information. So once we get to the Sol System, we'll use one of the Bronze facilities."

"I think, then, that we are as far along as we can get today," Sroonday said sibilantly. "Fleshing out the bones we have already put in place is a matter of details best left to staff. It will take some time, a few days at least, to acquire the materials you need. A freighter and a . . . discreet crew. And a captain."

"We have a captain," Roger said. "I'll get a list of the positions we'll need filled on the freighter. An old freighter, or one that *looks* old."

"Done," Sroonday said, rising. "I will not be directly involved in this further. It was hard enough to find a time when I could conveniently disappear as it is. Sreeetoth will be your liaison with me, and Admiral Ral will liaise with the War Minister."

"We thank you for your support, Minister Sroonday," Roger said, rising in turn and bowing across the table.

"As I pointed out, it is in our mutual interest," the Minister replied. "Alliances are always based upon mutual interest."

"So I've learned," Roger said with a thin smile.

Despreaux frowned and looked up from the list of stores she'd been accessing when the door beeped at her.

"Enter," she said, and frowned harder when she saw that it was the sergeant major and Eleanora O'Casey.

"Girl talk time again?" she asked more than a little caustically, swinging her station chair around to face them.

"You see what we meant," Eleanora said bluntly, without preamble, as she sat down in one of the room's float chairs and moved it closer to the desk. "I noticed you were really quiet in the meeting, Nimashet," she continued.

"I didn't have any contribution to make," Despreaux replied uncomfortably. "I'm already in way over my pay grade."

"Bullshit you didn't have a contribution," Kosutic said, even more bluntly than O'Casey. "And you know just what that contribution would be."

"Except that in this case, I halfway agree with him!" Despreaux replied angrily. "I think standing Adoula and his cronies, and everyone else associated with this plot, up against a nice, bead-pocked wall is a dandy idea!"

"And their families, too?" Eleanora asked. "Or are you going to let their relatives continue to have the positions of power their families held before the coup and also a blood feud with the Emperor? The point of courts and laws is to distance the individual from the act. If Roger has Adoula and everyone else summarily executed, everyone who disagrees with the decision will be after his scalp. And let's not even think about how the news media would play it! If he stands them all up against a wall and has a company of Mardukans shoot them, we *will* have a civil war on our hands. And a guerrilla war, and every other kind of war you can imagine."

"So we let them *walk*?" Despreaux demanded in exasperation. "Just like they always do? Or maybe they should get some quality time in a country-club prison, and then come out to make more minor mischief?"

"No," Kosutic said. "We arrest them, charge them with treason, and put them in jail. Then the IBI gathers the evidence, the courts do their work, and the guilty get quietly put to death. No passion. No fury. Calmly, efficiently, legally, and *justly*."

"And you think they won't walk with a passel of high-priced Imperial City lawyers?" Despreaux half-sneered. "With as much money as they have to throw at the problem?"

"Roger . . . didn't see all the data Sroonday had," Eleanora said uncomfortably. "With the things the Empress will have to say about . . . what's going on, I'd be very surprised if anyone were *willing* to be their lawyer, no matter what the fee. The difficulty will be keeping Adoula and New Madrid from being torn limb from limb."

"And just what," Despreaux asked carefully, "didn't Roger see?"

"I think that, for now, that will be kept to the Sergeant Major and myself," Eleanora said sternly. "You just focus on how to keep Roger from turning into another Dagger Lord. When he finds out, I think you'll have all you can handle keeping him from gutting New Madrid on the Palace steps."

"Welcome, Your Highness, to my home," Sreeetoth said, bowing to the prince as Roger stepped through the door.

"It's beautiful," Despreaux said in a hushed voice.

The home was a large plant—not exactly a tree, but more of a very *large* root. The top of the root-bole towered nearly twenty meters in the air and covered a roughly oval base which measured about thirty meters in its long dimension. Narrow branches clothed in long, fernlike purple leaves extended from the tops and sides, and the brown and gray moss which covered the surface of the root itself formed intricate patterns, something like a Celtic brooch.

It was placed against the slope of a low hill in a forest. Apparently, it had been positioned directly in the path of what had been a waterfall, for water moved among the twisting branches of the root, pouring out of the front of the "house" in a thousand small brightly sparkling streams. The interior, however, was snug and dry. There were some human chairs, but scattered around the main room were pillows and rugs made of some sort of deep-pile fabric.

"I was fortunate to acquire it while I was still a young officer,"

Sreeetoth said. "It is nearly two hundred of your years old. It takes only a decade or so for a *po'al* root to grow to maximum size, but they . . . improve with age. And this one is remarkably well-placed. May I offer drinks? I have human tea and coffee, beer, wine, and spirits."

"I'll take a glass of wine," Roger said, and Despreaux nodded in agreement.

"Thank you for joining me," the Phaenur said, reclining on one of the pillows, then widened its eyes as Roger and Despreaux sank down on others.

"Most humans use the chairs," it noted.

"We've been on Marduk for so long that chairs seem strange," Roger said, taking a sip of the wine. It was excellent. "Very nice," he complimented.

"A friend keeps a small winery," Sreeetoth said, bobbing its head in one of the abrupt, lizardlike gestures of its species. "*Tool* fruit wine is a valuable, though small, export of the Alphane Alliance. Most of it," it added dryly, "is consumed internally, however. Your health."

"Thank you," Roger said, raising his own glass in response.

"You are uneasy about being asked to join me in my home," the Phaenur said, taking a sip of its own wine. "Especially when I specifically invited the young Sergeant to accompany you, and no others."

"Yes," Roger said, simply. "In a human, that would be a guess. In your case, it's as plain as if I'd said it out loud, right?"

"Correct," it replied. "The reason for my invitation is simple enough, however. Much of the success of this operation depends upon you—upon your strength and steadiness. I wanted to meet with you in a situation uncluttered by other emotions."

"Then why not invite me to come alone?" Roger asked, tilting his head to the side.

"Because your own emotions are less cluttered when the Sergeant is near you," the Phaenur said simply. "When she leaves your side, for even a moment, you become uneasy. Less . . . centered. If you were Phaenur, I would say she was a *tsrooto*, an anchor. It translates badly. It means . . . one part of a linked pair."

"Oh." Roger looked at Despreaux. "We . . . are not so linked."

"Not in any official form or way," Sreeetoth agreed. "But you *are* so linked. The Sergeant, too, is uneasy when away from you. Her agitation does not show on her surface, but it is there. Not the same as yours. You become . . . sharp, edgy. In some circumstances, dangerous. She becomes . . . less focused, unhappy, worried."

"Are we here for couples counseling, then?" Despreaux asked dryly.

"No, you are here because your Prince is happier when you are around," it replied, taking another sip of wine. "On the other hand, if this *were* a matter for counseling, I would point out to both of you that there is nothing whatsoever wrong in requiring—or being—a *tsrooto*. The fact that the Prince is calmer, more centered, in your presence does not mean that he is weak or ineffectual without you, Sergeant. It simply indicates that he is in some ways still stronger and more effective *with* you. That the two of you have much strength to give one another, that together you become still more formidable. It is a reminder that—as I believe you humans put it—the whole can be greater than the sum of its two parts, not that either of you becomes somehow weak, or diminished, in the other's absence.

"But that is not why you are here. The Prince is here because I wanted to taste him, to know what we are wagering our trust upon. You are an odd human, Prince. Did you know that?"

"No," Roger said. "I mean, I'm quick—probably neural enhancements I didn't know I had—but . . ."

"I did not refer to any physical oddity," Sreeetoth said. "I have seen the reports, of course. Your agility and physical good looks, for a human, were noted in the reports we had from before your supposed death. As was your . . . untried but clearly capable mind. *Athroo* reports, samplings of your emotions, were few, but said that you were childish, disinterested in anything but play. Now we have this . . . other Prince. Before, you were normal; now we have someone who radiates more like an Althari than a human. There is no dissembling in you, none of the constant desire to hide your purpose we find among most humans. Fear of revealing your hidden faults, that overarching miasma of guilt that humans seem to run around in all the time. For the most part, you are as clear and clean as a sword. It is refreshing, but so odd that I was told to sample it fully and make a report."

It cocked its head to the side as if doing just that.

"There's no point in lying," Roger said. "Not with the Phaenur. I'll admit that was a pleasant change."

"Yet the Imperial Court is no place for a truly honest man," the Phaenur suggested.

"Maybe I can change that." Roger shrugged. "And if I can't, I have some truly dishonest advisers."

The Phaenur cocked its head to the side and then bobbed it.

"I sense that was a joke," it said. "Human and Phaenur concepts of humor are often at odds, alas."

"One thing I would be interested in," Roger noted, "to try to make the Court a more . . . honest place, is some Phaenur advisers. Not immediately, but soon after we retake the Palace."

"That could be arranged," Sreeetoth said, "but I strongly recommend that you contract with independent counselors. We like and trust the Empire, and you like and trust us. But having representatives of our government in your highest councils would be . . . awkward."

"I suppose." Roger sighed. "I'd like to do as much as possible in the open, though. The Court hasn't *been* a place for an honest man, and one way to change that might be to make sure that what's said in Court is honest. Among other things, it would place me in a position where I could work to my strengths, not my weaknesses. I've never understood the importance that's placed upon dishonesty in business and politics."

"I do," Despreaux said with a shrug. "I don't like it, but I understand it."

"Oh?" the Phaenur said. "There is a point to dishonesty?"

"Certainly. Even the Phaenurs and the Althari don't wear their thoughts on their sleeves. For example, Roger in command of the Empire will be a very restless neighbor. You have to know that. Surely there are others you'd prefer?"

"Well, yes," Sreeetoth admitted.

"But you don't bring it up, don't emphasize it. In it's own way, that's dishonest—or at least dissembling. And I have no doubt that you're capable of lying by omission, Mr. Minister." She looked directly into the Phaenur's eyes. "That there are things you have no intention of revealing, because to do so might evoke reactions which would run counter to the outcomes you're after."

"No doubt," Sreeetoth conceded, bobbing its head respectfully at her. "And you are correct. Roger's personality, the style of rulership we anticipate out of him, will not be . . . restful under the best of circumstances."

It made a soft sound their toots interpreted as quiet laughter.

"That may not be so bad a thing, however," it continued. "His grandfather, for example, was quite soothing. Also an honest man, but surrounded by deceit and virtually unaware of it. His lack of competence precluded the Empire's becoming a threat to us, which was restful, yet it also created the preconditions for the crisis we all face today.

"Still, that does not mean a restless human ruler is necessarily in our best interests. Roger's mother, unlike her father, is a very deceitful person, but not at all, as you put it, restless. She was solely concentrated on the internal workings of the Empire and left us essentially alone. From our reports, it is unlikely she will continue very long as Empress. That will leave this . . . restless young man as Emperor. We could prefer someone *less* restless, but he is the best by far of the choices actually available to us."

"How badly has Mother been injured?" Roger asked angrily.

"Quite badly, unfortunately," the Phaenur replied. "Calm yourself, please. Your emotions are distressing in the extreme. It is why we have not brought up the full measure of damage before."

"I'll . . . try," Roger said, as calmly as he could, and inhaled deeply. Then he looked directly at his host. "How damaged?"

"The nature of the reports on her condition we have received— their very existence—means that maintaining security to protect our source is . . . difficult," Sreeetoth replied. "We have been able to clear only one specialist in human psychology and physiology to take a look at them, but she is among the best the Alliance can offer in her specialty, and I have read her analysis. It would appear that the . . . methods being used are likely to cause irreparable long-term damage. It will not kill her, but she will no longer be . . . at the top of her form. A form of senility is likely."

Roger closed his eyes, and one jaw muscle worked furiously.

"I apologize for my current . . . feelings," he said after a moment in a voice like hammered steel.

"They are quite bloody," Sreeetoth told him.

"We'll handle it," Despreaux said, laying a hand on his arm. "We'll *handle* it, Roger."

"Yes." Roger let out a long, hissing breath. "We'll handle it."

He touched the hand on his arm very lightly for just an instant, then returned his attention to Sreeetoth.

"Let's talk about something else. I love your house. You don't have neighbors?"

"Phaenurs tend to separate their dwellings," his host said. "It is quite impossible to fully shield one's feelings and thoughts. We learn, early on, to control them to a degree, but being in crowds is something like being at a large party for a human. All the thoughts of other Phaenurs are like a gabble of speech from dozens of people at once. All the emotions of others are like the constant roar of the sea."

"Must be interesting working in customs," Despreaux observed.

"It is one of the reasons so much of the direct contact work is handled by humans and Althari males," Sreeetoth agreed. "Alas, that has been somewhat less successful than we had hoped. Your reports on Caravazan penetration have caused a rather unpleasant stir, with some serious political and social implications."

"Why?" Roger asked. "I mean, you're an honest society, but *everyone* has a few bad apples."

"Humans have been a part of the Alphane Alliance since its inception," Sreeetoth explained. "But they have generally been—not a lower class, but something of the sort. Few of them reach the highest levels of Alphane government, which has not sat well with many of them. They know that Altharis and Phaenurs are simply more trustworthy than their own species, but that is not a pleasant admission for them, and whatever the cause, or whatever the justification, for their exclusion, the fact remains that they do not enjoy the full range of rights and opportunity available to Altharis or Phaenurs.

"Althari males, however, most definitely *are* a lower class. Althari females, until recently, considered them almost subsentient, useful only for breeding and as servants."

"Barefoot and . . . well, I guess not pregnant," Despreaux said dryly, and grimaced. "Great."

"It is humans who have pushed for more rights for Althari males, and over the last few generations they have attained most of those rights. But it was humans and Althari males, and a single Phaenur who was supposed to be keeping an eye on them, who were corrupted by the Saints. I have already seen the level of distrust of the males growing in the females who work with them, those who know of their betrayal. Such a betrayal on the part of a *female* Althari would be considered even worse, and might shake their world view . . . and their prejudices. But, alas, only males were involved. And humans."

"So now both groups are under a cloud," Roger said. "Yes, I can see the problem."

"It is damaging work which has taken a generation to take hold," Sreeetoth said. "Most distressing. Admiral Ral has reinstituted communications restrictions on the males in her household, since you are staying there. That, in itself, is a measure of the degree of distrust which has arisen. She has lost faith in the honor of the males of her own household."

"Lots of fun," Roger said, and grimaced. "I almost wish we hadn't given you the information."

"Well, I cannot wish that," the Phaenur said. "But we have had to increase the level of counseling and increase the number of counseling inspectors. It is a difficult process, since they need to move about so that the counselors are unavailable for corruption. It is, in fact, something I had pressed for previously, but prior to your information the funds were unavailable. They are becoming available. Quickly."

"Sorry," Roger said with a frown.

"I am not," Sreeetoth said. "It helps me to ensure that the affairs of my department are in order. But you do seem to bring chaos wherever you go, young Prince. It is something to beware of."

"I don't mean to," Roger protested, thinking of the trail of bodies, Mardukan and human, the company had left behind on Marduk.

"You appear simply to be responding to your surroundings and the threats you encounter," Sreeetoth said, "not *seeking* to become a force of destruction. But be careful. However justified your responses, you *thrive* on chaos. That is not an insult; I do the same. To be in customs, it is a necessity."

"I think that was a joke," Roger said.

"You humans would consider it so, yes—an ironic reality," it replied. "There are those who manage chaos well. You are one; I am another. There are others who cannot handle chaos at all, and fold in its face, and they are much more numerous. The job of a ruler, or any policymaker, is to reduce the chaos in life, so that those who simply wish tomorrow to be more or less the same as today, possibly a bit better, can get on with their lives.

"The danger for those who manage chaos well, though, is that they seek what they thrive upon. And if they do not have it in their environment, they may seek to create it. I have found such tendencies in myself; they were pointed out to me early on, by one of my superiors. Since then I have striven, against my nature, to create placidness in my department. To find those who thrive on *eliminating* chaos. I have many subordinates, humans, Altharis, and Phaenurs, who also thrive on chaos—but those who cannot create order out of it, I remove. Their ability to manage the chaos is unimportant in the face of the additional chaos they create. So which will you do, young Prince? Create the chaos? Or eliminate it?"

"Hopefully eliminate it," Roger said.

"That is to be desired."

They ate, then, from a smorgasbordlike selection of the Phaenur foods that were consumable by humans, with several small servings of multiple dishes rather than one main entrée. Conversation concentrated on their travels on Marduk, the things they'd seen, the foods they'd eaten. Roger couldn't entirely avoid reminiscing about the dead—there were too many of them. And whenever he had a fine repast, and this was one such, it brought back memories of Kostas and the remarkable meals he had produced from such scanty, unpromising material.

When the meal was done, they departed, walking out of the grove to the waiting shuttle. It was the Phaenur custom, not a case of "eating and running." Phaenur dinner parties ended at the conclusion of the meal. In fact, the original Phaenur custom had been to conclude any gathering by the giving of foods to be eaten afterwards. That custom had been modified only after the Phaenur culture's collision with human and Althari customs.

Roger thought it was rather a good custom. There was never the human problem of figuring out when the party was over.

He and Despreaux boarded the shuttle in silence, and they were halfway through the flight back to the admiral's warren before Roger shook his head.

"Do think it's right?" Roger asked. "Sreeetoth? That I create chaos wherever I go?"

"I think it's hard to say," Despreaux replied. "Certainly there *is* chaos wherever we go. But there's usually some peace, when we're done."

"The peace of the grave," Roger said somberly.

"More than just that," Despreaux said. "Some chaos, to be sure. But an active and growing chaos, not just some sort of vortex of destruction. You . . . shake things up."

"But Sreeetoth is right," Roger noted. "There's only room for a certain amount of shaking up in any society that's going to be stable in the long-term."

"Oh, you generally leave well enough alone, if it isn't broken," Despreaux argued. "You didn't shake things up much in Ran Tai. For the rest, they were places that desperately needed some shaking. Even K'Vaern's Cove, where you just showed them they needed to get off their butts, and how to do it. It's not easy being around you, but it *is* interesting."

"Interesting enough for you to stay?" Roger asked softly, looking over at her for the first time.

There was a long silence, and then she nodded.

"Yes," she said. "I'll stay. If it's the right thing to do. If there's no serious objection to it, I'll stay even as your wife. Even as—ick!—the Empress. I do love you, and I want to be with you. Sreeetoth was right about that, too. I don't feel . . . whole when I'm not around you. I mean, I need my space from time to time, but . . ."

"I know what you mean," Roger said. "Thank you. But what about your absolute pronouncement that you'd never be Empress?"

"I'm a woman. I've got the right to change my mind. Write that on your hand."

"Okay. Gotcha."

"I'm not going to be quiet," Despreaux warned him. "I'm not going to be the meek little farm girl over in the corner. If you're going off the deep end, I'm going to make that really, really plain."

"Good."

"And I don't do windows."

"There are people for that around the Palace."

"And I'm not going to every damned ribbon-cutting ceremony."

"Agreed."

"And keep the press away from me."

"I'll try."

"And I want to get laid."

"What?"

"Look, Roger, this is silly," Despreaux said angrily. "I haven't been in bed with a guy—or with a female, for that matter—in nearly ten months, and I have needs, too. I've been waiting and waiting. I'm *not* going to wait for some damned matrimonial ceremony, if and when. And it's not healthy for you, either. Parts start to suffer."

"Nimashet—"

"We've discussed this," she said, holding up her hand. "If you're going to have a farm-girl as your wife, then you're going to have to be willing to have one that's clearly no virgin, if for no other reason than that she's been sleeping with *you*. And we're not on Marduk anymore. Yes, I'm one of your guards, technically, but we both know that's just a job description anymore. I guess I'm one of your staff, but mostly I'm there to keep the peace. There's no ethical reason, or moral one, come to think of it, why we can't have . . . relations. And we're *going* to have relations, if for no other reason than to take the edge off *you*. You're like a live wire all the time, and I *will* ground you."

"You always have grounded me," Roger said, patting her hand. "We'll discuss it."

"We already have," Despreaux said, taking the patting hand and putting it in her lap. "Any *further* discussion will take place in bed. Say 'Yes, Dear.'"

"Yes, Dear."

"And these tits are new, so they're still a bit sore. Be careful with them."

"Yes, Dear," Roger said with a grin.

"My, Your Highness," Julian said, looking up as a whistling Roger walked into the office he'd set up. "You're looking chipper today."

"Oh, shut up, Julian," Roger said, trying unsuccessfully not to grin.

"Is that a hickey I see on your neck?"

"Probably. And that's all we're going to discuss about the evening's events, Sergeant. Now, what did you want to tell me?"

"I've been looking into the information the Alphanes provided on our Navy dispositions." Julian was still grinning, but he spoke in his getting-down-to-business voice.

"And?" Roger prompted.

"Fleets can't survive indefinitely without supplies," Julian said. "Normally, they get resupplied by Navy colliers and general supply ships sent out from Navy bases. But Sixth Fleet is right on the edge of being defined as operating in a state of mutiny, with everything that's going on. So Navy bases have been ordered *not* to resupply its units."

"So where are they getting their supplies?" Roger asked, eyes narrowing in interest as he leaned his shoulders against the office wall and folded his arms.

"At the moment, from three planets and a station in the Halliwell Cluster."

"Food and fuel, you mean?" Roger asked. "I don't see them getting resupply on missiles. And what are they doing for spares?"

"Fuel isn't really that big a problem . . . yet," Julian replied. "Each numbered fleet has its own assigned fleet train service squadron, including tankers, and Sixth Fleet hasn't been pulling a lot of training maneuvers since the balloon went up. They haven't been burning a lot of reactor mass, and even if they had been, feeding a fusion plant's pretty much dirt cheap. I don't think Helmut would hesitate for a minute when it came to 'requisitioning' reactor mass from civilian sources, for that matter.

"Food, on the other hand, probably is a problem, or becoming one. Missile resupply, no sweat, so far—they haven't expended any of their precoup allotment. But spare parts, now. *Those* are definitely going to be something he's worrying about. On the other hand, you and I both know how inventive you can get when you're desperate."

"'Inventive' doesn't help if a capacitor goes out," Roger pointed out. "Okay, so they're getting resupplied by friendly local planets. What's that do for us?"

"According to the Alphanes, Helmut's supplies are being picked up by three of his service squadron's colliers: *Capodista*, *Ozaki*, and *Adebayo*. I was looking at the intel they have on Sixth Fleet's officers—"

"Got to love their intel on us," Roger said dryly.

"No shit. I think they know more about our fleets than the Navy does," Julian agreed. "But the point is, the captain of the *Capodista* is one Marciel Poertena."

"Any relation to . . . ?"

"Second cousin. Or once removed, or something. His dad's cousin. The point is, they know each other; I checked."

"And *you* know Helmut."

"Not . . . exactly. I was one of the Marines on his ship, once upon a time, but there were fifty of us. We met. He might remember me. Then again, given that the one time we really *met* met it was for disciplinary action . . ."

"Great," Roger said.

"Who the messenger is isn't really that important," Julian pointed out. "We just need to get him the message—that the Empress is in trouble, that the source of the trouble is provably not you, and that you're going to fix it."

"And that if we *can't* fix it, he has to disappear," Roger said. "That we're not going to crack the Empire over this. Anything is better than that, and I don't want him coming in after the fact, all guns blazing, if we screw the pooch."

"We're going to have a civil war whatever happens," Julian countered.

"But we're not going to Balkanize the Empire," Roger said sternly. "He has to understand that and *agree*. Otherwise, no deal. On the other hand, if he supports us, and if we win, he has his choice: continue in Sixth Fleet until he's senile, or Home Fleet, or Chief of Naval Operations. His call."

"Jesus, Roger! There's a reason those are all two-year appointments!"

"I know, and I don't really care. He's loyal to the Empire first—*that* I care about. Tell him I'd *prefer* CNO or Home Fleet."

"I tell him?"

"You. Turn over your intel-gathering to Nimashet and Eleanora. Then get Poertena. You're on the next ship headed towards the Halliwell System." Roger stuck out his hand. "Make a really *good* presentation, Julian."

"I will," the sergeant said, standing up. "I will."

"Good luck, Captain," Roger added.

"Captain?"

"It's not official till its official. But from now on, that's what you are from my point of view. There are going to be quite a few promotions going on."

"I don't want to be a colonel."

"And Nimashet doesn't want to be Empress," Roger replied. "Face facts, Eva. I'm going to need people I can trust, and they're going to have to have the rank to go with the trust. For that matter, you're going to be a general pretty damned quick. I know you think about the Empire first."

"That's . . . not precisely true," the Armaghan said. "Or, not the way it used to be." She looked him straight in the eye. "I'm one of *your* people now, Roger. I agree with your reasoning about the Empire, but the fact that I agree with it is less important than the fact that it's *your* reasoning. You need to be clear on that distinction. Call me a fellow traveler, in that regard."

"Noted," Roger said. "But in either case, you know what I'm trying to do. So if you think I'm doing something harmful to the Empire, for whatever reason, you tell me."

"Well, all right," she said, then chuckled. "But if that's what you really want me to do, maybe I should start now."

"Now?"

"Yeah. I'm just wondering, have you really *thought* about the consequences of making Poertena a lieutenant?"

"Pocking nuts, t'at's what t'ey are," Poertena muttered, looking at the rank tabs sitting on the bed. "Modderpocking nuts."

Poertena had spent most of his life as a short, swarthy, broad individual with lanky black hair. Now he was a short, broad, fair-skinned individual, with a shock of curly *red* hair. If anything, the new look fitted his personality better. If not his accent.

"How bad can it be?" Denat asked.

The Mardukan was D'Nal Cord's nephew. Unlike his uncle, he was under no honor obligation to wander along with the humans, but he did suffer from a severe case of horizon fever. He'd accompanied them to the first city—what he'd considered a city at the time—Q'Nkok, to help his uncle in negotiations with the local rulers. But when Cord followed Roger and his band off into the Kranolta-haunted wilderness, Denat (for reasons he couldn't even define at the time) had followed along, despite the fact that everyone *knew* it was suicide.

In the ensuing third of a Mardukan year, he'd been enthralled, horrified, and terrified by turns, each beyond belief. He'd very rarely been bored, however. He'd also discovered a hidden gift for languages and an ability to "blend in" with a local population—both of which abilities had been pretty well hidden among a tribe of bone-grinding savages—which had proved highly useful to the humans.

And in Marshad, he had acquired a wife as remarkable, in her own way, as Pedi Karuse. T'Leen Sena was as brilliant a covert operator as any race had ever produced, and although she was small—petite, actually—for a Mardukan, and a "sheltered city girl," to boot, she was also a very, very dangerous person. The fact that she'd seen fit to marry a wandering warrior from a tribe of stone-using barbarians might have shocked her family and friends; it did not shock anyone who knew Denat.

In addition to gaining adventure, wealth, fame, and a wife he doted upon, he and Poertena had become friends. Representatives of two dissimilar species, from wildly divergent backgrounds, somehow they clicked. Part of that was a shared love of gambling, at least if the stakes were right. The two of them had introduced various card games to unsuspecting Mardukans across half a planet, and done rather well financially in the process. To a Mardukan, cheating was just part of the game.

"Ask me if I trus' him," Poertena griped as he packed his valise. "He's a *Poertena*! I gotta say yes, but t'ey got no *idea* what an insult t'at would be. *Of course* you can' trus' him."

"I trust *you*," Denat said. "I mean, not with cards or anything, but I'd take you at my back. I'd trust you with my knife."

"Well, sure," Poertena said. "But . . . damn, you don' have to make a big t'ing about it. An' it ain't t'e same t'ing, anways. If Julian goes in all 'good of t'e Empire,' Marciel's gonna *preak*."

"Well, at least you're getting off this damned planet," Denat grumped. "It's a pocking ice ball, playing cards with these damned bears is *boring*, and the sky is overhead *all the time*. Doesn't it ever *rain*?"

Rain and overcast skies were constant companions on Marduk, one of the reasons the locals had evolved with slime-covered skin.

"You wanna come along, come along," Poertena said, looking up from his packing.

"Don't tempt me," Denat said wistfully. "Sena would kill me if I ran off without her."

"So?" Poertena snorted. "She also one of t'e bes' pockin' 'spooks' I know. Might be she come in handy in somet'ing like t'is."

"You really think Roger would agree to let both of us come?" Denat perked up noticeably, and Poertena chuckled.

"Hey, got's to prove somehow where t'e pock we been for t'e las' year, don' we? I t'ink a pair of Mardukans migh' be abou' t'e bes' pockin' proof we gonna find." He shrugged. "We can get more tickets. I don' know wha' we do por t'e passports, but we pigure out somet'ing. Ones we got are pretty good por complete pakes."

"Ask, please," Denat said. "I'm going crazy here."

"Well, we're moving." Roger pulled out a strand of hair, then tucked it behind his ear. "We can get an abort message to Julian, if it reaches him in time. But for all practical purposes, the die is cast."

"Second thoughts?" Despreaux asked. They were in Roger's quarters eating a quiet meal, just the two of them.

"Some," he admitted. "You don't know how good the 'government-in-exile' plan's looked to me from time to time."

"Oh, I think I do. But it was never really an option, was it?"

"No, not really." Roger sighed. "I just hate putting everyone in harm's way, again. When does it end?"

"I don't know." Despreaux shrugged. "When we win?"

"If we capture Mother, and New Madrid," he never called New Madrid "father," "and Adoula. Maybe everything will hold together. Oh, and capture the replicator, too. And if Helmut can checkmate Home Fleet. And if none of Adoula's cabal grabs a portion of the Navy and flees back to the Sagittarius Sector. If, if, if."

"You need to stop fretting about it," Despreaux said, and then smiled crookedly at the look he gave her. "I know—I know! Easier to say than to do. That doesn't keep it from being good advice."

"Probably not," he agreed. "But there's not much point giving someone advice you *know* he can't follow."

"True. So let's at least worry about something we might be able to do something about. Any news on the freighter?"

"Sreeetoth said maybe two more days," Roger replied with a shrug of his own. "They didn't have one that was quite right in-system. It's coming from Seranos. Everything else is ready to go, so all we can do is wait."

"Whatever will we do with the time?" Despreaux smiled again, not at all crookedly.

None of the crew recruited for the freighter were aware of the true identities of their passengers. They'd been recruited in spaceport bars around the Seranos System, one of the fringe systems of the Alphane Alliance which bordered on Raiden-Winterhowe, and they knew *something* was fishy. Nobody, no matter how rich and eccentric, charters a freighter, picks up a crew, and loads the freighter with barbarians, live animals of particularly nasty dispositions, and food that can't possibly recoup the cost of the voyage for reasons that weren't "fishy." But the crew, most of whom had some questionable moments tucked away in their own backgrounds, assumed it was a standard illegal venture. Smuggling, probably, although smuggling *what* was a question. But they knew they were getting paid smuggler's wages, and that was good enough for them.

It was twelve days to the edge of Imperial space, and their first stop was Customs in the Carsta System, Baron Sandhurt's region.

They intended to stop only long enough to clear customs, but it was a nerve-wracking time. This was "insertion," the most dangerous moment of any covert operation. Anything could go wrong. The Mardukans were all briefed with their cover stories. The Earther had hired them to go to Old Earth to work in restaurants. Some of them were soldiers from their home world, yes; but wars were getting short, which was leaving them unemployed, and unemployable. Some of them were cooks, yes. Would you like to try some roast *atul*?

Roger waited at the docking port as the shuttle came alongside, standing with his hands folded behind him and his feet shoulder width apart. Not entirely calm; total calm would have been a dead giveaway. Everyone was always uncomfortable at customs. You never knew when something could go wrong—some crewman with contraband, a change in some obscure regulation that meant a portion of your cargo impounded.

Beach appeared much calmer, as befitted her role. She was only a hired hand, right? Of course she was, and she'd been through customs repeatedly. And if anything was amiss, well, it wasn't her money, was it? The worst that could happen was a black mark against her and, well, that had happened before, hadn't it? She'd still be a captain on some vessel or another. It was just customs.

The airlock's inner hatch slid aside to reveal a medium-height young man with brown hair and slight epicanthic folds to his eyes. He wore a skin-tight environment suit and carried his helmet under his arm.

"Lieutenant Weller?" Roger said, holding out his hand. "Augustus Chung. I'm the charterer for the ship. And this is Captain Beach, her skipper."

Weller was followed by four more customs inspectors—about right for a ship this size. Most of them were older than Weller, seasoned customs inspectors, but not ones who were ever going to be promoted to high rank. Like Weller, they racked their helmets on the bulkhead, then stood waiting.

"Pleased to meet you, Mr. Chung," Weller said.

"Ship's documents," Beach said, extending a pad. "And identity documents on all the passengers and crew. Some of the passengers are . . . a little irregular. Mardukans. They've got IDs from the planetary governor's office, but . . . well, Mardukans don't have birth certificates, you know?"

"I understand," Weller said, taking the pad and transferring the data to his own. "I'll look this over while my team does its survey."

"I've detailed crew to show you around," Beach said, gesturing to the group behind her. It consisted of Macek, Mark St. John, Corporal Bebi, and Despreaux. "Go for it," she continued, looking at Weller's assistants. "I'll be available by com if you need me, but where I'll *be* is down in Engineering." She transferred her glance to Roger. "I'm going to make sure the damned TD capacitors aren't overheating this time, Mr. Chung."

She nodded to the customs party generally, then walked briskly away, and Weller looked up from the data on his pad to cock his head at Roger.

"Trouble with your ship, sir?"

"Just old," Roger replied. "Chartering any tunnel drive ship's bloody expensive, pardon my Chinee. There's little enough margin in this business at all."

"Restaurants?" Weller said, looking back down at the data displayed on his pad. "Most of this appears to be foodstuffs and live cargo."

"It was all checked for contamination," Roger said hurriedly. "There's not much on Marduk that's infectious and transferable. But, yes, I'm starting a restaurant on Old Earth—authentic Mardukan food. Should do well, if it catches on; it's quite tasty. But you know how things are. And the capitalization is horrible. To be successful in the restaurant business, you have to be capitalized for at least eighteen months, so—"

"I'm sure," Weller said, nodding. "Bit of an interesting group of passengers, Mr. Chung. A rather . . . diverse group."

"I've been in the brokering business for years," "Chung" said. "Like my investors, the people I picked to assist me in this venture are friends I've made over the years. It may look like a bit of a pickup crew, but they're not. Good people. The best."

"I can see what your captain meant about the Mardukans." Weller was frowning at the data entries on the Mardukans.

"They're all citizens of the Empire," Roger pointed out. "That's one of the points I've kept in mind—free passage between planets, and all that. No requirement for work visas, among other things."

"It all looks right," Weller said, holstering his pad. "I'll just go tag along with my inspectors."

"If there's nothing else, I'll leave you to your duties. I need to catch up on my paperwork," Roger said.

"Just one more thing," Weller said, taking a device from the left side of his utility belt. "Gene scan. Got to confirm you're who you say you are," he added, smiling thinly.

"Not a problem," Roger replied, and held out his hand with an appearance of assurance he didn't quite feel. They'd tested the bod-mods using Alphane devices, but this was the moment of truth. If the scanner picked up who he really was . . .

Weller ran the device over the back of his hand, then looked at the readout.

"Thank you, Mr. Chung," the lieutenant said. "I'll just get on with my work."

"Of course."

"We're cleared," Beach said as she came into the office.

"Good," Roger replied, then sighed. "This is nerve-wracking."

"Yes, it is," Beach agreed with a grin. "Covert ops are bloody nerve-wracking. I don't know why I don't give it up, but for now, things are looking good. A day more to charge, and we're on our way to Sol."

"Three weeks?" Roger asked.

"Just about—twenty and a half days."

"Time, time, time . . ." Roger muttered. "Ask me for anything but time."

"That damned inspector!" Despreaux groused.

"Problems?" Roger asked. As far as he'd been able to determine, the only trouble the inspectors had found was one of the pickup crew who'd had a stash of illegal drugs. The crewman had been escorted off the ship, and a small fine had been paid.

"No, he just kept trying to pinch my butt," Despreaux said angrily. "*And* asking me to reach up and get things from overhead bins."

"Oh." Roger smiled.

"It's not funny," Despreaux said, glaring at him exasperatedly. "I'll bet you wouldn't have enjoyed it if it'd been *your* butt, either! And I kept expecting him to say something like: 'Aha! You are the notorious Nimashet Despreaux, known companion of the dangerous Prince Roger MacClintock!'"

"I really doubt they'd put it like that, but I know what you mean."

"And I'm worried about Julian."

"So am I."

"If I never see another pocking ship, it be too soon," Poertena muttered as they stepped off the shuttle.

"Sorry to hear you feel that way, Poertena," Julian replied, "since with any luck, we'll see a few more. And try like hell not to talk, okay? Your damned passport says you're from Armagh, and that is *not* an Armaghan accent."

"How do we find this guy?" Denat asked. "I don't see anything that looks like a Navy shuttle."

Halliwell II was a temperate but arid world, right on the edge of Imperial space, near the border with Raiden-Winterhowe. Raiden had tried to "annex" it twice, once since the Halliwell System had joined the Empire. It was an associate world, a nonvoting member of the Empire, with a low population which consisted mostly of miners and scattered farmers.

Sogotown, the capital of Halliwell II and the administrative center for the surrounding Halliwell Cluster, boasted a rather mixed architecture. The majority of the buildings, including the row of godowns around the spaceport, were low rammed-earth structures, but there were a few multistory buildings near the center of town. The entire modest city was placed on the banks of one of the main continent's few navigable rivers, and the newly arrived visitors could see barges being offloaded along the riverfront.

Several ships were scattered around the spaceport—mostly large cargo shuttles, but including a few air-cargo ships, and even one large lighter-than-air ship. None of them had Imperial Navy markings.

"They might be using civilian shuttles," Julian said, "but it's more likely they're not here right now. We'll ask around. Come on, we'll try the bars."

Entry was informal. They'd asked about a customs inspector, but the shack where he should have been was empty. Julian left a data chip with their information on the desk, and then they walked into town.

The main road into town was stabilized earth, a hard surface that was cracked and rutted by wheeled traffic. There were a few electric-powered ground cars around, but much of the traffic (what of it there was) seemed to be tractor, horse, and even ox-drawn carts. It was midday, and hot (by human standards; Denat and Sena had their environment suits cranked considerably higher), and most of the population seemed to be sheltering indoors.

They walked through the godowns ringing the port and past a couple of hock-shops, then stopped outside the first bar they came to. Its garish neon sign advertised Koun beer and featured a badly done picture of a horse's head.

The memory-plastic door dilated as Julian walked up to it. The interior was dim, but he could see four or five men slouched around the bar, and the room smelled of smoke, stale beer, and urine. A corner jukebox played a whining song about whiskey, women, and why they didn't go well together.

"God," Julian whispered. "I'm home."

Denat pulled the membrane mask off his face and looked around, sniffing the air.

"Yeah," he said. "Guess some things are universal."

"So I've noticed," Sena said dryly, true-hands flicking in a body language gesture which expressed semiamused distaste. "And among them are the fact that males are all little boys at heart. Spoiled little boys. Try not to get falling down drunk, Denat."

"You just talk that way because you love me," Denat told her with a deep chuckle, then looked back at Julian. "First round's on you."

"Speaking of universal," Julian muttered, but he led the way to the bar.

The drinkers were all male, all of them rather old, with the weathered faces and hands of men who'd worked outside most of their lives and now had nothing better to do than to be drinking whiskey in the early morning. The bartender was a woman, younger than the drinkers, but not by much, with a look that said she'd been rode hard and put up wet and was going to keep right on riding. Blonde hair, probably from a bottle, with gray and dark brown at the roots. A face that had been pretty once, but a nice smile and a quizzical look at the Mardukans.

"What you drinkin'?" she asked, stepping over from where she'd been talking with the regulars.

"What's on tap?" Julian asked, looking around for a menu. All that decorated the room were signs for beer and whiskey and a few pinups with dart holes in them.

"Koun, Chika, and Alojzy," the woman recited. "I've got Koun, Chika, Alojzy, Zedin, and Jairntorn in bulbs. And if you're a limp-wrist wine drinker, there's red, white, and violet. Whiskey you can see for yourself," she added, jerking a thumb over her shoulder at the racked bulbs and plastic bottles. Most of them were pretty low-cost whiskey, but one caught Julian's eye.

"Two double shots of MacManus, and a full highball," he said, then glanced at Sena and raised an eyebrow. She flicked one hand in a gesture of assent, and he smiled. "Make that two highballs. And then, two glasses of Koun, and a pitcher."

"You know your whiskey, son," the woman said approvingly. "But those highballs're gonna cost you."

"I'll live," Julian told her.

"Who're your big friends?" the bartender asked when she came back with the drinks.

"Denat and Sena. They're Mardukan."

"Scummies?" The woman's eyes widened. "I've heard of them, but I've never seen one. Well, I guess you get all kinds. Long way from home, though."

"Yes, it is," Denat said in broken Imperial. He picked up one of the highballs and passed the second to Sena. Then both of them clinked glasses with Julian and Poertena. "Death to the Kranolta!" He tossed off the drink. "Ahhhh," he gargled. "Smooooth."

Sena sipped more sedately, then twisted both false-hands in a complicated gesture of pleasure.

"It actually is," she said in Marshadan, looking across at Julian. "Amazing. I hadn't expected such a discerning palette out of you, Julian."

"Smart ass," the Marine retorted in the same language, and she gave the coughing grunt of a Mardukan chuckle.

"What'd he say?" the barkeep asked, glancing back and forth between Sena and Julian.

"He was just observing that you should be glad Denat's past his heat, or there'd be blood on the walls," Julian said with a chuckle, grinning at both Mardukans. He took a more judicious sip of his own drink, and had to admit that it was smooth. "God, it's been a long time since I've had a MacManus."

"What are you doing in this godforsaken place?" she asked.

"Looking for a lovely bartender," Julian said with a smile. "And I got lucky."

"Heard it," the woman said, but she smiled back.

"Actually, we've been traveling," Julian replied. "Bit of this here and that there. Picked up Denat and Sena on Marduk, when I had a bit of a problem and they helped me out with it. I heard the Navy's been landing here, and that they've got some civilian crews in their service squadrons. I've got a clean discharge, and so does Magee here," he said, gesturing to Poertena. "Looking to see if there's any work."

"Doubt it." The woman shook her head. "Only thing that lands is cargo shuttles. They pick up supplies and take off again. Sometimes, the crews come in for a drink, but they don't stay long. And they're the only ones who land. Others've asked about work, but they're not hiring. You know what they're doing, right?"

"No," Julian said.

"They're waiting to see who wins in Imperial City. Seems there's a chunk of Parliament that's really gotten ugly about what's happening with the Empress."

"What *is* happening?" Poertena asked, with only the slightest trace of an accent.

"Yeah, the news is saying everything's peachy," Julian noted.

"Yeah, well, they would, wouldn't they?" The bartender shook her head.

"Only one seeing the Empress these days is that snake's asshole Adoula," one of the regulars said, sliding down a stool. "Won't even let the Prime Minister in to see her. They say they've toombied her. She's not in control anymore."

"Shit," Julian said, shaking his head. "Bastards. Calling Adoula a snake's asshole's insulting to snakes."

"Yeah, but he's got the power, don't he?" the regular replied. "Got the Navy on his side. Most of it, anyway. And he's got friends in the Lords, and all."

"I didn't swear my oath to Prince Jackson and his buddies when I was in," Julian said. "I swore it to the Constitution and the Empress. Maybe the admirals will remember that."

"*Sure* they will," one of the other drinkers said mockingly. "In your dreams! The officers're all for Adoula. He's bought them, and they know it. I heard he stepped on a *sierdo* once, and it didn't bite him because of professional courtesy."

There was a chuckle from the group, but it sounded weary.

"Well, just because others have asked, it doesn't mean we shouldn't," Julian said with a sigh. "If they're not hiring, somebody else will be. Any place to sleep around here?"

"Hotel up the road a few blocks," the bartender said. "Tuesday, Friday, and Saturday nights, we've got live entertainment. Strippers on Saturday. Don't be a stranger."

"We'll be back," Julian said, finishing his beer in one long pull. "Let's go look around, guys."

"You'll be back," the regular who'd slid over said. "Isn't much to see."

"And a round for your friends," Julian added, sliding a credit chip onto the scarred bar top. "See you later."

"So what do you think?" the bartender asked after the quartet had left.

"They're not spacers," the regular replied, sipping the cheap whiskey. "Don't move right. Hair's too short. If that guy's *got* discharge papers, they're from the Marines, not Navy. Probably casual muscle. Think they're planning on muscling in on Julio?"

"Doubt it," the bartender said with a frown. "But Julio's generally hiring. And even if he's not, he'll want to know about them. I'd better give him a call."

"You wanna gamble, there's a cut to the house," the bartender said. "Gotta have it to pay the local squeeze."

Poertena glanced up from his hand and shrugged.

"How much?"

"Quarter-credit a hand," she replied. "And here's why," she

added as a short, pale-skinned man stepped through the door to the bar.

The newcomer was apparently about thirty standard years old, with slick black hair and a thin mustache. He was dressed in the height of local fashion—acid-silk red shirt, black trousers, bolero, and a cravat. The line of the bolero was slightly spoiled by a bulge which might have been a needler or a small bead pistol. He was followed by three others, all larger, one of them massive. The short jackets they wore all bulged on the right hip.

"Hey, Julio," the bartender said.

"Clarissa," the man replied with a nod. "I hope you're doing well?"

"Well enough. You want your usual?"

"And a round for the boys," he said, walking over to the table where Poertena, Denat, and one of the regulars were playing. Sena sat nearby, reading what looked like a cheap novel but was actually a Mardukan translation of an Imperial Marines field manual on infiltration tactics and nursing a Mardukan-sized stein of beer.

"Mind if I take a seat?"

"Go ahead," Poertena replied. "Call."

"Two kings," the local said.

"Beats my pocking pair of eights," Poertena said, and the local scooped in the pot.

"New man deals," the "Armaghan" continued, and passed the deck to Julio.

"Seven card stud," the pale-skinned man said, riffling the cards expertly.

Just before he started to deal, Denat reached out one massive hand and placed it over the cards.

"On Marduk," he said solemnly, "cheating is considered part of the game."

"Take your hand off of me unless you want to eat it," Julio said dangerously.

"I wish to know if this is the case here," Denat said, not lifting his hand. "I have been told it isn't, so I haven't palmed any cards. Besides, it's difficult in an environment suit. I simply wish to know, is it the local custom to cheat?"

"You saying I'm cheating?" Julio asked as the most massive guard stepped forward. His move put Sena behind him, and she glanced up casually from her manual, then went back to her reading.

"I'm simply wondering out loud," Denat replied, ignoring the guard. "If it *isn't* the custom, perhaps you would like to remove that card you stuck up your sleeve and shuffle again."

Julio raised one hand to the guard, and then slipped the ace of diamonds from the cuff of the same wrist.

"Just checking," he said, sliding it back into the deck. "Julio Montego."

"Denat Cord," Denat said as the bar regular slid back from the card table.

"I'm just gonna—" the old man said.

"Yeah, why don't you?" Julio agreed without even glancing away from the Mardukan to look at him.

"As I said, on Marduk we have a saying: if you aren't cheating, you aren't trying," Denat explained. "I have no personal reservations about anything along those lines. Humans are so . . . picky about it, though. I was pleased to see you weren't."

"You wanna give it a try?" Julio asked, sliding the cards over. "Just a friendly hand? No money, that is."

"Doesn't seem much point," Denat muttered, "but if you wish."

He'd pulled off the environment suit's gloves and flexed his hands, then shuffled. He moved the cards so quickly they seemed to blur, then slid the deck over for a cut. After Julio had carefully cut the cards, he picked them back up and tossed out a three-way hand.

"Straight stud. No draw."

Julio picked up his cards and shook his head.

"What are the odds of getting a royal flush on the deal?" he asked. "Wow, am I lucky, or what?"

"Yes, very," Denat said. "Yours in diamonds would even have beaten mine, in spades."

"I t'ink maybe we don't play cards," Poertena said. "It's times like t'is I regret teaching t'at modderpocker poker."

"Or maybe, instead of playing, we just put the cards on the table," Julian said, sliding into the chair the regular had vacated. "What can we do for you, Mr. Montego?"

"I dunno," Julio replied. "What *can* you do for me?"

"We're not muscling in on your turf," Julian said delicately. "We're just looking for work with the Navy. If that's not available, we're just going to slide out. No muss, no fuss. No trouble."

"You aren't spacers."

"I've got a data chip says different," Julian pointed out.

"I can pick them up for a credit a pop," Julio scoffed. "And I've got local responsibilities to maintain."

"We're not going to cause any trouble with the locals," Julian said. "Just call us the invisible foursome."

"You've got two scummy bodyguards and a guy says he's from Armagh that's probably never even seen the planet," Julio said. "You're not exactly invisible. What's your angle?"

"Nothing that concerns you, Mr. Montego," Julian replied smoothly. "As I said, it would be better all around if you just ignored us and pretended we were never here. It's not something you want to stick your nose into."

"This is my turf," Julio said flatly. "Everything that goes on here concerns me."

"Not this. It has nothing to do with Halliwell or your turf."

"So what's the angle? You a drug contact for the Navy? Porno? Babes?"

"You're not going to let this lie, are you?" Julian said, shaking his head.

"No."

"Mr. Montego, do you have someone who you . . . deal with? Not a boss, not that. But someone to whom you, perhaps, forward a portion of your local income? For services rendered?"

"Maybe," Montego said cautiously.

"Well, that gentleman probably has someone with whom he deals in turn. And so on, and so forth. And at some level, Mr. Montego, well above what a friend of mine would refer to as our pay grade, there's a gentleman who probably should have mentioned that some of his associates were going to be sliding through your turf. We're not dealers, we're not mules. We're . . . associates. Conveyors of information. And before you ask, Mr. Montego, no. You're not going to find out what information. If you choose to get busy about that, Mr. Montego, things will get very ugly, very quickly. Not only in this bar, but at a level you don't even want to think about. The sort of level where people don't hire spaceport bouncers, but professional gentlemen who are familiar with the use of powered armor and plasma cannon, Mr. Montego."

All of this was said with a thin smile while Julian's eyes were locked on the local's.

"He's not pocking kidding," Poertena said, and rolled up his sleeve to reveal a thin scar line where an arm had been regrown. "Pocking trust me on t'at."

"I would, if I were you," Sena said in perfect Imperial from behind the mobster.

It was the first time she'd spoken anything but Mardukan, and Julio's head turned in her direction. She looked back at him with the closest thing to a smile a Mardukan's limited facial muscles could produce, and his eyes narrowed as he observed the heavy, military-grade bead pistol which had somehow magically appeared in her lap. She made no move to touch it, only went back to her book.

"One such professional gentleman, in his own way," Julian observed dryly, never so much as glancing in Sena's direction.

"You're correct," Julio said. "There should have been some word passed. But there wasn't. And there's a price for doing business on my turf; two thousand credits, and this meeting never happened."

"T'at's pocking—"

"Pay him," Julian said. He stood up. "Nice doing business with you, Mr. Montego."

He held out his hand.

"Yes," Montego replied. "And the name was?"

"Pay the man," was all Julian said, and walked over to the bar.

Poertena pulled out two large-denomination credit chips and slid them across the tabletop.

"I don' suppose you'd care por a priendly game of poker?"

"I don't think so," Montego said, standing up. "And it would probably be better if you kept your mouth shut."

"Story of my pocking life," Poertena muttered.

The stripper turned out to be a rather tired looking woman in her forties, and the live band was louder than it was capable. Sena and Denat, whose species' sexuality was rather different from that of humans, found the entire production bizarre, to say the very least, but they'd turned out to be quite popular with the regulars. Eight Mardukan-sized hands could set and maintain a beat for bumps and grinds that not even *this* band could completely screw up. And whatever else, the noise and crowd made for a decent place for a secure conversation.

Julian slid into the vacant seat beside the Navy warrant officer and nodded.

"Buy you a drink?" he asked. "Seems right for our boys in black."

"Sure," the pilot said. He was young, probably not too long out of flight school. "I'll take an alcodote before I lift, but, Christ, a guy's got to have some downtime."

"I've only seen shuttle crews come down," Julian said over the noise of the band and the Mardukans' enthusiastic clapping. Nobody in the bar had to know that Denat and Sena's contribution was the body-language equivalent of semihysterical laughter among their people.

"Fleet orders!" the pilot shouted back as the drummers started an inexpert riff. "No contact with the planet. Hell, even *this* is better," he said, pointing at the tired-looking stripper. "We've about run through the pornography available on the ship, and my right forearm is getting sort of overdeveloped."

"That bad?" Julian laughed.

"That bad," the warrant replied.

"You're from Captain Poertena's ship, right?" Julian said, leaning closer.

"Who wants to know?" The warrant took a sip of his drink. "Yes or no?"

"Okay, yes," the warrant said. "Man, I know I've had too much to drink. She's starting to look good."

"In that case, I need you to pass a message to your captain."

"What?" The warrant officer really looked at Julian for the first time.

"I need you to pass a message to your captain," Julian repeated. "Do it in person, and do it alone. Message is: The boy who stole the fish is sorry. Just that. And everything he's heard lately is a lie. Got it?"

"What's this all about?" the warrant asked as Julian stood up.

"If your captain wants you to know, he'll tell you," Julian replied. "In person, alone. Got it? Repeat it, Warrant." The last was clearly an order.

"The boy who stole the fish is sorry," the warrant officer repeated.

"Do it, on your honor," Julian said, and walked into the crowd.

"How was the run?" Captain Poertena asked. He was looking at data on a holo display and eating a banana. Fresh fruit was a precious rarity in Sixth Fleet these days, even in one of the supply haulers, like *Capodista*, and he was breaking it into small bites to enjoy it properly.

"Went fine, Sir," Warrant Officer Sims replied. "We got a full load this time, and I spoke with one of the Governor's representatives. They've been trying to fill our parts list, so far with no luck."

"Not surprising," Poertena said. "Well, maybe better luck next week. Sooner or later Admiral Helmut is going to have to fish or cut bait. Any new news from the capital?"

"No, Sir," Sims said. "But I had a very strange conversation on-planet. A guy came up to me and asked me to pass you a message. In person, and alone."

"Oh?" Poertena looked up from the holo display, one cheek bulging with banana while another piece rose towards his mouth.

"The boy who stole the fish is sorry," Sims said.

The hand stopped rising, then began to drop as Poertena's swarthy face went gray.

"What did you say?" the captain snapped, his mouth half-full.

"The boy who stole the fish is sorry," Sims repeated.

The piece of banana was crushed between two fingers, and then flung onto the desk.

"What did he look—No. Did this guy have an accent?"

"No, Sir," the warrant said, coming halfway to attention.

"Did he say anything else?"

"Just something about everything being a lie," Sims said. "Sir, what's this all about?"

"Sims, you do not have the need to know," Poertena said, swallowing and shaking his head. "Modderpocker. *I* don't have the need to pocking know." The captain had worked hard on his accent, and it only tended to show in times of stress. "I did not pocking *need* t'is. Where was t'is guy?"

"Well . . ." Sims hesitated. "In a bar, Captain. I know they're off limits—"

"Forget t'at," Poertena said. "Modderpocker. I've got to t'ink. Sims, you don't tell *anyone* about t'is, clear?"

"Clear, Sir." It was Sims' turn to swallow hard.

"I'll probably need you in a while. Get some chow and crew rest if you need. I t'ink we're going back to Halliwell."

"Sir, regulations state—"

"Yeah. Well, I t'ink t'e pocking regulations jus' wen' out t'e pocking airlock."

Julian looked up as a sizable shadow loomed over the restaurant table.

"Guy that looks a lot like a Poertena just walked into the bar," Denat said. "He's with that shuttle pilot. Sena's keeping an eye on them."

Julian had gone over to one of the local restaurants that served a really *good* bitok. He'd missed them on Marduk, and this place did them right—thick, cooked to a light pink in the middle, and with really good barbecue sauce. It was infinitely preferable to the "snacks" served in the bar, and Denat and Sena had remained behind to keep an eye on things while he ate it.

Now he set down the bitok and took a sip of cola.

"Okay, showtime," he said. "Where's Magee?"

"Dunno," the Mardukan said.

"Find him," Julian replied, and tried very hard not to be irritated by the little Pinopan's absence. After all, Julian hadn't expected Captain Poertena to show up this fast, either, and it was late at night by local time. *Capodista*'s skipper must have gotten the message and taken the first available shuttle back.

Julian dropped enough credits on the table to pay for the bitok and a tip and walked out. He glanced around as he stepped out of the restaurant's door. The street was somewhat more animated at night, with groups moving from bar to bar, and he felt mildly uneasy without backup. But there was nothing he could do about that.

He went to the bar and looked around. Despite the hour, the party was still in full roar, and the band had gotten, if anything, worse. At least the stripper was gone.

He moved along the edge of the crowd around the bar until he spotted Sena. She was by the bar, one lower elbow propped nonchalantly on its surface while a true-hand nursed a beer, where she could keep an unobtrusive eye on the two Navy officers who'd taken one of the tables at the back. Lousy trade craft. It was like signaling "Look over here! *We're* having a Secret Conversation!"

He chose a spot of his own at the bar, out of sight of them but where Sena could flash him a signal if they tried to leave. About ten minutes later, Denat loomed through the door, followed by Poertena.

"Where were you?"

"Taking care of some pocking personal business."

"You know that human who was taking off her clothes?" Denat asked.

"God*damn* it, P . . . Magee!"

"Hey, a guy's got pocking needs!"

"Well, you're not gonna have the equipment to do anything about them if you just wander off that way again," Julian said ominously, then sighed and shook his head at Poertena's unrepentant look.

"C'mon," he said, and led the way through the crowd towards the Navy officers' table.

"Captain Poertena," he said, sitting down and shifting his chair to a spot from which he could keep an eye on the bar.

"Well, I know *he's* not Julio," the captain said, pointing at the Mardukan. "And neither is he," he added dryly as Sena wandered over to join them. "And you're too tall," he continued, looking at Julian.

"Hey, Uncle Marciel," Poertena said with a slight catch in his voice. "Long pocking time."

"Goddamn it, Julio," the captain said, shaking his head. "What have you gotten yourself into? I should have had a team of Marines standing by, you know that? I'm putting my balls on the line here for you."

"They're not on the line for him," Julian said. "They're on the line for the Empire."

"Which one are you?" the captain snapped.

"Adib Julian."

"I don't recognize the name," the captain said, regarding him intently.

"You wouldn't. I was just a sergeant in one of the line companies. But get this straight, we've been on Marduk," Julian gestured with a thumb at Denat and Sena, "for the last ten months. *Marduk*. We can prove that a dozen different ways. We had *nothing* to do with it."

"This is about the coup!" the pilot blurted. "Holy shit."

"Sergeant—well, Captain, sort of, Adib Julian," Julian said, nodding. "Bronze Battalion of the Empress' Own. Currently, S-2 to Prince Roger Ramius Sergei Alexander Chiang MacClintock. Heir Primus to the Throne of Man."

Despite the racket all around them, a brief bubble of intense silence seemed to surround the barroom table.

"So," Captain Poertena said after a moment, "what's the plan?"

"I need to talk to Helmut," Julian said. "I've got encrypted data chips that prove beyond any reasonable doubt that we were on Marduk when the coup occurred, not Old Earth. This is *Adoula's* plot, not the Prince's. Helmut needs to know that."

"What's *he* going to do with it?" Sims asked.

"Warrant, that's between the Admiral and myself," Julian said.

"You realize, of course, that you're going to spend the next few weeks, at least, in solitary lockdown. Right?"

"Shit, this is what I get for talking to strangers in bars," the warrant said. "Let me get this straight. The Prince was on *Marduk*. Which means the whole line about him being behind the attempted coup so much bullshit. Right?"

"Right," Julian ground out. "Trust me on that one. I was there the whole time. Poertena and I are two of only twelve survivors from an entire Marine *company* that went in with him. We had to *walk* across that hot, miserable, rain-filled ball of jungle and swamp. It's a long story. But we didn't even know there'd *been* a coup until a month, month and a half ago. And *Adoula* is in charge, not the Empress."

"We'd sort of figured that out," the captain said dryly. "Which is why we're stooging around in the back of beyond out here. You're either a godsend or a goddammed menace, and I can't decide which." He sighed and shrugged. "You'll have to meet the Admiral. Sims, you and these other four go in solitary when we get to the ship. When we make rendezvous with the Fleet, I'll send them over in your shuttle to the *Zetian*. Why you four, by the way?"

"Julio to convince you," Julian said. "Me, because I've met Admiral Helmut before. And Denat and Sena because they're a counterpoint to proving we were on Marduk. And because Denat's a buddy of Julio's."

"Taught me everything I know," Denat said, shrugging all four shoulders.

"In that case, remind me not to play poker with you."

Admiral Angus Helmut, Third Baron Flechelle, was short, almost a dwarf. Well under regulation height, his feet dangled off the deck in a standard station chair, which was why the one in which he now sat was lower than standard. He had a gray, lined face, high cheekbones, thinning gray hair, and gray eyes. His black uniform was two uniform changes old—the pattern he'd worn as an ensign, and quite possibly the *same* uniform Ensign Helmut had worn, judging by the smoothness of the fabric. He wore his admiral's pips on one collar point, and the crossed cloak and daggers of his original position in Naval Intelligence on the other, and his eyes were slightly bloodshot from lack of sleep as he stared at Julian as if the Marine were something a cat had left on his doorstep.

"Adib Julian," he said. "I should have known. I noticed your name on the seizure orders and thought that treason would be about your *métier*."

"I've never committed treason," Julian shot back. "No more than you have by keeping your fleet out of contact. The traitors are Adoula and Gianetto and Greenberg."

"Perhaps. But what I see before me is a jumped-up sergeant— one I last met standing charges for falsifying a readiness report."

"There've been changes," Julian replied.

"So you tell me." The admiral considered him with basilisk eyes for several seconds, then tipped his chair very slightly back. "So, the wastrel prince returns as pretender to the Throne, and you want *my* help?"

"Let's just say . . . there have been changes," Julian repeated. "Calling Master Rog a wastrel would be . . . incorrect at this point. And not a pretender to the Throne; he just wants his mother back on it, and that bastard Adoula's head. Although his balls would do in a pinch."

"So what's the non-wastrel's plan?"

"I have to get some assurances that you're going to back us," Julian pointed out. "Not simply use the information to carry favor with Adoula, *Admiral*."

The admiral's jaw muscles flexed at that, and he shrugged angrily.

"Well, that's the problem in these little plots that run around the Palace," he said. "Trust. I can give you all the assurances in the universe. Prepare the fleet for battle, head for Sol. And then, when we get there, clap you in irons and send you to Adoula as a trophy, along with all your plans. By the same token, there could be Marines standing right outside my cabin, waiting for me to reveal my disloyalty to the Throne. In which case, when I say 'Oh, yes, Sergeant Julian, we'll help your little plot,' they come busting in and arrest me."

"Not if Sergeant Major Steinberg is still in charge," Julian said with a slight grin.

"There is that," Helmut admitted. He and the sergeant major had been close throughout their respective (and lengthy) careers. Which was one reason Steinberg had been Sergeant Major of Sixth Fleet as long as Helmut had commanded it. "Nonetheless."

"The Prince intends to capture his mother, and the Palace, and then to bring in independents to show that she's been held in duress, and that he had nothing to do with it."

"Well, that much is obvious," Helmut snapped. "How?"

"Are you going to back us?"

The admiral leaned further back and steepled his fingers, staring at the sergeant.

"Falsifying a weapons room readiness report," he said, changing the subject. "It wasn't actually your doing, was it?"

"I took the blame. It was my *responsibility*."

"But you didn't do the shoddy work, did you?"

"No," Julian admitted. "I trusted someone else's statement that it had been done, and signed off on it. The *last* time I made that particular mistake."

"And what did you do to the person who was actually responsible for losing you your stripes?"

"Beat the crap out of him, Sir," Julian replied after a short pause.

"Yes, I saw the surgeon's report," Helmut said with a trace of satisfaction. Then— "What happened to Pahner?" he rapped suddenly.

"Killed, Sir," Julian said, and swallowed. "Taking the ship we captured to get off that mudball."

"Hard man to kill," Helmut mused.

"It was a Saint covert commando ship," Julian said. "We didn't know until we were in too deep to back out. He died to save the Prince."

"That was his responsibility," Helmut said. "And what was his position on this . . . countercoup?"

"We developed the original plan's framework before the attack on the ship, Sir. It had his full backing."

"It would," the admiral said. "He was a rather all-or-nothing person. Very well, Julian. *Yes*, you have my backing. No Marines at the last minute, no double crosses."

"You haven't asked what you get for it," Julian noted. "The Prince will owe you a rather large favor."

"I get the safety of the Empire," Helmut growled. "If I asked for anything else, would you trust me?"

"No," Julian admitted. "Not in this. But the Prince authorized me to tell you that, as far as he's concerned, you can have Sixth Fleet or Home Fleet or CNO 'until you die or go senile.' That last is a direct quote."

"And what are *you* getting, Sergeant?" the admiral asked, ignoring the offer.

"As a *quid pro quo*? Nada. Hell, Sir, I haven't even been *paid* in over ten months. He told me before we left that I'm a captain, but I didn't ask for it."

Julian paused and shrugged.

"The safety of the Empire? Admiral, I'm sworn to serve the Empire, we both are, but *I* serve Master Rog. We all do. You'd have to have been there to understand. He's not . . . who he was. None of us are. We're Prince Roger's Own. Period. They call aides 'dog-robbers' because they'll rob a dog of its bone, if that's what the admiral wants. We're . . . we're *pig*-robbers. We'll steal slop, if that's what Roger wants. Or conquer the Caravazan Empire. Or set him up as a pirate king. Maybe Pahner wasn't that way, maybe he fought for the Empire, even to the last. But the rest of us are, we few who survive. We're Roger's dogs. And if he wants to save the Empire, well, we'll save the Empire. And if he'd told me to come in here and assassinate you, well, Admiral, you'd be dead."

"Household troops," the admiral said distastefully.

"Yes, Sir, that's us. And the nastiest group thereof you're ever likely to see. And that doesn't even count the Mardukans. Don't judge them by Denat; he just follows us around to see what mischief we get into. Rastar or Fain or Honal would nuke a world without blinking if Roger told them to."

"Interesting that he can command such loyalty," Helmut mused.

"That doesn't . . . fit his profile from before his disappearance. In fact, that was one factor in my disbelief that he had anything to do with the coup."

"Well, things change," Julian said. "They change fast on Marduk. Admiral, I've got a presentation on what we went through and what our plans are. If you'd like to see it."

"I would," Helmut admitted. "I'd like to see what could change a clothes horse into—"

"Just say a MacClintock."

"Well, well—Harvard Mansul." Etienne Thorwell, Editor in Chief of *Imperial Astrographic*, shook his head with an expression which tried, not entirely successfully, to be more of a scowl than a grin. "Late as usual—*way* past deadline! And don't you dare tell me you want *per diem* for the extra time, you little weasel!"

"Good to see you again, too, Etienne," Mansul said with a smile of his own. He walked across the office, and Thorwell stood to shake his hand. Then the editor gave a "what-the-hell" shrug and wrapped both arms around the smaller man in a bear hug.

"Thought we'd lost you for sure this time, Harvard," he said after a moment, stepping back and holding the reporter at arm's length. "You were supposed to be back months ago!"

"I know." Mansul shrugged, and his smile was more than a little crooked. "Seems our information on the societal setup was a bit, um, out of date. The Krath have undergone a religious conversion with some really nasty side effects. They almost decided to eat me."

"*Eat* you?" Thorwell blinked, then regarded Mansul skeptically. "Ritualistic cannibalism of 'great white hunters' by any sort of established city-building society is for bad novelists and holodrama, Harvard."

"Usually." Mansul nodded in agreement. "This time around, though—" He shrugged. "Look, I've got the video to back it up. But even more important, I got caught in a shooting war between the 'civilized' cannibals and a bunch of 'barbarian tribesmen' who objected to being eaten . . . and did something about it. It's pretty damned spectacular stuff, Etienne."

That much, he reflected, was certainly true. Of course, he'd had to do some pretty careful editing to keep any of the humans (or their weapons) from appearing in the aforesaid video. A few carefully scripted interviews with Pedi Karuse's father had also been added to the mix, making it quite plain that the entire war—and the desperate battle which had concluded it—had been the result of purely Mardukan efforts. The fact that it made the Gastan look like a military genius had tickled the Shin monarch's sense of humor, but he'd covered admirably for the human involvement.

"Actual combat footage?" Thorwell's nose almost twitched, and Mansul hid a smile. He'd told Roger and O'Casey how his boss would react to that. The official *IAS* charter was to report seriously on alien worlds and societies, with substantive analysis and exploration, not cater to core-world stereotypes of "barbarian behavior," but the editorial staff couldn't afford to ignore the realities of viewership demographics.

"Actual combat footage," he confirmed. "Pikes, axes, and black powder and the decisive defeat of the 'civilized' side by the barbarians who *don't* eat people. And who happen to have saved my own personal ass in the process."

"Hot damn," Thorwell said. "'Fearless reporter rescued by valiant barbarian ruler.' That kind of stuff?"

"That was how I figured on playing it," Mansul agreed. "With suitably modest commentary from myself, of course."

They looked at each other and chuckled almost in unison. Harvard Mansul had already won the coveted Interstellar Correspondents Society's Stimson-Yamaguchi Medal twice. If this footage was as good as Thorwell suspected it was, he might be about to win it a third time.

Mansul knew exactly what the chief editor was thinking. But what made *him* chuckle was the knowledge that he had the SYM absolutely sewed up once he was able to actually release the documentary he'd done of Roger's adventures on Marduk. Especially with the inside track he'd been promised on coverage of the countercoup after it came off, as well.

"I've got a lot of other stuff, too," the reporter went on after a few moments. "In-depth societal analysis of both sides, some pretty good stuff on their basic tech capabilities, and an update on the original geological survey. It really underestimated the planet's vulcanism, Etienne, and I think that probably played a big part in how some of the social developments played out. And a lot on basic culture, including their arts and crafts and their cuisine." He shook his head and rolled his eyes appreciatively. "And I've gotta tell you, while I don't think I'd care a bit for Krath dietary staples, the rest of these people can *cook*.

"Just before the wheels came off for the Krath, they made contact with these people from the other side of the local ocean—from a place called K'Vaern's Cove, sort of a local maritime trading empire—and I got some good footage on *them*, too. And the *food* those people turned out!"

He shook his head, and Thorwell chuckled again.

"Food, Harvard? That was never your big thing before."

"Well, yeah," Mansul agreed with a smile, "but that was when *I* wasn't likely to be winding up on anyone's menu. What I was thinking was, we play off the cuisine of the noncannibals when we start reporting on the Krath. Use it as a contrast and compare sort of thing."

"Um." Thorwell frowned thoughtfully, scratching his chin, then nodded. Slowly, at first, and then more enthusiastically. "I like it!" he agreed.

"I thought you might," Mansul said. Indeed, he'd counted on it. And it fitted in with the traditional *IAS* position—a way to use the shuddery-shivery concept of cannibalism by simply mentioning it in the midst of a scholarly analysis and comparison of the rest of the planet's cooking.

"All right," he said, leaning forward and setting his small, portable holo player on Thorwell's coffee table, "I thought we might start with this bit. . . ."

"Helmut's moving," General Gianetto said as Prince Jackson's secretary closed the prince's office door behind him.

The office was on the top occupied level of the Imperial Tower, a megascraper that rose almost a kilometer into the air to the west of Imperial city. Adoula's view was to the east, moreover, where he could keep an eye on what he was more and more coming to consider his personal fiefdom.

Jackson Adoula was man in late middle age, just passing his hundred and twelfth birthday, with black hair that was graying at the temples. He had a lean, ascetic face and was dressed in the height of current Court fashion. His brocade-fronted tunic was of pearl-gray natural silk, a tastefully neutral background for the deep, jewel-toned purples, greens, and crimson of the embroidery. His round, stand-up collar was, perhaps, just a tiny bit lower-cut than a true fashion stickler might have demanded, but that was his sole concession to comfort. The jeweled pins of several orders of nobility gleamed on his left breast, and his natural-leather boots glistened like shiny black mirrors below his fashionably baggy dark-blue trousers.

Now he looked up at his fellow conspirator and raised one aristocratic eyebrow.

"Moving where?" he asked.

"No idea," Gianetto said, taking a chair. The general was taller than the prince, fit and trim-looking with a shock of gray hair cut short enough to show his scalp. He was also the first Chief of Naval Operations—effectively, the Empire's uniformed commander in chief—who was a general and not an admiral. "The carrier I had watching him said Sixth Fleet just tunneled out, all at once. I've pushed out sensor ships. If they come back in anywhere within four light-days of Sol, we'll know about it."

"They can sit out eighteen light-*years* and tunnel in in six hours," Adoula said.

"Tell me something I don't know," Gianetto replied.

"All right," Adoula said, "I will. One of Helmut's shuttles picked up four people from Halliwell Two before he departed. Two humans and a pair of Mardukans."

"Mardukans?" The general frowned. "You don't see many of those around."

"The word from our informants is that they were heavies for an underworld organization. One of the humans had a UOW passport;

the other one an Imperial. They're both fakes, obviously, but the Imperial one is in the database. He's supposedly from Armagh, but his accent was Pinopan."

"Criminals?" Gianetto rubbed his right index and thumb together while he considered that. "That makes a certain amount of sense. Helmut has got to be hurting for spares; they're trying to get their ships refurbed off the black market."

"Possibly. But we don't want to assume that."

"No," the general agreed, but he was clearly already thinking about something else. "What about this bill to force an independent evaluation of the Empress?" he asked.

"Oh, I'm supporting it," Adoula replied. "Of course."

"Are you *nuts*?" Gianetto snarled. "If a doctor gets one look at her—"

"It won't come to that," Adoula assured him. "*I'm* supporting it, but every vote I can beg, bribe, cajole, or blackmail is against it. It won't even get out of committee."

"Let's hope," Gianetto said, and frowned. "I'm less than enthused by the . . . methods you're using." His frown turned into a grimace of distaste. "Bad enough to keep the Empress on a string, but . . ."

"The defenses built into the Empress are extraordinary," Adoula said sternly. "Since she proved unwilling to be reasonable, extraordinary measures were necessary. All we have to do is sit tight for five more months. Let me handle that end. You just keep your eye on the Navy."

"That's under control," Gianetto assured him. "With the exception of that bastard, Helmut. And as long as we don't get any 'independent evaluation' of Her Majesty. If what you're doing to the Empress gets out, they won't just kill us; they'll cut us into pieces and feed us to dogs."

"Now I'm a real estate agent," Dobrescu grumped.

"Broker," Macek said. "Facilitator. Lessor's representative. Something."

The neighborhood was a light industrial park on the slope of what had once been called the "Blue Ridge." On a clear day, you could see just about to the Palace. Or you would have been able to, if it weren't for all the skyscrapers and megascrapers in the way.

It had once been a rather nice industrial park, but time and shifting trade had left it behind. Its structures would long ago have been demolished to clear space for larger, more useful buildings, but for various entailments that prevented change. Most of the buildings were vacant, a result of the boom and bust cycle in commercial real estate. Fortunately, the one they were looking for was one such. They were supposed to be meeting the owner's representative, but she was late.

And, inevitably, it was a miserable day. The weather generators *had* to let an occasional cold front through, and this was the day that had been scheduled for it. So they sat in the aircar, watching the rain sheet off the windscreen, and watched the empty building with a big "For Lease" sign on the front.

Finally, a nine-passenger utility aircar sat down, and a rather attractive blonde in her thirties got out, set up a rain shield, and then hurried over to the building's covered portico.

Dobrescu and Macek got out, ignoring the rain and cold, and walked over to join her.

"Mr. Ritchie?" The woman held out her hand. "Angie Beringer. Pleased to meet you. Sorry I'm late."

"Not a problem," Dobrescu said, shaking the offered hand.

"Let me get this unlocked," she said, and set her pad against the door.

The personnel door led into a small reception area. More locked doors led into the warehouse itself.

"Just over three thousand square meters," the real estate lady said. "The last company that had it was a printing outfit." She pointed to the rear of the big warehouse and a line of heavy plasteel doors. "Those are secure rooms for ink, from what I was told. Apparently it's pretty hazardous stuff. The building has a clear bill of environmental health, though."

"Figures," Macek said, picking up a dust-covered flyer from a box—one of many—against one of the walls. "Escort advertisements. Hey, this one looks just like Shara!"

"Can it," Dobrescu said, and looked at Beringer. "It looks good. It'll do anyway."

"First and last month's deposit, minimum lease of two years," the woman said diffidently. "Mr. Chung's credit checked out just fine, but the owners insist."

"That's fine. How do we do the paperwork?"

"Thumb print here," the real estate agent said, holding out her pad. "And send us a transfer."

"Can I get the keys now?" Dobrescu asked as he pressed the pad to give his wholly false thumb print.

"Yes," Beringer said. "But if we don't get the transfer, the locks will be changed, and you'll be billed for it."

"You'll get the money," Dobrescu promised, holding his pad up to hers. He checked to make sure the key codes had transferred and made a mental note to change them. "We're going to take a look around," he said then.

"Go ahead," she replied. "If you don't need me?"

"Thanks for meeting us in this mess," Macek replied.

"What are you going to use it for, again?" she asked curiously.

"My boss wants to start a chain of restaurants," Dobrescu answered. "Authentic off-planet food. We need some place to store it, other than the ship it's coming in on."

"Well, maybe I'll get a chance to try it out," Beringer said.

"I'll make sure you get an invite."

Once the woman was gone, they went back out to the aircar and got the power pack, some tools, and a grav-belt.

"I hope like hell the modifications haven't covered it up," Macek said.

"Yeah," Dobrescu agreed. He took out a laser measuring device, checked the readout, and pointed to the center plasteel door. "There."

The room beyond was dimly lit, but what were clearly power lines stuck out of one wall near the ceiling.

"Nobody ever wondered about those?"

"Buildings like this go through so many changes and owners," Dobrescu said, putting on the belt, "that stuff gets rewired all the time. As long as it's not currently hot, nobody cares what it used to power."

He touched a stud on the belt and lifted up to the wiring, where he cautiously applied a heavy-gauge voltage meter. There were smaller wires for controls beside the power cables, and he hooked a box to them and took a reading.

"Yeah, there's something back there," he said. "Toss me the power line."

He caught the coil of heavy-duty cable on the second toss, and wired it into the power leads. Then he hooked up the control wires and lowered himself back down to the ground.

"Now to see if we're on a fool's errand," he muttered, and keyed a sequence into the control box.

There was a heavy grinding noise. The walls of the warehouse were set into the side of the hill and made of large, precast slabs of plascrete, with thin lines separating them for expansion and contraction. Now the center slab began to move backward, apparently into the solid hill. It cleared the slabs on either side, then began to slide sideways, revealing a tunnel into the hill. It moved surprisingly smoothly . . . until it abruptly stopped part way with a metallic twang.

"We need a lamp," Dobrescu said.

Macek went back out to the aircar for a hand light, and, with its aid, they found the chunk of fallen plascrete that blocked the door's track, levered it out of the way, and got the door fully open and operating. The air in the tunnel had the musty smell of long disuse, and they both put on air masks before they followed it into the hill.

The walls were concrete—real, old-fashioned concrete—dripping with water and cracked and pitted with extreme age. The door that sealed the far end of the tunnel was made of heavy steel, with a locking bar. Both had been covered in protective sealant, and when they got the sealant off, the portal opened at a touch.

The room beyond was large, and, unlike the approach tunnel, its air was bone-dry. More corridors stretched into the distance, and there was a small fusion generator on the floor of the main room. It was a very old model, also sealed against the elements. Dobrescu and

Macek cut the sealant away and, after studying the instructions, got it into operation.

Lights came on in the room. Fans began to move. In the distance, a gurgling of pumps started up.

"Looks like we're in business," Dobrescu said.

"What's the name of this place?"

"It used to be called Greenbrier."

"This one's not nearly as pretty as the last one," Macek said.

"Get what you're given," Dobrescu replied as they climbed out of the aircar. He'd been keeping a careful eye on a group of young men lounging on the corner. When the real estate agent landed and got out, they straightened up and one of them whistled.

The young woman—this one a short woman in her twenties, with faintly African features—ignored the whistle and strode over to the two waiting "businessmen."

"Mr. Ritchie?" she asked, looking at both of them.

"Me," Dobrescu said.

"Pleased to meet you," she said, shaking his hand, then gestured at the building. "There it is."

This area had once been a small town, before it was absorbed by the burgeoning Imperial City megalopolis. The town, for historical reasons, had managed to maintain its "traditional" buildings, however. This specific building had predated even the ancient United States . . . which had predated the Empire by over a thousand years. The home of an early politician of the unified states, it had a pleasant view of the small river that ran through the town. It had been maintained, literally, for millennia.

Yet shifting trade, again, had finally ruined it. The plaster walls were cracked and peeling, the roof sunken in. Windows had been broken out. The massive oaks which had once shaded the beautiful house of an early president were long gone, victims of the narrow band of sunlight available in a town surrounded by skyscrapers. The small town was now a drug and crime haven.

There were, however, signs of improvement. The pressure of real estate values this near the center of Imperial City had sent the outriders of a "gentrification" wave washing gently through it. Many of the ancient buildings were cloaked in scaffolding, and there were coffee shops and small grocers scattered along the narrow streets. The quaint old houses of what had once been Fredericksburg, Virginia, had become a haven for the Bohemians who survived in the urban jungle.

And they were about to get a new restaurant.

Dobrescu poked through the building, avoiding holes in the wood floors and shaking his head at the plaster fallen from the ceiling.

"This is going to take one helluva lot of renovation," he said, again shaking his head.

"I have some other buildings I can show you," the real estate agent offered.

"None of them meet the specifications," Dobrescu said. "This is the only one in the area that will do. We'll just have to get it fixed up. Fast." He consulted his toot and frowned. "In . . . fourteen days."

"That's going to be . . . tough," the young woman said.

"That's why the boss sent me." Dobrescu sighed.

Roger rolled over carefully, trying not to disturb Despreaux, and pressed the acceptance key on the flashing intercom.

"Mr. Chung," Beach said. "We've exited tunnel-space in the Sol System, and we're currently on course for the Mars Three checkpoint. We've gotten an updated download, including messages for you from your advance party on Old Earth."

"Great," Roger said quietly, keeping his voice down. "How long to orbit?"

"About thirteen hours, with the routing they gave us," Beach replied with a frown. "We're in a third-tier parking orbit, not far from L-3 position. Best I could get."

"That doesn't matter," Roger lied, thinking about how long that meant with Patty on a shuttle. "I'll go check the messages now."

"Yes, Sir," Beach said, and cut the connection.

"We're there?" Despreaux asked, rolling over.

"In the system," Roger replied. "Ten hours to parking orbit. I'm going to go see what Ritchie and . . ." He trailed off.

"Peterka," Despreaux prompted.

"Peterka have to say." He got to his feet and slipped on a robe.

"Well, I'm going back to sleep," Despreaux said, rolling back over. "I have to be insane to marry an insomniac."

"But a very cute insomniac," Roger said as he turned on his console.

"And getting better in bed," Despreaux said sleepily.

Roger looked at the messages and nodded in satisfaction.

"We got both buildings," he said.

"Mm . . ."

"Good prices, too."

"Mmmm . . ."

"The warehouse looks like it's in pretty good shape."

"Mmmmmmm!"

"The restaurant needs a lot of work, but he thinks it can be ready in time."

"MMMMMMMMMM!"

"Sorry. Are you trying to sleep?"

"Yes!"

Roger smiled and looked at the rest of the messages in silence. There were codes embedded in them, and he nodded in satisfaction as he scanned them. Things were going well. If anything, too well. But it was early in the game.

He checked out some other information sources, including a list of personal ads on sites dedicated to the male-friendly segment of society. His eyes lit at one, but then he read the signature and mail address and shook his head. Right message, wrong person.

He pulled out the schematic of the Palace again and frowned. All the surviving Marines, Eleanora, and his own memories had contributed to it, but he'd never realized how little of the Palace he actually *knew*. And the Marines, apparently deliberately, had never been shown certain areas. He knew of at least three semisecret passages in the warren of buildings, the Marines knew a couple of others, and he suspected that it was laced with them.

The original design had been started by Miranda MacClintock, and she'd been a terribly paranoid person. Successive designers had tried to outdo her, and what they'd created was something like the ancient Mycenaean labyrinth. He doubted that *anyone* knew all the secret passages, storerooms, armories, closets, and sewers. It covered in area which had once been home to a country's executive mansion, capital buildings, a major park, two major war memorials, and various museums and government buildings. All of that area—nearly six square kilometers—was now simply "the Palace." Including the circular park around it, grass only, with clear fields of fire. And there was talk of expanding it even further. Wouldn't that be lovely? Homelike.

Finally, realizing he was working himself into a fret, he went back to bed and lay looking at the overhead. After several minutes, he nudged Despreaux.

"What do you mean I'm getting better?"

"*Mwuff*? You woke me up to ask me that and you expect me to *answer*?"

"Yeah. I'm your Prince, you've got to answer questions like that."

"This whole plan is going to fail," Despreaux said, never opening her eyes, "in about thirty seconds. When I strangle you with my bare hands."

"What do you mean, 'getting better'?"

"Look, good sex requires practice," Despreaux said, shaking her head and still not turning over. "You haven't had a lot of practice. You're learning. That takes time."

"So I need more practice?" Roger grinned. "No time like the present."

"Roger, go to sleep."

"Well, you said I needed practice—"

"Roger, if you ever want to be able to practice again, go to sleep."

"You're sure?"

"I'm very sure."

"Okay."

"If you wake me up again, I'm going to kill you, Roger. Understand that."

"I understand."

"I'm serious."

"I believe you."

"Good."

"So, there's no chance—?"

"One . . ."

"I'll be good." Roger crossed his arms behind his head and smiled at the overhead. "Going to sleep now."

"Two . . ."

"Grawwwkkkkkk."

"Roger!?"

"What? Is it *my* fault I can't sleep without snoring?" he asked innocently. "It's not like I'm doing it on *purpose*."

"God, why me?"

"You asked for it."

"Did not!" Despreaux sat up and hit him with a pillow. "*Liar!*"

"God, you're beautiful when you're angry. I don't suppose—?"

"If that's what it takes for me to get some *sleep*," Despreaux said half-desperately.

"I'm sorry." Roger shook his head. "I'm sorry. I'll leave you alone."

"Roger, if you really are serious—"

"I'll leave you alone," he promised. "Get some sleep. I'll be good. I need to think anyway. And I can't think with that lovely nipple staring at me."

"Okay," Despreaux said, and rolled over.

Roger lay back, looking at the overhead. After a while, as he listened to Despreaux's breathing *not* changing to the regular rhythm of sleep, he began counting in his head.

"I can't sleep," Despreaux announced, sitting up abruptly just before he reached seventy-one.

"I said I was sorry," he replied.

"I know, but you're going to lie there, not sleeping, aren't you?"

"Yes. I don't need much sleep. It doesn't bother me. I'll get up and leave you alone, if you want."

"No," Despreaux said. "Maybe it's time for the next practice session. If you've learned anything, at least *I'll* get some sleep."

"If you're sure . . ."

"Roger, Your Highness, my Prince, my darling?"

"Yes?"

"Shut up."

"Old Earth," Roger breathed.

The ship was currently looking at the dark side of the planet. Relatively dark, that was. All of the continents were lit, almost from end to end, and a sparkling necklace of lights even covered the center of the oceans, where the Oceania ship-cities floated.

"Have you been here before, Mr. Chung?" the communications tech asked.

"Once or twice," Roger replied dryly. "Actually, I lived here for a number of years. I started off in intra-system brokerage right here in the Sol System. I was born on Mars, but Old Earth still feels more like home. How long to insertion?"

"Coming up on parking orbit . . . now," Beach said.

"Time to get to work, then," Roger replied.

"You look like you didn't get much sleep last night, Shara," Dobrescu observed brightly.

"Oh, shut up!"

"What's the status on the buildings?" Roger asked. Dobrescu had come up in a rented shuttle for a personal report and a quiet chat.

"The warehouse is fine; needs some cleanup, but I figured we had enough hands for that," Dobrescu said in a more serious tone. "The restaurant is going to need a few more days for renovations and inspections. I found out who to slide the baksheesh to on the latter, and they'll get done as soon as we're ready. There's a bit of another problem I couldn't handle on the restaurant, though."

"Oh?" Roger arched an eyebrow.

"The area's a real pit. Getting better, but still quite a bit of crime, and one of the local gangs has been trying to shake down the renovation teams. I had a talk with them, but they're not inclined to be reasonable. Lots of comments about what a fire-trap the building is."

"So do we pay them off or 'reason' with them?" Despreaux asked.

"I'm not sure they could guarantee our security even if we paid," Dobrescu admitted. "They don't control their turf that way. But I'm afraid if we got busy with them, it would be a corpse matter, and that could be a problem. The cops will look the other way on a little tussling, but they get sticky if bodies start turning up."

"The genius is in the details," Roger observed. "We'll try the famed MacClintock diplomacy gene and see if they're amenable to reason."

"It's going to be a really nice restaurant," Roger said as Erkum picked up one of the three-meter-long oak rafters in one false-hand and tossed it to a pair of Diasprans on the roof.

The building's front yard was being cleared by more of the Diaspran infantrymen. The local gang, whose leader was talking with Roger, eyed them warily from the street corner. There were about twice as many Mardukans in sight as gang members. The gang leader himself was as blond as Roger had been born, of medium height, with lanky hair that fell to his shoulders and holographic tattoos on arms and face.

"Well, in that case, I don't see why you can't afford a very reasonable—" he started to say.

"Because we don't know you can deliver," Roger snapped. "You can make all the comments you like about how inflammable this place is. I don't really give a good goddamn. If there's a suspicious fire, then my boys—many of whom are going to be living here—are going to be out of work. And they're not going to be really happy about that. I'd *appreciate* an 'insurance plan,' but the plan would have to cover security for my guests. I don't want one damned addict, one damned hooker, or one damned dealer in sight of the restaurant. No muggings. Better than having a platoon of cops. Guarantee me that, and we have a deal. Keep muttering about how this place would go up in an instant, and we'll just have to . . . What is that street term? Oh, yes. We'll just have to 'get busy.' You really don't want to get busy with me. You really, really don't."

"I don't like getting it stuck in any more than the next guy," the gang leader said, his eyes belying the statement. "But I've got my rep to consider."

"Fine, you'll be paid. But understand this. I'm paying you for *protection*, and I'd better receive it."

"That's my point," the leader said. "I'm not a welcome wagon. My boys ain't your rent-a-cops."

"Cord," Roger said. "Sword."

The Mardukan, who had, as always, been following Roger, took the case off his back and opened it.

Roger pulled out the long, curved blade, its metal worked into the wavery marks of watered steel.

"Pedi," he said. "Demonstration."

Cord's wife—who, as always, was following *him* about—picked up one of the metal rods being used for reinforcement of the new foundation work. She held it out, and Roger took the sword in his left hand and, without looking at the bar, cut off a meter-long section with a single metallic "twang."

"The local cops are right down on guns," Roger said, handing the sword back to Cord. "Sensors everywhere to detect them. You use guns much, Mr. Tenku?"

"It's just Tenku," the gang leader said, his face hard. He didn't answer the question, but he didn't have to. What his answer would have been was plain on his face, and in the glance he cast at the environment-suited Cord, who'd closed the case once more and gone back to leaning on the long pole that might, in certain circles, have been called a three-meter quarterstaff.

"You see them?" Roger pointed at the Diasprans who were picking up the yard. "Those guys are Diaspran infantry. They're born with a pike in their hands. For your information, that's a long spear. The Vasin cavalry who will be joining us shortly are born with *swords* in their hands. All *four* hands. Swords and spears aren't well-liked by the cops, but we're going to have them as 'cultural artifacts' to go with the theme of the restaurant. Mr. Tenku, if we 'get it stuck in' as you put it, then you are—literally—going to be chopped to pieces. I wouldn't even need the Mardukans. *I* could go through your entire gang like croton oil; I've done it before. Or, alternatively, you and your fellows could do a small community service and get paid for it. Handsomely, I might add."

"I thought this was a restaurant?" the gang leader said suspiciously.

"And I thought you were the welcome wagon." Roger snorted in exasperation. "Open your *eyes*, Tenku. I'm not muscling your turf. So don't try to muscle mine. Among other things, I've got more muscle." *And more brains*, Roger didn't add.

"How handsomely?" Tenku asked, still suspicious.

"Five hundred credits a week."

"No way!" Tenku retorted. "Five *thousand*, maybe."

"Impossible," Roger snapped. "I have to make a profit out of this place. Seven hundred, max."

"Why don't I believe that? Forty-five hundred."

They settled on eighteen hundred a week.

"If one of my guests gets so much as panhandled . . ."

"It'll be taken care of," Tenku replied. "And if you're late . . ."

"Then come on by for a meal," Roger said, "and we'll square up. And wear a tie."

Thomas Catrone, Sergeant Major, IMC, retired, president and chief bottle washer of Firecat, LLC, was clearing off his mail—deleting all the junk, in other words—when his communicator chimed.

Catrone was a tall man, with gray hair in a conservative cut and blue eyes, who weighed just a few kilos over what he'd weighed when he joined the Imperial Marines lo these many eons ago. He was well over a hundred and twenty, and not nearly the hulking brute he'd once been. But he was still in pretty decent shape. Pretty decent.

He flicked on the com hologram and nodded at the talking head that popped out. Nice blonde. Good face. Just enough showing to see she was pretty well stacked. Probably an avatar.

"Mr. Thomas Catrone?"

"Speaking."

"Mr. Catrone, have you been checking your mail?"

"Yes."

"Then are you aware that you and your wife have won an all-expenses-paid trip to Imperial City?"

"I don't like the Capital," Catrone said, reaching for the disconnect button.

"Mr. Catrone," the blonde said, half-desperately. "You're scheduled to stay at the Lloyd-Pope Hotel. It's the best hotel in the City. There are three plays scheduled, and an opera at the Imperial Civic Center, plus dinner every night at the Marduk House! You're just going to turn that down?"

"Yes."

"Have you asked your *wife* if you should turn it down?" the blonde asked acerbically.

Tomcat's hand hovered over the button, index finger waving in the air. Then it clenched into a fist and withdrew. He rattled his fingers on the desktop and frowned at the hologram.

"Why me?" he asked suspiciously.

"You were entered in a drawing at the last Imperial Special Operations Association meeting. Don't you remember?"

"No. They've generally got all sorts of drawings . . . but this one is pretty odd for them."

"The Association uses the Ching-Wrongly Travel Agency for all its bookings," the blonde said. "Part of that was the lottery for this trip."

"And I won it?" He raised one eyebrow and peered at her suspiciously again.

"Yes."

"This isn't a scam?"

"No, sir," she said earnestly. "We're not selling anything."

"Well . . ." Catrone scratched his chin. "I guess I'd better schedule—"

"There is one small . . . issue," the blonde said uncomfortably. "It's . . . *pre*scheduled. For next week."

"Next week?" Catrone stared at her incredulously. "Who's going to take care of the horses?"

"Sorry?" The blonde wrinkled her brow prettily. "You've sort of lost me, there."

"Horses," Catrone repeated, speaking slowly and distinctly. "Four-legged mammals. Manes? Hooves? You ride them. Or, in my case raise them."

"Oh."

"So you just want me to drop everything and go to the Capital?"

"Unless you want to miss out on this one-of-a-kind personalized adventure," the woman said brightly.

"And if I do, Ching-Wrongly doesn't have to pay out?"

"Errrr . . ." The woman hesitated.

"Hah! Now I know what the scam is!" Tomcat pointed one finger at the screen and shook it. "You're not getting me that easily! What about travel arrangements? I can't make it in my aircar in less than a couple of days."

"Suborbital flight from Ulan Bator Spaceport is part of the package," the blonde said.

"Okay, let's work out the details," Catrone said, tilting back in his desk chair. "My wife loves the opera; I hate it. But you can gargle peanut butter for three hours if you have to, so what the hell . . ."

"What a horribly suspicious man," Despreaux said, closing the connection.

"He has reason to be," Roger pointed out. "He's got to be under some sort of surveillance. Contacting him directly at all was a bit of a risk, but no more than anything else we considered."

The bunker behind the warehouse had the capability to artfully spoof the planetary communications network. Anyone backtracking the call would find it coming from the Ching-Wrongly offices, where a highly paid source was more than willing to back up the story.

"You think this is really going to work?" Despreaux asked.

"O ye of little faith," Roger replied with a grin. "I just wonder what our opposition is up to."

"And how is the Empress?" Adoula asked.

"Docile," New Madrid said, sitting down and crossing his long legs at the ankle. "As she should be."

Lazar Fillipo, Earl of New Madrid, was the source of most of Roger's good looks. Just short of two meters tall, long, lean, and athletically trim, he had a classically cut face and shoulder length blond hair he'd recently had modded to prevent graying. He also had a thin mustache that Adoula privately thought looked like a yellow caterpillar devouring his upper lip.

"I could wish we'd been able to find out what got dumped in her toot," Adoula said.

"And in John's," New Madrid replied with a nod. "But it was flushed, whatever it was, before we could stop it. Pity. I'd expected the drugs to hold back the dead man's switch longer than they did. Long enough for our . . . physical persuasion to properly motivate him to tell us what we wanted to know, at least."

"Always assuming it was the 'dead man's switch,'" Adoula pointed out a bit acidly. "The suicide protocols can also be deliberately activated, you know." *And,* he thought, *given what you were doing to him—in front of his mother—that's a hell of a lot more likely than any "Dead Man's Switch," isn't it, Lazar? I wonder what you'd have done to Alexandra herself by now . . . if you didn't need her alive even more than I do?*

"Always possible, I suppose." New Madrid pursed his lips poutingly for several seconds, then shrugged. "Well, I imagine it was inevitable, actually. And he had to go in the end, anyway, didn't he? It was worth a try, and Alexandra might always have volunteered the information herself, given that he was all she had left by that point. On the other hand, I've sometimes wondered if she could have told us even if she'd wanted to. The security protocols on their toots were quite extraordinary, after all."

"True. True." New Madrid pursed his lips poutingly for several seconds, then shrugged. "I suppose it was inevitable, actually. The security protocols on their toots *were* quite extraordinary, after all."

The Earl, Adoula reflected, had an absolutely astonishing talent for stating—and *re*stating—the obvious.

"You wanted to see me?" the prince asked.

"Thomas Catrone is taking a trip to the capital."

"Oh?" Adoula leaned back in his float chair.

"Oh," New Madrid said. "He's supposedly won some sort of all-expenses-paid trip. I checked, and there was such a lottery from the Special Operations Association. Admittedly, *anyone* who won it would be worth being suspicious of. But I'm particularly worried about Catrone. You should have let me take him out."

"First of all," Adoula said, "taking Catrone out would *not* have been child's play. He hardly ever leaves that bunker of his. Second, if the Empress' Own start dying off—and there are others, just as dangerous in their own ways as Catrone—then the survivors are going to start getting suspicious. More suspicious than they already are. And we *don't* want those overpaid retired bodyguards getting out of hand."

"Be that as it may, I'm putting one of my people on him," New Madrid said. "And if he becomes a problem . . ."

"Then *I'll* deal with it," Adoula said. "You concentrate on keeping the Empress in line."

"With pleasure," the Earl said, and smirked.

"Indian country," Catrone said as he looked the neighborhood over.

"Not a very nice area for an upscale restaurant," Sheila replied nervously.

"It's not so bad," the airtaxi-driver, an otterlike Seglur, said. "I've dropped other fares here. Those Mardukans that work in the place? *Nobody* wants to mess with them. You'll be fine. Beam down my card and call me when you want to be picked up."

"Thanks," Catrone said, getting the driver's information and paying the fare—and a small tip—as they landed.

Two of the big Mardukans stood by the entrance, bearing pikes—fully functional ones, Catrone noticed—and wearing some sort of blue harness over what were obviously environment suits. A young human woman, blonde and stocky, with something of a wrestler's build, opened the door.

"Welcome to Marduk House," the blonde said. "Do you have reservations?"

"Catrone, Thomas," Tomcat said.

"Ah, Mr. and Mrs. Catrone," she replied. "Your table is waiting. Right this way."

She led them through the entrance, into the entry room, and on to the dining room. Catrone noticed that there were several people, much better dressed than Sheila and he but having the look of local Imperial staff-pukes, apparently waiting for tables.

A skinny, red-headed woman held down the reception desk, but most of the staff seemed to be Mardukans. The restaurant area had a long bar at one side, on which slabs of some sort of meat were laid out. As they walked through the area, one of the Mardukans took a pair of cleavers—they would have been swords for a human—and began chopping a long section of meat, his hands moving in a blur. The sounds of the blades thunking into flesh and wood brought back unpleasant memories for Catrone, but there was a small ripple of applause as the Mardukan bowed and started throwing the chunks of meat, in another blur, onto a big iron dome. They hit in a star pattern and started sizzling, filling the room with the cooking noise and an odd smell. Not like pork or beef or chicken, or even human. Catrone had smelled them all in his time. Cooking human smelled pretty much like pork, anyway.

The table they were led to was already partially occupied. A big, vaguely Eurasian guy, and the blonde from the call. When he saw her, Tomcat almost stopped, but recovered with only the briefest of pauses.

"There seems to be someone at our table," he said instead to the hostess.

"That's Mr. Chung," she replied quietly. "The owner. He wanted to welcome you as a special guest."

Riiiight, Tomcat thought, then nodded at the two of them as if he'd never seen the blonde in his life.

"Mr. and Mrs. Catrone," the big guy said. "I'm Augustus Chung, the proprietor of these premises, and this is my friend, Ms. Shara Stewart. Welcome to Marduk House."

"It's lovely," Sheila said as he pulled out her chair.

"It was . . . somewhat less lovely when we acquired it," Chung replied. "Like this fine neighborhood, it had fallen into disrepair. We were able to snap it up quite cheaply. I was glad we could; this is a house with a lot of history."

"Washington," Catrone said with a nod. "This is the old Kenmore House, right?"

"Correct, Mr. Catrone," Chung replied. "It wasn't George Washington's home, but it belonged to one of his family. And he apparently spent considerable time here."

"Good general," Catrone said. "Probably one of the best guerrilla fighters of his day."

"And an honorable man," Chung said. "A patriot."

"Not many of them left," Catrone probed.

"There are a few," Chung said. Then, "I took the liberty of ordering wine. It's a vintage from Marduk; I hope you like it."

"I'm a beer drinker myself."

"What the Mardukans call beer, you would not care for," Chung said definitely. "There are times when you have to trust, and this is one of them. I can get you a Koun?"

"No, wine's fine. Tipple is tipple." Catrone looked at the blonde seated beside his host. "Ms. Stewart, I haven't said how lovely you look tonight."

"Please, call me Shara," the blonde said, dimpling prettily.

"In that case, it's Sheila and Tomcat," Catrone replied.

"Watch him," Sheila added with a grin. "He got the nickname for a reason."

"Oh, I will," Shara said. "Sheila, I need to powder my nose. Care to come along?"

"Absolutely," Sheila said, standing up. "We can trade our war stories while they trade theirs."

"Nice girl," Tomcat said as the two walked toward the powder room.

"Yes, she is," Chung replied, then looked Catrone in the eyes. "And a fine soldier. I'd say Captain Pahner sends his regards, but he is, very unfortunately, dead."

"You're him," Catrone said.

"Yes."

"Which one is she?"

"Nimashet Despreaux. My aide and fiancÈe."

"Oh great!"

"Look, Sergeant Major," Roger said, correctly interpreting the response. "We were on Marduk for *eight months*. Completely cut off. Stranded. You don't maintain garrison conditions for eight months. Fraternization? Hell, Kosutic—that's the hostess who led you over here—was carrying on for most of the time with Julian, who's now my S-2. And don't even get me *started* on the story of Gunny Jin. Nimashet and I at least waited until we were off-planet. And, yes, I'm going to marry her."

"You got any idea how easy it is to monitor in a restaurant?" Catrone asked, changing the subject.

"Yes. Which is why everyone entering and leaving is scanned for any sort of surveillance device. And this table, in particular, is placed by the fire pit for a reason. That sizzling really does a number on audio."

"Shit. Why the hell did you have to get my wife involved in this?"

"Because we're on a very thin margin," Roger pointed out. "Inviting just you would have been truly obvious."

"Well, I'm not getting involved in treason, whatever your reasoning," Catrone said. "You go your way, I'll go mine."

"This is not treason. I wasn't *there*. I was on *Marduk*, okay? I've got all the proof of that you could ask for. *Marduk*. This is all Adoula. He's holding my mother captive, and I *am* going to free her."

"Fine, you go right ahead." Catrone took a hard pull on the wine; his host was right, it was good. "Look, I did my time. And extra. Now I raise horses, do a little consulting, and watch the grass grow. What there is of it in the Gobi. I'm out of the Empire-saving business. Been there, done that, got *really* sick and tired of it. You're wrong; there are no patriots any more. Just more and less evil fatcats."

"Including my mother?" Roger demanded angrily.

"Keep your voice down," Catrone said. "No, not including your mother. But it's not about your mother, is it? It's about a throne for Roger. Sure, I believe you weren't in on the coup in the first place. But blood calls to blood, and you're New Madrid's boy. Bad seed. You think we don't talk to each other in the Association? I *know* you,

you little shit. You're not worth a pimple on your brother's ass. You think, even if it were possible, I'm going to walk in and give the Throne to *you?*"

"You *knew* me," Roger grated. "Yeah, you're right. I was a little shit. But this *isn't* about me; it's about Mother. Look, I've got some intel. What they're doing to her is *killing* her. And as soon as the can is popped, Mom dies. Bingo. Gone."

"Maybe, maybe not," Catrone said, then looked up. "Ladies, you're looking even better than when you left, if that's possible."

"Isn't he a lech?" Sheila said with a grin.

"He's sweet," Despreaux said.

"I'm not." Catrone winked. "I'm a very bad boy. I understand you can be a right handful, too."

"Sometimes," Despreaux said warily.

"Very dangerous when cornered," Tomcat continued. "A right bad cat."

"Not anymore." Despreaux looked over at Roger. "I . . . gave it up."

"Really?" Catrone's tone softened. "It happens . . . even to the best partyers."

"I . . . got very tired," Despreaux said. "All the partying gets to you after a while. Got to me, anyway. R—Augustus, well, I've never seen him turn down a party. He doesn't start many, but he's always the last man standing."

"Really?" Catrone repeated in rather a different tone.

"Really." Despreaux took Roger's hand and looked at him sadly. "I've seen him at . . . too many parties. Big ones, small ones. Some . . . very personal ones. Sometimes I think he lives a little too much for partying."

"Ah," Roger said. "Rastar's chopping up another joint. You have to watch this. He's a master with a blade."

"We saw it on the way in," Sheila said. "He's incredibly fast."

"Augustus," Despreaux said, "why don't you show Sheila a real master?"

"You think?"

"Go ahead," she said, catching Rastar's eye.

Roger nodded, then stood up and walked to the far side of the bar. Rastar bowed to him and stepped back as Roger reached under the bar and pulled out two slightly smaller cleavers. He set them down, put a long apron on over his expensive clothes, and stepped up on the raised platform even the tallest human required to work at a cutting surface designed for Mardukans.

The cleavers were more like curved swords, about as long as a human forearm. Roger slid them into sheaths on a belt and buckled the belt around his waist, then bowed to the audience, which was watching the demonstration with interest.

He drew a deep breath and crossed his arms, placing a hand on either sword. Then he drew.

The blades blurred, catching the firelight as they twirled around his body, close enough from time to time that his long hair rippled in the breeze. They whirled suddenly upward in free flight, then dropped, only to be caught by the tips of the blades between either hand's thumb and forefinger. He held them out at full extension by the same grips, and then they blurred again. Suddenly there was the sound of the blades hitting flesh, and perfectly sliced chunks of meat flew through the air to land on the dome in a complex dodecahedron.

The last slice flashed through the air, and Roger bowed to the applause as he cleaned the blades, then put all the tools away. He walked back to his table and gave another bow to the three diners.

"Very impressive," Catrone said dryly.

"I learned in a hard school."

"I'll bet."

"Would you like to see an example of the school?" Roger asked. "It's a . . . special demonstration we perform. You see, we slaughter our own meat animals here. That way everything's fresh. Caused a bit of a stink with the local animal lovers, until we showed them the meat animals in question."

"You probably don't want to watch this one, Sheila," Despreaux said.

"I'm a farm girl," Sheila replied. "I've seen slaughtering before."

"Not like this," Despreaux said. "Don't say I didn't warn you."

"If you're trying to impress me, Augustus . . ." Catrone said.

"I just think you should learn a little about the school," Roger replied. "See some of the . . . faculty I studied under, as it were. It won't take long. If Ms. Catrone wishes to sit it out . . . ?"

"Wouldn't miss it for worlds," Sheila declared, standing up. "Now?"

"Of course," Roger said, standing in turn and offering her his arm.

Catrone trailed along behind, wondering what the young idiot might think would impress him about killing some Mardukan cow. A few other diners, who'd heard about the slaughtering demonstration, attached themselves and followed "Mr. Chung" through a corridor and out into the back of the restaurant.

Behind the restaurant, there were a series of heavy-mesh plasteel cages, emitting a chorus of hissing. Three Mardukans stood by one of the cages, beside a door which led from it into an enclosed circular run, wearing heavy leather armor and carrying spears, two of them long, one short.

"There are several meat animals on Marduk," Roger said, walking over to a Mardukan who looked old for some reason and held a long case. "But for various reasons, we tend to serve one called *atul*. Humans on Marduk call them damnbeasts."

He opened the case and withdrew a really beautiful sword, fine folded steel, looking something like a thicker bladed *katana*.

"There's a local ordinance against firearms," Roger said, "so we have to take a more personal approach to slaughtering. In the jungle, and here, they use spears—rather long ones. Or a sword, for the more . . . adventurous. And there's a reason they're called damnbeasts."

What entered the run when one of the Mardukans opened the gate was the nastiest animal Catrone had ever seen. Three meters of teeth and claws, rippling in black-and-green stripes. It was low-slung and wide, six-legged, with a heavily armored head and shoulders. It darted into the light and looked at the humans on the other side of the run's mesh. Catrone could *see* the logic running through its head, and wondered just how smart the thing was.

One of the Mardukans with one of the long spears stabbed downward, but the thing moved aside like a cobra and caught at the

Mardukan with the other long spear. Its jaws slammed shut on the Mardukan's leg with a clearly audible clop, and it tossed the three-meter-tall ET aside as if he were no heavier than a feather. It whipped around the circular run, watching the two remaining spearmen with the same feral intelligence, then turned and leapt at the fence.

The plasteel held it for a moment, then the half-ton-plus beast was up and onto the sagging fence, facing the ring of former diners, who suddenly looked likely to become dinner, instead.

"Okay, this is just not on," Roger said. "Higher fences are clearly in order."

He sprang forward as Catrone wondered what in hell the young idiot was about. The ex-Marine was torn between training, which told him to put himself between the prince and the threat, and simple logic, which said he'd last barely an instant and do no damned good at all. Not to mention making people wonder why he'd risked his life for a businessman. Instead, he moved in front of Sheila, noting that Despreaux had taken a combat stance and was shaking her head at the prince's action as well. But she also wasn't blocking him, which was interesting.

The beast scrambled higher, rolling the fence over with its weight until the plasteel collapsed almost completely. Then it was outside the run, turned to the diners, and charged.

What happened was almost too fast for even Tomcat's trained eyes to follow, but he caught it. The prince slashed downwards with the sword, striking the beast on the tip of the nose and turning it ever so slightly. A quick flash back, and the sword ran across its eyes, blinding it. Now sightless, it continued straight ahead, just past the prince's leg, and the last slash—full forehand—caught it under the neck, where it was partially unprotected. The blade sliced up and outward, neatly severing its neck, and the thing slid to a stop in the dirt of the slaughter yard, its shoulder just brushing the prince's leg.

The prince had never moved from his spot. He'd taken one step for the final slash, but that was it.

Bloody hell.

The crowd which had followed them was applauding politely— probably thinking it was all part of the demonstration—as the prince flicked the sword to clear it of blood. The movement, Catrone noticed, was an unthinking one, a reflex, as if the prince had done it so many times it was as natural as breathing. He began an automatic sheathing maneuver, just as obviously an old habit, then stopped and walked across to the old Mardukan, who handed him a cloth to complete the cleaning of the blade. He said something quietly and put the clean sword back in the case while the headless monster lashed its tail in reflex, still twitching and clawing. Catrone sincerely doubted that Roger had learned that technique working on those things in a run.

Bloody *damned* hell.

"Is that what we're having for supper?" one of the audience asked as the two uninjured Mardukans dragged the thing away. The injured one was already on his feet, saying something in Mardukan that had to be swearing. The questioner was a woman, and she looked pretty green.

"Oh, we don't serve only *atul*," Roger said, "although the liver analog is quite good with *kolo* beans—rather like fava beans—and a nice light chianti. There's also *coll* fish. We serve the smaller, coastal variety, but it turns out they grow up to fifty meters in length in open waters."

"That's huge," a man said.

"Yes, rather. Then there's *basik*. That's what the Mardukans call humans, as well, because they're small, pinkish bipedal creatures that look just a bit like humans. They're basically Mardukan rabbits. My Mardukans refer to themselves as the *Basik*'s Own—bit of a joke, really. Then there's roast suckling damnbeast. Admittedly, it's the most expensive item on the menu, but it's quite good."

"Why is it so expensive?" Sheila asked.

"Well, that's because of how it's gathered," Roger said, smiling at her in a kindly fashion. "You see, the damnbeasts—that's those—" he added, jerking his thumb at the head which was still lying on the ground, "they lair in rocky areas in the jungle. They dig dens with long tunnels to get to them, low and wide, like they are. They dig them, by the way, because they, in turn, are preyed upon by the *atul-grack*."

"The what?" Sheila asked.

"*Atul-grack*," Roger repeated. "Looks pretty much like an *atul*, but about the size of an elephant."

"Oh, my . . ." the first woman whispered.

"Obviously, *atul-grack* are one of the hazards of hunting on Marduk," Roger continued. "But to return to the damnbeasts. One of the parents, usually the female—the larger of the two—always stays in the lair. So to get to the suckling damnbeast, someone has to crawl into the lair after it. It's very dark, and there's always an elbow in the tunnel near the den, where water gathers. So, generally, right after you crawl through the water, holding your breath, Momma," he gestured towards the pens again, "is waiting for you. You have, oh, about half a second to do something about that. One of my hunters suggests long, wildly uncontrolled bursts from a very heavy bead pistol, that being the only thing you can get into the den. You might have noticed they're armored on the front, however. Sometimes the bead pistol doesn't stop them. *Atul* hunters cannot get life insurance.

"And even if you do manage to kill Momma, there's a problem. The *atul* dig their tunnels about as wide and high as they are. So you have to . . . get past the defending *atul*. Generally using a vibroknife. But you're not done yet. Suckling *atul* range in size from about the size of a housecat to the size of a bobcat, and they trend towards the upper end of that range. There are usually six to eight of them, and they're generally hungry and look at the hunter as just more food. And, just as a final minor additional problem, you have to bring them out *alive*." Roger grinned at the group and shook his head. "So, please, when you look at the price for roast suckling damnbeast, keep all of that in mind. I don't pay my hunters enough as it is."

"Have *you* ever done that?" Sheila asked quietly as they were walking back to the table.

"No," Roger admitted. "I've never hunted suckling *atul*. I'm rather large to fit into the tunnel."

"Oh."

"The only time I've ever hunted suckling, it was an *atul-grack*."

After dinner, "Shara" took Sheila to show her some of the

interesting exhibits they'd brought back from Marduk, leaving Roger and Catrone over coffee.

"I missed this," Roger said.

"I still say this is a lousy spot for a private conversation," Tomcat countered.

"It is, it is. It's also the best place I've got, though. What do I have to do to convince you to side with us?"

"You can't," Catrone sighed. "And demonstrations of bravado aren't going to help. Yes, you have some people—some good people—who apparently think you've changed. Maybe you have. You were certainly more than willing to put yourself in harm's way. Too willing, really. If that thing had gotten you, your plan would have been all over."

"It was . . . reflex," Roger said, and made an almost wistful face. Tomcat had had a rather serious drink of wine after the "demonstration," but he'd noticed that Roger hadn't even appeared to have the shakes.

"Reflex," the prince repeated, "learned in a hard school, as I mentioned. I'm having to ride a fine line. On the one hand, I know I'm the indispensable man, but some chances—such as meeting with you—have to be taken. As to the *atul* . . . I was the only person there who was armed *and* knew how to take one out. Even if it had gotten to me, I'd probably have survived. And . . . it's not the first time I've faced an *atul* with nothing but a sword. A very hard school, Sergeant Major. One that also taught me that you can't do everything by yourself. I need you, Sergeant Major. The Empire needs you. Desperately."

"I said it once, and I repeat: I'm out of the Empire-saving business."

"That's *it*? Just that?" Roger demanded, and not even his formidable self-control could quite hide his amazement.

"That's it. And don't go around trying to recruit my boys and girls. We've discussed this—in much more secure facilities than you have here. We're out of this little dynastic squabble."

"It's going to end up as more than a dynastic squabble," Roger ground out.

"Prove it," Catrone scoffed.

"Not if you're not with us." Roger wiped his lips and stood. "It was very nice meeting you, Mr. Catrone."

"It was . . . interesting meeting you, Mr. Chung." Catrone rose and held out his hand. "Good luck in your new business. I hope it prospers."

When treason prospers, then none dare call it treason, Roger thought. I wonder if that was an intentional quote.

He shook Catrone's hand and left the table.

"Where's Mr. Chung?" Shelia asked when they got back to the table.

"He had some business to take care of," Tomcat replied, looking at "Shara." "I told him I hope it prospers."

"Just that?" Despreaux asked incredulously.

"Just that," Catrone said. "Time to leave, Sheila."

"Yes," Despreaux said. "Maybe it is. Sheila," she said, turning to Ms. Catrone, "this has been lovely. I hope we meet again."

"Well, we'll be back for supper tomorrow," Sheila said.

"Maybe," Catrone qualified.

"The *basik* was wonderful," Sheila said, glancing at her husband. "But it's been a long day. We'll be going."

Catrone nodded to the blonde hostess as they were leaving.

"Hell send, Mistress," he said.

"Heaven go with you, Mr. Catrone," the hostess replied, her nostrils flaring.

"What was that all about?" Sheila asked as they waited for the airtaxi.

"Don't ask," Tomcat answered. "We're in Indian country until we get home."

Tomcat didn't do anything that night except fool around with his wife a bit, courtesy of the bottle of champagne from the management. The all-expenses-paid trip he'd "won" had them in a very nice suite. Suites had not been high on his list of previous accommodations, and this one was really classy, more like a two-story apartment on the top floor of the hotel. He could see Imperial Park and a corner of the Palace from it, and when Sheila was asleep, he stood by the unlighted window for a while, looking at the place where he'd lived for almost three decades. He could see a few of the guards near the night entrances. Adoula's bully-boys—not real Empress' Own. And sure as hell not guarding the Empress, except against her friends.

The next day, their third in the city, they took in the Imperial Museums. Plural. It was a pain in the ass, but he'd married Sheila, his third wife, after he left the Service, and she'd never been to the Capital. They'd met while he was buying horses, shortly after he got out. He'd grown up on a farm, in an area in the central plains that was now chockablock with houses. He'd wanted to go back to a farm, but the only land he could afford was in Central Asia. So after gathering a small string, he'd set up the Farm. And along the way, he'd picked up another wife.

This one was a keeper, though. Not much to look at, compared to his first wife, especially, but a real keeper. As they walked through the Art Museum, with Sheila gawking at the ancient paintings and sculpture, he looked over at her and thought of what failure would mean. To her, not to him. He'd put it on the line too many times, for far less reason, to worry about himself. But if everything went down, they weren't going to target just him.

That evening, they ate in a small restaurant in the hotel. He made the excuse that they didn't have time to go over to Marduk house, not if they were going to make it to the opera.

They dressed for the evening, a classically simple black low-cut suit for her, and one of those damned brocaded court-monkey suits for him. The management had arranged the aircar for them, and everything was laid on. He added a stylish evening pouch to his ensemble, mentally swearing at the aforementioned monkey suit with its high collar and purple chemise.

As the second intermission was ending, he took Sheila's arm when they headed back to the box.

"Honey, I can't take much more of this," he said. "You stay. You like it. I'm going to go for a walk."

"Okay." She frowned. "Be careful."

"I'm always careful," he grinned.

Once out of the Opera House, with its ornate façade, he turned down the street and headed for one of the nearby multilevel malls. It was still open, still doing a fair business, and he wandered through, poking into a couple of clothing stores and one outdoor equipment store. Then he saw what he was looking for, and followed a gentleman down a corridor to the bathrooms.

The bathroom, thankfully, was deserted except for them. The guy headed over to the urinal, and Tomcat palmed an injector, stepped up behind him, and laid the air gun against the base of his neck.

The target dropped without a word, and Tomcat grabbed him under the shoulders, muttering at his weight, and dragged him into one of the stalls. He quickly stripped off his monkey suit and started pulling things out of the evening pouch.

There was a light, thin jumpsuit with dialable coloration. He set it to the same shade as the garments the target had been wearing. The target had also worn a floppy beret and a jacket, and Tomcat took those, as well as his pad and spare credit chips. He squirted alcohol on the target's shirt, then extracted the facial prosthetic from the pouch and slipped it on. It didn't look like the target, but anyone looking for Thomas Catrone wouldn't recognize him. There were thin gloves, as well, ones that disappeared into the flesh but would camouflage DNA and fingerprints.

He turned the pouch inside-out, so that it looked like a normal butt-pack, and stuck it up under the jacket for concealment, since the target hadn't been wearing one. Satisfied, he made one more sweep to ensure the site was clean, then stepped out of the bathroom. On the way out, he dumped the monkey suit into the incinerator chute. In one way, it was a damned shame—the thing had cost an arm and a leg. On the other hand, he was glad to see it gone.

He spotted the tail as soon as he left the dead-end corridor—a young male, Caucasian, with a holo jacket and a nose ring. The shadow paid no attention to the blond man in the jacket, his beret pulled down stylishly over one eye. The tail appeared to be enjoying a coffee and reading his pad, standing at the edge of the store with one leg propped up against the storefront.

Catrone walked on down the mall, slowly, strolling and shopping, searching for a certain look. He found it not far from a store which sold lingerie. Most women avoid eye contact with men they don't know; this young lady was smiling faintly at most of the passing men between glances at the pad she held in her lap.

"Hi, there," Catrone said, sitting down next to her. "You look like a woman who enjoys a good time. Whatever are you doing sitting around this boring old mall?"

"Looking for you," the girl said, smiling and turning off her pad.

"Well, I'm just a little busy at the moment. But if you'd like to really help me out in a little practical joke, I'd appreciate it."

"How much would you appreciate it?" the hooker asked sharply.

"Two hundred credits worth," Tomcat replied.

"Well, in *that* case . . ."

"My friend is waiting for me, but . . . I had another offer. I don't want him to feel dumped or anything, so . . . why don't you go take my place for a while?"

"I take it he goes both ways?"

"Very," Tomcat replied. "Dark hair, light skin, standing outside the Timson Emporium reading a pad and drinking coffee. Show him a *really* good time," he finished, handing her two hundred-credit chips.

"A lot of money for a practical joke," the hooker said, taking the chips.

"Call it avoiding the end of a wonderful relationship," Tomcat replied. "He can't know it was from me, understand?"

"Not a problem," the woman said. "And, you know, if you're ever in the mood for company . . ."

"Not my type." Tomcat sighed. "You're a lovely girl, but . . ."

"I understand." She stood up. "Light skin, dark hair, standing in front of the Emporium."

"Wearing a holo jacket. Drinking coffee—Blue Galaxy-coffee bulb."

"Got it."

The target was taking a long damned time on the toilet. Too long. Long enough that Gao Ikpeme was getting worried. But Catrone was wearing a damned evening suit; there was no way Ikpeme could have missed seeing *that* come out of the can.

He slid one leg down and lifted the other to rest it—then damned near jumped out of his own skin as a tongue flickered into his ear.

"Hi, handsome," a sultry voice said.

He whipped around and found himself face-to-face with a pretty well set up redhead. Keeping in fashion, she wore damned near nothing—a halter top and a miniskirt so low on her hips and so high cut that it was more of a thin band of fabric to cover her pubic hair and butt.

"Look," the redhead said, leaning into him and quivering, "I just took some Joy, and I'm, you know, *really* horny. And you are *just* my type. I don't care if it's in one of the restrooms, or in a changing stall, or right here on the damned floor—I just *want* you."

"Look, I'm sorry," Gao said, trying to keep an eye on the corridor door and failing. "I'm meeting somebody, you know?"

"Bring her along," the woman said, breathing hard. "Hell, we'll be *done* by the time she gets here. Or he. I don't *care*. I want you *now!*"

"I said—"

"I want you, I want you, *I want you*," the woman crooned, sliding around in front of him and up and down, her belly pressing against the world's worst erection. "And you want *me*."

"Geez, buddy, get a room," one of the shoppers said in passing. "There're *kids* here, okay?"

"Quit this!" Gao hissed. "I can't go with you right now!"

"Fine!" The woman raised one leg up along his body and rocked up and down. "I'll just . . . I'll just . . ." she panted hoarsely.

"Oh, Christ!" Gao grabbed her by the arm, darted into the store, and managed to find a more or less deserted aisle for what turned out to take about six seconds.

"Oh, that was good," the girl said, pulling her panties back into place and licking her lips. She ran her hands up and down his jacket and smiled. "We need to get together again and spend a little more time together."

"Yeah," Gao gasped, rearranging his clothes. "Christ! I've got to get back out there!"

"Later," the hooker said, waving fingers at him as he practically ran to the front of the store. There. She didn't even have to feel bad about the two hundred credits. Quickest trick she'd ever turned, too.

Gao looked up and down the mall corridors, but the target was nowhere in sight. He *could* have come out while he was off-post, but . . . Damn. Nothing for it.

Gao walked across the mall and down the corridor into the bathroom. There was nobody in sight inside. Feet in one of the stalls, though.

He pushed on the door, which slid open. There was a drunk sprawled all over the toilet; it wasn't the target.

Oh, shit.

He walked back out into the main passageway, hoping that maybe the target had just stepped into a store or something. But, no, there was nobody in sight.

He frowned for a moment, then shrugged and pulled out his pad. He keyed a combination, and shook his head at the person who appeared on the screen.

"Lost him."

Catrone tapped at his pad as if scrolling something and leaned into his earbug.

"I dunno, he went into the can. I watched it the whole time . . . No, I don't think it was a deliberate slip, I just lost him . . . Yeah, okay. I'll try to pick him up at the hotel."

Catrone consulted a directory, but the number the tail had called was unlisted. He could countertail him, and see what turned up, but that was probably useless. He'd have at least a couple of cutouts. Besides, Thomas Catrone had things to do.

Tomcat walked to a landing stage and caught an airtaxi across town. The taxi was driven by a maniac who seemed to be high on something. At least he cackled occasionally as they slid under and over slower cars. Finally, the cab reached Catrone's destination—a randomly chosen intersection. He paid in chips, some of them from the unfortunate citizen in the mall bathroom, and walked two blocks to a public access terminal.

He keyed the terminal for personal ads, and then placed one.

"WGM seeks SBrGM for fun lovin and serious crack romp. Thermi. *ThermiteBomb@toosweetfortreats.im*."

He did a quick check and confirmed that there were no identical ads on that site.

"Please pay three credits," the terminal requested, and he slid in three credit chips.

"Your ad in *Imperial Singles Daily* is confirmed. Thank you for using Adoula Info Terminals."

"Yeah," Catrone muttered. "What a treat."

He took the public grav-tube back to the hotel and sat by the window, watching the city go by. Even at this time of night, all the air-lanes were full, with idiots like that taxi driver weaving up and down and in and out of the lanes. The tubecars moved between the lanes, drawing their power from inductive current and surrounded by clear glassteel tubes, rounding the buildings three hundred meters in the air. You could see into windows, those that weren't polarized or curtained. People sitting down to a late dinner. People watching holovid. A couple arguing. Millions of people stacked in boxes, and the boxes stretching to the horizon. What would they think if they knew he was going past, with what was in his head? Did they care that Adoula was in control of the Throne? Did they want the Empress restored? Or were they so checked out that they didn't even know who the Empress was?

He thought about something someone had told him one time. Something like most men aren't good for anything but turning food into shit. But the Empire wasn't the Empress, it was all those people turning food into shit. They had a stake, whether they knew it or not. So what would *they* think? Anyone who tried to rescue Alexandra was risking a kinetic strike on the Palace, but just the civil disorder which would follow a *successful* countercoup would make all of those millions of lives about him a living hell. Air lanes jammed, tubes grounded, traffic control shut down . . .

He got out of the tube at a station a few blocks from the hotel and let himself in the back way. He'd dumped all the remaining credits from the target, along with the jacket and beret, in a public incinerator chute.

Sheila was sitting up in bed watching a holomovie when he walked into the suite. She raised one eyebrow at the way he was dressed, but he shook his head and took off the clothes. They, too, went into the incinerator. It was a room incinerator, moreover. This was a classy place that probably normally had staff-pukes and their bosses staying in its suites. It was as secure as anything he was going to find, and there probably wasn't anything incriminating on the clothes, anyway. But better safe than sorry.

He climbed into bed with his wife and laid an arm over her shoulder.

"How was the opera?"

"Great."

"I don't see how anything can be great that's all in a foreign language."

"That's because you're a barbarian."

"Once a barbarian, always a barbarian," Tomcat Catrone replied. "Always."

"Catrone was as clear as he could be that he won't help," Roger said. "And that the senior members of the Association aren't going to help, either. They're sitting this one out."

"That is so totally . . . bogus," Kosutic said angrily.

They'd come to the warehouse to "check on resupply." The restaurant was doing even better than Roger had hoped, almost to the point of worry. Even an interstellar freighter could carry only so much Mardukan food, and they were running through it nearly twenty-five percent faster than he'd anticipated. If he sent a ship back, *now*, for more goods, it might get back in time, but he doubted it. Fortunately, the Mardukans and their beasts could eat terrestrial food, and he'd been substituting that for the last few days. It didn't have all the essential nutrients they needed, though. The Mardukans were suddenly on the reverse side of what the Marines had faced on Marduk, but without Marine nanites which could convert some materials to essential vitamins.

It wasn't exactly what he would have called a "good" situation under any circumstances, but at least it gave them a convenient excuse to use the secure rooms in the underground bunker.

"The good news is that the first of our 'machine tools' have arrived from our friends," Rastar said. He was handling the warehouse and restaurant while Honal worked on another project.

"Good," Roger said. "Where?"

Rastar led them out of the meeting room and down a series of corridors to a storeroom which was stacked with large—some of them very large—plasteel boxes. Rastar keyed a code into the pad on one of them and opened it up, revealing a suit of powered armor plated in ChromSten.

"Now is when we need Julian and Poertena," Despreaux observed unhappily.

"These're Alphane suits," Roger pointed out, coming over to examine the armor carefully. "They'd be as much a mystery to Julian as they are to us. But we're going to have to get them fitted anyway."

"And they came through on the rest of it, too," Rastar said, making a Mardukan hand gesture which indicated amusement. He opened up one of the larger boxes and waved both left hands.

"Damn," Roger breathed. "They did."

This suit was much larger than the human-sized one in the first box, with four arms and a high helmet to accommodate a Mardukan's horns. The upper portion had even been formed to *resemble* horns.

"And this." Rastar opened up another long, narrow box.

"What in the hell is that?" Krindi Fain asked, looking down at the weapon nestled in the box.

"It's a hovertank plasma cannon," Despreaux said in an awed tone. "*Cruisers* carry them as antifighter weapons."

"It's the Mardukan powered armor's primary weapon," Rastar said smugly. "The extra size of the suit adds significant power."

"It had better," Fain grunted, hoisting the weapon out with all four hands. "I can barely lift this!"

"Now you over-muscled louts know how humans feel about plasma cannon," Roger said dryly. Then he looked around the human and Mardukan faces surrounding him.

"The Imperial Festival is in four weeks. It's the best chance we're going to have on the mission, and if Catrone and his fence-sitters aren't going to lift a lily-white finger, there's no reason to waste time trying for some sort of fancy coordination. Send the codeword to Julian, for Festival Day. We won't tell the Alphanes we don't need the additional suits—better we have more than we need than come up short. Start getting all the Marines fitted to them, and as many Mardukans as we have suits for. Training in close combat in *this* place is going to be easy enough. We'll plan around the details of the Palace that we know. It will have to be a surface assault; there's no other way in. At least the exterior guards are in dress uniform to look pretty. I know the Empress' Own's 'dress uniforms' are kinetic-reactive, but however good they may be against bead fire, they're not armor, which should let us kick the door open if we manage to hit them with the element of surprise.

"We'll initiate with the Vasin . . ."

Catrone sat at his desk, looking out the window at the brown grass where three horses grazed. He wasn't actually seeing the scene as he sat tapping the balls of his fingers together in front of him. What he did see were memories, many of them bloody.

His communicator chimed, and he consulted his toot for the time. Bang on.

"Hey, Tom," Bob Rosenberg said.

"Hey, Bob," Tomcat replied, grinning in apparent surprise. *Stay smooth, stay natural.* "Long time."

There was a slight signal delay as the reply bounced around from satellite to satellite. Any or all of which could be, and probably were, beaming the conversation to Adoula.

"I'm in-system for a bit. Thought you might be up for a party." Rosenberg had taken a job as a shuttle pilot on a freighter after resigning from the Corps.

"Absolutely," Tomcat said. "I'll call a couple of the boys and girls. We'll do it up right—roast the fatted calf."

"Works for me," Rosenberg replied after a slightly longer pause than signal delay alone could have accounted for. "Wednesday?"

"Plenty of time," Tomcat said. "Turn up whenever. Beer's always cold and free."

"I'll do about anything for free beer." Rosenberg grinned. "See you then."

"Catrone is throwing a party," New Madrid said with a frown.

"He's done it before," Adoula sighed. "Twice since we assumed our rightful position." As usual, he was up to his neck in paperwork—why couldn't people decide things on their own?—and in no mood for New Madrid's paranoia.

"Not right after a trip to Imperial City, he hasn't," New Madrid pointed out. "He's invited ten people, eight from the Empress' Own Association and two from the Raider Association, of which he's also a member. All senior NCOs except Robert Rosenberg, who was the commander of Gold Battalion's stinger squadron."

"And your point is?"

"They're *planning* something," New Madrid said angrily. "First Helmut moves—"

"Where did you hear that?"

"I was talking to Gianetto. I do that from time to time, since *you're* ignoring me."

"I'm not ignoring *you*, Lazar." Adoula was beginning to get angry himself. "I've considered the threat of the Empress' Own, and I'm ignoring *it*."

"But—"

"But *what*? Are they coordinating with Home Fleet? Not as far as we can see. Do they have heavy weapons? Most assuredly not. Some bead rifles, maybe a few crew-served weapons they've squirreled away like the paranoid little freaks they are. And what are they going to do? Attack the Palace?"

The prince shoved back in his chair and glowered at his taller, golden-haired coconspirator exasperatedly.

"You're putting two and two together and getting seven," he said. "Take Helmut's decision to move and Catrone's meeting. Helmut could *not* have gotten word to them, unless he did it by telepathy. We've been watching him like a hawk. Sure, we don't know where he is *now*, but he hasn't communicated with anyone in the Sol System. He hasn't even linked to a beacon. For them to have made prior contact and coordinated any sort of planning between Sixth Fleet and Catrone after we moved, they would have required an elaborate communications chain we couldn't possibly have missed. And there was no reason for them to have set up any sort of plan in advance. So the two events are *unrelated*, and without Sixth Fleet to offset Home Fleet, anything Catrone and his friends could come up with would be doomed. They have *no* focal point—the heirs are *dead*, Her Majesty is damned near dead, and *will* be, just as soon as the new Heir is born."

"That's not necessary," New Madrid said peevishly.

"We've discussed this," Adoula replied in a tight, icy voice. "As soon as the Heir is born—which will be as soon as possible for guaranteed survival in a neonatal care ward—she goes. Period. Now, I'm extremely busy. Do quit bothering me with ghosts. Understand?"

"Yes," New Madrid grated. He got up and stalked out of the office, his spine rigid. Adoula watched him leave, and then sighed and tapped an icon on his pad.

The young man who entered was pleasant faced, well-dressed, and entirely unnoticeable. His genes could have been assembled from any mixture of nationalities, and he had slightly tanned skin, brown hair, and brown eyes.

"Yes, Your Highness?"

"Ensure that everything is in place to remove the Earl when his utility is at an end."

"It will be done, Your Highness."

Adoula nodded, the young man withdrew, and the prince returned his attention to his paperwork.

Loose ends everywhere. It was maddening.

"Hey, Bob," Tomcat said, shaking hands as his guests arrived. "Lufrano, how's the leg? Marinau, Jo, glad you could make it. Everybody grab a beer, then let's head for the rec room and get seriously stinko."

He led them into the basement of the house, through a heavy

steel door, and down a corridor. Getting hold of the amount of land the Farm had needed to do things right had meant buying it in Central Asia, where prices had not yet skyrocketed the way they had in the heartland of North America. There was, of course, a reason prices were so much lower here, but even in Central Asia, there was land, and then there was *land*. In this case, he'd gotten the chunk he'd bought directly from the office of the Interior for a steal, given that it had "facilities" already on it.

The house sat on top of a command-and-control bunker for an old antiballistic missile system. "Old" in this case meant way before the Empire, but still in nearly mint condition, thanks to the dry desert air. There was a command center, bunk rooms, individual rooms for officers, kitchen, storerooms, and magazines.

When he'd gotten the place, those spaces were all sitting empty, except for the ones which had been half-filled with the fine sand for which the region was famous. He'd spent a couple of years, working in the time available, to fix a few of them up. Now the command center was his "rec room," a comfortable room with some float chairs and, most importantly, a bar. He used one of the bunk rooms as an indoor range. The kitchen had been fitted up to be a kitchen again, he'd fitted out a couple of bedrooms, and the storerooms—lo and behold—held stores. Lots of stores.

People joked that he could hold off an army. He knew they were wrong. He'd have a tough time dealing with more than a platoon or so.

And, ritually, once a week, he swept all the rooms for bugs. Just an old habit. He'd never found one.

"Hey, Lufrano," Rosenberg said as the rest filed into the rec room. He had a long metal wand, and he ran it over the visitors as he talked. "Been a long time."

"Yep," Lufrano Toutain, late Sergeant Major of Steel Battalion, agreed. "How's the shipping business?"

"Same old same old," Rosenberg replied. He ran the entire group, then nodded. "Clear."

"Fatted calf," Toutain, said in an entirely different voice, grabbing a beer. "Son of a—"

"Empress," Tomcat finished for him. "And a pretty impressive one. Boy's grown both ears and a tail."

"Now that would take some doing," Youngwen Marinau said, catching the brew Tomcat tossed him. Marinau had been first sergeant in Bronze Battalion for eighteen miserable months. He popped the bulb open and took a long drink, swilling it as if to wash the taste of something else out of his mouth. "He was a punk when I knew him."

"There's a reason Pahner got Bravo Company," Rosenberg pointed out. "Nobody better for bringing on a young punk. Where in the *hell* have they been, though? The ship never made it to Leviathan; no sign of them."

"Marduk," Catrone answered. "I didn't get the whole story, but they were there a long time—I can tell that. And Pahner bought it there. I took a look at what there is in the database about it." He shook his head. "Lots of carnivores, lots of barbs. I don't know exactly what happened, but the Prince has got about a company-plus of the barbs following him around. They're masquerading as waiters, but they're soldiers, you can tell. And they had some trouble with one of the carnivores they use as food. And that Roger . . ."

He shook his head again.

"Tell," Marinau said. "I'd love to hear that there's something in that pretty head besides clothes and fashion sense."

Catrone ran through the entire story, ending with the killing of the *atul.*

"Look, I don't shake, and I don't run," Catrone ended. "But that damned thing shook me. It was just a mass of claws and fangs, and Roger didn't even blink—just took it out. Whap, slash, gone. Every move was choreographed, like he'd done it two, three thousand times. Perfect muscle memory movement. Lots of practice, and there's only one way he could have gotten it. And fast. Just about the fastest human I've ever seen."

"So he can fight." Marinau shrugged. "Glad he had at least some MacClintock in him after all."

"More than that," Catrone said. "He's *fast*. Fast enough he could have left us all standing and let us take the fall. The thing probably would have savaged one of us, and then either fed or left. *He* could have gotten away while it was munching, but he didn't. He stood the ground."

"That's not his job," Rosenberg pointed out.

"No, but he was the one with the weapon and the training," Toutain said, nodding. "Right?"

"Right," Catrone said.

"Any chance it was a setup?" Marinau asked.

"Maybe," Catrone conceded with a shrug. "But if so, what does that tell us about the Mardukans?"

"What do you mean?" Rosenberg said.

"If it was a setup, one of them took a heavy hit for him," Catrone pointed out. "It didn't kill him, but I bet it was touch and go. If they set it up, they did so *knowing* the thing could kill them. Think about it. Would *you* do that if Alexandra asked you to?"

"Which one?" Marinau asked, his voice suddenly harsher with old memories and pain. He'd retired out of Princess Alexandra's Steel Battalion less than two years before her murder.

"Either," Catrone said. "The point's the same. But I don't think it was a setup. And Despreaux was interesting, too."

"She usually is." Rosenberg chuckled. "I remember when she joined the Regiment. Damn, that girl's a looker. I'm not surprised the Prince fell for her."

"Yeah, but she's trained the same way we are. Protect the primary. And all she did was get ready to back him up. What does *that* tell you?"

"That she's out of training," Marinau said. "You said she'd implied she'd lost it."

"She didn't 'lose it' in the classical sense," Catrone argued. "She stood her ground, unarmed, but she *knew* the best person to face the thing was Roger. And she *trusted* him. She didn't run, and she didn't go into a funk, but she also didn't move to protect the primary. She let *him* handle it."

"Just because he's brave," Marinau said, "and, okay, can handle a sword—which is a pretty archaic damned weapon—that doesn't mean he's suited to be Emperor. And that's what we're talking about.

We're talking about being a Praetorian Guard, just what we're not supposed to be. Choosing the Emperor is *not* our job. And if I did have a choice, Roger wouldn't be it."

"You prefer Adoula?" Catrone demanded angrily.

"No," Marinau admitted unhappily.

"The point is, he *didn't* do the deed. We already knew that." Catrone said. "And he's the *legitimate* heir, not this baby they're fast-cooking. And if somebody doesn't act, Alexandra's going to be as dead as John and Alex." His face worked for a moment, and then he shook his head, snarling. "You're going to let Adoula get *away* with that?"

"You're impressed," Rosenberg said. "I can tell that."

"Yeah, I'm impressed," Catrone replied. "I didn't know it was going to be him, just that something was fishy. And I wasn't impressed when I met him. But . . . he's got that MacClintock *thing* you know? He didn't before—"

"Not hardly," Marinau muttered grumpily.

"—but he sure as hell does now," Catrone finished.

"Does he want the Throne?" Joceline Raoux asked. She was a former sergeant major of the Raiders, the elite insertion commandos who skirmished with the Saint Greenpeace Corps along the borders.

"We didn't get into that, Jo," Catrone admitted. "I put them off. I wasn't going to give him an okay without a consult. But he was more focused on getting the Empress safe. That might have been a negotiating ploy—he's got to know where our interests and loyalties lie—but that's what we talked about. Obviously, though, if we secure the Throne, he's the Heir."

"And from our reports, he'll be Emperor almost immediately," Rosenberg pointed out gloomily.

"Maybe," Catrone said. "I'm not going to believe it until I've seen Alexandra. She's strong—I can't believe she won't get over it."

"I want her safe," Toutain said suddenly, his voice hard. "And I want that bastard Adoula's head for what he did to John and the kids. The damned *kids* . . ." His face worked, and he shook his head fiercely. "I want that bastard *dead*. I want to do him with a knife. Slow."

"No more than I want New Madrid," Catrone pointed out. "I *am* going to take that bastard, if it's the last thing I do. But Roger can give us more than just revenge—he can give us the Empire back. And that's important."

Rosenberg looked around at the group of senior NCOs, taking a mental headcount, based upon body language. It didn't take long.

"Catrone, Marinau, and . . . Raoux," he said. "Arrange to meet. Tell him we'll back him if he's got a real plan. And find out what it is."

"It won't include what we know," Catrone said. "It won't even include the Miranda Protocols."

"How do we meet him?" Marinau asked.

"Slipping our tethers will be harder than finding him." Catrone shrugged. "I know I'm being monitored. But finding him won't be hard; there's only a couple of places he can be."

"Meet him, again. Get a reading on him," Rosenberg said. "If you're all in agreement, we'll initiate the Miranda Protocols and gather the clans."

"Honal," Roger smiled tightly, controlling his gorge through sheer force of will, "the idea is to *survive* flying in a light-flyer."

The sleek, razor-edged aircar, a Mainly Fantom, was the only sports model large enough to squeeze a Mardukan into. It was also the fastest, and reportedly the most maneuverable, light-flyer on the market.

At the moment, Honal was proving that both those claims were justified, weaving in and out of the Western Range at dangerously high speeds. He had his lower, less dexterous, hands on the controls, and his upper arms crossed nonchalantly. There were some tricky air currents, and Roger closed his eyes as one of them caught the flyer and brought it down towards an upthrust chunk of rock. The flyer banked, putting the passenger side down, and Roger opened his eyes a crack to see the rocks of the mountainside flashing by less than a meter from the tip of the aircar's wing.

The car suddenly flipped back in the other direction, banking again, and stood up on its tail. Roger crunched his stomach, feeling himself beginning to gray out, as Honal left out a bellow.

"I *love* this thing!" the Mardukan shouted, rolling the car over on its back. "Look at what it can *do!*"

"Honal," Roger shook his head to clear it, "if I die, this plan goes to shit. Could we land, please?"

"Oh, sure. But you wanted to make sure we knew what we were doing, right?"

"You have successfully demonstrated that you can fly an aircar," Roger said carefully. "Most successfully. Thank you. The question of whether or not you can fly a stingship still remains; they're *not* the same."

"We've been working with the simulators." Honal shrugged all four shoulders. "They're faster than this, but a bit less maneuverable. We can fly stingships, Roger."

"Targeting is—"

"The targeting system is mostly automatic." Honal banked around another mountain, this time slower and further away from the rocks, and landed the car beside the more plebeian vehicle Roger had flown out to the site. "It's a matter of *choosing* the targets. Human pilots use mainly their toots, with the manual controls primarily for backup, but obviously, we can't do that. On the other hand—you should pardon the expression—humans only have one set of hands. *We're* training to fly with the lower hands . . . and control the targeting with the upper. I've 'fought' on the net with a few humans, including some military stingship pilots. They're good, I give you that. But one-on-one, I can take any one of them, and a couple of the rest of the team are nearly as good. Where they kick our ass is in group tactics. We're just getting a feel for those; it's not the same thing as riding a *civan* against the Boman. Go in against them wing-to-wing, and we just get shot out of the sky. The good news is that the squadron at the Palace isn't trained in group tactics, either. But they've got some pretty serious ground-based air defenses, and taking those out is another thing we're not great at, yet."

"Anything to do about it?" Roger asked.

"I've been reading up on everything I can get translated on

stingship doctrine. But we've got a lot of studying to do, and I'm not sure what's relevant and what's not. We're not as far along as I'd hoped. Sorry."

"Keep working on it," Roger said. "That's all we can do for now."

"They're using Greenbrier," Raoux said. The sergeant major no longer looked like herself. Like the Saint commandos, Raiders often had to modify their looks, and she'd gotten a crash retraining in old skills since the coup. "He's on his way there at the moment."

"Why Greenbrier?" Marinau asked. "It's just about the smallest of the dispersal facilities."

"Probably the only one Kosutic knew about," Catrone said. "Pahner would've known more, but—" He shrugged. "We'll shift the base to Cheyenne quick enough if it goes well."

"You ready?" Raoux asked.

"Let's get our mission faces on."

"All right," Roger said, looking at the hologram of the Palace. "Plasma cannon here, here, here, and here. Armored and embedded. ChromSten pillboxes."

"Won't take them out with a one-shot," Kosutic said. "But they can only be activated by remote command from the security bunker."

"Autocannon here and here," Roger continued.

"Ditto," Kosutic replied. "Both of them are heavy enough to take out armor, which we can't get into the area in the first assault anyway, because the sensors all over the City would start screaming, and the Palace would go on lock-down."

"Air defenses," Roger said.

"The minute stingers get near the Capital," Kosutic said, "air defenses all over the place go live. Civilian traffic's grounded, and the air becomes a free-fire zone. Police have IFF; we might be able to emulate that to spoof *some* of the defenses. It's going to be ugly, though. And that ignores the fact that we don't *have* stingships. We might have to mount weaponry on those aircars Honal is using for training."

"Wouldn't *that* be lovely." Roger grimaced and shook his head. "A formation of Mainly Fantoms going in over the parade . . ."

"We make the assault in the middle of the parade, and we're going to cause enormous secondary casualties," Despreaux pointed out unhappily.

"It's still the best chance we have of getting close to the Palace," Roger replied.

"And every scenario we've run shows us losing," Kosutic said.

"And if you ran a scenario of our making it across Marduk?" Roger asked.

"Different situation, Your Highness," Kosutic replied firmly. "There, we had zip for advance information on the tactical environment. Here we know the relative abilities, the mission parameters, and most of the variables, and, I repeat, *every single model we've run* ends up having us lose."

"I guess you need a new plan, then," Catrone said from the doorway. Heads snapped around, and his lips curled sardonically as he stripped off the mask he'd been wearing. The two people with him were doing the same.

"And how did *you* get in here?" Roger asked calmly, almost conversationally, then glanced at Kosutic. "Son of a *bitch*, Kosutic!"

"I'd like to know that, too," the sergeant major said tightly.

"We got in the through a well-shielded secret passage . . . the same way we're getting into the Palace," Catrone told her. "*If* you can convince us we should back you."

"Sergeant Major Marinau," Roger said with an extremely thin smile. "What a *pleasant* surprise."

"Hey, dork." The sergeant major waved casually.

"That's Your Highness the Dork, to you, Sergeant Major," Roger replied.

"Glad to see you've a gotten a sense of humor." The sergeant major sat at the table. "What happened to Pahner?" he continued, coming right to the point.

"Killed by Saint commandos," Kosutic answered as Roger worked his jaw.

"Now that hasn't been part of the brief," Raoux said. "Greenpeace?"

"Yeah," Roger said. "The tramp freighter we were jacking turned out to be one of their damned insertion ships . . . and we weren't exactly at full strength, anymore. Thirty remaining marines. They all got pinned down in the first few minutes. We didn't know who *they* were; they didn't know who *we* were. It was a pocking mess."

"*You* were there?" Marinau's eyes narrowed.

"No," Roger said flatly. "I was in the assault shuttles, with the Mardukans. Arm—Captain Pahner had pointed out that if I bought it, the whole plan was through. So I was sitting it out with the reserve. But when they found out it was commandos, I had to come in. So, by the end, yeah, I was there."

"You took Mardukans in against Greenpeace?" Raoux asked. "How many did you lose?"

"Fourteen or fifteen," Roger replied. "It helped that they were all carrying bead and plasma cannon."

"Ouch." Marinau shook his head. "They can handle them? I wouldn't put them much over being able to use rocks and sticks."

"Do *not* underestimate my companions," Roger said slowly, each word distinct and hard-edged. "All of you are veteran soldiers of the Empire, but the bottom line is that the Empire hasn't fought a major war in a century. I don't know you." He jabbed a finger at Raoux.

"Joceline Raoux," Kosutic told him. "Raiders."

"You're Eva?" Raoux asked. "Long time, Sergeant."

"Sergeant Major, Sergeant Major," Kosutic said with a grin. "Colonel, according to His Highness, but we'll let that slide."

"The point," Roger said, "is—"

He paused, then looked at Kosutic.

"Eva, how many actions did you have, prior to Marduk?"

"Fifteen."

"Sergeant Major Catrone?" Roger asked.

"A bit more," the sergeant major said. "Twenty something."

"Any pitched battles?" Roger asked. "A battle being defined as continuous or near continuous combat that lasts for more than a full day?"

"No, except one hostage negotiation. But that wasn't a battle, by any stretch. Your point?"

"My point," Roger said, "is that during our time on Marduk we had, by careful count, *ninety-seven* skirmishes and *seven* major battles, one of which had us in the field, in contact, for three days. We also had over two hundred attacks by *atul, atul-grack,* damncrocs, or other hostile animals which penetrated the perimeter."

He paused and looked at the three NCOs for a long, hard moment, and then bared his teeth.

"You may think you're the shit, Sergeants Major, but you aren't worth the price of a *pistol bead* compared to one of *my* troops, is that *clear*?"

"Easy, Roger," Eleanora said.

"No, I won't be easy. Because we need to be clear on this from the beginning. *Eleanora* has been in the middle of more battles than all three of you put together. From the point of view of combat time, I've got everyone in this *room*—except Eva—beat. Yes, we took on a Saint commando *company*. In *their* ship. And we smashed their ass. They didn't have enough people left to bury their dead. And compared to a couple of things we did on Marduk, it was a pocking *picnic*. *Don't* try to treat us like cherries, Sergeants Major. Don't."

"You'd used that sword before on those damnbeasts," Catrone said evenly.

"We had to *walk* across a *planet*," Despreaux said angrily. "You can't carry enough ammunition. The plasma guns blew up. And the damned *atul* just kept *coming!*" She shook her head. "And the Kranolta, and the Boman. The Krath. Marshad . . ."

"Sindi, Ran Tai, and the *flar-ke*," Roger said. "That damned *coll* fish . . . We have a little presentation, Sergeants Major. It's sort of the bare-bones of what happened, call it an after-action report. It takes about four hours, since it covers eight months. Would you care to view it?"

"Yeah," Marinau said after a moment. "I guess maybe we'd better see what could take a clotheshorse jackass and . . . make him something else."

Roger left after the first thirty minutes. He'd been there the first time, and he'd watched the presentation once already. Adventures are only fun if they happen to someone else a long way away.

Someday he might be able to just kick back and tell the stories. But not yet.

Despreaux followed him out, shaking her head.

"How did we do it, Roger?" she said softly. "How did we survive?"

"We didn't." Roger put his arm around her. "The people who went into that cauldron didn't come out. Some bodies came out, but their souls stayed there." He looked at her and kissed the top of her head, inhaling the sweet scent of her hair. "You know, I keep saying we need to do this for the Empire. And every time I do, I lie."

"Roger—"

"No, listen to me. I'm not doing this because I want the Throne. I'm doing this because I owe a debt. To you, to Kostas, to Armand, to Ima Hooker."

He frowned and tried to find the words.

"I know I need to protect myself, that it's all on my shoulders. But I don't want to. I feel like I need to protect *you*." His arm tightened around her. "Not just you, Nimashet Despreaux, but Eva, and Julian, and Poertena. We few who remain. We few who saw what we saw, and did what we did. You're *all* . . . special to me. But to do that, I have to do the rest. Rescue Mother—and, yes, I want to do that. I want Mother to be well. But I need to do the rest so *you* can be safe. So that you don't wake up every morning wondering if today they're going to come for you. To do that, I have to protect the Empire. Not a fragment, not a piece, not a remnant—the *Empire*. So that it's wrapped around you few like a blanket. And to do that, yes, I have to survive. I have to safeguard myself. But I think *first* about . . . we few."

"That's . . . crazy," Despreaux said, tears in her eyes.

"So I'm crazy." Roger shrugged. "Like I said, none of us survived."

"Well, that's enough of that," Raoux said, stepping into the corridor. She paused. "Oh, sorry."

"We were just discussing motivations," Roger said.

"Must have been a pretty intense discussion," Raoux said, looking at Despreaux.

"My motivation is pretty intense," he replied.

"I can see why," Raoux said. "I left when that . . . thing melted one of the troops."

"Talbert." Roger nodded. "Killerpillar. We figured out how to avoid them, and the poisons turned out to be useful." He shrugged. "You should have stuck around. You didn't even get to the Mohinga."

"The Mohinga?" Raoux's eyebrows rose. "That's a training area in Centralia Province. One nasty-assed swamp."

"We had one of our own." Roger looked at Despreaux. "Before Voitan, remember?"

"Yes," Despreaux said. "I thought it was bad. Until Voitan gave a whole new perspective to the word 'bad.'"

"Hey, you got to save my life. I still remember that really clear view of your butt. I thought I liked you before, but all I could think about all the time was what that butt looked like."

"Hell of a time to think of that!" Despreaux said angrily.

"Well, it was a very nice-looking butt." Roger smiled. "Still is, even if it's a bit . . . rounder."

"Fatter."

"No, not *fatter*, very nice . . ."

"Excuse me." Raoux folded her arms. "You guys want to get a room?"

"So, are we going to get your support?" Roger asked sharply. His smile disappeared, and he turned his head, locking onto her eyes. "From the Association?"

"Associations," Raoux said, turning slightly aside. "Plural."

The prince's expression, the way he moved and looked at her, reminded her uncomfortably of a bird of prey. Not an eagle, which had a certain majesty to it. More like a falcon—something that was no more than a swift, predatory shape wrapped around a mind like a buzz saw.

"We just call ourselves the clans," she continued. "Raider Association. Special Operations Association. Empress' Own Association. Lots of intermingling, what with people like Tomcat."

"All of them?" Roger asked.

"Why do you think I'm here?" Raoux countered. "I was never in the Pretty-Boy Club."

"And are we going to get the support?" Roger pressed.

"Probably. Marinau was a holdout, probably because he knew you. But if he can sit through that . . . briefing from Hell, I don't think he'll hold out for long. People change."

"That's what we were talking about," Roger said quietly. "I was just explaining to Nimashet that none of us got off Marduk alive, not really. Not the people that landed. We've all changed."

"Some for the worse," Despreaux said in a low voice.

"No," Roger said sternly. "You're my conscience, my anchor. You can't be my conscience *and* my sword. I've got people who can hold guns and pull triggers, and I can find more of them, if I have to. But there's only one you, Nimashet Despreaux."

"He's got a point," Raoux said. "And don't sweat combat fatigue—not after what I just watched. Anyone ever got hammered big time, it was you people. You've earned a change of duty assignments, and you've got your part to play."

"I suppose," Despreaux said.

"So what, exactly, are you bringing to the table?" Roger asked.

"Wait for the others," Raoux replied.

It didn't take long for Marinau to leave the room, as well, and Catrone followed shortly thereafter. Of the three NCOs, only Catrone was smiling.

"Christ," he said. "I wish I'd been there!"

"You would." Raoux shook her head. "You like nightmares."

"Okay, I'm convinced," Marinau said. "I kept looking for the special effects. There weren't any; that was real."

"As real as it gets," Roger said, his face hard.

Marinau cleared his throat, shook his head, and finally looked at the prince.

"I'm in," he said, still shaking his head. "But do you think you could have shown just a *little* bit of that when *I* was in charge?" he asked plaintively. "It would have made my job . . . well, not easier. More *satisfying*, I guess."

"Maybe I shouldn't have always shucked my guards when I went hunting," Roger said with a shrug. "But you all sounded like *flar-ta* in the woods."

"I'll tell you a secret," Marinau said, shame-faced. "We all figured it was your guides doing the hunting, and that you were just showing off and bringing back the heads. Shows how wrong I can be. And I'm man enough to admit it. I'm in."

"Raiders are in," Raoux said.

"Special Ops is in," Catrone said. "But only if we get a chance to get stuck in with some of those Mardukans. And I want the Earl of New Madrid. I'm going to spend the rest of my natural life torturing him to death. There's this thing you can do with a steel-wire waistcoat and a rock—"

"We'll discuss it," Roger said sternly. "Okay, back to the conference room."

"Here's the thing," Catrone said, when the playback had been turned down. Roger left the video playing, though, as a less than subtle point. "You know who the Strelza were, Your Highness?"

"No," Roger said.

"Yes," Despreaux, Kosutic, and Eleanora replied.

"What am I missing?" Roger asked.

"We got it on our in-brief to the Regiment," Despreaux told him, frowning at a distant memory. "Russian troops."

"Okay, ever heard of the Praetorian Guard?" Catrone asked.

"Sort of." Roger nodded. "Roman."

"Both the same thing," Catrone said.

"Not *exactly*," Eleanora said. "The Praetorians were originally Caesar's Tenth Legion, and—"

"For my point, they are," Catrone said, annoyed. "Both of them were guard forces for their respective Emperors. The equivalent of the Empress' Own. Okay?"

"Okay," Roger said.

"And both of them ended up deciding that *they* got to choose who was Emperor."

"I begin to see your point," Roger said.

"The Empress' Own is weeded *really* hard," Marinau said. "You can't just be able, you have to be . . . right."

"Pretty boys," Raoux said with a smile.

"That, too," Marinau agreed with a shrug. "But pretty boys that aren't going to be kingmakers. In a lot of ways, we're deliberately . . . limited. Limited in size—"

"And never up to full strength," Catrone interjected.

"And limited in firepower," Marinau continued. "Home Fleet can take us out anytime."

"If they want to kill the Empress," Roger said.

"True. But the point is that we *can* be taken down," Marinau said. "For that matter, garrison troops from outside NorthAm could do it the hard way, if they were prepared to lose enough bodies. As that bastard Adoula demonstrated."

"Some of this was deliberately set up by Miranda MacClintock," Catrone said.

"Who was one seriously paranoid individual," Marinau added.

"And a scholar," Eleanora pointed out. "One who knew the dangers of a Praetorian Guard. And while it's true you can be taken out, you're also the *only* significant Imperial ground force allowed on this entire continent. The brigade that attacked the Palace was a clear violation of Imperial regulations."

"But Miranda set up other things, too," Catrone said, waving that away. "This, for example." He gestured around himself at the facility. "You notice we're surrounded by skyscrapers, but none of them are here?"

"I did notice that," Roger agreed.

"Deliberate and very subtle zoning," Catrone told him. "To prevent this facility from ever being discovered. And you don't find out about some things until you've *left* the Regiment."

"Ah," Kosutic said. "Tricky."

"Some stuff has gotten passed down," Catrone said. "In the Association. Keywords. Secrets. Passed *from* former commanders and sergeants major *to* former commanders and sergeants major. Some of it's probably been lost that way, but it's been . . . pretty secure. You're out, maybe you've got some gripes with the current Emperor, but you've got this sacred trust. And you keep it. And you're no longer in a position to play kingmaker."

"Until now," Eleanora said, leaning forward. "Right?"

"Asseen," Catrone said, ignoring her and looking at Roger. "Are you Prince Roger Ramius Sergei Alexander Chiang MacClintock, son of Alexandra Harriet Katryn Griselda Tian MacClintock?"

Roger brushed his forehead, like a man brushing away a mosquito, and frowned in puzzlement.

"What are you doing?" he asked suspiciously.

"Answer yes or no," Catrone said. "Are you Prince Roger Ramius Sergei Alexander Chiang MacClintock, son of Alexandra Harriet Katryn Griselda Tian MacClintock?"

"Yes," Roger said firmly.

"Is there a usurper upon the Throne?"

"Yes," Roger said, after a moment. He could *feel* something searching his thoughts, looking for falsehood. It was an odd and terrifying experience.

"Do you attempt to take your rightful place for the good of the Empire?"

"Yes," Roger said after another pause. His quibbles about motivation didn't matter; it *was* for the good of the Empire.

"Will you keep Our Empire safe, hold Our people in your hands, protect them as you would your children, and ensure the continuity of Our line?" Catrone's voice had taken on a peculiar timbre.

"Yes," Roger whispered.

"Then We give unto you Our sword," Catrone said, his voice now distinctively female. "Bear it under God, to defend the right, to protect Our people from their enemies, to safeguard Our people's liberties, and to preserve Our House."

Roger dropped his head, holding it in his hands, his elbows on the table.

"Roger?" Despreaux said, putting her hand on his shoulder.

"It's okay," Roger gasped. "*Shit.*"

"It doesn't *look* okay," she said anxiously.

"God," Roger groaned. "Oh, God. It's all there . . ."

"*What's* there?" Despreaux turned on Catrone, her expression furious. "What did you *do* to him?!"

"I didn't do anything to him," Catrone said, his voice now normal. "Miranda MacClintock did."

★ ★ ★

"Secret routes here, here, here, here," Roger said, updating the map of the Palace through his toot. "This one is an old subway line. The control bunker is in the basement of an old *rail* station!"

"This was all in your head?" Eleanora asked in an almost awed tone as she gazed into the holo.

"Yes. Which—much as I hate to even think about it—makes me wonder if *they* could have gotten it from Mother."

"I won't say it's impossible," Catrone replied, "but it's set to dump if the subject is under any form of duress. Even harsh questioning would do it. I happen to know that *you* got updated, twice, after conversations with your mother."

"That figures," Roger said. "She always was one for . . . harsh questions. 'Why don't you cut your hair?' 'What do you *do* all day on those hunting trips?'" he added in a falsetto.

"The setup is incredibly paranoid," Catrone continued. "The doctors who handle the toot updates don't even know about it. It's a hack that's arranged by the Regiment, and the only thing *they* know is that it's an old mod. Hell, for that matter the hack that gave *me* the activation codes is handled the same way. Except—" his smile was crooked "—*our* toots don't just dump. They still have their active-duty suicide circuits on-line in case anyone tries to sweat us for what we know about the Protocols. As for the Imperial Family and the full packet, it's just one of the traditions of the Regiment. That's all most of us who know about it at all know. And the subjects aren't aware of it at all. None of them."

"You could slip anything in," Roger said angrily.

"So maybe we are kingmakers," Catrone admitted. "I dunno. But we don't even know what's in it. It's just a data packet. We get the data packet from the IBI. I think they're in charge of keeping the current intelligence info side of it updated, but even *they* don't know what it's *for*."

"It's more than just a data packet," Roger said flatly. "It's like having the old biddy in your head. God, it's weird. No, not having her in your head, but the way the data's arranged . . ."

His voice trailed off.

"What?" Despreaux finally asked.

"Well, first of all, the data's nonextractable." Roger was looking at the tabletop, but clearly not actually seeing it as his eyes tracked back and forth. "That is, I can't just dump it out. It's in a compartmented memory segment. And there's a lot more than just the Palace data. Assassination techniques, toombie hacks, poisons— method and application of, including analyses and after-action reports. Hacking programs. Back doors to Imperial and IBI datanets. Whoever caretakers this thing for the IBI's been earning his pay updating it with current tech and passwords. And there's more in here than I thought a toot had room for."

"Is there a way *in*?" Kosutic asked pointedly.

"I can see several. All of them have problems, but they're all better than what we'd been—" He held up his hand and shook his head. "Hang on."

He closed his eyes and leaned back in his float chair, swinging it from side to side. The group watched him in silence, wondering what he was seeing. Then he leaned suddenly forward and opened his eyes, crossing his arms and grinning.

Despreaux felt faintly uneasy as she studied that grin. It wasn't cold, by any stretch of the imagination. Quite the contrary, in fact. It was almost . . . mad. Evil. Then it passed, and he laughed and looked up at them.

"Now I know what Aladdin felt like," he said, still grinning.

"What are you talking about?" Kosutic sounded as uneasy as Despreaux had felt.

"Let's take a walk," Roger replied, and led them out of the room and down a series of corridors to the back of the south end of the complex. They ended up facing a blank wall.

"We swept this," Kosutic pointed out.

"And if it had been a normal door, you would've found it." Roger drew a knife out of his pocket and rapped on the solid concrete. "Asseen, asseen, Protocol Miranda MacClintock One-Three-Niner-Beta. Open Sesame!"

He slapped the wall and then stood back.

"Paranoid *and* with a sense of humor," Catrone said dryly as the wall started to slide backwards into the hill. The movement revealed that the "wall" was a half meter of concrete slab, pinned to the bedrock of the mountain ridge. The plug that had filled the corridor was nearly four meters deep, yet it slid backwards smoothly, easily. Then it moved sideways, revealing a large, domed room whose walls and ceilings reflected the silver of ChromSten armoring.

Ranked against the left wall were five stingships—a model Roger didn't recognize, with short, stubby wings, and a wide body—and a pair of shuttles. Opposite them were three light skimmer tanks, and both sets of vehicles were wrapped in protective covers.

"Wait." Roger held out his hand as Catrone started to step past him. "Nitrogen atmosphere," the prince continued as lights came on and fans started to turn in the distance. "You go in there now, and you'll keel over in a second."

"That up there, too?" Catrone asked, gesturing with his chin at Roger's head.

"Yep."

"Is there one of these at each dispersal facility?" Catrone asked.

"Yep. And a bigger set at the Cheyenne facility. You were the Gold sergeant major; you know about that one, right?"

"Yes. How many others?"

"Four, five total," Roger replied. "Greenbrier, Cheyenne, Weather Mountain, Cold Mountain, and Wasatch."

"Thirty stingships?" Rosenberg asked.

"Fifty," Roger told him. "There are ten each at Weather Mountain, Cold Mountain, and Wasatch, and fifteen at Cheyenne."

"I *knew* it didn't look right!" Catrone snapped. "That one's designated for the Empress, and I checked it out one time. The dome's too flat!"

"That's because the entire lower section is missing," Roger said. "All the stuff in there is *under* the known facilities. And this isn't part of the original facility; it was a later add-on." He glanced at a readout on the side of the tunnel and nodded. "That's long enough."

"I don't recognize those." Despreaux pointed at the stingships, as they crossed the chamber towards them. "Or the tanks, for that matter."

"That's because they're antiques," Rosenberg said, running his hand lovingly over the needlelike nose of the nearest. "I've only ever seen them in air shows. They date back more than a hundred years. Densoni Shadow Wolves—forty megawatt fusion bottle, nine thousand kilos of thrust, Mach Three-Point-Five or thereabouts." He touched the leading edge of one wing and sighed. "Bastards to fly. They used more aero-lift than modern ships—let them get away from you, and they went all over the sky, then hit the ground. Hard. They called them Widow-Makers."

"Not much good against Raptors, then," Roger sighed. "I thought we'd hit the jackpot."

"Oh, I dunno." Rosenberg pursed his lips. "It'll take good pilots, and I don't have fifty of those I can get in on this and be sure of security. It'd help if they're crazy, too. But basic stingship design just hasn't changed a lot over the last hundred years or so. Shadow Wolves are actually *faster* than Raptors, and, maybe, a tad more maneuverable because of the aero-surfaces. Certainly more maneuverable at high speeds; they'll pull something like thirty gees in a bank, before damping. But they sacrifice direct lift and gravity control, and the damping only brings it down to about sixteen gees at max evolution. The big difference is modern high-density fusion plants, which equates to more brute acceleration—better grav damping—and a considerably more powerful weapons fit. And, like I said, their out-of-control maneuvers are a bitch. No neural interfaces, either." He looked over at Roger and cocked an eyebrow. "Ammo?"

"Magazine." Roger pointed to the exit corridor. "And an armory. No powered armor. Soft-suits and exoskeletons."

"They didn't have the power-tech a hundred years ago that we have now," Catrone said, striding down the corridor. "Powering ChromSten armor took too much juice. Weapons?"

"Old—*really* old—plasma guns," Roger replied. "Forty-kilowatt range."

"That won't do it against powered armor," Kosutic said.

"And I'm not too happy about the idea of old plasma guns," Despreaux pointed out. "Not after what happened on Marduk."

"Everything's going to have to be checked out," Roger said. "Most of it should be pretty good; no oxygen, so there shouldn't have been any degradation. And the guns may be old, Nimashet, but they weren't built by Adoula and his assholes. On the other hand, some of the stuff was stashed by Miranda herself, people—it's damned near *six* hundred years old. Most of the other bits and pieces were emplaced later."

"So somebody's been collecting the stuff," Catrone said. "The Association?"

"Sometimes," Roger said. "And others. But usually the Family took care of it directly. Which left the entire process with some kinks Miranda couldn't really allow for. There are some . . . time bombs in this thing. Like I say, some of this stuff was put up by Great Gran, using the IBI, and some of the Family have followed up over the years with more modern equipment. Like your Shadow Wolves," he said, looking at Rosenberg. "But I think . . ."

Roger frowned and looked up at the ceiling, clearly considering schedules.

"Yeah," he said after a moment. "Mother should already have done some upgrades. I wonder why—" He paused. "Oh, that's why. God, this woman was paranoid."

"What?" Despreaux said.

"Bitch!" Roger snapped.

"What!?"

"Oh, not you," Roger said quickly, soothingly. "Miranda. Mother, for that matter. There are . . . familial security protocols, I guess you'd call them, in here. God, no wonder some of the emperors've gone just a touch insane." He closed his eyes again and shook his head. "Imagine, for a moment, a thought coming out of nowhere . . ."

"Oh, Christ," Catrone said. "'Do you trust your family? Really, *really* trust them?'"

"Bingo." Roger opened his eyes and looked around. "The protocols only opened up if the Emperor or Empress of the time fully trusted the people he or she was going to use to upgrade the facilities. And the people they were upgrading the facilities *for*. If they didn't trust them, from time to time they'd be . . . probed again. According to the timetable, Mother probably was being asked as often as monthly if she really trusted, well, *me*."

"And she didn't," Catrone said.

"Apparently not," Roger replied, tightly. "As if I didn't know that before."

"We pull this off, and she will," Marinau said. "Keep that in mind."

"Yeah," Roger said. "Yeah. And it wasn't just Mother, either. Grandfather's head just didn't work the way Miranda's—or Mom's—did. He didn't want to think about this kind of crap . . . so he didn't, and the Protocols jumped over him completely. That's why the stingships we've got here date clear back to before he took the Throne, although the ones at Cheyenne are more modern." His mouth twisted. "Probably because these were the ones *I* was most likely to get my hands on if it turned out Mom was right about me."

"But at least they're here," Despreaux pointed out.

"And because they are, we've got a chance," Rosenberg put in. "Maybe even a good one."

"We can't use the Cheyenne stingships," Roger pointed out. "Not in any sort of first wave; they're too far away. For that matter, they'd have to run a gauntlet even after the first attack. *Especially* after the first attack."

"And I've only got one other pilot I'd bring in on this," Rosenberg said.

"Pilots . . . aren't a problem," Roger replied evenly. "But we're going to have to get techs in to work on this stuff. It *should* be in good shape, but there's bound to be problems. There are spares here, as well."

"And we're gonna need more armor," Catrone said.

"Well, that's not a problem, either," Roger said. "Or modern weapons. The plasma guns here are ancient as hell, but they're fine for general antipersonnel work, and there are some heavy weapons the Mardukans can handle, for that matter. And we've got another source of supply. We've got over twenty heavy plasma and bead guns, and some armor, as well."

"Oh?" Catrone eyed him speculatively.

"Oh." Roger seemed unaware that the older man was looking at him. "But the big problem is, we're going to have to *rehearse* this, and this op's just gotten a lot bigger than we can squeeze into Greenbrier here. Somehow, we've got to bring everyone together in one place, and how the *hell* are we going to do that without opping every security flag Adoula has?"

"Tell you what," Catrone said suspiciously. "If you'll ante up your suppliers, we'll ante up how to rehearse. And where the techs are going to come from."

"Okay," Catrone said when he and Roger were back in the meeting room. Despreaux, Kosutic, and Marinau were going over weaponry, while Rosenberg was doing an in initial survey of the stingships and shuttles. "We need to get one thing out of the way."

"What?"

"No matter what, we're not going to oppose you, and we're not going to burn you," Catrone said. "But there are still some elements that don't think too highly of Prince Roger MacClintock."

"I'm not surprised," Roger said evenly. "I was my own worst enemy."

"They do, however, support *Alexandra*," Catrone continued, shaking his head. "Which could create a not-so-tiny problem, since when we take the Palace, *you're* going to be in control."

"Not if the Association is against me," Roger pointed out.

"We don't want a factional fight in the Palace itself," Catrone said tightly. "That would be the worst of all possible outcomes. But—get it straight. We're not fighting for Prince Roger; we're fighting for Empress Alexandra."

"I understand. There's just one problem."

"Your mother may not be fully functional," Catrone said. "Mentally."

"Correct." Roger considered his next words carefully. "Again," he said, "we have . . . reports which indicate that. The people who provided the analysis in those reports believe there will be significant impairment. Look, Tom, I don't *want* the Throne. What sort of lunatic *would* want it in a situation like this one? But from all reports, Mother isn't going to be sufficiently functional to continue as Empress."

"We don't know that," Catrone argued mulishly, his face set. "All we have are rumors and fifth-hand information. Your mother is a *very* strong woman."

Roger leaned back and cocked his head to the side, examining the old soldier as if he'd never seen him before.

"You love her," the prince said.

"What?" Catrone snapped, and glared at him. "What does that have to do with it? She's my Empress. I was sworn to protect her before *you* were a gleam in New Madrid's eye. I was Silver's battalion sergeant major when she was *Heir Primus*. Of course I love her! She's my *Empress*, you young idiot!"

"No." Roger leaned forward, resting his forearms on the table, and stared Catrone in the eye. "Being in that pressure cooker taught me more than just how to swing a sword, Tomcat. It made me a pretty fair judge of human nature, too. And I mean you *love* her. Not as a primary, not as the Empress—as a woman. Tell me I lie."

Catrone leaned back and crossed his own arms. He looked away from Roger's modded brown eyes, then looked back.

"What if I do?" he asked. "What business is that of yours?"

"Just this." Roger leaned back in turn. "Which do you love more—her, or the Empire?" He watched the sergeant major's face for a moment, then nodded. "Ah, there's the rub, isn't it? If it comes down to a choice between Alexandra MacClintock and the Empire, can you decide?"

"That's hypothetical," Catrone argued. "And it's impossible to judge—"

"It's an *important* hypothetical," Roger interrupted. "Face it, if we succeed, we *will* be the kingmakers. And people—everyone on Old Earth, in the Navy, in the Corps, the Lords, the Commons, *all* of them—are going to want to know, *right away*, who's in charge." He made a cutting motion with his hand in emphasis. "Right then. Who's giving the orders. Who holds the reins. Not to mention the planetary defense control codes. *My* information is that Mother's in no condition to assume that responsibility. What do *your* sources say?"

"That she's . . . impaired." Catrone's face was obsidian-hard.

"That they're using psychotropic drugs, toot controls, and . . . sexual controls to keep her in line."

"What?" Roger said very, very softly.

"They're using psychotropic—"

"No. That last part."

"That's why the Earl is involved," Catrone said, and paused, looking at the prince. "You didn't know," he said quietly after a moment.

"No." Roger's fists bunched. His arms quivered, and his face went set and hard. For the first time, Thomas Catrone felt an actual trickle of fear as he looked at the young man across the table from him.

"I did not know," Prince Roger MacClintock said.

"It's a . . . refinement." Catrone's own jaw worked. "Keeping Alex in line is apparently pretty hard. New Madrid figured out how." He paused and took a deep breath, getting himself under control. "It's his . . . style."

Roger had his head down, hands together, nose and lips resting on the ends of his fingers, as if he were praying. He was still quivering.

"If you go in now, guns blazing, Prince Roger," Catrone said softly, "we're all going to die. And it won't help your mother."

Roger nodded his head, ever so slightly.

"I've had some time to get over it," Catrone said, gazing at something only he could see, his voice distant, almost detached. "Marinau brought me the word. All of it. He brought it in person, along with a couple of the other guys."

"They have to hold you down?" Roger asked quietly. His head was still bent, but he'd managed to stop the whole-body quivers.

"I nearly broke his arm," Catrone said, speaking each word carefully, in a sort of high, soft voice of memory. He licked his lips and shook his head. "It catches me, sometimes. I've been wracking my brain over what to do, other than getting myself killed. I don't have a problem with that, but it wouldn't have helped Alex one bit. Which is why I didn't hesitate, except long enough for some tradecraft, when you turned up. I want those bastards, Your Highness. I want them so bad I can taste it. I've never wanted to kill anyone like I want to kill New Madrid. I want a new meaning of pain for him."

"Until this moment," Roger said quietly, calmly, "we've been in very different places, Sergeant Major."

"Explain," Catrone said, shaking himself like a dog, shaking off the cold, drenching hatred of memory to refocus on the prince.

"I knew rescuing Mother was a necessity." Roger looked up at last, and the retired NCO saw tears running down his cheeks. "But frankly, if the mission would have worked better, if it would have been safer, ignoring Mother, I would have been more than willing to ignore her."

"What?" Catrone said angrily.

"Don't get on your high horse, Sergeant Major," Roger snapped. "First of all, let's keep in mind the safety of the Empire. If keeping the Empire together meant playing my mother as a pawn, that would be the right course. *Mother* would insist it was the right course. Agreed?"

Catrone's lips were pinched and white with anger, but he nodded.

"Agreed," he said tightly.

"Now we get into the personal side," Roger continued. "My mother spent as little time with me as she possibly could. Yes, she was Empress, and she was very busy. It was a hard job, I know that. But I also know I was raised by nannies and tutors and my goddammed *valet*. Mother, quite frankly, generally only appeared in my life to explain to me what a little shit I was. Which, I submit, didn't do a great deal to motivate me to be anything *else*, Sergeant Major. And then, when it was all coming apart, she didn't trust me enough to keep me at her side. Instead, she sent me off to Leviathan. Instead of landing on Leviathan, which is a shithole of a planet, I ended up on Marduk—which is worse. Not exactly *her* fault, but let's just say that she and her distrust figure prominently in why almost two hundred men and women who were very close and important to me *died*."

"Don't care for Alexandra, do you?" Catrone said menacingly.

"I just found out that blood is much, much thicker than water,"

Roger replied, cheek muscles bunching. "If you'd asked me, and if I'd been willing to answer honestly, five minutes ago if I cared if Mother lived or died, the *honest* answer would have been: no." He paused and stared at the sergeant major, then shook his head. "In which case, I would have been lying to myself at the same time I was trying to be honest with *you*." He twisted his hands together and his arms shook. "I really, *really* feel the need to kill something."

"There's always those *atul*," Catrone pointed out, watching him work through it.

Frankly, the prince was handling it better than he had. Maybe he didn't care as much, but Catrone suspected that it was simply a very clear manifestation of how controlled Roger could be. Catrone understood control. You didn't get to be sergeant major of Gold Battalion by being a nonaggressive nonentity, and he could recognize when a person was exercising enormous control. Well, enough to prevent an outright explosion, at least. He wondered—for the first time, really, despite having seen the "presentation" from Marduk— just how volcanic Roger could be when pushed. Based on the degree of control he was seeing at this moment, he suspected the answer was *very* volcanic. Like, Krakatoa volcanic.

"Putting myself in the way of an *atul* right now would be stupid," Roger said. "If I die, the whole plan dies. Mom dies, and she . . . shit!" He shook his head again. "Besides, I've killed so many of them that it just wouldn't be *satisfying* enough, you know?" he added, looking at the sergeant major.

"Oh, yeah. I know."

"God, that hit me." Roger closed his eyes again. "At so many levels. Christ, I don't want her to die. I want to strangle her myself!"

"Don't joke about that," Catrone said sharply.

"Sorry." Roger sat motionless for another moment, then reopened his eyes. "We've got to get her out of there, Sergeant Major."

"We will," Catrone said. "Sir."

"I learned, a long time ago," Roger said, smiling faintly, his cheeks still wet with tears, "all of eleven months or so ago, the difference between being called 'Your Highness' and 'Sir.' I'm glad you're fully on board."

"Nobody is that good an actor," Catrone told him. "You didn't know. Your . . . sources didn't know?"

"I . . . think they did," Roger replied. "In which case, certain cryptic glances between members of my staff are now explained."

"Wouldn't be the first time staff held back something they didn't want their boss to know. Be glad it wasn't something more important."

"Actually, *this* is rather important. But I take your meaning," Roger said. "On the other hand, I think I'll just explain to them the difference between personal and important." He looked at the sergeant major, his face hard. "Don't get down on me, by the way, for considering Mother as a pawn. I saw too many friends die . . ."

"I watched," Catrone said, nodding to where the hologram had played.

"Yes, but even for someone who's been on the sharp end, you can't know," Roger replied. "You can't know what it's like to have to keep going every day, watching your soldiers being picked off, one by one, losing men and women that you . . . love, and the journey seems to never end. Seeing them dying to protect you, and nothing—*nothing*—you can do to help them that won't make it worse. So, I did. I did make it worse. I kept throwing myself out there. And getting them killed while they were trying to keep me alive. Until I got good enough that I was keeping *them* alive. Good enough that they were watching my back instead of getting between me and whatever was trying to kill us, because they knew I was, by God, the nastiest, most cold-blooded, *vicious* bastard on that entire fucking planet.

"I wasn't fighting this battle for Mother, Sergeant Major; I was fighting it for *them*. To get that damned Imperial Warrant off their heads. To make sure they could go to bed at night in reasonable certainty that they'd wake up in the morning. So that the *dead* could be honored in memory, their bodies brought home to lie beside the fallen heroes of the Empire, instead of being remembered only as losers in a failed coup. As incompetent traitors. That was no way to remember Armand Pahner. I'd use anyone—you, the Association, Mother, *anyone*—to keep them from—"

He shrugged angrily, and his nostrils flared as he drew a deep breath.

"But, yeah, I just found out that blood is thicker than water. Before, I only wanted Adoula . . . moved aside. He was another obstacle to be removed, period. Now . . . ?"

"New Madrid is the real bastard," Catrone ground out. "He's the one—"

"Yes, he is." Roger flexed his jaw. "I agree with that. But I'll tell you something else, Sergeant Major. You're not getting your wire waistcoat."

"Like hell," Catrone said uncomfortably. "You're not going to let him *walk*?"

"Of course not. And if the timing is right, you can shoot the bastard, father of mine though he is—genetically speaking, at least. Or I'll hand you my sword, and you can cut his pretty head off. But in all likelihood, if he doesn't get accidentally terminated during the operation, or if he's not in a position where early termination is the best course, we're going to turn him over to the courts and slip a nice little poison into his veins after a full and fair trial."

"Like hell!" Catrone repeated, angrily, this time.

"That's what's going to happen," Roger said sternly. "Because one of the things I learned in that little walk is the difference between the good guys and the bad guys. The good guys don't *torture* people just because they want vengeance, Sergeant Major. No matter what the reasoning. I didn't torture that damned Saint bastard who killed Armand Pahner after he'd 'surrendered.' I *shot* him before I left Marduk, and given the Saints' violation of Imperial territory and the operations those Greenpeace commandos carried out under his orders—not to mention killing so many Imperial Marines right there in Marduk orbit—it was completely, legally justified. I won't pretend for a moment that I didn't take a certain savage satisfaction out of it; as Armand himself once pointed out to me, I *am* a bit of a savage—a barbarian—myself. But I didn't torture even the sons of bitches who killed him and tried to kill me, and I never tortured a damncroc for killing Kostas. Killed quite a few, but they all went out quick. If there's a reason to terminate New Madrid as part of this operation, he'll be terminated. Cleanly and quickly. If not, he faces Imperial justice. Ditto for Adoula. Because we're the good guys, whatever the *bad guys* may have done."

"Christ, you *have* grown up," Catrone muttered. "Bastard."

"That I am," Roger agreed. "I was born out of wedlock, but I'm my *mother's* son, not my father's. And not even he can turn me into him. Is that clear?"

"Clear," Catrone muttered.

"I can't *hear* you, Sergeant Major," Roger said without a hint of playfulness.

"Clear," Catrone said flatly. "Damn it."

"Good," Roger said. "And now that that little *UNPLEASANTNESS*—" he shouted "—is out of the way, I'll give you one more thing, Sergeant Major."

"Oh?" Catrone regarded him warily.

"I've taken a shine to you, Sergeant Major. I didn't understand why, at first, but you remind me of someone. Not as smooth, not quite as wise, I think, but pretty similar in a lot of ways."

"Who?" Catrone asked.

"Armand Pahner." Roger swallowed. "Like I said, none of that trip would have worked without Armand. He wasn't perfect. He had a tendency to believe his own estimates that damned near killed us a couple of times. But . . . he was very much like a father to me. I learned to trust him more than I trust ChromSten. You with me, Sergeant Major?"

"Pahner was a hell of a man," Catrone said. "A bit of a punk, when I first met him. No, not a punk—never a punk. He was good, even then. But, yeah, cocky as hell. And I watched him grow for a bit. I agree, he was more trustworthy than armor. Your point?"

"My point, Tom, is that I've come to trust you. Maybe more than I should, but . . . I've gotten to be a fair judge of character. And I know you don't want to play kingmaker . . . which is why that's exactly what you're going to do."

"Explain," Catrone said, wary again.

"When we take the Palace," Roger said, then shrugged. "Okay, *if* we take the Palace. And we rescue Mother. *You* are going to decide—right then, right there."

"Decide who gets the reins?"

"Yes, who gets the reins. If Mother is even semifunctional, I'll step back. Give her time to get her bearings, time to find out how damaged she is. But you, Thomas Catrone, are going to make the evaluation."

"Shit."

"Do you think Adoula has this?"

Buseh Subianto had been in the IBI for going on forty years. She'd started out as a street agent, working organized crime, and she'd done it well. There'd been something about her fresh face and dark-green eyes that had gotten men, often men who were normally close-mouthed, to talk to her. Such conversations had frequently resulted in their incarceration—frequently enough, as a matter of fact, that she'd been quickly promoted, and then transferred to counterintelligence.

She'd been in the counter-intel business for more than twenty-five years, now, during which she'd slowly worked her way up the ladder of the bureaucracy. The face wasn't so fresh any more. Fine lines had appeared in her skin, and there was a crease on her brow from years of concentrated thought. But the green eyes were still dark and piercing. Almost hypnotic.

Fritz Tebic had worked for his boss long enough to know when to avoid the hypnotism. So he swallowed, then shrugged, looking away.

"He may have it," he replied. "He's seen the report on the Mardukans who met with Helmut's courier. And New Madrid was definitely having Catrone followed. Catrone went to the Mardukan restaurant here in Imperial city, and a week later, he's meeting with the hard-core members of the Associations. But . . . there are a lot of threads. Adoula's people might not have connected them. Might not."

"If they had, we'd already have an Imperial arrest warrant for treason for Catrone and . . ." she looked at the data, frowning, the thin crease getting deeper, "this Augustus Chung. What gets me is that the players don't make any *sense*. And where are the materials Chung's been receiving *coming* from?"

"I don't know," Tebic said. "OrgCrime Division's already looking at this Marduk House pretty closely—they think Chung is laundering money. But they don't have the information on the shipments. I haven't put any of this into the datanet. The original report on the meeting with Helmut's officers is in there, but none of the connections. And . . . there are a few Mardukans running around. They don't have any skills, so they tend to end up as heavies of one sort or another. Some *do* work for orgcrime, so basically, the Sixth Fleet link looks like a false-positive unless you also have the information on the equipment Chung's been receiving. Ma'am, what are we going to do?"

It was difficult to hide much from the Imperial Bureau of Investigation. Most money was transferred electronically, as were most messages, and everything electronic went past the IBI eventually. And the IBI had enormous computing power at its disposal, power that sifted through that enormous mass of data, looking for apparently unconnected bits. Over the years, the programs had become more and more sophisticated, with fewer and fewer false hits. Despite draconian privacy limitations which were—almost always—rigorously observed, the IBI had eyes everywhere.

Including inside the Imperial Palace. Which meant the two of them knew very well the actual condition of the Empress.

Tebic remembered a class from early in his Academy days. The class had been on the history of cryptography and information security, and one of the examples of successful code-breaking operations had been called Verona, a program from the earliest days of computers—even before transistors. The code-breakers had successfully penetrated an enemy spy network, only to find out that the other side had agents so high in their own government that reporting the information was tantamount to committing suicide. At the time of the class, Tebic's sympathy for them had been purely intellectual; these days, he connected with them on a far more profound level.

A few key people in the IBI knew that Adoula and the Earl of New Madrid had the Empress under their complete control. They even knew how. The problem was, they had no one to tell. The IBI's director had been replaced, charged as an accessory to the "coup." Kyoko Pedza, Director of Counterintelligence, had disappeared within a day afterwards, just before his own arrest on the same charges. It was five-to-one odds in their internal pool that he'd been assassinated by Adoula; Pedza had been a serious threat to Adoula's power base.

But the problem was that the IBI wasn't the Empress' Own. It wasn't even the Navy, sworn to defend the Constitution *and* the Empress. The IBI's first and only mission was the security of the *Empire*. Yes, Adoula had effectively usurped the Throne. Yes, he'd committed a list of offenses a kilometer long in doing so. Perjury, murder, kidnapping, and physical and psychological torture. Technically, they should lay out the data, slap a set of restraints on him, and lead him away to durance vile.

But realistically, he was too powerful. He had a major base in the Lords and the Commons, *de facto* control of the Empress, and control of most of the Navy, and Prime Minister Yang had obviously decided it wasn't time to challenge him too openly. Whether that was because of the chaos Yang feared would overwhelm the Empire if he did so, or because he was more concerned about his own power than he was about the Empress and the Constitution was impossible to say, although Subianto had her own suspicions in that regard.

But whatever the Prime Minister's thinking, as Navy Minister, Prince Jackson was effectively in control of all of the Empire's external and *internal* security organs, especially after he'd replaced Tebic and Subianto's superiors with his own handpicked nominees. If they wanted to arrest Adoula, they'd need to present a list of charges to a magistrate. And even if they found one stupid enough to sign a warrant, they'd never live to process it. Besides, Adoula had already done too much damage. He'd managed to *destroy* the Imperial Family, and Subianto and Tebic, unlike all too many citizens of the Empire, knew precisely how vital to its stability House MacClintock had been. Without it, there was only Adoula, however corrupt, however "evil," to hold things together. Without him, what did the Empire have? An Empress who was severely damaged. Probably civil war. And no clear heir to the Throne.

And now they had this. Smuggling of illegal and highly dangerous materials. Collusion with a foreign power—they were pretty sure about that one, although which foreign power was less clear. Conspiracy to commit treason—sort of; that one depended on the definition and whether or not it was technically possible to commit treason against someone who had treasonously seized power in the first place. Illegal monetary transfers—definitely. Falsification of identity without a doubt. Assault. Theft.

But...

"No chance of getting eyes and ears into the building?" Subianto asked.

"No," Tebic replied unhesitatingly. "Security is pretty unobtrusive, but very tight. Good electronics—very good, very professional. And those Mardukans literally sleep at the warehouse and the restaurant. The restaurant has countersurveillance devices—two agents have been asked to leave for trying to get floaters and directional mikes inside—but plenty of restaurants in Imperial City would've done exactly the same thing. Too many conversations nobody wants overheard."

"Who *are* they?" Subianto whispered to herself. "They're not the Associations. They're not with Adoula. They're not those idiots in the Supremacy Party."

"They're acting like they're going to counter Adoula," Tebic said. "But the Associations *have* to know the Empress isn't in the best condition, and there's no clear alternate Regent, much less a clear Heir, other than this fetus Adoula and New Madrid are growing." He paused and shrugged. "We've got three choices."

"I know." Subianto's face was hard and cold. "We can turn the data over to Adoula, and they disappear—or, maybe, get tried. We can do nothing, and see what happens. Or we can contact them."

"Yes, Ma'am," Tebic said, and waited.

His superior's face could have belonged to a statue—one of the old Persian emperors, the omnipotent semideities, often more than just a little insane, who had gifted humanity with such enduring phrases as "killing the messenger" and "maybe the horse will sing" and "the Sword of Damocles." *This* was a Sword of Damocles over both their heads, hanging by a thread. And the way those omnipotent emperors had wandered into the borderlands of sanity, Tebic knew, was from making decisions which would determine the fate of far more than just their own empire . . . and when they'd known their own lives, and their families', were on the line.

"I think," Subianto said, then paused. "I think, I'm in the mood to try some new food."

"When were you planning on doing this?" Catrone's voice was still cold, but he was focused again, had his mission face on once more.

"During the Imperial Festival," Roger replied. "We were going to have to do the attack fully on the surface—frontal assault. We were going to be in the parade that passes the Imperial Park. Mardukans in all their finery, *civan, flar-ta*, the works. We knew we could take down the outer perimeter guards with the Mardukans, but we couldn't get any further than that."

"Adoula's rarely at the Palace," Catrone pointed out. "He's either at the Lords, or in his offices in the Imperial Tower."

"I'll be honest," Roger said. "I've got a hard-on for Adoula, more than ever now, and I know we have to keep him from getting away. But mostly, I've been concentrated on getting to Mother and the replicator. Capture the queen and bring in impartial witnesses, and Adoula's out of power. Maybe he can make it off-planet, especially with his control of Home Fleet, but he's not going to be holding the Empire."

"True, but we have to take him out as well. We don't want him breaking off his own section of the Empire. And he's got a good many of the Navy's commanders in his pocket. For that matter, he's got *Greenberg* in his pocket. Taking the Palace isn't going to do us much good if Home Fleet drops a kinetic weapon on our heads. Or drops all their Marines on us, for that matter. The most we're going to be able to field is a very short battalion of guys who are mostly out of practice. We do *not* want to take on the Home Fleet Marine contingent supported by the ships."

"Okay," Roger sighed. "Cards on the table time. We're in contact with the Alphanes, and they have solid intelligence that Adoula intends to try to bring them into the Empire as soon as Mother is out of the picture."

"Is he *nuts*?" Catrone demanded. "No, he's not nuts; are *you* nuts? You're *sure*?"

"The Alphanes are—sure enough that if we don't get this working, they're going to jump Third Fleet. Adoula hasn't completely filled the command and staff there with his cronies, yet, but he's positively, according to them, planning on using Third and Fourth Fleets against them. Fourth is already his, but he can't divert too much of it from watching the Saints, or they may jump him from behind, so he needs Third, too. But once he's been able to make sure he has it, all the evidence says he's going after them. He doesn't believe they can't be conquered, and although they've got a sizable fleet, as Admiral Ral pointed out, the Empire has *six* fleets their size."

"Of course we do, but they won't back down," Catrone argued. "Not even if you take the orbitals. The bears are *nuts* about honor. They'll all die fighting, to the last cub."

"I know that," Roger said, shaking his head. "You know that. Adoula's *advisers* know that. But Adoula doesn't believe it. So if the command and staff of Third Fleet changes, the Alphanes are going active. That's something we have to keep an eye on."

"And they're your source of supply?"

"They're our source of supply," Roger confirmed. "Armor and weapons. Even armor for the Mardukans, which you'll have to see to believe. But nothing heavier than that, and it's been hard enough to hide even that much."

"I can believe that. Security on this is going to be a bitch. Somebody is *going* to notice, sooner or later. You do realize that, right?"

"We'll just have to hope it's later." Roger shrugged. "If the IBI starts sniffing around Marduk House, they'll discover what's pretty obviously a cover for money laundering."

"Show them what they expect to see?"

"Right. The only problem is, there *is* more money going out than coming in. But the money coming in is clean, too. So they're looking for a negative if they try to build a case. It's not exactly *clean*—it's from the Alphanes. But it's not anything they can tie to anything illegal."

"All right," Catrone said. Not because he was happy about it, but because he recognized that all they could do was the best they could do.

"Home Fleet," he continued, continuing his methodical examination of Roger's plans. "Any ideas there?"

"Well, how about a complete replacement of command and staff?" Roger replied lightly. Then his expression sobered. "The current plan is to take Greenberg out, simultaneous with the attack."

"Assassination?" Catrone said levelly.

"Yes," Roger replied unflinchingly. "There's no way to ensure we can simply grab him and move him out of the loop. And there are officers who will follow Greenberg just because he *is* the designated Home Fleet commander. Take him out of the loop, and they're going to have to make up their minds who to back. To be honest, if they're willing not to shoot at us, I don't care if they just sit the whole thing out. But I do *not* want Greenberg in charge, and the only way to ensure that, distasteful as it may be, is to kill him. There's already a team in place."

Catrone's face worked for a moment, and then he shrugged angrily.

"You're right, and I don't like it."

"Do you have a better solution?" Roger asked calmly.

"No," Catrone admitted. "And I agree it's necessary. But I still don't like it."

"We do a lot of things we don't like, because they're necessary. That's the nature of our business. Isn't it, Sergeant Major?"

"Yes," Catrone admitted again. "So . . . where are we?"

"Taking out Greenberg ought to put Wallenstein in command, as his exec," Roger continued, "but our intel says that whole thing's not as clear as it ought to be. Apparently, Captain Wallenstein . . . is not well thought of in the Navy. Something to do with his career track and the fact that he's never commanded anything bigger than a single cruiser.

"So with Greenberg gone, and Wallenstein labeled a paper-pusher in Adoula's pocket, that leaves Kjerulf with a damned good chance of taking over command . . . if he has a reason to try. And if we can prime him just a bit, I think he *will* try, which should at least muddle the hell out of Home Fleet's command structure. The other staff and commanders loyal to Adoula will want to intervene, but Kjerulf is going to wait and see what's going on. I'd expect some response from Home Fleet, but without Greenberg, it'll be uncoordinated."

"Even an uncoordinated response will be bad," Catrone pointed out. "Maybe worse. Desperate men will try desperate measures."

"Well, we've also got a fleet of our own," Roger said.

"Who?" Catrone asked, then nodded. "Dark Helmut, right?"

"Yes. We sent a team to contact him. They reported having made contact with one of his ship commanders, who'd arranged to transport them to meet with him, and Sixth Fleet's moved since then. It *might* be coming to warn Adoula, but if so, the warning should already have been here. If Helmut were working Adoula's side—which I doubt strongly—we'd already be in custody."

"So how do you get word to Sixth Fleet to coordinate things?"

"If they're on schedule, they'll pick up a standard data dump from the Wolf Cluster in—" Roger thought about it and ran some calculations on his toot, then shrugged. "In three days or so. They'll get a message that we're in place and preparing the assault, and they'll send a message telling us whether Helmut's on our side or not. But we won't know one way or the other until just before the assault. Time lag."

"Got it." Catrone looked unhappy, then grimaced. "Ever think how nice it must have been to be a general or admiral back in the good old days, when everyone was stuck on one planet and you didn't have to worry about messages taking days, or even weeks, to get to their destinations?"

"I'm sure they had their own problems," Roger replied dryly.

"Yeah, but a man can dream, right?"

"We'll have to send out our message giving the timing for the assault before we know whether or not Sixth Fleet is going to be available," Roger continued, ignoring Catrone's chuckle. "Impossible to avoid."

"Security on that?" Catrone asked more seriously.

"Personal ads," Roger said with a shrug. "What else?"

"You ever wondered how many of those personals are covert messages?" Catrone asked with another grin.

"Not until recently. A lot, I'd guess."

"I'm beginning to think they're the majority." Catrone's grin faded into a frown. "Security on covert ops gives me ulcers. There's a reason my hair is gray."

"Yeah," Roger agreed, then reached out through his toot to reactivate the updated hologram.

"We've been looking at the best schematic of the Palace we could put together before you and Great Gran Miranda came along, trying to come up with a plan that isn't suicide." He loaded the simulation of the best plan they had so far, and the two of them watched it in fast-forward as the attackers' blue icons evaporated. None of them even made it into the Palace.

"So far, we haven't found one," Roger observed dryly.

"Obviously," Catrone said with a wince. He sat back, scratching his nose, and frowned thoughtfully.

"There's a rhythm to taking the Palace," he said after a moment. "There are uniformed guards at these locations," he continued, highlighting the positions. Most of them had been filled in already, but he put in a few more that were in "Gold" and "Silver" sectors Kosutic hadn't known about. "But the real problems are the armored reaction squad you've got *here*," he highlighted the position, "the automated defenses, and the bulk of the guards, who are in the barracks."

He highlighted the other two threat locations briefly.

"I was in charge of the Palace's security for a long time," he said sourly, "and one of my background thoughts was always how *I* might take the place. I decided that, based on some of my own changes—

well, the various *commanders'* changes which I sort of suggested—it would be a bitch. But I also knew that no matter what I could do, there was a weakness. The key is Number Three Gate and the North Courtyard," he said, highlighting them.

"Why?"

"The North Courtyard has two manned defense posts." Catrone pointed them out, "but it's accessible via Gate Three. This assumes that the automated defenses are down, you understand that?"

"Yes."

"The courtyard is also the parade ground for the Empress' Own. It more or less severs the barracks and the outer servants' wing from the Palace proper. There are connecting corridors, but they're all covered by the courtyard. Take the courtyard, and you can use it as a landing zone for support forces. The only thing stopping them would be the defensive positions, but they're lightly manned, normally. Even upgraded security doesn't increase those guards, because they aren't guarding the principals directly, understand?"

"Yes." Roger was studying the schematic intently. "Take the gate, pin most of the garrison down in barracks, and seize the courtyard as an LZ. Then bring in your troops, use most of your support to reduce the bulk of the guards still in their barracks, and punch a group into the Palace. What about air support for the guards?"

"Stingship squadron." Catrone highlighted the hangar embedded in the sprawling Palace. "Only half strength, according to my information; it took a beating in the first coup, and finding more people for it is harder than finding the sort of grunts Adoula's been willing to settle for. It takes them at least fifteen minutes to go active. The reaction squad, if it's fully trained, can be armored up in three minutes, and react anywhere in the Palace within ten. Guards are full up in less than an hour. Completely down and surprised, when I was in charge, everyone was in armor and countering an assault in forty minutes, but an hour is the standard."

"Their communications will be dislocated," Roger said. "I can turn those off, scramble their internal communications, with the Protocols. Leave Temu Jin in place to keep them scrambled."

"Which means taking the command post *first*." Catrone

highlighted one of the new, hopefully secure routes. "You'll have to do it. You're the man with the codes, and most of them will only respond to you."

"Agreed."

"Send the first-wave Mardukans in to take the gate," Catrone continued, and Roger nodded.

"They can scale the wall if they have to. They've done it before. And I have codes for opening the gate, too."

"However they do it, they get in," Catrone said, "and take the courtyard away from the duty company before the rest of them get organized."

"With swords and pikes against bead guns." Roger winced. "But they can do it."

"Once they have the courtyard, the shuttles come in," Catrone continued. "Can they use human weapons? There'll be some lying around."

"Like pistols," Roger said. "Again, something they've done."

"This takes, say, five minutes," Catrone said. "More. They've got to cross the Park just to reach the gate."

"A thousand meters." Roger pursed his lips. "Two minutes for *civan* at a run; not much longer for the Diasprans. Say seven to ten minutes to take the courtyard."

"Which means the reaction team is up."

"Yeah, but they're busy dealing with an armored force that's already well into the Palace," Roger countered, highlighting the route from the command center to his mother's quarters.

"You're important," Catrone said warily. "Which means you're in the command post, right?"

"Wrong. Because *I* have to open doors here, here—lots of doors," he said, highlighting them. "That's why there will be fifteen armored troops—to protect *me*."

"Okay, okay." Catrone obviously didn't like it, but he recognized both necessity and intransigence when he saw them. "So *probably* the reaction squad is off chasing you when our forces land and punch into Adoula's mercenaries. One group detaches to take the Palace proper."

"The automated defenses will go to local control when the command post is compromised," Roger pointed out. "I can keep the secondary CP from going on-line, but I can't keep the automatics from going local."

"We'll deal with it," Catrone said, and stood back from the hologram. He and the prince studied it together for several silent seconds, then Roger tossed his head.

"I think we got us a plan," he said.

"Yeah," Catrone mused, still looking at the schematic. "You really trust the Mardukans that much? If they don't get that courtyard, we're going to have over a thousand heavily armed mercs swarming over us."

"I trust them with my life. More—I trust them with the Empire. They'll take the gate."

"Did you know that the Empress' Own Association's annual meeting is scheduled during the Imperial Festival?" New Madrid demanded as he strode into Jackson Adoula's office.

"Yes." Adoula didn't look up from the hologram on his desk.

"And so is the Raider Association's . . . and the Special Operations Association's," New Madrid continued angrily.

"Yes," Adoula replied calmly.

"You don't think there might be some minor problems stemming out of all that?" New Madrid asked, throwing up his hands.

"My dear Earl," Adoula said, still looking at his hologram, "we have the Saints poking around on the border in fleet strength. We have the Alphanes massing for what looks very much like an attack. There's another bill in Parliament for an evaluation of the Empress— this time pressed by my *opponents*, and thus much less easy to quash—and even that gutless trimmer Yang has stated that his last meeting with the Empress was less than satisfactory. Apparently our good Prime Minister considers that having her simpering at you during the meeting was . . . odd. As was the fashion in which she kept constantly referring all questions to your judgment."

"That bitch has got a mind like steel," New Madrid said tightly, "and her natural resistance to the drugs is high, and getting higher.

And I can't afford to leave any noticeable bruises. So even with the . . . other controls in place, we've got to keep her dialed down to the level of an amiable *moron* if we want to be sure she doesn't say something we can't spin the right way. She can't even remember how many *planets* we have, much less what sort of infrastructure is best where. And she certainly can't keep track of whose districts they're in."

"Neither," Adoula said angrily, looking up from the hologram at last, "can you, apparently. I gave very clear instructions on what she was supposed to say during the negotiations. We both know why *she* couldn't follow them; the question is why *you* couldn't either."

"Your 'instructions' covered sixty separate star systems!" New Madrid snapped.

"Then you should have brought *notes*!"

"You said nothing *written*!" New Madrid shouted.

"In this case, apparently," Adoula's cold, level tone cut through the earl's bluster like a scalpel, "we have to make an exception. And the point which apparently escaped you was that nothing that could be tied to *me* was to be written down. For the *next* meeting, however, I will ensure you have precise, written instructions as to what is to be spent, and where. I'll even ensure that they're written in very small words. In the meantime, your worries about those idiot Associations are duly noted. I'll have my guards on high alert in case they come over to make faces at the Palace. A Palace with walls, ChromSten gates, automated defenses, a squadron of stingships, and hundreds of armed guards. Is there anything else on your mind?"

"No." New Madrid thrust himself angrily to his feet.

"In that case, I have real work to do." Adoula waved at the door. "Good day."

He didn't bother to watch New Madrid flounce—that really was the only verb for it—out of his office. It was a pity, he thought, that the powered door couldn't be slammed properly.

He keyed up the next list and shook his head. There were far too many MacClintock loyalists in the IBI, but his supply of people loyal to *him* was finite. Getting reliable people into all of the necessary spots was going to take time.

Who was it who'd said "Ask me for anything but time"? He couldn't remember off the top of his head, but he knew he was asking himself for it.

Just a little time.

"You seem pretty tense," Despreaux said as she slid onto Roger's arm and rested her head on his shoulder.

"Uh-huh."

"It's going well," she added. "The Association, the supplies. This is as good as its looked in a long time."

"Uh-huh."

"So why in hell are you answering me in monosyllables? Something I don't know?"

"More like something I think you do know and didn't tell me," Roger said, jaw muscles clenching. "Something about my mother?"

"Shit." Despreaux sat up and eyed him warily. "The Association knew?"

"Catrone, at least. He assumed my so-capable sources had already informed me. I think he was wondering why I was so . . . calm about it."

"Why *are* you so calm about it?" she asked.

"I'm not," he replied. "I'm what you might call livid about what's been happening to my mother. And I'm almost as livid about the discovery that nobody told me about it. It wasn't like I wasn't going to find out. And if I'd first found out when New Madrid or Adoula were in reach—" He shook his head. "I don't want to think about what I might have done."

"I know," she said unhappily. "We've been discussing it."

"Yeah? Well, you were discussing it with the wrong person." He looked at her finally, and his eyes were hard. "You were *supposed* to discuss it with *me*. Remember me? The Prince? Boss-man? The Heir? The guy who's killed people for a whole hell of a lot less than torturing and raping his mother for months at a time? The guy who really needs to *not* start his reign by chopping off the heads of major political players out-of-hand? Roger? Me? Remember *me*, Nimashet?!"

"Okay, we pocked up!" She threw her arms up. "Maybe we're not as strong morally as we are physically! Do you really think we *wanted* to tell you? The Phaenurs were quite clear that they did *not* want to be around you when you found out. Neither did *I*, okay?"

"No, it's not 'okay.' The purpose of a staff is to manage the information so that the boss gets the information he or she *needs*. I *needed* that information. I needed to *not* be blindsided by it—not when we finally got my mother out, nor in negotiations with a still not particularly trustworthy ally!"

"You don't trust the *Association*?"

"I don't trust anyone but us and the Mardukans. And now I'm wondering if I should trust you."

"That's not fair!" she said angrily.

"Why is it not fair? Hello! You kind of forgot to tell me something *very* important about the operation, about postoperation conditions, about my responses . . . Why is it not fair?"

Her face worked, and it was obvious she was fighting not to cry.

"Damn it, Roger," she said quietly. "Don't do this. Don't *pound* me for this. Okay, we pocked up. We should have told you. But do *not* pound on *me* to get your mad out."

"Shit." He slid down and wrapped his head in a pillow. "Shit." He paused and shook his head, voice still muffled. "I'm sorry."

"I am, too," she said, openly crying.

"You're right," he said, still with his face in the pillow. "I did need to bring it up, but this wasn't the time or the place. I'm sorry. How the hell do you put up with me?"

"Well," she said lightly, even while tears still choked her voice, "you're good-looking. And you're rich . . ."

"God."

"Why didn't you bring this up earlier today?" she asked after a moment.

"The time wasn't right." Roger shrugged. "Too much going on. We sure as hell didn't need a big internal fight in front of the Association guys. But I couldn't keep it in once we got to bed. And I'm still angry, but now I'm angry at myself, too. Christ."

"Roger," Despreaux said quietly, "this is what's called a pillow-fight. There are rules for those."

"One of them being don't bring up business to beat up on your girlfriend?" he asked, finally pulling his head out of the pillow.

"No, the rules don't work that way. Not about what we fight about, so much as how we fight about it. And this is the rule you need to keep in mind—either we work it out while we're still awake, or you go sleep on a couch."

"Why do *I* have to sleep on the couch? I'm the prince. For that matter, this is *my* room."

"You sleep on the couch because you're the guy," she said, batting her eyelashes at him. "Those are the rules. It doesn't matter if this is your room or my room—this is my *bed*. And you can't use one of the other bedrooms. You have to sleep on a couch. With a blanket."

"Do I get a pillow?" he asked plaintively.

"Only if you're good. Otherwise, I get all of them."

"I . . . I don't *like* these rules."

"Too bad. Them's the rules."

"When I'm Emperor, I'm going to *change* them," Roger said, then shook his head. "God, that brings it up again."

"And so on, and so forth," she said. "Until one of us gets tired enough for you to go to the couch."

"Don't hide important things from me," Roger said quietly, "and I'll *try* not to use business to beat up on you. Okay?"

"Fair." Despreaux lay back down and leaned her head on his arm once more. "We'll discuss the more advanced techniques for quarreling another time. What's allowed, what's not, what works, what just makes things worse."

She yawned and snuggled closer.

"I get to sleep here?"

"Are we done?"

"I guess so," he said. "I'll take out the rest of the mad on Adoula."

"Do that."

"Hey, we just had a lovers' quarrel, right?"

"Don't go there . . ." she muttered, then yawned again. "So, other than that, is it *working*?"

"Too soon to tell. Too many things that can go wrong." It was his turn to yawn, and he pulled her closer to him. "For now, all we can do is keep to the path and hope nobody notices."

"Ms. Subianto," Roger said, stopping by the woman's table. "A pleasure to have you in Marduk House. I hope you're enjoying the *basik*."

"Lovely," Subianto replied, touching her lips with a napkin. "A truly new taste sensation. That's so rare these days."

"And this *atul* is great," Tebic said, cutting off another bite. "I can't believe it's so tender."

"We use a special tenderizer," Roger said with a quiet smile. "The rarest ingredients. Marinated for thirty-six hours."

Said ingredients consisted of killerpillar flesh-dissolving enzymes, diluted a hundred-to-one. One of Kostas' discoveries on the long march. The prince forbore to elaborate, however.

"You certainly got this restaurant up and running very quickly," Subianto said. "And in such a . . . prime location."

"Hardly prime," Roger demurred. "But the neighborhood does seem to be improving. Probably by example."

"Yes," she said dryly. "The physicians at Imperial General have noticed some of the . . . examples."

"I hope that's not an official complaint?" Roger raised one eyebrow. "Surely a lonely extraterrestrial has the right to self-defense?"

"It was not, in fact, a complaint at all," Subianto said. "The local PD's gang team thinks you're the best thing since . . . roast *basik*." She smiled. "And many of Parliament's staffers appreciate a restaurant with such . . . elaborate, if quiet, electronic security."

"The privacy of my guests is important," Roger said, smiling in turn. "As much a part of Marduk House's services as anything on the menu, as a matter of fact After all, this is a town with many secrets. Many of them are ones that you're supposed to protect, right?"

"Of course," she said smoothly, "others are ones we're supposed to penetrate. Such as who Augustus Chung really is? Why certain of his associates are meeting with an admiral who's been . . . remiss about responding to orders from central command? Why one

Augustus Chung has been receiving heavy weaponry and armor from an off-planet source? What Mardukans are doing training in stingship operations? Why Mr. Chung has been meeting with representatives from the Empress' Own Association? Why, in fact, such representatives—who are notoriously loyal to the Empress—are meeting with him at all?"

"I suppose I could say I have no idea what you're talking about," Roger replied, still smiling faintly. "But that would be a rather transparent, and pointless, lie. I guess the only answer is another question. Why haven't you reported this to Prince Jackson? Or, more to the point, to your superiors, which we both know would be the same thing."

"Because, whatever his current unusual position," Subianto said, "the IBI is in the service of the *Empire*, not Prince Jackson or his cronies. The evidence we have all points in one direction, Mr. Chung. So I'm here, sampling your excellent *basik*, and wondering what in the hell you think you're doing. And who you really are. Because simply capturing the Palace isn't going to help the Empire one bit, and if you have nothing more in your head than that—rescuing Her Majesty from her current admittedly horrible conditions—then . . . other arrangements will have to be made. For the Empire."

She smiled brightly at him.

"The IBI is a department of the executive branch of government, correct?" Roger asked carefully.

"Correct." Subianto eyed her host warily. She'd already noted that her normal charms seemed to slide right off of him. He'd noticed her as a woman, and she was sure he wasn't gay, but beyond that he seemed totally immune.

"And the Empress is the head of the executive branch, your ultimate boss, also correct?"

"Yes."

"And we might as well drop the pretense that the Empress is not under duress," Roger pointed out. "Which means the control of the executive branch goes to . . . whom?"

"The Heir," Tebic said with a frown. "Except that there isn't one. John and Alexandra, and John's children, are all dead, and Roger is reported to be at large and to have been instrumental in the supposed coup. But he's not. Adoula had him killed. The ship was sabotaged and lost in deep space. We know that."

"I hope like hell you found out *after* it happened," "Chung" said, showing signs of emotion for the first time.

"Afterward." Subianto frowned at the intensity of the reaction. "We found out through information received after Adoula took control, but we have three confirmations."

"In that case, Ms. Subianto, I will leave you," Roger said, smiling again, if somewhat tightly. "But in parting, I wish you would join Mr. Tebic in trying the *atul*. It really is as tender as . . . a fatted calf. Please ponder that. Silently." He smiled again. "Have a nice meal."

As their host walked away, Tebic looked at his boss and frowned.

"Fat—" he began. He could recognize a code phrase when he heard it, but this one made no sense to him.

"Don't," Subianto said, picking at the remaining bits of *basik* on her plate. "Don't say it."

"What . . . ?"

"Not here. I'm not sure where. I don't trust our secure rooms to not be monitored by *us*. You're a Christian, aren't you, Tebic?"

"Um." Tebic shrugged at the apparently total *non sequitur*. "Sort of. I was raised Armenian Orthodox. My dad was Reform Islam, but he never went to mosque, and I haven't been to church since I was a kid."

"I'm not sure it's translated into Armenian the same way," Subianto said, "and I'm Zoroastrian. But I recognize it. It's a phrase from the Bible—Emperor Talbot version, I think. That's still the most common Imperial translation."

"I can run a data search—" Tebic started to say, looking inward to activate his toot.

"Don't!" Subianto said, more sharply than she'd intended. Panicked might have been a better word. "Don't even think about it. Don't write it down, don't put it on the net, don't say it in public. Nothing. Understand?"

"No," Tebic said, going gray. "But if you say so . . ."

"I do," Subianto said. "Get the check."

★ ★ ★

The next day, late in the morning, Subianto walked into Tebic's office with a book in her hand. An actual, honest-to-God paper *book*. Tebic couldn't remember seeing more than half a dozen of them in his life. She set it on the desk and opened it to a marked page, pointing to a line of text.

> "And bring hither the fatted calf, and kill it;
> and let us eat, and be merry:
> For this my son was dead, and is alive again;
> he was lost, and is found."

At the top of the page was the title: "The Parable of the Prodigal Son."

"Holy . . ." Tebic's voice trailed off as his eyes widened.

"Yes." Subianto picked up the book, took out the marker, and closed it. "All that's holy. Let's hope it stays holy. And very, *very* quiet."

"You *told* her?" Catrone yelled.

"There wasn't much she didn't already know." Roger shrugged. "If they'd wanted to arrest us, we'd already be taken down or in a firefight."

"The Bureau won't be monolithic in these circumstances," Temu Jin said with a frown. The IBI agent had been managing the electronic and physical security aspects of the mission, keeping out of sight in the Greenbrier bunker. Of them all, he was the only one who hadn't had a body-mod. No one could possibly discover his connection to Roger without actually going to Marduk and piecing things together, and any attempt to do that would run into major resistance from the locals who were the prince's partisans. Those who'd been his enemies were no longer around to be interviewed.

There wasn't even much danger of Jin being noticed as "out of cover" by the IBI if that organization should happen to spot him. He was openly listed as a communications technician on the staff of the restaurant, and if the IBI used the right protocols, they *might* spot him as one of their own and realize they already had an agent in place. In which case he was in position to file a wholly false report on a minor money-trafficking operation, with no clue as to where the money was coming from.

Then again, he'd been a Counterintelligence and Imperial Security operative, and the head of that division had vanished under mysterious circumstances. He'd also sent out codes telling "his" agents they were in the cold, which meant, in all probability, that the records of one Temu Jin had been electronically flushed. So as long as no one who might recognize him by sight actually *saw* him, he was probably clean. But Buseh Subianto—who'd been in the same department, if not in his chain of command—might just possibly have been able to do exactly that. *He'd* certainly recognized the video of her and her companion, Tebic.

"Subianto is one of the really straight players," he continued. "Apolitical as anyone in Counter-Intel can get. It's why she's been in her current position so long; go higher, and you're dealing with policy, and policy *means* politics."

"She's playing policy now," Catrone muttered. "If she'd filed a report, we'd have Marines or IBI tac-teams swarming all over us. But that doesn't mean she's on our side, Roger."

"She was going to keep pushing," Roger said calmly. "She's an IBI agent, even if she doesn't work the streets anymore, and curiosity is what they're all about. But if I'm the Heir, then any decision she makes *is* policy. My estimate, based on her questions and the manner in which they were presented, was that she'd just keep her head down if she knew who I was. And I was the person handling it; I had to decide *how* I was going to handle it right then. It was my decision to handle it in that way."

"There's another aspect to consider," Eleanora said. "One of our big weaknesses is current intelligence. Up to date intel, especially on Adoula's actions and movements. If we had a contact in the IBI—"

"Too risky." Catrone shook his head. "She might be willing to keep her head down and ignore us. For that matter, I think Roger's probably right, that she is. But we can't risk bringing her in, or trying to pump her for information."

"Agreed," Roger said. "And if that's settled, let's move on. Are we agreed on the plan?"

"Home Fleet is still the big question," Catrone said with a frown.

"I know," Roger replied. "Macek and Bebi are in position, but we need a read on Kjerulf."

"Contacting him would tip our hand." Catrone was shaking his head again.

"That depends on Kjerulf," Roger pointed out. "And we're finding friends in the oddest places."

"I know him," Marinau said suddenly. "He was my CO when I was on Tetri." He shrugged. "I'd say he's probably more likely to be a friend than an enemy."

"You can't contact him, though," Catrone objected. "You're needed to arrange the rehearsals. Besides, we can be damned well certain Adoula's keeping an eye on you."

"Eleanora could do it," Roger said. "He's stationed on Moonbase. That's only a six-hour hop."

"Contacting him for a meet would be . . . difficult," Marinau pointed out.

"Is there some code he'd recognize as coming from you?" Roger asked. "Something that's innocuous otherwise?"

"Maybe." Marinau rubbed one ear lobe. "I can think of a couple of things."

"Well, even after everything else I've done, I never thought I'd stoop to this," Roger said, "but we'll send out a spam message, with your code in the header. He'll get at least one of the messages and recognize the header. I hope."

"I can set that up." Catrone grimaced. "The software's out there. Makes me sick, though."

"We've done worse, and we'll do it again," Roger said dryly. "I know that's hard to believe when we're talking about *spam*, but there it is. Are we in agreement otherwise?"

"Yes," Marinau replied. "It looks like the best we can cobble together to me. I'm still not happy about the fact that there's no reserve to speak of, though. You want a reserve for more than just somebody to retreat on."

"Agreed, and if I could provide one, I would," Roger said. "At least there's the Cheyenne stingship and shuttle force. If they can get here in time. And if it runs long, we can probably call on the Sixth Fleet Marines."

"How's the training on your Mardukans coming?" Catrone asked.

"From what I hear," Roger said with a grin, "the biggest problem is shoehorning them into the cockpits."

"This is pocking cramped," Honal complained.

The bay under the main Cheyenne facility was much larger than the one at Greenbrier . . . and even more packed with equipment. There were fifteen of the later and considerably nastier Bearkiller stingships, four Velociraptor assault shuttles, ten light hovertanks, and a series of simulators for all of them. Honal was currently stuffed into one such simulator, trying out the new seat.

"It's not my fault you guys are oversized," Paul McMahon said.

The stingship engineer had been between jobs when Rosenberg shanghaied him—hiring him off the net for "secure work at a remote location without the opportunity for outside contact." The salary offered had been twice his normal pay rate, but when he found out who'd hired him, there'd been a near mutiny, despite the fact that Rosenberg had been his CO before he retired from the Imperial Marines. He'd only agreed to help under duress and after receiving a sworn statement that he was *not* a voluntary participant. Rosenberg's recorded, legally attested statement probably wouldn't keep him out of jail, but it might let him at least keep his head, although he wasn't wildly enthusiastic about his prospects under any circumstances.

Of course, the engineer might have felt even less sanguine if he'd known who he was really working for. So far as he knew, Rosenberg was simply fronting an Association operation to rescue the Empress; he had no clue that he'd actually fallen into the toils of the nefarious Traitor Prince. Rosenberg didn't like to think about how McMahon might have reacted to that little tidbit of information.

At the moment, however, the man's attention was completely focused on his job, and he frowned as Honal popped the hatch and climbed out of the simulator—not without a certain degree of huffing, puffing, and grunting.

"It wasn't easy changing those seats, you know," he continued as Honal shook himself vigorously, "and the panel redesign and legroom extension were even tougher, in some ways. This model was already a bit like a whole-body glove when all they wanted to put in it was *humans*. And forget ejecting. The motivator is *not* designed for your weight, and we don't have time to redesign it. Not to mention the fact that you'd rip your legs off on the way out; they're in what used to be the forward sensor array."

"Hell with my legs—I can barely move my *arms*," Honal pointed out.

"But can you fly it?" Rosenberg asked. "That's the only thing that matters. We can't *hire* pilots for this, and I've only got a few I'd trust for it. We're really laying it all on the line. Can you *fly* it?"

"Maybe." Honal grimaced, lowered himself back into the simulator, and began startup procedures. "This isn't going to be fun," he observed.

"Tell me about it," Rosenberg sighed.

"How's the rest of the training going?" Honal asked.

"Nominal."

The team moved cautiously down the corridor, every sense strainingly alert, each foot placed carefully.

The corridor walls were blue plasteel, with what appeared to be abstract paintings every couple of meters. They'd looked at one of the paintings, and that had been enough. Within the swirling images, mouths screamed silently and demon faces leered. There was a distant dripping of water, and occasional unearthly howls sounded in the distance.

Raoux held up a fist as they reached an intersection. She pointed to two of their point guards and signaled for them to check it out. The first guard rolled a sensor ball into the intersection, bouncing it off the opposite wall, and then sprang forward, covering the intersection as the rest of the team bounded past. The second point moved down the corridor—then checked as a screamer abruptly appeared, apparently out of a solid wall.

The screamer was nearly as tall as a Mardukan, and had similar horns, but red skin and scales that were at least partially resistant to bead rifle fire. Despite that, the point engaged with a burst of low-powered beads which went downrange with a quiet crack and caught the screamer in the chest.

Unfortunately, the screamer lived up to its name and began howling. Alarms began to shrill in the background.

"We're blown," Marinau snarled. "Plan Delta!"

The team began to move faster, but as they passed a corridor, a blast of plasma came down it, and took out the team member who'd been covering the movement element's advance. Flamers—bigger versions of the screamers, with heavier armor that could at least partially resist the team's *heavy* weapons—came down the side corridor, while more flooded in behind them. Then things like flowers started popping out of the walls, throwing liquid fire that burned their armor.

Raoux blinked her eyes as she came out of the VR simulation, then cursed as more of the team members popped into the gray formlessness of "between" with her.

"Well, that didn't go too well," Yatkin observed with truly monumental understatement.

"No, it didn't," Raoux agreed dryly, shaking her head.

"There ought to be a way we can mimic the flamers, Jo," Kaaper mused.

"Paint ourselves red?" Raoux said bitingly.

"You know what I mean," Kaaper replied as two more figures formed.

One of them was a humanoid, tiger-striped tomcat, a bit short of two meters tall, cradling a bead rifle. The other figure was short, overweight, and young, with mussed hair and messy clothing. It was a standard Geek Mod One, the normal first-timer's persona avatar in the Surreal Battle matrix. He wore holstered, pearl-handled bead pistols for weapons.

"Hey, Tomcat," Raoux greeted, and looked over at the other figure. "Who's this?"

"I'm Sabre," the geek said. "Can I play?"

"Great," Yatkin said. "Just what we need. For cannon fodder."

"Can I play? Huh? Huh? Can I?" Sabre bounced up and down.

"Sure." Kaaper waved a hand, and a screamer appeared out of the air and turned towards the capering figure.

A bead pistol appeared, gripped in both of Sabre's hands. Even as he continued to bounce in excitement, the pistol began spitting beads. The screamer was spun in place as beads took off both arms, then the head. The rounds continued long after the magazine should have quit firing, and the head was blown into pulp before it even hit the ground.

"I got it!" Sabre squealed. "I got it!"

"Hacks are *not* going to help!" Yatkin snarled.

"No hacks," the human-sized tomcat said.

"Bullshit," Yatkin replied.

"No hacks," Sabre said, and changed. Again, it was an off-the-shelf mod, one styled to look slightly like Princess Alexandra. It could be used for male or female; Alexandra had been a handsome woman and made a damned handsome man. It looked very unlike Prince Roger, though, except in the eyes. The mod kept Alexandra's long, light brown hair, and now wore a torn, chameleon-cloth battle suit, patched with odds and ends of much less advanced textiles. Beside the bead pistols, which were now standard IMC military models, the figure carried a sword and had a huge chem-powered rifle across its back.

"Not hacks—experience. In a hard school," Sabre added in cold tones, and there was no trace of the excited kid anymore.

"Have to be a pretty damned hard school," Kaaper replied mockingly.

"Death planet, one each," Roger said to the VR system, and the formlessness changed. Now they were standing on a ruined parapet. Low mounds, the vine-covered ruins of a large city, stretched down the hill to a line of jungle. Rank upon rank of screamers were emerging from the jungle, and a voice spoke in the background.

"I'm sorry . . . *scriiiitch* . . ." the voice said, breaking up in static. "Forget that estimate of five thousand. Make it *fifteen* thousand. . . ."

A hot, moist wind carried the smell of jungle rot as the endless lines of screamers lifted their weapons and began a loud chant. They broke into a run, charging up the hill, soaking up the fire of the defenders, climbing the walls with rough ladders, swarming up the sides, pounding on the gate. Spears arced up and transfixed the firers, hands reached up and pulled them off the walls, down into the waiting spears and axes.

Through it all, Sabre left a trail of bodies as the sword flicked in and out, taking attackers in the throat, chest, stomach. Arms fell and heads flew as he carved the howling screamers into ruin, but they came on. The wall's other defenders died around him, leaving him practically alone against the screamer horde, and *still* the sword flashed and bit and killed. . . .

The scene changed again. It was dark, but their low-light systems showed a line of ax-wielding screamers, at least a thousand, charging a small group in a trench. Sabre spun in place, a large chemical pistol in one hand, sword in the other. Bullets caught the screamers— generally in the throat, sometimes the head—as the sword spun and took off a reaching arm, the head of an ax, a head. The trench filled with blood, most of the defenders were down, but still Sabre spun in his lethal dance.

A throne room. A screamer king speaking to Sabre, weird intonations, and a voice like a grave. Sabre nodding and reaching back, pulling each strand of his hair into place in a ponytail. He nodded again, his hands ostentatiously away from the bead pistols on his hips, not watching the guards at his back—not really looking at the king. Eyes wide and unfocused.

"You and what army?" he asked as the hands descended, faster than a snake, and the room vanished in blood.

"Lots of fun," Yatkin said after a minute.

"Oodles and oodles," Sabre replied.

"Yeah, but the firing *had* to be a hack," Kaaper pointed out. "Too many rounds. The old infinite-bead gun."

"Oh, please," Sabre said. "Watch." He summoned a target and

drew the bead pistol at his right hip. He didn't appear to be trying to impress them with the draw, but it simply *appeared* in his hand. And then he fired, rapidly, but not as rapidly as he had.

"Not particularly hard," Sabre said, lifting his left hand up for a moment to fire with a two-handed grip.

"You just reloaded," Yatkin said, wonderingly. "You'd palmed a magazine, and you reloaded on the fly. I caught it that time. Son of a bitch."

"Don't talk about my mother that way," Sabre said seriously. Then he lowered his arm and shook it, dropping a cascade of magazines onto the gray "floor."

"Sorry," Yatkin replied. "Sir. But can you really . . . ?"

"Really," Sabre replied.

"So . . ." the tomcat said. "He in?"

"I dunno." Raoux rubbed the back of her neck. "Can he handle armor?"

"Wanna death match?" Sabre inquired with a grin.

"No," Raoux said, after a long pause. "No, I don't think I want to death match."

"The VR training on the rest of the teams is going well," Tomcat told Sabre. "Can't bring in your oversized buddies very well, the sets aren't made for them, and they don't have toots, but their job is pretty straightforward, and they'll have trained teams leading them. I think our opponents are going to be remarkably surprised when we go for the big push."

"Gotta love net-gaming," Raoux said with a nasty smile. "And I've always thought Surreal Battle was the best around. How's our support coming?"

"Well, that's sort of hard to know," Tomcat said, frowning and waving a hand. "Sort of hard to know . . ."

"What fun," Helmut said, shaking his head. "During the Imperial Festival? Why not just put up a big sign: 'Coup in progress!' Security is always maxed during the Festival."

He sat behind the desk in his day cabin. Much as he trusted his personal command staff, this was one message he'd had no intention of viewing anywhere outside the security of his personal quarters. Now he looked across his desk at Julian with what could only be described as a glare.

"Roger will have his reasons—good ones," Julian replied. "I don't know what they are, but I'm sure of that. Anyway, that's the signal."

"Very well. Since Sergeant Julian is certain His Highness has good reasons for his timing, I'll prepare to move the Fleet." Helmut frowned as he consulted his toot and routed orders through it, then nodded. "We're on our way to the next rendezvous point."

Julian blinked. Given the movement schedule Roger's message had included, there was no need for quite that much rush. By his estimate, they had at least ten days' leeway, but he reminded himself that interstellar astrogation was definitely not his strong suit.

"What now, Sir?" he asked after a moment.

"Now we ponder what we'll find upon entering the system."

Helmut hopped off his station chair and walked across to the far side of his cabin, where a large section of deck had been cleared. The architect responsible for designing the admiral's flagship had probably intended the space for an intimate chair and sofa arrangement. Now it was simply a well-worn section of rug, and its function became evident as Helmut folded his hands behind him and started striding up and down it, nodding his head in time with his strides while he considered the skeletal plan and the intelligence updates on the Sol System which had accompanied the message.

"I have to admit," he said after several moments, whether to himself or Julian it would have been hard to say, "that Roger—or whoever put this together—isn't a complete idiot. At least he's grasped the importance of the KISS principle and applied it as far as anyone could in an operation this fundamentally insane. I think, however, that we might be able to improve on it just a bit."

"Sir?" Julian's tone was so cautious Helmut grinned tightly at him.

"Don't worry, Sergeant. We'll do exactly what His Highness wants. I simply think it may be possible to do it a bit more effectively than he envisioned. Or do you think he'd object to the exercise of a little initiative?"

"Master Rog generally thinks initiative is a good thing," Julian said. "Within limits."

"Oh, certainly, Sergeant. Certainly." The admiral's grin turned decidedly nasty.

"The key to his current plan," he continued, "is that we're to arrive four hours before the attack on the Palace kicks off, correct? We'll be almost ten hours flight time out from the planet at that point, but the system recon platforms will pick us up, and that should draw Home Fleet out to meet us. At the very least, given the dispositions in the intelligence packet, it will almost require them to concentrate well away from Old Earth, between us and the planet and out of range to interfere with the attack on the Palace when *it* kicks off, or risk letting us run over individual squadrons and mop them up in detail. Right?"

"As I understand it, Sir," Julian agreed, still cautiously, watching in fascination as the diminutive admiral began to pace faster and faster.

"Well, that's sound planning, given how many imponderables your Prince—or his advisers—had to juggle to come up with it. We'll pose a threat the other side *must* honor. But suppose we could find a way to simultaneously pose a threat they don't realize they *need* to honor?"

"Sir?" Julian was confused, and it showed.

"Roger intends to assassinate Greenberg," Helmut said. "Good start. Wallenstein's his XO, but everyone knows he's only there because Adoula owns him as completely as he does Greenberg. And unlike Greenberg, he's a chip-shuffler, never had a serious field command in his entire useless life. So he's not going to have a support base with Greenberg gone, and *that* ought to put Kjerulf in as temporary CO, at least until one of the other squadron commanders can get to Moonbase. Even then, the odds are that Kjerulf isn't going to just cede that command. So! There are—how many squadrons in Home Fleet, Sergeant Julian?" he barked, spinning on one heel to glare at the Marine.

"Six, Sir!" Julian replied.

"Very good." Helmut spun back to his pacing. "Always

remember that fleets and squadrons are *not* just machines, Sergeant; they're *human beings*! A regiment is only as good as its officers. Who said that Sergeant Julian?" he asked, spinning again to glower at the noncom.

"I don't . . ." Julian began, then frowned. "Napoleon?"

"You've been learning, Sergeant," Helmut said, and nodded and resumed his pacing.

"The Prince told me that, I think."

"Then he had good tutors." The admiral frowned thoughtfully. "So, six carrier squadrons, effectively without a head. In that situation, they devolve to local command, whatever The Book says. Which means we must read the minds of those local commanders if we want to predict their actions and reactions. Pro-Adoula? Pro-Roger? Sit it out? Neutrality? Informed neutrality? Nervous breakdown?"

His sentences came out in a staccato. Despite the relentless, machine-gun pace of his questions, it was clear they were rhetorical— that his thoughts were already racing far ahead of even his rapidfire questions.

"I don't even know, off the top of my head, who the squadron commanders *are*, Sir," Julian said, "much less anything about their personalities."

"Eleventh Carrier Squadron, Admiral Brettle," Helmut told him. "Recent promotion via Adoula. Impetuous, but not particularly bright. Two hundred and fifteen out of a class of two hundred and forty at the Academy. Classroom brilliance doesn't necessarily equate to brilliance in the field, of course, but he's done no better since. Unlikely to have made much advancement, for both personality and ability reasons, without pull from higher up. He had such pull, having long ago given his allegiance to Adoula. Owes one of the Prince's banks a bit more than five years' earnings for an admiral. No indications that he's behind on payments, but I'm sure he is. He spends too much not to be."

"Twelfth Carrier Squadron," Helmut continued. "Admiral Prokourov. Good deceptive tactician. Only middling at the Academy, but much better standing at Command and Staff College, and excellent in exercises. One command in a brief skirmish with the

Saints—Saints came off a distant last. I know him—as well as anyone does. Hard to say exactly where his loyalty lies, or what contact he had with Adoula pre-coup. I'd've thought he was loyal to the Empire, but he's still in command, so maybe I was as wrong about him as I was about Gianetto. Operationally, he started as a fighter pilot and likes fighters. Always look for his fighter wings to be where you don't want them to be. . . ."

"Sir, are you consulting your toot?" Julian asked quietly.

"If you have to consult records for this sort of thing, you don't deserve a command," Helmut snapped, and his eyes narrowed as he paced faster.

"Larry Gianetto, Larry *Gianetto*, Larry Gianetto," he half-sang, and did a slight skip in his pacing. "Ground force commander. Never particularly liked him, but that's neither here nor there. Good commander, well-liked in the Marines, considered a really honest man. Clearly a bad reading on many people's parts. But he's a *ground* commander, no experience running a space battle. Leaves the work of Home Fleet to Greenberg, by and large. Still a bit of a micromanager, though. Probably passes some orders, to known Adoula squadrons, directly—undoubtedly pissing Greenberg off. Last report has Fourteenth Squadron as the most solidly Adoula, so . . ."

He hummed the tune he'd been singing to himself for a moment, then nodded.

"Admiral Gajelis has the Fourteenth, and it's been reinforced by a third carrier division. Makes it fifty percent stronger than any of the other squadrons, and four of his six carriers have had their COs switched out since the coup. Very heavy-handed fighter. A cruiser officer—uses them for his primary punch. Thinks fighters are purely for defense.

"Gianetto," he sang again. "Gianetto's going to . . . put Fourteenth in somewhere near Mercury orbit. He'll figure they can react from there in any direction. A 'central reserve' to watch the inner system while he deploys the rest of his forces where they can close in behind any attacker. Very much in keeping with ground force tactics— ground-pounders don't think in terms of light-speed lag the way spacers do. He's overlooking the fact that his outer maneuver units won't know to start maneuvering until he *tells* them to. And if the intel's right, he's using Twelfth to sandwich Old Earth from the outside, same distance towards the periphery as Fourteenth to sunward. Which says things we may not like about Prokorouv's loyalties."

The admiral went back to his humming, eyes unfocused, then shrugged.

"On the other hand, it probably also means Gianetto doesn't trust Prokorouv quite as much as he does Brettle or La Paz, with the Thirteenth. Sure, he's got him in close to cover Old Earth, but by the same token, he's got Fourteenth close enough to cover *him*. So he's got his 'central reserve' either side of the planet and uses Gajelis to keep an eye on Prokorouv at the same time. Then he scatters the rest of Home Fleet out to watch the approaches.

"Greenberg may've squawked about that—he damned well should have!—but probably not. He knows about me, but he doesn't know about the Prince. So he also 'knows' that *I* know I don't have a hope in hell of accomplishing anything while Adoula controls the Palace and the Empress. *I'm* not going to hit Imperial City with KEWs—not when the Empress is the only person who could possibly rally resistance to him—and I don't have enough Marines to take the Palace against its fixed defenses before the entire Home Fleet closes in on me, signal-lag or no. So he's probably content to let Gianetto put Gajelis and Prokorouv wherever makes Gianetto—and Adoula—happy, while he covers the outer arc of the system with Eleventh and Thirteenth, which he can be confident will fight for Adoula if he needs them."

"What about Fifteenth and Sixteenth, Sir?" Julian asked.

"Out on the periphery with Eleventh and Thirteenth," Helmut said positively. "I'm not certain about Admiral Mahmut, with the Fifteenth. *He's* going to be an Adoula loyalist, but his carrier skippers may have other ideas. Hard to say. Admiral Wu, on the other hand, is not going to be one of Adoula's strong supporters."

Julian looked at him, and the admiral shrugged.

"Look, Sergeant, a lot of the officers who aren't actively opposing

Adoula right now are sitting it out because they simply don't see a viable alternative. The Prince is dead, as far as they know, and even if they knew differently, his reputation isn't one to engender confidence in him. So they may hate Adoula's guts and still see him as the only alternative to chaos the Empire simply cannot afford. I've taken pains for years—with, I might add, the Empress' explicit private approval— to build a cadre of ship commanders and senior officers here in Sixth Fleet which is prepared to blow hell out of Adoula and his lackeys anyway. Which is why Sixth Fleet 'just happened' to be stationed way the hell out on the frontier when the ball went up back at Sol. And also the reason Adoula's cronies at Defense HQ finagled ways for years to whittle Sixth down to the smallest carrier strength of the numbered fleets.

"But the point is, Wu's as apolitical as a flag officer can be these days. She's loyal to the Empire, but she's also cold-blooded enough to put the good of the Empire ahead of the good of the *Empress*. But she's also too good, and too popular with her officers and spacers— most of whom are going to follow her lead if the shit hits the fan—to fire without a really good reason. So Gianetto—and Greenberg—are making what they consider to be the best use of her. They figure they can count on her to resist outside attacks on the system, but maybe not to stay out of it if there's some sort of trouble planet-side. So they stick her out with Eleventh and Thirteenth, but covering a less critical section of the Tsukayama Limit."

"That . . . seems like a good idea," Julian said bemusedly.

"The target is *Old Earth*, Sergeant," Helmut snapped. "Yes, our fleet can come in from anywhere on the TD sphere. But if we come in from the other side of the system, or off-ecliptic, we've got a long drive across the system. That gives Gianetto all the time in the world to maneuver *inside* of us. *If* the squadrons are *near* Old Earth. But if they're still distributed the way they were when our last data packet was dropped, everything except Fourteenth and Twelfth is far too widely dispersed, trying to cover too much of the *system's* volume. Not concentrated. They're going to have to be assembled from all over the system from a cold start to defend the *planet* when we turn up. Figure four hours actual transit time to Old Earth orbit for

Fourteenth and Twelfth, but over twelve for the farthest out. We'll be *to* Old Earth in less than ten, and they won't even know to begin moving to intercept us till they get light-speed confirmation of our arrival. So we'll have had a lot of time to start building velocity for Old Earth before *they* do. That's precisely the weakness the Prince—or whoever thought this up—picked up on. They'll *have* to begin reshuffling their dispositions when we turn up, because they're so badly out of position to begin with.

"What Gianetto *should* be doing is worrying about covering the planet, and the hell with the outer system. And he should be putting only forces he knows he can *trust* in close. But Gianetto will go the other way, and Greenberg will let him. Instead of parking Fourteenth directly in Old Earth orbit, where it would already be in position, he's got it stationed way the hell in-system. And instead of allowing only forces he knows he can trust in-system, he's got Fourteenth double-tasked to keep an eye on Twelfth. Keep your friends close, and your enemies closer, where you can keep an eye on them—that's what he's thinking . . . when he should be concentrating on the fact that he's got the *rest* of his units so scattered that they'll find it harder than hell to concentrate before we get to Old Earth ourselves."

"What about Moonbase?" Julian asked.

"A point," Helmut conceded. "And to be fair—which I don't much want to be—probably the real reason Greenberg didn't bitch when Gianetto started spreading Home Fleet all over the backside of hell. Moonbase has the firepower of at least two carrier squadrons' ship-to-ship weapons all by itself, so in a way, he *does* have a task group—without cruisers, of course—in position to cover the planet at all times. But if Kjerulf can take over when Greenberg goes down, that gives *him* control of the Moonbase launchers and emplacements. Assuming he has the current release codes for them, at any rate. Best-case is for him to come in on our side and have the codes, but we can live with it if he only manages to deny Adoula's people access to them."

"That's fixed weapons, Sir. What about the Moonbase fighters?"

"They could be a problem. But there are two companies of Fleet Marines on Moonbase, and I've been careful to ensure that all the *worst* rumors I've gotten about the Empress' condition were dumped on the sites where Marines grouse to each other. I don't even have to guess what the response has been, do you?"

"No, Sir," Julian admitted.

"I've kept the Moonbase fighter wing in my thoughts," Helmut told him with a thin smile. "I'm sure the Marines have, as well. And Kjerulf, I know, has access to the same intelligence."

"Yes, Sir."

"Well, then," Helmut folded both hands behind him and frowned as he resumed his pacing. "The point is, Sergeant, that while Home Fleet will almost certainly move to concentrate between us and Old Earth, as predicted, when we arrive, the fleet's options are going to change rather abruptly when the planet goes up in flames behind them. What will they do then?"

"Turn around to go after the planet after all?"

"No," the admiral said firmly. "That's precisely why the Prince— or whoever—specified that we arrive so early. Gajelis is stationed a tad over four hours from Old Earth on a zero/zero intercept profile. That means that if he wants to stop and drop into orbit around the planet, he'll have to go to decel roughly two hours after he begins accelerating towards the planet. But he'll have been accelerating for *three and a half hours*—it'll take about thirty-five minutes for Perimeter Security to pick up our TD footprint and get the word to him—before anything happens on Old Earth. He won't be able to decelerate and insert himself into orbit. In fact, by the time he overran the planet, decelerated to relative zero, and then built a vector back towards it, we'd be running right up his ass."

"So they're screwed, Sir. Right?"

"Assuming—as I do—that Home Fleet's loyalty to Adoula is going to come unraveled in a hurry when Greenberg buys it and the fleet's officers realize someone's mounting an attempt to rescue the Empress, then, yes, Sergeant. Screwed is *exactly* what they'll be. But if they react quickly enough, they'll still be able to cut their losses and run for it. They'll be inside us, Sergeant. They can break for any point on the TD sphere, and the range will still be long enough for them to avoid us without much difficulty. Which means we could face a situation in which quite a lot of Adoula loyalists will get away from us. And if *he* gets away, as well—a distinct possibility, I submit; he's the sort of man who always has a rathole handy to dash down—we're going to be looking at a civil war whatever your Prince wants. In which case, I further submit, it would be nice if he didn't have any more ships on his side than we can help. Yes?"

"Yes, Sir," Julian said fervently.

"I'm so happy you agree, Sergeant," Helmut said in a dust-dry voice, then wheeled to give him another ferret-sharp smile. "Which is why we're leaving a little *early*, Sergeant Julian. I have a small detour I need to make."

"Who are these guys?"

"I dunno, Mr. Siminov," the gang leader said, standing as close to attention as he could manage.

Alexi Siminov referred to himself as a "businessman," and he had a large number of fully legitimate businesses. Admittedly, he owned only one of them—a restaurant—on paper; the rest he owned through intermediaries as a silent, and senior, partner. But the legitimate businesses of his small empire were quite secondary to its *illegitimate* businesses. He ran most of the organized crime in the south Imperial City district: racketeering, "protection," illegal gambling, data theft, illegal identities, drugs—they all paid Siminov a percentage, or they didn't operate at all.

"I thought they was just a restaurant," the gang leader continued, "but then I had to wonder. They smelled fishy. Then I guessed they was probably your people, and I made real nice to them. Besides, they've got heavy muscle. Heavier than I wanted to take on."

"If they were one of my operations, I'd have let you know," Siminov said, angrily. "They're laundering money. It's not *my* money, and I'm *not* getting my share of the action. That makes me upset."

"I'm sorry, Mr. Siminov." The gang leader swallowed. "I didn't know."

"No, you didn't," Siminov conceded. "I take it you shook them down?"

"We had to come to an agreement," the gang leader said with a slight but audible gulp. "They were pretty . . . unhappy about an . . . arrangement."

"And if they were one of *my* operations, do you think they would have *come* to an agreement?" Siminov's eyes flickered dangerously.

"Uh . . ."

"I suppose that logic was a bit too much for you." Siminov's lips thinned. "After all, you don't hold your position for your brains."

"No, sir," the gang leader said with a wince.

"You did come to an agreement though, right?" Siminov said quietly. "I'd hate to think you're losing your touch."

"Yes, sir. And you got your cut, sir."

"I'm sure. But not a cut of the action. Very well, you can go. I'll handle the rest."

"Thank you, sir." The gang leader backed out of the office, bowing jerkily. "Thank you."

Siminov rubbed his chin in thought after the gang leader's departure. The fool had a point; this group had some serious muscle. Mardukans were few off-planet, and of that few, quite a number of them worked as "muscle" in one organization or another, but always in tiny numbers. He didn't have *any*, and he'd never seen more than one of them at a time, yet this guy, whoever he was, had at least fifty. Maybe more. And they all had that indefinable air of people who could be unpleasantly testy.

Which meant the direct approach to enforcing his rules was out. But all *that* meant was that he'd need to use subtlety, and that was okay with him. Subtle was his middle name.

"Captain Kjerulf," Eleanora O'Casey said as she shook his hand. "Thank you for meeting with me."

They were in a fast-food establishment in the low-grav portion of Moonbase. She noticed that he showed no trace of awkwardness moving in the reduced gravity.

Kjerulf really did look a lot like Gronningen, she thought. Same size, just a shade over two meters, same massive build, same close-cropped blond hair, blue eyes, and square jaw. But he was older and, she could tell by his eyes, wiser. Probably what Gronningen would have been like if he'd had the time to grow up.

"There are people who handle supplemental supplies, Ms. Nejad," the captain observed, shaking his head as he sat down across the table from her. "I'm afraid I can't really help you in that."

His casually apologetic, meeting-you-to-be-polite tone was perfect, but he knew the meeting wasn't about "supplementary supplies." Not with that "roses are red and sauerkraut's yellow" message header.

"I realize that this isn't, strictly speaking, your area of responsibility, Captain," Eleanora said. "But you *are* a very influential individual in Home Fleet, and the Mardukan comestibles we can supply would be a welcome change for your spacers and Marines."

"I don't handle procurement, Ms. Nejad," Kjerulf said in a slightly cooler tone, and frowned.

"Perhaps. But I'm sure you have some influence," she said. "Left. For now."

He'd opened his mouth to reply before she finished speaking. Now he closed it, and his eyes narrowed. With Adoula replacing everyone who hadn't been bought and paid for, she had a point. But not one that a comestibles supplier would make. It might be one that . . . someone else would make, but whether that was good or bad would depend upon who she represented. On the other hand, Marinau had ended up as a sergeant major in the Empress' Own, he knew that. So—

"Perhaps," he said. "A few of the captains might accept a suggestion or two. But that would depend entirely upon the quality of the . . . supplies."

Eleanora considered the captain's background carefully, and hoped like hell that he'd had the same general upbringing as Gronningen.

"Some of our *atul*," she said, quietly, "are as moist as a fatted calf, Captain."

Kjerulf sat there for a moment, his face unchanging. Perhaps too unchanging.

"Impossible," he said finally.

"No, really," Eleanora replied. "They may be predators, but they're just as tasty—tasty enough even an Armaghan satanist would swear by them. I think you'd like one. They're vicious and deadly to their natural enemies, yes, but they provide a very fine . . . main course."

Kjerulf reached forward and picked a handful of fries off of her plate. He stuffed them into his mouth and masticated slowly and thoughtfully.

"I've never had . . . *atul*," he said. "And I've heard it's not very good, to be honest. And rare. To the point of extinction."

He dusted his fingers against each other to get the salt off, and looked at them distastefully. Finally, he wiped the grease off with a napkin.

"Your information is out of date," Eleanora replied. "They're very much alive, trust me."

"And you have them in-system, where they could be delivered promptly?" Kjerulf asked, still wiping his hands.

"Yes," Eleanora said. "And other fleets have added them to their supply list and found the taste quite acceptable. Much better than they'd expected from some other people's reports."

She picked up a fry of her own and squirted ketchup from a bulb down its length. As she bit delicately into the fry, her other hand squirted out the word "O'Casey" on her plate. Then she picked up another fry and wiped out the ketchup with it.

"I take it you're a senior member of this business venture?" Kjerulf said.

"I'm in charge of marketing and sales." Eleanora finished eating the fry which had erased her name. "And policy advising."

"And other fleets have found these supplies satisfactory?"

"Absolutely," Eleanora replied. "I want you to understand, Captain, that those people you can convince to try this new taste sensation will be in on the ground floor. We're planning on being a big name in the business here in the Sol System. Very soon."

"I'm sure you are," Kjerulf said dryly. "There are, however, many competitors in any business. And . . ." He shrugged and frowned.

"We realize that," Eleanora replied. "And, of course, there's the question of monopoly markets," she added, having thought long and hard about how *not* to use the words "Empress" and "Palace" in the conversation. "It's never easy to get started when someone else controls access to the critical markets. But we intend to break those monopolies, Captain, and free those markets. It's central to our business plan. Depending upon the quality of the businesses we find participating in the present monopolies, we might be interested in a buyout. That would depend upon the quality of those businesses' management, of course. We've heard they may have some internal problems."

"And your competitors?" Kjerulf said, puzzling over that rather complicated metaphor string.

"Our competitors are going to find out just how deadly to their future marketing prospects our ability to supply genuine *atul* really is."

"How are your projections?" Kjerulf asked after another pause.

"I'll admit that sales to Home Fleet are a big part of our expansion plans. But they're not essential. Especially since other fleets are already in our supply chain. But I'd hate to have any bickering between the various fleets' supply officers, and sales to Home Fleet would be very helpful. With them, our projections are excellent. Without them, they're . . . fair."

"I couldn't guarantee sales to the whole fleet," Kjerulf said. "I could make suggestions to some of the captains, but my boss—" He shrugged.

"During the expansion phase, your boss won't be an issue," Eleanora said coldly. "And if our expansion is successful, he won't become an issue, either. Ever."

"Good," Kjerulf said, and showed her his first smile. It was a little cold and thin, but it was a smile. She'd seen Gronningen smile that same way so many times it made her hurt. But, on the other hand, it also made her fiercely glad. Things were looking up.

Three days had passed since O'Casey's return from Moonbase. And the pace was picking up. Which explained why none of Roger's human companions were on-site when the visitors arrived at Marduk House.

The human in the lead was a pipsqueak, Rastar thought. The two guys following him were pretty big, for humans, but Rastar towered over them, and Fain and Erkum Pol were watching from the back door of the restaurant. One of the Diasprans was ostentatiously pitching live *basik* to the *atul*, for that matter; that usually tended to bring salesmen down a peg. But this guy wasn't backing up. One of his "heavies" looked a little green—glancing over his shoulder as one of the big female *atul* crashed into the side of her cage, ignoring the squealing *basik* as she tried to reach the Diaspran, instead—but the leader didn't even blink.

"It's really quite important that I speak with Mr. Chung," he said. "Important to him, that is."

"Isn't here," Rastar said, thickening his accent. He'd actually gotten quite fluent in Imperial, but the "big dumb barb" routine seemed the way to go.

"Perhaps you could call him?" the man suggested. "He really will wish to speak to me."

"Long way," Rastar replied, crossing all four arms. "Come later."

"Perhaps you could screen him. I'll wait."

Rastar stared at him for a moment, then looked over his shoulder.

"Call Mr. Chung," he said deliberately speaking in High Krath. "See what he wants me to do. Off the top of my horns, I'd say kick their asses and feed them to the *atul*." He turned back in time to see the leader twitch his face. So, they *did* have updated Mardukan language packs, did they? Interesting. He hoped Fain had noticed.

"Roger," Despreaux said, leaning in through the door to his office. "Krindi's on the com. We've got some heavies of some sort who want to see 'Mr. Chung.' They're pretty insistent."

"Crap." Roger glanced at Catrone. "Suggestions?"

They'd been refining the plan for the Palace assault and looking over the reports from VR training. So far, it was looking good. Casualties in the models, especially among the unarmored Vasin and Diasprans who were to make the initial assault, were persistently high, and Roger didn't like that one bit, but the plan should work.

"Play for time," Catrone advised. "Sounds like you're getting shaken down again."

"It's times like this I wish Poertena were around," Roger said. "Nimashet, rustle up Kosutic. Let's go see what they want. And tell Rastar to let them wait inside."

The visitor was dressed in an obviously expensive suit of muted bronze acid-silk, not the sort of garish streetwear Roger had anticipated. The two heavies with him, both smaller than Roger and nothing compared to the Mardukans, were sampling some Mardukan food at a nearby table. Their culinary explorations didn't prevent them from keeping a close eye on their surroundings, where Mardukans—most of them Diaspran infantry—were setting up for the evening. Erkum Pol and another Diaspran, in turn, were keeping an eye on them. Not at all unobtrusively.

"Augustus Chung." Roger held out his hand. He'd found a tailor who was accustomed to handling large customers, and he was dressed less formally, although probably at even greater expense, than his visitor.

"Ezequiel Chubais," the visitor said, standing up to take Roger's hand. "Pleased to meet you, Mr. Chung."

"And what can I do for you, Mr. Chubais?" Roger sat down, waving Despreaux and Kosutic to chairs on either side of his own.

"You've got a nice place here," Chubais said, sitting back down himself. "Very classy. We're both businessman, though, and we're both aware that the restaurant isn't all the business you're conducting."

"And your point, Mr. Chubais?"

"My point—more importantly, my boss's point—is that there's a protocol about these things. You don't just set up a laundering operation in somebody else's territory, Mr. Chung. It's not done."

"We're already paying our squeeze, Mr. Chubais," Roger said coldly. "One shakedown is all you get."

"You're paying your rent for operating a *restaurant*, Mr. Chung," Chubais pointed out. "Not a laundering operation. There's a *percentage* on that; one you neglected to pay. You've heard the term 'penalties and fines,' right?"

"And if we're disinclined to acquiesce to your . . . request for them?"

"Then we will, with great reluctance, have to take appropriate action." Chubais shrugged. "You've got a lots of muscle, Mr. Chung. Enough that it's a big question in our minds if you're just setting up a laundering operation, or if you're contemplating something a bit more . . . acquisitive. My boss doesn't like people horning in on his territory. He can get very unpleasant about it."

"We're not horning in on his territory," Roger said softly. "We've set up a quiet little operation that has so little to do with your boss that you wouldn't believe it."

"Nonetheless," Chubais said. "It looks like you've pushed through right on two million credits. The percentage on that would be two-fifty kay Penalties for failure to associate us with the operation, and failure to pay previously, are five hundred kay."

"Out of the question," Roger snapped. He paused and thought about it, frowning. "We'll ante up the percentage, but the penalties are out of the question."

"The penalties are nonnegotiable." Chubais stood and nodded to his guards. "We'll expect full payment within three days."

"Chubais, tell your boss that he really does *not* want to push this," Roger said very softly as he stood, as well. "It would be a very bad idea. Possibly the last one he ever has. He has no idea who he's pocking with."

"Pocking?" Chubais repeated, and one cheek twitched in a grin. "Well, Mr. Chung, I don't know where you come from, but you're in our territory now, and it's apparent that you have no idea who *you* are . . . pocking with. If you fail to pay, however, you'll find out."

He nodded, then left, trailed by his heavies.

"Roger," Despreaux said quietly, "our next transfer from our . . . friends isn't due until next week. We don't *have* seven hundred and fifty thousand credits available."

"I know." Roger frowned. "Kosutic, I know everyone's already on alert, but pass the word. They'll probably try to hit us either at the restaurant or the warehouse. I'd guess they'll try to stage something at the restaurant, probably when it's operating. Push the perimeter out a little bit."

"Will do," the sergeant major acknowledged. "It's going to play hell with our training schedule, though."

"Needs must." Roger shrugged. "If it was easy, it wouldn't need us, would it?"

"He was remarkably . . . unresponsive," Chubais said.

"Not surprising." Siminov touched his lips with a napkin. He was having dinner in his sole "legitimate" establishment and enjoying a very nice pork dish in wine sauce. "He's got enough muscle that we'd have to bring in every gang we have. And then we'd probably bounce."

"It would cause him a fair bit of trouble," Chubais pointed out. "Cops would be all over it."

"And they'd find a perfectly legitimate restaurant that was having gang problems." Siminov frowned. "Maybe they'd harass him a little bit, but not enough to shut him down. No, I want what's mine. And we're going to get it."

"Sergeant Major," Captain Kjerulf said, nodding as the NCO entered the secure room.

"Captain," Sergeant Major Brailowsky said, returning the nod.

"Have a seat," Kjerulf invited, looking around at the four ships' captains already present. "I've had my own people sweep the room. The posted agenda is readiness training and the next cycle of inspections. That is not, in fact, accurate."

No one seemed particularly astonished by his last sentence, and he turned back to Sergeant Major Brailowsky.

"Sergeant Major, do you know Sergeant Major Eva Kosutic?" he asked coldly.

"Yes, Sir," the sergeant major said, his face hard. "She was in my squad back when we were both privates. I've served with her . . . several times."

"So what do you think about the idea of her being involved in a plot against the Empress?" Kjerulf asked.

"She'd cut her own throat first," Brailowsky said without a trace of hesitation, his voice harsh. "Same with Armand Pahner. I knew him, too. Both as one of my senior NCOs and as a company commander. I was first sergeant of Alpha of the Three-Four-Two when he had Bravo Company. Sir, they don't come any more loyal."

"And I would have said the same of Commodore Chan, wouldn't you?" Kjerulf said, looking around at the other captains. One of them was . . . looking a tad shaky. The other three were stone-faced.

"Yes, Sir," Brailowsky said. "Sir, permission to speak?"

"You're not a recruit, Brailowsky," Kjerulf said, smiling faintly.

"I think I am," the sergeant major said. "That's what this is about, right? Recruiting?"

"Yes," Kjerulf said.

"In that case, Sir, I've known half the NCOs in Bravo of Bronze," Brailowsky said, "and I know what they thought of the Prince. And of the Empress. Between the two, there was just no comparison. That Roger was a bad seed, Sir. There was no *way* they were going to help him try to take the Throne."

"What if I told you they'd changed their minds?" Kjerulf asked. "That while you're right about their nonparticipation in the so-called coup attempt, they'd come to think rather better of Roger than you do? That, in fact, they're not all dead . . . and that he isn't, either?"

"You know that?" Captain (Senior-Grade) Julius Fenrec asked. He was the CO of the carrier *Gloria*, and he'd been listening to the conversation with a closed, set expression.

"I met someone who identified herself as Eleanora O'Casey," Kjerulf admitted with a shrug. "It *could* have been a setup to try to get me to tip my hand, but I don't think so. Can't prove it, of course . . . yet. But she says Roger is alive, and she used the parable of the prodigal son, which I think has more than one level of meaning. She also slipped to me that Eva Kosutic is alive, as well. And fully in the plan. I don't know about Pahner."

"That's not much to go on," Captain Atilius of the *Minotaur* said nervously.

"No," Kjerulf agreed, his face hard. "but I've seen the confidential reports of what's going on in the Palace, and I don't like it one damned bit."

"Neither do I," Fenrec said, "And I know damned well that Adoula thinks I'm too loyal to the Dynasty to retain my command. I'm going to find myself shuffling chips while some snot-nosed commander who owes Adoula his soul takes my ship. I don't like that one damned bit, either."

"We're all going to be shuffling chips." Captain Chantal Soheile was the CO of HMS *Lancelot*. Now she leaned forward and brushed back her dark hair. "Assuming we're lucky, and we don't have an 'accident.' And the rumors in the Fleet about what's happening to the Empress—I've never seen spacers so angry."

"Marines, too," Brailowsky said. "Sir, if you're going to make a grab for the Empress . . . Home Fleet Marines are on your side."

"What about Colonel Ricci?" Atilius asked.

"What about him, Sir?" Brailowsky asked, his eyes like flint. "He's a Defense Headquarters pussy shoved down our throats by the bastards who have the Empress. He's never had a command higher than a company, and he did a shitty job at that. You think we're going to follow *him* if it comes to a dynastic fight, Sir?"

He shook his head, facial muscles tight, and looked at Kjerulf.

"Sir, you really think that jerk Roger is alive?"

"Yes." Kjerulf shrugged. "Something in the eyes when O'Casey was dropping her hints. And I don't think O'Casey is the woman who left Old Earth, Sergeant Major. If the Prince has changed as much as she has . . . well, I'm going to be interested to meet him. Roast the fatted calf, indeed."

"Are we going to?" Soheile asked. "Meet him?"

"I doubt it," Kjerulf said. "Not before whatever's going down, anyway. I think they're getting ready for something, and since they seem to be planning on its happening soon, I'd say around the Imperial Festival."

"And what are we going to do?" Fenrec asked, leaning forward.

"Nothing. We're going to do *nothing*. Except, of course, to make sure the *rest* of Home Fleet does nothing. Which is going to take some doing."

"Hell, yes, it is," Atilius said, throwing up his hands. "We've got four carriers! We're talking about four carriers from three different squadrons taking on six full *squadrons*!"

"We're liable to get some help," Kjerulf said.

"Helmut," Captain Pavel of the *Holbein* said. He'd been sitting back, quietly observing.

"Probably," Kjerulf agreed. "You know how he is."

"He's nuts for Alexandra," Pavel said.

"So are you—which is why you're here."

"Takes one to know one," Pavel said, his face still closed.

"You in?" Kjerulf asked.

"Hell, yes." Not even the most charitable would have called the expression which finally crossed Pavel's face a smile. "I figure someone else will get Adoula's balls before I get there. But I'm still in."

"I'm in," Fenrec said. "And my officers will follow me. Regular spacers, too. They've heard the rumors."

"In," Soheile said. "If Roger doesn't move—and, frankly, I'd be astonished if he's changed enough to grow the balls for that—I say we do it ourselves. The Empress is better dead than what's going on, if the rumors are true."

"They are," Kjerulf said bleakly, looking at Atilius. "Corvu?"

"I've only got two more years to pension," Atilius said unhappily. "A desk is looking good about now." He looked miserable for a second, then straightened his shoulders. "But, yeah, I'm in. All the way. What's the line about sacred honor?"

"'Our lives, our fortunes, and our sacred honor,'" Pavel said. "That's what we're putting down for sure. But this had *better* be about restoring the Empress, not putting that pissant Roger on the Throne."

"If any of us survive, we'll see to that," Fenrec said. "But how are we going to signal commencement? I assume the idea is to keep the fleet from getting close enough to support Adoula's forces with kinetics and Marines."

"Ain't one damned Marine going to board a shuttle, Sir," Brailowsky said. "Except to kill Adoula."

"The Marines are going to have another job, Sergeant Major,"

Kjerulf said. "What the Marines are going to do is put down an attempted mutiny against the Throne by their own ships."

"Damn," the sergeant major said, shaking his head. "I was afraid it would be something like that."

"That, and certain duties on the Moon," Kjerulf said, and looked around at the others' faces, his own grim. "I don't know everything Greenberg and that weasel Wallenstein have been up to. I may be chief of staff for the fleet, but they've cut me out of the loop on a lot of stuff, especially right here on Moonbase. I've got a really bad feeling that Greenberg's changed the release codes on the offensive launchers, for instance, but there's no way to check without his knowing I've done it. If he has, I'll be locked out for at least ten to twelve hours while we break the lock. That's if everything goes well. And it's also why I need you and your ships in close to the planet."

"Speaking of Greenberg . . ." Soheile murmured, and Kjerulf smiled thinly.

"I have it on the best of authority that he won't be a factor. Ever again," he said.

"Oh, good," she said softly, showing her teeth.

"But for right now, he definitely *is* a factor," Kjerulf continued. "On the other hand, there are a few things *I* can get away with— routine housekeeping sorts of things—without mentioning them to him, either. Which is how the four of you got detached from your squadrons. I picked you because I figured I knew which way you'd jump, sure, but sliding you and Julius both out of CarRon 13 is also going to make a hole in one of the squadrons Greenberg's been counting on, Chantal."

"Umf." Soheile frowned thoughtfully, then nodded. "Probably the right call," she agreed. "I was thinking that having the two of us in the middle of his squadron might make La Paz think twice about jumping in on Adoula's side when he couldn't be sure who we'd fire on, but you're going to need us here worse, especially with the way Gianetto's reinforced Fourteenth."

"And not knowing which way Twelfth's going to jump," Fenrec agreed sourly, and looked at Kjerulf. "Any read on that?"

"No more than you've got," Kjerulf admitted sourly. "The one thing I'm pretty sure of is that Prokorouv's captains will back him, whatever he decides. And whatever I may think, *Gianetto* trusted him enough to give him the outer slot covering Old Earth."

"Yeah, but the one thing Gianetto's dispositions prove is that as an admiral he's a freaking wonderful ground pounder," Laj Pavel pointed out.

"That's true enough, and one of the few bright points I see," Kjerulf agreed. "We're still going to get the piss knocked out of us holding on, even if Prokorouv decides to sit it out with Twelfth. If I can get the launchers on line, Moonbase can cover the outer arc while you people fend Gajelis off, but in the end, they'll plow us under no matter what unless Helmut gets here on schedule."

"He will," Fenrec said, then barked a harsh laugh. "Hell! When was the last time any of us ever saw him miss his timing, however complicated the ops schedule was?"

"There's always a first time," Atilius pointed out dryly. "And Murphy always seems to guarantee that it happens at the worst possible time."

"Granted." Kjerulf nodded again. "But if I had to pick one admiral in the entire Navy to depend on to get it right, Helmut's the one, when all's said. No one ever called him a sociable soul, but no one's ever questioned his competence, either. And if he comes in where I expect he will, and if Thirteenth is already down fifty percent . . ."

"I see your logic," Chantal Soheile said, and gave him a tight smile. "You really are killing as many birds per stone as you can, aren't you?" She grinned at him again, then frowned. "But this is all still way too nebulous to make me what you might call happy. I know a lot of it has to stay that way, under the circumstances, but that brings us back to Julius' point about the signal to start the op. Was O'Casey even able to set up a channel to tell us when to move?"

"No. But I think we'll probably get all the signals from Old Earth we're going to need to know when to start the music. We'll just ignore the orders we don't like. The orders I've already had cut to move all your ships back to the L-5 Starbase, preparatory for overhaul, should be good long enough to get us through the Festival. If nothing actually happens, then we play things by ear. But that'll keep you all semidetached from your squadrons at least through the end of the Festival. Not to mention keeping you inside all the ships that aren't actually in dock. And I'll make sure all the ships in dock *stay* in dock.

"When the ball goes up, you four move to hold the orbital positions, and hold off Gajelis—and Prokourov, if it comes to that. You may have to deal with the Moonbase fighter force, if I can't get them to stand down. God knows I'm going to be trying like hell, as well as trying to get the missile batteries up *and* talking to all the captains that aren't bought and paid for by Adoula. All we have to do is hold the orbital positions, far enough out that they can't get accurate KEW down to the surface, until Helmut gets here. At that point, with Helmut outside and us inside, Adoula's bastards are either going to surrender or be blown to hell."

"If we don't get blown to hell first," Atilius said.

"Our lives, our fortunes . . ." Pavel said.

"I got it the first time," Atilius said.

"They're not going to be at their best, Sir," Brailowsky said. "Leave that to us. And when the time comes, you can bet we're going to be having some serious discussions with the Moonbase fighter force, Sirs." He wasn't grinning, but it was close.

"Glad you're enjoying yourself, Sergeant Major," Soheile said.

"Ma'am, I've been pretty damned mad about what was happening on Old Earth," Brailowsky said soberly. "I'm very happy to have a chance, any chance, to do something about it."

"Vorica, Golden, Kalorifis, and all the rest of CarRon Fourteen are Adoula's," Soheile said, shrugging at the sergeant major's elan. "Eleventh is going to be split, but I think it's going to go three-to-one for Adoula. Thirteenth won't be split anymore—not with me and Julius both here—but there's a good chance Fifteenth will be. Sixteenth . . . I don't know. Wu's been playing her cards as close as Prokourov has. But Brettle, La Paz, and Mahmut are as much Adoula's as Gajelis, and so are their flag captains. So figure all six of Gajelis' carriers, two of La Paz', three—at least—of Brettle's, and probably at least three of Mahmut's, from the Fifteenth. That's fourteen to our four, and all of them are going to fight like hell. That's damned near four-to-one odds. Even *if* the rest sit this one out. If Prokourov gets off the decicred and comes in on Adoula's side, as well, then we are truly screwed if Helmut doesn't get here right on the dot. And, sorry, Sergeant Major, that's going to be despite the Marines. There's only a squad or two on each of those ships."

"I didn't say it was going to be easy," Kjerulf said.

"How's he going to tell the sheep from the goats?" Ferenc asked. "Helmut, that is. Even if he's fast, we're going to be pretty mixed up at that point."

"Simple," Kjerulf said, grinning ferally. "We'll just reset our transponders to identify ourselves as the Fatted Calf Squadron."

Nimashet Despreaux was not, by any stretch of the imagination, a clotheshorse. Certainly not in comparison to her fiancé. She'd grown up on a small farm on one of the border worlds, where hand-me-downs had been the order of the day. A new dress at Yule had been considered a blessing during her childhood, and she'd never really felt any pressure, even after she joined the Marines and had a bit more spending money, to dress up. Uniform took care of any business-related sartorial requirements, and slacks and a ratty sweater were always in style off-duty, in her opinion.

Still, certain appearances had to be maintained under the present circumstances. She had only three "dressy" outfits to wear at the restaurant, and some of the regulars had to have noticed by now that she was cycling through them. So whatever her personal wishes, it was time to get a few more.

She stepped out of the airtaxi on a fifth-story landing stage and paused, frowning, as she considered the mall. She could probably get everything she needed in Sadik's. She hoped so, anyway. She'd never been one of those odd people who actively enjoyed the task of shopping, and she wanted to get this chore done and out of the way as quickly as possible. Thirty-seven seconds would have been her own preference, but this was the real world, so she'd settle for finishing within no more than an hour.

As she started for the mall, an alarm bell rang suddenly in her head. She was a highly trained bodyguard, and something about the too-casual demeanor of two rather hefty males headed in her general direction was causing a bit of adrenaline to leach into her system.

She glanced behind her as an airvan landed on the stage, and then whipped back around as the heavies she'd already spotted abruptly stopped being "casual." They moved towards her with sudden purposefulness, as if the airvan's arrival had been a signal—which it almost certainly *had* been. But they weren't quite as perfectly coordinated as they obviously fondly believed they were, and Despreaux flicked out a foot and buried the sole of her sensible, sturdy shoe in the belly of the one on her left. It was a hard enough snap-kick, augmented by both training and Marine muscle-enhancing nanites, that he was probably going to have serious internal injuries. She spun in place and slammed one elbow towards the attacker on the right. Blocked, she stamped down and crushed his instep, then brought her other elbow up, catching his descending jaw and probably giving herself a bone bruise. But both thugs were down—the second one just might have a broken neck; at the very least he was going to have a strained one—and it was time to run like hell.

She never heard the stunner.

"Has anyone seen Shara?" Roger asked, poking his head into the kitchen.

"She was going shopping." Dobrescu looked up from the reservation list. "She's not back?"

"No." Roger pulled out his pad and keyed her number. It beeped three times, and then Despreaux's new face popped up.

"Shara—" he said.

"Hi, this is Shara Stewart," the message interrupted. "I'm not available right now, so if you'll leave a message, I'll be happy to get back to you."

"Shara, this is Augustus," Roger said. "Forgotten we're working this evening? See you later."

"Maybe you will," Ezequiel Chubais said from the doorway, "and maybe you won't."

Roger turned the pad off and turned slowly towards the visitor.

"Oh?" he said mildly as his stomach dropped.

"Hello, Ms. Stewart," a voice said.

Despreaux opened her eyes, then closed them as the light sent splinters of pain through her eyes and directly into her brain.

"I really hate stunner migraines," she muttered. She moved her arms and sighed. "Okay. I've been kidnapped, and since I have little or no value as myself, you're either planning on rape or using me to get to . . . Augustus." She opened her eyes and blinked, frowning at the pain in her head. "Right?"

"Unfortunately," the speaker agreed. He was sitting behind a desk, smiling at her. "I suppose it might be 'b' and then 'a' if things don't go as we hope. There are certain . . . attractions to that," he added, smiling again, his eyes cold.

"So what are you asking? Penalties and fines?"

"Oh, the penalties and fines have gone up," the man said. "I'm afraid that, what with my costs associated with persuading your gentleman friend, you'd better hope you're worth a million credits to him."

"At least," Despreaux replied lightly. "The problem being that I don't think he has it on hand as spare cash."

"I'm sure he can make . . . arrangements," Siminov said.

"Not *quickly*," Despreaux said angrily. "We're talking about interstellar transit times, and—"

"—and, in case it's not clear to you, the money isn't all *mine* to distribute," Roger said angrily.

"Too bad." Chubais shrugged. "You'll have the money ready in two days, or, I'm sorry, but we'll have to send your little friend back. One small piece at the time."

"I've killed people for less than telling me something like that," Roger said quietly. "More than one. A great *many* more than one."

"And if I end up as food for your pets," Chubais said, his face hard, "then the *first* piece will be her heart."

"I doubt it." Roger's laugh could have been used to freeze helium. "I suspect she's worth more to me than you are to your boss."

★ ★ ★

"Chop away," Despreaux said, wiggling her fingers. "I'd prefer anesthetic, but if you'll just hold a stunner on me and toss me a knife, I'll take the first finger off right here. I might as well; we don't *have* a million credits sitting around at the moment!"

"Well, Mr. Chubais," Roger stood and gestured to Cord, "care to tell me where to send whatever remains there are?"

"You wouldn't dare."

Chubais glanced over at his guards, and the two men got up. They reached into their coats . . . and dropped as an oaken table, designed to seat six diners comfortably, came down on their heads. Erkum looked up at Roger and waved one false-hand.

"Was that right?" he asked.

"Just right," Roger said, without even looking at Chubais as he opened the case Cord held out and withdrew the sword. He ran one finger down the edge and turned it to the light. "Cleaning up the mess in here would be a bother. Take him out back."

Erkum picked up the no longer sneeringly confident mobster by the collar of his thousand-credit jacket and carried him through the restaurant, ignoring his steadily more frantic protests.

"Roger," Cord said, in the X'Intai dialect, which couldn't possibly have been loaded to Chubais' toot, "this is, perhaps, unwise."

"Too bad," Roger ground out.

He and his *asi* followed Erkum out into the slaughtering area, and Roger gestured to the *atul* pens. Erkum carried the mobster over and lifted him up against the pen. The *atul* inside it responded by snarling and snapping at what looked very much like dinner.

"Care to tell me where you're holding my friend?" Roger asked in a deadly conversational tone.

"You wouldn't *dare!*" Chubais repeated, desperately, his voice falsetto-high as the *atul* got one claw through the mesh and ripped his jacket. "Siminov will kill her!"

"In which case, I'll have precisely zero reason to restrain my response," Roger said, still in that lethally calm voice. "Gag him. And someone get a tourniquet ready."

When Chubais was gagged and Rastar had produced a length of flexible rubber, Roger took the mobster's wrist in his left hand and extended his arm. Chubais resisted desperately, fighting with all of his strength to wrench away from Roger's grip, but the prince's hand pinned him with apparent effortlessness. He held the arm rock-steady, fully extended, and raised the sword to take it off at the elbow.

But as he did, Cord put his hand on the sword.

"Roger," he said, again in The People's dialect, "you will not do this."

"Damn straight I will," Roger growled.

"You will not," Cord said again. "Your lady would not permit it. The Captain would not permit it. You will *not* do it."

"If he doesn't, *I* will," Pedi Karuse said flatly. "Des—Shara's a friend of mine."

"You will be silent, *asi*," Cord said gravely. "There will be another way. We will take it."

"Ro—Mr. Chung!" Kosutic came barreling through the door from the kitchen, followed by Krindi Fain. "What the *hell* is going on?"

Roger held the sword, still poised for a stroke, and began to tremble in pure, undiluted rage. Silence hovered, broken only by the *atul's* hungry snarls of anticipation and the gangster's ragged breathing. Finally, the prince twisted his sword hand's wrist, and the blade moved until its razor edge just kissed the mobster's throat.

"You have no idea who you are dealing with," he said, deadly calm once more. "No *pocking* idea at all. You and your boss are two slimy little problems which are less than a flea to me, and killing you would have about as much meaning to me. But a Mardukan barbarian just saved your ass, for the time being. He had more control, and more moral compunctions about chopping up a little piece of shit like you, than *I* ever will. Care to tell me where you're keeping my friend while I'm still inclined to listen to you?"

The mobster eyed the sword, obviously terrified, but shook his head convulsively.

"Fine," Roger said calmly. "I'll try another route. If, however, I'm unable to find the information that way, I'll give you to this young lady." He gestured at Pedi. "Have you ever read Kipling?"

Despite his fear, the mobster's eyes widened in surprise, and he produced another spastic headshake.

"There's a line from Kipling which you'll find appropriate if I don't find the information I want very quickly indeed." Roger's almost caressing tone carried an edge of silken menace. "It begins: 'When you're wounded and left on Afghanistan's plain, and the women come out to cut up what remains.'" He showed his teeth in a sharklike smile. "If the approach I'm about to try doesn't work, I'll leave you, as they used to say, 'to the women.' And she won't be cutting off your *arm*."

"Ms. Bordeaux," Roger said, after the three mobsters—one of whom would never again be a problem for anyone, thanks to Erkum's table—had been flown off to the warehouse in a van. "I need you to go see someone for me."

"Mr. Chung—" Kosutic began.

"I'm in no mood to be 'handled,' Ms. Bordeaux," Roger said flatly, "so you *will* shut the hell up and listen to my orders. You need to somehow arrange a meeting with Buseh Subianto. Now."

"Are you *sure* that's a good idea?" she asked, blanching.

"No. But it's the only idea I have short of chopping that silly little shit up into pieces. Would you prefer I do that, Ms. Bordeaux? Make up your mind, because I'd *much* prefer it!"

"No." Kosutic shook her head. "I'd really prefer that you avoided that."

"In that case, get with Jin and *find* her," Roger snapped. "If she knows where Ni—Ms. Stewart is, we'll go from there. If not, that guy is going to be walking and eating with stumps."

"I thought you said the good guys don't torture people?" Catrone said evenly.

"In the end, I didn't," Roger replied coldly. "And I might argue that there's a difference between torturing someone for vengeance and because you need information they won't give you. But I won't, because it would be an artificial distinction."

He looked at Catrone, with absolutely no expression.

"You should have listened more carefully, Tomcat. Especially to the part about Nimashet being my 'prosthetic conscience.' Because I'll tell you the truth—you'd rather have one of my Mardukans on the Throne than me without Nimashet."

Roger's eyes were cold and black as agates.

"Chubais is an operator for a rather larger fish named Alexi Siminov," Fritz Tebic said. His voice cracked at least a little of the tension between Catrone and the prince, and the IBI agent flashed a hologram of a face. "We have a long list of potential offenses to lay against Siminov, but he's rather . . . tricky in that regard. Nothing that we can take to court, in other words."

"I've known Siminov professionally for years," Subianto said.

It had been difficult for the two of them to disappear, especially without warning, but Buseh had worked undercover for years, and she hadn't lost her touch. They'd made it to the warehouse before Roger got there, and the two of them were now bemusedly working a sideline to what was apparently a countercoup.

"He was just starting his rise back when I was in OrgCrime," she continued. "Very smooth operator. Worked his way up in a very tough business. Did some strong-arm work to establish his rep, and clawed his way up, over the dead bodies of a couple of competitors, since. Polished on the surface, but more than a bit of a mad-dog underneath. Kidnapping is his style. So—" she glanced sideways at the prince "—is 'disappearing' the kidnap victim to avoid arrest or to punish an adversary."

"He's associated with several operations," Tebic said. "Theoretically, he could be almost anywhere, but he often uses this building for meetings." Another hologram appeared: a four-story building with some rather large men hanging around the front door. "It's a neighborhood association, technically. In fact, it's where he often meets with the groups he controls. We've tried to bug it several times with no success—very tight security. Armed security, by the way, legally authorized to carry weapons."

"What Fritz is saying," Subianto said, "is that because of our interest in Siminov, this particular building is always under electronic surveillance. And a woman matching the height and shape of your 'Shara Stewart' was seen being carried into the building. Since there was no missing persons report on her, it was assumed she was a street prostitute who'd run afoul of Siminov for some reason. The ImpCity PD wanted to do an entry on the basis that what we were seeing was a kidnap, assuming we could get a warrant. But the idea was shot down. If we did the entry and the presumed hooker had either 'disappeared' or refused—as she probably would—to swear out charges, we'd look like fools. Who is she, by the way?"

"Nimashet Despreaux," Roger ground out. "*Sergeant* Nimashet Despreaux. She's also my fiancée, which makes her a rather important person."

"But not an identity we can use," Subianto pointed out sourly. "Somehow I don't think you want me going to a judge to report that Siminov has kidnapped a woman wanted for high treason under an Imperial warrant. Which means we can't use ImpCity tac-teams to spring her."

"I wouldn't trust ImpCity SWAT to walk my dog," Catrone said contemptuously, "much less to do an entry with a principal this important."

"They're very good," Tebic protested.

"No, they're not," Catrone said definitely. "This is my profession. Trust me, they're not very good at all, Mr. Tebic."

"We know where she is," Roger said, "and we don't *have* the ransom. So I'd best go get her."

"Like hell," Catrone said. "Leave it to the professionals."

"Sergeant Major," Roger snapped, "again, get the wax out of your ears. I *am* the professional!"

"And you're *indispensable*!" Eleanora snapped back at him. "You're not going off on a Galahad mission, Roger. Yes, you'd probably be the best for the job, but you're *not* getting in the line of fire. Get that through your head."

"Try to stop me," Roger said coldly.

"We're on a tight schedule, here," Catrone pointed out, "and we don't have the personnel, associated with the main mission, or the time, to go rescue your girlfriend."

"We are *not* going to leave her to be chopped into pieces," Roger said, coming to his feet with dangerous grace.

"No, we're not," Catrone agreed calmly. "But *you* are essential for gaining entry to the Palace, and you can't be in two places at one time. If you walk out of this room, I'm walking out of the mission, and so is everyone I'm bringing to the table. *I* can handle this; you don't have to get any nearer. Do you know what I do for a living?"

"Raise horses," Roger said, "and draw your munificent pension."

"And *train* tac-teams," Catrone said angrily. "You can't get a weapon anywhere near Siminov's offices; *I* can. And he's got legal bodyguards that are *armed*; a sword isn't going to do you a damned bit of good!"

"You might be surprised," Roger said quietly.

"Maybe." Catrone shrugged. "I've seen you operate. But, as I said, let the *professionals* handle this—and I know the professionals."

"Ms. Subianto," Roger said, "I imagine it's pretty clear what's going on here."

"It was clear before our *first* meeting," Subianto said. "I wasn't aware it was this far along, but it was obvious what was going on. To me at least. I'm fairly sure no one else has connected the dots."

"We could use your help. Especially on current intelligence on movements and on details of Imperial City police security."

"I *hate* politics." Subianto shook her head angrily. "Why can't all you damned politicians solve your problems in council?"

"I wish it could be so," Roger said. "But it isn't. And I hate politics, too, probably more than you do. I tried to avoid them as hard as I could, but . . . some are born to them, some force their way into them, and some are forced into them. In your case, the last. In mine, the first and last. Do you *know* what they're doing to my mother?" he finished angrily.

"Yes," she said unhappily. "That was why I decided to ignore what was going on when you slid me that nice little 'fatted calf' code phrase. But that doesn't mean I want to help you. Do *you* know what sort of a nightmare this is going to cause in Imperial City? In the *Empire*?"

"Yes, I do. And I also know some of Adoula's plans that you

don't. But I also know what there is of you in the public record, and what Temu said about you—and that you're an honorable person. What's happening is *wrong*. It's *bad* for the Empire, and it's going to get worse, not better, and you know damned well which side you should be on!"

"No, I don't," Subianto said, "because I don't know that what you're doing is *better* for the Empire."

"Here we go again," Kosutic groaned. "Look, forget *everything* you think you know about Master Rog unless you're prepared to puke up your guts for about four hours."

"What does *that* mean?" Tebic asked.

"She's right," Catrone said. "Ms. Subianto, you know something about me?"

"I know quite a bit about you, Sergeant Major," Subianto said dryly. "Counter-Intel considers keeping an eye on the Empress' Own to be just good sense. You hear too many secrets to not be considered a security risk."

"Then trust my judgment," Catrone said. "And Sergeant Major Kosutic's. Roger isn't the worthless shit he was when he left."

"Why, *thank you*, Sergeant Major." Roger actually managed a chuckle. "Nicely . . . put."

"I'm starting to get that impression myself," Subianto said dryly, "although I'm not so sure he hasn't gone too far the other way. Almost cutting a suspect's arm off to get him to talk doesn't make me particularly thrilled about his judgment."

"You're going to need to block out four hours some time, then," Roger said. "After that, you'll understand what I consider 'appropriate'—and why. And that brings us back to Nimashet. Probably the only reason I didn't cut off the bastard's arm was Cord's very cogent point that Nimashet would not approve. Even to save *her*," he added bleakly.

"I need to speak to this IBI agent you have attached to you," Subianto said equivocally. "I don't recognize his name."

"And there's no record of him in the files," Tebic said. "He's a nonperson, as far as we're concerned."

"He's at the restaurant at the moment," Roger said. "We need to get this operation to pull Despreaux worked out, though. I'll get him headed over right away."

"I'll call my people," Catrone said. "Good thing we've got the datanet wired from here."

"This will *not* be a legal operation," Eleanora pointed out.

"I know. I'm not saying they'll be happy to do it; I said they *would* do it. I thought about bringing them in on the main op, but . . . Well, I trust them, but not that far. Besides, they're not combat troops— they're tac-teams. There's a fine line, but it's real. For *this*, though, they're perfect."

"Jin," Roger said, as the IBI agent stepped into the meeting room at the warehouse. "You recognize Ms. Subianto, and this is Mr. Tebic."

"Ma'am." Jin came to something like attention.

"Mr. Jin," Subianto replied with a nod.

"There's some question about your ID, Temu," Roger said, raising an eyebrow. "You don't appear to be listed in Mr. Tebic's records. Anything you'd care to tell me?"

"I was deep cover on Marduk," Jin said uneasily. "Kyoko Pedza's department. I got a coded message to go into the cold when this supposed coup occurred. I've sent two counter messages, requesting contact, but no response. Either Assistant Director Pedza has gone to ground, or he's dead. I would estimate the latter."

"So would I," Subianto sighed. "Which angers me. Kyoko and I have been good friends for many years. He was one of my first field supervisors."

"Assistant Director Pedza managed to dump lots of his files before he disappeared," Tebic pointed out. "It's not unlikely that Jin's was one of them."

"And Jin has been . . . an extremely loyal agent," Roger said. "He started covering for us long before we ever even met, and he was instrumental in getting us the weapons we needed to take the spaceport on Marduk. Capable, too; he cracked the datanet on the Saint ship in really remarkable time."

"Saint ship?" Subianto asked.

"It would take far too long to explain even a fraction of our story, Ms. Subianto. The point is that Jin has been an extremely loyal aide. Loyal, I think, to the Empire *first*. He's been assisting me because he sees it as his duty to the Empire."

"Yes, Sir," Jin said. "I'm afraid I'm not one of your Companions, Your Highness—only an agent assisting in what I see as a legitimate operation under Imperial law against a conspiracy of traitors."

"But," Subianto said, still frowning, "while I know a great many of our operatives, at least by name, I'm sorry to say that I don't recognize you at all."

"I'm sorry to hear that, Ma'am," Jin said politely.

"What was your mission?"

"Internal security monitoring," Jin replied. "Keeping an eye on what the local governor was doing. I'd been compiling a report I was pretty sure would have landed him in prison, at the very least. But that's not an issue anymore."

"No, it isn't," Roger said. "Based on the evidence against him, I gave him a field court-martial and had him executed."

"That was a little high-handed," Subianto said, arching her eyebrows. "I don't believe even the Heir Primus has the authority to arbitrarily order executions, however justified."

"It wasn't 'arbitrary,'" Roger said a trifle coldly. "You did hear me use the phrase 'court-martial,' didn't you? I'm also a colonel of Marines, who happened to be on detached—very detached—duty. I discovered evidence of treason while operating under field conditions in which reference to headquarters was not, in my estimation, possible. It's covered, Ms. Subianto. Every 'i' dotted and every 't' crossed."

He held Subianto's gaze for perhaps two heartbeats. Then the IBI agent's eyes fell. It wasn't a surrender, so much as an acknowledgment . . . and possibly a decision not to cross swords over a clearly secondary issue.

"Mr. Jin," she said instead, focusing on the other agent, "I'm sorry to say that Marduk is a fairly minor planet. Not exactly a critical, high-priority assignment, whatever the governor may have been up to. So I have to ask this—what is your IS rating?"

Jin cleared his throat and shrugged.

"Twelve," he said.

"TWELVE?" Roger stared at him. "*Twelve?*"

"Yes, Your Highness," Jin admitted. Twelve was the lowest Imperial Security rating possible for a field agent of the IBI.

"Agent Jin," Subianto said gently, "how many assignments have you had in the field?"

There was an extended pause, and then Jin swallowed.

"Marduk was my first solo field assignment, Ma'am," he said, gazing at the wall six centimeters above her head.

"Holy Christ," Roger muttered. "In that case, Ms. Subianto, I would say Agent Jin is one hell of a credit to your Academy!"

"And it also explains why I don't recognize your name." Subianto smiled faintly. "On the other hand, I have to agree with the Prince, Agent Jin. You've done well. Very well."

"Thank you, Ma'am," Jin sighed. "You understand . . ."

"I do," Subianto said, smiling openly now. "And, I'm sorry, but you're still officially in the cold until we can figure out some way to bring you in again."

"Oh, I think we can do something about that in about two days," Roger said. "God willing. And if nothing goes drastically wrong."

"Jesus, look at the signature on that van!" the monitor tech said. "Hey, Sergeant Gunnar, look at this!"

"Imperial permit IFF," the supervisor replied.

"I know, but . . . geez, that's some serious firepower."

The supervisor frowned and used her toot to dial the van.

"Vehicle Mike-Lima-Echo-Three-Five-Niner-Six, approaching Imperial City northeast, this is ImpCity PD Perimeter Security," she said. "Request nature of mission and destination."

Trey tapped the van's communicator and smiled at the female officer in the ICPD uniform who appeared in the HUD.

"Hey, thought you'd be calling," he said. "Firecat, LLC, Trey Jacobi. We're doing a demo for the Imperial Festival. Check your records."

The supervisor frowned and looked inward with the expression of someone communing with her toot, then nodded.

"Got it," she said. "You can understand why we were wondering. You're radiating wide enough they're probably picking you up at Moonbase."

"Not a problem." Trey chuckled. "Happens all the time."

"Mind if I come by for the demo?" Gunnar asked.

"Not at all. Monday, 9 a.m., Imperial City Combat Range. They say there's going to be a big crowd, so I'd get there early."

"Can I use your name to get a good seat?"

"Absolutely," Trey replied. "Take care," he added as he cut the connection.

"Be an even better demo tomorrow," Bill said from the passenger's seat. "And not at the range."

"Couldn't exactly invite her to that," Dave replied from the back. "Today, ladies and gentlemen, we're going to demonstrate how to smear a group of heavily armed mobsters and retreat before the police arrive," he added in a fast, high, weird voice. "Failure to properly plan and conduct the operation will result in severe penalties," he added in a deep, somber baritone. "If any of the members of your organization are captured, or killed, the department will disavow all knowledge of your existence. This van will self-destruct in five seconds."

"Could somebody *please* shut him up?" Clovis said from the seat next to Dave. "Before we're one short on the mission?"

"Well!" Dave said in a squeaky, teenaged female voice. "I don't think that's a very nice thing to say! I swear, some of the dates I agree to go on . . ."

"I'm gonna kill him," Clovis muttered "I swear it. This time, he's gonna bite it."

"B-b-but *Cloooovis*," Dave whined, "I thought you were my *friend*!"

The airvan pulled up in front of a hastily rented warehouse several blocks from the Greenbrier facility, then floated inside as the doors slid open. It eased to a stop in the middle of the empty warehouse, and Roger watched as Catrone's "friends" unloaded.

The driver looked remarkably like Roger had before his bod-mod. Shorter—he was probably 170 centimeters—but with long blond hair that was slightly curly and fell to the middle of his back, and a chiseled, handsome face. He moved with the robotic stride of a well-trained fighter, light on his feet, and had hugely muscled forearms.

"Trey Jacobi," he said, crossing to where Roger waited beside Catrone.

"Trey's a very good general operator," Catrone said, "and a former local magistrate. He's also our defense lawyer, so watch him."

"Who's my newest client?" Trey asked, holding out his hand to Roger.

"This is Mr. Chung," Catrone replied. "He's . . . a good friend. A very important person to me. He'd probably handle this on his own, but he has a pressing business engagement tomorrow."

The individual who climbed out of the driver's side rear door was a huge moose of a man, with close-cropped hair. He strode over like a soldier and stopped, coming to parade rest.

"Dave Watson," Catrone said. "He's a reserve officer with the San-Angeles PD."

"Pleased to meet you." Dave stuck out his hand, shook Roger's, and then resumed his position of parade rest, his face stern and sober.

"This is Bill Copectra," Catrone continued, as a short, stocky man came around the front of the van. "He does electronics."

"Hey, Tomcat," Bill said. "You're going to owe us one very goddammed big one for this. If you had a daughter, that would be the down payment."

"I know," Catrone replied, shaking his head.

"I had a hot date for this weekend, too," Bill continued.

"You've always got a date," the last man said. He was a bit taller than Bill, and wider, with oaklike shoulders, short-cut black hair, and a wide, flat face. He walked with a rolling stride which suggested to Roger either a sailor or someone who spent a lot of time on *civan*back. Make that horseback, this being Old Earth.

"This is Clovis Oyler," Catrone said. "Deputy officer with the Ogala department. Entry."

"That's usually my spot," Roger said, nodding as he shook Oyler's hand. "Charge?"

"Usually a modified bead gun," Oyler replied. "You can't stay on the door with a charge. And there's not many doors that won't go down with a blast from a twelve-millimeter bead."

"With a twelve-millimeter, you're not going to have many shots left," Roger pointed out.

"If you need more then three or four, you're in the wrong room," Oyler answered, as if explaining to a child.

"Tac-teams." Roger looked at Catrone and nodded. "Not combat soldiers. For your general information, Mr. Oyler, I usually do the entry in a tac-suit or powered armor and ride the entry charge through. Sometime we'll see who's faster," he added with a grin.

"Told you there was a difference," Catrone said. "And Clovis' technique does tend to leave more people alive and unmangled on the other side of the door."

He shrugged, then turned back to Copectra.

"Bill, we've got an address. We need a surveillance setup. Dave will emplace—taps and external wire. We need a schematic on the building and a count on the hostiles. Clovis, while Bill and Dave take care of that, you do weapons prep. Trey, you do initial layout."

"What are you going to be doing?" Trey asked with a frown. Catrone normally took layout himself.

"I've got another operation to work on," Catrone replied. "I'll be here for the brief, and on the op."

"What's the other op?" Trey asked. "I'm asking as your counsel, here, you understand."

"One of the kind where, if we need an attorney, he won't do us much good," Roger replied.

"Prince Jackson," General Gianetto said over the secure com link, "we have a problem."

"What?" Adoula responded. "Or, rather, what now?"

"Something's going on in Home Fleet. There've been a lot of rumors about what's happening in the Palace, some of them closer to reality than I like. I think your security isn't the best, Prince Jackson."

"It's as good as it can get," Adoula said. "But rumors aren't a problem."

"They are when the Navy gets this stirred up," Gianetto noted.

"But this is more than just rumors. CID picked up a rumor about a mutiny brewing among the Marines. They're planning something— something around the time of the Imperial Festival. And I don't like the codename one bit. It's 'Fatted Calf.'"

Adoula paused and shook his head.

"Something from the Bible?" he asked incredulously. "You want me to worry about a Marine mutiny based on the *Bible*?"

"It's from the parable of the *prodigal son*, Your Highness," Gianetto said angrily. "Prodigal son. You roast the fatted calf when the *prodigal son* returns."

"Roger's dead," Adoula said flatly. "You *arranged* that death, General."

"I know. And if he'd survived, he should have turned up somewhere within the first few weeks after his 'accident.' But it looks like *somebody* believes he's alive."

"Prince Roger is *dead*," Adoula repeated. "And even if he weren't, so what? Do you think that that airhead could have staged a countercoup? That anyone would have *followed* him? For God's sake, General, he was *New Madrid's* son! No wonder he was an idiot. What was the phrase you used about one of the officers I suggested? He couldn't have led a platoon of Marines into a brothel."

"The same can't be said for Armand Pahner," Gianetto replied. "And Pahner would fight for the *Empress*, not Roger. Roger would just be the figurehead. And I'm telling you, something is going down. The Associations are stirring, the Marines are contemplating mutiny, and Helmut is moving *somewhere*. We have a serious situation here."

"So what are you doing about it?" Adoula demanded.

"What's the most critical point we have to secure?"

"The Empress," Adoula said. "And myself."

"Okay," Gianetto replied. "I'll beef up security around Imperial City. Where I'll get it from is going to be an interesting question, since we don't have that many ground forces we know are loyal. But I'll figure it out. Beef up security around the Palace, as well. As for you, you need to be *moving* the day of the Festival."

"I'm supposed to be a participant," Adoula said with a frown. "But I'll send my regrets."

"Do that," Gianetto said dryly. "At the last minute, if you want a professional suggestion."

"What about the Marines?" Adoula asked.

"I'll replace Brailowsky," Gianetto said. "And have a little chat with him."

"Okay," Eleanora said, breaking into one of the final planning sessions. "We have a real problem."

"What?" Roger asked.

"Sergeant Major Brailowsky was just arrested, and the Marine web sites are all talking about Fatted Calf. I think Kjerulf was a little free with information."

"Shit." Roger looked at the clock. "Twelve more hours."

"Ask me for anything but time," Catrone replied.

"They're going to sweat him," Marinau said. "He's resistant to interrogation, but you can get anything out of anybody eventually."

"He's going to be in the Moonbase brig," Rosenberg said. "That's lousy with Navy SPs. We can't just spring him quietly."

"Greenberg is still in place," Roger pointed out. "If he knows Kjerulf is on our side, and Brailowsky would have to, since they're talking about 'Fatted Calf,' then we'll lose Kjerulf, as well. And they'll know it's going down sometime around the Festival."

"And Kjerulf knows it has to do with Mardukans," Eleanora said with a wince.

"And there's now a warning order on the IBI datanet," Tebic said, looking up from his station. "A coup attempt planned for around the Imperial Festival."

"They know everything important," Catrone said flatly, shaking his head. "We should abort."

Everyone looked at Roger. That was what Catrone realized later—much later. Even *he* looked at Roger. Who was looking sightlessly at the far wall.

"No," the prince said after a long pause. "Never take council of your fears. They know about Helmut, but that was obvious. They suspect I may be alive, but they don't know about Miranda."

He paused and consulted his toot.

"We move it up," he continued, his voice crisp. "It'll take time for them to do anything. Orders have to be cut, plans have to be made, squadrons moved, questions answered. Temu," he looked at Jin, "you've been managing the parade permits. Can we jump the queue? Get the Parade Marshal to move us forward to first thing in the morning?"

"We can if you're willing to risk slipping a little cash into someone's pocket," Jin said after a moment, "and I think I know which pocket to fill. But there's a chance he might smell a big enough rat to raise the alarm."

"Assess the odds," Roger said, and the extremely junior IBI officer closed his eyes for fifteen seconds of intense thought.

"Maybe one in five he'll smell something, but no more than one in ten that he'll do anything except ask for more cash if he does," he said finally, and Roger frowned. Then the prince shrugged.

"Not good, but under the circumstances, better than waiting for Brailowsky to be sweated," he decided, and turned to the other IBI agents.

"Okay, Fatted Calf is the codeword, apparently. Tebic, can you insert something covertly on the Marine sites—the ones they read?"

"Easy," Tebic said.

"Codeword Fatted Calf. Insert it so it will read out at oh-seven-hundred. That's seven hours from now. That's the kickoff time."

"What about Helmut?" Catrone asked.

"Nothing we can do about that," Roger said. "He was scheduled to turn up at ten, and that's when he'll turn up. I hope."

Catrone nodded at the prince's qualifier. Unfortunately, they still hadn't gotten any confirmation from Helmut that he'd even received Roger's instructions, much less that he'd be able to comply with them.

"We don't know anything for sure about Helmut at this point," Roger continued, "but we do know we *need* Kjerulf. He and Moonbase are right on top of us. If he can't at least confuse things up there long enough for us to take the Palace, we're all dead, anyway. And if we wait for Helmut, we lose Kjerulf."

He shrugged, and Catrone nodded. Not so much in agreement

as in acceptance. Roger nodded back, then returned his attention to Tebic.

"On the Moonbase net," he said. "Add: Get Brailowsky."

"Got it."

"You sure about that?" Catrone asked. "Security is going to be monitoring."

"Let them," said the prince who'd fought his way halfway around a planet. "We don't leave our people. Ever."

"We need one more thing," Roger said. It was a clear Saturday in October, the first day of the Imperial Festival. A day when the weather computers knew damned well to make sure the weather in Imperial City was *perfect*. Clear, crisp, and beautiful, the sun just below the horizon in Imperial City. The Day. Roger was staring unseeingly at the schematic of the Palace, fingering the skintight black suit that was worn under armor.

"Yeah, backup," Catrone said, looking at the plan one more time. It was going to be tight, especially with the Bad Guys expecting it. And they were all tired. They'd intended to get some sleep before the mission kicked off, but what with last-minute details and moving it up . . .

"No, I was talking about Nimashet," Roger said, and swallowed. "They're going to kill her the moment your team hits."

"Not if they think it's the cops," Catrone pointed out. "They're not going to want a dead body on their hands on top of everything else. I'm more worried about Adoula killing your mother, Roger. And you should be, too."

"We can't count on that," Roger said, ignoring the jab. "Remember what Subianto said about Siminov—a polished mad-dog, remember? And as much as you say your team is the best of the best, they're not *my* best. And my best, Mr. Catrone, is pretty damned good. And I do know one person I *can* count on."

"We don't need another complication," Catrone said.

"You'll like this one," Roger said, and grinned ferally.

Pedi Karuse liked to dress up. She especially liked the variety available on Old Earth, and she'd decided on a nice gold-blonde dress that matched the color of her horns. It had been fitted by a very skilled seamstress—she'd had to be to figure out how to design a dress for a pregnant Mardukan that didn't look decidedly odd. Pedi had matched it off with a pair of sandals that clearly revealed the fact that Mardukans had talons instead of nails on their feet. The talons were painted pink, to match the ones on her fingers. Her horns had also been expertly polished only a few hours before, by a very nice Pinopan woman named Mae Su, who normally did manicures. Humans had all sorts of dyes and colors, but she'd stayed with blonde this time. She was considering dying them red, since one of the humans said she was a natural redhead personality, whatever that meant. But for now, she was a blonde.

There was the problem of Mardukan temperature regulation, of course. In general, they had none. Mardukans were defined by Doc Dobrescu, who'd become the preeminent (if more or less unknown) authority on Mardukan physiology, as "damned near as cold-blooded as a toad." Toads, by and large, do not do well on cold mornings in October in Imperial City. Most of the Mardukans dealt with this by wearing environment suits, but they were so . . . utilitarian.

Pedi dealt with this sartorial dilemma—and the frigid environment—in several ways. First, she'd been studying *dinshon* exercises with Cord since she'd first met him. *Dinshon* was a discipline Cord's people used to control their internal temperature, a form of homeopathic art. Part of it was herbal, but most of it was a mental discipline. It could help in the Mardukan Mountains, where the temperatures often dropped to what humans considered "pleasant" and Mardukans considered "freezing." Given that this particular morning was what *humans* considered "freezing," Mardukans didn't even have a fitting descriptive phrase short of "some sort of icy Hell."

Dinshon exercises could help her manage even this bitter cold, but only for a few minutes. So she'd come up with some additional refinements.

Around her wrists—all four—and ankles, she had tight leather bands, with a matching collar around her neck. The accouterments made her look something like a Krath Servant of the Flame, which wasn't remotely a pleasant association, but the *important* part was that the bands covered heat strips that were hot enough to be on the edge of burning. More strips covered her belly and packed around the developing fetuses on her back.

With those and the *dinshon* exercises, she should be good for a couple of hours. And no icky, unfashionable environment suit.

All in all, she looked to be in the very height of style, if you ignored the slight reflection from the poly-saccharide mucoid coating on her skin, as she stepped daintily out of the airtaxi and pranced up to the front door of the Caepio Neighborhood Association Headquarters.

"My name is Pedi Karuse," she said in her best Imperial, nodding at the two men. One of them was almost as tall as she was. If she'd been wearing heels, she would have towered over even him, but he was big . . . for a human. "I'm here to see Mr. Siminov. I'm aware that he's in."

"The Boss don't talk to any scummy walk-in off the street," the shorter of the two said. "Get lost."

"Tell him I'm an emissary from Mr. Chung," Pedi said, doing her best to smile. It wasn't a natural expression for Mardukans, with their limited facial muscles, and it came out as more of a grimace. "And he'd really like to speak to me. It's important. To him."

The guard spoke into his throat mike and waited, then nodded.

"Somebody's coming," he said. "You wait here."

"Of course," Pedi said, and giggled. "It's not like we're going to wander around back, is it?"

"Not with a scummy," the bigger guard said with a scowl.

"You never know till you try it," Pedi said, and wiggled her hips. It was another nonnatural action, but she'd watched human females enough to get the general idea.

The person who came to the door was wearing a suit. It looked badly tailored, but that was probably the body under it. Pedi had seen pictures of a terrestrial creature called a "gorilla," and this guy looked as if he'd just fallen out of the tree . . . and hit his head on the way down.

"Come on," the gorilla look-alike said, opening the door and stepping aside. "The Boss is just up. He hasn't even had his coffee. He hates to be kept waiting when he hasn't had his coffee."

There was a loud buzz as Pedi stopped into the corridor, and the gorilla scowled ferociously.

"Hold it!" he said, surprise and menace warring in his voice. "You got *weapons*."

"Well, of course I've got weapons," Pedi said, giggling again as three more men stepped into the corridor. "I'm *dressed*, aren't I?"

"You got to hand them over," the gorilla said with the expression of someone who'd never understood jokes, anyway.

"What?" Pedi asked. "All of them?"

"*All* of 'em," the gorilla growled.

"Well, all right," Pedi sighed. "But the Boss is going to be waiting for some time, then."

She reached through the upper slits on her dress and drew out two swords. They were short for a Mardukan, which made them about as long as a cavalry sabre, and similarly curved. She flipped them and offered the hilts to the gorilla.

When he'd taken those, she started pulling out everything else. Two curved daggers, the size of human short swords. A punch-dagger on the inside of either thigh. Two daggers at the neck, and two more secreted in various spots that required a certain amount of reaching. Last, she handed over four sets of brass knuckles, a cosh, and four rolls of Imperial quarter-credits.

"That's it?" the gorilla asked, his arms full.

"Well . . ." She reached up and under her skirt and withdrew a long punch-stiletto. It was slightly sticky. "*Now* that's it. My father would kill me for handing them over so tamely, too."

"Just set it on the pile," the gorilla said. When she had, he offered the armload to one of the other guards and ran a wand over her, carefully. There were still a couple of things he didn't like. She had another roll of credits, for example, and a nail file. It was about two decimeters long, with a wickedly sharp point.

"I've got to have *something* to do my horns with!" she said, aghast, as he confiscated that.

"Not in here," the gorilla said. "Okay, now you can see the Boss."

"I'd better get it all back," she said to the guard with the armful of ironmongery.

"I'm going to love watching you put it all back," the guard replied cheerfully as he carted it into one of the side rooms and dropped it on a convenient table with a semimusical clang.

"So, what's it like, working for Mr. Siminov?" Pedi asked as they walked to the elevator.

"It's a job," the gorilla said.

"Anyplace in an organization like this for a woman?"

"You know how to use any of that stuff?" the guard asked, punching for the third floor.

"Pretty much," Pedi answered truthfully. "Pretty much. Always learning, you know."

"Then, yeah, I guess so," the gorilla said as the doors closed.

"She's in," Bill said.

"One more body to keep from killing." Clovis shook his head. "I hate distractions."

"'Just follow the yellow brick road!'" Davis said in a munchkin voice. "'Just follow the yellow brick road! Follow the, follow the, follow the, follow the, follow the yellow brick road! Just follow—'"

"I've got live ammo," Clovis said, shifting slightly. "Don't tempt me."

"Can it," Tomcat said, reaching up and lowering the visor on his helmet. "Forty-five seconds."

Honal wiggled to try to get some more space in the seat. He failed, and snarled as he began punching buttons.

"Damned dwarfs," he muttered.

"Say again, Red Six," the communicator said.

"Nothing, Captain," Honal replied.

"Outer doors opening," Rosenberg said. "Move to inner door positions."

"Dwarfs," Honal muttered again, making sure he wasn't broadcasting, and picked up on the antigravity. "A race of dwarfs."

But at least they made cool toys to play with, he thought, and pressed the button to transmit.

"Red Six, light," he said, then flipped the lever to lift the landing skids and pulled the stingship out of its bay, turning out to line up with the doors to the warehouse. They were still in the underground facility, but once out of the cover of the bunkers' concealing depth of earth, they were going to light up every beacon in Imperial City.

It was time to *party*.

"Three, four, five," Roger counted as he trotted along the damp passageway. Water rose up to the lip of the catwalk, and the slippery concrete surface was covered with slime.

The passage was an ancient "subway," a means of mass transit that had predated grav-tubes. Imperial City's unending expansion had left it behind long before the Dagger Years, and the Palace— whether by accident or Miranda MacClintock's design—was right over a spot that used to be called "Union Station."

Roger was counting side passages, and stopped at seven.

"Time to get the mission face on," he said, looking at his team of Mardukans and retired Empress' Own. The latter were mostly sounding a bit puffed by the three-kilometer run, but they checked their equipment and armed their bead and plasma cannon with the ease of years of practice.

Roger consulted his toot one last time, then opened what looked like an ancient fuse box. Inside was a not much more modern keypad. Hoping like hell that the electronics had held up in the damp, he drew a deep breath and punched in a long code.

Metal scraped, and the wall began to move away.

Roger stepped into the darkness, followed by twelve Mardukans in battle armor, a half-dozen former Empress' Own, likewise armored, and one slightly bewildered dog-lizard.

"Your first meeting is in twenty-three minutes, with Mr. Van den Vondel," Adoula's administrative assistant said as the prince entered the limousine. "After that—"

"Cancel it," Adoula said. "Duauf, head for the Richen house."

"Yes, sir," the chauffeur said, lifting the limo off the platform and inserting it deftly into traffic.

"But . . . but, Your Highness," the girl said, flushing. "You have a number of appointments, and the Imperial Festival is—"

"I think we'll watch the parade from home this year," he said, looking out the window. Dawn was just breaking.

The Imperial Festival celebrated the overthrow of the Dagger Lords and the establishment of the Imperial Throne, five hundred and ninety years before. The Dagger Lord forces had been "officially" beaten on October fifth; the removal of minor local adherents, most of whom had been dealt with by dropping rocks on their heads, was ignored. For reasons known to only a few specialized historians, Miranda MacClintock had stomped all over any use of the term "October Revolution." She had, however, initiated the Imperial Festival, and it remained a yearly celebration of the continuation of the MacClintock line and the Empire of Man.

The Festival was having a bit of a problem being festive this year. The crowds for the fireworks the night before had been unruly, and a large group of them had pressed into Imperial Park, calling for the Empress. They'd been dispersed, but the police were less than certain that something else, possibly worse, wouldn't happen today.

The Mardukans unloading from trailers, however, were simply a sight to boggle the eye. The beasts they were leading down the cargo ramps were like something from the Jurassic, and the Mardukans were supposedly—and the saddles and bridles bore it out—planning on riding them. The riders were big guys, even for Mardukans, wearing polished mail, of all things, and steel helmets. The police eyed the swords they wore—cultural artifacts, fully in keeping with the Festival and, what was more, tied in place with cords—and hoped they weren't going to be a problem.

The same went for the infantry types. They bore long pikes and antique chemical rifles over their backs. One of the sergeants from the local police went over and checked to make certain they didn't have any propellants on them. Scanners weren't tuned for old-fashioned black powder, and they looked as if they knew which end the bullet came out. They didn't have any ammunition, but he checked out the rifles anyway, just out of personal interest. They were complicated breechloaders, and one of the Mardukans demonstrated the way his broke open and was loaded. The ease with which he handled the rifle spoke to the cop of long practice, which was troubling, since they were supposedly a group of waiters from a local restaurant.

But when they unloaded the last beast, he nearly called for backup. The thing was the size of an elephant, and *clearly* not happy to be here. It was bellowing and pawing the ground, and the rider on its back seemed to be having very little effect on its behavior. It appeared to be searching for something, and it suddenly rumbled to life, padding with ground-shaking tread over to Officer Jorgensen.

Jorgensen blanched as the thing sniffed at his hair. It could take off his head with one bite from its big beak, but it only sniffed, then burbled unhappily. It spun around, far more lightly than anything that large should move, and bellowed. Loudly. It did *not* sound happy.

Finally, one of the big riders in armor gave it a piece of cloth that looked as if it might have been ripped from a combat suit. The beast sniffed at it, and snuffled on it, then settled down, still looking around, but mollified.

It was a good thing the crowds were still so sparse, Jorgensen thought. Maybe that was why the parade marshal had swapped these guys around to the head of the parade from somewhere near the tail? To get them and their critters through and out before the presence and noise of bigger crowds turned the cranky beasts even crankier?

Nah, it couldn't be anything that reasonable, he thought. Not with all the other crap going on this year.

But at least it was going to be an *interesting* Festival.

"Here he comes," Macek said, glancing up from the panel he'd pulled apart and sliding the multitool back into its holster on his maintenance tech's belt.

Macek and Bebi had both been stationed with the Moonbase Marine contingent in an earlier tour, which was why they'd been picked for this job. They didn't like it, but they were professionals, and they'd followed Roger through too many bloodsoaked battlefields to care about one bought-and-paid-for admiral.

"What about the aide?" Bebi asked.

"Leave her," Macek said, glancing at the attractive brunette lieutenant and pushing down his goggles. "Stunner."

Bebi nodded, withdrew the bead pistol from the opened maintenance panel, and turned. Greenberg had just enough time to identify the weapon in his assassin's hand before the stream of hypervelocity beads turned his head into gory spray. The lieutenant beside him opened her mouth as her admiral's brains and blood were deposited across her in a red-and-gray mist, but Macek raised his stunner before she could do anything more.

"Sorry about that, Ma'am," he said, and fired.

Both men dropped their weapons and put their hands on their heads as Marine guards pounded suddenly down the corridor, bead pistols drawn and very angry looks on their faces.

"Hello," Macek said.

"You mother-fu—!"

"Fatted Calf," Bebi interrupted conversationally, lowering his hands. "Mean anything to you?"

"Inner doors opening," Rosenberg said. "Initiate."

The Shadow Wolves swept forward, bursting from their hiding place in the very heart of Imperial City. As soon as he'd cleared the inner doors and had full communications capability, Honal keyed the circuit for all squadrons.

"Arise *civan* brothers!" he cried. "Fell deeds await! Now for wrath, now for ruin, and a red dawn!"

Roger had taught him that. He didn't know where the prince had picked it up—probably some ancient human history—but it was a great line, and deserved to be repeated.

"Oh, shit," Phelps said.

"What now?" Gunnar inquired with a yawn.

"Multiple signatures!" Phelps snapped. "Military grade. Three loca—four . . . *five* locations, two in the Western Ranges! Three of them are *inside* the city!"

"*What?*" Gunnar jerked upright in her station chair, keying up a repeater on her console. "Oh, my God! Not again."

"Where in the hell did they *come* from?" Phelps demanded.

"No idea," Gunnar replied. "But five gets you ten where they're *headed*." She started tapping in a set of commands, only to stop as her connection light blinked out. A fraction of an instant later, there was a rumble from the building's subbasement.

"Primary communications link down," Corporal Ludjevit said tersely. "Secondary down, too. Sergeant, we're cut off."

"Find out why!" Gunnar said. "Shit, can't we communicate at *all*?"

"Only if you want to use a phone," Ludjevit told her.

"Then use the fucking *phone!*"

"Luddite."

"Say what you will about all these human devices," Krindi Fain observed, blowing out the match, "there's a certain thrill to gunpowder."

The main communications node for the Imperial City Police Department had just encountered two kilos of the aforementioned gunpowder. The gunpowder had won.

"Humans taught us that, too," Erkum said, scratching at the base of one horn. "Right?"

"Oh, *be* a spoilsport," Krindi replied. "Time to get out of here."

"Right this way," Tebic said. "Getting in was easy." It had been, thanks to IBI-provided clearance for the "technicians." "Getting out, we have to take the sewers."

Imperial City was the best defended spot in the galaxy. Everyone knew that. What most were unaware of, however, was that it was defended primarily against *space* attack. Defensive emplacements ringed the city, and some were located in its very heart, for that matter. But they were designed to engage incoming hostile weapons at near orbital levels.

There were far fewer defenses near the ground.

The stingships used that chink in the capital's armor for all it was worth. Aircars had been grounded automatically, as soon as the city police network went down. That meant the traffic which would normally have been in their way was parked on the ground, drivers cursing at systems that simply wouldn't work. That didn't mean the air was free, just less cluttered by *moving* crap.

Honal banked the stingship around one of the city's innumerable skyscrapers and triggered a smart round. The round went upwards, then back, and impacted on Prince Jackson's office as Honal dove under a grav-tube and made another bank down 47th Street.

A police car at the intersection of 47th and Troelsen Avenue sent a stream of beads his way, but they bounced off the stingship's ChromSten armor like raindrops. Honal didn't even respond. The police, whether they knew it or not, were effectively neutrals in this battle, and he saved his ammo for more important things.

Such as the defensive emplacements at the edge of Imperial Park.

His sensors peaked as one of those emplacements locked onto him, and he triggered two HARM missiles at the radar. They screamed off the Shadow Wolf's wing racks, and he banked again—hard—to put another skyscraper between him and the defenses. The HARM missiles flew straight and true, riding the radar emissions into the defensive missile pods, and rolling fireballs blew the pods into scrap.

But one of the pods had already fired, and an anti-air missile locked onto his stingship and made the turn down 41st Street, howling after him.

A threat warning blazed in Honal's head-up display as the pursuing missile's homing systems went active. He glanced at the HUD's icons, then dropped the ship down to barely a hundred meters and kicked his afterburners to full thrust. The Shadow Wolf's turbines screamed as the stingship went hurtling down the broad avenue at the heart of the capital city of the Empire of Man, but the missile was lighter, faster, and much more modern. It closed quickly, arrowing in for the kill, and Honal waited carefully. He needed it close behind him, close enough that it couldn't—

He hauled up, riding his afterburners through a climbing loop on a pillar of thunder. His stingship's belly almost scraped the side of yet another skyscraper, and the semismart missile followed its target. It cut the corner to destroy the stingship, slicing across the chord of the Shadow Wolf's flight path . . . and vanished in a sudden blossom of flame as it ran straight into the grav-tube Honal had looped inside of.

"*Yes!*" Honal rolled the ship and headed for Montorsi Avenue and the next target on his list. "I am Honal C'Thon Radas, Heir to the Barony of—!"

"Red Six," Rosenberg said dryly over the com. "You've got another seeker on your tail. Might want to pay a little attention to that."

"Captain Wallenstein," the duty communications tech said in the clipped, calm voice of professional training. "We're receiving reports of a military-grade attack on Imperial City. IBI communications and Imperial City Police are down. The Defense Headquarters is in communication with us, and the defenses around the Palace are reporting attack by stingships."

"Contact Carrier Squadron Fourteen," Gustav Wallenstein said, turning to look at his repeater display as the same information began to come up there. "Have them—"

"Belay that order," a crisp voice said.

Wallenstein's head snapped around, and his face twisted with fury as Captain Kjerulf stepped into the Moonbase Operations Room.

"What?" Wallenstein demanded, coming to his feet. "*What* did you just say?!"

"I said to belay that order," Kjerulf repeated. "Nobody's moving anywhere."

"*Minotaur, Gloria, Lancelot*, and *Holbein* are moving," a sensor tech said, as if to contradict the chief of staff. "Course projections indicate they're moving to interdict the planetary orbitals."

"Fine," Kjerulf replied, never taking his eyes from Wallenstein. "What's happening on Old Earth is no concern of ours."

"The hell it's not!" Wallenstein shouted, and looked at the guards. "Captain Kjerulf is under arrest!"

"By whose orders?" Kjerulf inquired coolly. "I've got you by date of rank."

"By Admiral Greenberg's orders," Wallenstein sneered. "We've had our eye on you, Kjerulf. Sergeant, I *order* you to arrest this traitor!"

"Why does treason never prosper?" Kjerulf asked lightly, as the Marine guard remained at her post. "Because if it prospers, none dare call it treason. Well, Wallenstein, you've prospered for the last few months, but not today. Sergeant?"

"Sir?"

"Fatted Calf."

"Yes, Sir." The Marine drew her sidearm. "Captain Wallenstein, you are under arrest for treason against the Empire. Anything you say, etc. Let's save the rest until we have you in a nice interrogation cell, shall we?"

"Captain," the com tech said as a slumping Wallenstein was led out of the room, "there's a call on his secure line from Prince Jackson. He's asking for Admiral Greenberg."

"Is he?" Kjerulf smiled thinly. "That particular call might be a little difficult to put through, Chief. I suppose *I'd* better take it, instead."

He seated himself in the chair Wallenstein had vacated and keyed the communication circuit with a tap.

"And good morning to you, Prince Jackson," he said cheerfully as the prince's scowling face appeared on his com display. "What can I do for the Imperial Navy Minister this fine morning?"

"Can the crap, Kjerulf," Adoula snarled. The data hack in the display's lower corner indicated that it was coming from an aircar. "Get me Greenberg. And have Carrier Squadron Fourteen moved in close to Old Earth. Prince Roger's back, and he's trying another coup. The Empress' Own needs Navy support."

"Sorry, Prince Jackson," Kjerulf said. "I'm afraid that, as a civilian member of the government, you're not in my chain of command. And Admiral Greenberg is unavailable at the moment."

"Why is he unavailable?" Adoula demanded, suddenly wary.

"I think he just got a fatal dose of bead-poisoning," Kjerulf said calmly. "And before you trot out General Gianetto—who, unlike you Mr. Navy Minister, is theoretically in my direct line of command—you can feel free to tell him that he's up for the next dose."

"I'll have your head for this, Kjerulf!"

"You're going to find that hard going," Kjerulf told him. "And if we lose, you're gonna have to wait in line. Have a nice day, Your Highness."

He hit the key and cut Adoula off.

"Right, listen up, troops," he said, turning his command chair to face the Ops Room staff and tipping it back. "Does anyone really believe that the first coup was Prince Roger?" He looked around at the assembled expressions, and nodded. "Good. Because the fact is that Adoula led the coup, and he's been keeping the Empress hostage ever since, right?"

"Yes, Sir," one of the techs—a master chief with over twenty years worth of hash marks on his cuff—said. "I'm glad somebody's finally willing to say it out loud."

"Well, you can all make your decision right now," Kjerulf said. "Until very recently, Adoula thought Roger was dead. He's not. He's back, and he's got blood in his eye. Forget everything you've seen on the news programs about the Well-Dressed Prince. Bottom line, he's a MacClintock—and a *true* MacClintock, what's more. The Marines are with us. The captains of the *Gloria, Minotaur, Lancelot*, and *Holbein* are with us, and Admiral Helmut is on the way. He's probably going to be a day late and a credit short, because we had to start the ball early. Anyone who is *not* willing to stand his post—and that's probably going to mean missiles on our heads—head for Luna City, pronto. Anyone willing to stay is more than welcome."

He looked around, one eyebrow raised.

"I'm staying," the com tech said, turning back to her board. "Better to die like a spacer than work for that bastard Adoula."

"Amen," another of the petty officers said.

"Very well," Kjerulf said as the rest of them nodded and muttered their assent. "Send a message to all Fleet Marine contingents. The codeword is: Fatted Calf."

* ★ *

"I love Imperial Festival," Siminov said as Despreaux's float chair was wheeled into the room by the gorilla. "Bookies are busy, whores are busy, and drug sales are up fifteen percent."

Despreaux glowered at him over her gag, then turned to look at Pedi.

"So, as you see, Ms. Karuse," Siminov continued, "Ms. Stewart is unharmed."

"Well, Mr. Chung sent me over to negotiate," Pedi said, grimacing again in an attempt to smile and rubbing her horns suggestively with her fingertips. "You see, he just doesn't *have* a million credits sitting around at the moment. He's willing to offer a hundred thousand immediately, as what he calls the 'vig,' and pay the rest in a few days, if all goes well. In two weeks, at the outside."

"Well, I'm sorry you've come all this way for nothing," Siminov said. "The deal is nonnegotiable. Especially since my emissary went missing," he added harshly. "Perhaps *you* should go missing, Ms. Karuse," he suggested. "That would only— What was that?"

A distant explosion rattled the building, and Siminov and his gorilla looked at one another with perplexed expressions.

"Damn," Pedi said mildly, glancing at her watch. "Already?"

The gang lord and his bodyguards were still trying to figure out what they'd just heard when she slapped Despreaux's chair, throwing it across the room, and dropped forward. All four of her hands hit the floor in front of her feet, and she kicked back with both legs.

Gorilla and his brother went flying back against the wall. They slammed into it—hard—and Pedi pushed off with her lower hands and flipped backwards. She flew through the air, landing in front of the two guards even as they began to reach into their jackets for their bead pistols. Her upper elbows slammed back to connect with their faces, and her lower hands reached down and back. Her more powerful false-hands gripped tight, picked them up by their thighs, and threw them off their feet. They landed on the backs of their skulls with bone jarring force.

She somersaulted forward, thanking the gods of the Fire Mountains for a high ceiling, and flipped across the desk. All four hands balanced her on its surface as her feet smashed into Siminov, sending him backward to slam against the wall before he could raise the bead pistol he'd pulled from a drawer. He hit with stunning force, and the pistol went flying into a corner of the office.

Pedi somersaulted again, backwards this time, and ended up back between the guards. She grabbed gorilla's hair, tilted his head back so that his throat was extended and unguarded, and flipped the back of her horns across it with a head twist. The sharpened recurve opened it in a fountain of blood, faster than a knife, and she tossed the bleeding body aside and kicked the other guard on to his stomach. She stamped down with one foot to break his neck, then calmly reached over and locked the door.

"Roger thought you might underestimate a woman," she said gently as she strolled back across the room.

Siminov stared at her, stunned by his abrupt encounter with his office wall and even more by the totally unanticipated carnage about him. He was still staring when she picked him up with one lower hand and threw him across the room. He made the violent acquaintance of yet another wall and oozed down it to the floor in a heap, moaning and clutching an arm which had acquired a sudden unnatural bend just below the elbow.

"He especially thought you might underestimate a pregnant one, even if she was a Mardukan," Pedi went on genially. "And, I'll admit, if you were dealing with one of those beaten-down Krath wusses, you might have been having a different conversation."

She picked Despreaux up, heavy float chair and all, and used the sharpened side of her horns to cut the tape holding the human woman to the chair.

"But you're not dealing with one of them," she continued, walking over to where Siminov was trying to get to his feet. His eyes widened at the sight of the bloodsoaked Mardukan looming over him. "I am Pedi Dorson Acos Lefan Karuse, Daughter of the King of the Mudh Hemh Vale, called the Light of the Vales," she ended softly, leaning down so that her face was barely two centimeters from his, "and *that*, my friend, is a *civan* of a different color, indeed."

* * *

"You seem like a nice guy," Rastar said, lifting the inquisitive sergeant by his body armor in one true-hand as the earbud hidden under his cavalry helmet carried him Honal's message. He flipped his right false-hand in a gesture of apology and ripped the bead pistol off the cop's belt with his free true-hand. "I'm very sorry to do this."

He turned with the sergeant in front of him and pointed the pistol at the other police in the squad which had been watching the Mardukans.

"Please don't," he continued in excellent Imperial as hands jerked reflexively towards holsters. "I'm really quite good with one of these. Just toss them on the ground."

"Like hell," Peterson's second in command said, his hand on his pistol.

"Always the hard way," Rastar sighed, and squeezed his trigger. The bead blew the holstered weapon right out from under the corporal's hand, and the cop bellowed in shock—not unmingled with terror—and jerked his ferociously stinging fingers up to cradle them against his breastplate.

"No!" Rastar snapped as two of the other cops started to draw their own weapons. "He's not injured. But you have a very small area at the top of your armor where you're vulnerable. I can kill every one of you before you draw. Trust me on this."

"And you won't get a chance to, anyway," one of the Diasprans said, lowering a razor-sharp pike until it rested on one of the cop's shoulders. The small group of police looked around . . . into a solid wall of pikes.

Two more Diasprans stepped forward and began collecting weapons. They tossed them to Rastar, who caught the flying pistols neatly as the Diasprans secured the police.

"How many guns do you *need*?" Peterson demanded.

"I generally use four," Rastar said, "but larger caliber. They're on their way." He mounted his *civan* and looked at the Palace, a kilometer away. "This isn't going to be pretty, though."

"Two-gun mojo can't hit the broadside of a barn," one of the cops said angrily.

"Two-gun mojo?" Rastar asked, turning the *civan*.

"Firing two guns at once, you idiot," the sergeant said. "I cannot *believe* this is happening!"

"*Two* guns?"

Rastar turned to look at the police aircar, and his hands flashed. Four expropriated bead pistols materialized in his grip as if by magic and he emptied all four magazines. It sounded as if he were firing on full automatic, but when he was done, there were four holes, none of them much larger than a single bead, punched neatly through the aircar's side panel.

"Two guns are for humans," he said mockingly as he reloaded from one of the officers' expropriated ammunition pouches. Then he turned towards the Palace and drew his sword as the first explosion detonated in the background.

"Charge!"

Jakrit Kiymet keyed her communicator as an explosion rumbled in the distance.

"Gate Three," she said, frowning at the line of trucks setting up for the Festival.

"Military shuttles and stingships detected in Imperial City air space," the command post said tautly. "Be ready for an attack."

"Oh, great," she muttered, looking around. She'd been pulled from guarding Adoula Industries warehouses and made a member of the Empress' Own. That was usually a job for Marines, but she'd known better than to ask questions when she was told to "volunteer." Still, it didn't take a Marine to know that defending the Palace from stingships in her current position—standing in front of the gate, armed with a bead rifle—was going to be rather difficult.

"What am *I* supposed to do about stingships?" she demanded in biting tones.

"You can anticipate a ground assault, as well," the sergeant in the distant, and heavily fortified, command post said sarcastically. "The Palace stingship squadron is powering up, and the response team is getting into armor. All you have to do is stand your post until relieved."

"Great," she repeated, and looked over at Diem Merrill. "Stand our post until relieved."

"Isn't that what we do anyway?" the other guard replied with a chuckle. Then he stopped chuckling and stared. "What the . . . ?"

A line of riders mounted on—dinosaurs?—was thundering across the open ground of the Park. They appeared to be waving swords, and they were followed by a line of infantry with the biggest spears either of the guards had ever seen. And . . .

"What in the hell *is* that thing?" Kiymet shouted.

"I don't know," Merrill replied. "But I think you ought to tell them to go active!"

"Command Post, this is Gate Three!"

"And . . . time."

Bill swung the airvan out of traffic and dropped it like a hawk at the back door of the "neighborhood association."

Dave had opened the side door as they dropped, and Trey put two beads into each of the guards as Clovis rolled out of the vehicle under his line of fire. The entry specialist hit the ground before the airvan was all the way down, and crossed the alley at a run. He put the muzzle of his short, heavy-caliber bead gun against the lock of the door and squeezed the trigger. Metal cladding shrieked and sprayed splinters in a fan pattern as the twelve-millimeter bead punched effortlessly through it. One bead for the deadbolt, one for the handle, and then Dave kicked the door open as he hurtled past Clovis and charged through it.

Three guards spilled out of the room just inside the entryway. Their response time was excellent, but not excellent enough, and Clovis dropped to one knee, taking down all three of them as Dave went past.

"Corridor one, clear," he said.

Roger keyed the last of a long series of boxes and lifted the plasma cannon. He and his team were ninety seconds behind schedule.

"Show time," he muttered as the door slid backwards, and then up.

The power-armored guard outside the Palace command post door whirled in astonishment as the solid wall of the deeply buried corridor abruptly gaped wide. His reflexes, however, were excellent, and he was already lifting his own heavy bead gun when Roger fired. The plasma blast took off the guard's legs and sent him flipping through the air, and Roger's second shot took out the other guard while the first was still in midair.

That left the CP door itself. The portal was heavily armored with ChromSten, but Roger had dealt with that sort of problem before. He keyed the plasma gun to bypass the safety protocols and pointed it at the door, sending out a continuous blast of plasma. The abuse risked overheating the firing chamber and blowing the gun, and probably its user, to hell. It also made the weapon useless for further firing, even if it survived. But this time, the gun held up, and the compressed metal door ended up with a body-sized hole through its center, while the corridor looked like a rainy day on the Amazon—or a normal Mardukan afternoon—as the Palace sprinkler system came to life.

Roger dropped the now useless cannon and let Kaaper take the entry while he followed at the four position. It felt odd to follow someone else in, but Catrone had been right. Roger was the only person they literally could not afford to lose if some idiot decided to play hero. But there were no lunatics inside the command post. None of them were armored, and although they had bead pistols, they knew better than to try them against armor.

"Round 'em up," Roger said, and strode over to the command chair.

"Out," he said over his armor's external speakers.

"Like hell," the mercenary in the chair said.

Roger raised a bead pistol, then shrugged inside his armor.

"I'd really like to kill you," he said, "but it's unnecessary."

He reached out and picked the post commander up by his tunic. The burly mercenary might as well have been weightless, as far as Roger's armor's "muscles" were concerned, and the prince tossed him across the room contemptuously. The erstwhile commander slammed into the bunker's armored wall with a chopped-off scream, then slithered bonelessly down it. Roger didn't even glance at him. He was too busy punching a code on the command chair's console.

"Identification: MacClintock, Roger," he said. "Assuming control."

"Voiceprint does not match authorized ID," the computer responded. "MacClintock, Roger, listed as missing, presumed dead. All codes for MacClintock, Roger, deactivated. Authorization: MacClintock, Alexandra, Empress."

"Okay, you stupid piece of electronics," Roger snarled. "Identification: MacClintock, Miranda, override Alpha-One-Four-Niner-Beta-Uniform-Three-Seven-Uniform-Zulu-Five-Six-Papa-Mike-One-Seven-Victor-Delta-Five. Our sword is yours."

There was a long—all of three or four seconds—pause. Then—

"Override confirmed," the computer chimed.

"Deactivate all automated defenses," Roger said. "Lock out all overrides to my voice. Temporary identity: MacClintock, Roger . . . Heir Primus."

The automatic bead guns on the Palace walls opened up. They took down the dozen *civan* immediately behind Rastar in a single burst and traversed for a second.

Then they stopped.

"Thank you, My Prince," Rastar said under his breath. "Thank you for giving my people their lives, twice over."

Civan ran with long, loping strides, heads down and flipping tails balancing them behind. Rastar lay forward over his own beast's neck, all alone now and far out in front of the others. Only Patty had managed to keep pace with him, and the bead guns which had cut down his troopers had wounded her, as well. The big *flar-ta* was more enraged than hurt, however, and Rastar heard her thunderous bellows overtaking him from behind. He drew all four bead guns as they neared the gate, but the two guards at the gate, after a single burst of fire aimed at nothing in particular, turned around and hit the gate controls. The portal opened, and they darted through it.

The gate had opened just far enough to admit them, and it began closing immediately. Couldn't have that.

"*Eson!*" Rastar bellowed to the mahout on Patty's back.

★ ★ ★

Patty had had a very bad month.

First, the only rider with whom she'd ever had a decent sense of rapport had disappeared, replaced by someone who acted the same way, but just didn't *smell* right. Then she'd been loaded on ships—horrible things—prodded, led around, carted to different planets, unloaded, loaded again, and generally not treated at all as she'd come to expect. And most of the time the food had been simply *awful*. Worst of all, she hadn't even been able to let her frustration out. She hadn't been permitted to kill anything at all since before even the last breeding season.

Now she saw her chance. She'd been pointed at those little targets, and they were getting away. Yes, she'd been pinpricked, but *flar-ta* were heavily armored on the front, lightly armored on the sides, and rather massive. The bleeding wounds lined across her left shoulder, any one of which would have killed a human, weren't really slowing her down. And as the human guards tried to escape from her wrath, and the idiot on her back prodded at the soft spot on her neck, she sped into the unstoppable killing gallop of the *flar-ta* and lowered her head to ram the gate.

The twin leaves of Gate Three were marble sheathing over a solid core of ChromSten. If they'd been shut and locked, no animal in the galaxy could have budged them. But the integral, massive plasteel bolts had been disengaged to let the fleeing guards pass, and the only thing holding them at the moment was the hydraulic system which normally moved them. Those hydraulics were rather heavy—they had to be, to manage the weight of the ChromSten gate panels—but they weren't nearly heavy enough for what was coming at them.

The impact sound was like a flat, hard explosion. Marble sheathing shattered, one of Patty's horns snapped off . . . and the moving gates flew backward.

The mahout on Patty's back went flying through the air, and Patty herself stopped dead in her tracks. She rocked backward heavily as her rear legs collapsed, then sat there, shaking her head muzzily and giving out a low bellow of distress.

Rastar reached the gate, still far ahead of any of the others, and he reined in his *civan* and leapt from the saddle before it had slid to a stop.

The *flar-ta* had prevented the gates from closing, but her huge bulk had the archway *leading* to the gate half-blocked. There was little room to get past her—barely room for two or three *civan* riders at a time—and even as he watched, the hydraulics recovered and the armored panels started to close again. He darted forward, drew one of his daggers, and slammed it into the narrow crack under the left-hand gate. The panel continued to move for a moment, but then the blade caught. The gate rode up it, grinding forward, scoring a deep gouge into the courtyard's pavement. Then there was a crunching sound, and it stopped moving.

He repeated the maneuver with the right-hand gate, then drew his bead pistols as rounds begin to crack around his head. Humans in combat suits, which could stop rounds from bead pistols, were pouring into the courtyard from the Empress' Own's barracks. Most of them looked pretty confused, but the stalled *flar-ta* and the Mardukan were obvious targets.

More beads whipcracked past him, dozens of them. But if he allowed them to push him back, regain control of the gateway even momentarily, they would be able to unjam the gates and close them after all. In which case, the assault on the North Courtyard would fail . . . and Roger and everyone with him would die.

In the final analysis, human politics meant very little to Rastar. What mattered to him were fealty; his sworn word; the bonds of friendship, loyalty, and love; and his debt to the leader who had saved what remained of his people and destroyed the murderers of his city. And so, as the ever-thickening hail of fire shrieked around his ears and pocked and spalled the Palace's wall's marble cladding, he raised all four pistols and opened fire. He wasted none of his rounds on torso or body shots which would have been defeated by his foes' combat suits. Instead, he searched out the lightly armored spot at the throat, the vulnerable chink, no larger than a human's hand.

The combat-suited mercenaries recruited to replace the slaughtered Empress' Own weren't combat troops, whatever uniform they might wear. They were totally unprepared for anything like *this*, and those in the front ranks looked on in disbelief as bead after bead punched home, ripping through the one spot where their protective suits were too thin to stop pistol fire. *No one* could do what that towering scummy was doing.

Humans went down by twos and threes, but there were scores of them. Even as Rastar began dropping them, their companions poured fire back at him, and the calf of his left leg exploded as a rifle bead smashed it. Another bead found his lower right arm. His mail slowed the hypervelocity projectile, but couldn't possibly stop it, and the arm dropped, useless. Another slammed through his breastplate, low on the left side, and he slumped back against the *flar-ta*, three pistols still firing, still killing. More beads cracked and screamed about him, but he kept firing as his *civan* brothers thundered across the final meters of the Park to reach him. He heard their war cries, the sounds of the trumpets sweeping up behind him, as he had upon so many battlefields before, and another bead smashed his left upper arm.

He had only two pistols now, and they were heavy, so heavy. He could barely hold them up and a strange haze blurred his vision. He knew he was finally missing his targets—something which had never happened before—but there were still beads in his magazines, and he sent them howling towards his foes.

Another bead hit him somewhere in the torso, and another hit his lower left arm, but there were fewer humans now, as well, and his *civan* brothers were here at last. He had held long enough, and the riders of Therdan poured past him, forcing their way through the gate, taking brutal casualties to close with the humans where their swords could come into play. Combat suits might stop high velocity projectiles, but not cold steel in the hands of the Riders of the North, and Prince Jackson's mercenaries staggered back in panicky terror as the towering Mardukans and screaming *civan* rampaged through them and reaped a gory harvest.

And the Diasprans were there as well, climbing over the *flar-ta*, charging forward with level pikes while others picked up the weapons of fallen human guards. They were there. They were through the gate.

He set down his last pistol, the pistol that had been light as a feather and now was heavy as a mountain, and lay back against the leg of the *flar-ta* which had carried his Prince, his friend, so far, so far.

And there, on an alien plain, in the gateway of the palace he had held for long enough, long enough, did Rastar Komas Ta'Norton, last Prince of fallen Therdan, die.

"What's happening?"

"Looks like a dogfight in Imperial City, Sir," Admiral Prokorouv's intelligence officer said. "I don't know who against who, yet. And we've got the communications lag, so—"

A priority message icon flashed on the admiral's communicator console, and Prokourov tapped the accept key.

"Prok," General Lawrence Gianetto said from the screen, five minutes after the message had been transmitted from his office on Old Earth. "Roger's back. He's trying to take the Palace. We've got stingships and powered armor on our backs. Get into orbit and prepare to give fire support to the Empress' Own."

"Right." The admiral nodded unhappily. "I don't suppose I could get that order direct from the Empress, could I?"

Larry Gianetto scowled at the wallpaper in the two quadrants of his com display dedicated to CarRon 14 and CarRon 12. That bastard Kjerulf had locked him out of the Moonbase communications system completely, and the general made a firm resolution to have the system architecture thoroughly overhauled after the current situation had been dealt with. And after he'd personally seen Kjerulf dangling in a wire noose.

At the same time, and even through his fury, he knew it wasn't really the system's fault. His office was in Terran Defense HQ, which was the administrative heart of the Imperial military, but Moonbase was the Sol System's operational headquarters. That was why Greenberg had been on Luna instead of with one of his squadrons; because, in effect, Moonbase was the permanently designated, centrally placed flagship of Home Fleet. Every recon platform, system sensor, and dedicated command loop was routed through Moonbase, which was also the toughest, nastiest fortress ever designed by humans. Getting it back from Kjerulf, even after the attack on the Palace was dealt with, was going to be a gold-plated bitch, unless Gianetto had more loyalists in the garrison than he thought he did.

But for the moment, that meant that in a single blow, Kjerulf had blinded Gianetto's eyes. *He* was getting the take from every sensor scattered around the system; Gianetto and his loyal squadron commanders had only what their own sensors could see. And it also meant Gianetto had to individually contact each squadron commander through alternate channels. Channels which he was not at all certain were going to be proof against Moonbase's eavesdropping, despite their encryption software.

He drummed on his desk nervously. It was going to take five minutes for Prokorouv's and Gajelis' acknowledgments of his movement orders to reach him. And the signal-lag to his other squadrons was at least four times that long. He grimaced as he admitted that Greenberg had had a point after all when he'd pointed out that communications delay out to him. He'd brushed it aside at the time—after all, he'd known all about it for his entire professional career, hadn't he? But it turned out that what he'd known intellectually about its implications for naval operations and what he'd really understood weren't necessarily the same thing. He was a Marine. He'd always left the business of coordinating naval movements up to the Navy pukes, just as he'd left it to Greenberg. His own tactical communication loops had always been much shorter, with signal lag measured in no more than several seconds. He hadn't really allowed for order-response cycles this tortoiselike, and he wasn't emotionally suited to sitting here waiting for messages to pass back and forth with such glacial slowness.

He glowered at the other holographic displays floating in his superbly equipped office, and this time his scowl was a snarl. Light-speed transmission rates weren't the only things that could contribute to uncertainty. Finding someone—anyone!—who knew what the hell was going on could do the same thing. And despite all of the sophisticated communications equipment at his disposal, he didn't have a *clue* yet what was happening at the Palace. Except that it was bad.

Very bad.

★ ★ ★

"Plasma rifles!" Trey snarled, rolling back from the corridor as a blast cooked the far wall. "Nobody said they had *plasma guns!*"

"Plasma in the morning makes me happy!" Dave caroled in a high tenor. "Plasma in my eyyyyes can make me cryyyyyy!"

"Bill?" Catrone said.

"They just started popping up," the technician replied over Catrone's helmet com. "Seven sources. They must have had them shielded in the basement someplace. Three closing. Two in Alpha Quadrant, moving right."

"Then they've got the stairs," Catrone said. They'd made it to the second floor, but now they were getting pinned down and surrounded by heavier firepower.

"I'm down to twenty rounds," Clovis said, thumbing in another magazine. "Starting to see what your friend meant about combat troops. Which is the *only* reason I'm not killing Dave right now!"

"Yeah, we need some serious firepower," Catrone agreed tightly. "But—"

"Tomcat," Bill said. "Stand by. Help's on the way."

"Did *you* know they had plasma guns?" Despreaux asked as she triggered another burst at the left side of the doorway.

"No," Pedi said, aiming carefully at a leg which had exposed itself on the right side of the door. She missed . . . again. "Did you?"

"No," Despreaux said tightly.

"It's not like you could have told us, or anything," Pedi said, deciding to just spray and pray. Most of the rounds hit the wall, which they had discovered was armored plasteel. "So, if you did know, you can admit it. Just to me. Between friends."

"I *didn't*," Despreaux said angrily. "Okay?"

"All right, all right," Pedi said pacifically. "How do you reload one of these things, again?"

"Look, just . . . stay down and let me do the shooting," Despreaux said. "Okay?"

"Okay," Pedi replied with a pout. "I wish I had my swords."

"I wish I had my Roger," Despreaux said unhappily.

★ ★ ★

"Look, Erkum," Krindi said gently, eyeing the weapon his friend was carrying. "Let me do the shooting, all right? You just watch my back."

He looked up at the towering noncom one last time, while a small, still voice in the back of his brain asked him if this was *really* a good idea. Erkum was the only person, even among the Mardukans, who could have carried one of the light tank cannon the Alphanes had supplied—*and* its power pack—without benefit of powered armor. The sheer intimidation factor of seeing that coming at them should be enough to convince Siminov's goons to be elsewhere. Of course, there *were* possible downsides to the proposition. . . .

"Watch my back," he repeated firmly.

"Okay, Krindi," Erkum said, then kicked in the front door of the Neighborhood Association and stepped through it, tank cannon held mid-shoulder-high and leveled. The sudden intrusion froze the group of guards at the other end of the corridor for a moment as they turned, and their eyes widened in horror as they caught sight of him. Then he pulled the trigger.

The round came nowhere near the humans. Instead, it blew out the corridor's entire left wall, opening up half a dozen rooms on that side, then impacted on a structural girder and exploded in a ball of plasma.

Pol's finger, unfortunately, had clamped down on the trigger, and two more plasma bolts shrieked from his muzzle, blowing out a thirty-meter hole that engulfed the ceiling and most of the *right* wall, as well. The building was instantly aflame, but at least between them, the follow-up bolts had managed to take out most of the guards who'd been his nominal targets.

"Water *damn it*, Erkum!" Krindi dropped to one knee and expertly double-tapped the only human still standing with his bead rifle. "I told you *not* to fire!"

"Sorry," Erkum said. "I'm just getting used to this thing. I'll do better."

"Don't *try*!" Krindi yelled.

"Ooooo! There's one!" Erkum said as a guard skittered to a halt, looking at them through the flames of several eviscerated rooms on the right side of the mangled passageway. The human raised his weapon, thought better of it, and tried to run.

Erkum aimed carefully, and the round—following more or less the damage path to the *left* of their position—went through the room and hit a stove in the kitchen on the back wall, blowing a hole out the back of the building and into the one on the other side of the service alley, which promptly began spouting flames of its own. If the running guard had even noticed the shot, it wasn't evident.

Erkum tried again . . . and opened up a new hole in the ceiling. Then his finger hit the firing button to no avail as the cannon's internal protocols locked it down long enough to cool to safe operating levels.

"I'm out of bullets," he said wistfully. "How do you reload this thing?"

"Just . . . use it as a club," Krindi said, running to the end of the corridor with Erkum on his heels. Despite this planet's hellish climate, he was pretty sure he wouldn't have needed his environment suit anymore. The building was getting hot as hell.

"What the hell was that?" Clovis shouted.

"I don't know," Trey said, checking right, "but this place is *seriously* on fire!" He fired once, and then again. "Clear."

"I'm melting!" Dave shouted in a cracked falsetto. "I'm mellllting!" he added, taking down two guards who had just rounded a corner at the run.

"Up," Catrone said. "Whatever it was, it's given us an opening. Let's take it."

He tapped Dave on the shoulder and pointed right.

"Daddy, don't touch me there, please?" Dave said in a little kid's voice as he bounded down the corridor and skidded around the corner on his stomach. He cracked out three rounds from the bead gun and then waved.

"Corridor clear," he said in a cold and remote voice.

"Office of the Prime Minister," a harassed woman said, not

looking up at the screen. Sounds of other confused conversations came through from behind her, evidence of a crowded communications center without a clue of what was happening.

Eleanora cursed the fact that the only current number she had was the standard public line.

"I need to speak to the Prime Minister," she said pointedly.

"I'm sorry, Ma'am," the receptionist said. "The Prime Minister is a busy man, and we're all just a little preoccupied here. Perhaps you could call back some other time."

She started to reach for the disconnect key, and Eleanora spoke sharply.

"My name is Eleanora O'Casey," she said. "I am chief of staff to Prince Roger Ramius MacClintock. Does that ring any bells?"

The woman looked up at last, her eyes widening, then shrugged.

"Prove it," she said, her voice as sharp as Eleanora's. "We get all sorts of cranks. And I've seen pictures of Ms. O'Casey. They don't look a thing like *you.*"

"Are you aware that there's a battle going on in the city?"

"Who isn't?"

"Well, if Prime Minister Yang wants to know what's going on, you'd better put me through to him."

"Damn it," Adoula snarled into the com screen. "*Damn* it! It really is that little bastard Roger, isn't it?"

"It looks that way," Gianetto agreed. "We haven't captured anyone who's actually talked to him, but there's a widespread belief that he's back, and more his mother's son than his father's, if you get my drift. And they may be right. If I didn't know exactly where she's been and what her condition is, I'd say this plan had Alexandra's markings all over it. Especially the assassination of Greenberg. If it hadn't been for that . . ." He shrugged. "The point is, I'd say there's an excellent chance that they're going to at least get control of the Palace. And they've already taken out your office downtown. I'd be surprised if they hadn't made arrangements to deal with your other probable locations."

"Very well," Adoula said. "I understand. You know the plan."

He switched off the communicator and sat for just a moment, looking around his home. It was a pleasant place, and it pained him to think of giving it up forever. But sometimes sacrifices had to be made, and he could always build another house.

He stood up and went to the door, looking through it into the office on the far side.

"Yes, sir?" his administrative assistant said, looking up with obvious relief. "There are a number of messages, some of them pretty urgent, and I think—"

"Yes, I'm sure," Adoula said, frowning thoughtfully. "It's all most disturbing—*most* disturbing. I'm going to step out for a moment, get a breath of fresh air and clear my brain. When I come back, we'll handle those messages."

"Yes, sir," the woman said with an even more relieved smile.

She really was rather attractive, the prince reflected. But attractive administrative assistants were a decicred a dozen.

Adoula walked back to his own office, and out the French doors to the patio. From there it was a short walk through the garden to the back lawn, where a shuttle waited.

"Time for us to go visit the *Hannah*, Duauf," he said, nodding to his chauffeur/pilot as he stepped aboard.

The chauffeur nodded, and Jackson settled back into his comfortable seat and pressed a button on the armrest. The sizable charge of cataclysmite under his mansion's foundations detonated in a blinding-white fireball that virtually vaporized the building, all of the incriminating records stored on site, and his entire home office and domestic staff.

A tragedy, he thought, but a necessary one. And not just to tie up loose ends.

Admiral Prokourov spent the ten-minute delay while he waited for Gianetto's response to his own reply dictating messages to his squadron to prepare for movement. He also sent one other message of his own to another address while he waited. When the general's reply came, it was more or less what he'd anticipated.

"You've got the frigging order from *me*." Obviously, Gianetto had also been giving orders on another screen while he waited, but he snapped his head back to glare into the monitor and snarled the reply as soon as he heard the admiral. "And if you don't think you can do the job, I'll find someone who *will*! We don't have time to dick around, Prok!"

"Four hours-plus from our current position," Prokourov said with a shrug. "We'll start moving—"

The admiral paused as his shipboard office's hatch opened, and his eyes widened as he saw the bead pistol in the Marine sergeant's hand.

The Marine walked over and glanced at the monitor, then smiled.

"General Gianetto," he said solicitously. "What a pleasant surprise! You may be unhappy to hear this, but Carrier Squadron Twelve isn't going anywhere, you traitorous son of a bitch!"

He keyed the communicator off long before the general even heard the words, much less had a chance to formulate a reply. Then he turned to Prokourov. He opened his mouth, but the admiral gestured at the gun in his hand.

"Thank you, Sergeant," Prokourov said, "but that won't be necessary."

"Oh?" the sergeant said warily, and glanced over his shoulder. There was one other Marine at the hatch, but the rest of the flagship's Marine detachment was spread out attending to other duties, involving things like bridges and engineering spaces.

"Oh," Prokourov replied. "Do you *know* what's going on, Sergeant?"

"No, Sir," the sergeant replied. He started to lower his bead pistol, then paused, eyeing the admiral warily. "All I know is that we were supposed to do everything we could to prevent Home Fleet from moving to the support of the Palace and, especially, of General Gianetto."

"So what's your chain of command?" the intel officer asked with a frown.

"Dunno, Sir. Word is that the Prince's back, and he's taking a crack at getting his mother out. I know he's a shit, but, damn it, Sirs!"

"Yes, Sergeant," Admiral Prokourov said. "Damn it, indeed. Look, put down the pistol. We're on your side." He looked at the intel officer with a raised eyebrow. "Let me rephrase that. *I'm* on your side. Tuzcu?"

"I'd sure as hell like to know that whatever's going on has a *chance!*" The intel officer grimaced. "Certainly before I *commit*, for God's sake!"

"Sir," the sergeant said, lowering his pistol, "the whole Fleet Marine Force is on the Prince's side. Of the Empress', that is. Sergeant Major Brailowsky—"

"So that's why he was arrested," Prokourov said.

"Yes, Sir." The sergeant shrugged and holstered his pistol. "You serious about helping, Sir?" he added, keeping his hand close to the weapon.

"I'll admit I'm not sure *what* I'm helping, Sergeant," the admiral said carefully. "What we have right now is a total cluster fuck, and I would deeply like to get it unclustered. And as it happens, I've already contacted Moonbase to see what *they* have to say."

"I can guess Greenberg's reaction," the Marine growled sourly.

"That's assuming Greenberg is still in command," Prokourov noted. "Which I tend to doubt, since our movement orders came direct from Admiral Gianetto, not the fleet commander. It's possible, I suppose, that Greenberg was simply too busy doing something else to give us a call, but I expect he's suffered a mischief by now. And if he hasn't, you might as well just shoot me with that pistol, because if their planning—whoever 'they' are—is *that* bad . . ."

"Incoming call from Admiral Prokourov."

"My screen," Kjerulf said, and looked down as Prokourov appeared on his main com display.

"Connect me to Admiral Greenberg, please," the admiral said. "I need confirmation of instructions from the Navy Minister's office."

"This is Kjerulf," he said, looking at Prokorouv's profile. "I'm sorry, Admiral, but Admiral Greenberg is unavailable at this time."

Prokourov had his pickup off, and was speaking to someone

off-screen while he waited out the transmission delay. He didn't appear flustered, but, then, he rarely did, and Kjerulf turned off his own pickup as he noted a blip on his repeater.

"Carrier Squadron Fourteen is moving," Sensor Three reported. "Big phase signature. They're headed out-system at one-point-six-four KPS squared."

"Understood," Kjerulf said, and looked back down at Prokorouv's profile waiting out the interminable communications lag. He'd expected CarRon 14 to move as quickly as it got the word, but Prokorouv's CarRon 12 had become just as critical as he'd feared, because Greenberg *had* changed the lockout codes on the base's offensive missile launchers.

It was another one of those reasonable little safety precautions which was turning around and biting everyone on the ass in the current chaotic situation. Modern missiles had a range at burn-out of well over twelve million kilometers and reached almost ten percent of light-speed, and a few dozen of those fired against Old Earth—whether accidentally or by some lunatic—would pretty much require the human race to find a new place to call home, even without warheads. So it only made sense to ensure that releasing them for use was not a trivial process. Unfortunately, it had allowed Greenberg to make sure no one could fire them against any *other* target—like traitorous ships of the Imperial Navy supporting one Jackson Adoula's usurpation of the Throne—without the command code only he knew. And he was no longer available to provide it.

Fortunately, he hadn't done the same thing to Moonbase's countermissile launchers, so the base could at least still defend itself against bombardment. But it couldn't fire a single shot at anything outside the limited envelope of its energy weapons, which meant the four carriers of Fatted Calf Squadron were on their own. Things were going to be ugly enough against CarRon 14's *six* carriers; if CarRon 12 weighed in with four more of them, it would be bad. If they continued to sit things out, at least it would only be four-against-six, and that was doable . . . maybe.

The other squadrons were still too way the hell far out-system to intervene. So far. And they also had longer signal delays. Wu's

Squadron Six was all the way out on the other side of the sun, over forty light-minutes from Old Earth orbit. Thirteenth, Eleventh, and Fifteenth were all closer, but round-trip signal time even to them was over forty-three minutes. And, of course, their sensors had the same delay. They couldn't know yet what was happening on the planet, which meant none of them had had to commit yet. But they would. For that matter, they could already be moving, and he wouldn't know it until *his* light-speed sensors reported it.

He closed his eyes, thinking hard for a moment, then opened them again and glanced at his senior com tech.

"We still have contact with the civilian com net planet-side?"

"Yes, Sir."

"Then look up a number in Imperial city. Marduk...something. House, maybe. Anyway, it's a restaurant. Tell them where you're calling from and ask for anybody who has a *clue* what's going on! Ask for...ask for Ms. Nejad."

"Aye, aye, Sir," the noncom said in the tone of someone suppressing an urge to giggle hysterically.

"Marduk House," the Mardukan said in very broken Imperial.

"I need to speak to Ms. Nejad," an exasperated Kjerulf said.

"Kjerulf," Prokourov said on the other monitor, responding to Kjerulf's last transmission at last. "I'd sort of like a straight answer on this. Where's Greenberg? And what do you know about the fighting dirt-side?"

"She busy," the Mardukan said. "She no talk."

"Sir," a sensor tech said, "CarRon Twelve's just lit off its phase drive. It's moving in-system at one-six-four gravities."

Kjerulf's jaw clenched. So much for CarRon 12's neutrality. He glared at the Mardukan on his com display.

"Tell her it's Captain Kjerulf," the captain snapped. "She'll talk to me. Tell her!"

"I tell," the Mardukan said. He walked away from the pickup, and Kjerulf wheeled away from his own to the monitor with Prokourov on it.

"Greenberg's *dead*," he barked. He said it more harshly than he'd intended to, but he was a bit stressed. "As for the rest, Admiral, if you want to support Adoula, then you just *bring it on!*"

"Mr. Prime Minister, understand me. Roger is not the boy you knew," Eleanora said firmly, holding onto her temper with both hands. It had taken almost fifteen minutes just to get the pompous, self-serving jackass on the line, and he'd been fending off anything remotely smacking of taking a stand for at least five more minutes. "What's more important, you have to know what's been going on in the Palace."

"Know and suspect are two different things, Ms. O'Casey," Yang replied in his cultured Old Terran accent. "I've met with the Empress several times since the first of Roger's coup attempts—"

"That was *not* Roger," Eleanora said flatly. "I was *with* Roger, and he was on *Marduk*."

"So you say," the Prime Minister said smoothly. "Nonetheless, the evidence—"

"As soon as we take the Palace, all I ask is a team of independent witnesses to her Majesty's condition—"

"Guy named Kjerulf on the other line," one of the Diaspran infantrymen said. They'd moved to an office suite in an old commercial building, well away from the warehouse, which they'd known was going to be blown the moment the stingships lifted. All calls to the warehouse and restaurant were being forwarded, over deceptive links, to the office. "Says he wants to talk to Ms. Nejad. That's you, right?"

"Got it," Eleanora said, holding up her hand. "That's all I'm asking," she continued to the Prime Minister.

"And agreeing to it would be tantamount to supporting you," Yang pointed out. "We'll have to see what we see. I don't care for the Prince, and don't care to have him as my Emperor. And I've seen no data that supports your contention that he was on Marduk."

"Give me a more private contact number, and I'll dump you the raw file. And the presentation. Furthermore, we had Harvard Mansul from the IAS with us for part of it as independent corroboration, and an IBI agent for a third independent data source. There's plenty of documentation. And you *know* the Empress was being conditioned. You'd met her too many times before to think she was acting normally."

"As I said, Ms. O'Casey, it will be quite impossible for me, as Prime Minister, to . . ."

"Roger, this is Marinau, do you read?"

"Yes," Roger panted as he ran down the corridor. Automated systems had gone to local control, and he triggered a round at a plasma cannon that popped out of the wall. The cannon—and at least six cubic meters of Palace wall—disappeared before it could swivel and target his group. Another curtain of water erupted from overhead and splashed around his team's armored feet as they pounded onward.

"We've got the courtyard, but the shuttles are late," Marinau said over the sound of heavy firing.

"I've got the doors open up there," Roger snarled. "What more do you want?"

He paused and went to a knee, covering, as they reached another intersection and the team went past him. Plasma fire erupted from one of the side corridors, and the Mardukan who'd been crossing it was cut in half.

"Can you detach anyone?" Marinau asked. "We're getting slaughtered up here!"

"No," Roger said, his over-controlled voice like ice as he imagined the hell the unarmored Mardukans were facing. He'd fought with them across two continents, bled with them and faced death at their side. But right now, they had their job, and he had his. "Contact Rosenberg. See what the holdup is. Continue the mission. Roger out."

The corridor intersection had been taken, at the cost of another armored Mardukan and one of the Empress' Own. They were down to fifteen bodies, and less than halfway to his mother's quarters.

It was going to be tight.

Catrone held onto the desk as another titanic explosion rocked the building.

"What in the hell *is* that?" he asked as the armored room shuddered and seemed to lean to the right.

"I think I know," Despreaux said tightly. The rescue team had made it to Siminov's office, but they were pinned down again, with guards on both ends of the corridor covering the door.

"Me, too. And I'm going to *kill* Krindi for letting Erkum anywhere *near* a plasma gun," Pedi added, stroking her horns nervously.

"No way out, there, Boss," Clovis said, ducking back as bead rounds caromed off the doorway.

Trey was being tended to behind the desk after taking a bead through the thigh. The nasty hit had pulverized the femoral bone and cut the femoral artery, but Dave had an IV running and a tourniquet in place.

"A tisket, a tasket, a head in a basket," Dave said in a high voice. "No matter how you try, it cannot answer the questions you ask it!"

"Have you got any idea where we are?" Krindi asked over the crackling roar of flames. Fortunately, their environment suits were flame resistant, and they'd lowered their face shields and activated their filters. But the air was getting low on oxygen, and even inside the suits, it was bloody hot.

"Second floor?" Erkum suggested uncertainly. He was training the gun around, delighted to have it operational again as he looked for targets.

"Third floor, third floor," Krindi muttered, looking up. "Oh, hell. Erkum, look, very carefully . . ."

Catrone grabbed Despreaux as the rocking concussion of an explosion slammed into the room. The entire office seemed to lift and then drop, sliding downward and to the side in an uncontrolled fall as the desk toppled towards the right wall. It crunched to a halt at an angle, listing to the right.

Dave threw himself over Trey, trying to get a finger hold on the carpet.

Pedi rolled onto her stomach, gripped a fold of the deep-pile carpet in her teeth, and flung out all four arms. She managed to snag Catrone with her lower right, Dave and Trey with the upper left, and Clovis, as he slid past, with her upper right.

"Okay," she muttered through tightly clenched teeth. "What do we do now?" The floor her lips were pressed against was getting distinctively warm.

"Slip sliding away," Dave sang in a high tenor, holding onto the unconscious Trey with one arm and gripping the carpet between thumb and forefinger with the other hand. "Slip sliding away, hey!"

"I hate classical music," Clovis said as he drew a knife and very slowly lifted it in Dave's direction, then slapped it into the carpet as a temporary piton. "I really, really do . . ."

Honal banked left, almost clipping a building with his tail, then flipped right and down the next road, then left again, and pulled up sharply, rolling the stingship over on its back. As the Empress' Own stingship rounded the corner, he let it have a burst from his forward plasma guns and rolled back upright.

"Way's clear," he said. "Roll the shuttles!"

"Where's Alpha Six?" Flight Ops asked as Honal flew over the remains of the stingship sticking out of a building. Only the tail was visible, with the markings of a squadron commander.

"Alpha Six won't be joining us," Honal said, pulling up and over the building in salute to a fallen comrade. "Roll the shuttles."

Time to go and join Rastar. He was probably having fun at the gate.

"At least the Navy is still out of it," Ops said. "Rolling shuttles now."

"Citizens of the Empire!"

Prince Jackson Adoula's face appeared on every active info-terminal in Imperial city. He looked grave, concerned, yet grimly determined, and uniformed men and women bustled purposefully about behind him as he sat at a command station. Holo displays in the background showed smoke towering over the unmistakable silhouette of the Palace.

"Citizens of the Empire, it is my grave responsibility to confirm the initial reports already circulating through the datanet. The traitor, Roger MacClintock, has indeed returned to launch yet another attempt to seize the Throne. Not content with the murder of his own brother, sister, and nieces and nephews, he is now attempting to seize the Palace and the person of the Empress herself.

"I urge all citizens not to panic. The valiant soldiers of the Empress' Own are fighting courageously to defend her person. We do not yet know how the traitors managed to initially penetrate Palace security, but I fear we have confirmation that at least some Navy elements have been suborned into supporting this treasonous act of violence.

"All government ministers and all members of Parliament are being dispersed to places of safety. This precaution is necessary because it is evident that this time the traitors are targeting more than simply the Palace. My own offices in the Imperial Tower were destroyed by a precision-guided weapon in the opening moments of the attack, and my home—and my staff, many of whom, as you know, have been with me for years—was totally destroyed within minutes of the start of the attack on the Palace."

A spasm of obvious pain twisted his features for a moment, but he regained his composure after a visible struggle and looked squarely into the pickup.

"I swear to you that this monumental treachery, this act of treason against not only the Empire, not simply the Empress, but against Roger MacClintock's own family, shall not succeed or go unpunished. Again, I urge all loyal citizens to remain calm, to stay tuned to their information channels, and to stand ready to obey the instructions of the military and police authorities."

He stared out of the thousands upon thousands of displays throughout Imperial City, his expression resolute, as the image faded to a standard Navy Department wallpaper.

"Calm down, Kjer," Prokourov said ten minutes after Kjerulf's reply, calmly ignoring the outburst. "I'm *probably* on your side. Taking out Greenberg was a necessity, distasteful as it may have been.

But I want to know what *you* know, what you suspect, and what's going on."

"Ms. Nejad, she still busy," the Mardukan said, coming back into the monitor's field of view. "Gonna be staying busy."

"Tell her to get *un*busy!" Kjerulf snapped. "All right, Admiral. All I really ask is that you keep out of this. My main worry is CarRon Fourteen. We've shut down the Moonbase fighter wing, and it turns out that they're pretty unhappy with Gianetto, anyway. I've got a small squadron of loyal ships holding the orbitals. All I need is for the rest of the squadrons to stay out of it."

He turned off his mike and looked over at Tactical.

"Any more movement?"

"No, Sir," Sensor Five said. "But Communications just intercepted a clear-language transmission from Defense HQ to all the outer-system squadrons. General Gianetto's declared a state of insurrection, informed them that Moonbase is in mutinous hands, and ordered a least-time concentration in Old Earth orbit."

"Crap," Kjerulf muttered, and keyed his mike. "Admiral Prokourov, I take that back. We may need active support—"

"Captain Kjerulf," Eleanora O'Casey said, appearing on his other monitor. "What's happening?"

The door looked like oak. And, in fact, it was—a centimeter slab of polished oak over a ChromSten core. Most bank vaults would have been flimsy by comparison, but it was the last major blast door between them and Roger's mother. And, unfortunately, it was on internal control.

Roger lifted the plasma cannon—his third since the assault began—and aimed at the door.

"My treat, Your Highness," one of the Mardukans said, carefully but inexorably pushing Roger away from the door.

The prince nodded and stepped back, automatically checking to be sure the team was watching in every direction. They were down to ten, including himself. But there should be only two more corridors between them and his mother, and if the information in the command center's computers was correct, there were no automated defenses and no armored guards still in front of them. They were there. If only she was alive.

The Mardukan carefully keyed in the sequence to override the safety protocols, then triggered a stream of plasma from the tank cannon at the door. But that door had been intended to protect the Empress of Man. It was extraordinarily thick, and it resisted the blasts. It bulged inward, but it held stubbornly through seven consecutive shots.

On the eighth shot, the overheated firing chamber detonated.

Roger felt himself lifted up by a giant and slammed through the merely mortal walls of the approach corridor. He came to a halt two rooms away, in one he recognized in confusion as a servant's chambers.

"I don't sleep with the help," he said muzzily, picking himself out of the rumpled tapestries and ancient statuary.

"Your Highness?" someone said.

He tried to put a finger into one of his ears, both of which were ringing badly, but his armor's helmet stopped him. So he shook his head, instead.

"I *don't* sleep with the help," he repeated, and then he realized the room was on fire. The overworked sprinkler system was sending a fresh downpour over him, but plasma flash had a tendency to start *really* hot fires. These continued to blaze away, adding billowing waves of steam to the hellish environment.

"What am I doing here?" he asked, looking around and backing away from the flames. "Why is the room on fire?"

"Your Highness!" the voice said again, then someone took his elbow.

"Dogzard," Roger said suddenly, and darted back into the flames. "*Dogzard!*" He shouted, using his armor's external amplifiers.

The scorched dog-lizard came creeping out from under a mattress, a couple of rooms away, wearing a sheepish expression. She'd been following well behind the group. From her relatively minor damage, she'd probably run and hidden at the explosion.

"How many?" Roger said, shaking his head again and looking at the person who'd called him. It was Master Sergeant Penalosa, Raoux's second in command. "Where's Raoux?"

"Down," Penalosa said. "Hurt bad. We've got five left, Sir."

"Plus me and you?" Roger asked, pulling up a casualty list. "No, *including* me and you," he answered himself.

"Yes, Sir," the master sergeant replied tightly.

"Okay," Roger said, and then swore as a blast of plasma came *out* of the small hole his Mardukan had managed to blow in the door. So much for the CP's information that there were no guards beyond. "What are we on? *Plan Z?*" he said. "No, no, calm, right? Got to be calm."

"Yes, Sir," the sergeant said.

"Plan Z it is, then," Roger said. "Follow me."

"Sir, we just lost the feed from the system recon net," Senior Captain Marjorie Erhardt, CO HMS *Carlyle* said.

"We have, have we?" Admiral Henry Niedermayer frowned thoughtfully and checked the time display. "Any explanation of why, Captain?"

"No, Sir. The feed just went down."

"Um. Obviously something is happening in-system, isn't it?" Niedermayer mused.

"Yes, Sir. And it's not supposed to be," Erhardt agreed grimly.

"No, but it was allowed for," Niedermayer pointed out in return, with maddening imperturbability.

"Should we head in-system, Sir?" Erhardt pressed.

"No, we should not," the admiral said with just a hint of frost. "You know our orders as well as I do, Captain. We have no idea exactly what's going on on Old Earth right this minute, and any precipitous action on our part could simply make things enormously worse. No, we'll stay right here. But go ahead and bring the task group to readiness for movement—*low-powered* movement. Given the timing, we may need to adjust our position slightly, and I want strict emissions control if we do."

Larry Giancetto's face was grim as the icons and sidebars in his displays changed. Whatever his political loyalties, he was a professional Marine officer, one of the best around when it came to his own specialty, and keeping track of the apparently overwhelming information flow was second nature to him.

Which meant he could see exactly how bad things looked.

The attack on the Palace had been only minutes old when he ordered additional Marines into the capital to suppress it. Now, over half an hour later, not a single unit had moved. Not one. Some were simply sitting in place, either refusing to acknowledge movement orders or stalling for time by requesting endless "clarification." But others were stopped where they were because their personnel were too busy shooting at each other to obey. And most worrying of all, even in the units which had tried to obey his orders, the personnel loyal to him seemed to be badly outnumbered.

If the defenders already in the Palace couldn't stop these lunatics, then it was highly unlikely that anyone else on the planet would be willing to help him retake it afterward.

He looked at a side monitor, showing a fresh broadcast from Prince Jackson, and bared his teeth in a cynical, mirthless smile. The viewing public had no way of knowing that the bustling command post behind Adoula did not exist outside one of the most sophisticated VR software packages in existence. By now, Adoula was actually aboard the *Hannah P. McAllister*, an apparently down-at-the-heels tramp freighter in orbit around the planet. His public statements were recorded aboard the ship, beamed down to a secure ground station, plugged into the VR software, and then rebroadcast through the public information channels with real-time images from the Palace inserted. The illusion that Adoula was actually still in the city—or, at least, near at hand—was seamless and perfect.

And if things continued to to go to hell in a handbasket the way they were, it was about time Gianetto started considering implementing his own bug-out strategy.

"Christ, the cavalry at last," Marinau said as the first shuttle landed in the courtyard. He and what was left of his teams and the Mardukans had held the North Courtyard over twice as long as the ops plan had specified. They'd paid cash for it, too. But at least the bogus Empress' Own's armored reaction squad had gone in pursuit of Roger, thank God! And thank God the so-called troops Adoula had found as replacements weren't real combat troops. If they had been, there would have been *no one* left to greet the incoming shuttle.

It came under heavy fire, but from small arms and armor-portable cannon only. The heavy antiair/antispace emplacements had all been knocked out, and the shuttle was giving as good as it got. It laid down a hail of heavy plasma blasts on the positions which had the attackers pinned down, and as big—*huge*—armored Mardukans piled out of the hatches, more fire came from the sky, dropping across the positions of the mercenaries still holding the Palace.

"No," Kuddusi said, raising up to fire a stream of beads at the defensive positions. "The cavalry went in *first*."

"Let's move," Marinau said. "Punch left."

"Where are we going?" Penalosa asked as Roger led them down an apparently deserted corridor.

"To here." Roger stopped by an ancient picture of a group of men chasing foxes. He lifted an ornamental candlestick out of a sconce, and a door opened in the wall.

"This is a shortcut to Mother's room," he said.

"Then why in hell didn't we use it *before*?" Penalosa demanded.

"Because," Roger thumbed a sensor ball and tossed it into the passageway, "I'm pretty sure Adoula knows about it."

"Holy . . ." Penalosa muttered, blanching behind her armored visor as the sensor ball's findings were relayed to her HUD. There were more than a dozen defense-points in the short corridor. Even as she watched, one of them destroyed the sensor ball.

"Yep," Roger agreed, "and they're on Adoula's IFF." He keyed his communicator. "Jin, you getting anywhere?"

"Negative, Your Highness," Jin admitted. "I've been trying to crack Adoula's defensive net, but it's heavily encrypted. He's using a two-thousand-bit—"

"You know I don't go for the technical gobbledygook," Roger said. "A simple 'no' would suffice. You see what we see?"

"Yes, Sir," Jin said, looking at the relayed readouts.

"Suggestions?"

"Find another route?"

"There aren't any," Roger muttered, and switched frequencies. "God damn it." He hefted the replacement plasma cannon he'd picked up and tossed it to Penalosa. "If this doesn't work, get to Mother. Somehow," he added, and drew both pistols.

"*No!*" Penalosa dropped the cannon and grabbed vainly for the prince as he leapt into the corridor.

"That's it," Gianetto said. "I won't say it's all over but the shouting, but there are insertion teams deep into the Palace, they've secured an LZ inside the inner parameter, and they're lifting in additional troops. CarRon 14's moving, and so are Prokourov and La Paz. Unfortunately, I don't have a single goddamned idea what Prokourov is going to do when he gets here, and he's going to get here well before CarRon 13. The ground units here planet-side are either refusing to move at all, or else fighting internally about whose orders to take, and the commanders loyal to *us* don't seem to be winning. That means Gajelis is the closest available relief—with the head start he got, he's going to be here about twenty minutes before CarRon 12, even if Prokorouv's feeling loyal to us. And it's still going to take Gajelis another three hours-plus to get here. We may still be able to turn this thing around—or at least decapitate the opposition—if we can get control of the orbitals, but in the meantime, we're royally screwed dirtside. It's time to leave, Your Highness."

"I cannot *believe* that little shit could put something like this together!" Adoula snarled.

"It doesn't matter whether it was him, or someone else. Or even whether or not he's really still alive," Gianetto pointed out. "What matters is that the shit has well and truly hit the fan. I'll be issuing the official dispersal order in ten minutes."

"Understood," Adoula replied, and looked at his loyal chauffeur once again. "Duauf, go inform the captain that we'll be leaving shortly."

"At once, Your Highness," the chauffeur murmured, and Adoula nodded. It was so good to have at least *one* competent subordinate, he reflected. Then he pursed his lips in irritation as another thought occurred to him. One more thing to take care of, he thought irritatedly. Loose ends everywhere.

"We're holding the inner perimeter, Your Highness," "Major" Khalid said. "But we've lost the stingship squadron, and they're shuttling in reinforcements. They've got us cut off from the main Palace, and so far, they've thrown back every try to break out we've made. We need support, Sir. Soon."

"It looks bad," Adoula said, his face serious. "But the Navy units I control are on the way. They've got enough firepower to get you out of there. But given how complicated and fluid the situation is, I'm afraid these rebels may get their hands on the Empress and the replicator, and we can't have that. Kill the Empress at once. Dump the replicator."

"Yes, Sir," Khalid said, but he also frowned. "What about us?"

"As soon as the Navy gets there, they'll land shuttles to pull you out," Adoula said. "I can't afford to lose you, Khalid. We've got too much more work to do. Kill the Empress now, then all you have to do is hold out for—" The prince ostentatiously considered his toot. "Hold for another forty minutes," he said. "Can you do that?"

"Yes, Your Highness," the "major" said, squaring his shoulders. "I'm glad you haven't forgotten us."

"Of course not," Adoula said, and cut the circuit. He looked into the dead display for an instant. "Most definitely not," he said softly.

The defensive systems in the secret passage, light and heavy plasma and bead cannon, were momentarily confused. The figure was giving off the IFF of the local defenders, as last updated. In automatic mode, that didn't matter—not here, in *this* corridor. But the intruder had paused outside the systems' area of immediate responsibility, where matters were a little ambiguous. Did its mere presence in the corridor's entrance represent an unauthorized incursion? If not, its IFF meant it was not a legitimate target, but if it *was* an incursion . . .

The systems' computers were still trying to decide when beads started cracking down-range, destroying the first two emplacements. At which point, they made up their collective electronic minds and opened fire.

Roger considered it just another test.

Over the last year the Playboy Prince who'd set out so unwillingly for Leviathan had learned that life put obstacles in one's path, and one either went around them, if possible . . . or *through* them, if necessary. This fell under the category of "necessary," and there weren't enough bodies left to just throw them in and soak up the losses to take out the emplacements. More than that, he'd proven himself to be better at fast, close combat than any of the rest of the team. Ergo, this was one of those times when he *had* to put himself in jeopardy.

He'd killed three of the defensive weapons before they were all up and tracking on him. He killed a fourth, concentrating on the eight heavy emplacements, before the first stream of beads hit him. They knocked him backward, but couldn't penetrate the ChromSten armor. He got that bead cannon, and then a plasma gun gushed at his feet. He'd seen it tracking, and jumped, getting it while he was in the air. But when he came down, he stumbled, trying to avoid another stream of plasma, and fell to the side. He got the fifth emplacement before the first Raider could make it through the door.

Funny. He'd thought you were supposed to get cold at the time like this. But he was hot. Terribly hot.

"This really sucks," Despreaux said, coughing on smoke.

The wall, floor—whatever—of Siminov's office was too hot to touch now. So they'd climbed onto the edge of the desk, dragging Trey and the semiconscious Siminov with them. Some of the smoke came from the lower edge of the desk, which was beginning to smolder. When that caught fire, as it was bound to eventually, they were all going to be in rather desperate straits.

Despreaux happened to be the one looking at the door when the hand appeared.

It fumbled for a grip, and she raised her pistol before she

noticed that the hand was both very large and covered in an environment suit glove.

"Hold fire!" she barked as Krindi chinned himself up over the edge of the door frame.

"So, *there* you are," the Diaspran said, showing his teeth in a Mardukan-style pseudosmile behind his mask. "We've been looking all *over* for you."

"What took you so long?" Pedi asked angrily.

"I figured there was time," Krindi said, dragging himself fully through the doorway. "You were born to hang."

"Roger, just lie still!" Penalosa was saying.

"Hell with that." Roger got to his feet—or tried to. His lower left leg felt strangely numb, but he got got as far as his right knee, then pushed himself upright.

And promptly toppled over sideways again.

"Oh," he said, looking at the left leg which had refused to support him. Not surprisingly, perhaps, since it was pretty much gone just below the knee. "Now, that's a hell of a thing. Good nannies, though. I don't feel a thing."

"Just stay down!" Penalosa said sharply.

"No." Roger got up again, more cautiously. He looked around and picked up a bead cannon from a suit of armor with a large, smoking hole through its breastplate. "Let's go."

"God *damn it*, Your Highness!"

"Just a thing, Master Sergeant," Roger said. "Just a thing. Can I have an arm, though?"

"We've got the corridor suppressed," Penalosa said as the two damaged suits of armor limped slowly and painfully down the narrow passageway.

"I noticed," Roger said, when they came to the end. It was another ChromSten door.

"But there's this," Penalosa said. "And not only are we about out of plasma cannon, but these are awful tight quarters for trying your little trick. Not to mention that . . . nobody's too happy about trying it again, anyway."

"Nobody" being Penalosa herself and one of the Mardukans, since the other two suits had bought it destroying the last two installations after Roger had gotten the first six.

"Yes, understandable," Roger said. "But unlike the last door, Master Sergeant, this one is *original* installation." He bared his teeth behind his visor. "Open Sesame," he said.

And the door opened upwards.

"Attention all vessels in planetary orbit! This is Terran Defense HQ! Hostile naval units are approaching Old Earth, ETA approximately eleven-thirty-seven hours Capital Time. All civilian traffic is immediately directed and ordered to clear planetary orbit at once. Repeat, all civilian traffic is immediately directed and ordered to clear planetary orbit at once. Be advised that heavy fire is to be anticipated and that any vessel in a position to pose a threat to Imperial City will be deemed hostile and treated accordingly. Repeat, all civilian traffic is immediately directed and ordered to clear planetary orbit at once, by order of Terran Defense HQ!"

"Well, about damned time," Captain Kjerulf muttered as the grim-faced rear admiral on the display screen spoke. The recorded message began to replay, and he turned back to the thousand and one details demanding his attention with a sense of profound relief. He'd been more than a little concerned about the collateral damage which would almost inevitably occur when a full-scale naval engagement walked across the orbital patterns of the teeming commerce which always surrounded Old Earth. At least he didn't have to worry about *that* anymore.

"And it's about time," Prince Jackson Adoula muttered as *Hannah P. McAllister* made haste to obey the nondiscretionary order. There were, quite literally, hundreds of vessels in Old Earth orbit; now they scattered, like shoals of mackerel before the slashing attack of a pod of porpoises. Adoula's vessel was only one more insignificant blip amid the confusion of that sudden exodus, with absolutely nothing to distinguish her from any of the others.

Aside from the fact—not yet especially evident—that *her*

course would eventually carry her to *meet* CarRon 14 well short of the planet.

Getting to Siminov's office door was the biggest trick, since the floor was too hot to cross without third-degree burns. Fortunately, Krindi could walk on it in his environment suit, and he could lower them to Erkum, who was standing in a more or less fire-free spot on the ground floor. The gigantic noncom's height, coupled with the fact that the office had dropped most of the way through the second floor, made it a relatively easy stretch from that point.

Krindi got all of them out and down just before the last supports gave way and the armored room collapsed crashingly into the building's basement.

"God, I'm glad to be out of *there*," Despreaux said. "On the other hand, I really don't want to burn to death, either."

"Not a problem," Krindi said. "Erkum, gimme."

He hefted his towering sidekick's weapon only with extreme difficulty, but this wasn't something to be trusted to Erkum's enthusiastic notions of marksmanship. Despite its weight, he managed to get it pointed at the side of the building which was least enveloped in flames. Then he triggered a single round.

The plasma bolt took out the walls on either side and blew a nine-meter hole in the back wall. It would have set the building behind Siminov's on fire, if that hadn't already been taken care of some time ago.

"Door," Krindi observed as he pulled the power pack out of the plasma gun and tossed the weapon down into the flaming basement. "Now let's get the polluted water out of here."

They scrambled through the plasma-carved passage and into the alleyway between the blazing buildings, then turned and headed for the alley's mouth. Erkum carried Trey and the well-trussed Siminov, and all of them stayed low, trying to avoid flaming debris until they stumbled out into the fresh morning air at last.

And found themselves looking into the gun muzzles of at least a dozen Imperial City Police.

"I don't know who in the hell you people are," the ICPD sergeant in charge of the squad said, covering them from behind his aircar. "And I don't know what in the hell you've been doing," he continued, looking at the team's body armor and the Mardukans in their scorched environment suits, "but you're all under arrest!"

Despreaux started to say something, then stopped and looked up at the armored assault shuttle sliding quietly down the sky. A large crowd had gathered to watch the buildings burn, since the municipal firemen had wisely decided to *let* them burn as long as plasma fire was being thrown around, and the shuttle had to maneuver a bit to find a spot to land. Despreaux saw a very familiar face at the controls as it settled on its countergravity, and Doc Dobrescu tossed her a salute as the shuttle's plasma cannon trained around to cover the police holding them at gunpoint.

The rear hatch opened, and four Mardukans in battle armor unloaded. They took up a combat circle, two of them also sort of pointing their bead and plasma cannon nonchalantly in the general direction of the police.

And then a final figure stepped out of the shuttle. A slight figure, in a blue dress fetchingly topped off by an IBI SWAT jacket.

Buseh Subianto slid easily between the Mardukans and walked over to the ICPD sergeant . . . who was now ostentatiously pointing his own weapon skyward and trying to decide if placing it on the ground would be an even better bet.

"Good job, Sergeant," Subianto said, patting him on the shoulder. "Thank you for your assistance in this little operation. We'll just be picking up our team and going."

"IBI?" the sergeant's question came out more than half-strangled. "*IBI?*" he repeated in a shout, when he'd gotten his breath.

"Yes," Subianto said lightly.

"You could have *told* us!"

"Sergeant, Sergeant, Sergeant . . ." the Deputy Assistant to the Assistant Deputy Director, Counterintelligence Division, of the Imperial Bureau of Investigation said. "You *know* ImpCity data security isn't that good. Don't you?"

"But . . ." The cop turned and looked at the group by the flaming building. "*You burned the building down!* Hell, you set the entire *block* on fire!"

"Mistakes happen." Subianto shrugged.

"*Mistakes?!*" The sergeant threw his hands up. "They were using a *tank* cannon! A *plasma* tank cannon!"

Erkum ostentatiously interlaced his fingers in front of him and began twiddling all four thumbs. He also tried his best to whistle. It was not something Mardukan lips were designed for.

The sergeant looked at the Mardukans and the very old-fashioned combat shuttle.

"What in the hell *is* this?"

"Sergeant," Subianto said politely, "have you ever heard the term 'above your pay grade'?" The sergeant looked ready to implode on the spot, and she patted his shoulder again. "Look," she said soothingly, "I'm from the IBI. I'm here to help you."

Roger limped down the paneled corridor, using the bead cannon as a crutch and followed by Penalosa and the single remaining Mardukan. Dogzard, still in a deep funk, trailed along dead last. From time to time, Roger stopped and either broke down a door or had the Mardukan do it for him.

A guard in a standard combat suit stepped into the corridor and lifted a bead gun, firing a stream of projectiles that bounced screamingly off of Roger's armor.

"Oh, get *real*," the prince snarled, shifting to external speakers as he grabbed the guard by the collar and lifted him off the ground. "Where's my mother?!"

The strangling guard dropped his weapon and kicked futilely at Roger's armor, gurgling and making motions that he didn't know. Roger snarled again, tossed him aside, and limped on down the corridor as fast as he could.

"Split up!" he said. "Find my mother."

"Your Highness!" Penalosa protested. "We can't leave you unpro—"

"Find her!"

★ ★ ★

"Pity to waste you," Khalid said, flipping a knife in his hand as he approached the half-naked Empress on the huge bed. "On the other hand, you don't get many chances at Imperial poontang," he added, unsealing his trousers. "I suppose I might as well take one more. Don't worry—I'll be quick."

"Get it over with," Alexandra said angrily, pulling at the manacle on her left wrist. "But if you kill me, you'll be hounded throughout the galaxy!"

"Not with Prince Jackson protecting me," Khalid laughed.

He stepped forward, but before he reached the bed, the door burst suddenly open and an armored figure, missing part of one leg, leaned in through the broken panel.

"Mother?!" it shouted, and somehow the bead pistol holstered at its side had teleported into its right hand. It was the fastest draw Khalid had ever seen, and the mercenary's belly muscles clenched as the pistol's muzzle aligned squarely on the bridge of his nose. He started to open his mouth, and—

The bead pistol whined an "empty magazine" signal.

"*Son of a BITCH!*" Roger shouted, and threw the empty pistol at the man standing over his lingerie-clad mother with a knife. The other man dodged, and the pistol flew by his head and smashed into the wall as Roger stomped forward as quickly as he could on his improvised crutch.

Khalid made an instant evaluation of the relative value of obeying Adoula or saving his own life. Evaluation completed, he dropped the knife and pulled out a one-shot.

The contact-range anti-armor device was about the size of a large, prespace flashlight and operated on the principle of an ancient "squash head" antitank round. It couldn't penetrate battle armor's ChromSten, so it attacked the less impenetrable plasteel liner which supported the ChromSten matrix by transmitting the shockwave of a contact detonated hundred-gram charge of plasticized cataclysmite *through* the ChromSten to blast a "scab" of the liner right through the body of who ever happened to be wearing the armor. Its user had to come literally within arm's reach of his target, but if he could survive to get that close, the device was perfectly capable of killing someone through any battle armor ever made.

Roger had faced one-shots twice before. One, in the hand of a Krath raider, had badly injured—indeed, almost killed—him, despite armor almost identical to that which he was currently wearing. The second, in the much more skilled hands of a Saint commando, had killed his mentor, his father-in-truth, Armand Pahner. And with one leg, and out of ammunition, there wasn't a damned thing he could do but take the shot and hope like hell he managed to survive again.

Dogzard was still badly depressed, but she was beginning to feel more cheerful. Her God had gone missing, replaced by a stranger, but there was something about the rooms around her now—a smell, an almost psychic sense—which told her that her God might come back. These rooms didn't smell the *same* as her God, but the scents which filled them were elusively similar. There were hints all about her that whispered of her God, and she snuffled at the wood paneling and the furniture as they passed it. She'd never been in this place before, but somehow, incredible as it seemed, she might actually be coming home.

In the meantime, she continued to follow the stranger who said he was God. He hadn't seemed very much like God up until the past little bit. Just recently, however, he'd started acting much more as God had always acted before. The smells of cooking flesh and burning buildings were those she associated with the passage of her God, and she'd stopped and sniffed a couple of corpses along the way. She'd been shouted at, as usual, and she'd obeyed the might-be-God voice, albeit reluctantly. It didn't seem right to let all that perfectly good meat and sweet, sweet blood go to waste, but it was a dog-lizard's life, no question.

Now she was excited. She smelled, not her God, but someone who smelled much the same. Someone who might know her God, and if she was a good dog-lizard, might bring her back to her God.

She pushed up beside the one-legged stranger in the doorway. The smell was coming from the bed in the room beyond. It wasn't her God, but it was close, and the female on the bed smelled of anger, just like her God often did. Yet there was fear, too, and Dogzard knew the fear was directed at the man beside the bed. The man holding a Bad Thing.

Suddenly, Dogzard had more important things to worry about than impostors who claimed they were God.

Roger bounced off the wall as six hundred kilos of raging Dogzard brushed him aside with a blood-chilling snarl and charged into the room. He managed to catch himself without quite falling, and his head whipped around just in time to see the results.

"Holy Allah!" Khalid gasped as a red-and-black *thing* knocked the armored man out of its way and charged. He tried to hit it with the one-shot, but it was too close, moving too fast. His arm swung, stabbing the weapon at the creature's side, but a charging shoulder hit his forearm, sending the weapon flying out of his grasp. And then there was no time, no time at all.

Roger pushed himself off the wall as Dogzard lifted her stained muzzle. Her powerful jaws had literally decapitated the other man, and the dog-lizard gave Roger a half-shamed glance, then grabbed the body and pulled it behind the couch. There was a crunch, and a ripping sound.

Roger limped toward the bed, hobbling on his bead cannon and pulling off his helmet.

"Mother," he said, eyes blurred with tears. "Mother?"

Alexandra stared up at him, and his heart twisted as the combat fugue release him and the Empress' condition truly registered.

His memories of his mother included all too few personal, informal moments. For him, she had always been a distant, almost god-like figure. An authoritarian deity whose approval he hungered for above all things . . . and had known he would never win. Cool, reserved, always immaculate and in command of herself. That was how he remembered his mother.

But this woman was none of those things, and raw, red-fanged fury rose suddenly within him as he took in the scanty lingerie, the chains permanently affixed to her bed, and the bruises—the many, many bruises and welts—her clothing would have hidden . . . if she'd had any clothing on. He remembered what Catrone had said about the day they told him how Adoula had controlled her. Adoula . . . and his father.

He looked into her eyes, and what he saw there shocked him almost more than her physical condition. There was anger in them, fury and defiance. But there was more than that. There was fear. And there was confusion. It was as if her stare was flickering in and out of focus. One breath he saw the furious anger, the sense of who she was and her hatred for the ones who had done this to her. And in the next breath, she was simply . . . gone. Someone else looked out of those same eyes at him. Someone quivering with terror. Someone uncertain of who she was, or why she was there. They wavered back and forth, those two people, and somewhere deep inside, behind the flickering, blurred interface, she *knew*. Knew that she was broken, helpless, reduced from the distant figure, the avatar of strength and authority who had always been the mother he knew now he had helplessly adored even as he tried futilely to somehow win her love in return.

"Oh, Mother," he whispered, his expression as clenched as his heart, and reached the bed towards her. "Oh, Mother."

"W-who are you?" the Empress demanded in a harsh, wavering whisper, and his jaw tightened. Of course. She couldn't possibly recognize him behind the disguising body-mod of Augustus Chung.

"It's me, Mother," he said. "It's Roger."

"Who?" She blinked at him, as if she were fighting to focus on his face, not to find some sort of internal focus in the swirling chaos of her own mind.

"Roger, Mother," he said softly, reaching out to touch her shoulder at last. "I know I look different, but I'm Roger."

"Roger?" She blinked again. For an instant, a fleeting moment, her eyes were clear. But then the focus vanished, replaced by confusion and a sudden, dark whirlwind of fear.

"Roger!" she repeated. "*Roger?!*"

She twisted frantically, fighting her chains with all of their strength.

"No! *No!* Stay away!"

"*Mother!*" Roger flinched back physically from the revulsion and terror in his mother's face.

"I saw you!" she shouted at him. "I *saw* you kill John! And you killed my grandchildren! Butcher! *Murderer!*"

"Mother, it wasn't me!" he protested. "You *know* it wasn't me! I wasn't even *here*, Mother!"

"Yes—yes you were! You look different now, but I saw you then!"

Roger reached out to her again, only to stop, shocked, as she screamed and twisted away from him. Dogzard rose up, looking over the back of the couch, and growled at him.

"Mother," he said to the screaming woman. "Mother! *Please!*"

She didn't even hear him. He could tell that. But then, abruptly, the scream was cut short, and Alexandra froze. Her expression changed abruptly, and she looked at her son, cocked her head, and smiled. It was a terrible smile. A dark-eyed smile which mingled desire, invitation, and stark fear in equal measure.

"Are you here for Lazar? Did he send you?" she asked in a quieter voice, and arched her spine suggestively. "They told me someone would be coming, but I . . . forget the faces sometimes," she continued, dropping her eyes. "But why are you wearing armor? I hope you're not going to be rough. I'll be good, really I will—I promise! Tell Lazar you don't have to be rough, please. *Please!* Really, you *don't*," she continued on a rising note.

Then her eyes came back up, and the screaming began again.

"Penalosa!" Roger yelled, putting the helmet back on as his mother continued to scream and Dogzard rose from her kill menacingly. "*Penalosa!* Damn it! Get somebody else *in* here!"

When the police had secured the scene and the firefighters could get to work—mostly keeping the fire from spreading; Siminov's building and the two on either side of it were already a total loss—Subianto walked over to where Despreaux and Catrone were breathing something purple at the rear of a Fire Department medical vehicle.

"You two need to get moving," she said, bending down and speaking quietly into their ears. "There's a problem at the Palace."

* * *

"What do you think he's going to do, Sir?" Commander Talbert asked quietly.

He sat beside Admiral Victor Gajelis on the admiral's flagship, the Imperial Navy carrier HMS *Trujillo*, studying the tactical readouts. Carrier Squadron Fourteen had been under acceleration towards Old Earth for thirty-one minutes at the maximum hundred and sixty-four gravities its carriers could sustain. Their velocity was up to almost five thousand kilometers per second, and they'd traveled almost seven million kilometers, but they still had *eighty-five* million kilometers—and another three hours and thirty-eight minutes—to go. They could have made the entire voyage in less than two hours, but not if they wanted to decelerate into orbit around the planet when they reached it. On a least-time course, they would have gone scorching past the planet at over seventeen thousand kilometers per second, which would have left them in a piss-poor position to do anything about *holding* the planet for their admiral's patron.

At the moment, however, Talbert wasn't much concerned with what his own squadron's units were going to do. His attention was on the information relayed from General Gianetto about Carrier Squadron Twelve.

"What the hell do you *think* he's going to do?" Gajelis grunted. "If he planned on helping us out, there wouldn't have been any reason for him to cut off communications with Gianetto in the first place, now would there?"

"Maybe it was only temporary, Sir," Talbert said diffidently. "You know some of our own units had problems with their Marine detachments, and Prokorouv's squadron's personnel weren't anywhere near as handpicked as ours were. If his Marines tried to stop him and it took him a while to regain control . . ."

"Be nice if that was what happened," Gajelis growled. "But I doubt it did. Even if Prokourov wanted to take back control after he'd lost it, I don't think it mattered. I never did trust him, whatever the Prince thought."

"Do you think he was part of whatever's happening from the beginning, then, Sir?"

"I doubt it," Gajelis said grudgingly. "If he had been, he wouldn't have just sat there for almost twenty minutes. He'd have been moving towards Old Earth as soon as those other four traitors started moving."

He glowered at the frozen secondary tactical plot where the information relayed by Terran Defense HQ's near-space sensors showed the four carriers which had taken up positions around the planet. Those sensors were no longer reporting, thanks to the point defense systems which had systematically eliminated any platforms not hard-linked to Moonbase, but they'd lasted long enough to tell Gajelis exactly who was waiting for him.

Talbert glanced sideways at his boss. The commander didn't much care for the way this entire thing was shaping up. Like Gajelis, he knew who was in command over there, and he wasn't especially happy about it. Nor did he expect to enjoy the orders he anticipated once Carrier Squadron Fourteen managed to secure the planetary orbitals. But he didn't have much choice. He'd sold his soul to Adoula too long ago to entertain second thoughts now.

At least they didn't need the destroyed sensor platforms to keep an eye on Prokourov. Ship-to-ship detection range for carriers under phase drive was almost thirty light-minutes, and Carrier Squadron Twelve was less than ten light-minutes from *Trujillo*. They wouldn't be able to detect any of Prokorouv's parasites at this range—maximum detection range against a cruiser was only eight light-minutes—but they could see exactly what Prokorouv's carriers were doing.

Still, he'd have felt a lot more confident it he'd been able to tell exactly what was happening in Old Earth orbit. Corvu Atilius was a wily old fox, and Senior Captain Gloria Demesne, Atilius' cruiser commander, was even worse. Six-to-four odds or not, he wasn't looking forward to tangling with them. Especially not if Prokourov was about to bring a fresh carrier squadron in on their asses.

"Admiral," a communications rating said, "we have an incoming message for you on your private channel."

Gajelis looked up, then grunted.

"Earbud only," he said, then sat back and listened stolidly for almost two minutes. Finally, he nodded to the com rating at the end of the message and looked at Talbert.

"Well," he said grimly, "at least we know what we're going to be doing after we get there."

Francesco Prokourov leaned back in his command chair, considering his own tactical plot. The situation was getting . . . interesting. Not to his particular surprise, the other carriers of his squadron and his parasite skippers were more than willing to follow his orders. A few of them had opted to pretend they were doing so only out of fear of the squadron's Marine detachments, which was a fairly silly (if human) attempt to cover themselves if worse came to worst. But while Prokourov might not be another Helmut, he'd always had a knack for inspiring loyalty—or at least trust—in his subordinates. Now those subordinates were prepared to follow his lead through the chaos looming before them, and he only hoped he was leading them to victory and not pointless destruction.

Either way, though, he was leading them towards their *duty*, and that was just going to have to do.

But he had every intention of combining duty and survival, and unlike Gajelis, he had access to all of Moonbase's tactical information, which gave him a far tighter grasp on the details than Gajelis or the other Adoula loyalists in the system could possibly have. For example, he knew that Gajelis had not yet punched his cruisers (or had not as of ten minutes earlier), which made a fair amount of sense, and that Admiral La Paz's Thirteenth Squadron—or what was left of it after the original Fatted Calf defections—was coming in from astern of him. But La Paz was going to be a nonissue, whatever happened. His lonely pair of carriers wasn't going to make a great deal of difference after Gajelis' six and the combined eight of Fatted Calf and CarRon 12 had chewed each other up. Besides, CarRon 13 was at least six hours behind CarRon 12.

No, the really interesting question was what was going to happen when Gajelis crunched into Fatted Calf Squadron, and at the moment it was fairly obvious that Gajelis—who, despite his first name, was not a particularly imaginative commander—was hewing to a standard tactical approach.

Each of his carriers carried twenty-four sublight parasite cruisers and one hundred and twenty-five fighters, which gave him a total of one hundred and forty-four cruisers and seven hundred and fifty fighters, but the carriers alone represented thirty-eight percent of his ship-to-ship missile launchers, thirty-two percent of his energy weapons, forty percent of his close-in laser point defense clusters, and forty-eight percent of his countermissile launchers. Not only that, but the carriers were immensely more heavily armored, their energy weapons were six times the size of a cruiser's broadside energy mounts, and their shipkiller missiles were bigger, longer-ranged, and equipped with both more destructive warheads and far superior penetration aids and EW. And as one more minor consideration, carriers—whose hulls had two hundred times the volume of any parasite cruiser—had enormously more capable fire control systems and general computer support.

Cruisers, with better than three and a half times the huge carriers' acceleration rate, were the Imperial Navy's chosen offensive platforms. They could get in more quickly, and no ponderous, unwieldy starship had the acceleration to avoid them inside the Tsukayama Limit of a star system. But they were also far more fragile, and their magazine capacities were much lower. And outside the antimissile basket of their carriers, they were far more vulnerable to long-ranged missile kills, even from other cruisers, far less starships. So although Gajelis was essentially a cruiser commander at heart, he was holding his parasites until his carriers could get close enough to support them when they went in against Fatted Calf.

It was exactly what the Book called for, and given what Gajelis knew, it was also a smart, if cautious, move.

Of course, Gajelis didn't know *everything*, now did he?

"Find New Madrid," Roger said coldly.

He was out of his armor, but still wore the skin-tight cat-suit normally worn under it. The combination of the cat-suit's built in tourniquet and his own highly capable nanite pack had sealed the stump of his left leg, suppressed the pain, and pulled his body forcibly out of shock. None of which had done anything at all for the white-hot fury which filled him.

"Find him," he said softly. "Find him *now*."

He looked around at the human and Mardukan faces gathered about him in the Empress' private audience room. Their owners' smoke- and bloodstained uniforms and gouged and seared battle armor were as out of place against their elegant surroundings as his own smoke- and sweat-stinking cat-suit, but the bizarre contrast didn't interest him at all at the moment. His mind was too full of the woman, three doors down the hall, who screamed whenever she saw a man's face.

"Where's Rastar?" he asked.

"Dead, Your Highness," one of the Vasin said with a salute. "He fell taking the gate."

"Oh, God *damn* it." Roger closed his eyes and felt his jaw muscles ridge at the sudden spasm of pain he hadn't felt when he lost his leg. A spasm he knew was going to be repeated again and again when the casualty totals were finally added up.

"Catrone? Nimashet?" he asked, his voice harsh and flat with a fear he was unprepared to admit even to himself.

"They've got them," a master sergeant from the Empress' Own— the *real* Empress' Own—replied. "They're on their way. So are Ms. O'Casey and Sergeant Major Kosutic."

"Good," Roger said. "Good."

He stood a moment, nostrils flaring, then shook himself and looked back at his companions again.

"Find New Madrid," he repeated in an icy voice. "That slimy bastard will be skulking around somewhere. Look for an overdressed servant. And tell Kosutic, when she gets here—go to the Empress. My mother's safety is Kosutic's charge for now."

"Yes, Your Highness," the master sergeant said, and began whispering into his communicator.

"You know," Kjerulf commented to the command room in general, "I've decided I'm rather glad Admiral Prokourov is on our side."

"Amen to that, Sir," the senior Tactical rating said fervently, smiling admiringly at his readouts. Prokourov had punched his cruisers—*and* his fighters—twenty minutes after he got his squadron moving. For a cold-start launch with no previous warning, that was very respectable timing, and it spoke well of his people's readiness to accept his orders. Now those cruisers and fighters were boring ahead at four hundred and fifty gravities, better than two and a half times his carriers' acceleration, but barely three-quarters of their own maximum. At that rate, and employing strict emissions control discipline, shipboard detection range against them dropped to barely four light-minutes. But it meant that they would still reach Old Earth orbit in just over two hours, while CarRon 14 was still better than *three* hours out on its current flight profile. They'd get there far in advance of their own carriers, but they would double Fatted Calf's parasite strength, which would more than offset Gajelis' numerical advantage, especially with the Fatted Calf carriers to support them.

Of course, it was extremely probable that Gajelis would still pick them up before they got clear to Old Earth, but nothing he could do could get his *carriers* there any sooner, and knowing Gajelis . . .

"They've got the Palace," Larry Gianetto said bleakly from Admiral Gajelis' com display. His voice was inaudible to anyone else on *Trujillo*'s flag deck, but it came clearly over the admiral's earbud.

"Yes, Sir," Gajelis said aloud. He was aware of the need to pick his words carefully, lest one of his weaker-kneed subordinates waver in his duty, especially if he had time to stew over it.

"They're still playing it carefully. They haven't claimed or confirmed—or denied—that that little bastard Roger is back, but the rumors are spreading like wildfire, anyway. And they *have* sent out light armored vehicles and assault shuttles to bring in the Prime Minister, the other Cabinet ministers, and the leaders of the major parties in both the Lords and the Commons, as well as at least a dozen major journalists," Gianetto continued. "Once they've had a chance to get the Empress independently examined, we're all screwed. Unless, of course, we make sure that the results of that examination never become known."

"I understand, Sir."

"Be sure you do, Victor." Gianetto's voice was bleaker than ever as he gazed into the pickup of the com unit aboard the inconspicuous vessel carrying him away from the planet. "The only way to keep everything from falling apart is to take out the Palace and all of these bastards from orbit. Which is going to mean taking out an almighty big chunk of Imperial City, as well. It's on record that 'Roger' already blew up Prince Jackson's home and downtown office in an effort to kill him. If the Palace goes, as far as anyone will know once we get done spinning the story, it'll be because our valiant defenders managed to hold him off long enough for the Navy to arrive. At which point he either suicided to avoid capture, or—even better— hit the Palace with a KEW of his own and managed to escape in the confusion. You understand what I'm telling you, Victor? And that it has the Prince's approval?"

"Yes, Sir. I've already heard from Prince Jackson, and he entirely concurs."

Roger had gotten one of the Mardukans to find a broken pike, and he was leaning on that when New Madrid was brought in. Roger had to admit that he truly did look a good bit like his father. They'd never actually met before. Pity that the meeting was going to be so short, he thought coldly.

"Give me a sword," he said to the nearest Vasin as two Diaspran infantrymen threw his father at his feet.

The Earl of New Madrid was trembling, his terrified face streaked with sweat, and he stared mutely up at Roger as the Mardukan handed him the blade. The cavalry sabre would have been a two-handed sword for almost any human, but Roger held it in one hand, rock steady as he slid the tip of the blade under his father's chin.

"I'm curious, *Father*," he said. "I wonder why my mother would *scream* at the sight of me? Why she should *expect* to see men she can't even remember in her bedroom? Why she's covered in bruises and burns? Why she thinks someone who looks just like *me* killed my brother John in front of her? Do you think you might know the answers to those questions, Father?"

"Please, Roger," New Madrid whimpered, shaking uncontrollably. "*Please!* I—I'm your *father!*"

"'Bad seed' they called me," Roger half-whispered. "Behind my back, usually. Often enough to my face. I wondered what could make them *hate* me so? What could make my own *mother* hate me so? Now I know, don't I, *Father*? Well, Father, when a doctor finds a cancer, he cuts it out." Roger dropped the pike and raised the sword overhead in two hands, balancing on his good foot. "And I'm going to *cut you out!*"

"*NO!*" Nimashet Despreaux screamed from the doorway.

"I have the *right!*" Roger spat, not looking at her, trying not to see her, the sword held over his head and catching the light. "*Do you know what he's done?!*"

"Yes, Roger. I do," Despreaux said quietly. She stepped into the room and walked over to stand between Roger and his father. "And I know you. You can't do this. If you push me aside—if you *could* do it—I'll walk. You said it. Carefully, quietly. No muss. No fuss. We try him, and sentence him, and then slip the poison into his arm. But you *will not* cut off his head in a presence room. No one will ever trust you again if you do. *I* won't trust you."

"Nimashet, for the love of *God*," Roger whispered, trembling, his eyes pleading with her. "*Please*, stand aside."

"No," she said, in a voice of soft steel that was as loving as it was inflexible.

"Roger," Eleanora said from the doorway, "the Prime Minister is going to be here in about . . . oh, ninety seconds." She frowned. "I really think it would be better, in both the short and the long run, if you didn't greet him covered in your father's blood."

"Besides," Catrone said, standing beside her in the door, "if anybody gets him, I do. And you told me I couldn't do him."

"I said you couldn't *torture* him," Roger replied, sword still upraised.

"You also said we'd do it by the Book," Catrone said. "Are you going back on your word?"

Silence hovered in the presence room, a silence broken only by the terrified whimpers of the man kneeling at Roger's feet. And then, finally, Roger spoke again.

"No," he said. "No, Tomcat. I'm not."

He lowered the sword, letting it fall to a rest-arms position, and looked at the cavalryman who'd handed it to him

"Vasin?"

"Your Highness?"

"May I keep this?" Roger asked, looking at the sword. "It's a blade from your homeland, a blade you carried beside your dead Prince—beside my *friend*—for more kilometers than any of your people had ever traveled before. I know what that means. But . . . may I keep it?"

The Mardukan waved both true-hands in a graceful gesture of acceptance and permission.

"It was the blade of my fathers," he said, "handed down over many generations. It came to Therdan at the raising of the city's first wall, and it was there when my Prince hewed a road to life for our women and children as the city died behind us. It is old, Your Highness, steeped in the honor of my people. But I think your request would have pleased my Prince, and I would be honored to place it and its lineage in the hand of such a war leader."

"Thank you," Roger said quietly, still gazing at the blade. "I will hang it somewhere where I can see it every day. It will be a reminder that, sometimes, a sword is best not used."

The Prime Minister stepped into the room and paused at the tableau which greeted him. The soldiers, watching a man holding a sword. New Madrid on his knees, sobbing, held in place by two of the Mardukans.

"I am looking for the Prince," the Prime Minister said, looking at the woman who claimed to be Eleanora O'Casey. "For the *supposed* Prince, that is."

Roger's head turned. The movement was eerily reminiscent of a falcon's smoothly abrupt motion, and the modded brown eyes which locked on the Prime Minister were as lethal as any feathered predator's had ever been.

"I am Prince Roger Ramius Sergei Alexander Chiang Mac-Clintock," he said flatly. "And you, I suppose, would be my mother's Prime Minister?"

"Can you positively identify yourself?" the Prime Minister said dismissively, looking at the man in the soiled cat-suit, holding a sword and balancing on one foot like some sort of neobarbarian. It looked like something out of one of those tacky, lowbrow so-called "historical" novels. Or like a comedy routine.

"It's not something a person would lie about," Roger growled. "Not here, not now." He hopped around to face the Prime Minister, managing somehow to keep the sword balanced as he did. "I'm Roger, Heir Primus. Face that fact. Whether my mother recovers from her ordeal or not—the ordeal she went through while you sat on your fat, spotty, safe, no-risk-taking *ass* and did *nothing*—I *will* be Emperor. If not soon, then someday. Is that clear?"

"I suppose," the Prime Minister said tightly, his lips thinning.

"And if I recall my civics lessons," Roger continued, glaring at the older man, "the Prime Minister must command not simply a majority in Parliament, but also the Emperor's acceptance. He serves, does he not, at the Emperor's pleasure?"

"Yes," the Prime Minister said, lip curled ever so slightly. "But the precedent for removal by an Emperor hasn't been part of our constitutional tradition in ov—"

Roger tossed the sword into the air. He caught it by the pommel, and his arm snapped forward. The sword flew from his hand and hissed past the Prime Minister's head, no more than four centimeters from his left ear lobe, and slammed into the presence chamber's wall like a hammer. It stood there, vibrating, and the Prime Minister's jaw dropped as Roger glared at him.

"I don't much *care* about precedent," Roger told him, "*and I'm not very pleased with you!*"

"God *damn* it!" Victor Gajelis snarled under his breath as the new icons appeared suddenly in his plot. He knew exactly what they were, not that the knowledge made him feel any better about it.

"CIC confirms, Sir," Commander Talbert told him. "That looks like every single one of CarRon 12's cruisers. Prokourov must've punched them twenty-five minutes ago, because they're already up to almost eleven thousand KPS."

Gajelis' mouth tightened as he considered the tactical situation. Frankly, in his considered opinion, it sucked.

By sending his cruisers in at reduced acceleration, Prokourov had managed to get their velocity up to almost two thousand kilometers per second more than CarRon 14's. They were still seven million kilometers—almost eight—further from Old Earth orbit, but their greater velocity meant they would actually arrive well before Carrier Squadron Fourteen. Of course, they were *only* cruisers, but there were ninety-six of them.

No fancy cruiser tricks were going to get Prokorouv's *carriers* to the planet before Gajelis' own carriers, not with CarRon 14's twenty-minute head start. But CarRon 12's missiles would have the range to cover anything in orbit around the planet for over an hour before they actually reached the planet's orbital shell. Accuracy wouldn't be very good at such extended ranges, but to carry out his own mission orders, Gajelis had to get within no more than three or four hundred thousand kilometers of the planet. He couldn't guarantee the accuracy Gianetto and Adoula had specified from any greater range, even assuming that he could get missiles through the defensive fire of the ships already in planetary orbit. Besides, it was going to be difficult to make it look as if *Prince Roger's* adherents had done the deed if Moonbase had detailed sensor readings showing shipkillers from CarRon 14 hitting atmosphere. No, he had to get close enough to do it with KEW, and that meant advancing into Prokorouv's carriers' missile envelope.

Unless . . .

He thought furiously. Almost two hours had passed since the attack on the Palace began. His communications sections were monitoring the confused babble of news reports and speculation boiling through the planetary datanet, and it was obvious that opinion was hardening behind the belief that it was, indeed, Prince Roger. At the moment, however, most of the commentary seemed to incline towards the belief that it was simply a case of the nefarious Traitor Prince returning for a second attempt. The notion that it was an attempt to rescue the Empress was still being greeted with skepticism, but that was going to change as soon as the first independent report of the Empress' condition got out. That was going to take time, but there was no way to know how much of it.

"Punch the cruisers," he said flatly. "Maximum acceleration."

Talbert glanced at him, then passed along the order.

"What about the fighters, Sir?" he asked after a moment.

"Send them in, too," Gajelis said. "Configure them for CSP to cover the cruisers."

"Yes, Sir."

Gajelis didn't miss the brief hesitation before the commander's acknowledgment, but he ignored it. He didn't like committing his cruisers this early, but his own ships and Prokorouv's carriers were still eight light-minutes apart, which meant it would take eight minutes for Prokourov to learn that Cruiser Flotilla One-Forty had launched. Eight minutes in which Gajelis' cruisers would be free to accelerate at their maximum velocity. Even assuming Prokourov went to maximum acceleration on his own cruisers the instant they detected CruFlot 140—which he undoubtedly would—Gajelis' cruisers would have built enough acceleration, coupled with the distance CarRon 14 had traveled before launching them, to arrive four minutes before CruFlot 120. And CarRon 14 would be twenty minutes closer to the planet when that happened.

Gajelis' cruisers would be outside the effective range of his carriers' antimissile defenses, but they would be *inside* the basket for his carriers' shipkillers. The same thing would be true for Prokorouv's carriers, but Prokorouv's targeting solutions would be nowhere near as good. It wasn't an ideal solution, by any means, but, then, there *wasn't* an ideal solution to this particular tactical problem. And if he could get his own cruisers into energy range of the four so-called "Fatted Calf Squadron" carriers covering the planet, he could hammer them, especially with his own *six* carriers' attack missiles piling in on top of the cruisers' fire.

He was going to lose most of his own cruisers in the process, of course, especially with Prokorouv's cruisers coming in on them so rapidly. He had no doubt that that was what had prompted Talbert's hesitation. But it was also what cruisers were for. He didn't like it, but he'd come up through cruisers himself. He'd understood how the process worked then, and so would his cruiser skippers now.

Who also all knew they were dead men if Adoula went down.

"They've punched their cruisers," Kjerulf said from the com display.

"Yeah, we sort of noticed," Captain Atilius responded dryly. If the older officer had shown any hesitation about committing himself in the first place, there was no sign of it now. He was like an old warhorse, Kjerulf thought, faintly amused even now, despite all that was happening. Corvu Atilius probably should have made admiral decades ago, but he'd always been too tactical-minded, too focused on maneuvers and tactical doctrine to play the political game properly. "Roughhewn" was a term which had been used to describe his personality entirely too often over the course of his career, but he was definitely the right man in the right place as Fatted Calf Squadron's senior officer. He actually seemed to be looking *forward* to what was coming.

"I always knew Gajelis had shit for brains," Atilius continued. He shook his head. "He's going to get reamed."

"Maybe," Chantal Soheile said from her quadrant of the conferenced display. "But so are we. And it's not like he's got a lot of alternatives." She shook her head in turn. "He's got the edge in carriers and missile power. Basically, the only real option he's got is to pile in on top of us and tried to bulldoze us out of the way before Prokourov can get here."

"Sure," Atilius agreed. "But I guarantee you he'll be sending in his fighters configured for combat space patrol. It's the way his head works. He just doesn't see them as shipkillers—not the way he does cruisers. Besides," he bared his teeth, "his guys are going to have to deal with *Gloria*, aren't they?"

"CruFlot 140's punched, Sir," a sensor technician reported. "Max accel."

"Have they, indeed?" Senior Captain Benjamin Weintraub, CO, Cruiser Flotilla One-Twenty, replied. His ships were eighteen light-seconds ahead of their carriers, and he saw no reason to waste an additional half-minute waiting for Admiral Prokorouv's instructions. "Take us to maximum acceleration," he said.

Captain Senior-Grade Gloria Demesne, CO HMS *Bellingham*, narrowed her hazel eyes and considered the tactical plot as she leaned back in her command chair and sipped her coffee. It was hot, strong and black, with just a pinch of salt. Black gang coffee, just the way she liked it. Which couldn't be said for the tactical situation.

CruFlot 150—well, actually, it was component parts of four separate squadrons, but CruRon 153 was the senior squadron, Gloria was 153's CO, "CruFlot Fatted Calf" sounded pretty fucking stupid, and they by-God had to call it *something*—faced half again its own numbers. Not good. Not good at all, but what the hell? At least help was on its way, and if they couldn't take a joke, they shouldn't have joined.

Imperial cruisers carried powerful beam weapons, but for the opening phase of any battle, they relied on the contents of their missile magazines, filled with hypervelocity, fission-fusion contact and standoff X-ray missiles. They fought in data-linked networks, in which each ship was capable of local or external control of the engagement "basket." But for all their speed and firepower, their ChromSten armor was lighter than most military starships boasted and they lacked the multiply redundant systems tunnel drive ships could carry. The far larger FTL vessels were much more sluggish in maneuver, but they were undeniably powerful units, especially in defense. Although cruisers' acceleration meant they could chase the big bruisers down, doing so was always a risky proposition. And, despite the percentage of their internal volume given over to missile stowage, cruisers had much less magazine space than their larger motherships. Nor could they match a carrier's missile defenses, and that might be important. Because Carrier Squadron Fourteen was in the process of making a critical mistake.

Whether through simple stupidity—she'd never had thought much of Admiral Gajelis' brains—or because they were in a hurry, the hundred and forty-four ships of Cruiser Flotilla 140 were charging straight on in at 6.2 KPS^2.

Obviously, Gajelis wanted to get them into range for precision KEW strikes on the Palace, which meant brushing the four Fatted Calf carriers—and their cruisers—out of his way. But his more sluggish carriers were dropping further and further behind the speeding cruisers—they'd been almost eight and a half million kilometers behind when the cruisers made turnover. By the time CruFlot 140 entered effective missile range of Old Earth orbit, they'd be over *twenty-seven* and a half million kilometers back.

Of course, missile engagement envelopes were flexible. Both cruiser-sized and capital ship shipkillers could pull three thousand gravities of acceleration. The difference was that capital missiles, fired from the launchers which only ships the size of carriers mounted, could pull that acceleration for fifteen minutes, whereas cruiser missiles were good for only ten. That gave the larger missiles an effective range from rest of over twelve million kilometers before burnout, whereas a cruiser missile had an effective range before burnout of around 2,700,000 kilometers. Platform speeds at launch radically affected those ranges, however, and so did the fact that missile drives could be switched off and then on again, allowing lengthy ballistic "coasting" flight profiles to provide what were for all intents and purposes unlimited range . . . against nonevading targets. Against targets which could evade, and which also mounted the most sophisticated electronic warfare systems available, *effective* ranges were far shorter. Then there was little matter of active antimissile defenses.

Except that in this particular case, countermissiles from Gajelis' *carriers* weren't going to be a factor. CarRon 14's longer-ranged capital missiles could reach past its cruisers to range on Desmesne's ships and the Fatted Calf carriers, but their *counter*missiles would be unable to intercept the fire directed at their cruisers. That meant CruFlot 140 was more vulnerable than CruFlot 150, which was stuck in relatively tight to its own carriers, since a carrier mounted twenty-seven times the countermissile tubes a cruiser did. Gajelis' carriers and cruisers between them mounted roughly fifty-six hundred shipkiller tubes to Fatted Calf's combined thirty-seven hundred, but Fatted Calf had the cover of almost nine thousand *counter*missile tubes to CruFlot 140's seven thousand. And, even more importantly, no cruiser could match the targeting capability and fire control sophistication of an all-up carrier, which meant Fatted Calf's countermissile fire was going to be far more effective on a bird-for-bird basis. Not to mention the fact that each carrier mounted almost thirty-five hundred close-in laser point defense clusters, none of which would be available to CruFlot 140.

Gajelis had obviously decided to expend his cruisers in an effort to inflict crippling damage on Fatted Calf before his carriers came into range of Demesne's cruisers. He could "stack" shipkillers from his carriers to some extent by launching them in fairly tight waves, with preprogrammed ballistic segments of staggered lengths so that they arrived in CruFlot 140's control basket as a single salvo. It was going to be ugly if—*when*—he did, but the capital missiles would be significantly less accurate staging through the fire control of mere cruisers. And if something nasty happened to be happening to his advanced fire control platforms, it would throw a sizable spanner into the works.

It wasn't as if he had an enormous number of options, she reflected. For that matter, Fatted Calf didn't have a huge number of options, either. But a lot depended on the way the two sides chose to *exercise* their options.

The details. It was always in the details.

"Emergence . . . now," Astrogation said.

"It will take some time for us to get hard word on what's going on in the system," Admiral Helmut said, glancing over at Julian. They were in the Fleet CIC, watching the tactical plots and wondering if the trick was going to work.

"Sir, no response to standard tactical interrogation of the outer shell platforms," the senior Tactical Officer reported after several minutes. "We're getting what appears to be a priority lockout."

"Directed specifically against us?" Helmut asked sharply.

"I can't say for certain, Sir," the Taco replied.

"In that case, contact Moonbase directly. Tell them who we are, and ask them to turn the lights back on for us."

★ ★ ★

"Sir," Marciel Poertena's executive officer said just a bit nervously, "far be it from me to second-guess the Admiral, but do you really think he knows what he's doing here?"

"Don't be pocking silly," Poertena said. "Of course he does. I t'ink."

He looked at his display. HMS *Capodista* would never, in the wildest drug dream, be considered a *war*ship. She was a freighter. A bulk cargo carrier. The only thing remotely military about her was her propulsion, since she had to be able to keep up with the fleet elements she'd been designed to serve. Which, unfortunately, meant that her tunnel and phase drive plants were both powerful enough for the Dark Lord of the Sixth's current brainstorm.

At the moment, she, *Ozaki*, and *Adebayo* were squawking the transponders of HMS *Trenchant*, *Kershaw*, and *Hrolf Kraki*, otherwise known as Carrier Squadron Sixty-Three. Nor were they the only service ships which had somehow inexplicably acquired the transponder codes of their betters.

"Of course he does," Captain Poertena muttered again, touching the crucifix under his uniform tunic.

"What the hell is that?!" Admiral Ernesto La Paz demanded as a fresh rash of icons appeared in his tactical display. It was basically a rhetorical question, since there was only one thing it really could be.

"Major tunnel drive footprint astern of us!" Tactical called out at almost the same instant. "Eighteen point sources, right on the Tsukayama Limit."

"Eighteen." La Paz and his chief of staff looked at each other.

"It's got to be Helmut," the chief of staff said.

"And isn't that just peachy," La Paz snarled. He glowered at the display for several more seconds, then turned his head.

"Communications, dump a continuous tactical stream to all other squadrons."

"Aye, aye, Sir."

"Maneuvering, come twenty degrees to starboard, same plane. Astrogation, start calculating your first transit to Point Able."

★ ★ ★

"Sir," the Tactical Officer announced suddenly, "we have two phase drive signatures directly in front of us, range approximately four-point-five light-minutes. BattleComp reads their IFF as *Courageous* and *Damocles*. They're accelerating towards the inner system at one-point-six-four KPS squared. Current velocity, one-three-point-three thousand KPS."

"Ah, yes," Helmut murmured. "That would be our friend Ernesto. But only two ships? And already up to over thirteen thousand?"

He tapped his right thumb and forefinger together in front of him, whistling softly. Then he smiled thinly at Julian.

"It would appear that the party started without us, Sergeant Julian. How irritating."

"*Courageous* and *Damocles* are changing course, Sir," the Taco said. "They're coming to starboard."

"Of course they are," Helmut snorted. "La Paz isn't about to fight at one-to-nine odds! And he knows damned well we can't catch them if he just keeps running. No doubt he'd like us to try to do just that, though."

He glanced at Julian again and snorted at the Marine's obviously confused expression.

"I keep forgetting you don't know your ass from your elbow where naval maneuvers are concerned, Sergeant," he said dryly. "At least a part of what's happening is obvious enough. The attack on the Palace must have kicked off at least six hours ahead of schedule, because *we* arrived within one minute of our projected schedule, despite our little side excursion, and to have reached that velocity, CarRon 13 must have been underway for a bit over two and a half hours. And since it would have taken over twenty minutes for movement orders from Old Earth to reach La Paz, that gives us a pretty tight lock on when the balloon must have gone up. And we, unfortunately, are still nine-point-eight hours away from Old Earth. So it would appear that the plan to divert Adoula's squadrons away from the planet *before* the attack isn't really likely to work."

Julian's face tightened, but the admiral shook his head.

"Doesn't mean he's failed, Sergeant," he said, with a gentleness he seldom showed. "In fact, all the evidence suggests the attack on the Palace itself probably succeeded."

"*What* evidence?" Julian demanded.

"The fact that the system reconnaissance platforms have been locked out, that La Paz was obviously headed in-system just as fast as he could go, and that his carrier squadron is down to only two ships," Helmut said.

"The recon lockout had to have come from Moonbase—that's the only communications node with the reach to shut down the entire system. And if Adoula were in control of the situation, he certainly wouldn't be ordering his own units locked out of the system reconnaissance platforms. So the lockout order almost certainly came from someone supporting Prince Roger . . . which means *his* partisans have control of Moonbase.

"The fact that La Paz was headed in-system suggests the same thing—Adoula and Gianetto are calling in their loyalists, and they wouldn't be doing that unless they needed the firepower because of the situation on the Old Earth.

"And the fact that La Paz is down to only two ships—that half his squadron is someplace else—suggests that someone has been doing a little creative force structure reshuffling. My money for the reshuffler is on Kjerulf. Which would also make sense of Moonbase's detection from the Adoula camp."

"Sir," the Taco put in, "we're also picking up additional phase drive signatures. Looks like four carriers coming in from out-system—we're too far out for IFF—about half a light-minute out from Old Earth, decelerating towards orbit. We've got six more signatures coming out from the inner-system, decelerating towards the same destination."

"Gajelis and . . . Prokourov," Helmut said thoughtfully. He glanced at Julian again. "The six coming out from sunward have to be Gajelis and CarRon 14. I'm guessing the other four are CarRon 12, which *probably* means Prokorouv's decided to back your Prince. I can't think of any reason even Gianetto would think he needed ten carriers and over two hundred cruisers to deal with an attack on the Palace. Mind you, I could be wrong. He always did believe in bigger hammers."

"Incoming. Many vampires incoming!" Tactical announced.

Gloria Demesne only nodded to herself. It had been obvious what was coming for the last thirty minutes. CruFlot 140 was still over fifteen minutes out, just entering its own missile range of Fatted Calf, but Gajelis' carriers had started launching over a half-hour before. Now their big, nasty missiles were stacking up in CruFlot 140's control basket, and the cruisers themselves had just gone to maximum rate fire. No wonder even the computers were having trouble trying to tally up the total.

She understood exactly what Gajelis was thinking. This was a bid to overwhelm Fatted Calf with firepower while his own carriers were safely out of harm's way. Fatted Calf's carriers had the range to engage CarRon 14, but the chances of a hit at this range, especially without cruisers of their own out there to provide final course corrections were . . . poor, to say the least. And even any of their birds which might have scored hits would still have to get through CarRon 14's missile defenses. The term "snowball in hell" came forcibly to mind when she considered that scenario. So at the moment, he was free to concentrate *his* fire on the targets of his choice from a position of relative immunity.

For as long as his own cruisers lasted, anyway.

It might just work, but it might not, too, especially given the range at which his cruisers had opened fire. Their missiles would be coming in at high terminal velocities, but crowding the very limits of their designed fire control and with a ten-second signal lag in fire control telemetry, which gave away accuracy. The Imperial Navy's electronic warfare capabilities were good, even against people who had exactly the same equipment. It took the computational capabilities of a major platform to distinguish between real and false targets reliably. The sensors and AI loaded into shipkiller missiles were highly capable, but not as capable as those of the cruiser or carrier which had launched them, so firing at such extreme range meant Gajelis was accepting poorer terminal guidance due to the delay in telemetry corrections.

The sheer size of the salvos he was throwing was also going to have an effect. It wasn't going to catastrophically overwhelm the fire control capability of his cruisers, but it was going to overload it, which meant the computers would have less time to spend coaxing each missile into the best attack solution. If she knew Gajelis, he was going to concentrate a lot of that fire—especially the heavier missiles from his carriers—on Fatted Calf's carriers, instead of hammering the lighter cruisers. There were arguments in favor of either tactic, but Fatted Calf had no intention of wasting *any* of its birds on carriers. Not at this range. Demesne intended to kill cruisers, ruthlessly crushing the smaller, weaker platforms while they were out of their carriers' cover, and Captain Atilius, Fatted Calf's acting CO, just happened to be *Minotaur*'s skipper. Which meant the rest of the squadron's carriers, as well as its cruisers, were conforming to Desmesne's tactical direction.

Which was also why none of Fatted Calf's units had fired a single shot yet. At this range, it would take almost five minutes for CruFlot 140's missiles to reach Fatted Calf, and at their maximum rate fire the cruisers would shoot themselves dry in about fifteen minutes. They'd put a lot of missiles into space over those twenty minutes, but she had a lot of point defense to deal with them. If she waited to fire until the distance to Gajelis' cruisers fell to decisive range, *Bellingham* and her consorts would be able to control *their* missiles all the way in, which meant they'd be at least twenty-five percent more effective. Of course, they'd have to survive Gajelis' fire before they launched, but every silver lining had its cloud.

"Open fire, Captain?" Ensign Scargall asked. The young officer's taut voice was higher pitched than usual and her face was pale as she looked at her readouts, and Gloria didn't blame her a bit. There were already well over forty-five thousand missiles on the way, and *still* none of Fatted Calf's ships had opened fire.

"No, Ensign," Gloria said in a husky voice. She punched in a command, and the bridge was filled with a throbbing beat as she pulled out a pseudo-nic stick. She brushed a lock of red hair out of her eyes and puffed on the stick, lighting it.

"Hold your fire," she said. "Let them come. Come to me, my love," she whispered. "*Fifteen thousand tears I've cried...*" She'd had a hell of a singing voice, once. Before the pseudo-nic smoke had killed it. But every silver lining had its cloud. "*Screaming deceiving and bleeding for you . . .*"

"They're fighting dumb, Admiral," Commander Talbert said.

"Not much else they can do," Gajelis shrugged. "They have to come to meet us to keep us away from the planet. In fact, the only thing that surprises me is that they haven't cut the cruisers loose to intercept our cruisers even further out."

"They have to be worried about keeping us as far out as possible, Sir," Talbert said, "but they've had over three hours to get their forces deployed. They ought to be further out than this by now. And where are their fighters?"

"They probably didn't know exactly when this was coming," Gajelis said, and grimaced. "That's the problem with coups, Commander—it's harder than hell to make sure everyone's ready to kick off at the right moment. They're probably having to make this up as they go along, and they know we're just the first squadron they're going to have on their backs. So they're playing it as cautious as they can, but they still can't afford to wait us out and let us get into kinetic range of Imperial City. As for the fighters, they're obviously holding them aboard the carriers. Given the force imbalance, they'll want to send them in with maximum Leviathan loads. In a minute or two, they'll punch them to come in across the cruisers, from either system north or south."

"Atilius is tricky," Talbert pointed out. "And Demesne is worse. This isn't their style, Sir."

"There's no *style* to a battle like this, Commander," the admiral said, frowning. "You just throw fire until one side retires or is *gone*. We've got more firepower; we'll win."

"Yes, Sir," Talbert said, trying to project a little enthusiasm. It was hard. Especially knowing that Prokorouv's cruisers were going to be close enough to start "adjusting" the force imbalance in about another ten minutes. "I suppose there is a certain quality to quantity."

"Fatted Calf Squadron has just flushed its fighters," Tactical said.

"See?" the admiral said. "Flip a coin whether they go in over the cruisers, or under."

"Here they come!"

Not exactly a professional announcement, there, Demesne thought. But under the circumstances, a pardonable slip.

The volume of space to sunward of Old Earth was a hurricane of raging destruction. Countermissiles, roaring out at thirty-five hundred gravities, charged headlong to meet a solid wall of incoming shipkillers. Proximity warheads began to erupt, flashing like prespace flash guns at some championship sporting event. Stroboscopic bubbles of nuclear fury boiled like brimstone flaring through the chinks in the front gate of Hell. The interceptions began over a million kilometers out, ripping huge holes in the comber of shipkillers racing towards Fatted Calf, but the vortex of destruction thundered unstoppably onward. Eighty-four *thousand* missiles had been fired at only one hundred targets, and nothing in the universe could have stopped them all.

Point defense laser clusters opened fire as the range fell to seventy thousand kilometers, and the fury of destruction redoubled. CruFlot 140's missiles were coming in at twenty-seven thousand kilometers per second, which gave the lasers less than three seconds to engage, but at least tracking had had plenty of time to set up the firing solutions. Demesne's cruisers' point defense was lethally effective, and the four carriers' fire was even more deadly.

Laser heads began to detonate. Against ChromSten-armored ships, even those as light as cruisers, even the most powerful bomb-pumped laser had a standoff range of less than ten thousand kilometers; against a carrier, maximum effect of standoff range was barely half that. Cruisers began to take hits, belching atmosphere and debris, but Demesne and Atilius had been right. Over seventy percent of the incoming missiles were targeted on the carriers, a hundred thousand kilometers *behind* the cruisers.

CruFlot 150 turned, keeping its better broadside sensors positioned to engage the missiles which had already run past it, even as its ships took their own hammering. And they *did* take a hammering. Thirty percent of eighty-four thousand was "only" two hundred and sixty missiles per cruiser, and even with poor firing solutions and the carriers' support—what they could spare from their own self-defense—an awful lot of them got through.

Lieutenant Alfy Washington lay back in his seat, looking up at the stars through his glassteel canopy, his arms crossed. Fighters, and especially fighters on minimum power, had *very* little signature. Spotting them at more than a light-second or so required visual tracking, and space fighters were a light-absorbing matte black for a reason. But they were very, very fast. At an acceleration rate of eight KPS², they could pile on velocity in a hurry, and even their phase drive signatures were hard to notice at interplanetary distances.

He checked his toot and nodded silently at the data that was being fed to his division over the hair-fine whisker laser.

"Christ, Gajelis is dumb as a rock," he muttered, lying back again and closing his eyes. "And I'm glad as hell I'm not in cruisers."

HMS *Bellingham* rocked as another blast of coherent radiation slammed into her armored flank.

"Tubes Ten and Fourteen off-line," Tactical said tightly. "Heavy jamming from the enemy squadron, but we've still got control of the missiles."

For all their toughness, cruisers were nowhere near so heavily armored as carriers. Even a capital ship graser—or the forward-bearing spinal mount weapon of a cruiser like *Bellingham*—couldn't hope to penetrate a capital ship's armor at any range beyond forty thousand kilometers. Missile hatches and weapons bays were more vulnerable, since they necessarily represented openings in the ship's armored skin, but even they were heavily cofferdammed with ChromSten bulkheads to contain damage. For all practical purposes, an energy-armored combat had to get to within eighty thousand kilometers if it hoped to inflict damage, and to half of that if it wanted decisive results. Missiles had to get even closer, but, then again, missiles didn't care whether or not they survived the experience.

Cruisers, unfortunately, were a bit easier to kill, and *Bellingham* bucked again as yet more enemy fire smashed into her.

"Heavy damage, port forward!" Damage Control snapped. "Hull breach, Frames Thirty-Seven to Forty-six. Magazine Three open to space."

"That's okay. We got the birds out first," Demesne said, rubbing the arms of her station chair. Her tubes were flushed, and all she was doing now was surviving long enough to counter the Adoula squadron's ECM through the birds' guidance links. "Just let them stay dumb a *little* longer. . . ."

"Here comes anoth—" Tactical said, and then *Bellingham* heaved like a storm-sick windjammer.

The combat information center flexed and buckled, groaning as some furious giant twisted it between his hands, and Demesne felt her station chair rip loose from its mounts as the lights went out. The next thing she knew, she was on her side, still strapped to the chair, and one of her arms felt . . . pretty bad.

"Damage Control?" she croaked as she hit the quick release with her good hand. That was when she noticed the compartment was also in microgravity.

"XO?"

Nobody else in CIC seemed to be moving. Ensign Scargall was still in her station chair, sitting upright, but she ended just above the waist. What was left of her was held in place by a lap belt. The others looked to have been done by blast and debris. What a damn shame.

"Bit of a scar, there, Ensign," Demesne said. She was more than a little woozy herself, and she caught herself giggling in reaction.

"Captain?" her first officer replied in a startled voice. "I thought you were gone, Ma'am!"

"Bad pennies, XO. Bad pennies," she said. "How bad is it?"

"Heavy damage to Fusion Three and Five. CIC took a hit—I guess that's pretty obvious. Alternate CIC is up and functioning. Damage teams are on the way to your location."

"We're still fighting?" she asked, grasping a piece of scrap metal which had once been a million-credit weapons control station. Oh, well. There were others. Hopefully.

"Still in the game," the XO said. "Local gravity disruptions."

"Right." Demesne pushed herself across the shattered

compartment to the armored hatch. It was warped, and the readouts on the access panel were dead. She considered the problem for a moment, then pulled herself along the bulkhead to the large hole in the armor which had been supposed to protect CIC. She'd just about reached the ragged-edged hole when there was a flutter, and she got her feet under her just as gravity came back on. It was about half power, but better than floating.

She considered the breached bulkhead with a frown. The hole, while undeniably large, wasn't exactly what anyone might call neat. The passageway outside CIC had been pretty thoroughly chewed up, and there was a gap—over a meter wide—in the deck. That didn't seem all that far, but this particular gap lit up the darkened passageway like an old-fashioned light bulb with the cheery red of near molten metal. Besides, she was in no shape to jump any gaps under the best of conditions, and the jagged, knifelike projections fanging the bulkhead hole scarcely qualified as "the best" of anything. She didn't like to think about what they'd do to her unarmored shipsuit if she tried to get up a run to vault across the gap and didn't hit the hole dead center. She couldn't afford any nasty little punctures, any more than she could afford to come up short on that handy-dandy frying pan. The compartment's atmosphere had been evacuated—not surprisingly, since she could see stars through the meter-and-a-half hole in the passageway's deckhead if she leaned over and looked up. The frigging hole had been punched halfway through *her* ship! And it wasn't the only one, she suspected. That would have made her cranky, if she'd been the type.

But this wasn't the time to be thinking about that. The problem at hand was how to get out of CIC and to the alternate bridge. And, okay, admit it—she wasn't tracking really well. Probably the pain from the broken arm. Or maybe being thrown across the compartment.

She was still considering her condition—and the condition of her ship, which was just as bad or worse—when an armored Marine suddenly poked his head around the edge of the hole from the other side.

"Holy crap!" the Marine said on the local circuit. "Captain Demesne? You're *alive*?"

"Am I standing here?" she snapped in a gravel voice. "Is this a red suit? Does anybody *else* get a Santa suit?"

"No, Ma'am," the Marine said. "I mean, yes, Ma'am. I mean—"

"Oh, quit stuttering and lie down," Demesne said, pointing to the glowing edges of the gap.

"Ma'am?" the Marine said, clearly confused.

"Lie down across the gap," Demesne said, slowly and carefully, as it speaking to a child.

"Yes, Ma'am," the Marine said. He set down his plasma cannon and lay down across the gap obediently.

Captain Demesne considered him for a moment, then crawled carefully across his armored back, slithering out of CIC and towards her duty.

Commander Bogdan jinked her fighter to the side as a missile from one of the cruisers to planetary north flashed towards her squadron. But the cruisers weren't putting up their regular fight after the hammering they'd taken from CruFlot 140's fire.

That was good, but her business wasn't with Fatted Calf's cruisers. Her job was to intercept the Fatted Calf fighters before they got close enough to launch their Leviathan anti-ship missiles.

Fleet fighters were basically the smallest hull which could be wrapped around a Protessa-Sheehan phased gravity drive and the Frederickson-Hsu countergravity field which damped the man-killing effects of the phase drive. The size of the Navy's current Eagle III fighter also happened to be the largest volume which could be enclosed in a field capable of a full eight hundred gravities of acceleration.

All of that propulsion hardware, coupled with life support requirements, the necessary flight computers and other electronics, and a light forward-firing laser armament, left exactly zero internal volume, and the Eagle III was capable of only extremely limited atmospheric maneuvers. The phase drive would not function in atmosphere, and although the counter-grav could provide lift (after a fashion) it wasn't really configured for that, either. Nor did the fighter's emergency reaction thrusters begin to provide the brute power of something like an assault shuttle. Then again, the reaction drive assault shuttles had the internal volume for a *lot* of payload, whereas the volume requirements of the fighter's drive systems meant that all of its payload had to be carried externally.

Depending on the exact external ordnance loads selected, an Eagle III could carry up to five of the big, smart Leviathans. They were shorter-legged than ship-to-ship weapons. At 4,200 gravities, they accelerated forty percent faster than shipboard antiship missiles, but they had a maximum powered endurance of only three minutes. And, unlike ship-launched shipkillers, their stripped-down size left them with a drive which could not be turned on and off at will. Which meant they had a powered envelope from rest of approximately 667,000 kilometers and a terminal velocity from rest of 7,560 KPS. They were also much smaller targets . . . with *very* capable ECM and penaids. In short, they might be short-ranged and less flexible, but they were bastards to stop with point defense, so keeping them away from the carriers was a prime mission. And this time, everything was going right.

The fighters from the Fatted Calf units were slashing in at high acceleration, intent on closing the range to CruFlot 140 before launching, but Bogdan's fighters were armed specifically for an antifighter engagement, unburdened by the bulky shipkillers. They could have carried up to fourteen Astaroth antifighter/antishipkiller missiles in place of those five Leviathans. Or, as in Bogdan's fighters' case, eight Astaroths and two Foxhawk decoy missiles. That would give them a decisive advantage in the furball, and they'd punched with perfect timing to intercept the mission. The Fatted Calf fighters had another fourteen thousand kilometers to go before they could launch on the cruisers. And by then, Bogdan's squadron would be all over them, like a tiger on . . . a fatted calf.

"Coming up on initial launch," Bogdan said, prepping her Astaroths.

"Commander," Peyravi in Division 4 said suddenly. "Commander! Visual ID! *Those aren't fighters!*"

Bogdan blanched and set her visual systems to auto-track, trying to spot the targets. Finally, as something occluded a star, she got a hard lock, and swore.

"Son of a *bitch*." She switched to Fleet frequency. "Son of a bitch, son of a bitch, son of a—Mickey, Mickey, Mickey!" she shouted, calling for a priority override to the carrier squadron's CIC. "These are Foxhawk-Two *drones*! Repeat, they're Foxhawk-Deuces!"

"Blacksheep, Blacksheep," Washington's com said suddenly.

The Adoula fighter squadrons would have gotten close enough for a visual on the Foxhawks by now. The ship-launched version of the standard fighter decoys was big and powerful, but not big enough to fool sensors forever, and that meant it was time to go. Washington adjusted his chair to a better combat configuration and started bringing his systems online.

"Yes, Sir," he said, deepening his voice. "Three bags full . . ."

Admiral Gajelis had just heard the "Mickey" call when the lieutenant commander at Tactical nodded.

"Eagle fighters lighting off," she said. "They must've been blacked down. North polar three-one-five. Closing at four-three-seven-five! Range, two-five-three-two-five-zero!"

"Leviathan guidance systems coming on-line!" a sensor tech said. "Raid count is two hundred . . . five hundred . . . *fifteen* hundred bogeys! Vampire! Vampire, vampire—we have missile separation! Seven-five thousand—I say again, seven-five-zero-zero vampires inbound! Impact in six seconds!"

Commander Talbert's belly muscles locked solid. *Fifteen hundred fighters?* That was impossible! Unless—

"Punch all defense missiles, maximum launch!" Gajelis snapped. "And get the fighters back here!"

"Like there's time," Commander Talbert muttered as he passed on the orders.

Gloria Demesne charged into her alternate bridge just as the fighter ambush sprang. It wasn't just Fatted Calf's fighters. Prokourov had sent his own fighters ahead under maximum acceleration even before he got his cruisers into space. And Kjerulf's Moonbase fighters had reported for duty over an hour ago. There'd been plenty of time to get the speedy little parasites into position and shut down their emissions. Now they poured their heavy loads of Leviathans into the unsuspecting carriers from what amounted to knife-range.

Normally, fighter missiles had very little chance of significantly injuring a massively armored carrier. But, then again, normally the carrier's commander wasn't stupid enough to let fifteen hundred fighters get within twenty-five thousand kilometers of them with a closing velocity of over four thousand kilometers per second.

"Oh, no," Captain Demesne said softly. "You're not going *anywhere.*"

The Fatted Calf fighters, their racks flushed and empty, had gone to max deceleration on a heading back to their carriers leaving the field to the opposing cruisers. CruFlot 140, however, was badly out of position . . . and hopelessly screwed.

Both cruiser forces had taken heavy losses—Demesne had lost fifty-seven of her ninety-six ships—but CruFlot 140 had lost eighty-eight. They were down to fifty-six to her thirty-nine, they'd exhausted their own shipkillers, and even if their carriers had been in range to cover them with countermissiles, they were too busy fighting for their own lives against the fighter ambush to worry about their parasites. Which meant that the cruisers' only real option was to bore on in for the kill on CruFlot 150's remaining cruisers, hoping to reach beam range, where their numerical advantage could still make itself felt. Unfortunately for them, Demesne's readouts indicated that all of them were gushing air. Worse, from their perspective, they were well inside the missile envelope of the Fatted Calf carriers.

Those carriers hadn't gotten off unscathed in the missile holocaust. Captain Julius Fenrec's *Gloria* was out of it. She'd been shot to pieces—not such a good omen for certain cruiser skippers, perhaps; Demesne's mouth twisted wryly at the thought—and her surviving personnel were evacuating as rapidly as possible. It was an even bet whether or not they'd all get off before her runaway Fusion Twelve's containment failed. But the other three carriers of the improvised squadron were still in action, and unlike *Gloria*, their damage was essentially superficial. They'd lost very few of their missile launchers, and while their fighters hammered Gajelis' carriers, they were free to engage the surviving enemy cruisers undistracted by anything else. And that, Gloria Demesne thought, would be all they wrote.

Of course, in the meantime, there were all those missiles the fighters had sent scorching into CarRon 14's teeth. Which ought to begin arriving . . . right . . . about . . .

"Detonations on the carriers," the assistant tactical officer said. "Multiple detonations! Holy shit, *Melshikov* is just *gone!*"

"Admiral," Lieutenant Commander Clinton, at Tactical Two said, coughing on the smoke eddying about the compartment. CIC hadn't lost environment, and she still had her helmet latched back. "*Melshikov* is gone, and *Porter* reports critical damage. Everybody else is still intact . . . more or less."

Victor Gajelis ground his teeth together in fury. Fighters. Who would have believed *fighters* could inflict that much damage?

He glared at *Trujillo*'s damage control schematic. The fighter strike had concentrated heavily on *Melshikov* and *Porter*, and for all intents and purposes, destroyed both of them. *Porter* was still technically intact, but she'd lost two-thirds of her combat capability, her phase drive was badly damaged, and her tunnel drive had been completely disabled. She could neither survive in combat nor avoid it, and if he didn't order her abandoned, he might as well shoot her entire crew himself.

"It looks like *Gloria* is abandoning," Clinton added, and the admiral nodded in acknowledgment. At least they'd gotten one of the bastards in return, but that didn't magically erase his own losses or mean his other four carriers had escaped unscathed. *Trujillo* was probably the least damaged of the lot, and she'd been hammered hard. She'd lost a quarter of her missile launchers, almost as many of her grasers, and a third of her point defense clusters, and she was still an hour and a half short of Old Earth.

"Sir," Commander Talbert said quietly, "look at Tactical Three."

Gajelis' eyes flicked sideways, and his jaw clenched even tighter as the last of his parasite cruisers was blown apart.

"Three of Fatted Calf's carriers are still intact, Sir," Talbert pointed out in that same, quiet voice. "Prokorouv's cruisers will be in planetary orbit in another four minutes—with full magazines—and his carriers will be here in less than two hours."

Gajelis grunted in irate acknowledgment. A little voice deep inside told him it was time to give it up, but he could still do it. Yes, his ships were damaged, but *Gloria* was gone completely now—the explosion had been bright enough to be picked out clearly at twenty six million kilometers—and the three carriers still guarding the planetary orbitals were as badly damaged as his *four* surviving carriers. And the Fatted Calf cruisers had been effectively gutted, while their fighters were dodging around for their lives with his own in pursuit. He'd have to deal with Prokorouv's cruisers, as well as Atilius' carriers, but it would still have been little worse than an even fight, if not for Prokorouv's carriers. Still, if he went back to maximum acceleration, just blew past Old Earth and took out the Palace in passing . . .

"We have system recon platform access, Admiral," Tactical called out.

"Incoming encrypted message from Moonbase," Communications chimed in.

"Admiral," Tactical went on, without a break, "system platforms report heavy phase drive emissions closing on Old Earth," Tactical called out. "Lots of electronics, Sir. Electronics are encrypted, and we're having a hard time sorting it out. Looks like three squadrons. We're getting IFF off of them. One of them is CarRon 14, but the other two are squawking 'Fatted Calf One' and 'Fatted Calf Two.'"

"'Fatted Calf?'" Julian repeated with a puzzled frown.

"It's t'e pocking Bible," Poertena said excitedly. "You roast t'e pocking patted calp when t'e prodigal son returns."

"Indeed," Helmut agreed with a smile. "Sergeant Julian, you really need to brush up on your general reading." He studied the icons on his repeater plot. "Three ships in one squadron, noted only as Fatted Calf. And all of Twelfth Squadron, which is broadcasting as Fatted Calf Two."

"Intel update complete," Tactical said.

* * *

"Admiral La Paz reports a tunnel drive footprint, Sir. A bunch of them. It looks like another fleet." Silence hovered for a handful of seconds, and then Lieutenant Commander Clinton cleared her throat. "Confirmed, Sir. Admiral La Paz's count puts it at eighteen ships."

Gajelis looked at his own display as the central computers updated it, then shook his head.

"It's not going to be one of Prince Jackson's forces," he muttered. "Not that big and coming in from there."

"Helmut," Commander Talbert said.

"Helmut," Gajelis agreed bitterly. "Dark Lord of the Sixth. *Damn* that traitorous bastard!"

Commander Talbert wisely avoided pointing out that "traitorous" was, perhaps, a double-edged concept at this particular moment.

"We'll have to withdraw," the admiral continued.

"Withdraw to *where*?" Talbert demanded, unable to keep his anger totally out of his voice.

"Arrangements have been made," Gajelis said flatly. "Signal the squadron to break off and head for the TD limit. Flight Plan Leonidas. I need to make a call."

"So much for time," Helmut sighed, and punched a command into his repeater. A much larger hologram came up, covered with icons which were so much gibberish to Julian. "Ah, there's what we're after!" the admiral said, reaching into the hologram and "tapping" a finger through some of the symbols. The hologram's scale was so small that they scarcely seemed to be moving at all, but the vector codes beside them said otherwise.

"What is it?" Julian asked.

"Fourteenth Squadron," Helmut replied. "Well . . ."

He frowned and brought up a sidebar list and studied it briefly.

"It *was* Fourteenth Squadron," he continued. "Now, it's Fourteenth missing two carriers. Took a bit of a beating, apparently, but still the ones we want."

"Why them?" Julian asked.

"People, Sergeant. People," Helmut sighed. "It's not the ships, it's the minds within them. Fourteenth is Adoula's most loyal squadron. Where *else* would the Prince run to? The one squadron that would beat feet the instant my fleet turned up and Adoula got on board, which is why I had Admiral Niedermayer come in where he did."

"Is it going to work?"

"Well, we'll just have to see, won't we?" Helmut shrugged. "The bad guys aren't precisely where they should be—thanks to the fact that your Prince had to start early. Remind me to discuss the importance of maintaining operational schedules with him." The admiral bared his teeth in a tight smile. "As it is, we'll just have to wait and see. It'll be some time, either way." He banished the plotting hologram and brought up a 3-D chessboard, instead. "Do you play, Sergeant?"

"I wish I could have welcomed you aboard under better circumstances, Your Highness," Victor Gajelis said in a harsh, grating voice as Prince Jackson was shown into his day cabin. The admiral bent his head in a bow, and Adoula forced himself not to swear at him. It had become painfully obvious that Gajelis was not the best flag officer in the Imperial Navy. Unfortunately, all of the ones better than him seemed to be working for the other side, which meant the prince was just going to have to make do.

"You had no way of knowing Prokourov was going to turn traitor," he said as Gajelis straightened. "Neither did General Gianetto and I. And I still don't see how they coordinated this closely with Helmut. I know you could still have turned it around, if it hadn't been for *his* arrival, Victor."

"Thank you, Your Highness," Gajelis said. "My people gave as good as they got. But with Prokourov going over to the other side and bringing Helmut's numbers up even more—"

"Not just Prokourov, I'm afraid," Adoula said more heavily. "Admiral Wu turned *her* coat, too. She didn't have it all her own way. Captain Ramsey refused to obey the orders to go over to the other side, but all three of her other carriers supported her. *Hippogriff* is gone, but Ramsey hammered *Chimera* and *Halkett* pretty severely before she went. But that leaves only Eleventh, Thirteenth, and Fifteenth to support you—thirteen carriers for us, against twenty-six for them, counting the Home Fleet defections. No, Admiral, you were right to break off when you did. Time to get out with what we can and reassemble for a counterattack. General Gianetto and I have already transmitted the order to our other squadrons. Admiral Mahmut will rendezvous with you on your way to the Tsukayama Limit. Admiral La Paz and Admiral Brettle will proceed independently to the rendezvous."

"CarRon 14's changed course, Sir," Tactical said twenty-seven minutes later. "It's broken off."

"Has it?" Helmut replied without looking up from the chessboard as he considered Julian's last move. He moved one of his own rooks in response, then glanced at the Tactical officer. "He's headed for system north, yes?"

"Yes, Sir." The Taco seemed completely unsurprised by Helmut's apparent clairvoyance.

"Good." The admiral looked back at the chessboard. "Your move, I believe, Sergeant?"

"How did you know, Sir?" Julian asked quietly. Helmut glanced up at him, one eyebrow quirked, and Julian gestured at the tactical officer. "How did you know he'd go north?"

"Gajelis is from Auroria Province on Old Earth," Helmut replied. "He's a swimmer. What does a swimmer do when he's been down too long?"

"He goes for the surface," Julian said.

"And that's what he's doing—trying to break for the surface." Helmut nodded at the tactical display. "When he breaks vertically for the TD sphere, four times out of five he has his ships go up." He shrugged. "Never forget, Sergeant. Predictability is one of the few truly unforgivable tactical sins. As Admiral Niedermayer will demonstrate in about eight hours."

"Excuse me, Admiral, but we have a problem," a tight-faced

Commander Talbert said as he entered the briefing room where Adoula and Gajelis had been conferring electronically with Admiral Minerou Mahmut. The three carriers of Mahmut's CarRon 15 had rendezvoused with CarRon 14 less than ten minutes earlier. Now both squadrons were proceeding in company for the Tsukayama Limit, less than four light-minutes ahead of them.

"What sort of problem?" Gajelis demanded testily. On their current flight profile, they were less than twenty-five minutes from the limit.

"Seven phase drive signatures just lit off ahead of us, Sir," Talbert said flatly. "Range two-point-five light-minutes."

"Damn it!" Adoula snarled. "Who?"

"Unknown at this time, Sir," Talbert said. "They're not squawking IFF, but phase signature strengths indicate that they're carriers."

"Seven," Gajelis said anxiously. "And fresh, presumably." He looked at the prince and grimaced. "We're . . . not in good shape."

"Avoid them!" Adoula said. "Just get to the nearest TD point and *jump*."

"It's not that easy, Your Highness," Talbert said with a sigh. "We can jump out from anywhere on the TD sphere, but they're sitting almost bang center of where we were *going* to jump, and they were obviously prepositioned. They just fired up their drives—the best emcon in the galaxy couldn't have hidden carrier phase drives from us at this range if they'd been on-line. It's like they read our minds, or something."

"*Helmut*," Gajelis snarled. "The son of a bitch must've dropped them off at least four or five light-days out, outside our sensor shell. Then he sent them in sublight on a profile that brought them in under such low power the perimeter platforms never saw them coming! But how in hell did he know *where* to deploy them, damn it?!"

"I don't know, Sir," Talbert said. "But however he did it, they're inside any vector change we can manage. We've got velocity directly *towards* their position—forty-six thousand KPS of it. We can jink round a little bit, try to feint them off, but we're already nine million kilometers inside their missile range. The geometry gives even their *cruisers* over thirty million kilometers' range against our closing velocity, and we're only forty-five million out. By now they've already launched cruisers—probably their fighters, too—and they're only holding their missile fire till they can generate better firing solutions and get their cruiser missiles into range. And at our velocity, we're going to end up in *energy* range of them in another sixteen minutes."

"Launch decoy drones," Gajelis said. "Launch fighters for cover, and launch the cruisers, those that are spaceworthy. You, too, Minerou," he added to the admiral on his com display.

"Agreed," Mahmut said. "On my way to CIC. I'll check back in when I get there."

The display blanked, and Gajelis looked back up at Talbert.

"Go," he said sharply. "I'll join you in CIC in a minute."

"Yes, Sir." Talbert nodded and left quickly.

"You're going to fight?" Adoula asked incredulously.

"We'll *have* to," Gajelis replied. "You heard Talbert, Your Highness. We'll have to engage them."

"No, as a matter of fact, you *won't*," the Prince replied. "Have the rest of your forces engage, but getting me to Kellerman is the priority. This ship will avoid action and get out of the system. Have the others cover you."

"That's a bit—" Gajelis began angrily.

"Those are your *orders*, Admiral," Adoula replied. "Follow them!"

"This is going to be interesting," Admiral Niedermayer remarked. "Observe *Trujillo*," he continued. "Breaking off as predicted."

"Sometimes the Admiral scares me, Sir," Senior Captain Erhardt replied. "How did he know Gajelis was going to head *here*?"

"Magic, Marge. Magic," Niedermayer told the commander of his flagship. "Unfortunately, it would appear he was also correct about Adoula."

Niedermayer's flagship had been tapped back into the system recon net ever since Captain Kjerulf had reconfigured his lockout to allow Sixth Fleet access. He'd used that advantage to adjust his ships' position slightly, but it really hadn't been necessary. As Erhardt's last remark indicated, Admiral Helmut had called Adoula's and Gajelis' response almost perfectly. Only the timing had changed . . . and Helmut had gotten them here early enough for the timing not to be a problem.

"I can't believe the rest of them are just going to come right on in to *cover* him." Erhardt shook her head, staring at the plot where six of the seven enemy carriers had altered heading to accelerate directly towards them even as the seventh accelerated directly *away* from them. "The bastard is running out on them, and they're still going to fight for him?"

"Jackson Adoula is a physical coward, Marge," Niedermayer said. "Oh, I'm sure he's found some other way to justify it, even to himself. After all, he's the 'indispensable man,' isn't he? Without his stronghold in the Sagittarius Sector, it'd all the over but the shouting once the Prince retakes the Palace. So, much as I may despise him, there really is a certain logic in getting him away."

"Logic, Sir?!" Erhardt looked at him in something very like disbelief, and it was his turn to shake his head.

Marjorie Erhardt was very good at her job. She was also fairly young for her rank, and she had a falcon's fierce directness, coupled with an even fiercer loyalty to the Empress and the Empire. All of that made her an extremely dangerous weapon, but it also gave her a certain degree of tunnel vision. Henry Niedermayer remembered another young, fiery captain who'd suffered from the same sort of narrowness of focus. Then-Vice Admiral Angus Helmut had taken that young captain in hand and expanded his perspective without ever compromising his integrity, which left Niedermayer with an obligation to repay the debt by doing the same thing for Erhardt. And he still had a few minutes to do it in.

"The fact that they're fighting for a bad cause doesn't make them cowards, Marge," he said, just a trifle coldly. She looked at him, and he grimaced.

"One of the worst things any military commander can do is to allow contempt for his adversaries to lead him into underestimating them or their determination," he told her. "And Adoula didn't seduce them all by dangling money in front of them. At least some of them signed on because they agreed with him that the Empire was in trouble and didn't understand what the Empress was doing about it.

"And however they got into his camp in the first place, they all recognize the stakes they agreed to play for. They're guilty of High Treason, Marge. The penalty for that is death. They may realize perfectly well that their so-called 'leader' is about to bug out on them, but that doesn't change their options. And even without *Trujillo* they've got only one less carrier than we do. You think they are just going to surrender and face the firing squads when at least some of them may be able to fight their way past us?"

"Put that way, no, Sir," Erhardt replied after a moment. "But they're *not* going to get past us, are they?"

"No, Captain Erhardt, they're not," Niedermayer agreed. "And it's time to show them why they're not."

"Holy Mary, Mother of God," Admiral Minerou Mahmut breathed as his tactical plot abruptly updated. The icons of the seven carriers waiting for him were suddenly joined by an incredible rash of smaller crimson icons.

"Bogeys," his flagship's Tactical Officer announced in the flat, hard voice of a professional rigidly suppressing panic through training and raw discipline. "Multiple cruiser-range phase drive signatures. BattleComp makes it three hundred plus." More light codes blinked to sudden baleful life. "Update! Fighter-range phase drive detection. Minimum seven-fifty."

Mahmut swallowed hard. Helmut. That incredible bastard couldn't have more than a single cruiser flotilla with the force which would be settling into Old Earth orbit within the next twenty-five minutes. He'd dropped the others—*all* the others—off with the carrier squadrons he'd detached for his damned ambush!

Even now, with the proof staring him in the face, Mahmut could scarcely believe that even *Helmut* would try something that insane. If it hadn't worked out—if he'd been forced into combat against a concentrated Home Fleet—the absence of his cruiser strength, especially with the carrier squadrons diverted as well, would have been decisive.

Which didn't change the fact that Mahmut's six carriers, seventy-two cruisers, and five hundred remaining fighters were about to get brutally hammered.

He spared a moment to glance at the secondary plot where *Trujillo* was still generating delta V at her maximum acceleration. The distance between her and the rest of the formation was up to almost a million kilometers, and to get at her, Helmut's ships would have to get through Mahmut's. A part of the admiral was tempted to order his ships to stand down, to surrender them and let the Sixth Fleet task group have clean shots at *Trujillo*. But if he'd been in command on the other side, he wouldn't have been accepting any surrenders under the circumstances. His own small task group's crossing velocity was so great that it would have been impossible for anyone from the other side to match vectors and put boarding parties onto his ships before they crossed the Tsukayama Limit and disappeared into tunnel-space.

Besides, some of them might actually make it.

Commander Roger "Cobalt" McBain was a contented man. To his way of thinking, he was at the pinnacle of his career. CAG of a Navy fighter group was all he'd ever wanted to be.

Technically, his actual position was that of "Commander 643rd Fighter Group," the hundred and twenty-five fighters assigned to HMS *Centaur*. CAG was an older term, which had stood for the title of "Commander Attack Group" until three or four Navy reorganizations ago. There were those who claimed that the acronym's actual origin was to be found in the title of "Commander *Air* Group," which went clear back to the days when ships had battled on oceans, and the fighters had been air-intake jet-powered machines. McBain wasn't sure about that—his interest in ancient history was strictly minimal—but he didn't really care. Over the years, the position had had many names, but none of them had stuck in the tradition-minded Navy the way "CAG" had. If one fighter pilot said to another, "Oh, he's the CAG," whether the ships were old jets or stingships or space fighters, everyone knew what he meant.

From his present position, he might well be promoted to

command of an entire carrier squadron's fighter wing, which would be nice—in its way—but far more of an administrative post. He'd get much less cockpit time as a wing CAG, although it would look good on his resume. From there, he might claw his way into command of a carrier, or squadron, or even a fleet. But from his point of view, and right now it was damned panoramic, CAG was as good as a job got. A part of him wished he was with the rest of the squadron's fighter wing, preparing to jump Adoula's main body. But most of him was perfectly content to be exactly where he was.

And it was interesting to watch Admiral Niedermayer at his work. Obviously, the Old Man had learned a lot from Admiral Helmut . . . although McBain had never realized before that clairvoyance could be taught. But it must be possible. If it wasn't, how could Niedermayer have predicted where HMS *Trujillo* would be accurately enough to deploy the 643rd ten full hours *before* Gajelis and Adoula ever arrived?

"Start warming up the plasma conduits," Mahmut said. "Any cruisers that make it through are to be recovered by any available carrier."

"Yes, Sir," his flag captain acknowledged crisply, even though both of them knew how unlikely any of their units were to survive the next few minutes.

"Open fire," Admiral Niedermayer said, almost conversationally, and the next best thing to eleven thousand missile launchers spat fire. Four hundred fighters armed with antifighter missiles salvoed their ordnance at Mahmut's fighters, and another three hundred and fifty sent over seventeen hundred Leviathans at his cruisers. None of the ship-launched missiles bothered with the sublight parasites, however. Ultimately, the cruisers and fighters had no escape if the tunnel drive ships were crippled or destroyed, and Niedermayer's fire control concentrated on the carriers with merciless professionalism. He'd waited until the range was down to just over ten million kilometers. At that range, and at their current closing velocity, that gave him just under four minutes to engage with missiles before they entered energy range. In that four minutes, each of his cruisers fired a hundred and fifty missiles, and each of his carriers fired over four thousand. The next best thing to eighty thousand missiles slammed into the defenses protecting Minerou Mahmut's carriers.

At such short range, countermissiles were far less effective than usual. They simply didn't have the tracking time as the offensive fire slashed across their engagement envelope, and they stopped perhaps thirty percent of the incoming birds. Point defense clusters fired desperately, and there were thousands of them. But they, too, were fatally short of engagement time. They stopped another forty percent . . . which meant that "only" twenty-four thousand got through.

Maximum effective standoff range for even a capital shipkiller laser head against a starship was little more than seven thousand kilometers. At that range, however, they could blast through even ChromSten armor, and they did. Carriers were tough, the toughest mobile structures ever designed and built by human beings, but there were limits in all things. Armor yielded only stubbornly, even under that incredible pounding, but it *did* yield. Atmosphere streamed from ruptured compartments. Weapon mounts were blotted away. Power runs arced and exploded as energy blew back through them. Their own fire ripped back at their enemies, but Niedermayer's sheer wealth of point defense blunted the far lighter salvoes Mahmut's outnumbered ships could throw, and his carriers' armor shook off the relative handful of hits which got through to it.

By the time CarRon 15 and what was left of CarRon 14 reached energy range, three of its seven carriers and forty-one of its seventy-two cruisers had been destroyed outright.

By the time the traitorous carrier squadrons crossed the track of Niedermayer's task force, exactly eleven badly damaged cruisers and one totally crippled carrier survived.

"Admiral," Lieutenant Commander Clinton said with a gulp. "We just got swept by lidar! Point source, Delta quadrant four-one-five."

"What does *that* mean?" Adoula demanded sharply. He was sitting in a hastily rigged command chair next to the admiral's.

"It means someone's out there," Gajelis snapped. He'd left his handful of cruisers and fighters behind to assist Mahmut. His flagship was going to be fighting whoever it was with only onboard weapons.

"Captain Devarnachan is sweeping," Tactical said. "Emissions! Raid designated Sierra Five. One hundred twenty-five fighters, closing from Delta Four-One-Five."

"Damn Helmut!" Gajelis snarled. "*Damn* him!"

"Leviathans! Six hundred twenty-five vampires!"

"Three minutes to Tsukayama Limit," Astrogation announced tautly.

"They'll only get one shot," Gajelis said, breathing hard. "Hang on, Your Highness . . ."

"Damn and blast," McBain snarled as the distinctive signature of a TD drive formed. At such short range and with such short flight times, *Trujillo*'s countermissiles had been effectively useless, and over fifty of the Leviathans had managed to get through the carrier's desperately firing point defense lasers. They'd ripped hell out of her, and he'd hoped that would be enough to cripple her, but carriers were pretty damned tough.

"We got a piece of her, Cobalt," his XO replied. "A big one. And Admiral Niedermayer kicked hell out of the rest of them. Doesn't look like any of *them* got away."

"I know, Allison," McBain said angrily, though his anger certainly wasn't directed at *her*. "But a piece wasn't enough." He sighed, then shook himself. "Oh, well, we did our best. And you're right, we did get a piece of her. Let's turn 'em around and head back to the barn. Beer's on me."

"Damn straight it is!" Commander Stanley agreed with a laugh. Then, as their fighters swept around through a graceful turn and began decelerating back towards their carriers, her tone turned more thoughtful. "Wonder how things went at the Palace?"

"Your Highness, your mother's been through . . . a terrible ordeal," the psychiatrist said. He was a specialist in pharmacological damage. "Normally, we'd stabilize her with targeted medications. But given the . . . vile concoctions they used on her, not to mention the damage to her implant—"

"Which is very severe," the implant specialist interrupted. "It's shutting down and resetting itself frequently, almost randomly, because of general system failures. And it's dumping data at random, as well. It has to be hell inside her head, Your Highness."

"And nothing can be done about it?" Roger asked.

"These damned paranoid ones you people have, they're designed to be unremovable, Your Highness," the specialist said, with a shrug which expressed his helpless frustration. "I know why, but seeing what happens when something like this goes wrong—"

"It didn't '*go wrong,*'" Roger said flatly. "It was made to fail. And when I get my hands on the people who did that, I intend to . . . discuss it with them in some detail. But for right now, answer my question. Is there anything at all we can do to get this . . . this *thing* out of my mother's head?"

"No," the specialist said heavily. "The only thing we could do would be to attempt surgical removal, Your Highness, and I'd give her a less than even chance of surviving the procedure. Which doesn't even consider the probability of additional, serious neurological damage."

"And the implant, of course, responds to brain action, Your Highness," the psychiatrist noted. "And since the brain action is highly confused at the moment—"

"Doc?" Roger said impatiently, looking at Dobrescu.

"Roger, I don't even have a degree," Dobrescu protested. "I'm a *shuttle pilot.*"

"Doc, damn it, do not give me that old song and dance," Roger snapped.

"All right." Dobrescu threw his hands into the air almost angrily. "You want my interpretation of what they're telling you? She's totally pocked in the head, all right? Wackers. Maybe the big brains—the people who *do* have the degrees—can do something for her eventually. But right now, she's in one minute, out the next. I don't even know when you can see her, Roger. She's still asking for New

Madrid, whether she's . . . in or out. In reality, or out in la-la land. When she's in, she wants his head. She knows she's the Empress, she knows she's in bad shape, she knows who did it to her, and she wants him dead. I've tried to point out that you're back, but she's still mixing it up with New Madrid. With all the drugs and physical duress, on top of the way they butchered her toot, they've got her half convinced even when she's got some contact with reality that you *were* in on the plot. And when she's in la-la land . . ."

"I was there to see enough of that." Roger's face tightened, and he looked at Catrone. "Tomcat?"

"Christ, Your Highness," Catrone said. "Don't put this on me!"

"That was the deal," Roger told him. "As you asked me, not so long ago, are you going back on your word?"

Catrone stared at him for several seconds, then shrugged.

"When she's in, she's *in*," he said. "All the way in. She's still got a few problems," he conceded, raising a hand at Dobrescu, "but she knows she's Empress. And *she's* not willing to step aside." He looked at Roger, his face hard. "I'm sorry, Roger. It's not because I don't trust you, but she's my *Empress*. I'm not going against her, not when she still knows who she is. Not when it's too early to know whether or not she can get better."

"Very well," Roger said, his voice cold. "But if she's in charge, she needs to get back into the saddle. Things are in very bad shape, and we need her up," he continued, looking at the doctors. "There are people she *has* to meet."

"That would be . . . unwise," the psychiatrist said. "The strain could—"

"Either she can take it, or she can't," Roger said flatly. "Ask *her*. I'm out of this decision loop, starting right now."

"Like hell," Catrone said angrily. "Are you going to go off into one of your Roger sulks? You can't just throw the weight of the entire Empire onto her shoulders, damn it! She's *sick*. She just needs some *recovery* time, goddamn it!"

"Tomcat, I can't just make the galaxy *stop* while she gets better!" Roger snapped. "Okay. This was *your* decision—that was the deal. And for all I know, you've made exactly the right one. But if she's

Empress, she has got to *be* Empress, and that means *she* needs to determine what *I* do."

"But—"

"No '*buts*,' damn it! You know as well as I do how unsettled the situation is right now. Sure, we've got Helmut in orbit, and Prokourov and Kjerulf supporting us, but you've seen the coverage, just like me. Some of the newsies are doing their best to be dispassionate and impartial, but only a handful, and the *rest* of the rumors—"

He broke off with a frustrated snarl, then shook himself.

"Adoula did a damned good job of painting *me* as the one behind the first coup for public opinion," he said flatly. "Hell, you heard Doc—they've got *her* half-convinced! It's going to take time for everybody—*anybody*—to begin to understand what really happened. I know that. And I also know that's actually a pocking good argument in favor of Mother remaining in charge. If *she's* on the Throne, then obviously I'm not trying to take it away from her, right? So I *agree* with you about that, damn it! And I don't care if she makes me her one hundred percent alternate, which as Heir Primus *should* be my job right now, or just hands me the shit details to reduce her load while *she* tries to do the job. Hell, I don't care if she tells me to get off-planet and go back to Marduk! But for me to work for her, to help her, I have to at least be able to *talk* to her, Sergeant Major. And right now, I can't even do *that*!"

"Okay, okay!" Catrone held up his hands, as if he were physically fending Roger off. "Point taken, Your Highness—*point!*" He paused and drew a deep breath. "I'll see about a meeting. Not in private—that would probably be bad. A group meeting. You're right, there *are* people she has to see. The new Navy Minister. The Prime Minister. Helmut. I'll set up a meeting—an *easy* one," he added, looking at the doctors.

"A short meeting with people she knows," the psychiatrist said. "That may help her stabilize. It's an environment she understands. But *short*. Nonstressful."

"Agreed," Roger said curtly.

"And you'll be in it," Catrone said.

"I can't wait."

★ ★ ★

"Your clothes survived," Despreaux said from the bed.

"Sixty *million* credits worth of damage." Roger sighed, tossing his cane onto the foot of the bed and flopping down next to her. They'd gotten their old bodies back. Sort of. Despreaux had opted for . . . a bit of upper body enhancement, and she'd kept the hair. She'd decided that she liked being blonde, even if it didn't set off Roger's coloring as well as her earlier dark brown had.

Roger, on the other hand, was back to plain old Roger. Well, plain old Roger just starting to regenerate the calf of his leg. Two meters, long blond hair, green eyes. Deep frown . . .

"Sixty million," he repeated. "And that's just to the *Palace*."

"And then there's the rumor that there are dozens of secret ways in." Despreaux shuddered. "We need to get those blocked—and make damned sure everyone *knows* they're blocked."

"Working on it." Roger sighed again. "And we need a new Empress' Own. Replacement equipment. Work on the damage we did to the com facilities . . . Christ."

"If it were an easy job, it wouldn't take us," Despreaux told him with a crooked smile.

"And we need something else." Roger's tone was serious enough that her half-smile faded.

"What?"

"An heir," he said quietly.

The replicator had been found, turned over, the fetus poured out onto the floor and crushed. Roger had felt strange looking down at the pathetic, ruined body of the brother he would never know. They'd found the culprit among the surviving mercenaries—the DNA on his trousers had been a dead giveaway—and he was awaiting trial for regicide.

"Whooo," Despreaux said, letting out her breath. "That's a big thing to spring on a poor old farm girl! I'd hoped to have kids someday, your kids as a matter of fact, but . . ."

"Seriously," he said, sitting up on the bed. "We need an heir of the body, out of the replicator, viable to take the Throne. Hell, we need duplicates. Things are bad right now. I hope like hell that—"

"I understand," Despreaux said, reaching up to touch his cheek. "I'll stop in at the clinic tomorrow. I'm sure they'll take me in without an appointment."

"You know," Roger said, sliding down to hold her in his arms, "there's another way to get things started . . ."

"God, I thought once I got you in bed, it would be *easy*." She hit him with a pillow. "Little did I realize what a crazed sex maniac hid under that just plain *crazed* exterior!"

"I've got *years* of catching up," Roger replied, laughing. "And there's no time like the present."

"Sergeant Major Catrone," Alexandra VII sighed as Tomcat entered the sitting room.

She wore a high-necked gown, and her hair was simply but exquisitely styled. She looked every centimeter the Empress, but there were still shadowy bruises around her wrists. They had almost— *almost*—vanished, and he knew the medics had almost completely healed the . . . other marks on her body, as well. But they were still there, and something stirred and bared its fangs deep at the heart of him as she touched a control to raise the back of her float chair into a sitting position, and held out a hand.

"I'm so glad to see you," she said.

"All you need to do is call, Your Majesty." Catrone dropped to one knee instead of taking the proffered hand. "I am, and always have been, your servant."

"Oh, get up, Tomcat." Alexandra laughed, and laughed harder at his expression. "What? You thought I didn't know your nickname?" She grinned. "You were a bachelor for many years when you served me; I learned *all* about your nickname." She held out her hand again, fiercely. "Take my hand, Tomcat."

"Majesty," he said, and took it, dropping back to one knee again beside her chair and holding it.

"I haven't been . . . well enough to tell you," Alexandra said, staring at him, "what a *relief* it was to see your face. My one true paladin, there by my side once again. It was like a light in the darkness—and it was such an *awful* darkness," she ended angrily.

"Majesty," Catrone said, embarrassed. "I'm sorry it took us so long. We wanted—we *all* wanted—to move sooner, but until Roger—"

"Roger!" the Empress shouted, snatching back her hand and crossing her arms. "Everyone wants to talk about *Roger*! The prodigal son returned—ha! *Fatted calf!* I'd like to roast *him*!"

"Majesty, control yourself," Catrone said, gently but firmly. "Whatever you knew, or thought you knew, about Roger, you must take him as he is now. Fatted Calf would have been impossible without him. Not just because of the hidden protocols in his mind, either. Because of his leadership, his vision, his determination. His planning. He handled a dozen different actions as if they were one. Perfect combat gestalt, the best I've ever seen. And all he thought of was *you*, Your Majesty, from the first moment I told him what they were *doing* to you. His anger . . ."

The sergeant major shook his head.

"Only one thing kept him from killing New Madrid out of hand. I truly believe only one thing *could* have kept him from doing it, and it wasn't the Empire, Your Majesty. It was his fiancée. He loves you, Your Majesty. He loves his mother. He isn't his father's son; he's yours."

Alexandra looked at him for a moment, then looked away and shrugged, the movement angry, frustrated, possibly even a bit uncertain.

"I hear you, Tomcat. Maybe you really believe that. Maybe it's even true. But when I see him, I see his father's face. Why, of all my children, did *he* have to be the only one to survive?"

"Luck," Catrone said with a shrug of his own. "Excellent bodyguards. And perhaps most of all the fact that, I'm sorry, he's one of the hardest, coldest bastards House MacClintock has ever coughed up."

"Certainly a bastard," Alexandra agreed astringently. "But how I *wish* John were still alive! I knew I could trust him. Trust his good judgment, trust his reasoning."

"With all due respect, Your Majesty," Catrone said with a swallow, "John was a good man. A smart one, and as honest as he could be, working in this snake pit. A . . . decent fighter, and someone I would have been proud to serve one day as Emperor. But . . . Adoula got away. He's calling in all the fleets he controls, and proclaiming that *we're* the ones using drugs and torture to control you now that we've gotten you into *our* hands. We're in the midst of a civil war, and if there's one MacClintock, besides you, who I'd trust at the helm in a civil war, it's Roger. More than John. More even then Alex."

"So you say," Alexandra replied. "But I don't—"

"—why, Sergeant Major Catrone! What a pleasant surprise!" she said delightedly, her face blossoming into a huge smile. "Have you come for a visit?"

"Yes, Your Majesty," Catrone said evenly, his face wooden.

"Well, I hope you've had a good conversation with my friend, the Earl of New Madrid," Alexandra continued. "He's returned to my side at last, my one true love. So surprising that he's such a good man, with a son who's so evil. But, tell me, how are your horses? You raise horses now, don't you?"

"They're well, Your Majesty," he said, standing with a wince. His knees weren't what they used to be.

"I'm afraid I have a meeting in a few minutes with Our loyal servant, Prince Jackson," the Empress said, waving him to a chair. "But I certainly have time to speak to my most favored former retainer. So, tell me—"

"How is she?" Eleanora said, taking Catrone's arm to halt him briefly before they entered the room.

"Tracking," Catrone replied. "Fine at the moment."

"Let's hope this goes well," Eleanora sighed. "Please God it goes well."

"For your side or for her?" Catrone asked bitterly.

"We're on the *same* side, Sergeant Major!" Eleanora snapped. "Remember that."

"I know. I try, but—" Catrone shrugged, pain darkening his eyes. "But sometimes it's hard."

"You love her," Eleanora said gently. "Too much, I think."

"That I do," Catrone whispered. His face clenched for a moment, and then he shook himself. "Where's the Prince?" he asked in a determinedly lighter tone.

"Late," Eleanora said, her lips pursed in irritation.

They entered the conference room and took their seats. Their late entry did not pass unremarked, and they drew a stern look from the Empress at the head of the long, polished table. The room was lined with windows, looking out over one of the south gardens, and bright sunlight filled it with a warm glow. The Prime Minister had one end of the conference table and the Empress had the other. The new Navy Minister was also present; as was Admiral Helmut, who was temporarily holding down the position of CNO; the Finance Minister; Julian, who was still in some undefined billet; and Despreaux, who was in another. And, of course, there was one empty chair.

"And where is Roger?" Alexandra asked coldly.

The door opened, and Roger limped in. He wore a custom-tailored suit of bright yellow, a forest-green ascot, and a straw hat. The regeneration of his leg was still in its very early stages, and he leaned on a color-coordinated cane as he bowed.

"Sorry I'm late," he said, tugging on a leash. "Dogzard insisted on a walk, so I took her to visit Patty. And she didn't want to come back again . . . naturally. Come *on*, you stupid beast," he continued as he practically dragged the creature into the room. She hissed at most of the people sitting around the table, then saw the Empress and produced a happy little whine of pleasure.

Eleanora was watching Alexandra's face and sighed mentally as she saw the quick flicker of the Empress' eyes. In some ways, Eleanora wished Roger had retained his Augustus Chung body-mod. That had been impossible, of course, if only because of the public-relations considerations. But every time the Empress saw him, it was as if she had to remind herself physically that he was not his father even before she could deal with the ambiguity of her feelings where *he* was concerned.

"Sorry," Roger repeated as he finally managed to wrestle Dogzard across to the chair set aside for him. "Just because I let her eat one person . . . Sit," he commanded. "Sit! Quit looking at the Prime Minister that way, it's not respectful. Sit. Lie down. Good Dogzard."

The prince settled into his own chair, hung his cane over its back, looked around the table, and set his hat in front of him.

"Where were we?"

"I *think* we were about to discuss Navy repairs and consolidations," Alexandra said, raising one eyebrow. "Now that you're here . . ."

The meeting had been going on for an hour, which was longer than Catrone had feared, and far shorter than he'd hoped.

"Between making sure the Saints don't snap up systems and holding back Adoula, there just aren't enough ships to go around," Andrew Shue, Baron Talesian and the new Navy Minister, said, and threw up his hands.

"Then we make faces," Roger said, leaning sideways to pet Dogzard. "We bluff. We only have to keep them off our backs for . . . what? Eighteen months? Long enough for the shipyards to start pushing out the new carriers."

"Which will be *ruinously* expensive," Jasper O'Higgins, the Finance Minister said.

"We're at war," Roger replied coldly. "War is waste. Most of those expensive ships of yours are going to be scrap floating among the stars in two years, anyway. Mr. O'Higgins. The point is to have them, and then to use them as judiciously as humanly possible. But we have to have them, first, and to do that, we have to keep our enemies off our backs long enough for them to be built."

"They'll be used judiciously," Helmut said. "I know Gajelis. He's a bigger-hammer commander. 'Quantity has a quality of its own.' I'd be surprised if we couldn't give him at least two-to-one in damage levels. Admittedly, even those numbers are terrible enough. A lot of our boys and girls are going to die. But . . ."

The diminutive admiral shrugged, and the Empress grimaced.

"And Adoula has shipyards of his own," she said angrily. "I wish I could strangle my father for letting any of them get built outside the central worlds, especially in Adoula's backyard!"

"We could always . . . send an emissary to Adoula," the Prime Minister suggested, only to pause as Dogzard's hiss cut him off.

"Down!" Roger said to the dog-lizard, then looked at Yang. "Methinks my pet dislikes your suggestion, Mr. Prime Minister. And so do I."

"You yourself just pointed out that we have to buy time, Your Highness," the Prime Minister said coldly. "Negotiations—even, or especially, negotiations we don't intend to go anywhere—might be one way to buy that time. And if it should turn out that there actually was some sort of feasible arrangement, a *modus vivendi*, why—"

"Now I *know* I don't like it," Roger said, his voice several degrees colder than the Prime Minister's.

"Nor do I," Alexandra said. Her voice was less chill than her son's, but undeniably frosty. "Adoula is in a state of rebellion. If he succeeds in breaking off permanently—or even merely seems to have temporarily succeeded—others *will* try to do the same. Before long, the Empire will end up as a scattered group of feuding worlds, and all *we* may hold will be a few systems. And the expense at that point will be enormous. No, Roger has a point," she conceded, looking at him balefully nonetheless. "We can make faces. Bluff. But we will *not* take any step which even suggests we might ever treat with Adoula as if he were a legitimate head of state. Instead, we'll send—"

"—and I'm very much looking forward to the Imperial Festival, my love."

Her voice changed abruptly, crisp decisiveness melting into cloying sweetness, and she gazed at Roger with soulful eyes.

"As am I," Roger said. *His* expression had frozen into an iron mask as the Empress' had changed to one of adoration. "It is about that time, isn't it?"

"Oh, yes, my dear," the Empress crooned. "What will you be wearing? I want to make sure we're simply the *loveliest* couple—"

"I'm not sure, yet," Roger interrupted calmly, gently. "But I think, Alexandra, that this meeting's gone on long enough, don't you?" He waved to one of the guards by the door. "Let me call your ladies in waiting. That way you can make yourself fresh and beautiful again," he added, glancing sideways at Catrone, who gave a brief nod of approval.

When the docile Empress had been led from the room, Roger

stood and swept the people still seated around the conference table with eyes of emerald ice.

"Not a word," he said. "Not one pocking damned *word*. Meeting *adjourned*."

"Well?" Roger said, looking up from yet another of the endless reports floating in the holographic display above his desk. Decisions *had* to be made, and by default, he was making them, despite the fact that his mother had yet to define precisely what authority, if any, was his. Nobody was raising the issue, however.

Not more than once.

"It's a bad one," Catrone said.

His face was drawn, his eyes worried, as he sat down in one of the office's float chairs at Roger's wave.

"Really bad," he continued. "She's . . . changing. She's not asking for Adoula as much, not since we got the worst of the drugs scrubbed out of her system and told her he's gone off to his sector for a while. She still asking for New Madrid, but . . ." Catrone swallowed, and his face worked. "But not as often."

"What's wrong?" Roger asked.

"Christ, Your Highness," Catrone said in an anguished voice, dropping his face into his hands. "Now she's coming on to *me*! That *bastard*. That *stinking* bastard!"

"Pock!" Roger leaned back and grabbed his ponytail.

He stared at the older man for several seconds, then inhaled deeply.

"Tomcat, I know how hard this is for you. But you *have* to stay with her. You have to stay with us!"

"I will," Catrone said. He raised his head, tears running down his face. "If I leave, who *knows* what she'll latch onto? But, God! Roger, it's *hard*!"

"Be her paladin, Tomcat," Roger said then, his face set. "If needs be, damn it, be *more* than her paladin."

"Roger!"

"You just said it yourself. If you're not there for her, someone else will be. Someone who's not as good a man as you are. Someone

I can't trust like you. Someone *she* can't trust like you. You're on this post until relieved, Sergeant Major. Is that understood? And you'll do whatever it takes to stand your post, Marine. Clear?"

"Clear," Catrone grated. "Order received and understood, and I will comply. You bastard."

"That I am." Roger grinned tightly. "Literally and figuratively. The last bastard standing. The flag of the *Basik*'s Own wears a bar sinister proudly. We carried it across two continents, and to Old Earth, and into this very damned Palace, and we did *anything necessary* to complete the mission. Welcome to the Regiment. Now you know what it means to be one of us."

"And I think we should inform Mistress Tompkins that I'll need a new dress, don't you?" Alexandra said softly.

"Yes, Your Majesty," Lady Russell agreed.

They sat in a gazebo, watching cold rain fall beyond the force screen. Lady Russell was expertly sewing a tapestry, while the Empress mangled a needlepoint of a puppy in a basket.

"I'll never know how you do that so well," the Empress said, smiling politely.

"Years of practice, Your Majesty," Lady Russell replied.

"I'll have many years to practice—

"—two carrier squadrons to the Marduk System," Alexandra said, her face hard. "Given what Roger's said about—"

She stopped, and looked around, frowning.

"Where am I?" she asked in a voice which was suddenly cold and dead.

"The gazebo, Your Majesty," Lady Russell said softly, and looked at her half-fearfully. "Are you well?"

"I was in the conference room," Alexandra said tightly. "I was in a *meeting*! It was *sunny*! Where's the *meeting*? Where are the *people*? Why is it *raining*?"

"That—" Lady Russell swallowed. "Your Majesty, that was two days ago."

"Oh, my God," Alexandra whispered, and looked at the material in her lap. "What *is* this?"

"Needlepoint?" Lady Russell asked, reaching unobtrusively for her communicator.

"It's bloody awful, is what it is!" Alexandra spun the hoop across the gazebo. "Get me Sergeant Major Catrone!"

"Sit, Sergeant Major," Alexandra said, and pointed to the seat Lady Russell had vacated.

"Your Majesty," Tomcat said.

At Roger's order, Catrone had once more donned the blue and red of the Empress' Own, at his old rank of sergeant major. He wore dress uniform, and the golden aiguillette hanging from his shoulder indicated Gold Battalion, the personal command—and bodyguard—of the reigning monarch. Empress Alexandra VII, in this case.

"What happened in the meeting, Sergeant Major?" Alexandra rubbed her face furiously. "I was *in* the meeting, and then I was here, in the gazebo. What happened to me? Who's *doing* this to me?"

"First of all," Catrone said carefully, "no one is doing anything to you, Your Majesty. It's already been done."

She stopped rubbing and sat still, her hands still over her eyes, and he continued.

"Your Majesty, you have two mental states, as we've tried to explain to you before." He waved a hand at her. "This state. Alexandra the Seventh, Empress of the Empire of Man. Fully functional. As good a sovereign as I've ever served. Twice the sovereign her father ever was."

"Thank you for the soft soap, Tomcat," Alexandra said mockingly, eyes still covered. "And my other . . . state?"

"The other," he said even more carefully, then paused. "Well, Your Majesty, in the other you're . . . pliable. You still occasionally ask for your 'good friend,' the Earl of New Madrid, and refer to Prince Jackson as 'Our loyal Prince Jackson.'"

"Oh, God," she said.

"Do you really want it all?" Catrone asked. "Face facts, Your Majesty. You're still in a pretty delicate condition."

"I want it all." She sighed, lowering her hands at last. Then her face firmed, and she met his eye levelly. "All. What happened?"

"In your other state—"

"What do you call that?" she interrupted. "If you call . . . this one Alexandra. *Do* you call it Alexandra, Tomcat?"

"Yes, Your Majesty," he said firmly. "This is the Empress Alexandra. The woman I gave my service to long ago."

"And the other?"

"Well," Catrone winced. "We just call it la-la-land. The doctors have a long technical name—"

"I can imagine," she said dryly. "Do I know I'm Empress?"

"Yes, Your Majesty." Catrone's swallowed. "But, frankly, we just ignore anything you tell us to do. You generally don't give any orders, though."

He paused.

"What *do* I do?" she asked.

"Whatever you're told," Catrone said, his face hard. "About the only positive contribution you make is to ask when your very special friend will be back. And if he's not around, you hit on me, Your Majesty."

"Oh, Christ, Thomas." Her face went blank, and tears formed in her eyes. "Oh, Christ. I'm so sorry!"

"I'm not." Catrone shrugged. "I'm not happy that this has happened to you, Your Majesty, but I'm glad it's me. I've never seen you do it to any other male . . ." He paused again, then shrugged. "Except Roger."

"What?!"

"You think he's New Madrid," Catrone said. "You said *all*."

"And I meant it," Alexandra ground out. She inhaled deeply, nostrils flaring, and leaned back in her chair. "You said I was out for two days?"

"Yes, Your Majesty. We just left you with your ladies. You were . . . monitored by the guards to make sure none of them started giving suggestions."

"Good," Alexandra said firmly. Then she softened, and looked at him oddly. "Thomas?"

"Yes, Your Majesty?"

Her voice was much softer, and he watched her expression carefully, wondering if she'd wandered off again.

"I'm me," she said, and astonished him with a grin. "I could see the question in your eyes. But I have a very serious question of my own, one I'd like an honest answer to. What did my son tell *you* to do? About my come-ons?"

Catrone's hands worked on the arms of his chair, and he stared out at the rain for several long moments. Then he looked back at her and raised his eyes to meet her gray ones.

"He ordered me to do whatever was necessary to keep you from finding some other . . . gentleman companion," he said bluntly. "The doctors all agreed that any such . . . gentleman companion could tell you to give any order he thought up when you're in your la-la state."

"My God, he *is* a bastard, isn't he?" There was actually a bubble of delight in Alexandra's voice, and she shook her head and rubbed the bridge of her nose. "I'm having a hard time framing this next question, Thomas. Did he do that . . . ?"

"He did it for the good of the Empire," Catrone said, his tone as blunt as before. "And he did it knowing the trial I'd face. He told me my term of service is now until one of us dies."

"And you accepted that order?" Alexandra asked calmly.

"I've always served you, Your Majesty," Catrone said, looking suddenly very old and tired. "I always will. But, yes. When Roger gave that order, I obeyed it as if it had come from the mouth of my Emperor."

"Good," she said. "Good. If he can command that loyalty, that service from you—from my strength and my paladin—then, yes, perhaps I have misjudged him."

She paused, and her lips worked, trying not to smile.

"Thomas . . . ?"

"No," he said.

"You don't know what I was going to ask," she pointed out.

"Yes, I do," he said. "And the answer is: No. We never have."

"Tempted?" she asked.

He looked up, his eyes hot, almost angry, and half-glared at her. One cheek muscle twitched, and Alexandra smiled warmly.

"I'll take that as a yes," she said, leaning back in her chair, and cradled her chin in one hand, index finger tapping at her cheek. "You've remarried, haven't you, Tomcat?"

"Yes," Tomcat replied warily.

"Pity."

"What's this about, Catrone?" Roger demanded as he strode down the corridor. "Damn it, I'm up to my eyeballs in work. We're *all* up to our eyeballs in work."

"She's tracking right now," Catrone replied. "She has something she wants to say, and when she calls, you go."

"I'm just getting used to being treated like an adult," Roger snapped. "I'm not happy about being treated like a child again."

"You're not," Eleanora said as she joined them from a cross-corridor. Despreaux was with her, trotting to keep up with the shorter woman, and having a hell of a time doing so in court shoes.

"No, you're not," Roger's fiancée echoed, hopping on one foot and falling behind as she finally gave up and ripped the shoes off. "You're being treated like her Heir. She has something important to say."

The shoes came off, and she carried them in one hand by their straps as she hurried to catch back up.

"It's not just you, Roger," Eleanora said, nodding at Despreaux in thanks. "All of your Companions, your staff, Catrone, the Prime Minister, the full Cabinet, and the leaders of the major parties in both Lords and Commons."

"And in the throne room," Roger growled. "It's a pocking barn! Why the throne room?"

"I don't know," Julian said as he joined them, "but she called for the Imperial Regalia."

Krindi Fain, Honal, and Doc Dobrescu followed in Julian's wake, and Roger glanced at all four of them sourly.

"You guys, too?" he asked as they reached the doors of the throne room.

"Us, too," Julian agreed. "But the Prime Minister and a few of the others have already been in there for over half an hour."

"Crap," Roger said. "Tomcat, you're sure she's not in la-la-land?" he asked, holding up his hand to stop the footman who'd been about to open the door.

"Hasn't been for a day and a half," Catrone replied. "I don't think it's going to stick, but . . ."

"But we'd better get whatever this is over with while it does, right?" Roger said, lowering his hand and nodding at the flunky.

"Right," Catrone agreed as the throne room door swung open.

The throne room of the Empire of Man was a must-see on any tour of the Palace. It was a hundred meters long, and it had escaped the fighting almost completely unscathed. The soaring ceiling, with its magnificent fresco depicting the rise of Man and of the Empire, was intact, suspended sixty meters in the air by flying buttresses that seemed far too thin to support the weight. But they were ChromSten, representing the power and glory that had supported that rise.

More murals covered the walls, inlaid in precious gems. Spaceflight. Medicine. Chemistry. Trade. The arts. All that it meant to be "Man" was represented upon those walls, evoked by the finest artists humanity had produced. There was nothing abstract, nothing surreal—just the simple depiction of the works which made Man what he was.

The floor was a solid sheet of polished glasssteel, clear as distilled water, impervious to wear, unblemished and unmarred by the thousands upon thousands of feet which had crossed it in the half-millennium and more of the Empire's existence. It was two centimeters thick, that glistening floor, protecting the stone beneath. Strange, patchwork-looking stone. The stones composing that patchwork had been removed, carefully, one by one, from all of the great works of Terra. In each case, the stone which was removed had been replaced with one which matched it perfectly, and each of those irregular, varicolored stones—each tile in the throne room's true floor—was labeled and identified. The Parthenon. The Colosseum. The Forbidden City. Machu Piccu. Temples and theaters and cathedrals. Stones from the pyramids of Cheops and of the Mayans. Stones from the Inca, and from the great works of Africa. Stones from the walls where aboriginal peoples had worshiped their ancestors. Stones from the Great Wall, carrying with them, perhaps, the tortured souls of the millions who had died to build it. Thousands of stones, all of them bringing the souls who had worshiped at them and built them alive in this one place, the center of it all.

The Throne of Man itself was placed upon a dais formed by the ChromSten-armored hatch cover from a missile tube. That hatch cover came from *Freedom's Fury*, the renamed cruiser from whose command deck Miranda I, the first Empress of Man, had led the battle to throw the Dagger Lords off Old Earth and reestablish functioning and growing civilization in the galaxy. Fourteen steps led up to the throne, each of precious metals or gems. But the sere, scarred ChromSten of the ship outshone them all.

The Throne itself was even simpler, only an old, battered, antique command chair from the same ship. Over the years, it had been necessary to rebuild it more than once. But each master craftsman chosen for the task had taken meticulous care to reproduce exactly the same scarring, the same scorching, as the one Miranda the First, Miranda the Great, had sat upon through those awful battles. And it did have those scars, those burns. Right down to the clumsily carved initials, "AS," which had been cut into the side of the chair even before Miranda MacClintock and her followers cut their way to the flight deck of what had been a Dagger Lord ship to turn it against its erstwhile owners.

Alexandra VII, the seventeenth MacClintock in direct succession from Miranda I to sit upon that chair, sat upon it now. Roger saw her in the distance as they entered the room—a regal, distant figure, much like the mother he remembered of old. The Imperial Crown glittered upon her head, and she wore a long train of purple-trimmed, snow-white ice-tiger fur, and held the Scepter in one gloved hand. There were others present, dozens of them, although they seemed lost and lonely in the throne room's vastness, and Roger slowed his pace.

He walked forward, and his staff spread out to either side.

Despreaux walked at his right, holding her hated shoes in her hand and fidgeting with them. Then came Julian, tugging on the civilian suit he was just learning to wear. And Honal, wearing the combat suit of a stingship pilot.

Eleanora O'Casey walked to his left, calm and dignified, more accustomed to this room than even Roger. Then Doc Dobrescu, uncomfortable in formal clothes. Krindi Fain, still in his leather harness and kilt. And directly behind him was D'Nal Cord—slave, mentor, bodyguard, friend—and Pedi Karuse.

Thomas Catrone walked behind the two Mardukans, but Roger sensed still others behind him. D'estres and Gronningen. Dokkum, Pentzikis and Bosum. Captain Krasnitsky, of the *DeGlopper*, who'd blown up his own ship to take the second cruiser with him. Ima Hooker, and even Ensign Guha, *DeGlopper*'s unwitting toombie saboteur. Kane and Sawato. Rastar, waving a sword as his *civan* cat-walked to the side. The list went on and on, but most especially, he felt a friendly, fatherly hand on his shoulder. The sensation was so strong he actually looked to the side, and for a moment, with something other than his eyes, he saw Armand Pahner's face, calm and sober, ready to face any challenge for his Prince and his Empire. And beside Pahner, Kostas Matsugae stood looking on, wondering whether Roger was well-dressed enough for a formal audience, and tut-tutting over Despreaux's shoes.

He reached the first balk line, where a subject stopped and knelt to the Empress, and kept walking, pressed by an urgency in his mind, pushed forward by his ghosts. He passed the second line, and the third. The fourth. Until he reached the fifth and last, where his staff spread out on either hand behind him. And then, at last, he dropped to both knees and bowed his head.

"Your Majesty," he said. "You summoned; I am come."

Alexandra looked down at the top of his bowed head, then looked at the companions who had followed him into her presence. She paused in her perusal at sight of Despreaux's shoes and smiled, faintly, as if in complete understanding. Then she nodded.

"We are Alexandra Harriet Katryn Griselda Tian MacClintock, eighth Empress of Man, eighteenth of Our House to hold the Crown.

We have at times, lately, been unwell. Our judgment has been severely affected. But in this place, at this time We are who We are. At any time, this may change, but at this moment We are in Our right mind, as so attested by attending physicians and as proven in conversation with Our Prime Minister and other ministers, here gathered."

She paused, and looked around the throne room—not simply at Roger and his companions, but at all the others assembled there and nodded slightly.

"There have been eighteen Emperors and Empresses, stretching back to Miranda the First. Some of us have died in battle, as have our sons and daughters." She paused sadly as she remembered her own children and grandchildren. "Some of us have died young, some old. Some of us have died in our beds—"

"And some in other beds," Julian muttered under his breath.

"—and some in accidents. But *all* of us have died, metaphorically, right here," she said, thumping her left hand on the armrest of the ancient command chair. "No MacClintock Emperor or Empress has ever abdicated." She paused, her jaw flexing angrily, and looked again at Roger's bowed head.

"Until now."

She yanked the heavy train out of her attendants' hands and stood, wrapping it around her left arm until she had some capability of independent movement. Then she walked down the fourteen steps to the glassteel floor.

"Roger," she snapped, "get your butt over here."

Roger looked up, his face hard, and one muscle twitched in his cheek. But he stood at her command and walked to the base of the stairs.

"A coronation would take weeks to arrange," Alexandra said, looking him in the eye, her face as hard as his. "And we don't have the time, do we?"

"No," Roger said coldly. He'd wanted to have a conversation with his mother when he returned. This wasn't it.

"Fine," Alexandra said. "In that case, we'll skip the ceremony. Hold out your right hand."

Roger did, still looking her in the eye, and she slapped the Scepter into his hand, hard.

"Scepter," she spat. "Symbol of the Armed Forces of the Empire, of which you are now Commander-in-Chief. Originally a simple device for crushing the skulls of your enemies. Use it wisely. Never crush too many skulls; by the same token, never crush too few."

She struggled out of the heavy ice-tiger fur train and walked around to throw it over his shoulders. She was tall, for a woman, but she still had to rise on the balls of her feet to get it into place. Then she stepped back around in front of him and fastened it at his throat.

"Big heavy damned cloak," she snapped. "I can't remember what it's a symbol of, but it's going to be a pain in your imperial ass."

Last, she removed the Crown and rammed it onto his head, hard. It had been sized to her head for the day of her own coronation, and it was far too small for Roger. It perched on top of his head like an over-small hat.

"Crown," she said bitterly. "Originally a symbol of the helmets kings wore in battle so the enemy knew who to shoot. Pretty much the same purpose today."

She stepped back and nodded.

"Congratulations. You're now the Emperor. With all the authority and horrible responsibility that entails."

Roger's eyes stayed locked on hers, hard, angry. So much lay between them, so much pain, so much distrust. And now the steamroller of history, the responsibility which had claimed eighteen generations of their family, perched on *his* head, lay draped about *his* shoulders, weighted *his* right hand. Unwanted, feared, and yet his— the responsibility he could not renounce, to which he had given so many of his dead, and to which he must sacrifice not simply his own life, but Nimashet Despreaux's and their children's, as well.

"Thank you, Mother," he said coldly.

"Wear them in good health," Alexandra said harshly.

She stood, meeting his gaze, and then, slowly—so slowly—her face crumpled. Her lips trembled, and suddenly she threw herself into his arms and wrapped her own about him.

"Oh, God, my son, my only son," she sobbed into his chest. "*Please* wear them in better health than I!"

Roger looked at the useless club in his hand and tossed it, overhand, to Honal, who fielded it as if it were radioactive. Then he sat down on the steps of the Throne of Man, wrapped his arms around his mother and held her in his lap, with infinite tenderness, as she sobbed out her grief and loss—the loss of her reign, of her children, of her mind—on her only child's shoulder.